PRAISE FOR

# The Liberated Bride

"A magnificent, often comic, and humanely inexorable journey among Israel's Jews and their secret and denied sharers: the Arabs... The story splendidly branches and exfoliates... Yehoshua, who is near 70 and a dove, has written a novel that incarnates the message to extraordinary literary effect."     —*The New York Times Book Review*

"Above all, the book exhibits the pure craft of a writer in exceptional form and in near perfect control of his material."
—*The Washington Post Book World*

"Yehoshua, the most daring of the major Israeli writers, tells a simple story about a region that complicates all it touches.... The juxtaposition of a failed marriage and the turmoil of Israeli society suggests pointed commentary, but Yehoshua's portrait of the hesitant courtship between two peoples—sometimes tender and generous, sometimes grotesque and calamitous—remains, somehow, hopeful."
—*The New Yorker*

"Yehoshua has a great talent for mixing operatic drama with political and religious rumination without falling into moralizing or absurdism."
—*San Francisco Chronicle*

"Yehoshua is a keen observer of social and political realities, and a subtle writer capable of reflecting complex situations in events in daily life."     —*Publishers Weekly* (starred)

"This is a great read from one of Israel's premier authors, by turns profoundly funny and simply profound—there's a deep understanding of interpersonal relationships regardless of geography."
—*Library Journal* (Best Books of 2003)

"A sprawling, immensely moving, hugely entertaining and provocative novel of ideas, action and tragically missed opportunities."
—*The Montreal Gazette*

"A splendidly realized search for the causes of ruptures that rend families and nations: both timely and timeless."
—*Kirkus Reviews* (starred)

"Yehoshua, a writer deeply concerned with his country's destiny and its morality, has given us the gift of a new understanding of contemporary Israel and the problems of its citizens. But he has not written a polemic. He has written a powerful novel that breathes life on every page."
—*Hadassah Magazine*

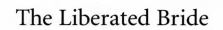

The Liberated Bride

# A.B. YEHOSHUA

# The Liberated Bride

*Translated from the Hebrew*
*by Hillel Halkin*

A HARVEST BOOK · HARCOURT, INC.
*Orlando   Austin   New York   San Diego   Toronto   London*

www.HarcourtBooks.com

This is a translation of *Kalah Ha-Meshaòhreret.*

Library of Congress Cataloging-in-Publication Data
Yehoshua, Abraham B.
[Kalah ha-meshaòhreret. English]
The liberated bride/A. B. Yehoshua;
translated from the Hebrew by Hillel Halkin.—1st U.S. ed.
p.      cm.
ISBN 0-15-100653-9
ISBN 0-15-603016-0 (pbk.)
I. Halkin, Hillel, 1939–   II. Title.
PJ5054.Y42K3513 2003
892.4'36—dc21   2003005360

Text set in Minion
Designed by Lori McThomas Buley

Printed in the United States of America

First Harvest edition 2004
A C E G I K J H F D B

PART I

# A Village Wedding

Had he known that on this evening, on the hill where the village held its celebrations, an evening suffused by the scent of a fig tree bent over the table like another, venerable guest, he would again be struck—but powerfully—by a sense of failure and missed opportunity, he might have more decisively made his excuses to Samaher, his annoyingly ambitious M.A. student, who, not content with sending him an invitation by mail and then repeating it to his face, had gone and chartered a minibus, after first urging the new department head to make sure the faculty attended her wedding. It wasn't just for her sake, she said. It would be a gesture to all the university's Arab students, without whom—the cheek of it!—the department would count for nothing.

His wife, Hagit, who knew all too well how weddings had depressed him in recent years, had warned against it. "Why do you need the aggravation?" she had asked. "But they're Arabs," he'd answered mildly, with the innocence of a man pursuing an academic interest. "As opposed to what?" she had wanted to know. "Human beings?" "On the contrary... on the contrary..." he had tried defending himself, at a loss to explain how Arabs, although not among the many objects of his envy, could be more human than anyone else.

Yet the snake of envy, his companion of many years, had slithered after him here too, to the little village of Mansura high up in the Galilee, near the Lebanese border. It had lain coiled in the incense of the glowing grilled lamb and writhed to the Oriental music that, despite its sobbing grace notes, secretly aspired to the savage disco beat of a Jewish wedding party—and now, as the student bride presented him not with the seminar paper she was a year late in finishing, but with her groom, it injected its venom.

Many hands had done their best to beautify Samaher, causing him to wonder for a moment whether he was looking at the same woman who had taken nearly all of his courses for the past five years. High heels and a swept-up hairdo had made her taller, and her usually restless eyes, chronically resentful when not anxiously scheming—the eyes of an active member of the Arab Student Committee—were smiling and relaxed. She was also without her glasses, and her eyes were heavily made up with a kohl so unusually tinted that he suspected it of having been smuggled across the border from Lebanon. A bright rouge masked the pimples that wandered as a rule from her cheeks to her throat and back again, and her long wedding gown bestowed a harmony, if only for a single night, on a figure not known for its sartorial coordination. Brimming with pride at having enticed him, the most senior and eminent of her teachers, to honor her and all Araby with his presence, she extended a hand quivering with excitement to his wife.

"So this is the teacher who's so annoyed at you," laughed the groom, pumping his hand in what could have been either an acknowledgment of Samaher's flightiness or a warning that she now had a protector. It was the same young man—taken by Rivlin for a maintenance worker rather than a future husband—who had stood every day last winter in the corridor outside the classroom waiting for their seminar to end. As if to atone for an error of which he alone was aware, he rose from his seat and congratulated the new husband cordially. Yet even as he did so, the cruel fate of his son, the young husband rebuffed, stung him sharply. So strong was the surge of resentment and jealousy that he at once sought out his wife—who, however, was laughing gaily at some remark. Such sentiments, although by rights she should have shared them, were unknown to her. Her glance, when he finally caught it, conveyed not so much sympathy as vague reassurance, plus a warning that he had better not get into one of his bad moods among all these people trying so hard to be hospitable.

It was being slowly spun out, Samaher's wedding, on the twilight of a bashful summer night, to the friendly warmth of young Arabs, many of them students from his and other departments at the university, who had gathered in their little autonomous kingdom, the borders of which were being drawn, stealthily but steadily, amid the pinkening hills of the Galilee. Now, telling a bearded young *qadi* in a gray cloak that she didn't want her Jewish guests to feel deprived, the bride asked him to repeat a shortened version of the wedding ceremony—which, they were surprised to hear, had already taken place in the bosom of her family a few days previously. It was an opportunity to still the wailing music, leaving the hill so shrouded in silence that the distant boom of an artillery shell fired across the border in Lebanon sounded like part of the reenacted rite.

## 2.

AS THE EVENING deepened and the music resumed its beat, and little lanterns were hung from grapevines trellised above tables spread with colorful piles of appetizers that were followed by copper trays of juicy, red-hot lamb, he was overcome by regret, not so much for having accepted Samaher's invitation as for having willingly surrendered his freedom of movement for the convenience of a prearranged ride. Two hours had passed, and none of the faculty showed the slightest sign of wanting to depart—least of all their organizer, Ephraim Akri. He was the new department head, a swarthy Orientalist who, though forced by the religious scruples proclaimed by the skullcap he wore to forage carefully through the little plates in search of kosher morsels, was so full of high spirits that he demanded—whether as a gesture to his hosts or as a boast of his own fluency—that even his Jewish colleagues speak to him only in Arabic. In fact, they were as taken with the bucolic atmosphere as he was. Hagit, always quick to adjust, was genially absorbed in the conversation around her, following it with interest and laughter and occasionally making a remark, or even uttering a single word, that was sure to leave an indelible impression.

Fated to spend more time at the wedding than he had intended, he decided to go for a walk—the sooner the better, before any more of the tender meat with which his plate kept being piled metamorphosed into his own flesh. He ambled over to the sweetly smoking spit to inspect the remains of the incandescent lamb, then joined a line of guests waiting by the rickety door of a makeshift outhouse. A nattily dressed young man, introducing himself as a construction worker who had labored on the professor's new duplex apartment in Haifa, tried escorting him to the head of the line. Before they could reach it, however, Samaher, who had been keeping him under surveillance, came to rescue him from the indignity of queuing up for an outdoor toilet by leading him to more dignified facilities.

"We live right near here, Professor Rivlin," she cajoled him, as if his presence at her wedding would be incomplete without a home visit. Before he knew it he was being led by the bride, hobbling on her unaccustomed high heels, past houses and courtyards and down a dark, narrow dirt lane. Her wedding gown showed signs of disarray, and its lace ruff, which had slipped from her slender shoulders, smelled faintly of fresh perspiration. In the pale moonlight, the polished nails of her hands and feet looked like large drops of blood. Barely two years ago, he recalled with amusement, this same vivacious young lady had had an attack of religion and sat sternly through his seminars in a long-sleeved black dress and large kerchief. It had been only a passing phase, however.

A horse whinnied. Once again he felt the ache of that other, wasted wedding that had come to naught. It made him want to rebuke his student guide.

"It embarrasses me, Samaher, to hear you tell people that I'm angry at you without your also explaining why."

She stopped in her tracks, blushing with pleasure. "But how can you say that, Professor? You're wrong. I not only explain why you're angry, I tell them you're right."

She studied his face and added with a smile:

"But so am I."

"You are?" he marveled bitterly. "How can you be right, too?"

"I can be right because how could I finish a seminar paper with a sick grandmother to take care of? And then, on top of it all, this wedding."

"That's enough excuses, Samaher," he said, loath to give this devious Arabic-studies major standing beside him in a wedding gown the chance to extort a new postponement.

Her smile brightened even more, as if she not only had been granted a postponement but had also been offered course credits for her wedding. Taking hold of his arm, she steered him with dexterous confidence toward an iron gate blocked by a large black horse.

Samaher scolded the horse in Arabic. When this made no impression on it, she seized it by its bridle and in her wedding gown, high heels and all, wrestled it out of the way. The battle was quickly over and left Rivlin struck by her determination. Raising her head proudly, she pulled the horse after them into the yard, shut the gate, put on her glasses after extracting them from a previously hidden case, and led him up the heavy, dark stone steps of her home.

He now found himself at another celebration, this one for women only. Squeezed together, in bright dresses, they sat on pillowed divans in a large guest room whose walls were covered with photographs of ancient elders wearing fezzes. A few old crones in a corner were puffing on glass narghiles. A younger, heavily adorned woman hurried over to him with a smile. "Professor Rivlin!" she exclaimed. This was Afifa, Samaher's mother, who long ago—back in the nineteen-seventies—had been a first-year undergraduate in the Near Eastern Studies Department. She had taken an introductory survey course of his and might have gone on to get a B.A. as her daughter would, had she not broken off her studies to have her.

"You know," Rivlin told the handsome woman, "it's not too late for you to go back to school. We'll readmit you. You can continue from where you left off."

She replied with an embarrassed laugh, as if he had made her an intimate proposition. Dismissing with a charmingly sinuous gesture the possibility of recovering lost time, she took possession of him from her daughter and led him to a large, spotless bathroom where he was given, as if he had come not just to relieve himself but also to take a leisurely bath, two fresh towels and a new bar of soap.

There was no lock or latch on the door. Quite apart from not wishing to worry his wife by his disappearance, this was sufficient reason for leaving the bathroom's contents uninspected, despite the opportunity afforded him to learn more about the private side of Arab life. He urinated in silence, washed his hands and face, took a large green comb from a shelf, rinsed it carefully, and ran it through his silver curls. Then, picking up a small bottle, he studied its Arabic label until satisfied that he understood it, and daubed a few drops from it on his forehead to sweeten the relentless bitterness assailing him.

The bride had returned to the wedding party on the hill without waiting for him, leaving her friendly mother to guard the bathroom door. It was an appropriate moment, he thought, to pay a sick call on Samaher's grandmother.

"Sick?" Afifa was startled. "Who told you she's sick?"

"But of course she is. The poor woman is bedridden." He deliberately mimicked Samaher's manner of speech.

"But who told you? She's not sick at all!" Triumphantly, Afifa pointed to a gaily dressed old woman puffing heartily on a narghile with her friends. Samaher's grandmother smiled back with a mouth full of smoke.

And yet, he decided, as Afifa—fearful he wouldn't find his way back by himself—went off to look for an escort, you didn't upbraid a lying bride on her wedding night. Samaher's mother returned with the bride's grandfather, a sturdy, taciturn old man in a gray satin robe and white kaffiyeh who stood waiting by the gate with his head bowed respectfully. Noticing the horse in the yard, he commanded it to join them. The three of them walked back up the lane, the solemn grandfather in the middle as he gallantly struggled to understand the Arabic of the Jewish professor.

The lit-up dance floor was now crowded with youngsters gyrating to the music. The Oriental wail had been replaced by Western tom-toms. From afar, Rivlin cast a yearning glance at his wife. She was where he had left her, seated beneath the fig tree, with her slender legs stretched in front of her, intent on the conversation. As always, especially in moments of distress, he was aware of how perfectly true and unquestioning was his old, faithful love for this woman, who was now engaged in tempting with a pack of cigarettes two departmental secretaries who had attached themselves to her. He knew that from now on, whenever they saw him, they would remember to send their special regards, coupled with words of admiration, to this woman whom they had just met, who sometimes said to him only half-jokingly:

"You're a lucky man! Luckier than you deserve to be."

## 3.

"YOU'RE FEELING BETTER."

It was a statement of fact, not a question, uttered with the precision with which she always diagnosed his moods. "You needn't be ashamed to admit that you're having a good time like the rest of us."

Admitting enjoyment, however, did not come easily to him—certainly not at a wedding, even an Arab one. Instead, omitting his visit to Samaher's bathroom—an episode that might strike his colleagues as unintelligibly bizarre—he began to relate with an odd relish his encounter with their old student Afifa. His proposal to reinstate her in the department met with cautionary remarks from the two secretaries. He should not, they warned him, arouse false Arab hopes. The Law of Return did not apply to abandoned studies. Afifa would have to start again from scratch.

"Sit down," his wife said good-naturedly. "Standing will get you nowhere."

She was right. It was pointless to hope that remaining forlornly on his feet might persuade anyone to set out for home. The refusal of their Arab hosts to be insulted by a premature departure was only part of the reason. The Jews, too, had lost all sense of time and of the long ride back to Haifa still ahead of them. Basking in the Oriental languor of the spring night, they were awaiting a final course of homemade ice cream. It did not escape him that his wife—for whom dessert, especially if it promised to be exceptional, was the raison d'être of every meal—had become the secret ringleader of a sweet-toothed conspiracy.

"I wish you'd sit down," she chided him again. "Stop making us nervous. You're not the driver. No one is leaving this wonderful wedding without dessert."

He sat, forced to yield to the popular demand for ice cream while attempting to follow, above the pounding of the rock music, an argument between the department head and some of the Arab students. Tensely but politely, the latter were listening to Akri's heated exposition of a theme that pained them despite its delivery in flawless Arabic—namely, that ever since the Arab world had been conquered by the Ottomans in the sixteenth century, Arab intellectuals had failed to confront the inner dysfunction of their society. Rivlin knew well that Akri, a Jew of Middle Eastern origin, was gracious to his Arab students, whose weddings he attended and whose language he went out of his way to speak, although less from admiration for their culture than from despair of it. Not that he had an aversion to Arabs. He felt no contempt or disdain for them. He simply had arrived at what he believed to be a scholarly conclusion: that they could never understand—let alone respect, desire, or implement—the idea of freedom. This was a theory, which Akri supported with an odd and astonishing assortment of facts morbidly assembled from the gamut of Arab history, that Rivlin firmly rejected. It smacked to him of racism, and he scoffed vehemently at it whenever it was mentioned by his colleagues. And yet tonight, whether because it fed or was fed by his own gloomy associations, he, too, felt Akri's despair, felt it to the point of paralysis. He sat there silently, one hand on the shoulder of his wife as she awaited her dessert.

The Arab students from the department, however, having listened respectfully to a man who was both their guest and their academic senior executive, were running out of patience, especially since they had been joined by other students who neither knew Akri nor needed to defer to him. Akri, continuing to deride the Arabs' history in an impeccable display of their language, was now surrounded by a shocked circle of listeners. The prospect of a row hung in the soft, mild air and threatened to spoil the gesture of their coming. Just as Rivlin, a full professor, was about to pull rank on Akri and nip the quarrel in the bud, there was a flurry of excitement. A chilled, glittering serving bowl was placed on the table while crystal dishes and golden spoons were handed out. How, Rivlin wondered as he tasted his first spoonful of the ice cream, could this remote little village, a bastion of chickens and donkeys, have produced such a magnificent last course, so lavishly creative in its flavors and deliciously chewy in its texture that he had to keep an eye on his ravenous wife, who had put on not a little weight in recent years? Not that this bothered him. He liked her company in any shape or form.

## 4.

DESPITE THE HOUR, it seemed entirely natural to Hagit, halfway home between Amihud and Shfar'am, to ask the Arab driver to stop by an illuminated greengrocer's stand, where she talked the two secretaries, as well as two young teaching assistants who had taken a fancy to her, into some late-night shopping, as if, Rivlin reflected, saddened to bid her Arab hosts good-bye, she were determined to bring home as a memento their freshly picked cucumbers, eggplants, squashes, and strawberries. His protests unavailing, he remained seated on the bus, boycotting the proceedings while regarding with amazement the sleeping Ephraim Akri, after his diatribe slumbering so sweetly that not even the sudden stilling of the motor could awaken him. Irritable and weary, he watched his wife circulate eagerly in the bluish light of a kerosene lamp. Several large dolls dangling from a thatched roof suggested idols in an ancient Canaanite temple. There she goes again, he thought angrily. Once more she was witlessly letting some shrewd merchant sell her a cornucopia of fruits and vegetables that would end up rotting in the refrigerator unless he ate them all himself.

A car drove up. Two young women climbed out and joined the midnight shopping spree. Despite his desire to intervene and put an end to it, the sight of the yellowish fog from a nearby gas station, into and out of which cars were pulling busily, had an immobilizing effect on him. Who would be left to rise early in the Jewish state, he wondered, if the Arabs, too, had begun to burn the midnight oil? His wife, meanwhile, having struck up a conversation with the two new-comers, added her spruce legs to theirs in another tour of the pagan greengrocery. The memory of the hale old grandmother sucking on the snake head of her narghile heightened his bile. How had he ever agreed to such a wasted evening? And especially when weddings, even of close family and friends, were becoming increasingly painful to him. Had he and Hagit stayed home tonight, they surely would have made the love that had disappointingly eluded them all week. And to-morrow he was expected to vacate his study for ten days in order to make room for Ofra, his sister-in-law from abroad, who would be staying with them until her husband joined her and they moved to a hotel. His prospects for the next week and a half were slim. The evenings without Hagit would be long, and the mornings with her short, not because she was attached to her only, elder sister by twin strands of love and guilt, but also because there would be no chance for him to make love to her while they were all together under one roof. A single item of Ofra's clothing in the next room, even a pair of her shoes, was enough to banish all thought of sex from Hagit's mind.

5.

RIVLIN'S BOYCOTT WAS dealt with by the simple expediency of having the greengrocer bring Hagit's bulging bags to the minibus and arrange them there carefully. "Here you are, Your Honor," he declared, having discovered who she was from the two lady passengers—recent law-school graduates entranced by their unexpected encounter with a dis-trict judge. Perhaps aware that, like all Arabs, he would sooner or later end up in court himself, whether in the dock or on the witness stand, the man seemed in awe of the genial magistrate who had chosen this time of night to patronize his stand.

"You should know better than to make friends with lawyers," Rivlin scolded her. "Don't you realize they're out to make a dishonest man of every judge?"

"Man, my dear," Hagit repeated with a grin. "You said so yourself. Not woman." Producing a small comb from her handbag, she invited him, as if the night's entertainment were just beginning, to run it through his hair. "Don't worry," she assured him. "I know where the bounds are. And I make sure others do, too." She could only have been referring to judicial bounds, because the minibus hadn't gone far before she was opening the paper bags at her feet to probe their contents. She popped into her mouth several cherries whose pink

globes must have reminded her of the munificent nipples she had
sucked when she was a child, and deposited the pits carefully in the
palm of her hand.

It was past midnight. The first guests to have been picked up by
their driver, they were the last to be dropped off. First they had to
awaken Akri. Although Akri's antics had nearly ruined the evening,
Rivlin watched him fondly as he walked with a springy gait to his
apartment building. He was pleased that he had used his influence
with the Appointments Committee to get Akri his promotion and
tenure—thus relieving himself of the long-standing burden of running the department.

On the East Carmel his wife parted with affection from one of the
secretaries, and, two blocks farther, just as lovingly from the other.
The minibus snaked through a new housing development, looking
for the street of a young instructor with a bright academic future.
Only now did Rivlin notice that the instructor's bashful wife was in
the early months of pregnancy.

The two merry young teaching assistants got off downtown. A Jew
and a Druze, they shared an apartment. At Carmel Center, Rivlin descended from the vehicle to lead an old professor emeritus, who never
missed a departmental event, to the front door of his old-age home.
They parted with unaccustomed warmth, as if an evening spent among
Arabs had reawakened their sense of Jewish solidarity. In years to come,
he knew, his wife's keen memory would preserve, if not the name, then
at least some identifying mark, of every person at the wedding.

Home at last in their new duplex on the French Carmel, to which
they had moved half a year previously, they were happy to see that,
as always, they felt no regret for the lush wadi that had abutted the
terrace of their old apartment, where they had lived for thirty years
before exchanging the wadi for the slow but sure elevator that now
brought them and their shopping bags to the fifth floor. The Arab
driver, a young man with almost sable skin and handsome, fiery eyes,
was distrustful of elevators but insisted on accompanying them to
their door and carrying their purchases inside. He was indignant when
Hagit sought to tip him. How could she think of such a thing? He,
Rashid, was one of the family. He was Samaher's cousin and would do

anything for her or her guests. Everyone in the village loved her and was proud of her. She had character and education and was one of Mansura's most prominent young people. Samaher would go far, despite having been ill all winter.

"Samaher, ill? Rivlin objected. "You must be mistaken."

Rashid stuck to his guns. Samaher had been ill.

"With what?"

He didn't know the name of the illness. He only knew it was a bad one. This was the reason Samaher had agreed to be married as soon as she had recovered: to make up for lost time.

## 6.

THEY MADE DO with giving the driver a cold drink, pleased with his *oohs* and *ahs* over the duplex. Informed that he intended to rejoin the festivities, which would go on all night, Hagit asked Rashid what the name *Samaher* meant in Arabic. Rivlin, indignant she hadn't turned to him, blurted:

"It means a javelin."

The young Arab begged to differ. *Samaher* meant a lance, not a javelin. His coal-black eyes glowed as he pointed out the difference. *Samaher*, he repeated solemnly, was a lance. A *samaheri* was a lancer. And with that he took his leave.

At last they were alone. The first thing they did was check the voice mail for a message from Ofer, their older son, who had spent the last four years in Paris. None of the three messages were from him. One, quick and bashful with an Arab accent, came from the cleaning woman's son, whose regular job it was to tell them she wasn't well, especially when her illness was imaginary. The second voice—clear, good-natured, and always a pleasure to hear—belonged to their younger son, Tsakhi; an officer in the army; he was calling to apologize for unexpectedly having to be on duty over the weekend, which meant that anyone wanting to see him would have to visit his base in the Galilee. The last message was from Hannah Tedeschi. In crisp, firm tones she announced that although she and her husband had returned to Israel a week ago from a long trip to South America, they were not yet installed in their Jerusalem home because before they could unpack, Professor Tedeschi's notorious asthma, having waited patiently for their vacation to end, had struck more cruelly than ever. If Rivlin wanted to see his old academic patron and doctoral adviser, he had better come to Bikkur Holim Hospital, where the barely conscious professor could be found on the third floor, in Room 8 of Internal Medicine. He needn't rush, though. This time, he was informed triumphantly by Hannah (an Orientalist herself and a first-rate translator of the poetry of the Jahaliya, the pre-Islamic "Age of Ignorance"), Tedeschi was in for a long hospitalization.

"It's unbelievable how she loves him to be sick," Rivlin said.

"Needs, not loves," his wife corrected him. Often a single word was enough to remind him of how admirably clever she was. "Come, let's go to bed," she urged when he wanted to listen to Hannah's message again, hoping to discern the difference between love and need with his own ears. "The house is a mess. And there's no cleaning woman tomorrow. You'll have to pitch in. I'll need your help to tidy up a bit...."

"A bit?" he repeated resentfully. He knew full well that in the end most of the work would fall on him. Unlike his wife, who had a prosecutor, a defense attorney, and a defendant all waiting for her to appear in court in her best judicial form, he had only the incomplete draft of a book that would be happy to be left for another day.

Hagit knew that her husband liked nothing better than to complain while taking refuge from his recalcitrant research in the chores of a malingering cleaning woman or an inadequate housewife. Careful to show no disrespect for the sacrifice demanded of him by her sister's visit, she let him go to the kitchen and—grumbling loudly about the food she had bought—switch on the dishwasher despite the late hour. When he finally climbed the stairs to their bedroom, she was sprawled on the bedspread fully clothed, watching the TV news with a bowl of cherries in her lap. Her "presomnial relaxation," as she called it, took precedence, like her postsomnial relaxation, over putting away the disorder of dresses, skirts, blouses, and shoes that testified to the difficulties of deciding what to wear to an Arab wedding.

"How can you possibly still be hungry?" Rivlin asked, scooping up a few cherries, more to help rid the bowl of them than because he was hungry himself.

"Why not?" She smiled serenely. "All I had to eat all night was ice cream. I never touched the lamb. That's more than I can say for some people, who ate half of it single-handedly."

"You're sure it was only half?" His own smile was glum. He was already feeling nostalgic for the juicy meat heaped unceasingly on his plate by the villagers. It was gone now, devoured without a trace, leaving only the faint strains of Oriental music pulsing inside him. He turned to regard his wife, whose face was pallid with fatigue. As of tomorrow he would have his childless sister-in-law on his hands, ten days' worth of advanced middle age. Though tired and dejected, he was determined as a matter of principle to assert his conjugal rights. Sitting at the foot of the bed, he lightly stroked the soles of Hagit's feet, so as to gauge his own desire before making any claims on hers.

## 7.

HIS DESIRE, HE CONCLUDED, even though the next day's chores were tediously waiting for him in a long line, would pass muster. He reached out, took the remote control from his wife's hands, and muted the TV. The pictures remained on the screen.

"Not now," Hagit said. "You won't enjoy it either. Don't force yourself. Let's wait until morning. You know what happens when I'm not in the mood."

"You will be," he promised, as if there were a switch he could press for that, too. Squirming free of him, however, she demurred. He couldn't tell if her resistance came solely from fatigue or also from something more ancient.

"In the end you'll leave me all alone."

"No, I won't." The stirring in his loins firmed his resolution. "Don't worry. I won't come without you." He switched off the overhead light, leaving only the reading lamp.

"Then talk to me!" she protested, with an inner anger that made her tense when he embraced her. "Say something! We're not animals.

You know how hard your silences are for me. You never have time for a loving or caring word."

And again there was no telling whether she was pleading with him to overcome her resistance or—already cradled by an exhaustion stronger than his arms—looking to fend him off. But he would not take no for an answer. Perhaps it was the sobbing grace notes of the music. Or else the lamb had been in heat, or he was haunted by the image of his attractive former student Afifa, now puffing on a narghile with Samaher's healthy old grandmother. He was not about to back down. As excessive as declarations of love seemed when he, too, wanted only to sink calmly into sleep, he managed to dredge a few sincere ones from his depths.

Hagit listened with eyes shut, a smile playing over her lips. She took words seriously. They counted with her even more in the bedroom than in the courtroom. Spreading heavy arms, she invited him to rise from his crouch by the bed and join her face to face. She kissed his forehead and eyes. Yet her kisses were lukewarm. Though there was a will, the way to her heart was blocked.

"What's wrong?" he asked, irritated.

"Nothing. I told you. I'm dead tired. Why insist on it? Did someone turn you on at the wedding?"

"How could you say such a thing?"

"I don't know. Forget it. You smell funny."

"I do? What are you talking about?"

"Don't take it personally. Something must have rubbed off on you in the village. Some strange perfume. Did you touch anything? Maybe it was the soap you used. It's nothing. Just wash your face. It's not a good smell. Perhaps we should both shower. We'll feel better if we do. You go first. We're both sweaty. It's been a long, sweaty day. We'll wake up fresh in the morning and have time for everything."

## 8.

FINIS. EVEN INTELLECTUALLY, the life had gone out of his lust. He stepped into the shower, thoroughly soaping his face and private parts. Unsure the smell was gone, he embraced his wife when their naked bodies collided outside the bathroom, menacingly offering her his forehead to smell. She burst into laughter and hugged him back, her marvelous breasts pressed against him. They would make love in the morning, she promised, kissing the proffered brow. It was a promise, he knew, backed by nothing. Who knew what the morning would bring? Things could go wrong even in their dreams.

And in fact the approach of her beloved sister, though still oceans away, roused Hagit from bed at dawn to vacuum the house, scrub and scour the windows and mirrors, refill the dishwasher repeatedly with dishes that had already been washed, and stoke the washing machine with clean towels and sheets. As a crowning touch, she made a bed fit for a princess, with starched, scented sheets, light, fluffy blankets, and brand-new eiderdown pillows—all in unspoken competition with the crisp and fragrant luxuriance that, carefully arranged by her sister, always awaited her on her visits to America.

Rivlin, whose wife was usually happy to let him and the cleaning woman manage the house, while she relaxed amid her dresses and fruit pits after a hard day in court, listened to her instructions without protest. He knew how much her sister's rare visits meant to Hagit. Like an old drill sergeant ordered about by a new officer, he helped hang another round of laundry while moving his belongings from his study. Although his sister-in-law would only be staying with them for ten days, this meant emptying all three drawers of his desk, clearing his books from a shelf, and transferring his computer to his small office at the university. He was actually fond of Hagit's sister and wouldn't have wanted her to be blamed for impeding his work, which had gone slowly since the move to the duplex.

The morning passed quickly. Soon the judge would don her black robe and join her colleagues waiting in the wings of the courtroom for the crier to announce them. Yet by working efficiently, he and Hagit had managed to accomplish more in two hours than the cleaning woman did in a day. The floors were spotless. The windows and mirrors gleamed. The guest room, its couch opened into a sumptuous bed, looked airy and inviting. Flowers, cakes, and other good things would arrive with the judge, bought on her way home from court. She would not accompany her husband to the airport. The trial was a long and secretive one, held behind closed doors, and there was no chance of an early recess.

## 9.

THE UPSHOT WAS that he had to start the second car for her—the little old model she wasn't used to driving—and once again explain the dashboard, the meaning of whose clocks and gauges she kept forgetting. Fortunately, Hagit was a relaxed but careful driver, which was the only reason she ever arrived anywhere in one piece. Nor was she in any hurry to depart now, even though she was late. First she had two requests of him. One was direct: as soon as her sister passed through customs, she wanted to be informed. The other was more complicated. Could he please, before leaving for the university, launder the curtain in his study? Only now had she noticed how filthy it was.

"What do you mean, filthy?"

"Filthy," she said gently, "really filthy. You, my dear, never notice such things."

"Suppose I don't. This is where I draw the line. I'm not laundering any curtains. The room is for your sister, not for some dowager queen."

"Dowager queen?" The expression struck her as oddly belligerent. What did queens have to do with her sister? It was his study. When he moved back into it in ten days' time, he'd appreciate a clean curtain too.

He didn't answer. This was always the best tactic to keep her from trying to change his mind. He wished she'd leave already. If you had made love to me yesterday, he whispered to himself, I might have laundered that curtain for you now. His silence was met with a hostile look. Parting from him, even for short periods, was always unwelcome to Hagit. Now, this morning of all times, a long court session was preventing her from going with him to the airport, which was one of her favorite places.

"What are you waiting for? You have to be in court."

"The court won't convict you for my lateness," she said with a smile, sure of her ability to disarm him with a deft remark. He said nothing. Changing the subject, she asked what he had thought of the Arab wedding.

"It was all right."

"It was more than all right." His brusqueness annoyed her. "It was marvelous. I had a wonderful time. You didn't seem to be suffering either. You must really think very little of the Arabs if their weddings don't make you envious."

He flared at that. "What are you talking about? What does envy have to do with it? Do you think I'm against people getting married?" It was a matter of memory, not envy. It pained him to be reminded. Of all that ruin and loss. Of what had been done to his son without justification. Why couldn't she understand that?

She let him talk. Late for a trial that couldn't start without her, she switched off the motor and said, not for the first time, "It's time you put all that behind you. It's been five years. How long can you go on feeling loss? Ofer was no innocent himself." Why brood when there was nothing to be done about it? She sometimes thought he was projecting onto their son feelings that had to do with other things.

"What things?"

"Your own self."

His own self? What did she mean by that?

"Not now," she said, restarting the motor. "We'll talk about it some other time. Just be nice to my sister. You know how sensitive she is."

"I'm always nice to her."

"Then be nicer than always."

The little car drove off. He knew it would brake immediately, however, for her to beckon to him and ask anxiously, as if she had never done it before, "Do you love me?"

A wave of love passed over him in spite of himself. Loath to send her off to the waiting courtroom with a clean conscience, he stared at the ground, weighing the question carefully before answering with a barely perceptible nod.

"How much?" she demanded, as though buying a kilo of fruit.

"A lot," he admitted honestly. Softly he added:

"More than you deserve."

The cross-examination wasn't over. "Why?"

He didn't know whether she was being coy or asking the most important question of her life.

"Tell me! Why do you love me so much?"

This was already too much. He laughed, thumped the roof of the little car, and exclaimed:

"Move! Enough already!"


## 10.

THE DAY PROMISED to be a long one. There were still eight hours left before his sister-in-law's plane landed. He returned to his study to get rid of more papers and decided to clear another shelf. Then he scrutinized the white net curtain on the window. Although it did not look dirty, he was prepared to wash it for his wife, who had a long, hard session on the bench ahead of her. He unhooked it, carried it carefully to the bathroom, like a bride across the threshold, and soaked it in lukewarm, soapy water. It took many rinsings for the water to run clear. Because it occurred to him that, in her eagerness to make her sister feel at home, Hagit might launder the clean curtain again while he drove to the airport, he left a note that he had cleaned it and would expect a commensurate reward. Then he erased the last sentence. His son might come home from the army unexpectedly and read it.

It was time to unplug the computer. He coiled its wires and packed it in two black traveling bags padded with small towels. Then, grinning foolishly, he stopped by the window of his study for a last look at his dead mother, who liked to putter around on the second-floor terrace of the building across the street. And indeed there she was, in a red, sleeveless summer dress. She had opened the venetian blind and was leaning on the railing while following a big garbage truck, which was proceeding slowly down the narrow street, with a glance cross, curious, and indifferent.

This ghost of his mother had begun appearing to him not long after they had moved into their new duplex. At first he had placed his desk against a wall so as to be able to concentrate better. It was his wife who had persuaded him to move it to a window. "If you run out of ideas," she said, "the wall won't give you any new ones. And if you don't, the view won't harm them."

He took her advice. A week passed before he tired of the panorama of the western Carmel, with its rich patches of green and red-tiled roofs immersed in pine trees. Shifting his gaze to the houses across the street, he scanned their windows and terraces. Suddenly, he spied the apparition playing solitaire on a terrace. Her straw-colored hair and her heavyset frame, hunched forward to preempt a hostile world, was the spit and image of the mother who had died three years ago. Dumbfounded and bemused, too distant to make out her features clearly, he imagined for a moment that she was the same lonely figure he remembered, withdrawn and sunk in a cosmic and trivial boredom.

The terrace across the street had four blinds. Only one of them was ever opened, and that, too, never more than halfway and for only a few hours a day. The woman was the only person he ever saw there. The rest of her apartment, which could not have been small, remained beyond his ken. She emerged from its gloom and vanished into it. Unlike his mother, who had liked to read old foreign-language magazines, this woman spent her time playing cards. Sometimes she appeared with a knife and a piece of fruit. Leaning on the railing, she sliced and ate the fruit quickly, spitting the pits into the garden below.

His youngest son and his wife, whom he, with mixed humor and anxiety, had apprised of the resemblance, were slow to acknowledge it. Hagit was actually indignant. "You're heartless!" she cried. "Your mother was never that ugly or awful-looking." Rivlin's sister, on the other hand, who had hated their mother, thought the double was better-looking. She understood her brother's fascination and stood for a long time by the window herself, smiling with grim satisfaction at the ghost as though viewing her in a peep show with no risk of a reprimand. Rivlin was so intrigued by the discovery that during their first month in the apartment he asked Tsakhi to bring him a pair of binoculars from his army base. Magnified, their neighbor resembled his mother—a strident peacock of a woman who had painted herself with flamboyant colors until her dying day—less closely. She used no makeup and had a yellowed, time-weathered face like that of an excavated sphinx. At first he took care to observe her from a place of concealment, afraid that he and his binoculars might drive her away or cause her to complain. Eventually, however, he realized that the danger was nil, since her gaze was always directed downward, as if the world lay only in that direction.

Now he would be parting from her for two weeks. He couldn't say he'd miss her. Yet sometimes, observing her in an idle moment, he had found a strange consolation in her manner, so familiar to him from his childhood. The difference was that this time, he felt no guilt or sense of obligation.

## 11.

ON THE TWENTY-THIRD floor of the university tower, on a desk in the office of the Near Eastern Studies Department, surrounded by student papers and faculty mail, sat a round copper tray filled with baklava. It was a gift from the attentive bride to the teachers who had missed her wedding, so that they wouldn't feel left out.

"It isn't fair," Rivlin protested. "The slackers shouldn't be rewarded."

"You can't deny that the effort was worth it," said the secretaries. They were treating him, the morning after, with an excessive friendliness. "It was a brilliant idea to go see our whining students in their natural habitat. They're so different in their own world. And how we enjoyed your delightful wife!" They already missed Hagit, who had vanished and left them once more with her morose husband.

"Yes. She knows how to have a good time," the professor admitted with a tight-lipped smile. "That's because I take such good care of her. Why shouldn't she?"

They chuckled at his outrageousness. They had tended to his needs for so many years that they couldn't imagine him doing the same for somebody else. Although it was awkward for him to be striking such an intimate note with these two women, with whom he had always been so formal, he knew that whoever was introduced to his wife did not quickly relinquish her. Perhaps she represented a path to him.

The door of the department head's office was shut. He was wondering whether to enter and tell Akri how pointless his previous night's harangue had been when the secretaries decided for him. "Professor Akri," they told him, "would like to see you."

Rivlin stepped into the large, brightly lit room that had long been his office. Even though he was glad to be relieved of the burden of running the department, he had left some of his books on the shelves and even kept a key as a way of retaining part ownership.

"Professor Tedeschi is in a coma," Akri greeted him. A normally taciturn man, he kept an orderly workroom. Mounted on his computer were photographs of his two grandsons, one blond and one dark like himself. Perhaps they had helped to inspire his theories about the wrong turn taken by Arab history.

"So I've heard," Rivlin answered dryly. He felt disappointed that Hannah Tedeschi, not content with his sympathy for her husband, had also turned to a more mediocre scholar than himself. If Tedeschi valued Akri, it was only for the thoroughness with which the new department head helped the old man to index and footnote his articles. "How come," Rivlin asked, "you're still afraid of his wife's hysteria after having been his teaching assistant in Jerusalem for so many years? Don't you realize that she needs and even enjoys her husband's attacks, which is why she's always so happy to tell us about them?"

Akri's head drooped slightly. Intrepid when battling Arabs, he was cautious about taking on Jews, especially insofar as it might affect his academic career. "This time it sounds serious," he said in defense of the SOS from Jerusalem. "He's been in a coma for two days."

"I know. He was in the exact same coma in April 1992. It didn't keep him from coming to his senses a few days later and giving the opening lecture at that big conference about Arabs and Turks at the Dayan Center. He was also in critical condition in February 1994. For four days he was in another world, but in the end he remembered to wake up in time for a sabbatical at Princeton. And I might remind you that here in Haifa, when he was our guest a few years ago at that mini-conference I organized on North Africa, he passed out after lecturing on the Turkish withdrawal from Algeria, spent the night in the emergency room, and caught a flight the next morning to the Israeli Academic Center in Cairo. The irrepressible Carlo Tedeschi is a devoted husband. As such, he knows that only his illnesses can keep his

"Yes, Ofer, you. You're the hero of his story, just as he is of mine."

A week after that winter night in Abu-Ghosh, Fu'ad returned to work at the hotel—as maître d' with a huge pay raise, though not yet as a partner. If Hendel's main worry was to keep the secret from his wife, Fu'ad's was now to keep it from Galya, the effect on whom, he feared, would be disastrous. And so when he was introduced one day to her fiancé, he was greatly relieved. Now, at least, there was someone to take her away from the danger zone.

He met the groom's parents too, the professor and the judge. As did everyone at the hotel, he considered this new family connection a source of pride and threw himself into the preparations for the wedding. And yet it quickly became apparent that, far from intending to carry the bride off to his own world, the new husband was being drawn into hers. He was already dreaming of a role in the hotel, where he sought to involve himself in the management.

The Arab's worries, far from decreasing, were now made worse. On top of everything, he had to keep Ofer's curiosity and enthusiasm within bounds. And so that morning, when Ofer insisted on descending to the forbidden basement, he did everything to stop him. Yet unable to defy Mrs. Hendel, he had no choice but to toss her the ring of keys, while thinking resentfully, "Before I've even been made a partner, I already have a partner of my own." Could he at least count on him to be discreet?

But Ofer's indiscretion was soon apparent. Before long he had risked his marriage by choosing honesty over love.

"It was the honesty *of* love that made me do it," Ofer murmured passionately. He suddenly regretted burning the letter he had written to Galya in Paris.

Fu'ad now faced a dilemma. Should he protect Galya's marriage by telling her the truth, or protect her family and his hoped-for partnership? He chose the latter, not realizing that this was the greatest fantasy of all. Hendel, saying nothing, quietly hiked his pay again without telling Tehila.

"And so they gave you the boot," Galya concluded, with an odd flourish. "You were driven from the hotel, from the family, from my life, and from my love. And two years later I found another husband, a very different one from you, who takes things as they come..."

"But how do you take things as they come?" Ofer pleaded in the darkness. "Explain that to me..."

"You just do. What shocked and outraged you wouldn't have mattered to Bo'az, because he accepts all that's twisted and perverse in life. He respects the privacy of others to a fault, even if they're close to him—even if it's his own wife. He's never intrusive or clumsy. Even when we make love, he's a world apart. If he had found out or guessed what you did—and perhaps he did—he would have kept it to himself. That's why Fu'ad, although he's not keen on him, is happy not to have to keep an eye on him or treat him as an obstacle."

"I wouldn't have been one either." It was extremely painful to him to think of her making love to someone else.

"Perhaps not. I suppose that's why he had such fond memories of you, even of the way you cried one night in the street. He even wrote a poem about it."

"A poem? About me?" Ofer got up and went tensely to the window. "What did it say?"

"I don't know. He never showed it to me. Anyway, it was in Arabic. He wouldn't let your father see it either."

And then, one day, Galya's father died. Although the whole staff feared for its future, Fu'ad's turmoil was especially great. While he had now taken over the dead man's responsibilities to the point of all but running the hotel, he was no longer guardian of the secret—and with it he had lost, not only his pay raise, but also all hope of becoming a partner.

"You tell it well," Ofer said softly.

"And then, in the middle of the bereavement, your father turned up. For five years, we hadn't seen him. We all felt he had come more to interrogate us than to console us. Even Fu'ad, who treated him like a new father figure and even made him write something in the condolence book, saw through him. "

"Yes. My father told us about that book. Do you remember what he wrote there?"

"More or less. It was addressed to my father. Something like, 'Despite the separation imposed on us, the memory of you still shines with light and generosity. We feel a keen and vivid sorrow at your death.'"

"He really wrote that? Light and generosity? How strange . . ."

"Why?" Galya protested. "Despite all that happened, you can't deny, Ofer, that it was that which attracted you to him, too. But my father wasn't Fu'ad's problem any more. Your father was. And at the same time, Fu'ad liked him. You see, your father sensed right away that he was the weak point in the protective wall around me. At first Fu'ad watched from a distance while your father questioned me twice. You tell me: What good would it have done to tell him about your crazy fantasy and what I thought of it? Would he have felt any better? Would it have helped him to make you less stuck? Believe me, I knew about that too and felt bad for you. I still do. But I wouldn't let him corner me, not even when he absurdly tried playing on my feelings for you. I did agree to answer your letter, so as not to frustrate him completely. I even answered your second one, though both were as nasty as they were anguished.

"Your father wouldn't give up. He came to the hotel a third time, when I wasn't there. And now he began a relationship with Tili, who makes friends easily, especially with older men. It was she, by the way, who sent him to sleep in the basement. To this day I have no idea what she knows or suspects about us, because I don't know whether she noticed you that day. Perhaps my father managed to hide it from her too. I was afraid to ask. It was easier, after talking to Fu'ad, to get up and run away."

"But what made him confess in the end? Was it my father?"

"No." Galya felt a new fountain of emotion welling up in her. "It wasn't your father, although it did have to do with him. Your father could have kept haunting the hotel forever and Fu'ad still wouldn't have talked. All the Arab-speaking professors and Orientalists in the world couldn't have wormed that secret out of him, because even though he lost his pay raise when my father died, he hoped his keeping silent would be chalked up to his credit. No, Ofer, what made him tell the truth was another Arab, one he met through your father. That's when he cracked . . . I mean, opened up. . . ."

"Another Arab?"

"Rashid or Rasheed. Have you heard of him?"

"No."

"Neither had I. But he made a big impression on Fu'ad. He's some kind of driver or guide your father employed. The haunt of the haunt, you might say. It was because of him that Fu'ad decided to discard what he called 'my veneer of being nice.'"

Ofer winced. "Is that what he says it was? Just a veneer?"

"I'm sure it was more than that. He just said it because he was desperate and wanted to provoke me. I've known him since I was a child. It's not a veneer, it's his true self. He's become cynical now because the promise my father made him is dead and buried. Tili isn't looking for partners. She'd go to bed with him before she'd go into business with him."

"But what did that other Arab have to do with it?"

"It started when he and your father talked Fu'ad into going to some poetry and music festival in Ramallah. Those Palestinians would like to be partners, too—in our country. Their own Palestinian Authority isn't enough for them. They can sing all the love songs they want, but in the end they'd like to pick us apart. Anyway, Fu'ad said it made him realize that working for Jews was getting him nowhere. And so he decided to take his severance pay and go back to his wife's figs and olives. Why be loyal to a dead man to protect a family from the truth that's making someone else suffer?"

"Me." Ofer shivered.

"You, Ofer, you. You see, I'm not the only one who kept thinking about you. So did Fu'ad. That Rashid reminded him of you. Not the way he looked, but the way he was. Fu'ad says he, too, has an old love he won't let die. He's a displaced, restless soul. Fu'ad feels sorry for both of you, the way he did when he found you crying by the hotel. Only now he's wised up. He knows that all the poetry of love doesn't mean anything. It won't help Rashid, and it won't help you. I'm the only partner Fu'ad has left. He thinks we should leave the hotel together. Three days ago he took me to that gazebo in the garden and told me everything. I started to shake. 'Go ahead,' he said. 'You have to ask forgiveness to cleanse the baby that should have been his...'"

## 23.

"MINE?" ENCHANTED, OFER TURNED to his ex-wife, clinging to their lost love. "So?" he asked. "You didn't bring me here from Paris just to tell me how Fu'ad scared you, did you?"

She raised her soft, weary eyes to him. "Perhaps," she said discouragingly.

On the lit terrace across the street, an old woman was carefully spreading a cloth on a card table to prepare it for the next day's game of solitaire. He remembered his grandmother's insistence that he ask Hendel for forgiveness. And he had done it. Now it was being asked of him.

He hesitated, then switched on the lamp on his father's desk. Casually, his hand brushed the shoulder of the women carrying the child that should have been his. Her confession done with, her face was tranquil and calm. Did she feel sorry? Had she acted out of love or only from pure calculation?

"Would you like to eat or drink?" he asked.

"Just a glass of water, please."

"That's all?"

"Yes."

He left the study and shut the door behind him, as if to keep her for himself a little longer. The outside world, temporarily erased from consciousness, regained its reality. His parents' duplex was dark and quiet. For a moment, he thought they had gone out. But no, they were in the living room, waiting quietly. Changing course, he went not to the kitchen but to their bedroom, where he found a plastic cup and filled it from the faucet in the sink. He drank, refilled the cup, and returned with it to the study. Galya sipped from it and put it down by the keyboard of the computer.

"You're not cold?"

"No." For the first time, she smiled at him. "My baby keeps me warm."

Why, he wondered, smarting, did she have to say "My"? Unless he breathed some life into the embers of intimacy that had begun to glow again, they would soon go out forever. He wanted to get her back onto the couch, to sit beside her and feel her body. He would have given anything for the kisses and caresses of which the truth had deprived him. But she was too ensconced in his father's chair to be moved—all but her white-stockinged feet, which dangled in the air.

"Can't you at least feel some hate for your father now," he asked, "for wrecking our love and marriage to save himself?"

"He was saving me too. I would never have survived your truth."

"There you go again! If it was *my* truth, what are you asking forgiveness for?"

"I can't judge him."

"But why can't you, damn it?"

"Because I pity him. I don't believe he wanted sex with her. He just couldn't get out of it."

"But what do you know about it?" He felt like weeping. "How can you say that? How can you defend a man who was so brutal to me? I never even told you that I met him one last time after our separation. I begged him in your very words. I said, 'I can't judge, I won't breathe a word of this. Just let me stay with Galya and your family.'"

"You did that after our separation?"

"Yes. I begged for my life. And he cynically blamed his betrayal on me."

"No, Ofer. You're wrong about that. He simply felt that your promises meant nothing. That you only made them because you confused the hotel with me. He didn't believe your love would last. And he was right..."

"But how can you say that? How can you even think it when you see me so torn up, stuck for years in my blind loyalty to you? I walk the streets of Paris without even noticing all the beautiful women around me. All I see is the curve of your breast, the sole of one of your feet..."

"That's just because you're far away. If we had stayed together, your love would have died. You can't accept the cruel, sick complexity of this world. You fight it all the time. Your hatred and envy of my father would have driven you crazy and poisoned us both."

"But your father is gone now. Why not come back to me?"

"Because the memory will haunt us. We'll never forget that you, too, were implicated. That's why you went poking in that basement, even though you were warned not to. There's nothing to regret. Our love was used up. You're just talking yourself into something."

"Don't you dare say that!" He jumped to his feet, pacing the room like a trapped animal unreconciled to its loss of freedom. "*I'm* talking myself into something? I, who go on paying the price for my loyalty and hope? What is it that you want? If I got down on my knees, would you believe me? You say you've come to ask forgiveness, but what does that mean? I kept my promise. I never said a word. Now give me some hope that you'll come back to me, if not now, then some day ... with your child that should have been mine ..."

"I can't. Watch it ..."

"The cup is leaking."

"No, it isn't. That's not where the water is coming from. You'd better call your mother. She'll know what to do...."

## 24.

THREE HOURS HAD PASSED and still the Rivlins didn't know to which hospital Ofer had taken his ex-wife or what was happening there. It was almost midnight. The French Carmel was quiet. The big searchlight in the navy base at Stella Maris shone with bright purpose in the thickening murk. Hagit undressed, got into bed, and switched on the TV. But the curly-headed newscaster whose smiles sweetened the hideous headlines was not on tonight, and she soon switched it off again.

"Come to bed," she told her husband tenderly. "Walking up and down all night won't make that baby get born any quicker."

"But suppose Ofer needs us?"

"At the delivery of another man's wife? You're too much! Come on, take off your clothes. You've had a hard day. And whatever happens, you'll have to take him to the airport tomorrow."

"But shouldn't we at least find out what hospital they're in? Suppose her mother or sister want to know. And where in the world did that husband of hers disappear to?"

"If he's not worried about her, you can relax too. You're not part of this birth."

"Why not?"

She raised her head from the pillow to regard him with amazement. Her hair disarrayed, her face wild with anger, she had lost her last shred of patience.

"Because you aren't! You'll wait for Ofer to get in touch—if he does. And you'll let him live out this day, and his meeting with Galya, and whatever is happening right now as he pleases."

"Of course. Naturally."

"Promise me you'll stay out of it from now on."

"I promise."

"Swear you won't phone or go looking for anyone while I'm asleep."

"All right. All right. . . ."

"No, it's not all right. Swear!"

"I swear."

She smiled. "And now get into bed. You'll sleep better for having sworn."

He undressed and got into bed, turning out the light and snuggling up to her. But the more regular her breathing grew as it carried her surely off to sleep, the more awake he became. His excitement getting the better of him, he disengaged himself and rose. Sleeping pills were out of the question on a night like this.

He entered his study apprehensively, as if the amniotic sac that had burst a few hours before might still be dripping. Hagit, with unusual alacrity, had mopped it up before he could get a look at it. Now, though, in the light of the desk lamp, he saw that his chair was still damp. Overcoming his qualms, he bent to sniff it. The stains had a slight, soapy scent. With a shiver of revulsion, he noticed what looked like bits of white, nearly colorless matter.

Galya had left her overnight bag on the couch. It was open. In it, beside her toilet articles and a book, were rolled her wet dress and underpants. He closed the bag and put it on the floor. Then, covering the chair with a sheet she had slept on as one covers the mirrors in a dead man's house, he sat down, switched on his computer, loaded a chapter of his book onto the screen, and set to work on it. He was getting closer, he thought, to the crux of things that he had been groping for since the spring. Though still not out of the woods, he felt confident that he was onto something real. Yet he wondered if he would ever find out what it was, or if he would remain like a faithful courier with no idea of the message he carried.

True to his pledge to Hagit, he waited to hear from Ofer. One might have thought his son could pick up a telephone and tell his parents, "Galya had the baby." Or, "We're still waiting." Or how the delivery was proceeding, or whether Jerusalem had been informed, or if Tehila and Bo'az were on their way. Or, at the very least, "I'll be home soon," or "I'm staying at the hospital," or "Go to sleep, Abba," or "Wait up for me." Hagit was asleep. He could easily phone every hospital in town and find out. But he had sworn not to.

The editing went well. He worked on the chapter and made such progress that he was almost up to the next one. It was nearly two o'clock. For a moment he imagined that Ofer and Galya would soon come home from a disco, as in those distant days before the wedding.

It took him a while to realize that the tapping on the front door was not imaginary. He hurried downstairs. Through the frosted glass he made out a blurry figure. It was Tehila, standing in the darkness. As though continuing a conversation, she remarked, without saying hello:

"Tell me, am I wrong or did you once live somewhere else, in a fantastic wadi all your own?"

"We moved," Rivlin said. She had hennaed her cropped hair, increasing her pallor.

"I'm told Galya made quite a scene." She gave him a mischievous look as he stood there, blocking her way. "Listen, I'm sorry it's so late, but she asked me to get her bag."

"But what's happening? Has she given birth?"

"There's still time, I suppose," Tehila said, with the nonchalance of an old maid who knows nothing about such matters. "The nurse in the delivery room says she's still not dilated. Bo'az wants to take her back to Jerusalem. We came in the hotel's tourist van, and there's plenty of room for her to lie down. It will be better for everyone."

"But where is she now?"

"Not far from here, at Carmel Hospital. It's nice and clean and she can give birth with a view of the sea. But we have a room reserved for her at Hadassah on Mount Scopus. She'll have to make do with a desert view there, but at least it's the one she grew up with."

"Who told you she was at Carmel?"

"Ofer. It was his decision to call us, because I think Galya would have been perfectly happy giving birth first and telling us later. But he didn't want the responsibility, so he left us a message, and we came running. Just imagine, we even brought my mother!"

"How is Ofer?"

"He's his usual excited, discombobulated self. And very sad-looking. Just see what you've done, Professor. Instead of liberating him as you planned, you and your Arabs have only complicated things. Now he has not only her but her baby to be attached to. Believe me, I still don't get why she had to make him come all the way from Paris. A nice letter would have been simpler and cheaper. But never mind. It's her right. It's even her right to buy him an expensive ticket and charge it to the hotel. As long as you're happy..."

"Me?" Rivlin mumbled. "Happy? I haven't the vaguest idea what it's all about."

She smiled brightly, satisfied with herself as always. "By the way," she added familiarly, "if your wife is awake, I'd love to say hello to her."

"She isn't," he said, horrified by the thought. He had to get rid of Tehila. "Wait here and I'll bring you the bag," he told her.

Yet no sooner had he left his post at the door than she was in the house. Nor did she wait for him in the living room, but instead followed him upstairs, as if he were showing her to a room in a hotel. He had to wheel and turn back when, respecting no bounds, she stopped by the open door of his bedroom to look at his wife—who, curled fetally in a tangle of sheets and blankets, was sleeping peacefully. Shutting the door angrily, he pulled her after him to his study, where she inspected the bookshelves, desk, and couch before reaching down wearily to take her sister's bag and return with it to the bottom floor.

He didn't invite her to sit. She asked for a glass of water, drank half of it, and left, clearly loath to depart.

What was he to make of it all? Although he felt calmer knowing that Galya's family was with her, he was still in the dark.

There was nothing to do but wait for Ofer. No longer in the mood to work at his computer, he sank onto the couch facing the TV and watched, with drowsy disinterest and the sound turned off, an old black-and-white thriller.

At four-thirty there was still no sign of Ofer. Had Galya stayed in Haifa to give birth? Or had they all gone back to Jerusalem together? It was a bad business either way. He went to the bedroom, determined to ask Hagit to absolve him of his pledge not to make phone calls. Although sound asleep, she so logically confuted the case he tried to make that he crawled into bed and dozed off beside her.

HE HAD HARDLY—OR so it seemed to him—plunged to the depths of sleep when he was dredged up from them again. His wife and son, both fully dressed, were standing by the bed.

"Go back to sleep," Hagit said. "Everything is fine. Ofer just wanted to say good-bye. He's promised to return this summer, perhaps for good. I'll take him to the airport. Don't worry."

Rivlin roused himself. This was no way to say good-bye.

"What happened?" he asked. "Did she give birth?"

"No," Hagit answered. "She still has time. They took her back to Jerusalem. Now say good-bye to your son and go to sleep. We don't want to be late."

But he wasn't about to miss the ride to the airport. "You can't leave me here by myself," he implored them. "Take me with you. I promise not to be a backseat driver."

They couldn't say no. Unwashed and unshaven, in a polo shirt and old jacket, he heaved himself like an empty sack into the rear seat. Ofer, his eyes shut and his head thrown back at an odd angle, sat next to Hagit, who gripped the wheel tensely. The traffic, although heavy despite the early hour, moved at a good clip. Rivlin, dead to the world, did not wake up until they arrived at the airport.

After Ofer had checked in, they went for coffee at a small, noisy corner counter.

Father and son, both groggy from their brief but deep sleep, regarded each other with wonder and suspicion, like two lawyers faced with summing up a case that had been thought to be interminable. Rivlin gulped some coffee, not knowing whether his son was as sad as he looked or merely tired and pensive.

"And so in the end," he said, a note of resignation in his voice, "you're leaving us without a clue to what happened or why anyone had to be forgiven."

"That's right," Ofer replied. He gave his father a faint smile, the first in recent memory. "Although you did your best to wreak havoc, you'll have to go on guessing, because you'll never know or understand more than you do now."

Hagit shifted her glance from one to the other, afraid of a last-minute row.

"But why?" Rivlin asked with bitter fatigue, refusing to accept defeat. "Why can't we know? Is it only because you still believe she'll come back to you?"

Ofer said nothing, avoiding his mother's pitying eyes.

Rivlin threw caution to the winds. "You'll be worse off than ever," he declared.

The judge squeezed her husband's thigh like an iron vise.

"No, I won't," Ofer answered serenely. He looked, Rivlin thought, less sad than lonely.

"Why not?"

"Because even if I'm still tied to her in my thoughts, and maybe in my feelings, I'm morally a free man. And that, Abba, is all you should care about."

He swallowed the rest of his coffee, got to his feet, hugged and kissed his father, and disappeared through the departures gate.

## 25.

IT WAS SPRING. The winter having been a real one, with rain, snow, storms, and floods, all Israel felt that it had earned the vernal scents and colors and was entitled to enjoy them before dun summer took over.

The spring semester had started. On his way to the university for the first meeting of his seminar on the Algerian revolution, Rivlin noticed a new traffic sign. The municipality, although not answering his letter regarding the corner of Moriah and Ha-Sport Streets, had acknowledged it nonetheless—not by accepting his suggestion to narrow the sidewalk, but by banning U-turns completely. And so, the professor thought self-mockingly, I only made things worse here, too. So much for citizens' initiatives! Yet on second thought, he had to admit that the new arrangement made better sense. Any U-turn at a busy traffic light like this was dangerous and pointless.

Before his seminar, he went to the departmental office for a list of its students. Knowing their names in advance helped him encourage them to be active. In the office, a new young secretary informed him that a middle-aged woman had been waiting for him all morning. They'd told her that he had no office hours today, but she had insisted on remaining.

He walked to the end of the corridor with a sense of foreboding. There, as he had guessed, was Afifa. Stripped of her jewelry, she wore a simple shawl draped over her head and shoulders that accented her femininity even more.

"Is it me you're waiting for?" he asked gently.

"Who else?" Her voice was anxious yet intimate, as though he were her family doctor.

"But..." He glanced at his watch. "I have a seminar."

"I know. I checked the catalogue. I've only come to give you Samaher's term paper and get her grade."

She wasn't requesting or beseeching it. She was asking for it as you might ask a bank teller for your money.

He made no reply. Leading her to his office, he sat her down unsmilingly, with none of his usual small talk in Arabic, and took the bright green folder. The translated stories and poems were neatly typed, with titles, notes, and two pages of bibliography. He leafed through them and looked up at Afifa, whose black shawl—more a moral than a religious statement, he assumed—deepened the glow in her eyes.

"It looks good," he said. "I'll go through it and give Samaher a grade."

"But what is there to go through, Professor? You already know everything that's in there, even if it was only read aloud to you. Take my word for it, it's everything you asked for. Now give her what she has coming to her."

"*Shu b'ilnisbilha?*"* He couldn't resist a few Arabic words.

Declining to collaborate in a fruitless ritual, she answered in Hebrew:

"Samaher will be fine. She's a strong girl. Her mind is all right again, like before her illness. And she's in a new house her husband built for her at the end of the village. There's no more grandfather and grandmother and everyone else looking over her shoulder. But the whole family and the whole village, Professor, want her to have her grade. I'm here to get it."

He smiled and leafed through the neatly typed work again, studying its matching pages of Arabic and Hebrew texts, the fantastical names of which reminded him of hours spent in Samaher's bedroom and in his own dimly lit office. He felt an old yearning for strange roads and a trusty driver.

"*U'feyn Rashid hala?*"† he asked. "*Lissato bubrum laf u'dawaran hawlkun?*"‡

But Afifa would not play the game. She gathered her shawl around her. "He's a poor devil, Rashid. He spends all his time in the hospital with that boy . . . the vegetable . . ."

"Vegetable? What vegetable?"

"Ra'uda's boy, Rasheed. He ran away to the hills one night, and some hunter with crazy ideas put a bullet in him. Only Allah knows how it will ever end."

"I didn't know!" Rivlin cried, rent by pain. "I remember Rasheed. I'm so sorry . . . Believe me, I loved that little boy."

"So did everyone," Afifa said angrily. "A lot of good it did him! A

* What's up with her?
† And where is Rashid now?
‡ Is he still hanging around you?

lot of good it did my mother, the boy's grandmother, who only wanted all her children home again! What has it brought us? A vegetable...."

Rivlin glanced at his watch. "And you?" he asked Afifa, who now had not only his sympathy but his esteem. "Don't you want to finish your B.A.?"

To his surprise, she didn't reject the idea.

"Allah is great...," she replied, leaving the matter open while continuing to regard him with suspicion, as if he were looking for another excuse to postpone Samaher's grade.

"Leave Allah out of this," he said bitterly, as if suddenly identifying the real problem. "Great or not, he has nothing to do with this. Go to the secretary and register. What's it to you? There's no obligation. Go on, don't be afraid. Now that Samaher has left home, you'll have time. Sign up for a course, mine or anyone's. Meanwhile, I'll grade this paper."

Although he hadn't meant to link the two things, this was how she understood it: Samaher's seminar grade swapped for her registration. A smile lit her face. She rose, tightened her shawl around her, held out her white, pudgy hand, and took her leave. Rivlin stayed in his chair, leafing through the paper a third time. Turning to the last page, he wrote an 80. Then, thinking better of it, he crossed this out, and wrote 90. Should he add some comment? He reflected briefly and wrote a sentence that he hoped was meaningful though addressed to no one in particular:

*"I have read, listened, accompanied, and lived with this paper and am pleased with it."*

Although this struck him as rather bland, it was too late to change it. Nor could he think of anything else to add. And so he simply signed his name.

## 26.

IN EARLY SUMMER, three months after Ofer's return from Paris, Tsakhi finished his military service. Remembering his fears when his youngest son went into the army with the thought of volunteering for a commando unit, Rivlin thanked his lucky stars for having enabled him to sleep well at night. The army, deciding it needed Tsakhi's brains more than his fighting prowess, had sent him from the induction center to an intelligence course that landed him in a secret base well-protected from the perils of the Jewish state. His officer's pay had even allowed him to squirrel away a tidy sum in the bank, there having been nothing to spend it on in the secret bowels of his mountain that he was forbidden to discuss even with his inquisitive father.

And yet since this high-interest savings account was a long-term one that could not be dipped into, the provident ex-soldier had no money to pay for the traditional post-army trip taken abroad by young Israelis—a problem aggravated by his intention of traveling, not on the cheap in the Far East or South America, but with his brother in France and Europe. And so, the day after his discharge, he wasted no time in finding a job. In fact he created one, going into business with the blond, baby-faced sergeant who had been his aide. Receiving permission to use Rivlin's computer, the two found room on it, between the professor's reflections on the disintegration of Algerian identity, to design an attractively colored ad for two experienced, responsible, and reasonably priced housepainters and plasterers.

"But what do you know about painting and plastering?" the amazed Orientalist asked. "Who would hire two nerds like you? And how do you know the walls you paint won't start peeling the day after?"

"Don't worry, Abba," Tsakhi assured him. "Nothing will peel." Without his uniform, he looked like the high-school boy he had been before being drafted.

Rivlin had grown accustomed, in the morning hours before Hagit came home from court, to a quiet house in which he was alone. Now he had a young partner—a most pleasant and much loved one, to be sure, but also a noisy and messy one who never switched off a light and who played strange, pounding music.

The blond sergeant arrived that same evening. He and Tsakhi ran off dozens of ads on the printer, waited until late at night for the municipal inspectors to be gone from the streets, and went to stick their notices on every electric pole, tree, traffic sign, storefront, bus station, and café they could find. Their coverage was so extensive that when a week later Rivlin glanced at a university bulletin board on which his colleagues had posted grades, he discovered a piece of paper with his own telephone number on it.

Another week went by, and one morning Tsakhi asked if the old jalopy could be spared so he and his sidekick could transport materials from a large hardware store, whose owners had promised to give them some professional tips. A few hours later, while Rivlin was hard at work trying to abstract a valid generality or two from Samaher's texts, the telephone rang. It was his son, asking whether he needed anything.

"Like what?"

The two youngsters were at the hardware store and wanted to know if he needed any tools, a new hammer or screwdriver, say, or perhaps some spare lightbulbs. They could get everything at a discount.

"No, Tsakhi," Rivlin said, delighted to have been thought of. "I don't need a thing, honestly."

"How about the car?"

"You can have it."

"You're sure?"

"Absolutely."

The main thing the ex-officer wanted to know was whether his father could direct him to the income-tax bureau.

"What do you need that for?" Rivlin asked.

He and his friend, Tsakhi explained, wanted to give their customers receipts. That meant registering with the tax authorities.

"You want to register before you've earned your first cent? Forget about it."

His son heard him out imperturbably and asked again:

"But do you know where they are?"

"Of course I do. But there's no point going there. You've just been discharged. You don't owe any taxes. Why register now?"

"Never mind," the young officer said soothingly. "Just tell me where they are."

"On Ha-Namal Street, near the outdoor market. Ask when you get there."

"Thanks," Tsakhi said, offering to buy fruit and vegetables for the house.

Rivlin was touched. "You needn't bother," he said. "You have enough on your mind. Do your thing."

"You're positive?"

"Well, if you insist, I suppose you could bring home some artichokes."

"How many?"

"You're asking me? Five or six."

"Fine. Anything else?"

"No. Just artichokes." He was impatient to get back to work.

Since their storeroom in the basement of their building was too small for all the ladders, paint cans, rollers, and brushes, some of this equipment was moved into Tsakhi's bedroom, along with a folding cot for the blond sergeant. The two got along well, at least to judge by the quiet, mutually respectful way they sat planning their business. Although the tax authorities were happy to open a file, and receipt books were printed, prospective customers were hard to find. The few who phoned often did so when Tsakhi was out, and Rivlin, who took to identifying himself as "the housepainter's father," had to take their calls.

The problem was the baby-faced sergeant, whose blond hair and blue eyes failed to win the confidence of potential clients, especially given the high prices the two asked for. This led to a revised marketing strategy, whereby Tsakhi's partner stayed below while his former CO, unshaven and wearing paint-spattered overalls, visited the apartment to be painted and gave a low estimate. Then, the deal concluded, he called in his expert assistant to go over everything with a fine-tooth comb and suggest a few extras for a slight increase.

This worked better. The two young housepainters soon acquired a reputation on the Carmel. Returning in the evening proud and pleased after a hard day's work, they lingered in their overalls, wearing them like a badge of distinction while cooking their supper and planning the next day. So great was their comradeship that Rivlin was tempted to come downstairs from his computer to join them. It was a chance to hear about small, old apartments with their rickety terraces and strange storerooms and funny owners, elderly pensioners or widows who, infected by the two young workers' enthusiasm, decided to do another wall or door . . . and then another and another . . .

"What a waste," Rivlin teased. "Here the army invests a fortune in teaching you high technology, and you end up painting walls."

But they didn't see it that way. Heatedly they defended the house-painter's profession, which needed skill and judgment and rewarded them with the bright colors and good smells that they had been deprived of all the years that they had lived, while staring at flickering screens, like moles in the belly of their mountain.

## 27.

THE DAYS WERE GETTING warmer. Rivlin, opening his study window as far as it would go, tried longingly to remember the aroma of spring flowers that had bathed their old apartment in the wadi. His eyes, tired from hours at the computer, instinctively sought out the old woman across the street. She, too, had raised all the blinds on her terrace. A large ladder was standing there. On it, Rivlin was astonished to see the blond sergeant. He was talking to the young officer, who was seated at the card table, while slapping plaster on the wall.

Without thinking twice, or even saving the text on his computer, Rivlin left the duplex and hurried excitedly to the building across the street, in which he had never been before.

He didn't know the ghost's name. But he did know her floor, and he knocked on her door without looking at what was written there. The old woman, wearing a large apron and a hairnet, opened it. The smell of some cheese dish came from the kitchen. A radio on the terrace was playing the rock music his son liked. The ghost's face was soft and smiling, unlike the time he had met her in the pharmacy. Perhaps this was because she was in her own territory, protected from all harm by two sturdy young workmen newly discharged from the army.

"Good morning, ma'am," Rivlin introduced himself. "I'm the boss of the two painters working for you. I came to see how they're doing and to ask if you're satisfied."

The ghost's weather-beaten face gaped at him. She looked back into the apartment, as if racking her brain for something to complain about.

Meanwhile Tsakhi, hearing his father's voice, appeared in the hallway, a lively mixture of amusement and astonishment in his big, brown eyes.

Rivlin warned his son with a look not to give him away. "I want you to be entirely satisfied with my staff and their work, ma'am," he continued. "You should feel you're getting the best possible service. That's why I need to know if you have any complaints. Think carefully. Perhaps they've been noisy, or impolite, or not neat enough. Just tell me. I'll give them a piece of my mind and change them immediately. Why, if you'd like I'll take their place myself. Just say the word and I'll put on my work clothes...."

This was already too much for the ghost. The smile of pleasure fracturing her face was positively alarming. So much consideration could be fatal for a hard-bitten woman like her.

"There's no need," she murmured, thrilled and grateful to be getting such attention. "Everything is fine. Don't put yourself out. Your workers can stay. Just tell them to hurry up and finish..."

"You're sure? Perhaps you'd like to think about it."

"Oh, no." She was suddenly worried she might lose them. "They're just fine. They're nice boys..."

Brimming with pride that his younger son had vanquished so fearful an apparition, he strode quickly out to the open terrace, which was bright with morning sunlight. Curiously, he glanced at the window of his study across the street. Through it he could spot his computer. He went over to the red card table. Despite all the flying plaster, a deck had been dealt for a game of solitaire. He carefully picked up a card. The old woman, though concerned that the strange contractor might ruin her game, said nothing. It was too beautiful a morning to be angry at the world. She stared at the middle-aged man with the gray curls, who did not seem to fit his own job description.

"Tell me," she said, "don't I..." Her clear khaki eyes squinted at him. "Don't I know you from somewhere?"

"No," he said, giving her a firm, friendly smile of encouragement. "You don't know me from anywhere. But now, ma'am, if you don't mind my saying so, you do know me a little bit...."

*Haifa, 1998–2001*

# ALSO AVAILABLE OCTOBER 2004

*Five Seasons*
0-15-601089-5 • $14.00

---

OTHER TITLES FROM CELEBRATED ISRAELI
AUTHOR A. B. YEHOSHUA

*A Journey to the End of the Millennium*
0-15-601116-6 • $14.00

*A Late Divorce*
0-15-649447-7 • $14.00

*The Lover*
0-15-653912-8 • $14.00

*Mr. Mani*
0-15-662769-8 • $14.00

*Open Heart*
0-15-600484-4 • $15.00

wife sane in our morbid Israeli reality. That's why he's always in perfect health when he's abroad. Relax, Ephraim. A week ago he returned from a trip to Tierra del Fuego. It would never have occurred to him to have a coma there."

"Tierra del Fuego?" Although the skullcapped department head found the Tedeschis' far-flung itineraries bizarre, he was not prepared to surrender his concern. "But suppose this time it's real," he persisted, wary of dubious psychological explanations that subverted the rabbinic commandment to visit the sick, hypochondriacs included. "Even if he's only doing it for his wife, shouldn't we be supportive?" He wished to propose to Rivlin that the two of them, after the afternoon's departmental seminar, drive to Jerusalem to see their old teacher. It would give them an opportunity to talk about business and perhaps discuss his little sermon at Samaher's wedding, which was admittedly not beyond challenge. Even if neither of them succeeded in convincing the other, the department head said with a hint of a smile, they would keep each other awake.

But Rivlin had family commitments. Even without them, he would not have been inclined to spend a second long evening with Akri, much less join him in a sick call as if they were equals, either academically or in their relationship with a revered teacher.

Now, however, standing by the window of his little office at the university, which was to be his sole work space for the next ten days, his back to the reinstalled computer on whose screen was not yet flickering the problematic book he had been struggling with for the past year, his glance drifted longingly from the plaza at the foot of the tower to the grayish folds of the mountains of the Galilee where last night's Arab wedding had died out toward morning, and he wondered whether Ephraim Akri might be right. Perhaps this time Hannah Tedeschi's distress call was genuine, more even than she suspected. If he set out for Jerusalem immediately, he would be able to warn the old professor and his wife that one too many make-believe departures from this world might result in a real one, and still manage to get to the airport on time.

Certainly, he was in no mood to switch on the computer in his little office and view his crabbed work, which lacked a core, a justification, and any apparent relationship to the panoramic view outside. Tele-phoning the district court, he left a message for Judge Rivlin, who was in closed chambers, telling her that he was leaving early for Jerusalem before going to the airport and that there would be nowhere to contact him during her noon recess. He knew this would displease her, not so much because she would fear his coming late to the airport or think he was taking Hannah Tedeschi too seriously, as because she liked to be privy to all his whims. If he was going to play hooky from work while she sat in a black robe weighing the fateful dramas of the awe-stricken actors in her courtroom, she at least wanted to know about it.

He stopped by the departmental office on his way to see if there was any mail for him. There was nothing, however, except a polite re-minder to pay his share of Samaher's wedding gift. He settled the debt and consumed the last squashed piece of baklava, glancing idly through Akri's now open door to his desk, at which, undistracted by his departmental chores, the department head sat peacefully im-mersed in his scholarship. Asking a secretary to check the plane's final arrival time, he went to inform Akri that, feeling real alarm for the spuriously ill Tedeschi, he had decided to prod him into conscious-ness by setting out for Jerusalem at once. "That way, Ephraim," he re-marked, "he'll be ready with a bibliographical favor to ask of you when you turn up there tonight."

Akri smiled faintly, the deep flush of his dark face disclosing the umbrage he took. Now that he had tenure, he had nothing to fear from a senior colleague. And yet two promotions from assistant to full professor still lay between them, too great a distance for him not to be stung by Rivlin's sarcasm.

## 12.

"YOU'RE RIGHT ABOUT one thing." Rivlin paced freely around the new department head's office while trying to decide whom Akri resembled more, his blond or his dark grandson. "That harangue of yours needs to be challenged. I'm sure we'll have a chance to debate it sometime soon. For the moment, I'd just like to inquire whether you don't think it was tactless, perhaps even—you'll forgive my saying so—imprudent, to lecture Arabs at an Arab wedding on your theory of ... what is it that you call it? Your Theory of Arab Failure? An Orientalist's Theory of Despair? Yes, your Theory of Despair. I might ask whose despair, though—ours or theirs?"

"Everyone's ..." Feeling his colleague's hostility, Akri braced for a confrontation.

"Well, you should realize that not everyone understands what it is that you've despaired of." Rivlin stared at the photographs on Akri's computer, bitterness welling inside him not only at the grandfather, but at the grandsons too. "You don't have to give me your whole speech again. I've already heard it: your despair is pure, intrinsic, theoretical, with no tendentious political content or ideological agenda. But if I, who have some knowledge of your ideas and your articles, have difficulty discerning their purity of intent, what can you expect of others? The students at the wedding weren't all from our department, you know. Those who were are accustomed to your baroque style and have their semiallegorical, semihumorous way of interpreting it. But there were students from elsewhere as well. Why provoke and confuse them at an idyllic village wedding?"

"But that's precisely the place for it!" Akri declared with unexpected tenacity. "On their own turf, where they feel most at home, surrounded by their favorite foods, totally connected to themselves and to their land. It's only there that you stand a chance of getting them to admit the truth. You know me well. You know I don't look down on the Arabs. I only want to call their attention to a fundamental flaw in their conception of freedom that has spelled tragedy and disaster for them. What did I do wrong last night? I livened up a wedding party with an intellectual discussion in a perfectly civilized way. Didn't our rabbis say that a table without words of wisdom is no better than a pagan altar?"

"Words of wisdom?" Rivlin looked at Akri as if he thought the usually quiet department head had gone mad. "Whose wisdom? You demolished their past, you defamed their ancestors, you attacked their honor, you enumerated their every weakness, you told them they have no future. Do you really think they're a merrily self-flagellating band of masochists like us Jews?"

"No one is a masochist." Akri retained his composure. "I was being objective. I was speaking respectfully and with the best of intentions. Precisely because there were so many young people there, engineers and science majors and future intellectuals, I said to myself, here's a chance to give them a different perspective on their own history— and in their own language, a rich, fluent Arabic such as they love. If we're ever going to learn to get along with them, going to their weddings and making small talk while eating barbecued lamb won't be enough. We have to reach out and touch the truth, even if it hurts. Even if it may be futile."

"You don't say!" Rivlin glanced at his watch. "Well, in the first place, the truth is not so simple. And second, you don't flaunt it at a wedding, not even in fancy Arabic."

This time the hurt flashed from the lenses of Akri's metal-framed glasses. Rivlin patted his shoulder.

"Look, now isn't the time for it. I have to get going. We'll postpone the discussion—but not for long. I'll be your next-door neighbor for the next few weeks. My sister-in-law is arriving in Israel today, and my wife has kicked me out of my study. Tomorrow or the day after we'll have a nice, quiet chat. Not about your truth, or about my truth, but about truth in general."

## 13.

ALTHOUGH HIS SISTER-IN-LAW'S flight was scheduled to land in five hours, there was still, the secretary told him, no arrival time—a first indication of a possible delay. This made it possible for him to drive to Jerusalem with his mind at rest. Indeed, after leaving his car in the hospital parking lot, he detoured to the cafeteria for a bite to eat before taking the large elevator to the third floor. Not that he was hungry. However, he feared that his encounter with his old teacher's illness might spoil his appetite for later.

At first he thought he had been given the wrong room number. The room he entered was small and dark and had only one bed, its bare mattress folded in half as though someone had recently died. His heart sank. Could Tedeschi have made a terrible mistake and gone too far? A moment later, though, he heard the low drone of a radio and noticed that the room had a niche in which the patient, hooked up to three brightly colored transfusions, was lying with his eyes shut. The tops and bottoms of Tedeschi's pajamas did not match. The pants, on which were stamped the name of the hospital, hung agape around his private parts. The shirt was his own; Rivlin recognized it from previous sick calls. The renowned Arabist seemed to be in a state not so much of unconsciousness as of anticonsciousness. His round face, branded by the Argentine sun, was flame red. Only his thinning but still boyish hair, dancing lightly in the breeze of a small fan aimed directly at him, looked untouched.

The female broadcaster finished the news bulletin and began to interview several politicians, seeking to embroil them in an argument. It seemed doubtful that Tedeschi could hear the altercation, much less follow it, although he was usually addicted to the airwaves, which was why his wife had left the transistor on in her absence. He was breathing with difficulty, choked by a severe asthma that was either holding back or forcing up—Rivlin could not tell which—the phlegm gurgling from his depths, prevented by the blue oxygen mask on his face from clearing his lungs with one of the violent coughing fits, commonly commenced after finishing a lecture and taking his seat in the hall, that had shocked many an audience of Orientalists. Although Rivlin had seen the old mentor from whom he had learned so much (however dated some of it now was) in such twilight zones before, and although he had always been able, by pressing on the lever of Tedeschi's fine sense of irony, to lift him over the awkward hump of his self-pity, now, facing the red flame kindled in the Argentine, he felt less sure of himself.

"Carlo?" he whispered, calling the old man by his first name, as had Tedeschi's teachers, Professors Benet, Maier, and Goitein, who had taught the young Italian in the delicately arched buildings of the Hebrew University campus on Mount Scopus in the days of the British Mandate. Although he had been forced to take a Hebrew name upon joining a mortar unit at the outbreak of Israel's War of Independence, during which the old campus was lost, Tedeschi, now a rotund, energetic young teaching assistant, became Carlo again in the university's temporary postwar accommodations and remained so at the new campus at Giv'at Ram, where he soon received his professorship.

The sick man opened one eye and shut it immediately. Rivlin thought Tedeschi recognized him but lacked the strength, or so it seemed, to emerge from his fog and explain (let alone justify) his condition. Most likely he was waiting for his wife—the loyal impresario of his illnesses—to return and bring Rivlin up to date, with her usual brutally frank histrionics, on her husband's condition and hopeless prognosis. Once she had gone on long enough, she would let Rivlin range far afield to the latest academic gossip. That alone, he knew, was capable of rousing his old mentor, not only from his stupor, but even from the grave.

And yet he restrained himself and said nothing, his eyes taking in, with a mixture of curiosity and slight nausea, the ugly yellow puncture marks from the intravenous needles in the arms of this man who as a youngster, in 1939, after the signing of the Hitler-Mussolini pact, had fled Turin for Palestine and wandered there from one lonely asylum to another before beginning the career that was to win him an international reputation as an expert on the decadent but long-lived Ottoman Empire.

"Just what do you call this, Carlo? What's going on?" Rivlin asked softly again, somewhat frightened by the fiery shade of unfamiliar, astonishingly strong red in Tedeschi's face. It was as if the Israeli Orientalist, having gone to the end of the world, had there been transformed into an Oriental himself.

Again one eye opened. Weary and irritable, it quickly shut once more, to protest the impatience that refused to wait for the woman who, with true dramatic flair, would tell the tale of his latest attack. Meanwhile, he stretched his short legs. From between his feet, still clad in the blue plimsolls given to travelers on El Al's business class, fell an anthology of Jahaliya love poems. Finely penciled in its margins were the notes of Hannah Tedeschi, who just a year ago had published a selection of wonderfully translated verse from this same volume.

Rivlin glanced at his watch. If his sister-in-law's flight was on time, he would have to leave for the airport in half an hour. Who would give him credit for his visit if the sick man went on clinging to his comatose state? Leaving the room, he roamed the corridor until he found Hannah, who was talking animatedly to one of the nurses.

"Yochanan? Here so soon? What was the rush? I told you in my message that Carlo wasn't going anywhere."

The visitor smiled at this strange woman, Tedeschi's second wife, who had been smitten by him as a student, after his first wife was committed to a mental hospital. As young as she was, she soon adopted her stormy husband's eccentricities. Cultivating his medical problems was her way of avoiding her predecessor's fate.

"This time," Rivlin said, embracing her loosely, "you've managed to scare me. I thought it best"—a trace of sarcasm crept into his voice—"to get here before Carlo jumped out of bed for some new conference or expedition."

"What on earth are you talking about?" Hannah Tedeschi said indignantly. "What conference? What expedition? Stop being so cynical. Can't you believe what you see with your own eyes?" The cold glitter in her own eyes signaled her satisfaction that Rivlin, Tedeschi's oldest student and close and loving friend, did not take her husband's condition too seriously.

"But I do believe it," he replied, hugging her more tightly. "I certainly do. He looks terrible. He has the most awful color. What do the doctors say?"

"The doctors," Hannah snorted, "don't know a thing. That's the whole problem." Only the constant need to minister to her husband had kept her, the wonderful translator, from an academic career as brilliant as his.

"It's the same story each time," Rivlin could not resist pointing out. "You go from doctor to doctor, and from one treatment and medicine to another, and nothing ever comes of it. That's because you won't face up to the truth."

"And just what might that be?" Hannah snapped, aggressively opening the door to the sick man's room.

"That it's purely psychological. It's entirely in your heads, his and yours." The eternally rebellious pupil regretted his words immediately.

## 14.

RIVLIN, WHO SOON had to leave for the airport, was beginning to fear he wouldn't be able to exchange a word with the defiantly unconscious man, whose wife was now describing, with cruel academic exactness, their tribulations since returning to Israel. In Tierra del Fuego, she told Rivlin, Tedeschi's breathing had been normal, despite the hardships of the trip.

Rivlin, who had no idea why such a trip had been taken, tried to interrupt her torrent of words long enough to understand. "But what were you doing in Tierra del Fuego?" he asked. "What possessed you to go there?"

Tedeschi, it seemed, had been invited to Argentina for a lecture series. And since the government of Italy, many years ago, had volunteered to honor its responsibility toward the young victim of fascism by treating him to an annual week of convalescence from his asthma at any rest home of his choosing—anywhere—the Tedeschis had decided on a Patagonian adventure. After journeying all the way to the bottom of the world, they thought it a shame not to explore what lay beneath it.

Tedeschi's eyelids flickered with humorous anticipation. Having listened with enjoyment to his wife's account of his sufferings, he was now ready for the ironies of his loyal student, his first teaching assistant, whom he had sent to establish a new department of Near Eastern Studies in Haifa before the two of them could get on each other's nerves—get in each other's way—in Jerusalem. With a wave of his hand he signaled his wife to remove his oxygen mask, so that he might converse with this visitor he was fond of—who, however, was more alarmed than ever by the old man's voice, weak and unrecognizably groping.

"How is Her Honor?" Tedeschi managed to whisper before choking almost at once. It was his way of conveying, Rivlin thought, that he would have liked a visit from Hagit, too. At heart, the old man esteemed her more than he did the husband now bending compassionately over him.

Thirty-three years had gone by since the winter evening on which Rivlin, then writing his master's dissertation, had brought an aspiring law student doing her army service to his professor's home. He was already considering marriage and remembered exactly what she wore that night—a black pleated skirt, which made her look fuller than she was, beneath a soft red woolen sweater. Although Hagit hardly spoke and seemed ill at ease in the presence of the great scholar, Rivlin, by now familiar with Tedeschi's overbearing manner, noticed the sweet but ironic smile with which she regarded him. The great scholar, for his part, struck by some force in the young woman, kept trying to impress her with his wit. When, in a display of interest that was considered good manners in those days, she rose and went to the professor's large bookcase to inspect its contents, Tedeschi enthusiastically wagged his head behind her back and winked singularly to tell his pupil that he had made a good choice and should not let her get away.

Years later, when relations between the two men were sometimes strained by mutual accusations of academic betrayal, criticism, and neglect, their memories of this evening, on which the older man gave his fateful and sage nod of approval to the younger one, were still able to reconcile them. Besides being Rivlin's doctoral adviser, Tedeschi had also been partly his matchmaker.

Now, as the conversation continued to proceed along medical lines, including the results of Tedeschi's latest blood and urine tests, Hannah Tedeschi removed the plimsolls from her husband's feet to show Rivlin that, far from having just another attack of asthma, the famous Orientalist was suffering from a new and aggressive form of inner rot. Rivlin, unable to bear the sight of the chipped, yellowing nails on the old man's toes, reached for the volume of Bedouin love poems.

"I see you're working on a new book of translations," he said, in an attempt to change the subject to more intellectual matters. Hannah, annoyed to have her case history interrupted, sent him a sharp glance.

"I read the five translations that recently appeared in *2000*. They're not only incredibly faithful, they're true poems in their own right, works of art. It's unbelievable how perfectly you captured the two aspects, the comic and the chilling, of Al-Hajaji's great opening salutation. I've recited your rendition to my students several times in order to make them see that, one thousand four hundred years ago, the despotism of an Arab tyrant could also be delicately ironic."

He positioned himself in the center of the room and recited:

"I, a man of much renown, still aspire upward. When I strip off my turban you shall know who I am....

"O inhabitants of Al-Kufa! I see heads ripe for plucking. I, their master, see the blood between the turban and the beard...."

"*As though* I see the blood...." The translator corrected him gently.

"Of course. *As though*. What a marvelous version of the line, *Waka'ani anzaru ila al-dimai' bayna 'l'amami w'al-laha.* You've done a great thing, Hannah. We'll never forgive you if you go adventure-hunting again in Tierra del Fuego instead of giving us more ancient Arab poetry in such wonderful translations. Who else could do it so well?"

Standing in the middle of a hospital room with her husband's plimsoll in her hand, kept from finishing her stirring account of his maladies, the translator, though her work had already been acclaimed in a weekly literary supplement, was unprepared for such kudos from a full professor. Granted, Rivlin's field was history, not poetry, but he was a connoisseur of the latter, too. The bitter resentment on Hannah's face yielded to a look of surprise. She seemed not to know what to make of Rivlin's sudden panegyric. The bright flush in the sick man's face, however, left no room to doubt that he took pleasure in the compliments lavished on his wife. He broke into a cough that grew steadily more violent.

## 15.

WHETHER TO CALM her husband or merely keep him from talking, Hannah hurried to replace the oxygen mask.

Tedeschi shut his eyes painfully, his cough burbling out in a fresh supply of oxygen. Unbuttoning his pajama top, he bared a chest that rose and fell like a bellows.

"Where," sighed the translator, "am I to find the peace and quiet to translate love or battle poems? You know that Carlo's jubilee volume is supposed to be coming out soon. All the material is ready except for the article you promised."

Rivlin scratched his head. "Yes. That article. I can't seem to finish it. . . ."

Tedeschi's eyelids fluttered again. Choking or not, he wanted to hear his ex-student explain why it was so difficult to finish an article.

"We've just moved to a new apartment in a new building. The whole transition, not to mention the actual construction, has been brutal. Hagit can't take time off from her trials, and the whole burden has fallen on me. I've actually become stupider this past year. My brain has shrunk. I've lost my concentration. And the Arabs have driven me to despair. How can you write with any sympathy about the Algerian freedom fighters of the nineteen forties and fifties when you see the terrible carnage going on there now? It's insane, the terror they've let loose."

"But what do you care if they're murdering each other now?" Hannah Tedeschi rebuked him. "You're writing about the past. And who says you have to love Arabs to write about them? You promised us an article. Don't you see the state Carlo's in? We can't put out a jubilee volume in his honor without the participation of his best-known student. Think of how it would look. . . ."

Rivlin smiled uncomfortably. "Most successful student" or simply "best student" would have made him happier. He did not always like having his name linked to that of the Jerusalem scholar, whose recent work was rather weak. He glanced at his watch again. It was time to leave for the airport. Relieved that he had eaten before being exposed to Tedeschi's feet, he laid his arm on the old man's shoulder in farewell. "It's all psychological," he almost reiterated, feeling impelled to repeat his diagnosis. But he caught himself in time.

"You can expect another visit tonight. A ritual one. Ephraim Akri wishes to do his religious duty. And Hagit and I may come together on Saturday."

Tedeschi looked agitated, as if unwilling to part so soon.

"What is it?" asked his ex-student with genuine concern. The old professor did not reply. His face was angry and tense. Fearful of another

spasm, he kept on his oxygen mask and pointed, with an arm connected to an IV drip, to the empty bed by the door.

What does he want of me now, Rivlin wondered: to become the
patient next to him? If the amusing farce of Tedeschi's illnesses
turned into a soap opera, little would remain of the old man's charm.

But Hannah understood better. "Carlo is right," she said, happily
remembering. "We forgot to tell you who just died. We watched him
fading all night from a stroke. What's the name of your son's father-
in-law?"

"My son's father-in-law?" Rivlin took a backward step and regarded the folded mattress as if the death might still be hiding in its
crevice. "Who are you talking about? My sons aren't married."

Tedeschi, who was following the conversation intently, began to
strangle beneath his mask.

"But you know who I mean. Your in-law!" Hannah fought to uphold the death that had taken place. "Don't be stubborn, Yochanan.
Listen to me. I'm telling you a fact. They brought him here a few days
ago, at night. It only lasted a few hours, but we both recognized him.
He was your in-law. Your ex-in-law, anyway. I just can't remember his
name...."

"Hendel?"

"Hendel? Let it be Hendel. We weren't told his name. It went with
him when they wheeled him out of here."

"But where did you know him from? How did you know who he
was?"

"What do you mean, how? We remembered him from the lovely
wedding you made for Ofer here in Jerusalem. The tall man who
owned a hotel. It was him. You can check for yourself. How could you
not have known? Don't you read the newspapers? You haven't been
in touch with the family?"

## 16.

"WHY SHOULD I have been?" Rivlin answered angrily, his departure
now strained. "What for? There were no grandchildren to share with
them. We haven't heard from them for five years. There was no need

to stay in touch. Not that we have anything against them. But there's nothing going for them either. I must have told you: the marriage ended suddenly, after a year. There were no explanations. Ofer's wife simply left him...."

A few minutes later he was in the corridor. Without waiting for the elevator, he dashed excitedly down the stairs as if in hot pursuit of this latest death, one half-suspected by him of being purely imaginary, the joint hallucination of two hypochondriac Orientalists who, not satisfied with the real patients, doctors, and medical instruments all around them, had gone and invented even more.

He hurried to the parking lot, stopping at a public telephone to make sure before driving back down to the coastal plain that his sister-in-law's flight was on time. Not only was it not on time, however, it was delayed, he now was informed, by a shocking four hours, as if it had run out of gas in midair. His first thought was of how annoyed his wife would be when she found out that he had left early for Jerusalem. Had he remained in Haifa, her usual good luck would have enabled her, with this assist from the airplane's engines, to join him at the last moment on the ride to the airport that she liked so much.

For a moment he considered not calling her. However, knowing that she would later interpret this as a deliberate evasion, perhaps even an admission of guilt to an indictment he could not foresee, he phoned home, and felt relieved when no one answered. Leaving a short, vague message on her voice mail, to strengthen his alibi he dialed the court. There he was informed that Hagit's session had ended and she had set out for home. He knew she would take her time making the rounds of the bakeries, delicatessens, and flower shops that would turn their immaculate home into a sumptuously festive one.

Keys in hand, he stood uncertainly by his car. Should he leave Jerusalem, the city of his childhood, and drive to his sister Raya's home, which was near the airport, where he could rest? Or should he remain here and take advantage of the blank hours at his disposal to renew some old tie that had lapsed or carry out some neglected obligation?

Already, however, his legs were carrying him back to the hospital to confirm the Tedeschis' cheerfully delivered obituary. Doing so was easy. Considering the obstacles put by large hospitals in the way of those trying to locate the living, the process of uncovering the well-documented fate of the dead posed no problems. Before long he had all the information he wanted. Tedeschi and his wife had not misled him. The folded mattress had indeed belonged to his former in-law, who had hastily departed the world three days earlier. Rushed to the hospital in the evening with an excruciating headache, he had lost consciousness that night and died the next morning.

There was, Rivlin thought, something fitting about the freedom, even the sense of mission, with which the hospital's officials disclosed the details of Mr. Hendel's death. With these details in hand he adjourned to the cafeteria, where he sat trying to put in order his welter of emotions. Above all, he felt sad for the deceased, an impressively optimistic man his own age who left behind—Rivlin remembered her well—a delicately attractive, childishly dependent wife. She could easily, he imagined, feel lost and driven to despair. There flickered in him an old regret for the loss of his burgeoning relationship with her gentlemanly husband. Warm, although restricted to practical matters, it had been cut short abruptly five years ago.

And yet as he sipped his Turkish coffee, which he was counting on to keep him awake through the long day still ahead, he was not surprised to detect in his regret, like the grain of cardamon in his drink, the sweet, subtle taste of revenge. He felt it not only toward the daughter of the dead man, now deprived of a father to whom she was greatly attached, but toward the deceased himself, who had refused to join him in preventing the bitter divorce or even understanding the cause of it. Rivlin shuddered, struck by the realization of a new loss. Besides the friendship written off five years ago, he was now deprived of his last link to what had happened. Ofer himself behaved as if the young wife who left him was forgiven, perhaps even forgotten. But a father's heart knew better. His son was only pretending to have gotten over it.

## 17.

WHICH WAS WHY he felt an urge to leave the hospital and go to the place itself, the family hotel surrounded by pine trees at the southern end of the city. To cross the thick carpet of sighing pine needles, descend the reddish stone stairs flanked by oleanders and laurels, catch the sudden glimpse of the blue nugget of Dead Sea beyond the wilderness of the Judean desert, and knock on doors of the wing of the building where the family now sat in mourning: mother, sister, brother, and others he had got to know in that brief year—an aunt, an uncle, several cousins, and even, if she had not meanwhile died before her son, the dowager grandmother who was the establishment's first proprietress. On their infrequent visits to Jerusalem in the five years since the divorce, he had felt that his wife, without admitting it or perhaps even being conscious of it, had thwarted all his attempts to approach not only the hotel but even Talpiyot, the neighborhood in which it stood. Once, two years ago, while strolling on the promenade overlooking the old walled city from the south, he had suggested visiting the Talpiyot home, now a museum, of the author S. Y. Agnon. Hagit had refused. "Why risk running into someone who doesn't want to see you?" she had said, with characteristic bluntness. "What does that mean?" he shot back angrily. "That we're barred from Talpiyot forever?" "Not forever," she'd answered, slipping an arm around him. "Just for now." But now he was in Jerusalem with time on his hands and no one to judge him or tell him what to do, and with a valid reason to stop by the hotel of his former in-law, whose death had provided him, if not with the duty, at least with the right, to pay a call during the seven days of bereavement.

He debated whether to phone home again in the hope of finding Hagit or simply to tell her about it back in Haifa. By now, though, he was in Talpiyot, scouting the familiar surroundings. The pine wood, in which he had often played as a child, were the same, yet changed, as were the garden and the yard. He hadn't thought he would be so moved by them. All that had been rendered impossible by the divorce, it appeared, was still preserved in the sweetness of memory, sealed against being opened by a golden film of anticipated pain. How terribly easy it was for him to relive the unforgettable night of the wedding, so private and so public at once, just as was the garden with its catered events and the hidden home in which Galya, Ofer's bride, had grown up. It was this combination that so appealed to Rivlin—who, together with Hagit, was warmly treated as family whenever he was sighted by the staff on the garden's paths. Already during their first meeting, when the marriage was a foregone conclusion, Galya's father had generously offered them the freedom of the grounds. Indeed, he told them, he had decided to expropriate the hotel from its customers not only for the wedding ceremony, but for three whole days of festivities. Moreover, by writing off the costs as a business expense, he would shift the groom's parents' share of the costs onto the income-tax authorities.

At first Rivlin tried turning down this unexpected perk. Mr. Hendel, however, stood firm. "Don't worry," he said. "We'll find other things for you to pay for. I promise I won't lose on the transaction." Rivlin and Hagit, he said, had an open invitation to stay at the hotel at his expense whenever there was a room available. A phone call to the desk clerk was all that was necessary, and there would be no social obligations attached.

Hagit was for resisting temptation. "We can afford to pay for our own hotel room," she told him. Yet in the end she, too, gave in to their future in-laws' entreaties, and on their next visit to Jerusalem, which was to see the young couple's new apartment, a month before the wedding, they had spent the night at the hotel in a modest but tasteful room whose window looked out majestically on the desert and on the great salt sea in its folds. Needless to say, they stayed at the hotel again during the three hectic days of the celebration, when they were given a suite facing the Old City.

And yet in the course of the brief year between the wedding and the divorce, Hagit had managed, however politely and apologetically, to keep Galya's parents and their enticements at arm's length. In the end Rivlin feared being taken by them for a snobbish intellectual. And so, arranging to appear at a meeting of the Jerusalem Orientalists' Society, he used the opportunity, much to Hagit's chagrin, to spend the night in his in-laws' hotel. There he had been showered with attention sufficient for both himself and his missing wife.

## 18.

THE MANY DEATH notices by the entrance and at the reception desk with its old lithographs of Palestinian landscapes, and arrows pointing the way to the mourners' quarters, spelled out the demise of the family's privacy. Rivlin was reminded of the first question he had asked Galya's father on being introduced to him. How, he had wanted to know, could a family live a normal life in the middle of a hotel? In reply he received an exact description of Mr. Hendel's formula for separating the two spheres. As it was unnecessarily wasteful, in the proprietor's opinion, to keep them totally apart, and since he had at his disposal attractive rooms, a kitchen that had to stay operational, and a staff of chefs, waiters, and chambermaids without always enough to do, he had decided long ago to lodge his family in the hotel. However, he had made it clear from the start to his three children—especially to the youngest, the spoiled little girl who was to be Ofer's future bride—that their right to a life of luxury, with serviced rooms and daily meals chosen from a first-class menu, depended on their self-restraint, it being incumbent upon them to conceal the existence of their private lives from the guests, who needed to maintain the illusion that is cherished by each guest, even if paying for a single night alone: that the establishment is as exclusively devoted to his comfort as if he were its sole owner.

It was, thus, astonishing to see this inviolable rule rudely shattered by the death of the man who had decreed but could no longer defend it. Plastered over the entrance, the lobby, and the door to the dining room were sorrowfully worded death notices in English and in Hebrew, as if all at once the family had decided to tear down the curtain hiding it and permit—no, compel—the guests to share its unexpected grief.

It was 3:20 P.M. His sister-in-law's flight would not land before seven. Rivlin had time to spare. Resisting the printed invitations to the bereavement, he decided to wait until four and let the mourners enjoy their afternoon nap.

He wouldn't have minded a nap himself. The day was turning out to be longer and more tiring than he had anticipated. He went over to an armchair in the lobby and swiveled it around to face the garden— the same garden full of flowers, lit by a pure Jerusalem noonday sky, that he remembered from his anxious childhood. Had it been this rich with color the last time he saw it, or had it been enlarged and transformed over the past five years with new flowerbeds and shrubs? His eyes followed a path that led to the lawn. On that lawn, close to midnight, the bride, her veil and bridal train discarded, had enticed him to dance with her. Thrilled, he had moved cautiously but freely to the music. He had not danced since his student days, he explained to Galya's family, because his wife, afraid, perhaps, that she might blur her judicial boundaries, would not go along with it. This made Galya turn to Hagit and demand that she join them. Most of the wedding guests had gone home. Only close family and friends remained, and Hagit yielded and danced, first with him and the bride and then with their two sons. Though shy and hesitant, she was graceful. He had felt a deep surge of happiness. It was as if his son's marriage, more than any book or article he had written or could write, were his life's great achievement.

Now, although he had made up his mind to pay his respects, he lingered in the armchair, to give Hagit time to return home, unpack the treats she had bought, and set the table. It wasn't that he needed to ask permission for something he knew would seem pointless to her, but simply that he wished to be aboveboard. The last twenty-four hours had been full of good deeds: first his attendance at the Arab wedding, then his visit to his old professor, and now this condolence call on a family to which he no longer belonged.

He sat regarding the flowers and the light on the lawn, his fond memories of the wedding mixed with thoughts of the failure that had followed and the death that had just taken place. Actually, a great deal had changed in the last five years. Evidently, the hotel had done well. The little knoll that had been part of the desert beyond the hotel grounds was now annexed to the garden, and the old dance floor, with its grapevine-trellised gazebo that had served as the wedding canopy, had been replaced by a new swimming pool and a small amphitheater. Even five years ago the term "family hotel" had struck him as overly modest. Now it seemed more like a boast: that amid so much luxury an intimate touch could still be preserved.

Rivlin let himself be drawn into the garden, as if he were in search of the vanished gazebo. In fact, it had not vanished at all. Rather, it had been thoughtfully moved to higher ground, its ancient foliage of grape leaves replaced by bright bougainvillea. Beneath it they had stood that night, all six of them: the groom, the bride, and two sets of parents. He walked warily toward it. New spotlights were hidden in the bushes. He shut his eyes and remembered the long-ago twilight in which he, the father of the groom, had felt like a newlywed himself. And why not? There, by his son's side, he had pledged anew his troth to his wife and forged a new blood-tie to a young bride he hardly knew. Now he strode to the spot on which Ofer had stood and where he had reached out instinctively, midway through the ceremony, for his mother's hand. Humiliation and anger mingled with the sweetness of the memory.

## 19.

HE LOVED HIS wife's way of answering the telephone. Her soft, cultivated "Hello" was alive and attentive. There was nothing remote or fuzzy about it. And now it also tingled with the expectation of hearing a sister's voice. Hence her angry gasp of disappointment when she heard that the flight was late.

"Why didn't you call me before?"

"You weren't home. I tried you at court, but you were gone."

"Where are you now?"

"In Jerusalem."

"Still in Jerusalem? What are you doing there? Are you with Tedeschi in the hospital?"

"No. I left."

"How is he?"

"It's a more serious attack than usual. You should see him. He's red as a beet."

"Is he really unconscious?"

"I'd say half-conscious."

"Which half?"

"He has difficulty talking. But he listens. He can follow."

"But what was so urgent about seeing him? You're always complaining that you have no time for work. Why look for still more things to do?"

"As long as I was going to the airport, I thought I'd make the gesture. I had a hunch the flight would be late."

"What kind of hunch?"

"At eleven o'clock there was still no arrival time on the recorded announcement at the airport."

"But if you thought the flight would be late, you should have waited for me. I would have gone with you. You know how upsetting it is for me not to be there."

"I never imagined the delay would be for four whole hours. I thought it would be a small one."

"You could have waited to find out. What made you rush off to Jerusalem? Since when is Tedeschi so urgent? You keep saying his problems are psychological, and suddenly you're in a panic over him."

"In the first place, psychological problems deserve attention too. And second, Hannah's telephone call yesterday worried me. Sometimes people just go and die on you."

"Not Tedeschi. You can count on him. And even if you had nothing better to do, you could have waited for me. Or at least let me know. I would have come with you. I care about Tedeschi too. I'm shut up in a dark courtroom with all kinds of shady characters and you're gallivanting around the world."

"What kind of gallivanting? I went to the hospital."

"Hospitals can be fun, too. You might have waited. It was another of your premature ejaculations...."

"Are you out of your mind? What kind of way is that to talk? Me...?"

"I didn't mean it like that. I was talking about life. About living. You know how I love going places and seeing things."

"Nothing will be gone tomorrow. What have I done? It's not my fault the flight was delayed. It inconvenienced me too."

"But what are you doing now? You still have three hours left. Go to Raya's. You can rest there until the plane lands. Does your back still hurt?"

"My back?"

"This morning you said you had a backache."

"It's gone."

"You should rest at Raya's anyway. You can lie down there. I just spoke to her fifteen minutes ago. Start out now. We rose early today.

You're not a young boy anymore. You can't just keep going. Take a nap. By the way, it was nice of you to wash the curtain."

"Especially since it wasn't dirty."

"Nothing is ever dirty, in your opinion. But what counts is that you washed it. Start out now. Raya is expecting you. I'll phone in an hour."

"Wait. Listen. Something's come up. Listen to this. Her father died."

"Whose father?"

"Yehuda."

"Yehuda who?"

"Hendel."

"Yehuda Hendel died? When?"

"A few days ago."

"Who told you?"

"Carlo. Hendel was in the bed next to him. He had a stroke one night. He was gone in a matter of hours...."

"But why should Carlo have mentioned him?"

"He remembered him from Ofer's wedding."

"From six years ago? He sounds pretty conscious to me. How old was Hendel?"

"He must have been about my age. Maybe half a year older."

"How terrible. When did you say it happened?"

"Three days ago. Believe me, at our age you have to read the obituaries every day. If I hadn't gone to see Tedeschi, I'd never have heard about it."

"In the end we hear about everything."

"The question is what you do with what you hear. By my reckoning, they're still sitting shiva at the hotel. As long as I'm in Jerusalem, I might as well pay them a little condolence call."

"Forget it. Why get involved? Send them a letter. You write such lovely condolence notes. That way they'll have a permanent record."

"A letter isn't enough. This calls for something more personal. They must be devastated. Just think of Galya's mother, of how dependent she was on him."

"That's why it's better to write and not barge in on them. They won't understand what you're doing there after five years of being out of touch. And it will look strange for you to turn up by yourself, without me...."

"What's there to understand? It's a condolence call. I can tell them the truth. I happened to be in Jerusalem, and you were in court."

"Listen. Do me a favor. Don't go. You're overdoing it. They're not friends of ours, and they're no longer relatives either. You're getting involved for no good reason. What's got into you? I thought you were angry at them."

"I was angry at her, not at him. He never wronged me."

"But he's dead. If you go there now, it's to see her."

"Hagit, sometimes we have to extend ourselves. She was our daughter-in-law. You can't erase the past."

"No one is erasing anything. Write them a nice letter. You're the last person she needs to see now. What can you do for her?"

"I don't have to do anything. I only have to say how I feel. If I died, wouldn't you appreciate her coming from Jerusalem to see you?"

"You know I can't stand your fantasies about dying. That was your family's favorite occupation, imagining how you'd all die and mourn for each other. In my family, death wasn't talked about."

"Like sex."

"Maybe. Not that it ever kept anyone from having children or dying. Listen to me. Forget about it. Go to your sister's, and we'll write them a letter together. Suppose you hadn't gone to Jerusalem and happened to hear that he was dead?"

"But I'm in Jerusalem. I'm even in Talpiyot. Right next door to their hotel."

"You are? What are you doing there?"

"I must have secret longings for the place."

"Longings for what? I thought you wanted to relax. Wasn't that Arab wedding enough for you?"

"Definitely. It was tediously long. That lamb is still sitting in my stomach. It was probably that wedding that made me long for Ofer's. Listen, Hagit. There's no point in arguing. I'm here, and it's my to duty drop in on them."

The judge paused to assess her husband's intentions and reevaluate the battlefield before answering.

"All right. But remember. Condolence calls are short and sweet. You don't want to hold up the line behind you. Don't overstay your visit."

"Why should I overstay it? I'll say a few words and leave."

"And remember to give them my condolences too. And to explain that you did all you could to keep me from coming with you."

## 20.

HE HEADED FOR the third floor, where the family residence was tucked away in a wing of the hotel, but the arrows directed him to a reading room on the second floor, which had been converted into a receiving room. He was surprised to see how many callers there were, among them even some hotel guests. In a corner stood a huge table with some bottles of water and a large condolence registry tended by an elderly Arab waiter in a black suit and bow tie. His presence added a solemn formality to the occasion.

Rivlin did not wish to be recognized at once. First he wanted to spot the ex-daughter-in-law on whose account he had come and to observe the state she was in. To his disappointment and curious relief, however, a quick glance around the room revealed that she wasn't there. He had had no idea whether his sorrow for her could get the better of his old anger. On a leather couch, lugged upstairs from the lobby, sat Tehila and Ohad, her older sister and brother, supporting their widowed mother. Dressed in black, Mrs. Hendel was stonily gripping the shoulder of a small boy of about four, apparently a grandson, who had been set on a stool at her feet to help her maintain her equilibrium. For a moment, Rivlin considered beating a retreat. Mrs. Hendel, absorbed in her grief, still hadn't noticed him. Yet a second later Tehila, a tall, unmarried woman who had managed the hotel with her father, gave him a friendly smile, and with a look of respect in her whiskey-colored eyes rose to greet him.

Rivlin shook his head in commiseration and hurried to the widow, who glanced up at him with lovely blue eyes reddened and widened by tears, sorrow, and guilt. The sight of her discharged in-law come from afar to share her grief only reminded her of it anew, causing fresh tears to trickle down her cheeks. More like a lost child than a grown-up woman, she fell into his arms, for the past five years no longer a kinsman's, asking only that he, too, like the others, embrace her tightly and understand, by the limpness of the flesh and bones in his grasp, that the inner kernel of her being had dissolved with the death of her husband.

Of course, anyone aware of the devotion that Mr. Hendel had demanded of his wife and bountifully received from her could have predicted the crushing effect of his abrupt disappearance. But what Rivlin saw now was a total collapse—for instead of feverishly reciting for the umpteenth time, as the newly bereaved are wont to do, the many details of her husband's death and the shock it had given her, she fell back out of his arms and onto the couch in a speechless daze, so utterly absorbed in her sorrow that, as if it concerned someone else entirely, she let her daughter tell Rivlin about it.

"But where is Galya?" he asked, interrupting Tehila, whose account was as long as her father's passing had been brief. "Does she still live in Jerusalem?" Apart from the news of her remarriage, which had reached him and Hagit belatedly, he knew nothing about her.

Galya, it seemed, still lived in Jerusalem. Indeed she lived quite close to the hotel, which was why she had taken a noonday break from the shiva and gone home to rest. Not, Rivlin was told, that he shouldn't wait for her. On the contrary, Mr. Hendel's youngest daughter, having been the closest to her father, was most in need of consolation, especially from someone who had traveled from Haifa for her sake.

Rivlin sat there dejectedly, with a wary brevity giving this family that was no longer his, a résumé of the recent life of its ex-son-and-brother-in-law, before taking advantage of the arrival of a delegation of somberly dressed Mormons, descended from Mount Scopus, to obey his wife's warning against tarrying too long. Rather than leave all at once, he withdrew to the bow-tied waiter, who recognized him and even addressed him by his name and title while pouring him a glass of water. Perhaps the professor, he said, would like to look at the condolence book and its messages, written in several languages, and add a few words of his own. Actually, Rivlin thought such a volume seemed grandiose for a man of Hendel's rank and station. Nevertheless, addressing it not to the survivors but to the dead man himself, he penned a sentence:

> Despite the separation imposed on us by your younger daughter, the memory of you over the years still shines with your light and generosity. We feel a keen and vivid sorrow at your death.
>
> The Rivlin Family, Haifa.

## 21.

HE REGRETTED THE words as soon as he had written them. Yet so great was the appreciation with which the old Arab waiter read them that he was embarrassed to cross them out, and merely turned a few pages of the book to keep them from being the first thing to strike the next person's eye. New callers kept arriving, increasing the noise in the room. The conversation, veering from the subject of Mr. Hendel's death, now touched on the family's plans for the future. His wife, Rivlin thought, had been right. As always. What had made him insist on coming? A brief letter would have been enough. In half an hour the telephone would ring at his sister's and his wife would be on the line, wanting to know why he still hadn't arrived from a visit that he never should have made. He went back to the widow, who sat up like a wind-up doll at his approach. More than words she appeared to need physical contact that could be placed as a warm compress over her dislocated self. Next he said good-bye to Tehila, who seemed upset, even aggrieved, by his departure.

"I'm terribly sorry," he said. "It's by pure chance that I came to Jerusalem, and I have a sister-in-law to pick up at the airport. I'll wait outside a little longer. If Galya doesn't come, please be sure to tell her I was here."

"But of course she'll come."

He went back down to the lobby. A gray light from the desert deepened the somberness of the late Jerusalem day. Springtime clouds, not yet fled before the rainless summer, made intricately changing patterns in the sky. The air was astir with something. Scanning the guests in the lobby for a familiar face and noticing that each was seated before an identical piece of cake, he realized that they were a group of Christian pilgrims from America, Mormons or Evangelicals, of the kind Mr. Hendel had specialized in. Feeling excluded, he retreated farther—not, however, out to the street, but rather back to the garden, with its red gravel path leading to the flowering gazebo. He stood gazing at the entrance to the hotel. Should his ex-daughter-in-law arrive, he would have a chance to scrutinize her from afar before deciding whether to approach her or—relinquishing her forever—slip quietly away.

It was four-thirty. Although there was still plenty of time before the plane landed, he was beginning to feel guilty toward his wife. She had been more farsighted than he had been. What was he to the Hendels, or the Hendels to him, anymore? Nothing tangible in memory could compensate for the ignominy of what had happened or assuage the longing that had reopened like an old wound. It was time to depart the magic of Jerusalem and set out. The dead man wasn't worth the gesture he had made. Rivlin remembered the bitter taste left by their last conversation, five years ago, when—telephoning without Hagit or Ofer's knowledge—he had made a fool of himself trying to find out why the marriage had so shockingly broken up. "Even if I accept it," he had said to Hendel imploringly, "I'll have no peace until I understand the real reason. And I don't think Ofer understands it either. You're the person Galya trusts most. I think you should find out the truth from her and share it with me."

Mr. Hendel had flatly refused. He and his family, he said, were just as pained by the sudden rift, which no one could possibly feel happy about. But if it had to happen, it was better happening sooner than later. Better, too, quickly, rather than nerve-rackingly bit by bit. He had faith in his children and would never want to know more than they wished him to. Besides, anything his daughter might tell him would be treated with strictest confidence. And sensing that Rivlin, who wanted only to cut short the conversation, felt hurt, he had ended on an optimistic note.

"You needn't torment yourself. In a year or two it will all be forgotten. Why worry about it? They're young. Their life is still ahead of them. Each of them will find someone else."

## 22.

AND IN FACT, he had no cause for complaint. The optimist willing to wait for the truth to emerge in time could not possibly understand the sufferer driven in the depths of him to breathe it into life all at once. It gave him a feeling of pleasure, therefore, when Tehila, who took after her father physically as well as in a business sense, now hurried after him along the garden path to beg him to wait for Galya. She was sure to arrive any minute. He couldn't allow himself to miss her after coming so far to see her.

"But I'm the last person she would want to be consoled by."

"How can you say that? Even after the separation, she always spoke of you in the friendliest tones when you were mentioned. She was in awe of your wife. I think she must have been afraid of her."

"Afraid of Hagit?" The thought amused him. "Why not of me?"

Tehila leaned smilingly toward him. "How could anyone be afraid of you? She had warm feelings for you. More than warm. If you ask me, she loved you."

"She did?" Rivlin felt a tremor. "Come on! The way she broke off all ties with us was heartless. It was totally out of the blue. She never bothered to explain anything."

"I'm sure she meant well. She just didn't want to cause you more pain. I want you to know that if, God forbid—God forbid!—it were your wife to whom something had happened..." Tehila crimsoned. "If it had been the opposite, God forbid...your wife or someone close to you...she would have gone straight to see you, just as you have come to see her."

He weighed her words and nodded in gratitude, as if the return call paid by his son's ex-wife on the Carmel had already taken place. Affectionately, he reached out to touch her shoulder. She had inherited not only her father's hard, bony face but also his lanky, aristocratic frame.

"Well then, I give in. But only for a few minutes."

"Why don't you rest while you're waiting? You can even stretch out in this gazebo. How do you like the changes we've made? The place is a lot pleasanter now. I'll bring Galya as soon as she arrives. In the meantime, Fu'ad will be at your service."

## 23.

EVEN THOUGH HE had no wish to cause his wife, who would soon be speaking to his sister, the slightest concern, he decided not to phone her. The longer he could put off the accounting she was sure to demand of him, the better. Meanwhile, over an emptied coffee cup and the last crumbs of his cake, he pondered the encounter awaiting him. The bougainvillea flowering on the old gazebo, which had changed its location but not its charm, and the Jerusalem air freshening toward evening gave him new hope that it still might be possible to redress, if only in small measure, the consequences of the parting five years ago. There were still two hours before his sister-in-law landed, and in any case, she was a woman who took her time and divided her luggage into many small pieces that never arrived on the conveyor belt all at once. Keeping on the safe side, he had at least an hour to get to the airport.

It was twenty after five when Tehila returned with Galya. With them was Galya's new husband, a tall fellow with a short ponytail. One glance at Galya was enough to make Rivlin understand why Tehila had insisted that he wait, for he could see at once that her mourning was of a different and more passionate nature.

She was dressed in black, like her mother, and still wearing her ritually torn funeral blouse. He couldn't tell whether it was the thinning of her hair or her lack of sleep, or something else that had happened over the years, but she struck him as less pretty and more awkward than the image preserved in the wedding album in his Haifa home. The satisfaction this gave him softened his sense of grievance. Hurriedly, before he could say a word, her outstretched little hand still in his, she apologized for her lateness, as though they had had an appointment she had not come on time for.

How different was the stormy bereavement of Hendel's youngest daughter from the quiet composure of her unmarried sister, who stood smiling beside her! Even the new husband, judged by Rivlin to be older than his son, appeared startled by his wife's agitation, at which he slowly wagged his ponytail back and forth.

"There are people," Galya said to Rivlin, "who, because they can imagine their own death, can also imagine the deaths of those they love. It helps prepare them for it when it strikes. But not me, Yochanan. Nothing could have prepared me for this. I keep feeling it as if my father were dying in front of me over and over. There's no net to hold me. Our family—we were more like Hagit's than like yours— we never talked or even thought about death. It was as if life would go on forever. Maybe our brains were addled by all those Christian tourists talking about eternal bliss."

The perfect naturalness with which she mentioned his and Hagit's families gave him a sensation of fresh, intimate directness, as if the separation of five years ago had never taken place. Heartening too, for some reason, was her failure to introduce her husband.

"Has Ofer heard?"

"How could he have?" Rivlin simpered at the childish question. "I myself only found out today—and by pure chance. I was visiting an old teacher who was hospitalized in the bed next to your father's. He remembered him from the wedding. That's the only reason I'm here. Honestly."

The contingency of it, he could see, displeased her. Full of her father's death, she wanted the world to have room for nothing else.

Tehila interrupted them. "I'll leave you two here and go back to my mother," she told Rivlin. She had her father's small, shrewd eyes. "The next time you're in Jerusalem, Yochanan, don't overlook us again. You needn't wait for someone else to die."

She turned to Galya's husband, whose birdlike face wore a worried frown. "You," she said to him, stating a fact, "will come with me."

## 24.

EMBARRASSED BY THEIR failure to introduce him to the new husband, who appeared to have been entirely forgotten by his wife, Rivlin said hesitantly: "You must be..."

"Bo'az." Tehila, answering for him, prodded the young man to come with her.

"... her new husband." With a sheepish smile Rivlin pointed to his ex-daughter-in-law, who nodded in confirmation.

"I'm pleased to meet you. You may know...that I'm..." He choked on his words.

"Of course I know," the new husband said tactfully, smiling back with a pleasant, rarefied mien. "I know everything."

"Everything? But how?"

"I mean, everything I've been told."

Bo'az and Tehila returned to the hotel. Galya went to fetch a metal chair from beside the pool. The old waiter, who had followed Rivlin to the garden, hastened to help her.

It was five-thirty. He would leave at six, come what may. Meanwhile, every second that passed only made him angrier at the silence in which they were sitting. And yet how could he have refused such a rare opportunity, even if opposed by his wife? Galya, too, seemed to have grown suddenly aware of the situation. With a movement he found touching, she fingered the rip in her blouse as if to protect herself against this comforter who had come not only to comfort.

He studied her pale, slightly swollen face, on which, the day Ofer announced their engagement, he had allowed himself, following his wife's lead, to plant a kiss—the first of many whenever they met.

"The fact is," he began, "that you don't deserve this visit from me." His openly aggressive tone surprised and pleased him. "You caused us a great deal of sorrow and disappointment. Not so much by the separation you imposed on Ofer—you had every right to do as you saw fit—as by running away without saying good-bye, let alone explaining why you broke up a marriage we mistakenly thought was a happy one."

Galya was caught off guard. The hand fingering the blouse fell to her side.

"Even if that's so," she admitted in a low tone, "and I did run away, it was because of the friendship and trust we had between us. There was nothing I could tell you. Not because there was nothing to say, but because there was no way of saying it...."

"I don't understand."

"Ofer must have told you something."

"No. Nothing concrete. Nothing that made any sense. . . ."

A wave of relief appeared to pass over her. She blushed with emotion. "Then he must have had his reasons."

"Not at all," Rivlin protested vigorously. "He wasn't evading us or hiding anything, I'm sure of that. He simply had no idea what made you walk out on him with no warning."

"No warning?" She smiled mockingly. "As if that were possible."

"There were signs in advance?"

"Of course there were. There had to be."

"Well, they must have been too subtle for us. In any case, I'm telling you—listen carefully—that Ofer couldn't explain it. That was the reason he didn't want to talk to us."

"Then why keep trying to make him?" She was upset now.

"We stopped doing that long ago. It's a subject we avoid. But even then, he feels our sadness and keeps away from it. . . ." He paused to phrase it more exactly. "I suppose I should say my sadness. I'm less able than Hagit to live with it, perhaps because Ofer is closer to me and more like me. I identify with him more. Listen. I'll say it again. A long time has gone by. We've come to accept your divorce. But I still refuse to accept its mysteriousness. It keeps Ofer from freeing himself like you and meeting someone else."

"You're overstating it," she accused him boldly, almost contemptuously. "There was nothing mysterious about it."

"If there wasn't, so much the better. Then you can explain to me right now what happened, and I'll free myself, too."

And he added softly after a brief silence:

"From you."

"But why from me?" She seemed exasperated. "Why can't you let things be? Maybe we discovered that we simply weren't compatible. Isn't that enough for you?"

"But you were compatible!" exclaimed the ex-father-in-law. "You still are. . . ."

"That's not up to you to decide." She narrowed her large, pretty eyes despairingly. "What do you want from me? If *he* didn't tell you why we separated, he had his reasons."

"Then you tell me!" He was growing more heated. "If it's too intimate, or even...forgive me...too deep or complicated...perhaps
sexual...something you don't want me to know about...then tell
Hagit. You know what a good listener she is. She's wise and she's honest and she's loyal. Believe me, she keeps the darkest secrets from me
as if she had been told them behind closed doors in a courtroom.
She'll keep yours, too."

He felt relieved. Not simply because he had got it off his chest at
last, but because his unstinting praise of his wife, who was no doubt
furious at his disappearance, made up in part for this strange conversation that would only have aggravated her even more.

Galya tossed her head, eyeing him with distrust.

"What happened? Tell me!" He was losing his temper. "Why can't
you give me a straight answer? Or is it that you, too, don't understand
what you did?"

His open refusal to believe her set her on edge. She had lost a dearly
loved father three days ago and now, still overwhelmed by it, needed
all the tenderness she could get, not this cruel rebuff.

"But who says I owe you anything?" Her eyes blazed. "It's over with.
It's all over with. I've remarried. If it were not for my father's death, I
could consider myself a happy woman. It's your son's own problem if
he can't free himself of me. It's not mine. How old is he now, thirty-
two? Thirty-three? If he still doesn't know why I had to leave him,
even though...even though I loved him a lot...then he has a problem. Maybe you do too. Maybe—who knows?—you're even the cause
of it...."

## 25.

A QUARTER OF an hour had gone by. He had to stick to his schedule,
especially because he might yet be caught in the rush-hour traffic
leaving Jerusalem. But if this singular encounter ended now, with no
resolution, he simply would have added to his old torment a new
sense of missed opportunity.

His glance wandered to two pink-skinned Holy Land pilgrims
who, undaunted by the chill evening air, were diving into the swim-

ming pool that had replaced the old dance floor. On that floor, six years ago, a happy and ravishing young bride had determinedly approached a cerebral, middle-aged couple who hadn't danced for so many years that they were as intimidated by the old dances as they were by the new ones. Hesitantly, Rivlin had let himself be coaxed, encouraged by the young people around him. He needn't fear looking foolish, they assured him, because nowadays there were no rules. Next came the turn of his wife, dragged laughing onto the floor by her sons, so that midnight found the two of them pawing the air with their hands and feet like two endearingly wary bears. Mr. and Mrs. Hendel, whose long years in the hotel business had made them excellent dancers, cheered them on. After a while the same bride who now sat sullenly hunched before him had made them all join hands and dance in a circle around her.

"Suppose you're right," he said, trying to outflank the swift passage of time with a hurried admission. "Suppose, indirectly, we too had to do with the failure of your marriage. Isn't that a reason why we deserve to understand what happened? It's painful to think we've been kept in the dark when even your new husband knows all about it. It doesn't matter if you've been inconsiderate or simply scared. As far as I'm concerned, it's all the same."

She said nothing, her resentful glance protesting—justifiably, he knew—the pitiless way he had turned a condolence call into a bill of indictment. His wife had been right again. The visit was ending with a pointless exacerbation of past wounds. In his despair he thrust a lance he hadn't known he possessed.

"Listen, Galya. I'm in a hurry to get to the airport. And you have to rejoin your family. I just want to say that, though we haven't spoken for five years, your father's death is truly hard for me.... We're no longer one family, and I wasn't obliged to come today. Still, you see that I did anyway. This death is a double blow for me, because for five years—secretly, without telling Hagit, because she's too proud to acknowledge her feelings—I've kept hoping that one day it would be possible to ask your father to help me to understand. I've always thought that he of all people, who loved you so much and was so attached to you, was the one to do it...."

His reference to her dead father, he saw at once, only heightened her distress. She rose, the setting sun red on her eyes.

"My father knew nothing. And even if he had suspected something, he would never have revealed to anyone, not even my mother, a secret having to do with me. He respected me totally."

"I know he did. Yet I'm convinced he would have agreed had he known.... What I'm trying to say is . . . had he known the truth about me...."

"What truth?"

He made a supreme effort to pretend that his next words were no more his than the gray birds flying heedlessly above the pine trees he had played among as a child.

"The truth about my situation. I'm talking about my illness . . . because I don't have much time left to live. I'm sure he would have taken that into account...."

"You're ill?"

"Yes," he said. Unforeseen and absurd, the declaration was made calmly. "I haven't much time left."

In the time that remained his imagination wove a narrative of intricate arabesques out of the secret illness of Samaher, the pretended illness of her narghile-puffing grandmother, the actual and deadly illness of Mr. Hendel, who was presently hovering above the two believers in his resurrection who were splashing in the swimming pool, and the illness that he now invented, with its real pain and imaginary symptoms, for an internationally renowned Orientalist improvising a lecture on it from his fantasies.

"Yes," he said again, lowering his gaze to avoid the eyes of the young woman he had forced to factor his death into her father's. "It's a fatal disease that my wife alone knows about—and believe me, she too doesn't know everything. We haven't told Ofer or his brother yet. For the time being, I'd rather spare them. I'm telling you this, while swearing you to secrecy, only to prick your conscience, if you have one, into helping me get at the truth, or at least your version of it. It's not only for my son's sake. It's for my own inner peace as well."

## 26.

STRANGELY, HOWEVER, HE did not insist on an immediate answer. As if they both needed time to recover from the shock of his revelation, he held out his hand in farewell while expressing the hope that his dramatic confession would not keep them from meeting again. The final moments were devoted by him to a few appreciative words about the deceased. Then, adding the wish that the family's sorrow and bereavement might become a source of creation and strength, he gave Galya a light hug, as casually as in the old days, and planted a fatherly kiss on her cheek in testimony to the memories and reckonings that time could not erase. Her body clung to his warmly, as if his approaching death were now one with the death that had just taken place. Pressed against her, he realized with a start that she must be pregnant. He said nothing and hurried to his car. Although it was already five after six, he was sure he would make it to the airport on time.

The traffic out of Jerusalem wasn't bad. At the Kiryat-Ye'arim gas station he stopped to phone the airport. The final time, it turned out, had retreated from its finality by forty more minutes, thus enabling him, if the traffic continued to flow, to drop by Raya's. Apprehensive about contacting his wife, who might cross-examine him about the whys and wherefores of having stayed too long in a place he should never have been in, he preferred to call his sister. To his amazement, she told him that Hagit hadn't tried to get in touch with him. Raya was in the middle of making cheese fritters, a favorite dish from their childhood, and impatient to know when he would arrive. "Are you sure you have enough time?" she inquired. That, he told her, depended on road conditions. "Even if I come," he warned her, "it will only be to wash my hands and face and pop a fritter into my mouth. Then I'll be off."

## 27.

THE TABLE AT his sister's was already set. Rinsing away the sick and the dead at the sink, he called Hagit before sitting down to eat—and found, not an anxious, irritated wife, but a soft and sleepy one, freshly awakened from a delicious afternoon nap, lengthened past the usual span of her naps by her fatigue and the absence of her husband's habitually restless body from her side. "What's happening? What time is it?" she asked, with the innocence of a pampered child granted a special indulgence. "How are you?" Her voice was full of concern for him. "Did you sleep or at least rest at Raya's?" He maneuvered carefully between maintaining a fog of uncertainty around his movements and complaining about the world's many demands on him. "How is your back?" Hagit wanted to know. "Is it better?" "A little," he answered grudgingly, loath to forfeit her sympathy for a condition that had vanished and been forgotten long ago. There was no knowing when it might come in handy again.

"I want you to promise me one more time, darling. Be patient and nice with my sister."

"Don't worry. She's one person I'm always nice to."

"Be nicer than nice."

"Trust me."

"How was the shiva?"

"I'll tell you later."

"Just a hint."

"It's hard for them. Hendel's wife is still in shock, just as I thought she'd be. She's a wreck."

"Did you talk to Galya?"

"Yes."

"What about?"

"What does one talk about at such times? About her father. About death."

"That's all?"

"More or less."

He shut his eyes, recalling his outrageous lie.

"I hope you didn't raise the subject of Ofer."

"Not exactly."

"Not exactly what?" The judge was waking up.

"We'll talk about it later, Hagit. Not now. You don't want me to miss your sister's flight."

## 28.

HE WAS STILL prying open with a finger the shiny eyes of his sister's granddaughter's doll when a plate of golden fritters, their crisp warmth enclosing little slabs of fried cheese, was set before him. It never ceased to amaze him how, despite his sister's indefatigable and never ending hatred of their mother, she continued to make all her dishes, as if determined to demonstrate how simple and even improvable they were. It wasn't easy for him to resist an improved taste of his childhood. In the end he had to plead with her—just as he had pleaded with his mother in her day—to stop plying him with more fritters and to wrap them in aluminum foil for his sister-in-law, who was by now probably circling overhead.

As he had feared, however, it was half past eight before, weary and exhausted, he was able to hold yet another woman in his arms—the fifth of the day by his count, although without a doubt the prime mover of the five. He embraced her gingerly, knowing that her youthful-looking body, which, after a single miscarriage, had borne no children, was thin and fragile at the age of sixty. Five years his wife's senior and a year older than himself, she stiffened self-protectively in the innocent embrace of a devoted brother-in-law who had spent the day on his way to the airport to welcome her.

Ofra herself had been en route from British Columbia for thirty hours. Yet her small, delicate face, rather than showing signs of tiredness, was lit by a spiritual elation only further refined by the six-hour delay for repairs in Dublin. She and her husband, Yo'el, who worked for the United Nations as a consultant on the agricultural economies of developing countries, were not only frequent flyers who had accumulated zillions of points with four different airlines, but also conscientious travelers who loved wandering through the duty-free shops of the world, the details of which they studied as intensely as if they were back in the Zionist youth movement, in which they had met in Tel Aviv, memorizing the clues of a treasure hunt.

What was the point of commiserating with an abused traveler who had enjoyed every minute of the flight and even managed to catch two or three catnaps that, however brief, more than rid her of her jet lag? And so without further ado they set out on the road to Haifa, over which the spring night had scattered its scents and lights, while he told her the latest news of his family, but especially of the young Army Intelligence officer, her favorite (if only because he was named for her father).

"Yo'el and I worry about him each time there's an incident in Lebanon," she said.

"It's not him you need worry about," Rivlin rebuked her, as if annoyed that the two Israeli émigrés didn't convey their concern over the situation in Lebanon to a more appropriate address. "I've explained to you several times that he's at a well-guarded base in the Galilee. If this entire country were to go up in smoke, he'd be the last to be affected. He wouldn't even hear the screams."

Ofra didn't crack a smile. Like her sister, she disapproved of fantasies of violence, even ones designed solely to illustrate how safe her nephew was. She and her husband, though gone from Israel for over thirty years, still considered themselves temporary absentees entitled to demand of those who had remained behind that they take good care of the country.

"I still don't understand what he does there."

"You can't get anything out of him. If you ask me, he's listening to the radio communications of Syrian pilots. Maybe they'll tell us what's going to happen in the Middle East."

"All in Arabic?"

"Unfortunately, that's the language the Syrians use."

"He knows it that well?"

"Well enough to know he's hearing it. And also, I hope, to understand it."

"You wait and see, Yochi. He'll end up an Arabist like his father."

"What for? So that he can be driven to despair? Who needs it?"

She dropped her eyes without answering. "Despair," as his brother-in-law Yo'el told them candidly, was a taboo word at the conferences on developing economies, which were held in the most hopeless of deteriorating countries, that he regularly attended in the loyal company of his wife.

Rivlin switched on the radio. Perhaps a brief exposure to the hourly news bulletin would help acclimatize his passenger to the homeland she hadn't been in for three years. In fact, he doubted whether she would have come now, had it not been for a wedding in Yo'el's family. The two of them were inseparable. If he, for his part, took her along with him into his conference rooms as if she were an agricultural expert herself, she returned the compliment by letting him attend her sessions at the beauty parlor, where he sat reading a newspaper on a revolving chair by her side while giving advice to the hairdresser. Their mutual dependence was so great that he had taken to putting his driver's license and credit cards in her purse, leaving only a few coins in his pocket like a small boy's allowance. He had agreed with reluctance to Ofra's coming to Israel two weeks before him, during which time he would have to go around with his own wallet.

"It's a lucky thing," Rivlin teased his sister-in-law good-naturedly, "that you people have an occasional wedding in this country. Otherwise we'd never see you at all...."

Ofra acknowledged the justice of his reproach. And since he knew she was too tactful to mention Ofer's wedding festivities of six years ago, to which she and Yo'el had dedicated a month of their lives, he took the liberty of telling her about his former in-law's sudden death. Unlike Hagit, she took in stride his desire to revisit the original site of Ofer's botched marriage. She remembered it vividly and listened attentively to his descriptions of the new swimming pool, the refurbished garden, the bereaved ex-daughter-in-law, and her tall second husband with the ponytail.

He was tempted to relate his conversation with Galya. It might serve, he mused, as a trial balloon to gauge Hagit's probable reaction. But Ofra had already shut her eyes and was enjoying, between Zichron Ya'akov and Atlit, one final nap, as though on the last leg of her flight. He glanced at her slender sixty-year-old form. The years were embalming her as an eternal adolescent. He really should get up the courage someday, Rivlin thought as the lights of Haifa came into view, to ask Yo'el about their married life. Perhaps there were a few useful lessons in it for him.

## 29.

THE APARTMENT HAD even more sparkle now than in the morning. Brightly lit and adorned with flowers, it awaited the arrival of the guest who, having followed via floor plans and telephoned reports the tortuous drama of its construction, was now seeing it for the first time.

The two sisters threw their arms around each other. Happy tears mingled with sad ones. Rivlin deposited the cheese fritters on the food-laden table and went to bring Ofra's suitcases to his top-floor study, which had been further transformed in his absence. The big desk had been pushed to one side, the table lamp was replaced by a reading light, and a third pillow now graced the royal bed. Beside it lay folded a new woolen blanket from which the price tag had yet to be removed.

He proceeded to the bedroom, turning off two or three unnecessary lights on the way while grumbling about the lengths to which his wife was prepared to go in order to appease the critical eyes of visitors, even her own sister's. Without taking off his shoes he lay down on the bed, careful not to rumple the covers before his sister-in-law's tour of inspection was over.

He thought with a smile of Akri. At this very moment his skull-capped colleague was bending cautiously over Tedeschi's rotting feet to confirm the dark prognosis of the translator of Jahaliya poetry. He let his thoughts wander. Across them fell the shadow of the bereaved hotel.

What bizarre inner devil had driven him, in his quest for sympathy, to invent a fatal disease? Would this succeed in extracting his ex-daughter-in-law's secret? Yet perhaps she herself had no comprehension of what she had done.

One way or another, he would have to warn her to say nothing.

Gently and reasonably.

Had she believed him? Or had she thought he was hallucinating? But hallucinations are an illness too.

Take the asthmatic Tedeschi in his oxygen mask. Or Samaher and her grandmother with the narghile.

Hagit would hit the ceiling.

How could he have sunk so low?

A trap. That was what it was. And his wife wanted them to wait patiently until their son-in-exile found someone else, even though the five years that had gone by had led to nothing. Ofer was at the end of his rope. He was nearly thirty-three. What good was patience? It wasn't time that freed you from traps. It was truth. And he would fight for it. Cunningly and untiringly.

He mustn't give up. Never mind the eternal judge below, whose ringing laughter was now calling him to come down and join them for supper.

"Don't you first want to show your sister the bedroom and the Jacuzzi?" he called down from above.

"Soon. There's no hurry. Let's have a bite first."

She was in a good mood, wide awake from her long nap and her sister's arrival. Rivlin turned on his side to reflect on an ancient and unrealized ambition that thirty-five years of marriage had not quelled. He still hoped one day to persuade his wife to share a bubble bath with him.

It was midnight when they remembered him and went to look for him.

"So you conked out, eh?" laughed Hagit. "My poor darling... and with your shoes on, yet. You didn't even shower."

He opened his eyes, feeling their radiant sisterly warmth.

"How do you like the apartment?" he asked his sister-in-law of the brightly jet-lagged cheeks.

"It's much nicer than I imagined from the floor plans."

"Well, I paid for it with my mental faculties," he said, not for the first time. "I've lost my power of concentration. While Hagit was having a fine time with her criminals in court, I was jousting over every brick, faucet, and electric socket with a crooked Jewish contractor and his wily Arab workmen."

"At least it ended well," Ofra said comfortingly.

"It wasn't as bad as all that," Hagit added. "Go to sleep. You ran yourself ragged today with all your needless expeditions. And last night," she told her sister with satisfaction, "we went to an Arab wedding in the Galilee and came home late."

"An Arab wedding?" marveled Ofra. "How come?"

He tried picturing Samaher's wedding. It seemed to have taken place, not a day, but a year ago.

PART II

# Jephthah's Daughter

A<small>ND YET IF</small> there had been advance signs, as Galya claimed, how had he and Hagit failed to notice them? Had they been so subtly concealed? Or had Ofer and Galya, too, not wanted to see them?

And what made a sign a sign? His meeting with Galya in the hotel garden had been so hurried and emotional that he had had no chance to ask. The time she had refused to wake up, for example: was that a sign? Now, thinking about it, he was inclined to believe it was.

A few weeks before the separation, Rivlin took part in a day's conference at the Hebrew University in Jerusalem. Bored by the lectures, all rehashes of familiar material, he'd decided to skip the concluding session and visit his son and daughter-in-law. Galya answered the telephone. "We'd love to see you," she told him. "Let's have an early supper." "Make it a light one," he cautioned, not because he wasn't hungry but because he didn't wish to inconvenience her.

Yet when he arrived, Galya was in the bedroom, asleep or pretending to be. A glum-looking Ofer gave him an absent-minded hug. The kitchen was full of dirty dishes, the living room was untidy, and there was no sign on the table of even the lightest supper. "I'm really not hungry," he reassured his son, who seemed upset by something. "I just wanted to say hello. A glass of tea will be fine. Although maybe," he added quietly, "we should wait for Galya to wake up. After all, she knew I was coming."

But Galya did not wake up. They sat in the living room over tea and cake, listening to the sounds that came intermittently from the bedroom. Ofer made no attempt to investigate them and responded curtly to his father's attempts at conversation, as if keeping him at arm's length. "It's certainly an odd time of day to sleep," Rivlin remarked after a while, with a smile, albeit in an injured tone. "Isn't she afraid of being kept up at night?" "Would you like me to wake her for you?" Ofer asked. "For me?" Rivlin said. "What for? I'll be heading home in a minute."

Was this a sign?

He arrived back in Haifa and was told by Hagit that right after he'd left Jerusalem Galya had telephoned to apologize for her ill-mannered slumber. Ofer got on the phone, too.

"How did they sound to you?" he asked anxiously.

"The usual. Nice and friendly."

"Are you sure?" he persisted. "Are you sure?"

OR PERHAPS THIS was a sign.

At the opera in Tel Aviv, during the intermission, they suddenly noticed, a few rows ahead of them, their daughter-in-law sitting with her father. Her long hair, usually done up in a bun, fell glamorously over her shoulders. He and Hagit had hurried over, uncertain whether to be delighted or worried by this unexpected encounter. Where, they asked, was Ofer? Hagit gave Galya a kiss. Rivlin, self-conscious in her father's presence, made do with a comment about her hair. Galya blushed awkwardly. Her father came to her defense. It was his idea to let it down, he said.

They returned to their seats. As the lights slowly dimmed, Rivlin saw his daughter-in-law throw him a fearful glance, as if feeling guilty for the husband left at home. Her hands quickly gathered her hair into a bun.

Was this what she meant by a sign?

OF ONE SIGN, at any rate, he had no doubt.

Some three weeks before the separation, Galya spent a weekend with her parents in the Galilee. There was a small hotel there that her father was thinking of acquiring. Having been to see their in-laws in Haifa only once since the wedding, the Hendels suggested dropping by on their way back to Jerusalem. That morning, however, a few

hours before they were due, Galya telephoned to say they would not
be coming. She offered no explanation and no apology.

Which was why, on the terrible Saturday when Ofer broke the
news of the divorce, Rivlin had remarked cuttingly, "Maybe you just
found out, but her parents knew long ago." Ofer denied it. "They
didn't know a thing," he insisted. "They were in shock just like you.
Her mother burst into tears right in front of me."

A sign? Or a coincidence?

AND PERHAPS SHE meant subtler signs, like the Friday night a month
before the separation.

The young couple had slept over at their home. In the middle of
the night, on his way to the bathroom, Rivlin spied the glimmer of a
white nightgown in the living room. Although the intimate circumstances made him shy of approaching her, he felt Galya's eyes on him.
"How long have you been awake?" he asked. "I never fell asleep," she
answered brusquely. He took a step toward her. "Is anything wrong?"
As though he were to blame for her insomnia, she shrugged like a
stubborn child and looked at him accusingly. "Why don't you wake
Ofer?" he asked. She shrugged again. "Would you like me to sit up
with you?" he inquired gently. "You needn't bother," she said. "It's no
bother," Rivlin replied. He sat down across the room from her, at first
silent and then feebly trying to make conversation. Her head
drooped. Her eyes shut, and her breathing grew deeper. Slowly she
drifted back to her lost sleep. Yet when he suggested she go back to
bed, she refused. All she wanted was a blanket, she said.

Was that a sign of things to come? But how?

HE REMEMBERED, TOO, a strange dream of Ofer's. It was Galya who
told it to them, as if to warn them of something.

In his dream Ofer was in an inner room of the hotel, sitting by the
bed of Galya's father, who lay pale and indisposed. No one else in
the family was there. Not knowing how to call for help, he roamed the
hotel. There were no guests. The staff had vanished, too. The rooms
were empty. Some were missing their tables and beds. Fixtures were
ripped from the bathrooms.

He returned to the inner room, in which the sick man had risen from his bed and was sitting in an armchair. Deciding to bring him a glass of water, he went to the bathroom to see if the sink had a faucet. It did, but only one. As he wasn't sure whether it was for hot water or cold, he abandoned the idea and picked up an old electric shaver from the marble counter. He blew away the hairs that adhered to it, went to the sick man, and started shaving him.

It must have been a dream with signs, Rivlin thought. Why else would he remember it so many years later?

## 1.

THAT SATURDAY MORNING they were back in the Galilee. Hagit's sister, who had yet to see her favorite nephew in uniform, let alone with his officer's bars, had gently but firmly turned down several weekend invitations in order to visit Tsakhi at his army base. Not that the Rivlins needed a special reason to make the trip. Even their car, to judge by the alacrity with which it took the twisting road to the large intelligence base on Mount Canaan, was eager to see their youngest son.

They were not the first parents to park outside the base, whose green gate had a double entrance in keeping with its top-secret nature. A few early birds had arrived before them and were already feeding their fledglings snacks, soft drinks, and even hamburgers.

"The army has gone soft," Rivlin observed disdainfully. "If anyone like us had turned up at the gate of an army base in my soldiering days, they would have been mowed down at once."

Half-hidden behind the gate, surrounded by ferns in a thick stand of oak trees, was a small shack whose pastoral innocence camouflaged the real entrance to the underground base. Carved into a mountain, the installation was covered by tall antennas and giant satellite dishes that ran in a silver forest to a nearby second hilltop. Rivlin, amused by the thought of an elevator inside a mountain, had once asked his son whether there was one. But Tsakhi had only smiled, refusing to disclose even so innocent a fact. Nor had he reacted when Rivlin accused the army of being "hysterically hush-hush." Without bothering to defend either it or himself, he had merely dipped his head in sorrow at being unable to satisfy his father's curiosity.

"Sometimes," the judge liked to remark, in a doting tone very different from her clipped severity on the bench, "I think I gave birth to a saint."

"What's so saintly about him?" Rivlin would protest, while hoping that his son's beatification might reflect creditably on him, too. "What good does it do to be a saint nowadays? Let's just hope that nothing spoils him."

Despite having been on duty all night, the young officer who emerged from the mountain in crisp, spotless fatigues did not look spoiled at all. Beaming in the dewy morning light, he hurried—oblivious to the glances of other soldiers, some of them under his command—to give his notoriously fragile aunt a gentle hug.

"So he's not a saint," the judge had conceded. "But he does have a sense of boundaries. He knows right from wrong, and he doesn't care what others think of him, unlike you and Ofer. You needn't worry about him. Compliments don't go to his head. Nothing will spoil him or throw him off stride."

As if to prove her right, the saint, approached by a blond, baby-faced sergeant hoping to take advantage of the family reunion by asking his commanding officer for a favor, cut him off sharply and sent him on his way.

## 2.

"As long as I'm here, why don't we take a little walk and see the spring flowers. What do you say?"

The son to whom Rivlin extended this invitation was being fawned upon by a fond mother and aunt, who no doubt saw in him the reincarnation of an old photograph of their father mounted on a horse in a Russian cavalry uniform.

"But why take a walk?" objected Hagit, who had already placed a large bag of cherries on the grass. "Ofra has come especially to see Tsakhi. If you're restless, go yourself."

The young officer glanced ingenuously from one parent to the other, wondering how to satisfy two such contradictory desires at once. Rivlin, who wanted to be alone with his son in order to get his appraisal, or even approval, of the conversation in the hotel garden in Jerusalem, was forced to yield. Making his way among picnicking parents spreading checked tablecloths and coaxing blue flames from gas burners, he wandered off on his own.

Deprived of a conversation partner, he soon found himself on the mountainside, slowly but steadily climbing a path. For a while his rapid pace seemed about to carry him to the summit—where perhaps, he mused, amid the silent chatter of the antennas, satellite dishes, and smart sensors, he might find inspiration for his unfinished book. But the summit was farther away than it looked, and he soon came to a high military fence in a field of flowering bindweed and squirrel grass. Fearing mines, he picked a spot beneath an old oak tree and sat down quietly in the fresh grass, the last of the morning dew glinting on his shoes. Far beneath him, the entrance to the base looked like the opening of an anthill. His affectionate glance made out his son. Seated between his aunt and his mother, the young officer was probably being fed a banana.

Despite Hagit and Ofra's twice-weekly international phone calls, the two never tired of retrieving from oblivion, with an intimacy born of the bedroom shared by them as children, all that had fallen since their last meeting into the stormy crevices of time. They never had looked like sisters, and they resembled each other even less after so many years of being apart. Tall, thin, and stooped, Ofra, the eternal product of the left-wing youth movement in which she had met her husband, dressed with a mousy simplicity. Plump, merry, vivacious, opinionated, and pampered Hagit, on the other hand, wore fancy clothes, liked expensive makeup and perfumes, and smoked with the flair of a juvenile delinquent. Perhaps she was still trying to compensate her father for his disappointment in having a second daughter.

Early that morning, at a dawn hour rarely suitable for love, Rivlin had overcome her defenses. "I hope you've noticed how nice I've been to your sister," he had begun, following up on this advertisement for himself by quickly stripping off his pajamas and diving beneath the blankets. Forced to admit his model behavior, Hagit, thinking she heard a noise from her sister's room, tried fending him off with hugs and kisses. But Rivlin would not take no for an answer. "If you use your sister as an alibi, I'll end up hating her," he said. "But can't you hear that she's up?" Hagit whispered. "You've gone deaf from thinking too much." Throwing off the blanket, he ran naked to the door of his expropriated study and put his ear to it to demonstrate that she was imagining things.

Whether despite or because of this, their lovemaking was especially delicious. He rose from it contented, while his wife resumed from beneath the blanket her investigation of his frowned-upon condolence call. In her years as a district attorney, before being appointed to the bench, she had acquired a reputation as a shrewd cross-examiner, and he now answered her questions warily without denying that he might have, between expressions of sympathy for the bereaved, alluded to the painful mystery of Ofer and Galya's separation.

Hagit put on her glasses to study the defendant she had made love to.

"That's all there was?"

"More or less."

"What else was there?"

"That's all."

"I hope you realize even that was too much."

"What was?"

"Mentioning Ofer to her. Wanting to know and understand everything. Come to my courtroom some day and you'll see the terrible things people do because they don't stop to think."

He made no reply.

"Let it go," she urged him gently. "Let it go. It only causes you grief. It's time you separated from her, too."

"Me?" Rivlin laughed and reddened. "I'll never see her again."

"I mean psychologically. That's why I was against your going to the hotel and wallowing in your old misery and begging for explanations. It's demeaning. For me, too. And most of all, for Ofer. It's over with. Let her be. She has a new husband."

"Yes," he murmured, delivering a counterstroke. "I think she's pregnant."

"Pregnant?"

"Unless she's just put on weight. She's lost her good looks, by the way."

"But what makes you think she's pregnant?"

"It just struck me ... when we were saying good-bye...."

"What struck you?"

"Nothing. You know what I mean. Forget it. She's really broken up over her father. I felt it when I said good-bye...."

"Felt what?"

"Just for a second. It was like the old days. I hugged her ... just to comfort her ... and I thought I felt ... this heaviness...."

"A heaviness?"

"Forget it. It's only an image. Don't pounce on every word."

"But what made you hug her in the first place?"

"I just felt like it. It wasn't really a hug. I was feeling sorry for her. Why are you so hard on her?"

"It's you, not me, who's been angry with her all these years."

"That's so. I was. I still am. But she suddenly seemed so sad to me. She's too young to lose a father. What did I do wrong?"

She threw off the blanket, rose from bed naked, and put on a bathrobe. Going over to him, she took him in her arms and kissed him so hotly that he trembled.

"I just can't...." He choked. "I can't stop thinking about it. Ofer has been in limbo for five years, without a woman in his life. That's the reality. Why shouldn't I try to understand what happened ... to make some sense of it...."

She rested her hands on his shoulders and shook him lightly, the bounty of her breasts showing through her robe.

"I know how it hurts you." Her loving tone had a reprimand in it. "I'm on your side. That's why I'm asking you to put it behind you. All your worry and anxiety just make it worse for Ofer, even if you're far away and think he doesn't know. If you don't free yourself of that woman and stop trying to understand more than she does, he'll never be free, either. Not of her and not of you."

"But he has to know."

"Know what?"

"That her father died."

"Why? Why does it concern him?"

"He can't not write a condolence note."

"Why not?"

"Because the first thing she asked was whether he knew. She expects to hear from him."

"Let her expect. Sooner or later he'll hear about it and do what he wants. Whatever that is, it will be right for him. It's his affair, not yours. Do you hear me? It's none of your business!"

"But how can I not tell him I went to the hotel?"

"Just don't. Why should you? To make him want what's lost forever?"

## 3.

SOMETHING RUSTLED IN the bushes. Rivlin reached for a stone in case it was a snake. An animal, mole or rabbit, peeked worriedly from underneath some branches and took a step toward the Orientalist as if meaning to ask something, before changing its mind and darting off.

A soldier emerged from the hidden entrance of the base with a message for Tsakhi. The young officer rose, embraced his aunt, kissed his mother, and glanced at the mountainside in search of his father. Rivlin waved. Although the gesture meant, "Don't worry, son, get back to work and we'll see you soon," Tsakhi came running toward him.

"You didn't have to run all this way to say good-bye," Rivlin scolded him warmly. "You'll be home on leave in a few days. War won't break out before then."

"I suppose not." The young officer blushed. "Well, I'll be seeing you," he said, touching his father's arm lightly.

Although the housekeeper had risen from a sickbed to prepare a large lunch for them, Hagit preferred as usual to eat out. Her one concession to the pot roast waiting at home was to choose a dairy restaurant with a fancy menu. Rivlin, undeterred by the elaborate descriptions, ordered at once and hurried off to the rest room. He knew his sister-in-law needed time to deliberate, turn the pages, and make inquiries of the waitress. Although she and her husband were inveterate travelers and diners out, she still harbored the pristine illusion that every restaurant had its culinary apotheosis if only one knew what to ask for.

Finally the decisions were made. Even the waitress seemed satisfied. A first round of wine was poured, and the judge lit a slim cigarette and persuaded her nonsmoking sister to join her. Far removed from the depressing memory of their mother's cooking, they were happiest together in restaurants. Now, after summarizing the virtues of the gallant young officer, they proceeded to the wedding that was the formal, if not the sufficient, cause of Ofra's coming to Israel. Hagit wished to plan her sister's outfit and appearance.

"But why don't you come with us?" Ofra sought to persuade them. "Yo'el says his family sent you two invitations that weren't confirmed."

"Yo'el is mistaken," Rivlin said, regarding the dish put before him with disappointment. It looked small and insipid, and he stole a glance at his wife's plate to gauge her appetite and the prospects of sharing her meal. "We confirmed that we weren't coming."

"But why not? Wouldn't you like to be with us? Yo'el needs your help to get through the evening with his horrid family."

"How horrid can anyone be at a wedding?" Rivlin chuckled. He had heard more than one juicy story about the crudity of his brother-in-law's clan.

"Horrid enough. They'll ask nosy questions about why people our age have to go traveling to the ends of the earth, or what happens if Yo'el gets sick somewhere...."

"But they have every right to be worried," he warmly rebuked the girlish frequent flyer.

Rivlin's sister-in-law, however, refused to equate his and Hagit's genuine concern with the spiteful criticisms of Yo'el's envious family. "We need you there to defend us," she insisted.

Hagit wavered. "After all, we don't really know them ... and we didn't invite them to Ofer's wedding...."

"Who remembers Ofer's wedding?" Rivlin's sister-in-law exclaimed aggravatedly, heedless of the feelings of the two people in the world she felt closest to. "All that matters is that they invited you and want you to come. It will be a big, outdoor affair at a new caterer's. We'll spend the evening together. There's so little time on this visit to be with you."

Rivlin cast a warning glance at Hagit, who was already asking about this new caterer.

"It's called Nature's Corner. It's in a woods on the banks of a stream."

Hagit was weakening. "For my part..."

But Rivlin, having foreseen the danger, had already taken preemptive action. He and Hagit, he announced, had tickets that evening for the theater, for a new play, on a biblical theme, that had opened to rave reviews.

"You can change them to another night," Ofra pleaded. "We'll come with you. Yo'el loves mythological subjects. We need you at the wedding. You don't have to buy a gift. Ours will be from you too."

"It's not a matter of a gift. The last thing I need is more weddings."

"Actually, I wouldn't mind going," Hagit told her sister. "But weddings make this man of mine so depressed that he's a menace to the bride and groom. The only weddings he can put up with, more or less, are Arab ones...."

"More less than more," Rivlin said. "I felt depressed even at that Arab wedding in the middle of nowhere two days ago. I can't help it. I was programmed that way by a cruel mother. Never to forget. Never to let go. Never to give in. Always to fight on. And after talking to Galya and meeting her new husband, the need to know what happened to Ofer's marriage is eating away at me like a cancer.... Why go to a wedding in Nature's Corner just to be miserable?"

"I hope you're not about to cry," Hagit said, with a smile.

"Suppose I am?"

"Well, don't. Do it some other time."

"Not even a little?"

"Not even. I warned you against going to that bereavement."

"But how could I not have gone?" He appealed hotly to his sister-in-law. "How could I have overlooked his death? It's simple courtesy for an ex-in-law to express his sympathy in such circumstances."

But the judge was not inclined to be judged.

"A condolence note would have done nicely. You should have seen," she told her sister, "the touching letter he sent not long ago to the widow of an academic rival who died unexpectedly."

She cut a large slice from her quiche and placed it, without asking, on her husband's empty plate.

It failed to placate him. His confession of fatal illness in the hotel garden now filled him not with guilt but with compassion—for himself and for the young woman in black who had sat, shocked, across from him.

"Hagit wants nothing to do with them. She's too . . . I don't know what. Proud, or secretly angry. She doesn't even want to tell Ofer that Hendel died."

"You don't?" The visitor turned to her sister timidly, reluctant to interfere in a family squabble that had broken out when they were having such a good time.

Hagit didn't answer. Pushing away her plate, she lit a cigarette and signaled the waitress to bring the dessert list.

Rivlin persisted. "You be the judge. Should we tell Ofer or not?"

"But what difference does it make?" Hagit asked, glaring to let him know that no matter how great the intimacy between her and her sister, no one in the world could or should settle their disputes for them. Angrily he snatched the proffered menu while informing his sister-in-law, who was regarding them with mild anxiety:

"Nature's Corner will do without us. Weddings get me down so that I could wreck not only a corner of nature, but the whole works. If it isn't too late, we'll come after the theater to rescue you."


## 4.

A COUPLE THEIR own age, an overdressed woman and a man with a goatee, entered the restaurant and recognized Ofra with cries of joy.

"Look who's here! Are you back in Israel?"

Ofra squirmed, as if reluctant to admit that she knew them. However, once they had demonstrated a knowledge of her name and Yo'el's, and given proof that all four of them had recently been together at an Aztec ruin in Mexico, she abandoned the pretense.

"Just for a wedding. Yo'el is coming in a few days."

Eager to reestablish a tie forged by a chance meeting far away, the couple asked to be introduced to the Rivlins.

"We were on this wonderful Geographic Society tour," they explained, "when who did we run into on a godforsaken hacienda in Mexico but Ofra and Yo'el?"

They held out their hands in a show of friendship, hungry, so it seemed, for new relationships at home as well as abroad. Or so Rivlin construed their insistence on giving their names and occupations and asking for his and Hagit's.

Near Eastern studies made no impression. But a judge was something else.

"A justice of the peace?" they asked avidly.

Hagit chose to reply to the question with an indifferent exhalation of smoke.

"A district judge," Rivlin answered for her.

"You don't say! We're thinking of suing a Jerusalem hospital for price-gouging. Maybe your wife could tell us what our chances are."

Hagit's continued silence was a sign that her inner radar was blipping strongly.

Rivlin, with an embarrassed smile, tried thinking of how to cut the conversation short without offending anyone. Although he sensed the shudder that ran through his sister-in-law, who seemed to know what was coming next, he couldn't resist inquiring what the court case was about.

"You've probably guessed," the man with the goatee said intimately to Ofra. "It was your husband who placed the call to Israel for us. Perhaps he even remembers and would like to testify on our behalf."

"But what's it all about?" Rivlin asked, deliberately ignoring his wife's restraining hand.

There was no longer any stopping the couple from telling their story, which they related while standing between two tables and forcing the waiters to detour around them. The husband was an accountant, the wife a teacher of music. With a mixture of cynical amusement and dense innocence, they told how, two days before they set out on a grand tour of Central America for which they had registered with friends and made a hefty down payment, the music teacher's octogenarian father had died in an old-age home. Because the week of bereavement would have caused them to miss their dream trip, they decided to postpone the funeral by freezing the deceased—a nonbeliever who would have raised no religious objections—in the hospital morgue. Nor was the reason they gave—namely, the need to give relatives abroad sufficient time to get organized—entirely imaginary, since the deceased's son, the music teacher's brother, had pressing business in Chicago and preferred a later date. "Enjoy your trip," he'd told them. He was sure their dead father would not have wanted to spoil their plans. He would have all the time in the world to spend in the ground; meanwhile, the worms could dine on someone else.

Rivlin glanced at his wife. She had been served her dessert, a chocolate parfait topped with maraschino cherries, and was staring over it at the standing couple. The obvious repugnance they aroused in her having failed to head them off, she now confronted them directly, head up, eyes riveted to them, mouth slightly open in concentration.

At the hospital the couple had had good luck. The morgue pathologist, a slightly alcoholic Russian, agreed to accommodate the deceased in his freezer with no time limit or questions asked. He had an available drawer and was willing to charge a fair price.

"How much?" Rivlin asked curiously.

"Less than a hundred shekels a day, VAT included."

"Not bad."

And so the orphaned music teacher and her husband set out on their tour with their friends. Between one Mayan temple and the next, they planned the fine funeral they would have. Unfortunately, several days after their departure from Israel an inquisitive hospital official, an observant Jew, dropped in on the morgue and discovered that one of its occupants was overextending his stay. A fuss was made, the Russian pathologist was reprimanded, and a search began for the next of kin. When these were discovered in Central America, they were encouraged to return at once—by a steep price hike.

"How much?" asked the professor, suddenly brimming with high spirits.

"Five hundred shekels a day, without VAT."

"That's pretty stiff."

"Disgraceful. Criminal. Unjustifiable," complained the man with the goatee. "Pure vengeance. And when we got home and demanded the original price, that little religious bastard, with all his talk about the dignity of the dead, wouldn't let us bury my wife's father until we forked up the extra cash."

"How was the funeral?"

"Grand! My brother-in-law came with his whole family. Lots of cousins and friends were there, too. We told them the whole story. After all, we're enlightened, rational people. Well, what do you think?" the man asked the judge, whose spoon was suspended in midair. "If you tried the case, would we stand a chance?"

"A very good one," Hagit pronounced.

"You don't say!" The two were thrilled.

"Of going to jail."

"To jail?" They were dumbfounded. "But why?"

"For excessive enlightenment."

They crimsoned and laughed.

"We're onto you!"

Hagit did not take her eyes off them.

"You're so enlightened that you're a public danger."

No one spoke.

As usual, Rivlin found himself full of admiration for his wife. Yet when he turned amusedly to Ofra, he was surprised to see a frightened look on her face. Anyone capable of freezing his own father-in-law, she no doubt thought, might do even worse things in the middle of a restaurant on a peaceful Sabbath in the Galilee.

"Well," the man said, a sly smile above his goatee, "it's a good thing there are courts of appeals."

"For sure," the judge agreed. "They'd not only acquit you, they'd declare you national heroes."

She lifted a cherry from her parfait with two careful fingers. The situation was now decidedly awkward. With a brisk farewell, the couple retreated to a table. Rivlin was about to swear at them when the judge, extricating her spoon from the chocolate parfait, silenced him by passing him her dish.

"Have some, it's very good," she urged him gently. Yet when he handed it back to her after two spoonfuls, she waved it off, her appetite gone, and stared at it as if it were the corpse of the music teacher's father.

"But why make *me* eat it?" Rivlin protested.

"Because you're paying for it. It's a shame to leave it. Cheer up and have another spoonful, my love. It's not like you to be so squeamish."

## 5.

LATE THAT SATURDAY night, after many long conversations, endless rounds of tea and snacks, numerous phone calls to near and distant cousins, and a visit from a friend who dropped by "for a minute" and didn't leave, Ofra went downstairs to shower and Rivlin summoned his wife to the bedroom, shut the door, and declared:

"Before you and your sister become any more symbiotic, I want to know what your plans are and where I fit into them."

"Fit in?" wondered the tired woman stretched out on her bed. "How do you mean?"

"You heard me. What are your plans, and where do I fit in?"

But there were no new plans, Hagit said, only old ones. On Tuesday they had a concert. On Thursday the two sisters were going to the movies. And on Saturday they were all driving to Jerusalem to visit their aunt in her geriatric institution, whence they would proceed to the airport to pick up Yo'el.

"And apart from that? What more do I have to do for your sister?"

"What do you have to do? Nothing. Be patient and kind."

"That's what I have been."

"Until this afternoon. You were snappish and sarcastic with her when we returned from the Galilee."

"How can you say that?"

"You know exactly what I mean."

"I don't like a whole day to go by without a chance to talk to you in private."

"To talk about what?"

"There's always something."

"But why didn't you use the time to nap this afternoon? We made sure the house was quiet."

"I tried. I can't fall asleep without you."

"Read something. A story. A novel."

"I can't. Life is too turbulent."

"Life is too turbulent? That trip to Jerusalem did you in."

"It wasn't the trip. It was your reaction to it. Your hostility."

"I hardly said a word. There was nothing to upset you."

"It just wasn't like you, a strange notion like hiding Hendel's death from Ofer."

"I wish you'd stop poking around in dead ashes."

"If they're dead, what do you care?"

"It takes one live spark to start a new fire."

"What kind of fire?"

"It's been five years. The divorce is final. Galya is remarried. You knew she was pregnant when you hugged her."

"I never hugged her. I put my hand on her shoulder. And I never said she was definitely pregnant. . . ."

"It doesn't matter. If she's not, she will be. What do you want? For Ofer to be burned all over again?"

"For him to catch on. To understand."

"There's nothing to understand. Some things just have to be accepted. Even your Algeria, which you've spent years studying and writing about, keeps surprising both itself and you to the point of writer's block. Why can't a young woman surprise herself and break up her marriage?"

He said nothing. The bathroom door opened below. Their guest had finished her shower. Hagit listened alertly, seeking to determine whether her sister might need an extra towel or anything else.

"So what about tomorrow?"

"What about it?"

"Do you need me in the morning, or do I have a free day?"

"Of course you do. I'd just be grateful if you dropped Ofra off at Pesi's boutique in the mall on your way to the university, so that she can try on some clothes. It opens at nine-thirty. I'll be late for court if I take her myself."

"I was thinking of leaving earlier."

"When is your class?"

"At noon."

"Then you're in no hurry. She has to find something nice for the wedding. All that traveling has made her neglect herself. Yo'el has forgotten how to dress, too."

"All right."

"She'll try on a few things and then show me what she likes."

"All right."

"There's a little café next to the boutique. You can have something to drink and read the paper there."

"Are you trying to tell me I'm supposed to bring her back here?"

"Of course. How else would she get back?"

"What do you mean, how else? By bus."

"Two buses."

"So two buses."

"With all those clothes from the boutique."

"How heavy can they be?"

"Ofra isn't taking any buses. I can't ask her to do that."

"She's traveled all over the world, she's crossed whole continents— and she can't take a bus in her own country?"

"All over the world she has Yo'el. He looks after her. Here I'm responsible."

"For what?"

"Her pleasure and well-being."

"But what's wrong with a bus? Just because I've arranged your life for the past thirty years to keep you away from public transportation, do you think having to take a bus is a tragedy?"

"It's not a tragedy. But no sister of mine who is here on a short visit will be made to get on and off buses with packages. If you can't wait half an hour, then don't. I'll adjourn the trial, take a taxi, and bring her home myself."

"I surrender. I'll bring baby home. But only on the condition that she doesn't have to decide what clothes to buy. You'll help her make up her mind. Because if she has to do it by herself, I really will miss my class."

"You're an optimist. If she had to make up her own mind, you'd miss the rest of your life. But don't panic. She doesn't want to. She'll pick out a few things, and we'll decide here. You'll help, too. Why shouldn't your opinion count?"

"Forget my opinion," Rivlin said, with a modest grin. "Let her blame you, not me, for making her buy what she doesn't want or not letting her buy what she does want."

"She won't blame you if you don't pressure her, my dear. She's not your wife. Just be helpful."

"By the way, I tried phoning Ofer an hour ago. There was no answer. I left him a message on his voice mail."

"What did you say?"

"Nothing."

"Nothing?"

"Nothing special. Nothing."

## 6.

3.4.98

*Galya,*

*Yesterday my father left a message on my voice mail that your father died unexpectedly a few days ago. He said he was at the bereavement and that you asked him whether I knew and how I had reacted. He also said he was telling me against the better judgment of my mother, who thought it pointless to involve me.*

*Of course, she was right. We haven't exchanged a word since we broke up, and it's best that way. Not that your father's death isn't a serious matter, but it, too, should have been spared me.*

*That's why I debated whether to break the vow of silence that both of us have kept honorably until now. But since I realize how terrible all this must be for your mother, I thought I would (should?) let her know that, despite our divorce and my estrangement from your family, I understand what she's going through and wish to express my sympathy.*

*She's a woman I always liked. (And who liked me, if I'm not mistaken.) I won't say anything about your father. He's gone now. Quite apart from the horrible things he did, it's frightening to hear about such a sudden death. At least (or so I understand) he didn't suffer. And so if you, too, Galya, need a word of sympathy (or however you call it) from me, here it is.*

*Although only on the condition that you don't write back.*

*Ofer*

# 7.

EXCUSE ME. Are you new here?

There used to be another salesgirl...

Pesi, of course! Pesi.

This is my wife's sister. She spoke to Pesi about her.

They agreed she could try on a few things, take home what she liked, and return what she didn't want this evening. My wife can't come now because she's at a trial... I mean, she's the judge... and so we thought we'd do with my sister-in-law what we do with her: pick out a few things and decide in a relaxed way at home.

No, this is my sister-in-law from abroad. But my wife buys here all the time. Practically all her new clothes come from here. I'm sure you'd recognize her.

You do? That's odd. I suppose I'm the only man who ever walks in here.

For sure. If you'd like me to leave a check as a deposit, there's no problem. Pesi knows us.

This way, Ofra. Everything in this section is on sale, isn't it? You see, I'm an expert on this place.

She'll tell you what she's looking for.

Israeli. Of course.

But it has to be suitable for other occasions, too. Not just weddings.

Look at this, Ofra. It's gorgeous. What do you think? It's certainly dignified enough.

Do you have a skirt that goes with this?

Two weeks ago you had a tunic, with a three-quarter-length sleeve—light brown velvet, with a strip of green embroidery. My wife tried it on. It was a bit tight on her, but it might fit her sister. She's much thinner.

I wouldn't call it summery. More *demi saison*, as the French say. . . .

Something along these lines. Not this, though. The fabric was richer. With a strip of green embroidery. Maybe it's been sold. It was lovely. But my wife said it was too tight. Ofra, how about this ensemble?

For goodness' sake! What are you afraid of? You can't keep dressing as though you were in the youth movement all your life.

It's not fancy at all. It's cute. Try it on. Listen to me. What are you afraid of?

I'm in no hurry. Don't worry about me. As long as we're here, let's take a little longer and pick out some nice things that we can think about afterward.

You'll find a bigger dressing room to your right, Ofra.

In the time I've spent dodging women in this store, I could have written at least two more articles. But it's been worth it. We've bought some nice things here. There's something about the design, the way you cut things, that suits Hagit's figure. It hides what needs to be hidden. I must say that your prices are high. But as long as she listens to me, what we buy doesn't end up forgotten in the closet.

Go on, try it on. You can't tell a thing just by looking.

Of course. I'll wait out here.

Me?

She lives abroad. Her husband works for UNESCO. He's an adviser on Third World economies. They spend more time on airplanes than you do in your bedroom.

I suppose you could call them émigrés, even though they'd never admit it. They've been globe-trotting for thirty years. But they'll make sure to be buried here.

Of course. Where else, in Africa?

So you do remember my wife.

Exactly.

Yes. She's very nice.

A district judge. There are six of them in Haifa. She's one.

In the past few years we've bought nearly all her clothes here. When I retire from teaching, I can open a rival boutique of my own. But only with clothes made by your designer.

No. She's a few years older than my wife.

Because she's so thin and girlish. She never had children to make her go to seed. And she has a husband who looks after her. He's not in Israel now, which is why I've been drafted in his place. It takes two shrewd sisters to have found such devoted caretakers.

Let's have a look, Ofra. It's not bad.

Turn the other way.

She's right. The hem needs to be shortened.

Too see-through? I don't see anything. Believe me, Ofra, I have a good eye. It looks fine on you. It's classic. It just needs to be shortened and taken in at the back. You don't want to look like you're on your way to Yom Kippur services.

I sometimes drive my wife crazy too. But I have to. Everyone needs somebody to keep an eye on them. She could buy some catastrophe that would go straight into her closet and never come out. It's my job to veto that. It's the husband who suffers most when his wife buys the wrong clothes. . . .

What did you say your name was?

If you could pin up the hem for us, Na'ama, we'll take it home. My wife will convince her.

There's no obligation, Ofra. You heard what Na'ama said.

You like this one? But it's so dreary! You'll be the only person dressed in mourning at the wedding. It will make you stand out, which is just what you don't want.

Trust me.

Yo'el is a wonderful man, but he's no judge of clothes. Just look at how he dresses himself.

Never mind. Forget I said it.

All right. Try it on, if you must.

They're close even for sisters. She and her husband come for short visits every two or three years. We give them the royal treatment.

I teach at the university.

In the Near Eastern Studies Department.

Of course. Mostly Arabs. But also Turks and Iranians and various other madmen.

We Jews still suffer from the delusion that we're not part of the Middle East. We think we've stumbled into it by accident.

Rivlin. Professor Yochanan Rivlin.

Really?

In what department?

That's a good one to be in if you're looking for a husband.

Ours is a good one if you're looking for a wife. An Arab one.

Let's have a look. I don't like the combination. The other was much nicer. It's not bad in front, but we also have backs. And from the back you look like a receptionist in a mortician's office. In fact, this color makes you look like a receptionist with jaundice.

Not if you ask me. But I'm only the driver. If you feel you must, we'll take it home for consultation. Meanwhile do yourself a favor and try on this little item. It won't cost you anything.

What do you mean, too loud?

It's cheery, not loud.

This flower?

Can't it be removed?

But she can if she wants to, can't she?

You see? It's a lovely dress. You'll come alive in it. Try it on for my sake.

Don't worry about me. I have time. My class isn't until noon. But we do have to get a move on. You should try on a few more things. Don't forget, the wedding is next week. And whatever you choose will need alterations...

## 8.

THEIR GUEST RETURNED home in a dither with three shopping bags full of dresses, skirts, pants, and blouses. Pesi, arriving on the scene at the last moment, added a few items for the judge. "Your sister," she told Ofra, "is my best and favorite customer. Her husband is fun, too, even if his taste is a bit conservative."

Ofra thanked him profusely for his efforts. Her gaunt face was ruddy from the morning's adventure, which had been more exhausting than a transoceanic flight, not only because of the colorful array of clothing set before her, a Spartan woman accustomed to her wardrobe of what her husband liked to call her "uniforms," but also because of her officious brother-in-law, who kept trying, rather insensitively, to talk her into buying what he liked. The freedom with which he told the salesgirl what alterations to make left her feeling that her body, so fragile and delicate, was a plaything in his hands.

Rivlin, too, felt he had gone too far. Had his wife known how he would behave, she might have preferred sending her sister in two buses. And yet he was satisfied. Even Ofra needed a face-lift now and then. It would keep her from drying up too fast.

## 9.

THERE WERE TWO messages on the voice mail. One was from Professor Tedeschi in person. In a despondent tone, he informed the Rivlins that the doctors had again despaired of diagnosing his condition and were sending him home to let it make up its own mind. The second message was from Ephraim Akri. With an insistence not typical of his pliant Oriental nature, he requested his colleague to stop by the departmental office on his way to class.

The secretaries in the office were waiting for him. Clearing out the students who were hanging around, they shut the door and ushered him with secretive glee into an inner room. There he was presented with two nameless term papers and asked to confirm that the comments in the margins were his own.

They were in his handwriting. Obviously, he had read the papers thoroughly and thought little of them. Yet, idiotically, the secretaries informed him, they had then been photocopied and submitted for another course with his marginal notes still on them.

"I just wanted to make sure," one of the two said triumphantly. "I knew the comments were yours."

"From their handwriting or their brilliance?" Rivlin asked, with a smile. He glanced at the gloomy Akri, whose pessimistic view of the Arab conception of freedom was in no way lessened by so primitive a deception.

"Can you identify the student who wrote these papers?" Akri asked. Rivlin shrugged.

"Whoever it was could have copied them from someone else," said the older of the two secretaries, who took pride in seeing through students in general and Arab students in particular. "They just might have done a better job."

"I've been told that in the English department," the younger secretary volunteered, "they've got papers that were written in Beirut and Damascus, even Baghdad. There's a market all over the Middle East, especially for Shakespeare."

"Shakespeare?"

"He's the safest bet." The younger secretary had studied English literature herself for two years. "Every day someone publishes a new book about him. There's no way to tell what's original and what isn't."

"Then how do they know these aren't?"

"They're too good. And their bibliographies list Arabic books that aren't available in Israel. There are hard-up instructors and even professors in Arab countries willing to sell term papers on *Hamlet*, *Othello*, or *Romeo and Juliet* to the highest bidder."

"Not to mention *The Merchant of Venice*," Akri put in. "Dr. Dagut once told me that he was given a term paper on Shylock by an Arab student that was full of anti-Semitic remarks."

"I hope he didn't flunk him because of it."

"God forbid. The liberals in the English department love anti-Semitic remarks. These just seemed suspicious because they were so extreme...."

Rivlin sank slowly into the armchair in which, as department chairman, he had frequently napped. The battle of the boutique had been tiring, though by no means unpleasant. He leafed through the two term papers, trying to guess their author by their style and subject. He thought of Samaher.

"Well, what do you think?" Akri asked.

"I'd turn it over to the disciplinary committee. They'll find out who sold what to whom."

"That could get nasty. It will make the student newspaper, and the Arab students will raise a rumpus."

"Let them."

"I wouldn't want to impugn their honor."

"You?"

"Me above all. There's a difference between historical generalizations and personal accusations. The rules call for expulsion in a case like this. It will end badly."

Akri glanced at the two secretaries. His sudden solicitude for the misconceivers of freedom did not seem to please them. "Whatever we do, we mustn't be hasty," he declared heatedly. "Before we make our staff happy by besmirching our own department, let's try to work this thing out. Why step on toes if you don't have to?"

"By doing what?"

"Something stupid."

"You sound like a politician."

"There's nothing wrong with politics if it can prevent conflict."

The new department head adjusted his steel-rimmed glasses and politely signaled the two secretaries to leave him alone with his colleague.

## 10.

"CAN YOU GUESS who wrote these two papers?"

"You say they were written by the same person?"

"Yes. They're in the same style."

Rivlin leafed through them. How, he wondered aloud, could he possibly know? He had graded so many papers in his life.

"But these were written recently," Akri said.

"How can you tell?"

"Your handwriting dates from the last two years."

"What do you mean?"

"I compared it with your writing from previous years in some old files. It's changed. Your letters used to be larger, more upright and decisive. Lately they've become . . . well, a bit scrawled- and scrunched-looking. The lines are crooked, as though something were pressing on them."

"If ever they make you a cabinet minister, Ephraim, I'd suggest the ministry of police."

"I'll consider it."

"Since when have you become graphologist?"

"We all agreed that the marginal comments were yours. I wanted to know when they were from."

"But why all this sleuthing around? It's a waste of time. Get the two students to talk."

But the Oriental Akri was so sensitive to the feelings of his Arab students that he was concerned even for the cheats among them. He didn't want to make use of informers. This was a Jewish method, far worse than discrimination or neglect, that had left a festering sore in Arab society. He preferred to solve the case by himself.

Out of the corner of his eye Rivlin noticed, beside the two photographs on top of the computer, a new picture of an infant in a crib. Did Akri have another grandson? Until officially informed of this, he decided bitterly, he would ignore the newcomer and assume him to be an earlier version of Grandson One or Two.

He rose awkwardly from his chair. "I have a class," he said. But the department head continued to detain him.

"We have to determine whether, when she gave those papers to someone else, she knew what would be done with them."

"How do you know it was a she?"

"Because she uses the feminine case for herself."

Rivlin pictured a young woman in a wedding gown, pulling a black horse away from a gate. "Sometimes I don't know what to make of you, Ephraim," he said, with a patronizing smile. "On the one hand, you speak about Arabs with the most awful despair. And on the other, you coddle them like a social worker."

"It's all connected," the department head replied, flattered to be considered a paradox. "It's our human and scholarly responsibility. The better we understand the Arabs, the better we can defend ourselves against them. We have to distinguish the crucial from the trivial, what's important to them from what isn't. That's the only way we'll ever know what to expect from them. We have to honor their feelings and realize what hurts them in order to guard against betrayal and lies. It's a question of patting their backs with one hand while squeezing their balls with the other. Without romantic or egotistical illusions. Because it's the purest egotism on the part of their so-called friends—I'm talking about our own bleeding-heart colleagues—to treat the Arabs as our clones who share our values and hopes. It exasperates me how the same types who are always accusing our Jewish society of decadence and fanaticism expect the Arabs to think just like them. If you don't like your own self, at least don't impose its norms on others."

"Do you know who wrote those papers?" Rivlin asked, interrupting. "It was our bride, Samaher. The one whose wedding you made us go to."

"I thought as much." Akri was not surprised. "I was waiting to hear it from you. Something about them reminded me of a paper she wrote for me as an undergraduate."

"That was the only time she wrote anything. She hasn't done a thing since entering the M.A. program. I've given her three extensions, and the only requirement she's met is getting married."

"That's not an unimportant one," Akri said seriously. "Nothing terrible has happened. Now that we've caught her red-handed, we'll make her fulfill her other requirements."

"Well, then, I wash my hands of her. She's all yours."

"They're all mine," the new department head replied, confirming his position of authority. "But let's be discreet about it. And first of all, that means getting our secretaries to keep their mouths shut...."

## 11.

ON TUESDAY EVENING, at seven-thirty, half an hour before he and Hagit were due to leave for a concert at the Israel Philharmonic, Rivlin's sister phoned and asked to speak to Hagit about a strange dream she had had that day. Ever since attending a course in forensic psychology a few years previously, Hagit had liked interpreting dreams.

"Not now, Raya," Rivlin told her. "We have a concert, and Hagit isn't dressed yet. And Ofra hasn't decided what to wear, either...."

"All I need with her is five minutes. Otherwise, I'll forget the dream."

"It can't be that important if it's so forgettable."

"Two minutes..."

"Sorry. I know how long your two-minute conversations can last. I'm tired of arriving at concerts after all the parking spaces have been taken."

"Two minutes, I promise," his sister pleaded. "She doesn't have to interpret it. Let me just tell it to her so that she can think about it during the concert."

"Hagit dreams her own dreams during concerts. I'd be a rich man if I received a refund for every concert she's fallen asleep at."

"Just a few words."

"You can tell your dream to me. I'll pass it on to her."

"My dreams crumble when I tell them to you."

"Just the gist of it. I'm already dressed. For a small fee, I'll even be your analyst. Who can understand your childhood neuroses better than I?"

But his sister did not want to tell him her dream or have him for her analyst. As children they had fought frequently, just like their parents. Only after his marriage was their relationship put on a more even keel. And since Hagit's feelings of guilt toward her childlessly globe-trotting sister had room in them for Rivlin's sister too, she had let herself become Raya's confidante, the sole person capable of shaking golden coins from the pockets of her dreams. Now, overhearing the conversation, she picked up the receiver.

"I'm warning you," Rivlin whispered, removing the covers from their king-size bed and folding back the blanket for a quick plunge after the concert.

"Don't be so mean. Give me a minute with her. We've never come late for a concert yet...."

And so Rivlin's sister, a divorcée of many years who never talked about her ex-husband, told Hagit of a short, powerful dream about him. In it she was holding a baby, a little toddler, while imploring her former partner in English, *"Please, don't hurt the child."* He merely laughed, climbed into his big car, and drove off while leaving her standing in the street. Still clutching the little boy, she hurried off to the house of her ex-husband's old friends to look for some baby food. Yet all they gave her was half a glass of milk, and she ran desperately back out to the street, boarded an empty bus, and sat the hungry baby beside her.

That was the whole dream. As he had feared, Raya now wanted it interpreted on the spot.

"Your brother is having a fit," the half-naked judge told her. "Off-hand, though, I'd say that the baby is you."

"Me?"

"Well, parts of you."

"Parts...?" The idea both delighted and alarmed her. "What parts?"

"Let's talk about it in the morning."

## 12.

THE CONCERT WAS sold out. The only seats available were onstage. Rivlin, feeling sorry for his pale-faced sister-in-law, who was still ago-nizing over her dress for the wedding, gallantly surrendered his place beside Hagit and went to sit behind the orchestra.

The program was structured around several unknown young soloists making their debuts and consisted of a number of shorter works and several excerpts from longer ones—an approach that Rivlin found annoying. Apart from being opposed on principal to vi-olating the aesthetic integrity of a musical composition, he feared that the Philharmonic's renowned Indian conductor might try to fit so many young talents into the evening that it would become unduly long. These fears were dispelled by a quick glance at the program notes, which listed the length of each piece; after totaling them up and adding time for applause and intermissions, he concluded that the concert would end on schedule. Leaning back in his seat, he cast a benevolent glance at the overflow audience on the stage, which was young and unpretentiously dressed. Several rows ahead of him sat a man with a ponytail. For a moment he thought it might be his ex-daughter-in-law's husband. Come to think of it, though, the ponytail was as gray as the coat of a mouse.

He gazed down at the auditorium, looking for the wife who must already be missing him. Would she notice him and wave back? Or feel comfortable enough beside her sister to doze off? Lately she was suffering from fatigue, no doubt from the stress of a long closed-door trial that she was barred from talking about. At concerts, plays, and even movies she was soon so entangled in the cobwebs of sleep that were it not for her husband, who made sure to wake her at critical junctures, and especially before the end, she would not have known what she had sat through.

The opening soloist was a Russian immigrant, a tall, blond adolescent with a self-effacing manner, who played the first movement of the Tchaikovsky violin concerto. Rivlin, though fancying himself a lover of music, did not pretend to judge the caliber of the performance. Still, he had a melancholy tendency to doubt the staying power of young prodigies. "Time alone will show what will become of them," he liked to grumble as they took their bows. "Maybe someone knows what happened to last year's prodigies. Where are they now?"

Deep down he knew that his cynicism was caused by his worry for his stranded son. The night before, they had talked briefly with Ofer on the phone, after which Rivlin had insisted on going over every word of the conversation with Hagit. Resigned to Ofer's telling his mother that he knew of Hendel's death, he was surprised when it went unmentioned. Now, as a long orchestral prelude coaxed the violin from its silence, he wondered whether this was a sign of indifference to his ex-wife or of a secret pact with the father fighting to rescue him, even at the price of more pain, from the tyranny of an old wound.

The sentimental music of the Russian composer—who, the program notes said, was almost driven to suicide each time the critics panned his work—made its sure, swift way toward the final cadenza. From his vantage point behind the orchestra, Rivlin could see the back and shoulders of the young violinist, quivering with feeling. As his anxiety for his son, an exile mourning his marriage in a distant place, mounted in tandem with the trumpets, flutes, horns, and strings, he sought out the reassuring presence of his wife. Yet the passionate movements of the dark-skinned conductor, his baton pointed from time to time straight at Rivlin, as if he too were expected to contribute a few bars, hid Hagit from sight.

The orchestra fell silent. Having run out of both patience and emotion, the Russian violinist attacked the cadenza with a coldly calculated technique, as if wishing to have done with it as quickly as possible. Now that the musicians seated next to him were idle, Rivlin studied them for a clue to what they thought of the young soloist. Yet he could not tell whether they were even listening. The members of the wind section, busy cleaning their instruments, were whispering and smiling to each other with an old rapport. No doubt they had heard and would hear this concerto dozens of times, and this performance did not appear to have been one of the more impressive. From time to time they glanced at the conductor, whose limp, motionless stance, head down and hands at his sides, cleared the way for the yearning husband to search once more for his wife—only to look away in confusion upon discovering that he was staring at the wrong woman.

"You have to respect his bounds. You have no right to trespass, not even in your thoughts."

"Not even in my thoughts? What's wrong with you? How can anyone control such painful thoughts?"

"You can if you want to. And if you can't, at least keep them to yourself. Be careful. Ofer isn't you. You don't own him. You have no right to interfere in what happened between them. It can't do any good."

"But time is passing. . . ."

"Don't exaggerate. It's only four years."

"Five! Five! What makes you say four?"

"It doesn't matter. He'll find someone. A woman who suits him better. Stop conjuring up old ghosts. Let him breathe."

Several months after Ofer's sudden divorce, their son had stored his possessions in their apartment and gone to Paris to study hotel and restaurant design, a field he had become interested in after his marriage. That was more than four years ago. He had worked as an apprentice, without pay, for various architects, most of them Jews, while auditing classes at a cooking academy in order to "get the feel," as he put it, of the relationship between a kitchen and its diners. Meanwhile, he supported himself by working as a night security guard at the Jewish Agency in the 17th arrondissement—a situation shortened by his parents, in response to casual inquiries, to "Ofer works for the Jewish Agency in Paris."

The conductor lifted his baton and spurred the orchestra, as if it were a pack of hunting dogs, to race to the end of the movement. Rivlin did not join in the applause. Aloof, he watched the flustered soloist take his curtain call and vanish into the wings. Near the exit, by the kettledrum, were some empty seats. Rivlin decided to move to one of these, so as to improve his view of both the soloists and his wife.

The two sisters were chatting happily. Hagit, noticing his new location, seemed pleased that he would be visible for the rest of the concert. She waved, then signaled him with a smile to comb his hair.

The Tchaikovsky interpreter was followed by a parade of young female performers, most of them daughters of Philharmonic musicians. The first was a pianist with eyeglasses. Her long silver dress trailed past him across the floor while he read about her, her studies, and her accomplishments in the program, which announced that she was to play Rachmaninoff's *Rhapsody on a Theme by Paganini*. Alas, now all he could see, from his vantage point by the bald kettledrummer, were two bare shoulders and a white back with silver ribbons. What, he wondered, was the musical significance of such décolletage? Was there a connection between the low-necked dress and the rhapsody? Were this pianist and the tender young soloists who followed her—bare of shoulder, flowing of hair, alluring of bosom, slyly slit at the leg—offering their carnal bodies in compensation for possible lapses in their renditions, for notes misplayed or omitted, or was this their consolation prize to a sense of sight forced to play second fiddle to the sense of hearing? And what, then, of the performers with pimples and bad complexions? Of what use were they to an audience promised visual as well as audial pleasures?

As the father of two sons, he had been deprived, once the wife of the elder one left him, of paternal access to young maidenhood. Now, as a steady procession of it passed before him, nubile, fluid, and flushed with excitement, a violin, clarinet, oboe, cello, or flute in its bravely vestal hands, he could not listen to the second concerto of Karl Maria Von Weber or to Ravel's *Les Tsiganes* or Chausson's *Poeme,* without an old sorrow welling up in him. Borne on the alternating waves of the music, his fictional confession in the hotel garden throbbed in him like a real disease.

This time the applause found him ready to join in, and he exchanged smiles with the bald kettledrummer, who had crossed his sticks in the symphonic gesture of approval for a job well done. Yet as he sought to leave the hall at the concert's end, the Orientalist's way was blocked by the ushers, who had shut the doors to prevent the early-to-bed-and-to-rise Haifaites from rushing for the exits.

There was a surprise finale. Never since he and Hagit had taken out their Philharmonic subscription could Rivlin remember such a thing. At the special request of the conductor, a musician rose and asked the audience to remain seated. As much as he loved the local musical scene, the Indian maestro had not forgotten his native land—which, poor, vast, and suffering, had young talents, too, who deserved a hearing. With a sharp wave of the baton, an Indian lad was thrust upon the stage. A fat, bespectacled ten-year-old in a baggy black suit, he stepped forward with a little violin that reminded Rivlin of the instrument once bought for him by his mother, who had dreamed of raising another Yehudi Menuhin.

The solemn boy, looking more like a despondent dwarf than a child prodigy, paid no attention to the applauding audience. Like a well-trained baby elephant, he took his place beside the smiling maestro, who patted him lovingly, as if reminded of his own self fifty years earlier. Leaving the orchestra to its own devices, the big Indian put the little one through his paces, leading him gently and attentively down the enchanted paths of Mendelssohn's First Violin Concerto—

paths that would take him assuredly Westward if only he remained a true son of the East.

## 13.

YO'EL, UNLIKE HIS WIFE, chose to arrive on a Saturday, thus giving the judge the pleasure of an airport reunion. Invoking recent precedent, the Rivlins decided to detour first to Jerusalem, where Hagit and Ofra's old aunt was impatiently awaiting a visit from her nieces— especially from the fragile émigré, whose Third World peregrinations she had faithfully followed from the inner sanctum of her little room in a geriatric institution. And as long as they would be in the capital anyway, Hagit said, why not recoup the chance, lost the week before, to succor that dubious invalid Professor Tedeschi, now home from the hospital? The judge was never averse to the lavish praise that the illustrious polymath was sure to bestow on her.

Since family meetings in Jerusalem had a way of unfolding with an inner rhythm of their own that made their outcome difficult to fore-see—especially when they involved two sisters eager to reminisce about their dead parents with an old aunt who was hard to stop once she got started—it was decided to put the sick call first, which would make it possible to cut short the visit to the aunt with the imperative of setting out for the airport. And so, on a crisp, sky blue Saturday morning, the three travelers were admitted to the Tedeschis' apartment by the translator of Jahaliya poetry, who shook a stern head at them as if to say: "Although you may find us at home and not in the hospital, don't delude yourselves for a moment that our afflictions have passed, much less that they are—the thought of it!—imaginary. On the con-trary, the doctors' refusal to face the facts only makes matters worse." Introduced to Ofra, she gave her a bitter smile, satisfied with this new addition to the anxious circle of her husband's well-wishers, before leading them into the old living room into which, thirty-two years pre-viously, a young instructor had brought his girlfriend, then in the army, for the approval of his academic mentor, the sound of whose slippers was now heard as he came padding from an inner room.

The flame red color of Tierra del Fuego that Rivlin had noted in Tedeschi's cheeks had faded to the ruddy suntan of an Alpine skier, and the hospital pajamas had been replaced by a pair of old corduroy pants. Only the pajama top, flecked with medicinal stains, was unchanged. Tedeschi's skinny arms, proudly bearing the yellow marks of the infusion needles, protruded from the sleeves. He entered the room slowly, ignoring his old student and making straight for Hagit, who kissed him warmly on both cheeks and handed him a bouquet of flowers. Bowing slightly to Ofra, he asked Hagit, with ironic pathos:

"To what do I owe the privilege of Your Honor's coming all this way just to see me?"

"Not just," Rivlin corrected him. "Also."

"Come, come, Carlo," Hagit said, with a smile. "Don't you think you're worth a trip to Jerusalem?"

The old polymath shrugged genuinely skeptical shoulders and sank into a large armchair that had slightly deformed itself to accommodate his shape. The translatoress, on guard lest her husband stray from the subject of his medical condition, thus collaborating with the enemy, who made light of it, kept an irritable eye on him.

"He looks much better than he did last week," Rivlin told her. Sarcastically he added, "He must be in training for the conference at the Dayan Center later this month."

The Jerusalem scholar, while regarding Rivlin's two women with approval, dismissed the conference with a disdainful wave and began to cough with gusto, the phlegm rattling so loudly in his chest that Ofra winced in her corner. He winked, still without looking at Rivlin, and declared:

"Who cares about that conference in Tel Aviv? Unless, that is, you'll be presenting something new there that I owe it to myself to listen to...."

"I'm afraid," the visitor from Haifa replied glumly, "that I have nothing new to present."

"Those Tel Avivans just want to make a splash. I've informed them that I'll have to feel better than I do now before I give them the benefit of my latest insights."

The old professor modestly shut his eyes.

"Then you're considering giving a paper?" Rivlin, out of sorts, glared at Hagit, who had insisted on this visit. *You see?* his expression seemed to say. *Why bother when it's all just a big act?*

"What paper?" Hannah Tedeschi protested, rallying to the side of the man's illness. "Carlo is fooling himself if he thinks he'll be back on his feet in two weeks. The only conference he'll attend will be about the results of his tests."

"Rubbish," Tedeschi murmured, glancing from the wife fifteen years his junior to his ex-student, the pitiable professor from Haifa. "What's the matter with you? Don't tell me your book is still bogged down. Can't you throw the conference some juicy little bone, something heartwarming about the Algerian psychosis?"

"I have no bones to spare," Rivlin replied, with a hostile air. "You know me. I don't need to go to conferences just to remind the world of my existence. If I have nothing to say, I say nothing."

Tedeschi shut his eyes again and nodded in vague confirmation.

"But you've been working on that material for years!" exclaimed their hostess, distressed not for the conference in Tel Aviv, but for her husband's jubilee volume. "Don't tell me you can't get a single article out of it!"

"One can always toss something off, Hannah. But you, of all people, who work so hard and have only three or four poems to show for it at the end of the year, should understand the difficulty of producing something solid that will withstand the test of time. I can't write about the fifties and sixties in Algeria, which were a period of vision and hope, without taking into account the insane terror going on now. A scholar with some integrity doesn't just closet himself with old documents and materials. He reads the newspapers and connects the past to the present. It's his job to show that today's developments have their roots in yesterday's."

"It's hopeless," Hagit said with a smile, recrossing her legs for the benefit of the old polymath, who, though wheezing a bit, was listening raptly. "I'm married to a man who is convinced that everything has a logical reason. He can't fall asleep at night until he finds it."

"Tea or coffee?" asked a chagrined Hannah Tedeschi.

The two sisters chose tea. The unkempt house and the state of its upholstery suggested that the milk in the fridge might not be fresh. The professor from Haifa, knowing the Tedeschis better than the women did, asked for brandy, hoping it might disinfect any dirty glass given him.

Tedeschi wagged a half-threatening, half-approving finger. "He's right," he said of Rivlin, as though to justify having considered him his successor. "We must never write about the past as if the present didn't exist. On the contrary, we have to look for the hidden symptoms of impending disorder even before it breaks out. Historical research is like prostate cancer: we need a blood test to detect the antibodies that signal the malignancy still contained in one little gland, before it invades the entire body. We must measure both kinds of cholesterol, the good and the bad, to determine the secret relationship that blocks the blood vessels and leads to a sudden heart attack. There are subtle signs that show up in newly coined speech, in imaginative combinations that occur only to poets and novelists. And at the same time, we must not be taken in by mere decadence, by the whiners and complainers who speak only for themselves."

Rivlin's head began to droop. He was familiar with the latest theories about the tendency of art and literature to signal social transformations. Yet all the studies concocted from such ideas, unless made solid by government protocols, political declarations, and legal and institutional decisions, were too frothy to merit a response.

"Yochi has no time for novels," Hagit announced. "He says life is too turbulent."

She was enjoying her visit with the hypochondriac so much that, forgetting to refuse the grayish slab of cake placed before her, she bit politely into it and even praised it. But yet the translatoress, well aware of her shortcomings in the kitchen, shrugged off the hypocritical compliment, while turning impatiently to the recalcitrant Rivlin.

"Surely you could write something about a poem or two."

"Only if translated by you," Rivlin warmly answered the tense, severe woman, whose blue eyes, magnified by thick spectacles, were the same as those of the mischievous student he had attended classes with back in the sixties. Knowing it would give her pleasure, he again recited Al-Hajaj's grand soliloquy, this time in Arabic.

"But what," he lamented, "would the know-it-alls say if I used a wonderful poem written fifteen hundred years ago to explain the murders of terrorists today?"

"Then choose a modern poem. Something hot off the press." Tedeschi sounded as if he were running a fast-food stand. "Listen, Rivlin. We have something authentically new for you. Hannah, tell him about that friend of yours...the poor fellow who was killed...."

## 14.

ONCE AGAIN, THE Tedeschis—needing, so it seemed, the constant presence of real death—had a surprise corpse for him. This time it was an unknown young scholar from the Arabic Department in Jerusalem, who, stimulated by a literary, sociological, and ethnographic interest, had undertaken a study of popular literature in North Africa. The translatoress, no mean student of Arabic literature herself, had helped her friend unravel the subtle historical allusions hidden in the intricacies of contemporary Arab writing. And he, an observant Jew intimately familiar with religious sources, had repaid her with many an elegant rabbinic phrase that came in handy in her renditions of Jahaliya poetry. So productive had their collaboration over the past year been that they had even toyed with the idea of putting out a joint anthology of Arabic verse in Hebrew translation, he doing the moderns and she the ancients. And then he was killed.

"How?" Rivlin asked.

"In that bus bombing near Pisgat Ze'ev."

"That's the first university teacher killed by a terrorist that I've heard of."

"He wasn't just a teacher," Tedeschi protested angrily. "He was a first-rate scholar who burned the midnight oil to understand the Arab mind. Not that that stopped them from snuffing him out one fine day."

"Those aren't the same Arabs," Rivlin protested.

"Yes, they are, yes, they are!" bitterly declared Hannah Tedeschi, who generally avoided political arguments. "Don't be naive, Yochanan.

Anyone who has burrowed through ancient Arabic poetry as much as I have knows it's all one world."

"How can you let her say such a thing?" Rivlin scolded his old professor.

Tedeschi waved him off. "Let her say what she wants. She loved that young man. And rightly so, because he belonged to that scholarly nobility that, far outside the limelight, does the dirty work that clears the way for the rest of us, correcting old errors and pointing out new directions."

"It was horrible," their hostess told the two sisters. "He was carrying a briefcase full of rare Arabic newspapers and magazines, and they were all spattered with blood. I cried when his wife showed them to me—I, who have gone through hell with Carlo and never shed a tear. What a loss to the world of scholarship. And to think of what those sons of bitches in the department made him go through to get a lecturer's rank!"

"What was he doing on a bus? Didn't he own a car?"

"What car? He gave his all to his work and barely made a living. If it hadn't been for Carlo, who managed to arrange a small fellowship for him last year, he would have been on welfare. You should have seen his apartment."

"What did you say his name was?"

"Yosef Suissa."

"An Orthodox Jew?"

"One of the decent ones."

"The field has recently been flooded by such types."

"Flooded?"

"Enriched." Rivlin corrected himself while signaling his wife that the visit was over. Hagit, however, paid no attention and even agreed to a second cup of tea, as an antidote to the ghastly cake.

"So what do you say?" their hostess demanded. She looked so weary and distracted at this hour of the morning that Rivlin wondered whether Tedeschi's first wife wasn't making a comeback in her.

"About what?"

"About having a look at Suissa's material. You never know. Perhaps you'll find a spark of inspiration for your book."

"In old poems and stories? No thanks. They're not my line."

"No, but they're not far from it," Tedeschi said. "You can spice your work up with them. Believe me, it's not a bad recipe...." He winked again at the two sisters. "Not bad at all. At Cambridge, when I illustrated the Turks' casual attitude toward state corruption with examples from popular nineteenth-century theater, it went down rather well."

"But you're asking me to look at things written in a local dialect that I would have a hard time translating."

"Do as some of your colleagues do and find an Arab student to help you," their hostess suggested. "Carlo always has a few talented young Arabs doing the drudgery."

"What makes you think they'll understand Algerian dialect?"

"They will if you give them a reason to—say, a research assistant-ship. They'll use far-flung family connections to find out what they don't know. Take a look at Suissa's material. It's a shame to let it go to waste."

"But why not find someone in his own department?" Rivlin asked, trying to get out of it. "There must be someone who wants to carry on his work and publish. I'd just be muscling in."

Hannah Tedeschi was relentless. "No one gives a damn about pop-ular culture. They think it's beneath them. They'd rather write about that blind Egyptian who won the Nobel Prize."

"I thought he was deaf."

"Deaf, blind, who cares? They don't have Suissa's feel for everyday life."

"That's enough talking," Tedeschi told his wife. "Call Mrs. Suissa and tell her that Yochanan is on his way over now to take everything. She's so swamped by all the papers her husband left behind that she's liable to torch them in desperation."

"But it's Saturday...."

"Don't worry about it. His wife is no longer a Sabbath observer. The religious one in the family was him. Look here, Yochanan. Listen to your moribund old professor. Do it. You know I'm your loyal friend, whatever our mutual reservations and recriminations. Take my advice. Don't miss the chance to see what Suissa had. It has nothing to do with my jubilee volume. I couldn't care less about that. It's only making me sicker. Phone her, Hannah. As long as you're already in Jerusalem, you might as well benefit from it. . . ."

Rivlin felt a wave of the same affection that had moved him in the distant days of his doctoral studies, when he had sat for hours in this room under the strict but patient tutelage of the dedicated teacher who had pinned great hopes on him. Back then the smells from the kitchen came from the cooking of Tedeschi's first wife, cooking that alone was sufficient evidence that she was losing her mind. He cast a questioning glance at Hagit and Ofra.

Hagit threw up her hands in cheerful surrender. "What do you have to lose?" she asked. Even his sister-in-law, who always minded her own business, nodded ever so slightly in agreement.

## 15.

SINCE MORNING SHE had been waiting under the carob tree at the geriatric home, a hundred meters from her old apartment in the neighborhood of Bet ha-Kerem. She had left the apartment twenty-five years ago to wander from one mental institution to another, either physically ill or else punishing herself with a Pirandellian, profoundly phantasmagorical madness that, alternately under and out of control, withstood the many assaults of electric shock and drugs. Her older sister, having attended her in her disturbance with anxious devotion, died and left two daughters to carry on. The elder of these took pains to keep in touch with her aunt writing from the remote lands she traveled in, while the younger and jollier one made sure, despite her own numerous obligations, to phone regularly and visit once a month. Deferring with a smile to the old woman's many delusions—old and new alike—she kept reminding her of what no one else dared tell her, namely, that all things are permitted the insane except the abdication of love. And if their sick aunt truly loved her two nieces, she would bestow on them the gift of memory, telling them all they had known and forgotten, or had never known at all, about the dead.

Indeed, in recent years their aunt had begun to mine from her melancholy glittering diamonds forged in the darkness of time. With a renewed curiosity about the past, she had plunged to astonishing depths to retrieve these bright, hard nuggets. A first harbinger of this change was the sweetly ironic tone in which she took to speaking to Rivlin, the faithful driver who accompanied her niece to their meetings and sat in the shade of the trees by the front gate, reading a newspaper and fending off the mental patients seeking to approach him, until the time came to retrieve his wife, gently but determinedly, from the sick woman's clutches. In the early years of her institutionalization, these appearances of his had so stricken her with fear that he had had to be instantly ejected. Slowly, however, her attitude yielded to a quiet resignation, which was in turn transformed, at first behind his back and eventually to his face, into a coquettish coyness. Hagit, encouraged, kept her aunt informed of all Rivlin's activities, as though by dangling the bait of him before the old woman's reawakening sense of humor she might lure the silken butterfly of sanity from its grim cocoon.

Gradually, their aunt emerged from her fortress of self-imposed oblivion with a great desire to know. So reinvigorated was her interest in the numerous details, large and small, of the lives of friends and relatives that Rivlin wondered whether—listening, making connections, cross-referencing, and double-checking—she didn't know better than he did what went on in his wife's courtroom or what the young officer was up to in the depths of his mountain. And so, having driven the two sisters to their midday rendezvous and spied from afar their aunt's white tresses beneath the large carob tree—where, leaning on her cane, she had been standing in anticipation for over an hour beside a table transported for the occasion from the dining room and set for four—he yielded to his wife's entreaties to donate a few minutes of his time to the soothing effect of allowing her aunt a few jibes at his expense.

And in fact, no sooner had Ofra embraced her aunt and Hagit gaily presented her with a bar of chocolate than the observant old lady began teasing Rivlin for his impatience to be gone.

"You can't wait to get away from me, can you?"

He joined his palms together, Indian-style, to signify having come in peace.

"I'd be superfluous today. You have a special guest. I wouldn't want to rob you of your time with her."

She smiled wanly in agreement. Like a powerful computer scanning his file for recent entries, she asked in her deep, rehumanized voice:

"How was the wedding of your Arab student Semadar?"

"Samaher. . . ."

"Of course. Samaher. Was it as difficult for you as usual?"

He flushed awkwardly and cast a reproachful glance at his wife for having revealed his secret, as a gambit to enhance her aunt's mood.

"Not quite. . . ."

"He doesn't envy Arabs as much," Hagit explained.

"Not yet," Rivlin added lamely.

## 16.

IT WASN'T EASY to find the address in Pisgat Ze'ev. The Jerusalem chapter of Rivlin's life had ended with the 1967 war, before the appetite of the victors had pushed back the bounds of the city in one compulsive new neighborhood after another. Although the buildings of the development in Jerusalem's far north were new, the streets meandered unclearly, and the house numbers owed more to poetic license than prosaic logic. For a moment, he was tempted to abandon the whole wild-goose chase, telephone a Hebrew University colleague, and settle for a whiff of what was cooking in the academic kitchens of Jerusalem. But since he had time to spare, the two sisters' aunt having insisted they stay for lunch, he decided to obey his old teacher and take a look at Yosef Suissa's files. Perhaps something of the man's brilliance had rubbed off on them.

At least this time he wasn't paying a condolence call. The first days of the Suissa family's bereavement were long over with. He had never even met the deceased—who, however, or at least so he hoped, must have known about him. Polite small talk or patient listening to how the dead man had breathed his last would be unnecessary. He would introduce himself and wait by the door for Suissa's research to be delivered, with a sigh of relief, to his capable hands—which, sorting through it to detect its interrupted purpose, might manage to breathe some life into it.

He stood on the third-floor landing, the same wilderness of Judea that he had gazed at from the hotel in Talpiyot visible through a dusty window in the corridor. This time, however, the Dead Sea did not glint in the distance. Not trusting Tedeschi's assurance that the widow was no longer a Sabbath observer, he refrained from ringing the bell and rapped lightly on the door, at a point beside the dead man's name.

The decision proved to be a wise one. The door was opened by the deceased's father, a short, somber, religious Jew with a hat and a scraggly mourner's beard that appeared to have grown on top of a previous one. A prayer book lying on the dining-room table testified to his having recently returned from the synagogue, perhaps in the hope of saving the threatened sanctity of the Sabbath, which Rivlin could hear being thrashed in a washing machine. To help get over his discomfort, the Orientalist introduced himself with his academic title, apologized for intruding, and added a few words of commiseration for the death of the lately departed. Nodding morosely, Suissa senior opened the door of a bedroom, from which sprang a small, wildly laughing, bare-bottomed orphan, the imprint of a potty on his behind. Without further ado the child threw himself on the visitor, who was not sure whether he was being physically attacked or appealed to for protection and love. On the orphan's heels came the young widow. Barefoot, unkempt, and dressed in shorts, a naked infant in her arms, she proclaimed by her appearance that her husband's tragic death had released her, not only from the bonds of religion, but from those of civilization itself. It was as if, Rivlin thought, the savage soul of the terrorist had taken possession of the wife of his victim.

Little wonder that the bereaved father, his hat still on his head, had made a beeline back from synagogue to ward off the evil spirit let loose in the house.

"I'm Professor Rivlin." He leaned compassionately forward toward the widow, one hand patting the naked infant clinging to her neck. "I believe Dr. Hannah Tedeschi told you about me."

"Yes. I've prepared a package for you. But come to the bedroom and have a look. Perhaps there's still more there."

The visitor's face burned as hotly as if he were being shanghaied to the Land of Fire. He followed the woman, trailed after by her father-in-law, with the bare-bottomed child running ahead. Tossing the infant onto the blankets of a large bed, in which he began to crawl and entangle himself, she led Rivlin to a modest desk, wedged between the bed and a closet, that was piled high with papers, folders, and books. One had the impression of a work in progress interrupted not months but mere minutes ago. A screen and a keyboard stood alone, without their computer. The latter, the widow told Rivlin, had been taken by an Arab research assistant who hoped to salvage what was on it. Her large, pretty eyes rested anxiously on him, as if inquiring whether she had done the right thing by letting a junior member of the department—and an Arab, yet—make off with the computer.

"They'll build their careers on his blood," Suissa senior muttered, with a hatred that made Rivlin shiver, as though he too were a vulture feeding off the dead man's corpse.

"So what? What do you care? Let them." The widow's scolding tone made it clear that her father-in-law was getting on her nerves.

"How old was your son?" Rivlin asked the man sorrowfully.

"Thirty-three. The age at which they crucified the Christian. Except that my son, may he rest in peace, was a good man...."

It was odd to hear a Jew just back from synagogue comparing his son to Jesus.

The visitor wished to avoid misunderstanding.

"I have to tell you that I'm in a different academic field. I deal with Arab history, not literature or poetry. I have no idea whether any of this material, which Professor Tedeschi and his wife wanted me to look at, is related to my work. I'll take it home for a week or two. If anything interests me, I'll have it photocopied. You'll get it all back...."

The thought of the large package of newspapers being returned to her only made the widow more depressed.

"No," she said. "Please don't. There's no need. You can donate it all to the library."

"His brain went squish!" the bare-bottomed child shouted happily, scrambling underfoot. He stuck out his little hand to touch the package, which was wrapped in brown paper tied with rough twine.

His grandfather grabbed at him to silence him. Leaping onto the bed, the boy vanished with his naked brother among the blankets.

The Orientalist lifted the package, careful not to inquire whether the bloodied pages had been removed or were inside. Before leaving, he yielded to temptation and asked to see a photograph of the deceased. The young widow hurried to bring him several, each of which revealed someone else.

## 17.

AS THE SCANTILY attired widow was about to walk her visitor to his car, if only to flee the apartment, her mother-in-law—short and hatted, like her husband, though her hat was a bright bonnet—appeared with a large pot of Sabbath stew to shore up the crumbling dikes of the Day of Rest. Promising to stay in touch, Rivlin thanked them all again and returned to his car. He debated opening the package, decided not to, and thrust it into the baggage compartment, which he had rearranged to make room for Yo'el's suitcase, even though he knew the latter would be small.

Again he had time on his hands. Better yet, no guilt was attached to it. And so before driving back into town to find a restaurant that was open in the desolation of the Jerusalem Sabbath noon, he made a U-turn onto a winding street from which he could compare the desert view from the city's north with that from the south. Not only, however, was the blue patch of the Dead Sea missing here too, the noble yellow vista of the Judean wilderness was bleak and dreary, perhaps because of a large Bedouin settlement whose shacks and black tents defended the hillsides against the city's ravenous encroachment.

Nevertheless, a path descending between two buildings lured him down it with the promise of detecting a sliver of the inland sea that in his Jerusalem childhood had fired his imagination as the city's answer to the Mediterranean—that far destination of summer vacations. But bleakness still curtained the gray horizon. Looking back up at the third-floor window of the little apartment, he tried to imagine what the dead scholar had seen as he sat at the desk squeezed into his bedroom: not a tiresome old crone like the one Rivlin saw sitting on her terrace in Haifa, but the play of wind and light on the desert, and Arabs, unwilling citizens of the Israeli-ruled city, strolling among the shacks and tents in which burned their hearth and cooking fires. Surely this was a better perspective from which to study the Arab soul and understand, as Ephraim Akri had put it, what mattered to it and what didn't. Again he felt tempted to inspect the package in the baggage compartment. As it was unlikely that Yo'el would be in any hurry to take his wife to a hotel, many days would go by before he could sit down in his study to determine whether Suissa's material might indeed provide a spark of inspiration.

He had tried not to grumble about his expulsion from his workroom and to be as patient as possible with their fragile and likable guest. This was not merely to calm his wife's nagging anxieties about her hospitality. It was also to justify, if only to himself, the new and clandestine freedoms that he was taking.

## 18.

THIS TIME, THERE being no suitable pretext for another call, it took creativity and courage to avoid the twin embarrassments of being a nuisance to the Hendels and in defiance of his wife. And who could promise him that Galya would even be there? There was no guarantee, on this bleak, sleepy afternoon, of finding his ex-daughter-in-law in the hotel whose threshold he was crossing.

His last visit, with its heated conversation beneath the gazebo by the swimming pool, had made him a familiar figure to the clerk at the reception desk, who regarded him, a guest needing no directions, with approval. But although he knew the way to the Hendels' quarters, he feared that his unexpected reappearance might be taken as a bizarre or even unbalanced regression, rather than as the sober determination to clear up an ancient mystery. Therefore, he headed for the crowded dining room, in which he lingered despite the unlikelihood of his son's ex-wife turning up there. Taking a tray, he joined the line by the food counter, whose steamy dishes made him feel slightly queasy. If nothing else, he would enjoy a good meal whose tastes brought back better days. The talk around him informed him that, this time too, he was surrounded by a group of Christian pilgrims.

Well, then, I'll be a pilgrim myself, Rivlin thought, placing his loaded tray on a table occupied by two outsize Americans, tall, hefty men despite their elderly appearance. They welcomed the Israeli diner and sought to strike up a conversation, which Rivlin joined by proudly informing them, Christian Zionists, that he was not only a Jewish professor but the scion of an ancient Jerusalem family. Inquiring about their itinerary, he pointed out its advantages and shortcomings and responded to their praises of the hotel by mentioning that his son had been wed to the owner's daughter, albeit not for long. This led the two pilgrims, in the charitable spirit of their journey, to consider his visit and partaking of a meal with them as an act of religious benevolence.

A young Arab waiter came to clear the table. Uncertain of the new pilgrim's identity, he discreetly sought to establish it and—unauthorized to issue a free meal ticket—went to fetch the maître d'. This turned out to be the old Arab who had recognized Rivlin at the bereavement and encouraged him to write in the condolence book. "What's the problem?" he scolded. "Professor Rivlin is one of the family. He can eat all he wants on the house." "You mean I was one of the family," Rivlin corrected with a laugh while the waiter blushed with embarrassment. But this merely evoked a dismissive wave of the hand. Families were to be entered, not exited.

"You did the right thing by coming here for a rest, Professor," the maître d', whose name was Fu'ad, observed. "This is the best season."

Rivlin had to explain that he had not come to rest or even to eat. He had returned because his wife and sister-in-law were lunching in the city with an aunt. The heart had its reasons. And as though it were an afterthought, he murmured:

"Is Galya by any chance here?"

"You didn't finish talking to her the last time, did you?"

The man's powers of observation surprised him.

Fu'ad sighed proudly. "If I didn't notice such things, who would? She was the one of Mr. and Mrs. Hendel's children whom I spent the most time with. He and his wife, the poor woman, used to go once a week for a night out in Tel Aviv and leave Galya with me. If she was upset, I'd take her home to Abu-Ghosh to play with my nephews. After a while she'd calm down. Believe me, no one knows her as I do. She's a smart young lady, but moody and stubborn. Sometimes, I would take her out for an ice cream or a falafel when I had free time at the hotel. She liked that. It always cheered her up. Now she's taking Mr. Hendel's death hard, maybe even harder than the missus. Harder than her sister, that's for sure. She seemed so sad after that conversation with you last week. What made you leave in such a hurry?"

"I had to be at the airport. I have to be there again today."

"You Jews are always at the airport. Always coming and going. You can't sit still. It will make you sick in the end."

"To tell the truth, I already am sick," the guest said with a smile, looking through the window at a lovely white cloud sailing by. The thought of the illness born here ten days ago made him feel a sweet pang. Stricken, he bowed his head and whispered to the man in the dark suit and black bow tie:

"I'm quite ill."

The maître d' looked at the Orientalist suspiciously.

"Ill, Professor? But that can't be."

"Why not?"

"Is that what you told Galya last week?"

"Among other things."

*"Mish ma'ool, ya eyni."**

*"Leysh la? Ma'ool jiddan."†*

*"Ma t'zalnish al-fadi. Kulna minhibak k'tir hon."‡*

*"Shu ni'mal, hada min Allah."§*

*"Shu Allah? Ma lak uma l'Allah? Ma tistahbilnish."‖*

The two elderly pilgrims, surprised by the change of language in mid-conversation, sat up like two pinkish, blue-eyed elephants given a secret command and took their prudent leave.

---

\* It can't be, my friend.
† Why not? It can definitely be.
‡ Don't distress me like that. We're all very fond of you.
§ What can I do? It's God's will.
‖ What God? What does it have to do with God? Don't mock me.

"Where is Galya?"

"Perhaps with her mother."

"And husband?"

"Of course."

"Could you bring her here? *Bas hi. B'sif.*"*

"*Ala rasi.*"†

## 19.

It wasn't just from crying, Rivlin decided cheerfully upon seeing his ex-daughter-in-law, still dressed in black, emerge hesitantly from a side door. She really had lost her looks, and the short haircut she had got since their last meeting only emphasized this. He rose to greet her from the dark corner of a little lounge set off from the dining room. It was here that Hendel, seated before a full-length mirror in which he watched the smoke spiral up from the cigars that his wife couldn't stand, had come when he'd wanted to indulge. Any man, friend, foe, neighbor, or stranger had the right to appear at a bereavement and offer his consolation to the mourners. Yet her ex-father-in-law's insistence on a second meeting perplexed the young woman who, regarding him with a mixture of pity and fear, now slipped into the chair by his side.

"I've received a letter from Ofer," she said at once, using the son to shield her from the prying father.

He shivered with joy.

"A short one. And a nasty one. He was very hard on me. That's no way to comfort anyone. But it doesn't matter. I took it for what it was."

"You see?"

"See what?"

"Despite all the time that's gone by, he hasn't given up."

"But on what?"

"On wanting to know. To understand. Like me."

---

\* Just her. Secretly.

† Trust me.

She shook her cropped head angrily. "You're wrong. His letter had nothing to do with that. I've already told you that he understands all he needs to."

He felt his confidence shaken by her firmness. He reached out a fatherly hand that fell short of touching her. In the mirror he saw Fu'ad moving slowly across the empty dining room. The maître d' cast a glance at their dark corner and disappeared.

"Listen carefully, Galya. If I thought for a moment that he understood why you left him, or had come to terms with it, I'd never have stooped to come here again."

"But why is it stooping?" she protested hotly. "You mustn't say such things, Yochanan. I was very touched by your last visit. I'm touched by this one, too. We're all grateful. If only there were some way I could help.... But you mustn't try to make me feel guilty or take your anger out on me. I have enough problems."

A desert wind riffled the curtain. Rivlin took the plunge.

"I've already told you..."

"What?"

"That I haven't much time left."

"How do you mean?"

"I told you."

"But what's wrong with you?"

"The details don't matter. I don't like to discuss them. I'm not asking for pity, only for justice."

"But what does this have to do with justice?"

He bowed his head and said nothing, feeling a stirring in her.

"You're torturing yourself for no reason. What does it matter? People get together and break up all the time. I left your son because we couldn't go on the way we were. Because it would have been wrong to. Ask him. Why should I tell you what he won't?"

"He would like to. He can't."

She made no reply.

In the mirror behind her Rivlin saw her ponytailed husband peer into the dining room.

"Fine. I won't bother you again. Just do me one last favor. Answer his letter."

"But he told me not to," she said with a triumphant gleam. "Those were his last words."

"Never mind." His anger turned against his son. "Write him. It doesn't matter what. Just give him a sign. If he swallowed his pride enough to send you a condolence note, he must want an answer even if he denies it. Give him one. Anything. A few words. It makes no difference what they are. Do it for my sake. You owe me that much."

"Owe you?" He felt her waver.

"Morally. We treated you like a daughter from the minute you set foot in our home. We couldn't have loved you more. Whatever you wanted, whatever you asked for, even hinted at, was yours. We never said a word when you broke up the marriage. We just gritted our teeth, Hagit and I. We tried being high-minded about it."

She nodded slowly in confirmation. The word "high-minded" swept him along.

"Even if you think you owe us nothing, do it for your father's sake. Don't leave me in the dark. I won't come again, I promise. This is the last time. Not even Hagit knows I'm here. She would be furious if she saw me pleading with you like this. Promise you'll write to Ofer. Even if he doesn't want you to. Just this once."

"But what should I say?" she whispered despairingly, like a student bewildered by a teacher's demands.

"Anything. Make him realize he understands."

She weighed his words carefully before making a movement with her head. He couldn't tell if she was nodding it or shaking it. Her eyes were damp with what looked like old tears. Again, something told him that she was pregnant.

The tall husband passed again across the mirror. The two blue-eyed, evangelical elephants reentered the dining room and wandered slowly through it, lifting the tablecloths as though looking for something they had lost.

## 20.

"YOU DIDN'T BELIEVE me. Well, now you've seen for yourself. She gets more lucid from day to day. She even remembered the names of places in South America that Yo'el told her about three years ago. It's not just her memory, either. She can explain things, see connections. And she's so funny! She has a sense of humor she never had before. Did you hear what she said about Yochi? It's too bad, Yochi, that you weren't there. Where were you all that time? You would have enjoyed her. Imagine: she not only thought of asking about your work, she even remembered it had to do with Algeria. At first she said Morocco and then she caught herself. When I told her you were stuck she asked me to tell you she understood. She has real empathy. I'm sorry you didn't stay. Where on earth did you disappear to? To think that for years the psychiatrists sent her from one institution to another without holding out any hope! It's no wonder I bristle whenever one of them gets on the witness stand and spouts some diagnosis."

"Don't generalize."

"You're right. One mustn't. But I've seen enough to be skeptical about the experts. I can understand wanting to make a science of mental disorder. But do it modestly, with a sense of proportion. After all, they're not pathologists analyzing DNA in a lab. How can they label every hoodlum psychotic or schizophrenic or posttraumatic?"

"Give us the bottom line," Rivlin said, accelerating as they came out of the last turn of the descent from Jerusalem. "What are you saying, Hagit? That your aunt was making believe? That all the time we ran after her from asylum to asylum we were really going from theater to theater?"

"She wasn't making believe. I'm not saying that. Her torment was real. She didn't believe she deserved the love that our mother and all of us gave her, and that drove her to extremes of anxiety. It never occurred to her that we needed her love, too. Did we ever tell you, Ofra, how we first realized she was getting better?"

Ofra nodded. Although she had heard the story many times, she was always ready to hear it again.

The road to the airport was lightly traveled on Saturday afternoons. The anticipation of seeing Yo'el made the trip a pleasant one. Hagit was still too full of the lunch with her aunt and the family anecdotes to probe where her husband had been. It was just as well,

Rivlin thought. Although he could have padded his account of the time he had spent with the Suissas, he preferred not to. His failure at the hotel only made him feel more guilty.

"Actually," he said, interrupting his wife's entertaining but familiar account of her aunt's recovery, "Hagit owes her aunt a great deal."

"How is that?" Hagit asked.

"Didn't she once shock some sense into you as a child by telling you how awful you were?"

Like a healthy person recalling past illnesses, the judge liked to be reminded of a time when she hadn't been nice. Now, she looked lovingly at the husband who—if only to tease her—remembered her childhood so well.

"When was that?" Ofra asked, glowing in the backseat at the thought of Yo'el's arrival.

"Don't you remember how our parents used to send me to her in Jerusalem during summer vacations? I spent weeks there. Once she told me I wasn't nice to be with. It made a big impression."

"How old were you?"

"About twelve. I worshiped her then. Every word of hers was holy. It had a great effect."

"It's too bad it didn't last," joked her husband.

"But it did. Really. You could have used an aunt like that, someone to hold up a mirror to you. Yochi's mother"—Hagit turned around to her sister—"kept him tied to her apron strings, summer vacations included. He wasn't insurable, and she never gave him a chance to grow up."

A jumbo jet passed overhead, in one line with the road. For a second they seemed to keep up with it.

"Maybe that's Yo'el's plane," Ofra said.

"Perfect timing!"

But Yo'el's plane had landed a quarter of an hour early, and since he had only hand luggage, he was out of the terminal and perched on a low wall by a fountain, looking suntanned and refreshed, when they arrived. Reading a Hebrew paper, his toes sticking out of his biblical sandals, he did not look as if he had been away for three years.

## 21.

HER HUSBAND'S LARGE hands alone, in Ofra's opinion, could handle her fragile body without breaking it. Although they had been separated for only ten days, she and Yo'el clung to each other tightly, as if also embracing the children never born to them. It was a while before Yo'el turned to Hagit and gathered her, too, in his arms, after which he clapped Rivlin on the back and asked what was new in Algeria.

A spring dusk was descending when they reached Haifa. Gazing from their terrace at some trees bordered by two streets that ran down toward the sea, the distant gleam of which was invisible in the twilight, Yo'el—having been taken on a tour of the duplex by his now knowledgeable guide of a wife—acknowledged that the loss of their old wadi was not so grievous. Then, over bowls of grapes and cherries, the forgotten taste of which quickened the senses of the Israeli émigré, Rivlin decided that the time had come to relate the story of their moving.

"It's pure theory until you have to do it. You know, we lived in our old place for nearly thirty years. We thought we had some control, or at least some idea, about what went into it. A total illusion! Even the mover, who came to give us an estimate, turned out to be a wild optimist.

"The day before we packed was a Saturday in spring, just like now. We were sitting on our terrace overlooking the wadi, saying good-bye to our view of the sea. The apartment was still in one piece behind us. The pictures were still on the walls, the wineglasses were in the cupboard, the cheeses and the soft drinks and the containers of food were in the refrigerator, the books were on the shelves next to the photo albums—just the way it is now. Except, that is, for the sacks and the folded cartons, which were waiting in a corner for the packers to arrive the next day. Suddenly I had a mild attack of panic. 'Hagit,' I said. 'How can we be sitting here sitting here so calmly? Before the storm strikes, don't you think we should at least sort through what we're taking?' But in the immortal words of Oblomov in the Russian novel, 'If there's work to be done, let someone else do it.' We went on sitting on the terrace.

"Early the next morning, we're drinking our coffee and reading the newspaper while listening to the birds in the wadi, not at all like two people whose our lives are about to be turned upside down, when in walk two packers. They looked like two little ants, a dark woman of about thirty-five, a chain-smoker as thin as a match, and her scrawny twelve-year-old son, a boy with a black skullcap on a black head of hair. 'How will just the two of you manage?' I asked. 'Don't worry about us,' the woman says. 'Just tell us where to start.'

"Well, they attacked the house like two locusts. A pair of zombies couldn't have gone around with less plan or method, stuffing everything into sacks the way they did. The boy flew everywhere without a sound. He was like some blind, wingless grub, grabbing one thing after another and filling sack after sack. Imagine, I'm shaving in the bathroom when he walks in after me and scoops up whatever he can, the toothbrushes, the shaving cream, my bifocals, everything. I barely managed to retrieve my glasses from his sack. We spent the first two weeks after moving trying to figure out into which of dozens of sacks and crates our lives had been thrown by those maniacs and sprinkled with the mother ant's cigarette ashes.

"But I'm getting ahead of myself. The next morning six Arab moving men show up with a big truck and a little Jewish driver. Our new apartment was so close by that I was sure we'd be done by the afternoon. Well, by the time the first truckload pulled out it already was the afternoon, and the apartment was as full as ever. And when evening came and a second big truckload left, we still hadn't made a dent in anything, I started to cringe every time I saw a moving man. Something, humanly, had gone wrong. I mean, naked we come into this world and naked we leave—what were we doing with so many things? Were they all to prove our existence or simply to maintain it?

"The movers, every one of whom we now knew by name, address, and individual moving style, were getting restless. Halfway between the two apartments, the Jewish driver, who had been declaring all day that he had never been given such a job in his life—four flights of stairs from the wadi to the street, and four more from the street to the duplex, and with 'all those goddamn books'—threatened to quit on us. And when the new owner turned up with three workers with hammers, who began knocking down the walls for his renovation while we were still moving out, I began to feel my whole life was a mistake. Luckily, Hagit took command at that point and calmed the mutiny with a smile and a pay raise. The extra money did wonders. By midnight the old apartment was empty, and the last truckload had arrived with that big bookcase over there. The only problem was that it didn't fit into the stairway and had to be hoisted onto the terrace with ropes and pulleys.

"It was now two A.M. I was standing on the terrace with the head mover, who was having a fine time giving orders how to maneuver a bookcase that no one could see in the darkness. You could only hear it lifting off the ground, gaining altitude, and banging into things as it rose. I was too happy we were finished to give a damn. I felt so grateful to the movers for not abandoning us in the middle that I said to them in Arabic, 'You're fantastic! We could conquer the world between us. Let's draft you all into the Israeli army and march on Iraq.'"

"Iraq?"

"Iraq."

"Why Iraq?"

"Why not? Search me. I was punch-drunk by then. That must have been when I began losing my faculties. Since then I've lost a little more of them every month trying to get this place into shape."

"What did they say?"

"Who?"

"The Arab movers."

"What should they have said? They were so glad to be done that they would have taken on Iran too...."

22.

AS DARKNESS DESCENDED, Yo'el fell merrily asleep in the middle of a sentence, and Hagit went hurriedly off to make a second bed in the study—which, Rivlin announced, hoping thus to prevent the long-dreaded judicial inquiry into his free hours in Jerusalem, he was donating to his in-laws for the remainder of their stay. Not that he could work in his office at the university, where the students, secretaries, and teachers gave him no peace. But in any case, he intended to spend the next few days in the library with the journals and newspapers he had brought from Jerusalem, even though they were unlikely to be of great value.

The judge, stretched out fully dressed on their bed after a delightful day, agreed at once to his proposal. However, not only did she appear to take it quite for granted, but it did nothing to prevent her from wanting to know what he had done in Jerusalem. By way of reply, Rivlin invented a long stroll taken by him on the promenade south of the Old City. Since the two of them had once walked there together, he would not be asked for an account of it.

But Hagit was not through with him. "Is that all you did?"

For good measure he decided to throw in a visit to the Agnon House in Talpiyot, if only to demonstrate that he didn't need her agreement to go there.

"The Agnon House? It wasn't nice of you to go by yourself."

"But you never wanted to come."

"Only because I didn't want to run into Galya or her parents."

"What would have happened if you did?"

"Nothing. I just didn't want to see her."

"And now?"

"Now I don't care. She's ancient history."

"You can't mean that."

"Of course I can." Hagit yawned. "What's the Agnon House like?"

"I don't know. It was closed," he said, realizing in the nick of time that he would have to describe a place he had never been in.

"So what did you do then?"

"Then I rejoined you and Ofra."

## 23.

IN HIS ROOM in the university tower, facing the bald top of Mount Hermon in the distance, he tore open, with a slight trepidation, the wrapping paper containing the scholarly remains of the Jerusalem prodigy. The old, moth-eaten pages, many from the house organs of North African trade unions, were mimeographed or printed on rough paper. How could he tell the old stains from new ones made by blood or spattered brain? Since, like the blots in a Rorschach test, the dim yellow marks could tell him only about himself, he decided to ignore them and concentrate on the printed words.

The Tedeschis had been right. The amount of fiction and poetry in old North African newspapers and publications from the 1950s and '60s was amazing. It left the impression that the Arabs of the Maghreb had cared less for their struggle for independence than for their own private lives—their personal loves, friendships, and griefs, and the villages and landscapes they inhabited. Many of these compositions, marked in red by the murdered scholar, had been singled out by him for analysis.

But an analysis pointing to what?

A spark of inspiration, Rivlin concluded after leafing through the old pages, which left his fingers smelling of an unfamiliar spice, would not be found here. He was too much a believer in the tried-and-tested approaches to history to have much faith in the potential of such writings. Still, it might be possible, as Tedeschi had suggested, to use the odd poem or story to illustrate popular attitudes discussed in his book. Yet this called for precise translation, and the marked passages, though written in standard literary Arabic, had, as he had anticipated, expressions in local dialect that would give his critics a field day if he misconstrued them. Of course, he could always consult Ephraim Akri, who was a better philologist than intellectual historian. Yet a full professor had to be careful about exposing his academic weaknesses to a junior colleague eager for promotion.

So intense was his concentration as he labored to decipher, without noticeable success, the murdered Arabist's motives for singling out certain passages, the strange smell of whose paper was now on his face as well, that he failed to hear the light knock on his door. As though in a dream, a nervously smiling woman in her middle forties, well groomed and perfumed, slipped into the seat across from him and began to inquire, in typical Arab fashion, about him and his family without bothering to introduce herself or explain why she had come.

He pushed away the newspapers and cast a friendly glance at the woman, whose attractive features caused an old memory to flicker pleasantly. Sure from his smile that he had recognized her, she was now telling him how hard it was to find his room. It wasn't clear whether she was complaining or expressing her wonder at the size of the university. Still groping for her name, he suddenly remembered her standing guard outside a clean, fragrant bathroom and exclaimed happily, "Why, it's . . ."

"Afifa." Her modest smile bared two rows of marvelously white and flawless teeth.

Judging by his response, the name pleased him greatly. His interest in her feminine ripeness, which spoke more to an aging heart like his own than did the flaunted sexuality of the young students who flitted down the university's hallways, was indeed growing. Was it possible, he wondered with amused alarm, that this middle-aged Arab woman had taken seriously his casual suggestion that she return to her studies?

"How is the newlywed?" Rivlin asked. "We haven't seen her since the wedding."

"That's why I've come. . . ." Afifa's face fell. "Samaher isn't well again."

"Not well?" He snickered incredulously, rocking back and forth in his chair. "Don't believe her. She's just afraid to show her face. There's a small criminal case awaiting her."

"A what case?"

"Criminal. *Jina'i.*"

"I know what that means." She was insulted by the idea that she needed the word translated. "But what has she done criminal? She's an honest girl, Samaher. Ever since she was a baby. . . ."

"Why don't you ask her? She can tell you all about how she gave old term papers of hers to friends who copied them and handed them in as their own."

"Copied them?" Samaher's mother apparently knew all about it. "She just let those bums read them, to see how it's done. Why blame her? She has a good heart. She's too kind. That's always been her problem. We could never even slaughter a chicken or a sheep without her crying and calling us names. . . ."

"*Shu ma l'ha issa? Shu m'dayi'ha?*"*

"Pardon?"

"*Shu indha il'an?*"†

"She has that sickness of hers again," Afifa answered, declining to speak to Rivlin in Arabic. "She wants me to ask you for another postponement for that composition she owes you."

Who, Rivlin wondered, did the woman think he was—a grade-school teacher on Parents' Day? Yet, loath to offend her, he asked gently again in Arabic:

"*Shu maradha?*"‡

The attractive woman crimsoned as brightly as if she had been to Tierra del Fuego herself. A tear, dabbed at in vain with a little handkerchief held in her hand, dropped from her large, almond-shaped eyes. The handkerchief was torn by a wail, a primitive bleat of pain that burst from her throat and sent a seductive shudder through his loins.

When had a woman last cried like this in front of him? Only on television. Hagit was too accustomed to the sobs of her defendants to indulge in such a thing herself, while his sister cried only over the telephone—hardly the place for the cleansing, eye-dilating tears he was looking at now. As if reluctant to let go of them, Afifa went on dabbing at them with her little handkerchief even when he carefully nudged toward her a box of tissues.

But at least now she gave in and switched to her own language. In a colorful village patois, she described Samaher's depressions, which had grown so bad a year ago that her daughter had had to be hospitalized for a while in Safed and put on powerful drugs, which affected her concentration and ability to write. Ashamed to tell her professor about it, his M.A. student had blamed her grandmother, who loved her dearly and would do anything for her.

Rivlin thought of, but did not mention, his wife's opinion of psychiatrists. Why undermine the Arabs' faith in the Jews' ability to cure

---

* But what's the matter with her now? What's troubling her?
† What's wrong with her now?
‡ What is she ill with?

them? It surprised him that he had not noticed anything amiss in Samaher, who, her usual chatty self, had sat in the second row of his seminar class. Even in her "Hamas period," as she referred to the year when she'd come to his classes in a long dress and white shawl, she had retained her vivaciousness. Was his knowledge of his students that superficial? Or had he become so detached from reality himself that the aberrations of others seemed normal?

"But what is it that you want?" he asked, reverting to Hebrew before their intimacy could grow too great.

"*Iza b'ti'dar, Elbrofesor Rivlin, aazilhha shwoy elwaza'if.*"*

"Another postponement? I've already given her too many. . . ."

"Then *ahsan shi tilghi'ha bilmara.*"†

"But I can't just forget about it!" He rocked again in his chair, amused by the impudence of it.

"Because she'll never finish it. She'll lose a whole year's credit. And she's pregnant and has to stay home because the doctor says school is bad for her depressions. Why can't you? What difference would it make? Give her an exam instead of a paper, anything to help her get the degree. *Maskini, ishtaghlat ketir lisanawat adidi.*"‡

"It's out of the question. *Shu fi hon, su'?*"§

"But why a marketplace?" The affront made her flush. "Why can't you give her an exam instead of a paper? Isn't it the same?"

"Not at all."

"But you can make it the same. Samaher says so. Professor Rivlin is the best and most important teacher, she says. Everyone listens to him."

"Ha!"

"Everyone does. They all say so. You're the one who has the power. The head of everything. That's what she told us from her first day as a student. He's the man, she said. The one worth studying for. The most interesting and important. Much more important than that dark, nasty man who was at the wedding. She's always talking about you. At first her father was afraid for her. He thought she'd gone and

---

* Perhaps, Professor Rivlin, you could give her a postponement.
† The best thing would be to waive it entirely.
‡ The poor child worked so hard for so many years.
§ What is this here, a marketplace?

fallen in love with some young teacher. 'But he isn't that at all,' she told us. 'He's an elderly, dignified man. He could be a grandfather.'"

Rivlin smiled a melancholy smile.

"Listen," he said. "It's no use. This is a university. I'm not the one who makes the rules. You can't change a paper to an exam. If it's too much for her, she can put the M.A. off. She already has a B.A. That's enough for the time being. She can continue later. We'll help her."

"How? Once you drop out, you're out."

"Not necessarily."

"What about me? The secretaries at the wedding said I'd have to start all over again."

"If you really wanted to go back to school, we could make a special arrangement."

"You see? You can do it if you want to."

He grinned.

"Well? What do you say?"

"I'm sorry. First she needs to shake off her depression. Let her have some children. Then we'll see. Trust in Allah."

He didn't know what in the world had made him say that. And yet why not? Allah was a handy word.

The little room fell silent. The woman, refusing to accept defeat, remained in her seat. Her glance drifted past him to the hills of the Galilee, returning to regard him with a quiet hostility that only increased her beauty.

"It's no tragedy," he said soothingly. "Unless you're interested in an academic career, there's no great difference in Near Eastern studies between a B.A. and an M.A. Samaher can get a government job with just the B.A."

Her mother placed a soft white hand despairingly on the table.

"You're making fun of us, Professor. Samaher, a government job? You think she needs to work? The degree is for her honor. For ours, too. We promised the groom's parents. They didn't like her depressions. They only agreed to the marriage because we explained how educated she was to be getting her M.A."

He shut his eyes for a moment, wishing she would cry some more.

"I'll tell you what."

Afifa regarded him.

"Tell Samaher to come see me. I'll give her a new subject. An easier one."

But she just kept at him.

"Samaher can't come to the university now. Her husband won't let her leave the village. *Hayif ti'malu-lo doshe.*"\*

"*Ay doshe?*"†

"*Ma ba'aref. Huwa bahaf min el-habl.*"‡

This time the bleat was stifled. Rivlin reached out cautiously and gave the moist, pudgy hand on his desk a friendly pat.

"I'll give Samaher something in place of a paper. Something from the newspapers you see on this desk. She'll read some passages and summarize them. Nothing complicated. Just a few stories and poems. She can do it at home. She won't need a library. Maybe it will even help get her out of her depression."

"I'll take them with me now."

"Easy does it! In the first place, they're too heavy for you. And second, I have to photocopy them. They're rare material and not mine. Why don't you send Samaher's husband to make copies?"

"Forget about her husband. He has no time. I'll send someone else. The cousin who drove you to the wedding."

"Rashid."

"Rashid." She was surprised Rivlin remembered the name. "Rashid is best. He'll take care of everything. Stories and poems are just the thing for her."

## 24.

THAT MONDAY THE young officer was supposed get leave so that he could see his newly arrived uncle. At the last minute, however, he yielded his turn to a friend, a romantic soul with an urgent need to talk a girlfriend out of leaving him. Not knowing when he might get

---

\* He's afraid she'll do something foolish.

† Like what?

‡ I don't know. He's afraid of foolishness.

another pass, Tsakhi asked his parents to bring Yo'el and Ofra to the base that evening.

And so once again they drove the winding roads of the Galilee. While the two sisters sat in back recollecting childhood trips, Rivlin patiently questioned his brother-in-law about developments in the Third World. Although these were enough to drive anyone to despair, he thought a knowledge of them might help him to understand his own tortured Algeria.

Early for their rendezvous on Mt. Canaan, they stopped for a bite at the same restaurant in which they had met the two corpse freezers. But Yo'el did not seem upset when told the story, perhaps because his travels in impoverished lands had inured him to the fate of corpses.

It was getting dark when they reached the double gate of the intelligence base and parked in its improvised picnic grounds, now ominously deserted. Rivlin opened two director's chairs for the women and took the émigré, who had never lost his love of the Israeli landscape, along the fragrant goat path running up the mountain. A full moon risen in the east bathed the mountains in a generous light that enabled them to keep an eye on their wives below, sitting near the gate. Confident that they would spy Tsakhi when he appeared, they walked on in the brightening night.

A large lizard scurried across their path.

"Watch out nothing bites you," Rivlin warned his lanky brother-in-law, who was still wearing his biblical sandals.

"After all the times I've been bitten in Africa and Asia, what do you think the Middle East can do to me?"

Rivlin felt a wave of warmth for the man.

"I'm afraid you don't take us very seriously."

"I do. But you're all terribly spoiled. You think all the tears in the world belong to you. As if there weren't a big, suffering universe all around you."

The Orientalist lowered himself onto the same large rock that he had sat on ten days before and cast a glance at the two sisters below, who were looking lonely and abandoned. He was about to shout something encouraging down to them when his wife, catching sight of him and Yo'el, waved first.

The silence around them was profound. Little animals, satisfied that the invaders meant no harm, resumed their hidden munching. Yo'el looked around and breathed deeply, taking in the approach of the Israeli night. It occurred to Rivlin that he and Hagit hadn't made love in a week, nor could they possibly do so until their two guests departed. It was remarkable how, as the years went by, his desire for his wife grew stronger, as if their psychological intimacy only increased their physical passion.

Yo'el sat chewing on the stem of a plant. Now was the time, Rivlin decided, to talk about the facts of married life. If the two sisters were at all alike in their makeup, some pointers might be gained from it.

"I've been wanting to ask you," he said, broaching the topic. "It's a small thing ... you needn't answer if you don't want to ..."

"Answer what?"

"Just don't get annoyed."

"But what is it?" The longer Rivlin's prologue, the more bewildered Yo'el became.

"I've been wanting to ask you ... just don't get annoyed ... it's an odd question, I know ... but do you and Ofra ... ever shower or bathe together ... I mean would she agree ... because Hagit, you see ..."

"But what makes you ask?" Yo'el gave him a puzzled smile. "I've never tried. How could I? You know Ofra. Half an hour in the shower is her minimum. My maximum is five minutes."

An armed soldier emerged from the hidden entrance to the base.

"That must be Tsakhi," Rivlin said, cutting the conversation short even though he knew it wasn't his son. And indeed, back in the parking lot, they saw it was the blond, baby-faced sergeant. He had been sent to inform the visitors that something had come up to prevent the young officer from leaving his post. There was no point in waiting.

"But what happened?" Rivlin asked, disappointed.

"There's a problem with some instrument."

"What instrument?"

The sergeant gave him a forbearing smile.

"Tell him to come for just a few minutes," Rivlin tried cajoling the messenger. "Just to say hello. His uncle has come especially to see him. He's leaving the country in a few days."

"He knows that," the sergeant replied calmly. "Don't think he doesn't feel bad that..."

Rivlin interrupted him brusquely. "Go tell him anyway."

"Forget it," Hagit said. "If he can't come, he can't come. Take his word for it."

The sergeant nodded in approval at her common sense.

## 25.

AT THE UNIVERSITY the next day, in the narrow hallway of the twenty-third floor, he found the messenger from Samaher. Sturdily built, sable-skinned, Rashid was eagerly awaiting his mission. Rivlin placed a pile of North African journals and newspapers in his arms and sent him to the library to photocopy the excerpts marked by the murdered Jerusalemite, plus some additional passages checked by himself.

Three hours later the Arab returned, with two thick binders of photocopies, red for the poems and green for the stories. Each entry had been indexed by author, with the date and place of publication in red ink. The originals, too, had been reorganized and were now arranged chronologically. Explanatory flags in Hebrew and Arabic, written in a clear, curling hand, were attached to them.

"About these stains, Professor..." Rashid pointed to the yellow flecks on the newspapers. "I didn't make them...."

"Of course not."

Rivlin revealed the awful truth.

Rashid cursed the suicide bomber roundly. "That's life," he said.

Rivlin was taking a liking to the young man. "Tell me," he asked him confidentially, "what really is the matter with Samaher?"

"*Ya'ani,* she has moods. It's her nerves. She's feeling low. But she'll get over it. She's strong. And smart as a whip. Believe me, I tell everyone: Just wait, in a few years you'll see Samaher in the Knesset."

"The Knesset?"

"Yes. Someone like her belongs there."

"Because she's so depressed?"

Rashid laughed.

"Because it's so depressing."

His handsome eyes, the color of coal, had a hypnotic warmth.

"But really, what's the matter with her?" This time his tone was sterner. "What's going on?"

"She's tired. Exhausted. And her husband is the nervous type. He has no patience for her."

"She should have married you," Rivlin blurted unthinkingly. "You seem patient enough."

"Me?" The blood rushed to Rashid's face, as if a leak had sprung inside him. He gave a start. "Why not?" he laughed. "Her father would never have agreed, though...."

"Because you're cousins?"

"Because I'm dark. Too dark for his taste."

The Orientalist asked the affable young Arab about himself. For two years, Rashid said, he had been a university student too, in the electrical-engineering department of the Haifa Technion. Then he left. Engineering didn't interest him, nor did he believe he could find work in the field. He had bought a minibus and made good money transporting passengers. Perhaps next year he would audit a few classes.

Rivlin handed him a sheet of paper and dictated the demands he was making of his ailing student.

One: A precise but literary translation of all the poems into Hebrew.

Two: A Hebrew summary of all the stories.

Three: A list of motifs common to both.

That was all. It was pitifully little for an M.A. seminar paper. Yet what else could he do? He was beginning to feel sorry for Samaher. And there was all the more reason for her to hurry, because he was tired and ill himself and no one else in the department would put up with her shenanigans.

"Ill? With what?"

"Never mind. Just don't tell anyone. Not everything has to be public knowledge. That's something we Jews need to learn. Life needs its little secrets. Just see to it that Samaher is warned. There'll be no more postponements or excuses. Let her do what I've asked within a few weeks and she'll get her grade. And please—let's leave her mother, father, and grandmother out of this."

## 26.

*18.4.98*

*Ofer,*

*It would have been the right thing not to reply. Not only so as not to vi-olate our "honorable silence," as you call it, but also because a condolence letter with poisoned arrows in it doesn't deserve a reply. You've forced me to violate, not only our silence, but the sacred vow of fidelity made to my hus-band, since I am concealing this letter from him.*

*And in the dark night of my sorrow, which knows no consolation, noth-ing but longing for a beloved man (and only a man), you still won't give an inch. Again you allude to your unspeakable fantasies.*

*(To think I once loved you so much.)*

*Your father, with whom I genuinely sympathize, is still tormented by our failed marriage. He believes that you don't understand what happened.*

*You?*

*You don't understand?*

*I've conveyed your condolences to my mother. She thanks you. For some reason, she still grieves for you.*

*Please, don't answer this letter. Let's return to our old silence. It may not be so honorable anymore, but it's just as important.*

*Galya*

## 27.

RIGHT UP TO the day of the wedding, Ofra, fearful of being left alone with Yo'el's family, tried persuading her sister and brother-in-law to join them. Yet having had the foresight to purchase two tickets for a biblical play in Tel Aviv that evening, Rivlin was not going to let even an exemption from gift-giving force him to attend a wedding he didn't have to be at. Hagit's efforts to sway him, born of sympathy for her sister's plight, only led him to deliver a harangue. What did Ofra want of him? She spent her life traipsing around the world like a middle-aged princess, with no worries or family duties. It would not be so terrible if for once she had to meet her obligations un-assisted. At most, he was prepared to drive her and Yo'el to the wedding. Perhaps even to drive them back, although this was already going too far.

Now, nearing Nature's Corner, he found himself growing gloomier by the minute as his car followed the lanterns waved in the fading light by the young parking attendants whose job it was, before changing costumes and turning into waiters, to divert him from the highway onto a dirt approach road that looped through fields of crackling stubble. He stepped on the brakes as soon as he reached the parking lot—whence, pounded by music that would grow more savage as the night progressed, a stream of elegantly dressed guests flowed toward a green buckboard propped decoratively on its shaft as though on loan from an old Western, beyond which a bridal gown and bright glasses of wine glimmered through the branches of trees. This was as far as he went. Putting his foot down, he refused even to congratulate or greet the parents of the bride, fearing to encourage the illusion that he might stay. Although his sister-in-law, wearing the dress he had failed to talk her out of, delayed their parting as if still hoping to change his mind, he swung the car determinedly around, wove through a phalanx of arriving vehicles, and sped back to the highway and their biblical drama.

The audience entered slowly, advancing toward a stage in the round, on which they were invited to sit as though part of the performance. To heavy but clear-toned music, twelve young actors and actresses dressed in black took their places, microphones attached to them so that they might speak, or even whisper, the words of the ancient text naturally and from the right inner place.

## 28.

My heart is sore pained within me,
And the terrors of death are fallen on me.
Fearfulness and trembling are come upon me,
And horror hath overwhelmed me.
And I said, Oh that I had wings like a dove!
For then would I fly away and be at rest.
Lo, then would I wander far off, and remain in the wilderness.

Selah.

ALTHOUGH RIVLIN HAD no idea how the play would develop or what was in store for them, the somber prologue from the Book of Psalms, cast into the black space of the auditorium, made him sit up. He smiled encouragingly at his wife. She nodded back, secretly pleased to have been rescued from a wedding that, even if it did not arouse her envy, was eminently forgoable.

Two actors began to recite? declaim? read? speak? act? passages from the story of the Creation. *In the day the Lord God made the earth and the heavens....* The story of Cain and Abel... *This is the book of the generations of Adam.* The grand biblical language soared with contemporary freshness. Though hardly a sentence or word did not come from Scripture, the female director had taken liberties, rearranging and editing the text for the benefit of the spectators, who sat in the dark with quiet yet skeptical attention, slowly sipping old wine, its taste unfamiliar to many of them, from a new bottle.

And Adam lived an hundred and thirty years, and begat a son in his own likeness, after his image; and called his name Seth: And the days of Adam after he had begotten Seth were eight hundred years: and he begat sons and daughters: And all the days that Adam lived were nine hundred and thirty years: and he died.

And Seth lived an hundred and five years, and begat Enos. And Seth lived after he begat Enos eight hundred and seven years, and begat sons and daughters. And all the days of Seth were nine hundred and twelve years: and he died.

And Enos lived ninety years, and begat Cainan. And Enos lived after he begat Cainan eight hundred and fifteen years, and begat sons and daughters.

Emerging from a far corner, a solemn young actress enumerated the generations while crossing the stage in a long, slow diagonal, her floating gait trancelike. In the middle of her path several young men lay twisted on the floor, tormented by the venerable ages of the endlessly begetting ancients. Slowly, the tedious list of names and numbers, accompanied by a distant peal of bells, took on meaning and drama, perhaps because of the way the young actress enigmatically paused before each repetition of "... and daughters."

Rivlin sought to catch his wife's eye, to convey that he liked the performance so far and hoped it would continue to hold his interest. But Hagit's gaze was riveted to the stage—to which he, too, turned intently back so as not to miss a movement or a word. He admired the director for seeking to breathe life into forgotten and unpoetic biblical texts that were tediously plain: dry laws, harsh commandments, blessings, warnings, curses, lists of clean and unclean animals—all backed by electronic music and made amusingly real by sprightly actors in striking costumes.

Now, as two shaven-headed actors leaned over a large table, discussing between them, with the cackling pedantry of old men, ancient sexual prohibitions both commonsensical and bizarre, a tall, striking actress with golden curls falling to her shoulders took out a small white handkerchef and alternately brandished and tore at it with dancelike, repetitive movements as though it were a flag of protest or surrender. With sorrowful irony she joined the exchange, reciting the mordant laws, intricate and outrageous, meted out by the biblical legislator to the virgin raped by a stranger in a city or a field:

If a damsel that is a virgin be betrothed unto an husband, and a man find her in the city, and lie with her; then ye shall bring them both out unto the gate of that city, and ye shall stone them with stones so that they die; the damsel, because she cried not, being in the city; and the man because he hath humbled his neighbour's wife; so thou shalt put away evil from among you.

If a man find a damsel that is a virgin, which is not betrothed, and lay hold on her, and lie with her, and they be found; then the man that lay with her shall give unto the damsel's father fifty shekels of silver, and she shall be his wife; because he hath humbled her, he may not put her away all his days.

"Marvelous!" he whispered to his wife, watching with pleasure as a barefoot actor and actress sat down near them to lament the childlessness of Abraham and Sarah prior to the birth of Isaac.

"*Now Sarah and Abraham were old,* the plump actress related, *and well stricken in age; and it ceased to be with Sarah after the manner of women.* She moved contortedly in her envy of the concubine who bore Ishmael to her husband, describing in a deep, sobbing voice not only her own anguish, but that of the bondmaid she tormented:

"*And Abram said unto Sarai, Behold, thy maid is in thine hand; do to her as it pleaseth thee. And when Sarai dealt hardly with her, she fled from her face.*"

All at once, without knowing how or why, the Orientalist felt a lump in his throat. It was as if the sobbing of the barren Sarah were meant for him, were in him. And while Abraham, the defiant believer, promised Sarah in God's name that she would have a son before the year was out, the plump actress writhed on the floor, clinging to her despair and renouncing all hope in a tragic, sardonic voice:

"*After I am waxed old, shall I have pleasure, my lord being old also?*"

So powerful and convincing was her renunciation that a wordless sorrow moistened his eyes. He froze, afraid to let his wife see. She, however, aware of his tears, laid a light hand on his knee.

## 29.

"THAT'S THE END of the first act," Rivlin said. "Now there's an intermission."

He leafed through the program, looking for the name of the actress who played Sarah. Putting his arm around his wife, he declared with satisfaction:

"I was on the verge of tears."

"Do you know why?"

"It touched me. It hit a nerve. Didn't you feel that way too?"

"Yes. I did."

They headed for an opening in the human wall besieging the buffet. Suddenly Rivlin saw his wife stop short and duck.

"What's the matter?"

"Don't move," she whispered.

But it was too late. The burly man ahead of them had caught sight of her and was staring at her in astonishment.

"Don't I know you?"

Hagit said nothing.

"You're the judge!"

She was unable to move.

"Don't you remember me?" He reddened, the bills he was holding to give the counterman trembling slightly in his fingers.

Although she shook her head, the shadow of a smile crossed Hagit's face. Rivlin sensed that she knew this handsome, well-dressed man.

"Is this your husband?" The man pointed, staring at Rivlin.

Hagit said nothing. The Orientalist nodded.

"I'm Amnon Peretz." The man whispered his name dramatically, as though it were a dark secret. "You still don't know who I am?" He grinned. "You gave me twelve years."

Solemn and pale, Hagit bobbed her head. It wasn't clear what she was confirming—her memory of the trial or the length of the prison term.

"You're out?"

"For the past three years. For good behavior."

"I'm glad to hear it."

She bobbed her head again, regaining her composure. Gently she asked:

"Are you enjoying the play?"

Eager to discuss other things, the man was surprised by the question.

"Very much," he answered with a smile. "And you?"

"Also," Rivlin replied, heading for a new opening at the buffet.

Back in the dark auditorium, on whose stage silhouettes were slowly moving, Hagit whispered that the man had been a chronic wife- and child-beater until brought to trial. There was no time for further details, for the Children of Israel, having left Egypt with the battered suitcases of European refugees, were now beginning their trek through the desert.

And the children of Israel removed from Rameses, and encamped in Succoth.

And they departed from Succoth, and encamped in Etham, which is on the edge of the wilderness.

And they removed from Etham, and turned again unto Pi-hahiroth, which is before Baal-sephon; and they encamped before Migdol.

And they departed from before Pi-hahiroth and passed through the midst of the sea into the wilderness, and went three days' journey in the wilderness of Etham, and encamped in Marah.

And they removed from Marah, and came unto Elim; and in Elim were twelve fountains of water, and threescore and ten palm trees; and they encamped there.

And they removed from Elim, and encamped by the Red Sea.

And they removed from the Red Sea, and encamped in the wilderness of Sin.

And they took their journey out of the wilderness of Sin, and encamped in Dophkah.

And they departed from Dophkah, and encamped in Alush.

And they removed from Alush, and encamped at Rephidim, where was no water for the people to drink.

And they departed from Rephidim, and pitched in the wilderness of Sinai.

And they removed from the desert of Sinai, and pitched in Kibroth-hataavah, which meaneth Appetite's Grave.

Once again, with slow movements and crystalline words, the actors held the audience in thrall, pulling after them strips of fabric on journeys that crisscrossed to far places and peoples, conquered cities and smoking ruins, while listing, besides the laws of illnesses, abscesses, lesions, leprosies, offerings, and priests, the numbers of men under arms in each of the twelve Israelite tribes. With a mixture of horror and glee, the astounded Orientalist noted how—transfixed by a zealous and restless God who, unable to leave them alone, promised and threatened, pummeled and soothed, resolved and decreed—the Jews never wearied of their wanderings.

And then, the journeys, wars, lesions, deaths, burials, homicides, and cities of refuge having come to an end, a thin actress with black tresses licking at her face like little snakes strode to the middle of the stage. Kneeling, she told the story of Jephthah's daughter with soft, sinuous gestures.

Then the Spirit of the Lord came upon Jephthah, and he passed over Gilead and Manasseh, and he passed over Mizpeh of Gilead, and from Mizpeh of Gilead he passed over unto the children of Ammon.

And Jephthah vowed a vow unto the Lord, and said, If thou shalt without fail deliver the children of Ammon into mine hands,

Then it shall be, that whatsoever cometh forth of the doors of my house to meet me, when I return in peace from the children of Ammon, shall surely be the Lord's, and I will offer it up for a burnt offering.

A muffled drumming accompanied the maiden as she hurried innocently out to greet her victorious father with a dance, never guessing that she was about to fall victim to his inexorable vow. A tense Rivlin hung on every word as she submitted to her fate.

My father, if thou hast opened thy mouth unto the Lord, do to me according to that which hath proceeded out of thy mouth; forasmuch as the Lord hath taken vengeance for thee of thine enemies, even of the children of Ammon.

And she said unto her father, Let this thing be done for me: let me alone two months, that I may go up and down upon the mountains, and bewail my virginity.

And yet by the end of this wrenching tale, the thin maiden with the snakelike tresses had not exactly submitted, for she now told her story again. The drumming grew faster. Her movements, stylized and measured the first time, were now sweepingly defiant.

*Then the Spirit of the Lord came upon Jephthah, and he passed over Gilead and Manasseh, and he passed over Mizpeh of Gilead, and from Mizpeh of Gilead he passed over unto the children of Ammon.*

For the second time she came to her cruelly loving father's words as he rent his clothes: *Alas, my daughter! Thou has brought me very low and art my downfall! For I have opened my mouth unto the Lord and cannot go back.* The lump was back in Rivlin's throat. The tears almost shed for the childless Sarah stung his eyes for the senselessly sacrificed maiden.

And yet in her despair, Jephthah's daughter—having gone with her friends to bewail her virginity upon the mountains before being sacrificed by her father because of the vow he had vowed without stopping to think who might run excitedly to greet him—was not content with telling the story twice. As the drums' frenzy mounted and the music gathered force, she told the tale of her immolation a third time. The staid, obedient child of the first version was now a proud, wounded tigress, snarling ferociously at her father's mad vow and the vile deed about to be done her. Her at first sinuous and then sweeping movements turned out to have been but preliminary sketches for the savage paroxysm of her slender body, now lashing out at the world.

And so, when for the third time she uttered her father's cry as he rent his clothes and blamed not himself but her—*Alas, my daughter! Thou hast brought me very low and art my downfall*—a shudder convulsed Rivlin's being. Quickly, he removed his eyeglasses and hid his face.

## 30.

DESPITE THE PLAY'S length, it was not yet midnight when the Rivlins' car groped its way along the dirt road strewn with sputtering lanterns in order to bring Ofra and Yo'el back from their corner of nature to the glitter of civilization. Although the parking lot was mostly empty, the savage music still shook the tall eucalypti as if a great multitude were continuing to dance.

Yo'el and Ofra sat off to one side at an empty table. The former youth-movement counselors, eternally young themselves, looked weary, old, and sad. Their clothes damp from the night vapors rising from the stream, they ignored the commotion on the dance floor with its melee of fat aunts capering with small nephews and grandchildren and ecstatic youngsters hoisting on their shoulders not one bridelike figure but three, all in various states of undress.

Loath to let the last gasps of the wedding spoil his high spirits, Rivlin was for making a quick getaway with his exhausted brother- and sister-in-law. Genuinely indignant, however, the bride's father insisted that the two shirkers at least have some dessert.

It didn't take much to persuade the laughing judge to agree, especially as the tray handed to her held not one dessert but many, each more scrumptious-looking than the last.

"How was the play?" Yo'el asked. In twenty-four hours he and his wife would be far away.

"Wonderful. It's a must. If I were you, I'd postpone my flight just to see it."

But the two émigrés were anxious to leave their muggy native land.

"He actually cried," Hagit told on him merrily, licking whipped cream from a long golden spoon.

"He did?" Yo'el and Ofra marveled.

"Buckets." Hagit grinned. "With every word."

"That isn't true. I only cried in a few places," Rivlin asserted with an odd pride, helping himself to a piece of chocolate cake. "The story of Jephthah's daughter broke me up especially."

## 31.

23.4.98

*Galya,*

*You answered me even though I asked you not to. So much for your right to tell me whether or not to answer you. (As for our lost and entirely imaginary "honor," let's leave such things for others.)*

*You should be thankful that I wrote what I did and not worse. If you're so sure of yourself and of your family, both the living and the dead, why violate your "sacred vow of fidelity" to your husband by hiding my letter? If the "truth" is on your side, you should want him to see it, since it's the perfect chance to prove to him how truly mad your first husband is and how right you were to leave him. (Just be careful, though. My insanity is a boomerang. Who falls in love with a madman but a madwoman? And you did love me. Terribly.)*

*Do you want to know what made my father visit you during the bereavement? It had nothing to do with feeling sorry for you or your family. The man is quite simply still tortured by our separation, because he doesn't understand what happened. He's a historian who has to understand everything. His own self too, because, despite his position, he's consumed by doubt about himself and anyone he suspects of being like him.*

*It's a good thing my mother, at least, has some faith in me.*

*If my father is foolish enough to try to make contact with you again, don't let him. I'll try to restrain him, too. Sometimes I wonder why I chose to spare my parents by not telling them what happened between us. Was I afraid that they, like you, would be unable to believe me and would end up begging you to forgive me? Or did I keep my promise because of the accursed hope you held out to me?*

*Enough. Too much. Every word is superfluous. You can go back to mourning the man I never could mourn for.*

*Ofer*

### PART III

# Samaher's Term Paper

Y ET THERE HAD to have been signs, early warnings, by which a serious scholar looking unflinchingly at the present could unlock the past. How could the simple desire to avenge the 1991 elections, whose canceled results robbed the Islamic Salvation Front of victory at the polls, have so inflamed Algeria's religious fundamentalists and army that they fought a ten-year civil war in which armed bands repeatedly attacked their own people and massacred simple villagers like themselves, women, children, and old people?

Writers in academic journals, scholars from the Universities of Montpelier and Aix-en-Provence, in which were deposited the archives of the colonial rule that turned Algeria into a French province in the early nineteenth century while disenfranchising the country's population, had racked their brains over questions like: "Where did we go wrong? What was it that made Algeria incapable of institutional stability? What have we not accounted for in the ledger of the past? What still veils the violence of the Terror of the 1990s?"

Reading these SOSs sent by his colleagues across the sea, he had felt obliged to help. His scholarly conscience rose to the challenge posed by the slashed throats of infants.

Prudently, he had opened a new computer file and begun a long essay entitled "Early Warnings of the Horror of the Disintegration of National Identity." Then, as a responsible historian who thought in sober categories, not a hack journalist, he erased "Horror" and substituted "Shock to" for "Disintegration of."

———

FOR EXAMPLE: was it possible to see in the riots that broke out in October 1934, at the tomb of the Muslim saint Ibn Sa'id, between Berber pilgrims and the reformists of the Salafia movement in the Constantine district, a first warning of the indiscriminate Terror of the 1990s? A report recently discovered in a military archive in Toulon, filed by the French officer who had rushed to the scene, suggested a surprising perspective, worthy of careful consideration.

Certainly an Israeli Orientalist, no matter how secular, might be expected to sympathize with the reformist vision of the Salafia, which sought to return Islam to its pristine origins by purging the dross from its monotheistic core. Nor could an enlightened or rational person fail to be repelled by the pilgrims' superstitious revels and commerce in amulets and holy water. Even though, as the latest studies showed, the reformists too had their fanatical side, their leaders' high intellectual level, rhetorical gifts, and staunch defense of Algerian nativism against French military brutality and colonial rapacity had to appeal to a liberal observer like the Orientalist.

In the course of the Constantine riots, two men were killed, and many more wounded. Based on the assumption that the reformists were waging a moral and spiritual war against the pilgrims' paganlike practices, which distracted the faithful from the struggle for individual and communal self-betterment, it seemed natural to blame the violence on primitive Berbers clinging to otherworldly beliefs. And yet, surprisingly, this was not the picture painted by the French officer summoned to restore order between the warring parties. It was the Berbers, he reported, who were attacked first, the opening shots having been fired from the ranks of the reformists, who were led by prominent clerics and intellectuals. The shots were aimed at a slender, white-cloaked Sufi monk capering by a sacred tomb.

Was this an early warning, subtle but unmistakable, of the ruthless Terror that would come sixty years later? Could the reformists' descendants, the supporters of the Islamic Front, be venting their wrath not only on their traditional enemies—heretics, Westernizers, corrupt army officers, writers and journalists—but also on innocent villagers who, rather than joining the political struggle, remained benightedly mired in pilgrimages, amulet peddling, and necromancy? Did the fundamentalists, in the chaos following the cancellation of the elections, turn on their own illiterate brethren as if to say: "So it's graves, saints, and holy men that you want? Be our guests! We'll fill your villages with the graves of so many old men, women, and children that you'll never have to flock to a saint's tomb again, since you'll have plenty of your own."

Or take this forgotten item, found in a transcript of court proceedings from the Eyn-Sifra district bordering on the Sahara: perhaps it, too, was an early warning of the senseless brutality now taking place. In 1953, inspired by a recently published story by Albert Camus, three French students from the University of Marseilles, two young men and a woman, set out with an experienced local guide named Hamid el-Kadr to get a sunset view of the Sahara. Camus's story concerned a depressed Frenchwoman named Jeannine who accompanies her husband, a traveling salesman, on his rounds in the Algerian countryside. One day the childless couple find themselves in a small town at the desert's edge, where they climb to a hilltop fort with a view. So shattered are the remote, frozen depths of Jeannine's being by the vast empty spaces she sees that she undergoes an inner revolution. In the middle of the night she awakes with an unsettled feeling, leaves her hotel room, and climbs back to the fort, from which she stares longingly at the Bedouin tents in the distance, her unfulfilled femininity thirsting for the infinite freedom of the Sahara.

It was under the influence of this story that the three French students decided to spend their Christmas vacation on a quest for Camus's heroine, hoping to relive her experience. Their guide even managed to find a hilltop fort and brought them to its panoramic vista. There they saw, like the childless Jeannine, the black tents of nomads and the silent camels nibbling at the edge of infinity. Unwilling to make do with mere longing, they asked their guide to take them to the encampment. Having reached the edge of the desert, why not push a bit farther into the cold night for a meatier taste of its eternal essence?

Hamid el-Kadr was agreeable and took them to the encampment, where their unexpected appearance met with a warm welcome. They were fed and given a place to sleep under the desert sky, huddled beneath layers of blankets. Yet in the morning, when they awoke, the Bedouin had vanished, tents, camels, flocks, and all. Going to wake

their guide, asleep in his blanket roll, they discovered to their consternation that the Bedouin had made off with his head.

The three terrified tourists ran for their lives, uncertain whether
to report the brutal murder to the local Berber gendarme or to go
straight to the French garrison in the district capital. In the end, duty
prevailed over fear, and they went to the gendarme, who did not seem
overly surprised. To ensure their personal safety, he locked them in
his house until a French officer arrived.

It took three months to find the murderer, who was caught when
he returned with his family and livestock to the foot of the fort, confident that all was forgotten and perhaps even hoping to attract new
tourists. When asked by the French judge what his motives had been,
he answered that the guide's French was too good for a believing
Muslim and Algerian patriot like himself, and that not knowing to
what lengths such a treacherous tongue might go, he had cut it off
with the rest of the head. And in reply to the judge's astonished query
as to how someone ignorant of French could assess its fluency, the
Bedouin pointed to the freedom of the young Frenchwoman's laugh
when Hamid el-Kadr spoke to her.

AND PERHAPS HE, Professor Rivlin, had found another harbinger of
the Terror now rampant in Algeria. To be sure, one had to be careful
about going all the way back to the 1850s, when the French, having
commenced their colonial administration, disbanded the guilds
known as the *jama'at*. Yet having recently supervised a doctoral dissertation on the subject that suggested some curious conclusions, he
decided to return to it.

During the long period of Turkish rule in North Africa, many Algerian villagers, especially in times of drought or economic hardship,
migrated to the cities for their livelihood. They did not settle in them
permanently, however, or mingle with the urban population. Rather,
organizing themselves by place of origin and occupation—that is,
flour miller, butcher, perfume merchant, bathhouse keeper, and so
on—they formed cooperative guilds, each led by an elected official,
recognized by the Turkish authorities, called the *amin*. Each *amin* was
empowered to judge and discipline the members of his *jama'a*, bach-

elors unwilling to marry out of their tribe or village who accepted his decisions without challenge. This arrangement officially ended in 1868, when the French government, after considerable debate, revoked the autonomy of the *jama'at* and the authority of the *amins*. At first the *jama'at* refused to accept the French decree. Particularly angered were the now unemployed *amins*, who had derived many benefits from their position. For years the guilds struggled to maintain themselves on an unofficial basis, the members continuing to obey the *amins* despite their unrecognized status. Not until the early twentieth century did these voluntary cooperatives lapse completely, leaving the French exclusively in control.

And yet the ancient memory of these independent guilds stayed with the villagers from the desert, who were now an urban proletariat dependent on French colonial rule. The longing for the little *jama'a* with its strongman was passed down. From time to time, it even induced certain simple villagers to imagine that they were the new *amins* and to blame the failure of their dreams not on the authorities but on their illiterate neighbors, whom they accused of refusing to submit to them. This situation culminated in 1927, in a bizarre incident that took place in the village of Mezabis, on the fringe of the desert, 560 kilometers from the capital. There, a local resident, in a throwback to Turkish times, gathered a small *jama'a* that appointed him its *amin* and launched a punitive campaign that only came to an end when the French caught him and put him to death.

Had the elections of 1991, held during a conflict between a brutal, disorganized army and furious fundamentalists, led to a new outbreak of atavism? Were its new, self-fantasized *amins* taking back the power they had lost one hundred years before? Were the vicious bands formed by them none other than the old *jama'at*, sallying forth once more to judge and punish at night?

# 1.

ONCE THE MERRY émigrés, having filled their suitcases with the Israeli pharmaceuticals they always took back with them, were gone, Rivlin wondered whether his fears of their visit had not been exaggerated. It had passed slowly, yet in a tender Chekhovian ambience, full of mellow conversations over glasses of tea on the large terrace, and in leisurely walks on the beach. Although being exiled from his study to the university had not unstuck his blocked book, perhaps some wisdom had rubbed off on it from all the computers humming on the top floors of the tower overlooking the Galilee—from which his own computer, having sat quietly for two weeks, had been carried home again wrapped in soft towels. As he watched it light up against the background of his mother's ghost playing solitaire on her terrace, the breeze teasing the Carmel seemed to whisper, "Be of good cheer! Steady at the keyboard!" To bolster his and the computer's spirits, he made the words "Be of Good Cheer!" float across his display screen.

Meanwhile, a letter had arrived from Samaher. Written for some reason in Arabic, it informed him in a patronizing tone—as if she were doing her favorite professor a favor by accepting his offer to help her salvage the semester—that she had begun the new project assigned her. Indeed, she appeared to be enjoying it, for the stories and poems brought to her by her cousin, she wrote, were so interesting that she was actually "wild" about them. (Samaher wrote "wild" in Hebrew, as if Arabic lacked a word to express the cuddly Israeli concept of wildness.) For the first time, she was discovering the grandeur of the Arab nation that stretched from the Euphrates to the Atlantic, and the pride she felt in it. She had already translated two love poems and would soon finish summarizing two stories. One of these was realistic, the other, a naively sentimental (although, in her opinion, highly political) bit of folklore. If allowed by the doctor—for she was happy to inform Rivlin that she was pregnant and temporarily restricted to her bed—she would bring everything to the university when it was ready.

"Damn!" Rivlin swore under his breath. "What made me get involved with her? All I've done is given her a new batch of excuses." Worse yet, he no longer possessed Yosef Suissa's original collection, which had been returned to Jerusalem at the urgent request of the murdered scholar's father, who wished to see for himself what in the Arab soul had so intrigued his beloved son. Not that Rivlin had any illusions that Suissa's texts might rescue his own book. Still, now that they had been brought to his attention, he felt obliged to deal with them. It was even with a feeling of relief that he turned to them, as they gave his marooned project an immediate direction that it lacked.

He telephoned Samaher to reprimand her, only to be told by Afifa, who sounded alarmed by his angry demand to be sent at once whatever was finished, that her daughter was bedridden. Two days later, Rashid brought him two short love poems translated into a fluent Hebrew. The first went:

Who has seen her in the morning, When her brow opens like a flower, / Restful with dew and lilies, / Roses, violets, / Flowers, and the nests of ruins? / Who has seen the dawn of her glory? / Who has seen her nightclothes, / Woven among mulberries, / On which hang two berries, / And half a berry again, / Two kingdoms of silk / And half a kingdom? / Matchless among unmatched women, / Who can see her hips / And stay sober? / O follow the curve/ And the slide of them / To a different star! / They are a way-point of the future, / A journey from death / To life. There they stand and lament / The ruins of the Arabs, / The desert of the Arabs.

The hypnotic, coal black eyes of the messenger stared intently at the baffled professor, who failed to fathom the swift transition from the curves of an unmarried woman awakening in the morning to the ruins of lamenting Arabs.

"Where is the Arabic original?" he asked.

The messenger had brought the translation alone.

The second poem was written by the same poet, Farouk el-Janabi, and was about the same mystery figure:

How stunning is night's color in her eyes! / In them she hides a note from her lover, / And a cool ring with which to cheat Time. / How stunning is night's color in her eyes! / She paints a tattered flag, / A black cloak, / For those turned back / By the gates of her glory. / She paints the night / So that none are seen by none. / O unmatched woman.... / How beauteous is her misfortune!

"What about the stories?" Rivlin asked disappointedly.

"Samaher is still working on them," her cousin said. "She spends all her time in bed. It's easier for her to do short poems. But don't you worry, Professor. She'll have it all in good time."

"Can she really be pregnant so soon?" he asked incredulously.

"That's what her mother says," was the noncommittal answer.

## 2.

MEANWHILE, THERE WAS a new development in the closed-door trial. A key witness for the prosecution, who, fearing for his life, had fled to an Asian republic of the former Soviet Union, had now agreed after concerted pressure to testify, but only on condition that the court, in whose closed doors he had no faith, hear him in a place of his own choosing outside of Israel. At first, a single judge had seemed sufficient. But the defense, worried that the testimony might be highly damaging, had insisted that all three judges attend. This meant Hagit too.

"The court agreed without knowing where it's going?"

"That was the condition. But there's no need to worry. We'll be told the exact location as soon as we get to Vienna. And the Israeli embassy will know where we are."

"But suppose I were to abscond like that?"

"I'd be annoyed," Hagit admitted with an unflappable smile. "But that's only because you could always take me with you. I can't take you. But why should you care? Won't it be nice to be rid of me for a while?"

"Not like this."

"Then like what?"

"I'd need a more thorough break from you."

Taken aback, she laughed and went to kiss him.

"Don't imagine it's going to be all fun and games. This is a working trip."

Yet she did not seem put out by the prospect of it. Her mood was one of excitement. Besides the adventure itself, there was the prospect of new evidence deciding a case that had dragged on inconclusively for months. And surrounded by male colleagues, she would surely be getting at least as much attention as could be provided by a single husband.

Rivlin felt an anxious sadness, coupled with an unfamiliar aggressiveness. Their impending separation, though short, was a rare event, and his wife's forensic talents, marshaled to convince him that it was a blessing in disguise that might revive his powers of concentration, did not reassure him. He grumbled not only about the fancy restaurants and good meals she would enjoy without him and the new places he would not get to see with her, but about the chronic disorder she always left behind. This was why he insisted, on the eve of her departure, on her keeping an old promise, made earlier in the year and repeated before her sister's visit, to go through the clothing in her closet and throw out what wasn't needed. It was time they gave their stuffy life an airing.

## 3.

EVEN THOUGH HAGIT was leaving the next day and hadn't yet decided what to pack, so that she swore she would do "anything" for her husband if only he put off closet-cleaning until her return, he was determined to have his way. And so at 10 P.M., two chairs were set up in their bedroom, one for the clothes whose fate had been sealed and one for those granted a temporary reprieve. Hagit hated parting with her old things, which were an inseparable part of the self she felt comfortable with. Not surprisingly, the Rivlins were at loggerheads at once.

"First of all, what about this?" He grabbed a faded gray coat by its fur collar as though it were a beggar caught panhandling in the closet. "The last time I wanted to throw this out you promised to wear it, but I'm still waiting for that to happen. All it did was spend two more years growing moldy in the closet and infecting everything else."

"You can't blame me if we haven't had any real winters."

"You wouldn't have worn it if we had. A heavy coat with a fur collar is an absurdity in this country."

"But I love it."

"Strictly platonically. The time has come to part."

"We'll regret it the first cold winter that we have."

"Bye-bye, sweetheart," Rivlin said, depositing the folded coat on the first chair. "And now, before we do anything else, the moment has come, ten years after her death, to pay our last respects to your mother's woolen skirt."

"Don't you dare touch it!"

"But why not? You've never worn it, and you never will. Give it to some new immigrant from Russia."

"Don't Russia me. It stays right here."

"Why?"

"I've already told you. It has sentimental value."

"I'll be damned if I understand what sentiments an old black skirt of your mother's can arouse."

"You would understand better if you had ever felt any sentiments for your own mother."

"I certainly never felt any for her old skirts. How long does this skirt have to hang over us like a black fate?"

"What's fateful about it? It's a memento."

"It doesn't look like we're going to get far tonight."

"I told you we wouldn't. I'm tired. Why do we have to do this now? I have to be up at three in the morning. I promise to go through everything when I get back."

"I've heard such promises before. You'll come back exhausted, and that will be the end of it. Here, let's give it one more try. Fifteen more minutes. I deserve a less cluttered house. Look at this embroidered blue blouse. It's lovely, but it's reached the end of the road. It's much too tight on you."

"Do you remember when we bought it?"

"In Zurich."

"No. In Geneva. In a little store near the lake. It cost a fortune, and you were against spending the money."

"I wasn't. I just had my doubts."

"That was so long ago. And look how alive this purple embroidery still is! Do you have any idea how often I've worn this? How much use I've got out of it?"

"Of course I do. It's one of your uniforms."

"Then let's spare it. For a blouse like this, I'm ready to lose weight."

"Hagit, you know you'll never lose weight. Bye-bye, blouse. It's been good to know you. Now lie down and let yourself be folded like a good girl."

"I can't stand giving it away."

"And now, Hagiti, look this brown suit in the eye and admit that it's been five years since you last touched it."

"No, it hasn't. I wore it to the party you were given by the Oriental Society."

"So you did. But my partying days are over."

"It's not my fault if it's out of fashion."

"That's what you said the day you bought it."

"It could come back in."

"Not a chance."

"You're a hard man. What's it to you if I own another suit?"

"I told you. It clutters up your closet and hides the clothes that are wearable."

"Then let's put it in your closet."

"Are you out of your mind? Come on, bite the bullet! This suit will make a perfect gift to some poor, penniless woman who can't afford to be in fashion. And she can also have these old velvet pants of yours...."

"Never!"

"But there's a hole in them."

"I can wear them around the house."

"With a hole? I don't deserve the honor."

## 4.

YET THOUGH YOU knew you would have trouble sleeping the night before she left, you never thought such desolate sorrow would chip away at you, slowly and dully, minute by minute. Already at ten-thirty, feeling the impending signs, you hurriedly put on your pajamas, threw another pillow on the bed, turned off the lights, and lowered the blinds to shut out the moon, as if in it lay the threat to your sleep. And even then, still not reassured, you preemptively swallowed a blue sleeping pill to stun the day's anxieties and the morrow's premonitions. Not that you were reckless. Afraid of sleeping through the alarm, you divided the pill in two, taking half for yourself and giving the other half to the guileless traveler, a stranger to worry and insomnia. Excited by her adventure and protesting the loss of the newspaper that you snatched from her hands while switching off the reading light, she kissed you gently and curled herself, to the serenade of her musical snores, into her usual, peaceful ball of sleep.

How could you have been so slow then to recognize the poison dripping into you as you tossed for a whole hour in bed, dozing fitfully, rumpling sheets and kicking off blankets, until you went to lie down on the convertible couch in your study, the royal bed from which you vainly tried to shake the leftovers of your fragile sister-in-law's sleep, until at midnight, with a desperate hope, you swallowed another sleeping pill, this time a whole one ingested with a glass of brandy that, though it hit you like an uppercut, merely poured more fuel on the stubborn flame inside you?

Can it be that your beloved's folded clothes, now lying resigned to their fate in a higher pile than you had counted on, reminded you of happier times? Because Hagit, after fighting tooth and nail for each item, suddenly reversed course and joined your clearance campaign with such ardor that you had to stop her in a panic, uncertain whether this was a shrewd ploy to make you back down or a genuine decision to prune her wardrobe, which would inevitably be followed by a demand for its massive renewal.

And so, fatigued and confused by new and old desires, you return after midnight to reconsider the old dresses, skirts, and blouses. By the glow of the reddish night-light between the two floors of the duplex, you run your hand over worn velvet, finger beloved embroidery, caress light wool, and sniff at a never-worn pair of red high-heeled shoes that you called "whorish" because you thought their provocative nature would bring a blush to the cheeks of defendants and plaintiffs alike. Their straps shamelessly seductive, they have fled from drawer to drawer, closet to closet, and apartment to apartment before being apprehended at last and added to the pile of castaways waiting to be sent to some charity.

You know what is the one thing capable of chaining to your bed the recalcitrant sleep now wandering about the apartment. But you know, too, that your mate of many years will never allow you to mix love with slumber, lest she lose control over an act that is in her opinion more spiritual than physical. And so, reduced to raising the blinds again in the hope that the rebuffed moonlight may dispel the darkness of the room, you whimper (though not to tomorrow's traveler, whose sleep is precious, but to the sky, the stars, the sleeping ghost across the street, the blue pill that has been swallowed by your anxiety rather than vice versa):

"I haven't slept a wink. Not for one minute."

And you lapse into silence, not knowing whether your voice has made a dent in the woman beside you. After a while comes her faint but clear answer. It is on automatic pilot, that unconscious critique born of pure judgment that enables her, in all times and places, no matter how deep the night or her sleep, to utter words of reassurance or reproach that not only are unremembered by her in the morning, but amuse her greatly when she is told of them.

"Never mind, my love. There's nothing sacred about sleep."

"Look who's talking."

"Ben-Gurion slept four hours a night and was the best prime minister the country ever had."

"Give me four hours and I'll be a happy man."

"You can sleep all you want when I'm gone."

"How? When? What are you talking about? The housekeeper is coming tomorrow. How can I sleep with her around? And that goddamn Samaher is sending me her cousin with her material. What made me get involved with her? God Almighty, how did I let it happen?"

"Never mind. You'll sleep afterward."

"I'm a wreck."

"What's the matter with you tonight? Don't tell me you envy me too."

"Of course not. There's nothing enviable about you. It's just the injustice of it. You can abscond all the way to Europe, while I can't even do it for a few hours to Jerusalem without feeling guilty."

"When did you abscond to Jerusalem?"

"I didn't."

"Then what do you feel guilty about?"

"You. Wherever I go makes you jealous and angry."

"Because I don't like being without you. Tomorrow will be hard for me too. But what was I supposed to do? You mustn't mind my going. I had no choice. Believe me, I'm not looking forward to it."

Astonished, you stare at this woman making perfect sense in her sleep, from the depths of which she talks like an obedient fetus.

"All right, all right. It doesn't matter. Go on sleeping. You only have an hour and a half left."

"Would you like me to put you to sleep too?"

But already her breathing grows regular, and she sinks back under, beneath the straight blanket, upon the crisp sheet, her fist against her mouth like the last trace of an old habit of thumb-sucking. You snuggle up to her from behind, one hand on her stomach, trying but failing to access her warmth, to cling to her, fetus-to-fetus, your breath in one rhythm with hers, sucking in the generous bounty of her calm, untroubled sleep—only to give up and, with a sudden movement, despairing and reconciled at once, free her of the burden of you. Oddly, your mood improves at once. Slipping out of bed, you put on your bifocals, shut the bedroom door behind you, turn the light on in the kitchen, put up some water up to boil, and go to switch on your computer, across whose screen float the words "Be of Good Cheer."

## 5.

ONLY WITH THE first glimmerings of dawn was Rivlin permitted to shut the suitcase and stand it by the front door. Hagit, wearing makeup and her regulation black suit that no number of clearance campaigns would eliminate, joined him for coffee. Beaming and expectant, she agreed to help finish an old piece of cake left over from her sister's visit. The two of them sat looking at each other with a deep and weary affection, surprised to discover that their rare, if brief, separation was really about to take place.

"What would you like the housekeeper to cook for you today?"

"Nothing. The fridge is full of leftovers."

"Will you come downstairs with me?"

"Of course."

"It's not necessary. The suitcase isn't heavy."

"What's necessary is to get a coherent explanation from you of how we're going to be in touch and how I'll know when you'll be back. This whole trip is a little too mysterious for me."

"Mysterious? It's only for three or four days. And I won't be alone."

"But who will be responsible for all of you?"

"Why does anyone have to be responsible? The embassy in Vienna will know where to contact us. Just don't expect a phone call today. Maybe tomorrow. Are you going to change that shirt?"

"What's wrong with it?"

"It's creased. You can't come down with me in that. And please shave, too."

"I never shave this early."

"Shave anyway. You can't expect everyone to be familiar with your habits."

He shaved, put on a fresh shirt, and took down her suitcase while she lingered to check her makeup, in an assertion of her feminine prerogative to be late. A sleek Corrections Authority van was waiting in the narrow street. The driver, dressed in a prison warder's uniform, had switched on the revolving blue police light to proclaim the importance accorded by the state to its judicial institutions. The district court secretary, a tall, lanky man, greeted Rivlin and moved quickly to take the suitcase. Recognizing the Orientalist at once, Hagit's two colleagues on the bench shook his hand. Soon she appeared, her eyes aglow with adventure, wearing an old cardigan salvaged at the last moment from the pile of cast-off clothes. Two young men, the prosecutor and the defense counsel, scrambled from the van to salute her and make the professor's acquaintance.

His wife was now surrounded by a full-court press of five attentive men. Overhead, a first cloud was turning pink in the dawn light above the Carmel. Drunk from his sleepless, lovelorn night, Rivlin took his wife in his arms and kissed her before everyone. Then, suddenly relaxed and smiling, he turned to the travelers and declared, as if it were he who was dispatching them:

"It's time you ended this damn trial."

A head movement of the judge's told him he had gone too far. Trying to make up for it, he said gallantly:

"And try to enjoy yourselves if you can...."

Only upon returning to the apartment, where he noticed that Hagit had taken the unusual step of washing the breakfast dishes, did he realize how guilty she had felt, not for leaving him, but for the moment of parting. At once he picked up the phone and dialed Ofer, the night guard sitting behind a heavy green security door in Paris. Although the switchboard of the Jewish Agency was shut down after work to prevent the off-hours from being whiled away on the phone, Ofer had an emergency line that could be used in a pinch. If he ever fell asleep while on duty, Rivlin told himself, it was better for him to be awakened by his father than by his boss.

He began the call by relating Hagit's dawn departure, the feverish preparations for which had turned him into a night watchman like his son, although one who watched only himself. With a touch of irony he described the Corrections Authority van, into which an entire courtroom had fitted. Next he asked Ofer about the weather in Europe, his latest exam, and the date of the next one—and since the emergency line could not be used for long, he inquired casually before hanging up whether a reply had arrived from Jerusalem to his son's condolence letter.

The voice at the other end was startled. "How did you know I sent Galya a letter?"

"I suppose you told me."

"I couldn't have, Abba. I never said a word to you."

"Well, then I suppose I assumed that's what you would do," Rivlin said, trying to keep his presence of mind. "Don't forget that she was once your wife."

There was a heavy silence behind the green door, on the other side of which an early-morning Parisian breeze was perhaps already blowing. Then came the unexpected query:

"Have you told Ima?"

"Told her what?"

"What you've been hiding from her. That you told me about Hendel even though she asked you not to...."

"Not yet."

"But why not, Abba?" Ofer's laugh was cynically provocative. "It's not like you to act behind her back. In the end you'll have to pay for that."

"Don't worry about what I'll have to pay for. And don't romanticize your parents. We're good friends, not Siamese twins. Your mother is a judge. It's her job to put a line through the past by passing sentence. I'm a historian. For me the past is a gold mine of surprises and possibilities."

"A gold mine?" Rivlin heard a note of scorn. "A dunghill is more like it."

"Dunghills have their surprises too." He spoke softly, the telephone pressed to his ear like a rifle tracking a bird. "So? Did you get an answer from Galya?"

"What does it matter to you?"

"It doesn't. But I had the feeling she wanted you to know about her father's death. The first thing she asked when I came to the hotel was, 'Does Ofer know?'"

Silence. Then:

"She did? How strange."

"Yes. In the garden. Don't get me wrong, Ofer. I'm angry at her, too. But it pained me to see her in such grief. She was devastated, desperate for comfort. Even from you."

"Devastated. The poor thing...." There was vindictiveness rather than compassion in those words. "Yes, that's what she said in her letter."

"So she answered you." He had bagged the bird with a single, well-aimed shot.

"Yes. With a very sad note. And a nasty one."

"Nasty?" He gave a start, excited to hear the same word that had been used by Galya to describe his son's condolence note. Perhaps so much nastiness between a couple that hadn't spoken for five years held out hope for new understanding. In a soft but authoritative voice, like that with which he had soothed his son when, cranky and troubled, he had been wakened as a child by bad dreams, Rivlin asked:

"Nasty? Why? What did she say?"

"Never mind."

"But what? Explain yourself. You can't just leave it like that. Why don't you ask her what she wants?"

That did it. Ofer suddenly let loose with a bitter grievance that became a harsh tirade.

"That's enough, Abba! There's a limit. What do you want from me? What are you trying to do? You should listen to Ima. She knows better than you what is and isn't possible. You think you can call up ghosts and control them. When will you realize there are things that you don't have to understand? There are things I don't understand myself. Have some faith in me. . . . No, no," he continued when his father sought to apologize. "Please, don't. I know what you're going to say. Listen to me for once. Ima is right. It's annoying how uptight you are. You're always poking at things. Well, poke at your Arabs, not at me. And don't be angry. I don't want to hurt your feelings. But you should talk to Ima. You're wrong about her. She doesn't want to put a line through anything. She wants boundaries. And that's something you're a world champion at crossing and getting others to cross. I'm not blaming you. But it's amazing how naive you can be despite all your education and knowledge. And when you start being stubborn about your naïveté, you become impossible. . . .

"No, don't," he went on, not letting his father reply. "Please. Don't tell me you're worried. Worry can be real and smothering anyway. I've told you a thousand times, but you won't listen. . . . Yes, I have! More than a thousand! Get it into your head that I know exactly how and why my marriage broke up. I may not have been happy about it, I may not have come to terms with it, but I know why it happened. I do! Do you hear me? I do! And if I decided to spare you what I know and keep silent for five years, don't think I'm going to start talking now. . . .

"No, no. . . . You mustn't be upset. You know that I love you, even if I'm angry. But it gets harder all the time, believe me. Maybe that's because I'm like you.... No, listen. Don't start in on that again. I have to hang up. It's nearly morning, and there are things to be done before opening the office. We're on an emergency phone. Take my word for it, none of this has been an emergency for quite some time...."

## 6.

GHOSTS? HE LET the word run through his racing mind. Perhaps. But this ghost was pregnant. The fact that he had got Galya to answer, however "nastily," an equally "nasty" letter from his son took the sting out of Ofer's rebuke. He leafed through the morning paper, took off his clothes, and strode around the apartment while waiting for the Jacuzzi, installed as a prize for the ordeal of moving, to fill with foam that would consign the night to oblivion by caressing private parts never touched by others underwater. Once in the bath he shut his eyes and let its currents churn past him while imagining himself on the airplane with his wife. Soon he was swooning in the arms of the accursed slumber that had eluded his advances all night long. Here, of all places, water jetting all around him, his soul was at last trapped in its embrace...

It was thus that the coal-eyed messenger, arriving at the appointed hour, was required to demonstrate his faith by persisting in short, polite rings of the doorbell, reinforced at intervals by a thoughtfully civilized drumming of his knuckles in various rhythmic measures, to which the duplex responded with a stubborn silence. Indeed, had Rivlin surmised that the empty-handed Arab had come not to deliver but to fetch—and first and foremost, to fetch the Orientalist himself—he would never have risen in the end to throw out the love baby of sleep with the golden bathwater rippling in the early-morning light by running to the front door, dripping wet and blind, and petitioning abjectly from his side of it:

"Is that you, Rashid? You'll have to excuse me. I'm a bit woozy because my wife had to catch a plane this morning and I didn't sleep all night. Just leave Samaher's material behind the big flowerpot and tell her I'll get in touch."

The Arab, however, had precious little material to leave. On the contrary, since it was too immaterial to be left behind a flowerpot, he was prepared to wait for the professor to make up for lost sleep and to return that afternoon or evening. "It makes no difference," he declared from his side of the door. "The day is shot anyway."

Rivlin felt a new burst of anger at Samaher, who was now enlisting her entire family to make a fool of him. Yet before he could tell the messenger to go shoot himself along with the day, it occurred to him that Suissa's texts were still in Mansura. Slowly, the leaden crust on his eyes was dissolving. Rashid, he decreed, should return in an hour.

"Only an hour? Are you sure, Professor? You don't want to sleep more than that?"

"An hour will be fine. Don't make it any longer."

An hour later, fully dressed and ready to cope, the slippers on his feet the only sign of his untimely abduction from the bosom of sleep, he sat in the living room looking irritably at the sable-skinned young man, who had refused all refreshment except for a glass of water, which had not touched his lips. On the table lay a Hebrew translation of a poem by a Berber from Oran, Hatib Abu el-Slah. Written in the early 1940s, it had been excellently translated by Samaher:

The world, sharp as a razor, / Slashes my cheeks. / Pursued by the
law as though by a whale, / I amuse myself by making a paper star. /
Fire worshipers gather around its light. / An Ethiope attendant fans
me. / I rise on straws toward the windows, / Snuff out the
honeymoon lamp, / And climb on the radiant beams of teeth /
While incense ascends from me. / I sculpt an angel that is eaten like a
raisin along the way, / Sit chewing on ice like a ball rolled off the
playing field, / Travel on a reed, / And transport painted eggs, chicks,
and kerosene. / In pants as short as an entry in a diary, / I jump to
the stars through the glass panes of the observatory. / I unbutton my
shirt, breathe the pure air, / And create a lion of stone / Infested by
fleas and the secrets of the microcosm.

"Where is the Arabic?" he asked, surprised by the poem's playful tone.

This time too, however, there was only a translation.

"Tell me, Rashid, what's going on here? Is Samaher subjecting me to Chinese water torture by dripping one poem at a time on me? And where are the stories?"

The young man's sense of truth and justice was unshaken by Rivlin's sarcasm. With a candid look that demanded credence, he swore that his cousin had read everything marked by the murdered scholar and even filled a copybook with her notes and summations. It was just that, being bedridden, she found it difficult to write. Her handwriting was so bad and full of spelling mistakes, in Arabic as well as in Hebrew, that she was embarrassed to let her professor see it.

"But this poem is perfectly legible."

"That's because I wrote it. The poems are easy. She learns the Arabic by heart, goes over it with her mother, puts it into Hebrew, learns that by heart too, and dictates it to me on Saturday when I have the day off."

"But how long is this going to go on?" the sleepy Orientalist wanted to know. "Is she really pregnant?"

"So her mother keeps saying," Rashid said again without indicating whether he believed it.

The messenger sat straight in his chair, the glass of water still untouched. He was, Rivlin thought, a devoted, sensitive young man. The coal black eyes were neither cunning, sardonic, nor obsequious.

"Well, what now?"

"Both Samaher and her mother think an oral exam would be best."

"An oral exam?"

"Yes. She'll tell you what's in the stories, and you'll write it down for your research. Dictating them to me in Hebrew would take too long."

"I've had quite enough of this," the professor snapped, though not in genuine anger. "Samaher and her lovely mother have gone bonkers. They think they can make a soft touch like me rewrite the rules of the university."

Rashid, solemn, said nothing. Like a sorrowful but obedient disciple, he crossed his arms and waited for the professor to think better of it.

"So when will she come to take these orals of hers?"

"But how can she come?" Rashid spread his arms in amazement. "The doctor won't even let her go to the bathroom. That's why her mother wants you to come to us . . . to the village. . . ."

"*I* should drive to the village?"

"Of course not. I'll drive you. I'll bring you back, too. Whenever you like. It could even be now. That's what Samaher's mother says."

Why did Rashid keep bringing her into this? Did he suspect him of having a crush on the attractive woman who had cried in his office?

Rivlin glanced at the translated poem. Could so sophisticated a piece of free verse have been written in the Algeria of the 1940s, or was this a hoax concocted for his benefit in Samaher's Galilee village? In either case, he had to retrieve the photocopies of Suissa's texts before they disintegrated between the sheets of her bed . . . unless, that is, the promised spark of inspiration depended on direct contact with the rare originals returned to Jerusalem.

And yet the dawn parting from his wife, without even a definite reunion to look forward to, coming on top of a sleepless night that weighed on him like a sick, heavy cat on his shoulders, had turned him into such a passive, malleable, and perhaps even seducible creature that, instead of terminating his special arrangement with Samaher and demanding the material back, he sat drowsily contemplating her jet-colored intercessor, whose noble and refined manner reminded him of his younger son's. Although sensing the professor's bewilderment, Rashid did not avert his glance. Willing to put up with a reprimand but not a refusal, he cocked a guileless head. One might have thought, from the way he kept his gentle eyes on the Orientalist while awaiting a reply, that he had all of Araby behind him. He did not even turn to look when a key scraped in the door and the housekeeper, in tight jeans and high heels, made her bored appearance.

## 7.

WAS AGREEING TO his Arab driver's suggestion to take along a blanket and two small pillows an early warning of the depth of the seduction? For although Rivlin protested that he never slept in cars, Rashid insisted on making a bed of the backseat for the comfort of the Jewish professor, who would travel "just like in an ambulance."

Before turning onto the Northern Highway, the minibus entered a gas station on a side road. The station's name appeared only in Arabic, the pennants decorating it were colored an Islamic green, and each driver was given a copper tray with Turkish coffee and a piece of baklava instead of the usual mudslinging Hebrew newspaper. Rashid handed these to his passenger. It was the holiday of Ramadan, and besides, he never felt hungry before evening.

"You're right, it's Ramadan," Rivlin said, remembering that it was the month in which Muslims fasted by day and ate at night. "I would never have come today if I had realized that."

"But why not, Professor? Why should Ramadan bother you? It's a time when guests are especially welcome."

The sleepless night, coupled with the infusion of morning slumber, had left him fuzzy-headed. He emptied the coffee cup, catching sight, as he threw back his head to drain the last drops, of the university tower in Haifa, a thin needle on the horizon.

"Still, Rashid," he said, "tell me the truth. I need to know it before we reach the village. What's wrong with Samaher? Is she depressed?"

Samaher's cousin put his head in his hands, as if to think the matter through.

"Sometimes. But sometimes she's happy and even sings songs."

He took out a pocketknife and strode to a field behind the gas station. Finding a bush with blue flowers among the dry brambles, he deftly cut a few fresh branches and made a bouquet of them.

"You can give this to Samaher's grandmother," he said, with a twinkle. "We Arabs never give flowers. That's why we're always so glad to get them."

The village lay silent, struck by a withering noon light. The minibus climbed a small hill and parked between the wrecks of two fifties pickup trucks, near which red Arab chickens of an obsolete stock were pecking at the ground. Rivlin, his head aching, stopped by a large, dusty fig tree, trying to remember something.

"Yes, the wedding was here," Rashid said with a hint of melancholy. There was no telling whether his doleful tone had to do with the event itself or with its being over so soon. "We put all the Jewish guests by this tree. Your wife sat over there. She laughed all evening. We even talked about it afterward, how a woman could be a judge and laugh so much."

"But these old trucks weren't here then, were they?"

"They were, but we covered them with a tarpaulin. We spread olive branches on it and put the D.J. and his equipment on top of them."

Here was the narrow lane down which Samaher's wedding dress had rustled as she resolutely transferred her illness to her grandmother. In broad daylight it was a short, simple path. The black horse rubbing its head against the bars of the front gate was familiar, too.

Rashid stroked the animal's unbridled neck. Gently gripping its intelligent head, he gave it an odd, quick kiss. Samaher's mother opened the door of the large stone house. Either because of the holiday, or to distance herself from the Jewish professor who had acceded rather too quickly to her request, she was wearing a traditional peasant dress. Soon the sturdy, silent grandfather, his bald head no longer hidden by a kaffiyeh, was summoned to the scene too. Giving the Orientalist what looked like a Turkish salute, he unscoldingly led the friendly horse to its stable, as though it were a slow-witted but likable child.

By now, several women had congregated by the front door along with Afifa and the grandmother. Some young and some old, they greeted the visitor respectfully.

"*Allah yehursak.*"*

"*Barak li'lah fik, ya mu'alim.*"†

"*Kadis!*"‡

"*Low kunt ba'aref ino 'l-yom Ramadan,*" Rivlin replied, "*ma kuntish bawafe' bilmarra aaji el-yom la'indikon.*"§

"But why not, Professor? Why let Ramadan stop you?" Afifa scolded him in a friendly Hebrew. "You're not a Muslim, and Muhammad didn't make the fast for you. And even if you were, it's a free country...."

Samaher's grandmother sniffed the flowers Rashid gave her. Kissing her eldest grandson's hands, she blessed him for bringing "Samaher's important teacher." No one, it seemed, had really expected him to come.

---

* God save you.
† Welcome, Teacher.
‡ The man's a saint.
§ Had I known it was Ramadan, I would never have agreed to come here today.

# 8.

HE WAS LED to a spacious bedroom, in which stood a black lacquered chest, a closet, a large table, several smaller ones, and some chairs. Half-lying and half-leaning on pillows in a big bed, his student of many years looked pale and thin. Her hair was gathered in a net and traces of red polish from the wedding were still on her fingernails and toenails, which stuck out from beneath the blanket. He gave her a suspicious, pitying look. Expecting a child, he told himself, as though he had lately become an expert on false pregnancies, she was not. It looked more like a case of depression.

"You really came." She blushed and smiled wanly. "Thank you. Thank you, Professor, for coming to our village."

"*Sad'uni*," * he said, addressing not only Afifa and the grand-mother, who had followed him into the room, but the women outside in the hallway, "I've been teaching at the university for thirty years, and this is my first house call. *Bil sitta ow marid.*" †

"*Tiwafakt bil'aml es-saleh.*" ‡

"*Allah yibarek fik.*" §

Meanwhile, the sable-skinned impresario was arranging the stage by plumping up the squashed pillow behind his cousin, bending down to retrieve a pair of slippers from beneath the bed, throwing some wrinkled napkins into a wastepaper basket, and handing the grandmother two dirty glasses. Turning to Samaher's medicines, with which he seemed familiar, he restored some order to them before pulling out two notebooks and pens from the lacquered chest. All this was done deftly and knowledgeably, in a code composed of short, swift sentences, as if he alone knew the desires of the recent bride.

"How's the new husband?" Rivlin asked cautiously, putting the question to no one in particular.

"Working hard for his father."

"What at?"

---

* Believe me.
† In good health or illness.
‡ You've done a great deed.
§ God bless you.

"He's a building contractor."

Rashid now placed Suissa's texts in their colored binders on the large table. At least, Rivlin thought with relief, he could take them back to Haifa with him.

The messenger was not yet done. Moving a large armchair close to the bed, he placed a small table next to it and spread this with an embroidered cloth just as a girl entered the room with a knife and fork.

"*Min fadleku, la.*"* The guest returned the silverware to the hands of the frightened girl. "Don't serve me any meals now. We have plenty of time. And what's this about food, anyway? *N'situ Ramadan?*"†

"*Shu Ramadan? Kif faj'a nat lak Ramadan?*"‡ The women laughed, amused by how easy the Jew thought it was to become a Muslim. "You have your Yom Kippur, Professor. What's Ramadan to you? *Er-ruz matbuh, u'lahm el-haruf ala 'lnar.*"§

The Orientalist stuck to his guns. He was not eating now. He had already told Rashid. His wife had flown abroad early in the morning, as a result of which he hadn't slept all night. If he ate now, he would need to sleep, which was not the purpose of his visit.

But why shouldn't he sleep? The women took to the notion enthusiastically. "In fact, why don't you do it the other way around, Professor, and sleep first? If your wife is out of the country, you're in no hurry to get home. Have a light snack, and we'll give you a nice, quiet room to lie down in. That way you'll be fresh for the exam."

"The exam? What exam?"

"The oral exam for Samaher's final grade...."

But the Orientalist, well aware how Arab guile was concealed behind the innocence of the desert, was quick to squelch, even at the risk of his newly won popularity, the illusion of a final grade.

"I'm not giving Samaher any exam. She knows as well as I do that she's still a long way from a final grade. I came here today to hear the oral summaries that she can't write. And to take back the material."

---

* No, thank you.
† Have you forgotten it's Ramadan?
‡ What Ramadan? What do you have to do with Ramadan?
§ The rice is cooked, and the lamb is already on the grill.

The messenger gasped. "You're taking back the material?" So that was why the professor had agreed so easily to come to the village.

"Why shouldn't I?"

It was an awkward situation. Rivlin turned to his student, who, though she hadn't missed a course of his in five years, lay staring at him as though she had never seen him before.

"You can still finish your assignment," he said to her. "Rashid can photocopy a new set for you. The poems you've translated aren't bad at all. In fact, you've done a good job. In a minute we'll see what you've done with the stories."

There was a ripple of relief that the professor was not proposing to reject Samaher's term paper. Fearfully, the young girl returned again to place a jug of cold water and an infusion of herbs in front of Rivlin. "Even the greatest saints," Afifa assured him, "have been known to drink during the fast." A small boy, dressed in a fez and a festive holiday robe, entered proudly bearing a narghile, which Samaher's grandmother had ordered as an antidote for the Jew's hunger. The growing acceptance of his determination to observe the fast caused Rivlin to fear that he might have to leave the village in the end on an empty stomach.

Meanwhile, Samaher, greatly cheered by his compliment, dismissed not only the women, but her cousin as well. Before shutting the door behind him, Rashid pulled down the colored blind on the window, leaving the teacher and his student pleasantly bathed in a golden Galilean gloom.

## 9.

"Do you have enough light, Professor?"

"That remains to be seen."

He leaned back in his armchair and smiled at his student, who removed her hairnet and shook her hair out with a brisk, free movement. Above her bed was a picture of an ancient dignitary, a patriarch belted with a dagger. How, he wondered, had she managed to lure him, first to her wedding, and now into her bedroom?

"Well?" He could not resist taking a dig at all the lies. "This pregnancy of yours—is it definite?"

"Almost..." The answer was diplomatic.

"How are you feeling?" he asked in a fatherly tone.

"Better." A tear shone in her eye.

"Then let's begin." He took some of the herbs, crushed them between his fingers, and inhaled their scent. "First, where are the originals of the poems you've translated? I don't doubt you've done a faithful job, but I have to check whether the Arabic is quite so modern."

"But why shouldn't it be, Professor? Do you think we're always going to remain...primitive?"

"What a word to use, Samaher!" Her forwardness startled him. "Who said anything about primitive? I merely wanted to see the originals."

"They're in the binders on the table. I'll call Rashid and tell him to find them."

"That can wait. By the way, I like your cousin. He's a fine fellow and very devoted to you. How come someone like him isn't married?"

Samaher shrugged. "He hasn't found a wife." In an irritable whisper she added, "He doesn't want one. What can I do about it? Nothing."

"You're quite right," the Jewish professor admitted. "There's nothing you can do. Let's move on. You say that you've read two stories..."

"Two? A lot more than that."

"You mentioned two in your note to me: a realistic one about a feud between village clans, and one that's more like a folktale."

"A parable."

"Of a political nature."

"In my opinion."

"Let's start with that. Do you remember where you summarized it in your notebook, or do we have to call Rashid?"

She was insulted. "Why Rashid? Of course I remember."

She leafed through some pages and found it.

The story had appeared in a mimeographed periodical, a quarterly or biannual named *Katarna*,* put out with French backing in the

---

* Our Train.

1940s by the Railway and Post Office Workers Union of Algeria. Besides information on the postal and railway services and their development, the volume included articles, stories, and poems written by union members. In January 1942, one Ibrahim Ibn Bakhir, a ticket clerk at the Sidi Bal-Abbas station, published a tale titled *"El-Tifl el-Faransi el-Murafrif."*

" 'The Floating French Baby'?" Rivlin translated doubtfully.

"That's correct. It's one of the stories you marked, Professor."

Forbearing to point out that most of the markings were Suissa's, he sat back in his chair.

### The Tale of the Floating French Baby

In a small village near Sidi Bal-Abbas lived a hardworking farmer named Yusuf with his wife, Ayisha. Although the two were good, fine-looking people who loved each other greatly, they had no children. "I'm afraid," Yusuf said to Ayisha, "that I'll have to take another wife to bear me children." "That," Ayisha replied, "is only natural. But to prevent my life from being consumed by jealousy, let me first travel through the countryside. Perhaps I can find an abandoned orphan to be mine." "You're right, my beloved wife," the farmer said. "Go look for an abandoned child. Just make sure you return to me. Although by then I will have taken a second wife, my love for you is assured until your dying day."

The farmer's wife decided that the best place to look for an abandoned child was a railway station. People in stations are always in a hurry and often forget suitcases, bags, and even babies. So as to remove all suspicion from herself, and escape being molested because of her beauty, Ayisha cut her hair short, dyed it white, and stuck a beard on her face. Then she sewed herself a short cloak, found a big walking stick, and began wandering from station to station, disguised as a Sufi holy man, in search of an abandoned child.

At first all went well. The old Sufi was treated with respect, and no one suspected a thing. After a while, however, attracted by the Sufi's bare legs, which were unusually smooth and shapely, people began to follow him and seek his blessing. Afraid of being given away by her soft voice, Ayisha stopped talking and only smiled. But this only increased the number of her devotees, who accompanied her from station to station.

Meanwhile the train management, seeing that the silent Sufi had increased the number of passengers, gave him a free lifetime ticket.

"How very strange," Rivlin chuckled. "You can see the author was a ticket clerk."

Yet how was Ayisha, now surrounded day and night by loyal disciples who expected her to work wonders, supposed to find an abandoned baby to comfort her for the many children that her husband's second wife would bear? And so one night, hatching a plan, she talked. In a thick, slow voice like an old man's, she told her disciples that she was planning to work a wonder such as no one had ever seen. She would make a little baby too small to stand on its feet float outside the window of a train. Yet who would agree to volunteer their offspring for such a risky miracle? She had to find an orphaned or abandoned child with no mother. If her disciples would bring her such an infant, she would do the rest.

Several days went by, and then Ayisha's disciples kidnapped a baby. It wasn't an orphan, however. It was French, because only the French leave their babies lying in baby carriages. It was far easier to steal an infant from a Christian pram than from the shoulder sling of a Muslim mother.

This frightened Ayisha greatly. She had intended to get hold of an abandoned child, a poor, dirty little waif whom she could save from hunger, and now she had been brought a big, fat, blond, well-dressed, conspicuous baby. And the police were already searching for its kidnapper!

Nor was that all. Ayisha had planned to wait for her disciples to fall asleep at night and then rip off her beard, change her hermit's cloak for a dress, veil her face, and slip away to her husband's village. How, surrounded by boisterous disciples, with the French police and army on her heels, was she going to do that with a fat, blond French baby?

And what would she tell her angry followers when they discovered
that they had kidnapped a baby for a wonder she couldn't work? And
so, sitting down beneath a distant tree, she prayed to Allah to have
pity on the French child, whose miracle was planned for the next day.

Samaher was leaning cross-legged against the plumped pillows, her
long hair grazing the embroidered flowers on her nightgown. There
was new color in her cheeks, and her voice had grown stronger, as
if this bizarre and tedious tale were now carrying her along with
Ayisha's disciples and the trains.

The next day, Ayisha boarded a train with several of her disciples.
As soon as it picked up speed, she took the French baby and tossed it
out the window. Yet Allah had heard her prayer and had pity. He did
not let the child fly away but kept it floating outside the window,
laughing and playing with the wind until Ayisha took it back into the
train. At the next station it was given to a ticket clerk and brought to
the police, who had posted a large reward.

"There's that ticket clerk again," laughed the visitor.

Ayisha, now a famous—though still childless—wonder-worker,
was very sad. Everyone who heard about the floating French baby became more devoted to her than ever. A house was built for her on a
mountaintop, and pilgrims came to kiss the hem of her cloak and the
dainty soles of her feet. Even her husband's second wife, who also was
childless, came to kneel before her without knowing who she was.

"That's the end. Nice, isn't it?"
"Let's not exaggerate," he said, his headache back again. It was a
story for *One Thousand and One Nights.* "What strikes you as political about it?"
"Well, you see, Professor, I thought that if it was written in 1942,
during the Second World War, when the French were as helpless as
babies, it was a story about how sorry the Arabs felt for them."

"Sorry? Didn't they throw the French baby out the window?"

"Yes, but only because Allah would save it. The God of the Muslims," Samaher said gently, "who has mercy on the whole world. I think that's the point of the parable, don't you?"

He recalled how, in her first years as an undergraduate, she had kept getting into political arguments until, tired of them, she had stopped.

There was a profound silence.

"Tell me, Samaher," he asked. "Do you believe in God?"

She blushed, her eyes flashing. "Why ask me? Ask the man who wrote this story, Ibrahim Ibn-Bakhir. Ask his readers. They were believers."

"That may be. But are you one, Samaher?"

"In God?" She smiled her Mona Lisa smile. "Not exactly. . . ." Realizing where she was, she checked herself. "But during Ramadan, when we're fasting, I do try to believe . . . And when I'm not feeling well, too. . . ."

## 10.

RIVLIN ROSE FROM his chair and began to pace up and down as though he were in a seminar room at the university. His sleepless night pounded in his temples. What had made him come to this place?

He stumbled across the narghile on the floor. Lifting it, he gave it a sniff, put it carefully down in a corner, went to the tray of medicines by Samaher's bed, picked up a small bottle that rattled with blue pills, and stood there assessing their purpose. "Are these for your depression?" he bluntly asked his student, who was following his every movement with concern.

"I'm not depressed . . . just moody. . . ." She smiled anxiously at the Jew standing so close to her bed. "My mother and grandmother take them sometimes, too. They're good for when you feel blue."

Did he feel blue? He took a pill from the bottle, licked it with the tip of his tongue, and popped it into his mouth without asking permission. It had a bitter and sour but clean taste.

The pleasant gloom was pierced by the coal black eyes of the trusty messenger, sent to inform Rivlin that his bed was ready. An afternoon nap was a welcome prospect. Before retiring for it, however, the Orientalist wished to hear the second, realistic story, the one about the feuding clans. Perhaps realism was better suited to uncovering the spark that had kindled the Algerian conflagration.

"Your cousin," he told Rashid, possibly hoping that his praise would spur the young Arab to continue his efforts on Samaher's behalf, "has quite an original interpretation of the story of the French baby."

Not that Rashid's loyalty or admiration needed spurring. "Leave it to Samaher," he said. "She has a B.A. in Arabic language and literature."

"Then this will be an interdisciplinary project," Rivlin said. And to prevent them from thinking that he was being ironic at their expense, he suggested that he stay until the end of the day's fast. "After all," he added, "if you've lured me all the way to your village, I may as well enjoy some good food."

"A baby lamb, slaughtered just for you!"

Rashid was ecstatic. Going to the table, he carefully collected the large binders to bring to Ma'alot, the nearest town with a photocopier. He did not want a single day to be lost in the career of his cousin, by whose bed he hovered like a dark bird, gently helping her to ease the pressure of the pillow crumpled behind her back. The visitor watched the coals of his eyes burn hypnotically into themselves as he bent over her, as though examining the pimples on her throat. Recklessly turning her on her side, he scooped her up in one arm before she could stop him, while airing and straightening the sheets with his other hand. Rivlin, enthralled and aghast at the passion between the two young Arabs, could not bring himself to turn away.

But it was time for the second, realistic story, which he hoped would be more plausible than the first. If it lacked the rumble of trains and the din of stations, which the author of the first tale knew well, at least it would have no miraculous babies or beautiful women disguised as saints. Set in a remote village in the mountains, it had been written by an author named Yassin bin Abbas and published in the spring 1948 issue of a short-lived Oran literary magazine called *Al-Huriya al-Thalitha*, or "The Third Freedom." (What the first and second freedom were remained unclear.) Its language, according to Samaher, was highly colloquial, with so many odd local expressions that Rashid had gone with it to a relative in the Gaza Strip who had spent years working for the PLO in North Africa.

### The Story of the Poisoned Horse

There was once, *Samaher began enthusiastically,* a small village on a mountain called Jebl Musa. *She had abandoned her prone position and was now sitting up in bed with her notebook on her knees and her bare feet dangling.* Its poor, simple farming families barely eked out a living from the arid soil. Yet one of them, the Sidik family, had sheep, goats, and two horses. The other farmers hated the Sidiks, whose flocks and horses, they were convinced, ate the villagers' crops at night. No matter how often the Sidiks promised to keep their animals out of the neighbors' fields and graze them only in natural pasture, the farmers did not believe them. It got so bad that hardly anyone even spoke to them.

The Sidiks had a daughter, a lovely girl who had been named Leona after a French prime minister called León who was a great friend of the Muslims in Algeria. Yet so great was the village's hatred and suspicion of her father and brothers that none of its young men could think of marrying her, despite her good looks and good nature. "Never mind," her father said to her. "If we can't find you a husband in the village, we'll find one somewhere else." And so he sent one of her brothers to an old uncle in a far-off place, hoping that someone there, perhaps a cousin, might agree to marry her.

Samaher looked up from her notebook to see whether her teacher was listening. He had removed his eyeglasses and was wearily sprawled in his chair, fascinated as always by the Hebrew spoken by her generation, which alternated between a clumsy translation of her native Arabic and a true command of Israeli idiom.

Meanwhile, this plan became known to a fine young man named Ahmed ed-Danaf, the son of farmers in Leona's village. Ahmed ed-Danaf was secretly in love with Leona and was tormented by the thought that she would marry someone else far away. Leona, too, had set her eye on this young man, even though she never spoke to him. How, thought Ahmed ed-Danaf, could he keep his beloved from marrying? Not that he believed that his father would let him marry her himself. But at least, so he hoped, she would not be taken someplace else, where he could never see her again. And so he did something desperate.

Not far from the village was a large French estate whose owners raised wheat and fodder and scattered rat poison in their fields to protect their crops. Although the Frenchmen had tried convincing the Muslims to do the same, the farmers were afraid that their little children, who roamed the fields freely, might eat the poison and die. Now Ahmed ed-Danaf went to the Frenchmen and told them that he wished to do as they did. They were happy to see such a modern Arab and gave him a sack full of poison pellets. But he did not scatter these pellets in his fields. He hid them.

Meanwhile, a husband was found for Leona. He was indeed a cousin, a middle-aged widower who lived in France and had come to Algeria on a brief visit. He was ready, he said, to take an Algerian woman back to France with him, and the rumors made the rounds that the Sidiks would soon be holding a betrothal ceremony. And so Ahmed ed-Danaf made up his mind to put poison in the Sidiks' stable. It didn't kill their horses, but it made them very sick.

Of course, the Sidik family also had donkeys, which could have been harnessed to the betrothal wagon, too. But a donkey was not as dignified as a horse—and the horses were sick. This grieved the Sidiks greatly, especially since something told them that their horses were not the victims of Allah but of a curse someone had put on them. The question was who.

Meanwhile, Ahmed ed-Danaf, seeing the great sorrow of Leona's family, let alone the suffering of the horses, who lay miserably in their stable, all grassy-eyed and foaming at the mouth, began to feel sorry for his evil deed.

The phrase "grassy-eyed," uttered in the heat of the narration, brought a faint smile to Rivlin's lips, even though his head was now lolling to one side and his breathing had grown heavy. It was one of those comic slips that sound natural.

"Hold it, Samaher," he said. "Isn't Ahmed ed-Danaf also the name of a character in *One Thousand and One Nights*, the one in Scheherazade's story about the old woman?... You know who I mean ... Delilah!"

But the name meant nothing to Samaher. Nor did she remember any such story in the great prose classic of the Arabs.

And so Ahmed ed-Danaf decided to make amends. He found his courage and lay in wait for Leona and said to her, "I've heard that someone has cursed your horses and made them sick. If your family is afraid to leave them alone in order to go to your betrothal, I'm willing to look after them, because I love horses and it hurts me to see them. You can't blame the horses for our village feud, because they aren't part of it."

The Sidiks did not know what to do about Ahmed ed-Danaf's offer. But Leona, who felt he had made it because he was in love with her, persuaded her father to take it in good faith.

And so it was. The Sidiks harnessed plain donkeys to their wagon and set out for the betrothal. Yet on the night after their departure, one of the horses died. When Ahmed ed-Danaf arrived at the stable in the morning and saw this, he was frightened and even cried. Then he called for his two brothers, and they dragged the carcass away to keep it from saddening the other horse, which was fighting for its life. From that day on, Ahmed ed-Danaf was determined to stay by its side day and night, thinking only of it and of his beloved, who was being betrothed far away.

"Actually, Professor Rivlin," Samaher said, "I haven't got to the main part yet. I've only summarized the beginning. The rest is awfully long and gruesome. It tells how Ahmed ed-Danaf fights with all his strength to save the life of the horse he poisoned, because it belongs to the family of his beloved, who will go to France and never see him again.... Are you still listening, Professor? Perhaps it's too much for you."

This remark was well timed, because the last sentences, entwined in the sweet faintness mounting within him like a rampant ivy, had been dissipated in a desperate struggle with a fatigue of such uncommon violence that he slumped sideways in his chair and nearly stretched out on the Persian rug on the floor by the bed of his M.A. student, who had infected him, it seemed, not only with her depression, but with the fatigue of her false pregnancy.

## 11.

SINCE RASHID, NOT trusting Rivlin's patience to hold out until the end of the day's fast, had hurried off to Ma'alot to photocopy the Jerusalem scholar's material, the bedridden M.A. student had to summon her mother, who whisked the Orientalist off to sheets as white and soft as any his wife had ever made his sister-in-law's bed with. Assisted by Samaher's grandfather, who bent to remove his shoes, Rivlin felt the flame of his tiredness welding him to his lost sleep of the night before, which had doggedly followed him all the way to the village.

Later that evening, seeking to apologize for his attack of somnolence, he blamed it on the pill for "feeling blue," which he confessed to having sampled from Samaher's tray of medicines. Afifa, however, ruled this out.

"No pill could knock you out like that, Professor. Your tiredness came with you from Haifa. You were a sight when you arrived. If you had listened to us and gone right to sleep after *El-Tifl el-Faransi il-Murafrif*, we wouldn't have had to drag you off to bed more dead than alive. Believe me, Professor, *il-habbeh illi a'tatak iyaha Samaher hiya* friendly *l'il-nas.** It's just a pill to cheer you up a bit. I sometimes even let my little girls have one. It gets them through their homework."

And indeed, curious to find out whether Ahmed ed-Danaf had saved the life of the horse he had poisoned, he returned with the last, fading light to his armchair by Samaher's bed not only showered and refreshed, but greatly cheered. He felt as if the entire narcoleptic afternoon had been cranked out musically inside him in something called the Symphony of the Great Sleep. The first movement had been a brutally violent fortissimo: In it, a man, stripped of identity and

---

* The pill Samaher gave you is friendly to people.

consciousness, had lain fully dressed without knowing whence he had come, to what or whom he belonged, or whether he would ever wake again. An occasional errant dream notwithstanding, he had been as impermeable as a block of black stone. Yet after a while, his titanic stupor pierced by the scent of a strange soap that energized him sufficiently to pull off his shirt and pants in the hope of a more intimate contact with the wonderfully friendly sheets, the Jewish Orientalist had detected the theme of a second movement, which took command of a slumber made doubly delicious by the absence of his beloved wife. Whisked away that morning by a party of competent and responsible men, she had taken with her all worry for her welfare and even all worry for her worry for him. Guaranteed a minimum twenty-four-hour exemption from his daily accounting to her, he reached down and pulled off his socks.

Nor could the sounds of children returning from school or the glow of two o'clock on the alarm clock convince him that the time had come to wake up. After all, if the first prime minister of Israel, with all his many obligations, had nevertheless asked—or so said the Orientalist's wife—for four hours of sleep, why should he, whose obligations were few, make do with less than three? And so even upon rising from his cozy bed he left the lights off and refrained from any noise that might encourage members of the household to look in on him. With every intention of falling asleep again, he turned his temporary attention to the room he was in, hoping to make out, by the shimmering slivers of light that fell through the slats of the shutter, where and in whose realm he was.

Much to his pleasure, he saw that Samaher's wise mother had put him in the bed of the trusty cousin and not in that of some elderly aunt or uncle forced to forfeit an afternoon's nap for his sake. He was in a small wing of the house that included a shower and a bathroom, the abode of an independent, stouthearted, and—so it seemed— passionate young man. Perhaps this was why the door was equipped with a large bolt, which the Orientalist immediately slid into place while debating whether or not to return to full consciousness.

He chose not to. His rightful quota of sleep was not yet exhausted, and besides, he was feeling hungry and did not wish to show weakness by reneging, scant hours before sunset, on his apparently poignant but absurdly inappropriate pledge to fast on Ramadan. Groping his way in the dark to the toilet, he sat down on it slowly and encouragingly whispered to himself:

"As a human gesture, it's the least you can do."

## 12.

THE THIRD MOVEMENT began at 3 P.M. Rondo? Andante? Allegro? Although the visitor was still celebrating his exemption from reporting in, not only to his widely scattered family, which was not about to go looking for him, but even to the patient Arabs who had hushed for his sake the children playing in the yard, the second movement's keen, anarchic sense of freedom had faded. Thoughts he had driven away came creeping back from beneath the pillow.

And yet he was determined to hold the line and not wake up. As though rising to the challenge, he now stripped off his underpants and surrendered the last fraction of himself to the accommodating bed. Lying naked between the sheets and under a light blanket, he recalled the case of a Haifa accountant, a recent widower sent to audit the suspicious books of a Galilean township not far from Mansura. Entering the house of the town council's treasurer, the accountant had soon found himself immersed, not in the books, but in the bed of the man's youngest daughter, in which he fell fast asleep.

And yet this accountant was a public servant who had nodded off on the job among Jews, whereas Rivlin, though no widower, was his own master and among Arabs. Why not, then, doze a little longer in the bed of this young man the age of his eldest son while delving in its sheets for his old dream of tasting the essence of Araby? Curling up like a fetus beneath the blanket, therefore, he took firm possession of the pillow, but his thoughts, slipping from his grasp, dragged him back to Ofer's dawn rebuke. Surprisingly, he felt no pain or resentment. If anything, his position had been strengthened. If both son and ex-daughter-in-law had been truthful enough with each other to be nasty, the venom of the past retained its potency, and there were boundaries to be crossed.

Thus it was that, in this Galilean village, in this cool stone house, the thick walls of which muffled all superfluous sound, Rivlin, while continuing patiently to pursue the fluttering nymph of sleep, reassured himself that he had been right to overrule his wife, and even to risk her ire, by forcing a confrontation between two young people who had agreed too lightly, as if they were all alone in the world and responsible to no one, to separate, five years ago.

He knew how infinitesimal was his influence over his ex-daughter-in-law, now remarried and about to give birth, and even over his distant son, who, though suffering, refused to concede injury or accept help. Still, he was not prepared to forego the understanding that every parent has a right to demand. How strange that here, in this far corner of the country, secluded in willful sleep in a remote Arab village, his desire to know remained as great as ever, so that he seemed to hear his hosts encouraging him as they moved silently from room to room. "Keep it up, Professor," their inaudible voices said. "Don't give in. Here, among us Arabs, you can bathe in the true river of time."

And so, confident that time would continue to flow from the underground springs of Mansura, Rivlin curled up once more to catch the nymph of sleep in his bosom. And since Samaher's cousin had left no dream for him, he created a nude apparition of his own and made love to himself.

## 13.

YET ANOTHER HOUR passed in symphonic slumber. Young and old, the members of the household kept as silent as if the visitor were not Samaher's professor from Haifa but the Caliph of Baghdad in person. Awakening for some reason at the end of the third movement more exhausted than at the end of the second, Rivlin realized that it was only polite to get over his ill-mannered sleeping sickness, for which his insomnia of the night before was but a pretext, one that had unleashed an ancient weariness that must have been handed down from his earliest progenitors.

He rose, switched on the bed light, and studied the space around him. A photograph of Rashid stared down at him from the wall opposite the bed. The messenger looked younger and sat on a horse while gazing into the distance. Prior to dressing, Rivlin folded the sheets and tucked them into the pillowcase. Next, he folded the bare mattress and laid the blanket on top of it, as he had been taught to do in basic training before a furlough. Then he washed, soaping himself and rinsing his mouth with toothpaste to freshen up before rejoining the Arabs.

It was a pity, he thought, that he had not managed to dream a single dream of his own in the intimate atmosphere so generously provided him, now lambent with the soft, coppery light of a village afternoon astir with the shouts of children. Limply, he sat down at a small, old-fashioned secretary covered by a plastic map from Beirut showing the countries of the Middle East in bright colors. The State of Israel, though included, had been shrunk to the borders of the 1947 United Nations partition resolution, marked by a dotted line, like an illusion waiting to be dispelled. Above the little cubbyholes of the desk, each with its handsome brass handle, an empty artillery shell served as a vase for some artificial flowers, their dusty plastic blossoms inclined toward a gold-rimmed glass containing sharpened pencils in different colors. Behind the secretary, a bulletin board had bright notes from a memo pad pinned to it—reminders, scrawled in a clear, curling hand, of jobs for the minibus. The messenger, a tidy tenant, clearly liked his surroundings to be cheerful, as evidenced also by the lively book jackets with which he had covered not only the old Arabic novels, published in Beirut and Damascus, that stood in orderly rows on the shelves, but also two stray volumes of the *Hebrew Encyclopedia* and a book called *The Israelis.* A heavy black photograph album, on which some faded blue receipt books had been neatly stacked, contributed a more somber note.

Rivlin reached for the album, whose black binding reminded him of the condolence book in which several weeks ago he had written a sentence, no longer regretted by him, to a dead man. He was curious to see how Samaher's family had looked when younger.

To his disappointment, however, the photographs were of no one he could recognize. No youthful Afifa or middle-aged grandmother stared out at him, not even Samaher as a child. There was only page after relentless gray page of an unfamiliar, dark-skinned woman with eyes that resembled Rashid's. Her stony face was unsmiling and grave, both as a stiff young girl and as a married woman surrounded by sad, frightened-looking children—at first two or three of them, then four or five. In the background was a village, less picturesque than Mansura, sometimes seen from the courtyard of a run-down house and sometimes through two olive trees or from the window of a large kitchen full of big black pots. There were shots without it, too—one was of the woman standing by the bed of a sick-looking man in pajamas. Rivlin had the sense that this mysterious woman, with her solemn, frozen air, had been photographed not for her own sake but for some ulterior motive.

He sat leafing through the dreary album in the cheerful room of the bachelor tenant, amazed at the patience of the Arabs who, having laid an exhausted Jew to bed three hours before, hadn't checked to see if he had risen from the dead. The Ramadan sun streaked the wall with a first, golden hope of day's end as the fourth and final movement of the symphony began. Strong yet soft as fur, the tail end of his slumber now stroked the roots of his consciousness, from which ancient brain-children, the fossil relics of his doctoral days, shuddered to life and carried him off to an Asiatic country of fertile steppes. A huge, open shed stretched to hills on the horizon. It was a giant barn, full of large, quiet cows with golden spots, the markings of a breed long thought to be extinct, which here, thousands of miles from the sea, were gathered in noble silence in a global, cosmic farm bristling with snow white udders whose bountiful milk fed the calves and lambs that descended, naked and shorn, from the hills. One of these, spotted from afar by Rivlin's sharp eye, raised a cropped head: its expression, sad, suspicious, and lost, was his eldest son's. Spying its dreaming father across the wide expanse, it wagged a stubby tail in recognition. Not only did it look like his son, it was his son, who had undergone, unknown to his parents, a horrid transformation that had compelled him to wander with a Turkish flock from Europe to Asia.

The dreamer's heart went out to the lamb. He would have liked to approach it and ascertain whether, as seemed to be the case from afar, it was unhappy in its metamorphosis. Yet fearful that it might flee in shame or misunderstanding, he knelt instead and threw it a stick to retrieve while clucking his tongue as though it were a dog or stray cat. This proved a miscalculation. The stick only frightened it, turning innocent anxiety to alarm. Rearing on its hind legs, the lamb broke away from its huddled companions and retreated to the hills, its little tail forlornly still.

## 14.

ALTHOUGH SO HARSH a dream could not but put an end to the final movement, it did not detract from the splendor of the lengthy nap wrested from the no-man's-time of afternoon. Even if it had only lasted four hours, like the legendary sleep of the first prime minister, its exotic intimacy made it seem twice as long.

He urinated and washed up, and unbolted the door in the hope of finding at least one Arab waiting worriedly for him in the hallway. There was no one. His long nap seemed to have made him one of the family. The old grandmother, whose open door he now passed, was seated beside the grandfather, she listening to Arabic music on the radio while he dozed on a divan beneath a wall clock. She nodded to Rivlin as though he were an old friend and nothing could be more natural than a reputable Jewish professor wandering around her house at twilight. Pointing to the clock, she said:

"*Iza inta ju'an, ya eini, il-akl hadr. Ka'yahudi, inta sumt an kul hatayak u'hatay eiltak. Lakin iza inta m'samim innak t'kamel, lazim ti'raf inno ba'd akal min sei'ah b'tiji il-kunbila taba Sadal.*" *

The air flowing through the open window had a clear, dry Palestinian tang such as he remembered from his childhood. Grinning with curiosity, he let himself be lured into the old couple's room as if he were their middle-aged son.

"*Il-kunbilah taba Sadal? Shu hada?*" †

"In British times there was an old cannon in the next village that

---

\* If you're hungry, my dear, there's food. For a Jew, you've fasted enough for all your own and your family's sins. But if you don't want to stop now, you should know that the SLA cannon shot [ending the fast] will be in less than an hour.
† The SLA cannon shot? What's that?

fired each day at the end of the fast. Now Israel lets the soldiers of the Southern Lebanese Army across the border shoot a mortar shell. We eat on Lebanese time."

The old lady chortled toothlessly.

"My mother won't eat on Ramadan unless something goes boom first," laughed Afifa, entering the room in a large apron that smelled tantalizingly of cooking. "How are you, Professor? Are you sure you've slept enough? A person might have thought you had missed three nights' sleep, not just one. Is that how worried you were about your wife's trip?"

He nodded amiably, feeling a profound serenity, in a world that was not of this world. Even his hunger, no longer nagging, was pleasantly vague. Could the pill against "feeling blue" have given him a high?

"Where is Rashid?" he asked. "Has he finished photocopying?"

"Long ago. Don't worry, the material is ready. We'll call him the minute you want to leave. *Bas leysh bidak t'safir? Ma n'halik.** Absolutely not. We're sitting down to our holiday dinner in an hour, and you're one of the family. And the bathtub is free if you want to use it. Samaher just bathed and is waiting to finish the story of Ahmed ed-Danaf and the sick horse. She has other stories for you, too. One is about an absurd man who killed two Frenchmen, '*El-Gharib El-Mahali.*' How would you translate that?"

"The Local Stranger."

"Exactly."

Was he, then, personally and professionally, on the verge of a long-craved intimacy with the Arabs, one much greater than the merely literary one proposed by his old mentor in Jerusalem, an intimacy that would prolong the day into a stirring, eventful night? And was the freedom of knowing that his movements could not be tracked by his wife so seductive that he was prepared to abandon himself to it? Not that these Arabs were the same as the Algerians whose crisis of identity had hobbled his computer for over a year. Yet surely the translatoress of the Age of Ignorance was right about their belonging to

---

* But why leave? We won't let you.

"one world," a world sometimes cruel and sometimes indulgently hospitable.

And indeed, in that case why not bathe in the tub remembered fondly from the night of Samaher's wedding and now put at his disposal by a ruddy and buxom Arab woman redolent of holiday aromas, who had taken a course of his twenty years ago? Let the distinguished Jewish Orientalist be pampered by the same Arabs who brimmed with grievances against the crimes of Western colonialism and frustrated him by their refusal to accept any responsibility for their condition.

"*Inti bidal'ini aktar min zojti*," * Rivlin said to Afifa, the white lie making him blush.

"*Kif ti'dar el-maskini t'dal'ak, iza-ma kan andeha wa't?*" †

Touched to hear this unexpected defense plea for the judge uttered in a remote Arab village, he happily went off to bathe, accompanied by two towels, a bottle of fragrant liquid soap, and a young girl, who had been appointed to guard his privacy outside a bathroom door that would never, so it seemed, be locked or bolted.

## 15.

HE SOAKED IN the foamy water, examining the ceramic tiles on the walls with the expertise of a man who had recently been through the construction of a new apartment. The truth was trite but sad: the Arab workers did a better job of tiling in their own homes than they did in the homes of their Jewish customers. And why, really, should this be surprising?

He dried himself with both towels and dressed. As the sun went down to the smells of dinner from the kitchen, he stepped into Samaher's room, reinvigorated and shiny-faced, to continue her "term paper," which now seemed to him a marvelous invention.

Her own bath, to judge by an empty washtub in a corner and a puddle of water on the floor, had taken place in her room. Though

---

* You spoil me more than my wife does.

† How can that poor woman spoil you if she never has any time?

she had changed to a brighter robe, she looked pale, worn, and anything but refreshed. Propped exhaustedly on a large pillow, she suggested—perhaps because her hair was now done up in two braids—a suffering child more than an M.A. student. Her sorrowful eyes reproached him for abandoning her for his monumental sleep in the middle of her story.

"Where's Rashid?" he asked of his now indispensable sidekick.

"Why do you need him?" she answered sullenly, as if to erase the smarting passion of being swept up in her cousin's arms.

"Never mind. It's not important."

"I can tell him to come right away."

"There's no hurry."

Through the large window, a last, vivid drop of sun sizzled in the cleft between two distant hills.

"Don't worry, Professor. He'll take you home whenever you want." There was a new, hurt note of disappointment in her voice.

"But there's no hurry, Samaher," he repeated serenely, seated in the armchair by the open window, through which he caught a first whiff of the dialogue of hot coals and meat. "I'm not worried in the least. I've already caught a bad case of nirvana from all of you."

She reddened at what seemed another of his anti-Arab digs. Looking tense and miserable, she wriggled anxious legs beneath the blanket.

"Well, what happened in the end with Ahmed ed-Danaf?" he asked, like a teacher encouraging a stuck pupil. "Did he save the horse he poisoned?"

"Do you really want to know?" Her eyes flashed with resentment. "I thought you found it so silly that it put you to sleep."

"Silly?" He was amused. "Not at all. It was no sillier than the other story."

"The other one?" she repeated dreamily.

"The literary value of these stories doesn't matter. I'm looking for something else—the spirit of the times, some sign of the future."

"The future?"

"The insane Terror, for example."

"What Terror?"

"The one in Algeria. They've been butchering one another there."

She gave him a guarded look, as if searching for a mysterious new drift that five years of his courses had not revealed to her.

"I've never heard of it. Is there a book about it?"

The Orientalist stared hard at the young Arab.

"It's been going on for eight years."

"*Masakin* . . ."* Dismissing the butcher and the butchered alike, she reached out with a thin hand for her bed lamp. The bulb beneath the red lampshade lit up like a little sun in place of the real one that had vanished. Opening her notebook, she softly continued the tale of the young villager who fought to save the life of the horse he had poisoned.

Ahmed ed-Danaf's unhappy love for Leona, the daughter of a family of hated shepherds betrothed to a relative from France, was now joined by the suffering of the poisoned horse sprawled on its straw in the stable. Samaher's summary was so full of detail that Rivlin couldn't tell what was in the story and what had been invented by her. Descriptions of lights and shadows, smells and sounds accompanied the drama of the horse, which failed to grasp why the strange young man who had poisoned it two days ago was now sitting up with it all night, hand-feeding it mashed oats and kissing and petting it with loving words. After a few days Ahmed ed-Danaf tied a thin rope around its neck and led it daintily around the stable. In the end it recovered and even carried its rescuer to a hilltop above the village, from which he was the first to greet his beloved upon her return from the betrothal that would take her to France. And that was the end.

"The end?"

"Of the story."

"Very good," the professor said, with an approving glance at his student. She was definitely not pregnant. No doubt her mother had confined her to bed to keep her from doing something rash.

Samaher, calmed by her teacher's patient attention, stopped wriggling her legs. Her long lashes drooped. Evening shadows clung to the walls of the room.

---

* The poor things.

"Can you use such a story, Professor?" she asked with a ghostly smile.

As he was reassuring her that there was value even in a folktale, written at the height of Algeria's struggle for independence, about unhappy love and a sick horse, the sound of a shell rang out. Soon afterward, Samaher's husband, still in his plaster-spattered work clothes, warily entered the room. Acknowledging Rivlin with a nod, he turned anxiously to see how his new wife's depression was doing.

## 16.

THE HOLIDAY DINNER, announced by the setting of the sun, was held in the courtyard. Joining them was Samaher's father-in-law and his two sons, as well as several neighbors and village notables who had come to break the fast with the Jew *illi bisum zay il-mu'amin, lakin al-fadi.* * Now that his marathon slumber in Rashid's bed, already famous throughout the village, had been interpreted not only as a sign of great weariness brought from afar, but also as a vote of confidence in the Arabs, he was greeted with warmth as well as respect, like a potential kinsman who might become a real one if plied with enough food.

Yet oddly, though he hadn't touched a thing since his cup of coffee and piece of baklava in the gas station that morning, Rivlin was not very hungry. So lackluster and almost abstract was his appetite that it was satisfied with a bit of pita bread dipped in warm hummus, thus compelling Afifa to provide him with a special carver, a mysterious old man named Ali who was either somebody's uncle or Samaher's second grandfather. A punctilious, square-shouldered man, he came and went grandly from the kitchen bearing a copper tray of choice morsels plucked from the head, ribs, rump, and inmost organs of the lamb and arranged by him on Rivlin's plate, from which he sternly force-fed them to the Jewish professor.

It was hard for the Orientalist to say no, especially since the guests, although deriving no benefit from Ali's labors, urged him to obey the old man, brought from another village to coax him out of a fast un-

---

* Who had fasted, for no good reason, like a believer.

required by Allah. Moreover, the morsels put on his plate being few and select, Rivlin had to assume them to be a mere prelude, a symbolic tasting meant to lure him back, stomach and all, from the ominous steppes of his dream.

The village was coming to life. Passersby stopped to peer through the iron gate at the Jewish professor. A few entered to introduce themselves—elderly teachers, brawny high-school graduates, even some old students who had had children and grandchildren since taking his courses at the university. All seemed pleased by his long sleep and gratuitous fast. Someone wanted to know about Samaher. Was it true, as her mother claimed, that he had made her his research assistant? And what, precisely, was the research?

It was a calm Galilean evening. Rivlin, clear of mind and unlimited of patience, gladly answered the villagers' questions. Who could say whether they, too, might not provide a spark of inspiration? His research met with general approval. Algeria was a country dear to the Arabs. Its inhabitants had suffered almost as much as the Palestinians. You couldn't blame them if bad things had rubbed off on them from the French. "But when will you write something about us, Professor Rivlin?" they all asked.

Good-humoredly he explained that even when writing about Arabs in far-off times and places he looked for the connecting link with what was nearby. "After all," he told them, "you all have the same roots and come from the same desert." While this was still being digested, there was a whinny from the black horse. Sticking a bridleless head between the bars of the gate, it had come to remind Samaher's grandfather to take it back to the stable.

"What's the bottom line, Professor? Will Samaher get her final grade?"

The impatient question came from the contractor, Samaher's father-in-law, who had been eating silently beside him.

The man's two sons tried silencing him. Rivlin, however, gave him a friendly pat on the back.

"Of course she'll get it," he said. "In time to be given her M.A."

"But what can anyone do with an M.A.?" the contractor wondered out loud. "What good is it?"

"Every case is different," Rivlin reassured him. "Samaher could continue for her next degree."

"Her next degree?" The man turned despairingly to his son. "*Fi kaman thaleth?*"*

"It's called a doctorate," Samaher's sad husband whispered back.

## 17.

WHERE IS RASHID?

Yet not even the thought of your missing driver can prevent you from calmly dismissing all worries. Whether it's your magical sleep that has scrambled your biological clock and muddled the hours, or the absence of your wife, even the greenish stars in the village sky now patiently await your confirmation that night has arrived.

Rashid, it seems, is lying low because of Samaher's husband. Hence the repeated reassurances that he'll drive you where and when you want. "Rashid is all yours, Professor. Relax," Afifa half-scolds, half-soothes you, as if you'd been given a black slave, rather than a citizen, albeit a displaced one, of the state of Israel—one who, on the way out of Ma'alot this morning, pointed to a Jewish community center and some tennis courts on a hillside and said, "That's our village, Dir-el-Kasi." "Was your village," you corrected him. "Right," he conceded after a moment's thought. "Was."

In a corner of the courtyard Afifa now kindles a savage fire and throws blackening eggplants in it. Enveloped in bitter smoke, you find yourself defending the political acrobatics of a right-wing prime minister you didn't vote for. "It will take a shrewd operator to get the right to cross the Rubicon," you say, and a college graduate who remembers Caesar explains the image with an Arabic proverb that has to be explained once more in Hebrew for your benefit.

Afifa has an idea. "Since your wife, Professor, is out of the country, why not sleep here tonight in the bed you've gotten used to? Rashid won't need it because he works nights during Ramadan, and you'll

---

* Is there a third one, then?

have all evening and tomorrow morning to make more progress with Samaher."

"Sleep here?" You run a hand through your gray curls. "It's very tempting, but *inni el-yom azuz, marbut fi 'l-leil fi frasho.*" *

The glitter of a smile in her eyes tells you that once again you've made a comic blunder in your Arabic, which you learned from texts and documents at the university and not, like the new department head, whose supple, serpentine speech transfixes his listeners before biting them, in the streets of Mesopotamia. Still, you insist on dropping an Arabic sentence or expression here and there, not just to keep your listeners on their toes, but to let them know that their world is your second home.

And all this while fierce old Ali won't let you alone, coming and going with his little tray and refusing to take no for an answer, as if the barbecued lamb would be mortally injured unless you consumed its innards. Having eaten, as your wife put it, "half a lamb" at Samaher's wedding, you'll soon have eaten the other half unless you stop now. And so, though you wouldn't mind another helping, you deem it best to rise and call for your displaced citizen, although only after first asking Samaher, promoted by her mother to the position of your research assistant, for one last story, that of the moonstruck murderer.

## 18.

SAMAHER'S ROOM WAS unexpectedly crowded. The full moon, the only light apart from her little reading lamp, sketched on the walls the shadows of the young women, some wearing Islamic kerchiefs, who had come to see how their friend had survived the fast in her confinement. Samaher had changed clothes again and was wearing a loose, colorful peasant dress like her mother's. A tray of food, most of it left uneaten, lay on the lacquered chest beside the new photocopies of Dr. Suissa's material.

Samaher gave him a timid smile. Her pale face, sallow by day, was

---

* I'm an old man tied every night to his own bed.

now as heavily made up as on the night of her wedding. The Lebanese kohl around her eyes hid any sign of tears.

"I see you have visitors," Rivlin said.

"They're here for you, not me, Professor," she answered with her old impishness. "They want to get a look at you and hear you speak Arabic."

The young women giggled shyly. The more religious tightened the kerchiefs on their heads.

"There are even two students here from your survey course. Don't you recognize them?"

"That's not so easily done," he murmured, afraid of being approached with yet another request for a change of topic or extension. "Well, do we have time for another story? Perhaps we should make it 'The Local Stranger,' as your mother suggested."

"Yes. It's special and not very long. If you don't mind, my visitors would like to hear it, too. I think it's the perfect story for your research, Professor. I came across it in the photocopies this afternoon, while you were sleeping. That poor man who was killed in Jerusalem didn't notice it. To tell you the truth, it was Rashid who did. 'The Local Stranger'—that's an eye-catching title, isn't it? It was written by a journalist named Jamal bin el-Maluh as an attack on an important French author. He's mentioned in the introduction—Albert Camus. Have you ever heard of him, Professor? But what a question! Of course you have. Who hasn't? Rashid even found books of his in Arabic right here in the village, and his novel *The Stranger* was published in Syria. Just imagine: even the Syrians know him and honor him! I took a look at it just now, while you were eating. Jamal bin el-Maluh's story starts out exactly like it, but it's also a criticism of it...."

She spoke animatedly, smiling at her guests. Rivlin recalled how years ago, in the same survey course, she had been one of the first students whose name he had mastered. Thin, alert, and adversarial, from her regular seat at the front of the large lecture hall, she had frequently raised her hand to argue with him, making up for her lack of knowledge with a keen, if sometimes perverse, intelligence. Although he had tried being patient with her, he had secretly hoped that the more practical-minded Jewish students in the course would silence her—as, eventually, they did.

It was eight o'clock. From the village mosque, the prayer call of the muezzin came pleading over the rooftops. Was he still in a Jewish state? Or had he been, like his wife, transported to a far land? He wondered whether the new department head would be more pleased or appalled to know how he had spent the day. Once more turning Samaher's quarters into a seminar room, he explained to her and her guests why the Syrians were right to not to fear the French writer's philosophy of the absurd. Meanwhile, they were joined, his clothes clean and his hair wet from the shower, by Samaher's husband, who waited for her to make room for him on the edge of her bed. He, too, wanted to hear the story of the Local Stranger. So did Afifa and Samaher's grandmother. Even the large contractor peered in bewilderedly from the hallway. Everyone was there but the black horse.

### The Story of the Local Stranger

Jamal bin el-Maluh, a Tunisian journalist and author, had written a rather sardonic preface for this story, which was published in 1949 in a small magazine called *El-Majaleh*. "Not long ago," he wrote, "on a visit to France, I noticed that all Europe was praising a short, absurdist novel by a French colon named Albert Camus. It told the story of how, one hot day on the beach, for no reason at all, a young Frenchman named Marseault murdered an Algerian he had nothing against. 'The sun was too much for me,' he casually told the court. And yet if that young Frenchman had no reason to murder anyone, and reality is absurd, as our philosophical author claims, why would it have been any less absurd of him to kill a Frenchman like himself? Why must he absurdly kill an Arab?"

And so Jamal bin el-Maluh decided to invent an absurd Arab to balance the absurd Frenchman. If everything was absurd, let the absurdity be equal. His story, a parody of Camus's novel, began in almost the exact same words: "Today my father died. Or maybe it was yesterday. I can't remember."

204 ·

"In *The Stranger*, it's his mother," Rivlin mused.

"Yes, I noticed that, Professor. But here it's the father, because it would be hard to imagine a young Arab who didn't mourn the death of his mother. A father is something else. The character's name, Musa, even sounds like Marseault. He lives in Algiers, and he puts his dead father in a car and takes him to his village to bury him without feeling any grief. That same night he returns to the city for a date at the movies with his girlfriend. And the next day he takes off from work and goes swimming, just like the character in Camus. But he doesn't go for an afternoon walk on the beach, because who can take the midday sun in Algiers? He waits for it to be evening—say, like now—and then strolls on the sand looking at the waves. After a while he approaches a nice French couple, a boy and a girl sitting on a bench, and asks how they are and what time it is. They tell him the time but not how they are and go on talking to each other. He's standing near them, staring at the moon rising over the bay. It's like a big egg yolk, and it scares him, and he can't take his eyes off it. And so he decides to wait for the two French to start kissing in the moonlight. That's what the French like to do, and he thinks it will calm him. But they just go on talking, and he gets more and more scared, because now the moon is overhead and could fall on him at any minute. So he goes over to the couple and asks in French, 'What do you think of that moon?' 'It's a very nice moon,' they say. 'You don't think it will fall on me?' he asks. That makes them laugh. Let them laugh, Musa thinks, at least they'll die happy. And he takes out a big knife, slits their throats because it's absurd, and goes home for a nap."

"For a nap?" Rivlin asked. He couldn't tell whether that, too, was part of the story or one of Samaher's embellishments.

There was a stir in the room. From a corner of it, the coal black eyes of the messenger signaled his readiness to set out and at the same time stole a glance at Samaher's husband—who, seated on the edge of the bed, was as curious as anyone to know whether the Arab murderer would stick to his absurdity in court or come up with explanation for his deed.

The shrewdly ironic Jamal bin el-Maluh kept his hero faithful to the absurd. Like Camus's stranger, the Arab refused to say he was sorry or ask the court for mercy, and blamed it all on the moon. The one difference was that in the Arabic version, the judge, too, was so affected by the spirit of absurdity that he acquitted the defendant. And so, Samaher concluded triumphantly, Jamal bin el-Maluh proved that the Arabs could be even more absurd than the French.

The room laughed at the French defeat.

"But how could he have acquitted him?" Rivlin chided her, as if Samaher had made the whole thing up. "Are you sure that's the end?"

"I'm afraid so," she said, with a complacent smile. "I can't help it, Professor."

The Jewish Orientalist felt a tremor of delight. Though weakly and dully perhaps, the spark of inspiration promised by his Jerusalem mentor was beginning to glow like a dusty coal. He rose, took a cup of Turkish coffee from a tray brought by Samaher's sister, downed it in a gulp like a shot of brandy, and asked the jet-colored messenger if he could locate Jamal bin el-Maluh's wonderful and important story in the photocopied material waiting in the minibus.

"Of course he can," Samaher answered for him. "I told you, it was he who found it."

The young ladies bowed their heads, fearful of being blinded by the dazzling light of illicit love that flashed past the tired husband.

## 19.

"DID YOU MANAGE to eat?" Rivlin asked his driver, who stepped on the gas as they left the village.

"There's plenty of time for that, Professor. Don't worry about me. During Ramadan I eat all night. After I return you to Haifa, I have to pick up some workers in Jenin and bring them to their jobs in the morning. Have you ever been to Jenin, Professor?"

"Maybe once, thirty years ago. After the 1967 war."

"I have a sister not far from there, in a village called Zababdeh. I'll drop in on her tonight too. That's the custom. On the nights of

Ramadan, a brother visits his married sisters and brings them gifts. Money, food, whatever he can..."

"That's something I never knew."

"For sure. It's to keep her from feeling low that she has to be with her husband's family and not with her own kin on the holiday. Who knows, maybe I'll have a pig for her tonight...."

"A pig?"

"A wild boar. There's a forest after Elkosh where I want to stop, if you have no objection, and look for some hunters."

"Pork on Ramadan? What are you talking about?"

"Relax, Professor. My sister is a Muslim, but she lives with a Christian. Most of Zababdeh is Christian. They'll eat anything you bring them: chickens, pigs, sharks, frogs, you name it. The pig isn't for her. It's for the school run by the Abuna, the Christian priest. She works as a cook there. He's a good man, the Abuna, always ready to lend her a hand, because her man is sick and not so young anymore. She had to raise the children by herself, away from her family. She doesn't eat pork, but she'll cook it for the Abuna."

"But where is she from originally?"

"Where should she be from, Professor? She's Israeli, born in Mansura. Her bad luck was to marry someone from the West Bank twenty years ago and lose her Israeli ID. Now Israel won't let her back in. We've filled out forms and begged Knesset members to intervene—nothing helps. They won't even allow her to return with just the children, without her sick husband. They say she has to leave them behind, too. You'd think they were lepers or something. How can she leave them? You tell me, Professor. But that's the West Bank for you. It's a trap. The poor woman walked into it and can't get out.... After Elkosh, if you don't mind, we'll take a dirt road, half a kilometer at most. It goes to an old grave that's being renovated because it's some rabbi's from the Torah. We'll see if there's a pig or not. It won't take more than half an hour. But only if it's all right with you. If you're in a hurry or feeling tired, just say so. I heard in the village that you slept for a while...."

"For a while?" He grinned at Rashid's tact. The driver must have heard of his marathon. "It was more than a little. It was four whole hours—and in your bed..."

"It's an honor, Professor." The Arab lowered his head almost to the steering wheel and murmured, "My bed is your bed."

Rivlin's head throbbed, as if the gentle but powerful erotic force that had lifted Samaher from her bed, grazing the pimples on her face, might make demands on him too.

The windows were open. The dry fragrance of the summer night filled the minibus, which took the curves swiftly but surely, braking before the turn-off to the dirt road. Newly blasted, to judge by the red soil still seeping from the rock on either side of it, it wound to a small structure awaiting the pouring of a concrete dome, its venerable sanctity's seal of approval. In the meantime, while the ancient rabbi's new home was under construction, a large jeep was parked beside it.

"There they are!" the Arab cried happily. "You can either wait for me here, Professor, or climb that hill up ahead with me. Take it from me, it's not far, one hundred and twenty or thirty meters at the most."

The Jew, needless to say, was not about to wait in the darkness by an empty grave. Knowing Rashid's estimates of time and distance to be accurate, he joined him in scrambling up the steep, rocky hill. "I hope no one thinks we're pigs," he joked as he followed his agile guide, who looked back from time to time to see if the middle-aged Orientalist needed help.

"What a thought, Professor!" Rashid said. "They're licensed hunters. They know enough to get a degree in it. One is a lawyer, and the other is a dentist. They only shoot what they're allowed to. Besides, I'll give them a warning whistle when we get close...."

All the same, though the moon was bright enough to highlight the yellow flowers of the prickly pears, the Orientalist, afraid of being taken for a prowling animal, stayed close to Rashid, who sounded some shrill whistles in the direction of a clump of trees on the hilltop.

"If they're tracking something, they won't answer," he whispered. "Let's wait and see."

A call came from the branches of the trees:

"Rashid?"

"Yes, Anton. It's me."

"*Walow,*\* 'Yes, Anton, it's me.'" The hunters guffawed at the Hebrew answer. "*Weyn inta, ya az'ar kushi?*"†

"Cut it out, Marwan. You too, Anton," Rashid said good-naturedly. "I'm not alone. I have a distinguished Jewish guest. And he speaks Arabic, so watch yourselves."

"*Min hada?*"‡

"First come on down from those trees."

"*Lakin min jibtilna?*"§

"Come on down."

The hunters were perched in harness seats up near the tops of the trees, double-barreled shotguns in their hands.

"Tell us who you've brought."

Rashid introduced the Jewish professor. The strong beam of a flashlight was aimed at them from a tree.

"Jesus Christ!" the lawyer said. "Are you Judge Rivlin's husband? Believe it or not, I once tried a case before her. . . ."

"Will you two come down!" Rashid scolded. "We can't have a conversation with you sitting in a tree."

"Marwan is ashamed to be seen."

"Why is that?"

"Don't ask! I hate to admit it, but an hour ago he shot and killed a piglet. A little baby."

"It was an accident," Marwan apologized. "I didn't mean to. I can't even look at it."

"He thought it was a jackal. But how could it have been a jackal, when the jackals were killed off long ago?"

"I never said it was a jackal, you dope! I thought it was a partridge. Watch out behind that tree, Rashid. *Dir balak! La tit'harak ula t'sib ishi. . . .*"‖

---

\* What the hell!

† Where are you, you little black bastard?

‡ Who is it?

§ But whom have you brought us?

‖ Be careful! Don't move or touch anything.

The two hunters clambered slowly down, their shotguns snagging on the branches. Despite the hot night, they were wearing military flak jackets; their pockets bulged with shells. The gray-haired man was the dentist. The lawyer was younger and taller. Both had pistols strapped to their waists, as if they were manhunters too.

"Welcome to Hunter's Hill, Professor," said the lawyer, who spoke a racy Hebrew. He gave Rivlin a cheerful handshake. "No kidding, I once appeared before your wife in a libel suit. She made mincemeat of me."

"Deservedly?"

"Who knows what's deserved and what isn't, Professor?" The lawyer sighed and shouldered his gun. "Ask your wife. She always thinks she's right. A tough woman, I'm telling you!"

Rashid came to the judge's defense. "She's not always so tough. You should have seen her laughing at Samaher's wedding. The village will never forget her."

"Maybe she laughs at weddings. But in court she has a tongue like a knife. A first-rate judge. Even the losers respect her."

Rivlin, stung by longing, nodded modestly. Where are you now, my love? Are you in your hotel? Can you—uncomplaining, uncomforted, unable to switch rooms—cope with the tacky accommodations? Who will open your suitcase for you, hang up your clothes, make bearable your world while you sit huddled on the bed, staring glumly at the ugly, dirty walls?

"What brings you here?" the hunters asked.

Rashid told them about his cousin's promotion to research assistant on an important scholarly project.

"Is Samaher still ill?" The question, asked by the lawyer, was addressed to Rivlin, as if it took a Jew to verify such things.

"Not unless pregnancy is an illness," Rashid interposed angrily. Afraid the Orientalist might talk too much, he changed the subject to the Jew's Ramadan solidarity fast.

The two hunters threw Rivlin wondering looks.

"But what will you do for us Christians, Professor?"

"I'll fast during Lent."

They laughed and led him and Rashid to a large rock. Behind it, underneath a black tarpaulin that they removed, a piglet lay in the moonlight.

"I don't know how it happened," the dentist lamented. "I'm always so careful."

Rivlin had never seen a wild boar up close. The little creature lay peacefully on its bristles, its snout agape as though letting out a last sigh.

Rashid knelt and looked for the entry wound. He turned the piglet over, exposing a smooth, pink belly. It was three or four months old, he reckoned. He held it up by its hind legs to gauge its weight.

"How in hell could I have thought that was a partridge?" the dentist asked.

"The mother pig took off with the first shot," Anton told them. "She's still hanging around. We saw her from the trees, fifty or sixty meters off. Maybe she's waiting for her baby to come back."

"Are you going to shoot her too?" Rashid asked.

"If she insists."

"On what?"

They laughed. "Dying."

"What do you say?" Rashid asked. "Should we give the piglet to the Abuna?"

"Just take it as it is, unskinned and uncleaned. It's our gift. *Il-banduk hatamli kalbi.** It will bring us bad luck."

Rashid turned to Rivlin. For the first time in their travels, he laid a light hand on the Jew's shoulder.

"You won't mind, Professor, if we put the piglet in the back of the minibus? Don't worry. It's fresh and won't smell. But if it will bother you, forget it. You're the passenger. It's up to you."

Rivlin looked at the piglet, deep within which, like a powerful sleeping pill, was a bullet. It seemed to be poignantly hugging itself, its forefeet crossed, when dangled by Rashid. The Orientalist gingerly stuck out a foot to touch the curious tail, stiffly erect in the moonlight. Dreamily he rocked the carcass with a toe, suddenly struck by the realization that he was in for another sleepless night. "All right,"

---

* The little bastard's broken my heart.

he said glumly to Rashid, who was awaiting his decision. "Wrap it up, and we'll take it to the Abuna."

Odd, his using the Christian title of respect for a priest he had never met.

## 20.

AND HOW, REALLY, did you manage to stay up that whole night? What kept you going? Wanting to meet the Abuna? Or was it the Song of Paradise that enticed you from your bed to a foreign adventure needing no passport?

You may as well admit it: the displaced and irreplaceable Arab with the coal black eyes, who is the age of your eldest son, though more like your youngest in his sure and easygoing sense of himself, has an influence over you. And not at all a bad one, though it has made his concerns and adventures yours too. A transporter of men who are at home in the give-and-take of human commerce, he finds it entirely natural to transport you, an introverted old professor, across a dotted green line on the map that, imaginary demarcation, will be haggled over until the end of time.

One way or another, now that the minibus is again speeding along the main road with a prematurely and sorrowfully shot piglet in its backseat, you can check your clarity of mind and powers of endurance—both, despite (or is it because of?) the bizarre day, amazingly keen and looking forward to the night plans of your driver, which include, so it seems, not only a charitable Abuna and a needy sister awaiting her holiday gift, but a Song of Paradise sung by an angel in a church.

"An angel?"

"A Greek Orthodox nun brought from Lebanon to sing in the Abuna's church so that the Christians won't feel left out during Ramadan."

"Your Abuna sounds like a wise man."

"He can't be mine if I'm a Muslim," Rashid tactfully corrects you. "But he is a wise and good man. He helps everyone. And I tell you, Professor, the Song of Paradise is heavenly. You can ask the Muslims from Nablus and Kalkilya who came to hear it last year."

"What do they know about Paradise?" you ask, to take the young man down a peg.

"They haven't been to it yet," Rashid admits. "But if the angels there sing like she does, they'll have no complaints when they get there."

"What does she sing?"

"Byn ... Bynza ... how do you say it?"

"Byzantine."

"Right. Byzantine chants. They say she makes the heart tremble. Sometimes she faints at the end. That makes it even better."

"Faints?"

"Yes. She has these dizzy spells. That's why they send her here and to Jordan, because they don't like her to faint in Lebanon. They think she does it for effect. But what effect can fainting have in Palestine? None at all."

You laugh. You're beginning to like this young Arab more and more. He must be aware of it, too, if he wants to take you to church with him tonight.

It's nine o'clock. No one is waiting for you at home. You haven't been this free in ages. If you were in Jerusalem, you could return to the Hendels' hotel.

But you're in the western Galilee, with a driver who will take you anywhere. It's a time to sit back and to think, not about your wife and sons, or even about your stuck book, but only about yourself. A full moon, the moon of Arab absurdity, casts its royal glow on Haifa Bay and the Carmel. Not only will it not fall on you, it will light your way wherever you go.

"But tell me, Rashid. Can we cross the Green Line and drive into Jenin in the middle of the night just like that?"

The Arab is surprised by your question.

"We're Israelis, Professor, have you forgotten? Why would anyone stop us at a checkpoint?"

## 21.

As on the night of Samaher's wedding, this time too the minibus pulled into the all-night vegetable stand with its colorful dolls that made him think of Canaanite household gods. Its Arab owner, now revealed to be a Christian, recognized Rivlin at once. But it was Rivlin's wife whom he missed and to whom—after helping to load a sack of beans, a gift to the Abuna and his flock, onto the minibus— he sent a small bag of cherries as both an offering and a warning that, if she did not return as a customer, he might turn up as a plaintiff in her court.

At Yagur Junction, before turning left for Arab Nazareth rather than continuing on to Jewish Haifa, Rashid glanced at his passenger to make sure he hadn't changed his mind. In Nazareth's crowded downtown, they stopped to pick up some cartons of eggs and a crate of canned goods, a present from the Church of the Annunciation to the Church of the Temptation in Zebabdeh. Then, the engine purring softly, they glided down into the Valley of Jezreel with its good old Jewish farming villages laid out in neat arrangements of lights. They sped through Adashim Junction; passed Mizra and Balfouria; drove through the broad, deserted streets of sleeping Afula, which made no attempt to detain them; and headed south on an empty road to the whir of the sprinklers of Kibbutz Yizra'el. The lights of the Israeli settlements grew fewer, and the plastic frames of greenhouses alone gleamed white in the faithful moonlight that was prepared to cross the border, if such it was, together with them.

For now the Arab was saying:

"The army checkpoint is right ahead of us, Professor. Getting through it is no problem. It's just that if they see a darky like me with a high-class type like you, they may think you're being kidnapped. It's better to take a detour. It will add ten more minutes, but we have time."

"What if I really am being kidnapped, Rashid?"

"Then it's only to Paradise," the Arab laughed. "That's for your own good, Professor."

The minibus turned right toward Mukibla and then left onto a harvested field, jolting lightly. Rashid maneuvered it slowly over a narrow ditch, reached a fence, switched off the engine, and got out. Several kicks and a section of fence was down. Shadowy in the moonlight, he wiped his hands and climbed back into the driver's seat. It was the moment chosen by Rivlin to touch the shoulder of the messenger and ask, in the silence of the night, whether Samaher was really pregnant. The unexpected question, as though given urgency by the border they were crossing, made Rashid start. "That's what her mother says," he answered, as evasively as before. This time, though, he added hesitantly: "Who knows for sure, Professor? Only God and the ultrasound." He looked dolefully down at the floor of the car, as if having said too much.

"Then what keeps her in bed?"

"She's confused. It started before the wedding. Maybe her soul is looking for another body. But don't be angry at Samaher, Professor. She's always liked you, from the first day of her first class with you. I swear, she's in love with you."

"Don't be ridiculous...."

The Arab gave him a searching look, puzzled why this should make him angry. Starting the engine, he crossed the fallen border with his parking lights on. "We're in Zone C," he explained, gesturing at the vagaries of the Oslo Agreement in the darkness around them. "Two kilometers from here we'll enter Zone B, and in Jenin we'll be in the middle of A. Then, on the way to Kabatiyeh, we'll cross back into B and come to Zababdeh, which is one half B, one quarter C, and one quarter none of the above, because a small Jewish settlement has squeezed itself in there."

Jenin was full of life, a wild festivity of Ramadan lights. Its shops and markets were open despite the late hour, and a steady stream of cars and horse- and donkey-drawn wagons clogged the streets. Slow-moving men stood in groups; women, cloaked and uncloaked, hurried laughing through the smoke of charcoal grills. And children, no end of children, clung to the minibus, which Rashid steered with great patience, yielding right-of-way to all comers. The city seemed engaged in a great orgy of eating that took place in the dark passageway between one day's fast and the next. Two armed Palestinian policemen peremptorily flagged down their vehicle, but only to banter with the Israeli Arab, who was known and liked on this side of the border, too. The Jew was looked through as if he weren't there.

If here, too, Rivlin thought, not for the first time, the Arabs stay up all night partying, who, really, will look after us Jews by day? Not sure how Rashid would respond to such a reflection, however, he watched in silence as the latter excused himself politely and drove as far as the city's last street lamp, whose light fell on a macadam road that had once been part of a British Mandate highway running the length of Palestine. The bright Israeli man in the moon had now been transformed into a cloud-veiled Palestinian woman—who a few kilometers further on bared her face to shine on two more armed Palestinians wearing camouflage suits and carrying black Kalachnikov assault rifles. This time Rashid was grilled about his passenger before being allowed to head southeast for Kabatiyeh, a town notorious during the Intifada for the long and cruel curfews imposed on it. Perhaps this was why its inhabitants, refusing to go to sleep, were still up and about with pots, trays of food, and holiday gifts, vanishing and reappearing in the lit doorways of shops and houses and sometimes thumping the Israeli vehicle with a jovial or hostile fist. The minibus made its way through twisting side streets, emerged in a cool, dim valley, and climbed a hilltop to a village whose houses were half hidden by trees behind empty streets. At the top of the hill, in front of a drowsing iron gate that opened on the courtyard of a church, Rashid stopped and pulled a rope that rang an old gong.

The gate creaked. Slowly, laboriously, it was opened by a boy of about ten, who must have been waiting for them all evening. He threw his arms around Rashid and clung to him tightly while a second child leapfrogged over him to embrace his beloved uncle and a third, materializing from nowhere, shouted something and pushed his brothers aside before a quickly crawling black baby could reach them across the white flagstones of the courtyard. There being nothing left of her uncle to grab hold of, the baby clutched at Rivlin, who was peering through the open door of the church, past rows of empty pews, at a crucified Jesus made of light-colored wood—a rugged, thoughtful, rather likable young man hanging from a cross behind a handsome altar decorated with fresh branches and lit by a reddish light. Now a plump priest wearing a cassock and eyeglasses appeared.

This was the Abuna, who came hurrying out of the church in the moonlight that shone through a gap between two Samarian hills. Using one hand to free the Jew of the infant clinging to his feet, he offered him a hearty handshake with the other, while babbling in English as if he had just met an old friend.

"We've been in touch with Mansura and know everything about you, Professor. How wonderful that a Jew should come to our church at the end of a fast day during Ramadan! I assure you, you haven't come in vain. Our prayers have been answered, and Sister Suheyr feels well enough to sing a mass for us tonight. You'll see for yourself, sir: it's not to a church in Zababdeh that you've come, but to Paradise. And not just to Paradise, but to Paradise on a night when an angel is giving a concert."

## 22.

Prior to entering Paradise, however, it was necessary to pass through the purgatory of a basement apartment at the rear of the church, which consisted of two rooms and a kitchen. In the innermost room, beside a crib, lay the sick Christian husband. The outer room had a low table, set for a meal and surrounded by cushions on the floor. While the two older boys continued to grip their Israeli uncle to keep him from escaping, the younger one, having no Arab to take hold of, lifted the baby onto his shoulders and bashfully reached for the hand of the Jew so as to lead him to his dark-skinned mother— who, on this night of dreams within dreams, proved to be none other than the woman Rivlin had seen in the album.

She looked taller and more robust than in her photographs. Overcome by emotion, she buried her face in her hands, hiding her tears from the younger brother freshly arrived from the place of her nativity. Rashid gave his sister a staunch, comforting hug and deftly slipped, like a reverse pickpocket, several bills of money into the unprotesting pocket of her gown.

"*Bikafi, Ra'uda. Mish ajeina lahon minshan d'mu'eik. Kaman jibtilak deif m'him k'thir. Bikafi tibki, ahsan yuhrub min hon. Ana jit aakol*

*andik. U'ana ju'an k'thir, u'izza b'tittahri, b'yohod il-deif abuna. Leish
il-buka, ya uhti? Hada 'id, hata il-yahudi hada sam min shana 'l-yom."*\*

She looked at the guest with wonder. Getting hold of herself, she
wiped the tears from her hypnotic, coal black eyes and apologized in
Hebrew:

"Forgive me—and welcome. How can I not feel sad when I know
you're coming from Mansura? How can I not cry? My whole family is
there, my grandfather and my grandmother and everyone. And Israel, it won't even let me visit her, because it's afraid my children will
come too.... Maybe you know someone...."

"*Bikafi, bikafi!*" her brother interrupted. "*Mish bidna nirja lal'awal.*"†

"But how come your sister knows Hebrew?" Rivlin asked.

"Why shouldn't she? She lived in Israel until she was married at the
age of fifteen. She even went to high school there. Tell the professor,
Ra'uda, what you learned in Hebrew class."

"The poems of Bialik."

"You see? She studied Hebrew poetry. And she practices speaking
so that she can convince the authorities she's Israeli and should be allowed to return. When there were Israeli soldiers in the village, she
used to talk to them all the time. She would translate their orders for
the Abuna."

"They should have stayed," Rashid's sister said despairingly.

"Don't even say it! They might hear you and come back," Rashid
joked, urging his sister to serve the soup before the Abuna came and
snatched them away as guests for his dinner.

"But I'm not hungry," Rivlin protested.

"You have to eat something," Rashid said softly. "It's for her honor.
You'll shame her by not tasting anything."

"Don't be bashful," the woman told Rivlin, returning from the
kitchen with some serving dishes. The three boys were already tucked

---

\* That's enough, Ra'uda. We didn't come here for your tears. I've brought you a very important
guest. If you don't stop crying, he'll run away. I've come to eat with you. And I'm good and
hungry. If you don't get a move on, the Abuna will feed our guest himself. Why cry, my sister?
It's a holiday. Even this Jew fasted today in its honor.

† Enough, enough! Don't start all over from the beginning.

in at the table with big spoons in their hands. Even the black baby, wearing a little apron, was standing at one end of the low table, watching her mother ladle out red lentil soup from a large pot. Speedy Rashid, having already washed up and changed his shirt, attacked the soup as voraciously as if he had come all the way from Mansura for it.

The sick Christian husband now appeared from the back room, too. A pale, gangling man with long hair, an unshaven face, watery blue eyes, and hands marked by sores, he shook a weary head as he took his seat and produced from his pajama top a shiny mess kit, left behind by the Israeli army, that he handed to his wife to be filled. Tasting a spoonful of the soup, he made a nauseated face and inquired of his jet-colored brother-in-law if their visitor was the dreamed-of Jew who would return Ra'uda to her family in Israel.

## 23.

AND NOW THE Abuna descended to the basement to thank Rashid for the gifts sent by the Christians of Israel. He was especially touched by the Galilean piglet, which, shorn of its bristles and tail, was about to be put in the oven. Yet he was unhappy, the Abuna was, to find the Orientalist in the basement, staring at a bowl of soup, when up above in the teachers' room all was ready for a feast that was to be attended by Socrates and Plato, two seminarians thus nicknamed because they had studied in Athens.

"Who could object to being called Socrates even in jest?" the Abuna asked, spreading his arms with a cross-eyed twinkle. Taking the baby's spoon, he tasted the soup and praised it highly, a necessary preliminary to receiving permission from the lady of the house to spirit away her Jewish visitor.

The Abuna left with Rivlin in tow. On their way, to demonstrate that the midnight oil was burned on Ramadan in Zababdeh too, they made a moonlit side trip to a classroom. There, seated at small desks, was a group of female students, who immediately straightened up and veiled themselves. The Abuna patted their heads and showed their notebooks to Rivlin, who was asked to approve the penmanship of these poor Muslim girls from a village near Nablus. They had been sent to the Christian school after Abuna promised to display no crosses or icons—he had these replaced with colorful posters extolling the universal virtues in English and in Arabic.

Next, the Abuna lit a pocket flashlight and led Rivlin down a corridor filled with scaffolding, to show him his dream: a new wing of the school, unfortunately still unfinished because "We Greek Orthodox are stingy, like you Jews, but also poor." From there he took him to the roof and proudly pointed out a valley below, spectral in the light of the moon. "It's the Vale of Issachar," he said. "Zababdeh is the Issachar of your Torah."

Rivlin nodded in agreement while stealing a glance at his watch. It was eleven-thirty.

Where are you now, my beloved wife? Did your cotravelers take good care of you today? Have you made your peace with your hotel room, or are you still huddled beside an unopened suitcase, yearning for your bed and the man you think is in it? And yet, light of my life, I am not. I, too, have been condemned to spend this night in a strange land, though nearer to home than you. Our unslept-in apartment must be wondering what to say, should anyone come looking for the addled Orientalist now dutifully following the flashlight of a stout and jolly Christian priest.

The Abuna led him to a large kindergarten full of colored blocks and old pillows, creatively refashioned into human and animal dolls. On the walls still hung pennants of the Israeli Border Patrol unit that, sent to pacify the village, had commandeered the room during the Intifada.

"And was the village made peaceful?" Rivlin asked curiously, fingering a doll to see what its shiny eyes were made of.

The Abuna's eyes twinkled merrily. "Only toward the end, when the soldiers were too exhausted to pacify anyone...."

It was the hour for the late news on Israeli TV, regularly watched every night by Hagit. She liked the way its cultured, curly-headed newscaster did his smiling best to make the world's sorrows more palatable before sleep. Here in the newborn Palestinian autonomy, however, sleep was out of the question, perhaps because the modest freedom won by its inhabitants was most apparent in the wee hours of the curfewless nights. And the Jewish visitor felt free, too—free enough to tease his hosts, assembled in warm welcome at the table:

"*Izan ya muhtaramin, il-muslamin b'yoklo fi 'l-leil, il-yahud fi 'n-nahar, u'intu in-nasara, kaman fi 'n-nahar u'kaman fi 'l-leil.*"*

The Christians laughed, pleased to belong to a religion so cunning as to dispense with the restrictions of both Judaism and Islam. Shy but beaming, they introduced themselves. Some wore clerical collars. There were women, too, laughing and vivacious in the middle of the night.

"But how did you know I was coming?" the Orientalist asked in bewilderment. "I myself had no idea that I was crossing the Green Line with Rashid until the last minute!"

Yet Rashid, it turned out, had telephoned the Abuna from Samaher's home in Mansura to inform him that his gifts would include a Jew, a professor from Haifa who was a specialist on Algeria. Had the sable-skinned Arab so easily manipulated him? Rivlin wondered with a slight feeling of alarm, taking his place between Socrates and Plato—who, happy to be called by their sobriquets, asked what he was looking for in the North African folktales he had found in old publications.

"For warning signs of the insane brutality that later broke out in Algeria," he answered with a smile, breaking off and putting in his mouth such a small crust of warm pita bread that one might have thought he was commencing another fast. The Abuna, not yet settled into his seat, put this answer into lengthy Arabic while offering Rivlin an unfamiliar purple sauce full of little leaves in which to dip the next piece of his bread.

"But what good will finding such signs do, Professor?" The Hebrew question, asked with a sigh, came from a teacher wearing a large golden cross over the cleft above her heart.

"None at all, Madam," the Orientalist answered, his smile sadder this time. "*U'lakin min wazifti inno ma asa'id, bas a'raf.*"†

---

* And so, gentlemen, the Muslims eat by night, the Jews eat by day, and you Christians eat by both.
† But my job is to know, not to help.

"Know thyself..." Socrates confirmed in English.

"*Lakin leysh?*"\* The Abuna put a positive face on it. "*Yimkin nit'alem 'an il-zawahir hadi, ya'ani min halno'a, hon fi Filastin....unu'iti tahdir lalra'is.*"†

"*Le'min?*" There was laughter. "*'Njanet? Ahsan shi ma-nihkish ishi, la tahdir u'la il-Jaza'ir, hata ma-yurkubhinish afkar min il-Shaitan, la-samahallah.*"‡

But the academic brain, its gray curls now tilted at a downward angle, had no interest in the future, only in the past.

## 24.

THE LEBANESE NUN now made her entrance. She was dressed, not in angelic white, but in a plain brown habit, in whose deep pockets she kept her hands. Young and slim, she wore simple sandals and a small silver cross that hung down on a long chain to her bosom, which looked ample beneath the heavy cloth that covered it. Her face was framed by a white clerical collar and a wimple, from which a few strands of hair had escaped. Pale and delicate, she peered tensely at the company that rose in her honor. It was not a face that asked to be patronized. The Orientalist, intrigued by the hush that greeted her, which brought the Abuna hurrying excitedly to her side, put down his fork and got to his feet, too.

The nun hesitated at the sight of him. A slight bob of her head disclosed her concern that contact with a Jew, especially before a performance, might compromise the mission she had been sent on by her convent in Baalbek—namely, to spend the month of Ramadan in Jordan and the suffering Holy Land firming up the spirits of the diminishing faithful by means of the old Byzantine liturgy.

Muslims, too, had come to hear the voice of Paradise dwelling within the nun's habit. Not that a Muslim had any reason to be

---

\* But why?

† Perhaps if we learn these signs here, in Palestine, we can warn the president [Arafat].

‡ Whom? Are you out of your mind? It's best to say nothing. No warnings and no Algeria! Let's not go giving the Devil ideas, God forbid.

dissatisfied with life on earth, where Islam was doing well. Yet there were believers in Allah, worried that the Palestinian autonomy might end up as a stale fantasy rather than as a viable state, who preferred keeping one eye on the higher spheres. And since the Abuna did not wish to arouse unwanted religious tensions in broad daylight, he had invited the Muslim audience for a midnight concert because that could not be confused with an actual mass and—even more important—because the Lebanese's fainting fits were best kept in the dark.

As for the Jews, they had grabbed more than their share of the terrestrial Eden from the Arabs, the celestial one was not for them, and they were represented tonight by a surprise Orientalist. Naturally enough, therefore, the singing nun, now carefully sipping a beverage spiked with honey, averted her pretty eyes from a man who might cast an evil spell on her vocal cords.

Might he? Yet even if it was the witching hour, Rivlin was feeling quite rational. Indeed, after an adventurous day spent chasing the chimerical spark of inspiration in the Land of Israel and Palestine without a loving but critical wife to set him bounds, he was considering demanding a retroactive research grant. And in any case, the real wizard, who was now entering the teacher's room and asking Rivlin with fatherly solicitude how he was, was his sable-skinned driver, whose protean identities also numbered enamored cousin, faithful brother, many-armed messenger, swift kicker of fences, and multidirectional crosser of borders.

Everyone knew Rashid and was in thrall to his enchantments. He, for his part, having eaten his fill of the childhood dishes cooked for him by his sister, was now ready for seconds from the Christians. "*Il-kenisi 'am-tint'li, ya uhti,*" he gently told the nun. "*Aju min Kabatiyeh u'min Tubas, hatta fi sharkas min Dir el-Balad, tarkin en-nom min shanik, kulhom bistanu il-leili l'al-mt'a 'l-k'biri.*"*

The nun smiled wearily at the Arab from Israel who had room in

---

* The church is filling up, my sister. They've come from Kabatiyeh and Tubas, and there are even Circassians from Dir el-Balad. They've all given up their sleep for you and are expecting a night of delights.

his heart for everyone. She shut her eyes and shook her head back and
forth like a baby lulling itself to sleep.

"*Inshallah...*"* Her voice, heard by the Orientalist for the first
time, had a striking spiritual presence. "*Inshallah...*"

The diners began hurriedly rising from the table to find a place in
the church. Taking his passenger aside, Rashid whispered:

"Relax, Professor. You have a reserved seat. You'll sit with the
Abuna and the notables. The one thing you need to know," he
warned, "is that the church has no bathroom and this nun can sing
nonstop for an hour or more. You don't want to miss any of it, because she's top-notch, and the aisles will be so packed that you'll
never get back in if you've gone out. So if you think you might have
to... I suggest you take my advice... there's a very clean bathroom
right here..."

Rivlin thought of being led by Samaher up the narrow lane to her
house on the night of her wedding. For a moment, his spirits flagged.
He would have liked to go home, climb into bed, and pull a familiar
blanket over him. But how was it possible, not only to miss the Song
of Paradise, but to ask Rashid to drive him back to Haifa now? And
on the other hand, was not this the test of Afifa's promise that his
driver would take him anywhere, anytime?

The driver himself was engaged in gently pushing Rivlin into a
bathroom that locked with a key. Unable to find the light switch, he
made do with the unveiled moon, which illuminated a large bathtub
whose claw-footed legs, like the Devil's cast in lead, reminded him of
his parents' old-fashioned tub in Jerusalem.

He felt dizzy. As though in a dream, he urinated silently and briefly,
wet his face and hair with cold water from the tap, and leaned halfway
through the open window, outside of which was hanging some
freshly laundered underwear, to take a deep breath of the Palestinian
countryside. The door handle rattled. Opening it to make way for the
next in line, he saw the Lebanese singer standing in the dark corridor.
He bowed his head in homage, feeling himself redden as he said:

---

* God willing.

224 ·

*"Shaifi sayid'ti, hatta il-yahudi biddo yi'raf shu b'ghanu il-leili b'il-janeh."* \*

Laughing in her strong, sure voice, she dismissed, with a charming gesture, the Jew and Paradise equally.

*"Il-janeh... il-janeh... kulhon honi bi'Filastin b'balghu, majanin shwoy. Min hakalhon inno b'il-janeh 'am b'ghanu?"* †

The professor laughed, too. Emboldened by her friendly tone, he begged to differ. Why should there not be song in Paradise, he said, and inquired in what language she would be singing that night and whether it would be possible to obtain the words.

The nun answered that she planned to sing the Easter Mass in Greek and Arabic.

*"Hasan jiddan,"* he responded enthusiastically. *"Ana 'l-an bash'ur b'il-mut'a abl-ma tiji alay."* ‡

Her pale face seemed to twitch in the moonlight, her remote glance turning to an ironic compassion. Extending a finger toward the Jew's heart, she said in French, as though embarking with him for new territory:

*"Mais vous n'êtes pas trop fatigué, Monsieur?"* §

## 25.

EVEN THOUGH, GIVEN the history of the previous twenty-four hours, he should have been not only tired but thoroughly wiped out, he did not doze off, even once, the way he did during Philharmonic concerts. Deeply moved, he sat beside the Abuna, listening intently while holding some creased pages that contained the Arabic program notes and the text of the Mass. His front-row seat, which offered no visual distractions, forced him to keep his eyes on the singer, who stood erect in her habit and sandals on a step near the altar, accompanied by

---

\* You see, Madam, even a Jew wants to know what you'll sing tonight in Paradise.
† Paradise... Paradise... Everyone in Palestine gets carried away, they're all a bit crazy. Who told you anyone sings in Paradise at all?
‡ Very good. I can already feel, Madam, the pleasure in store for me.
§ But aren't you terribly tired, Monsieur?

four white-haired men. It wasn't clear whether she had brought them from Beirut or assembled them locally.

Her rich coloratura voice showed the influence of the Arab scale, its vibrato tendencies kept in check by a religious austerity. Though distilled in her to an abstract emotion, the soulfulness of Arab vocalism retained its erotic sweetness. Despite the monotony of the Byzantine chants, she gave their transitions a dramatic power, her strong, sure voice rising to stirring heights. The accompanists, standing behind her by a flickering candle, backed her with a steady, unobtrusive drone that reminded Rivlin of the hum of a generator or the rush of water past a boat. At times, as though yielding to the current, she let her voice drop and joined them, or at other times fell mute during the choir's recitative. Then would come a moment of silence, while she considered what had been said before framing her reply.

Rivlin made no attempt to comprehend the Greek. But the nun's soft Arabic sent a shiver through him, as though an ancient matriarch were speaking to him. Under his breath, he translated the words to the chant for Holy Thursday.

"Include me, O Son of God, in this mystic dinner with its holy bread. For I will not reveal your secret to the enemy, nor give you the kiss of Judas. Like the thief on the cross, O Lord, I beseech you to remember me when you come into your Kingdom."

The spiritual uplift often noticeable in performing musicians shone redoubled in her face. Yet her singing was no more a religious rite than it was a concert to be greeted by applause. Halfway between prayer and art, it belonged to the domain of memory or of hope for an uncertain redemption.

"Many of the Muslims have come to see her faint," the Abuna whispered to Rivlin in English, perhaps to prevent those near them from understanding. "But she won't tonight. She's already told me."

Proud that so many believers in Allah had come to his church to pass the time between the post- and the prefast meals, he was also a bit apprehensive of them.

The Jew turned cautiously around in his seat. How could he tell the Muslims from the Christians? Perhaps Rashid, standing in the aisle behind his somber sister, could enlighten him. But his driver merely flashed him a V sign, as if to say, *Admit that I've kept my word.*

"But why won't she?" Rivlin whispered, disappointed.

"You embarrass her."

"Me?"

"That's a fact, Professor. She's a real Lebanese, not a Palestinian refugee. She comes from way up in the mountains and isn't used to crying or fainting in front of Jews."

The Abuna laid a hand on the Orientalist's knee to comfort him, or perhaps to end their conversation, since the singer, who was looking straight at them, had a note of annoyance in her voice.

Rivlin's cheeks burned. It piqued him to think of the nun being embarrassed to faint in front of him. She was now singing about the sacrament of the washing of feet. Would she let him wash hers— which, glimpsed through the straps of her sandals, were carnally petite? Or would he first have to become a Christian?

## 26.

THE EXCITEMENT IN the church was building. The candle in its tall candelabrum had begun to sputter. As the ancient Byzantine chants quavered more and more with Arab grace notes, the mostly male audience swayed and joined the droning chorus. The little sailboat had entered stormy waters.

The Abuna, his moon-shaped face bright with satisfaction, was unfazed. Removing his eyeglasses and rubbing his eyes, he let half a cross-eyed squint roam the throng of rhapsodic Muslims while the other half winked at the Christians. Although the upsurge of emotion threatened to swamp the church's sanctity, frowning upon it too openly might strike the Muslim notables in the front row as Christian impudence. One of them, a bearded young imam, was staring at the Lebanese with burning eyes, as if plotting to steal her voice at the concert's end.

"*T'safrani, ya ruhi, t'safrani, ya idisi ayuha il-batul....*"*

---

* Faint, my dear soul! Faint, O holy virgin!

The murmur was Plato's. Alarmed by the sharp tilt of the sacred toward the profane, he prayed for a dignified fainting fit that might calm the clamorous crowd and bring the evening to a peaceful end.

The nun, however, showed no sign of swooning. Determined to stay conscious for the Jew, she confidently let her unclouded coloratura plunge to more masculine depths. A note of grief crept into the chant for Palm Sunday:

"I inspect the bridal chamber, O Lord. But although it is adorned in glory, I have no garment with which to enter it. I beg you, lave the garment of my soul, enlighten me, save me."

Once more he felt a lump in his throat, as on the night of the biblical drama in Tel Aviv. Was he about to succumb, in this godforsaken church near Jenin, to the same strange need to cry that had overcome him while watching the thrice-repeated dance of Jephthah's daughter? And there was no one here, not even Rashid, who could calm him with the wisdom of his wife.

He lifted the program to his eyes to hide them. What was it that moved him almost to tears? There were no human conflicts or relationships here, only the bliss of an ancient Jew's moonstruck disciples discovering he was gone from the grave. Yet the magical voice of the Lebanese nun soared with such power that he turned in wonder to the Abuna, who nodded with approval at the Jew's damp eyes. It's perfectly natural, Professor, he might have said had he been inclined to say anything at all. Cry, weep all you want. Such is the Song of Paradise. Sometimes it's in Arabic, sometimes in Greek. *Inshallah*, the day will come when you Jews, too, if only you show some magnanimity, will sing it in Hebrew.

But Rivlin did not want to look foolish in front of these nocturnal Arabs. This was not the opera house in Tel Aviv, after all, in whose great auditorium a tear could be concealed, but a simple village church, brightly lit to keep the Muslims from complaining that the Christians were stealing their souls in the darkness. Resolved to keep his tears to himself, he turned his glistening eyes to the nun, whose robe was girded by a rope belt. With a long, piercing cry she strove to subdue an audience that was increasingly confusing the Passion of God with the passion of Um Kulthoum. Rivlin feared that his night out in the

Palestinian Authority was ending in another of his infatuations. He leafed through the program notes with their thumbnail biography.

"Sister Suheir Sharuan was born in Dir el-Amhar, Lebanon. She has degrees in religion and musicology, with a specialization in Oriental and Occidental song, from St. Joseph's University in Beirut and the Université de Saint-Esprit in France. For the past ten years she has studied Byzantine and Gregorian chant in Lebanon and Athens and has performed with choral accompaniment in the Church of Saint-Julien-le-Pauvre in Paris. A member of the Basilite Order, she spends summers on evangelical missions to the Christian communities of Jordan and Palestine."

## 27.

GET A GRIP on yourself. You're not the only one awake on this long night. So is your eldest son, studying for another pointless exam behind his heavy green door. So, perhaps, is your youngest son, patrolling his mountain fastness to make sure that the signs of war and peace are read correctly. Even your wife—who knows?—may be tossing and turning. You have nothing to complain about. The spark of inspiration, though still not trapped, is flickering closer, and you have heard the Arabs' Song of Paradise and even passed the test of their acceptance—no small achievement for a pedantic Jewish Orientalist.

And now, in the courtyard of the little church, you are surrounded not only by the Abuna and his flock, but by young Muslims who, having heard the music of the Christians, wish to know what the Jews have to say. Why draw boundaries in the first place, they want to know, if the peace they bring is an illusion?

As you try to reassure them, you are approached by Rashid's sister. Before you know it she is on her knees, begging you in Bialik's Hebrew to use your Jewish influence to help her retrieve her ID card so that she can return to her native village.

"*Bas ma'a 'l-ulad, mish bidunhum,*"* her brother warns her, struggling to pull her to her feet.

---

* Only with the children. Not without them.

But the dark woman strikes her head despairingly and insists:
"Even without them!"

"*Abadan la!*" Her brother loses his patience. "*Kif b'tihki, ya majnuna. Bifsadu aleiki!*"*

He yanks her up violently, then regrets losing his temper, embraces her, and compassionately leads her back to her basement at the rear of the church.

The soft, autonomous Palestinian moon vanishes in nebulous folds. A fresh night breeze cools the blood warmed by Paradise. The door is locked on the darkened church. In the parking lot reclaimed by the murky night, Christians and Muslims crowd around the nun, whose bell-like voice has not a trace of faintness. You, too, would like to thank her for a moving experience, but you don't wish to be pushy, a Jewish stranger deep in a long-destroyed kingdom of vanished Israelite tribes. And so while you wait for Rashid to return, you wander off to a fence with a view of the Vale of Issachar. A lone car heads down a dirt road toward a Bedouin encampment, beside which two tall horses graze in profound tranquillity.

The old anxiety has you in its clutches.

Stop! Give it up, you stubborn fool.

Whether he knows or not, understands or not, is stuck or not, protests or not—let him be. Leave him alone. It isn't you who will release him from the net of lost love he is thrashing in.

Yes, Hagit. You knew better than I did.

Set him free even in your thoughts.

See how far I've come tonight to free you, Ofer.

Will you laugh at this story of your father's?

Are we, too, knowingly or not, to blame for the breakup of your marriage?

Five years. What are you protecting yourself from, my son? The disgrace? The humiliation? The error? The betrayal? Look around you. It's a vulgar, shameless striptease of a world that can't wait to confess what never happened even in fantasy.

And you won't give an inch.

---

* Never! Just listen to yourself, you madwoman! People will talk about you!

Stop! Let him be....

For the thousandth time....

How often did you have to be told? He's his own person. Let him live his own life. Set him free.

Give it up.

You too, Galya. You too, O bride of pain. Set him free, lost bride....

There. It's done. I swear by the stars above. No more imaginary ill-nesses. No more visits to the hotel. No more inquiries, questions, lies. But you, too, my son, for the love of God, stop being so sad and depressed. I don't want you, wild and wretched, in my dreams anymore.

## 28.

RETURNING TO THE basement, Rivlin was surprised to find the metal door locked. Rashid had vanished into thin air.

He hurried back to the courtyard of the church. It was empty. The Abuna and the nun were gone. Two sole figures, young men with long hair, remained by the gate. They supposed the Israeli Arab must have gone to see the skit about the Jewish kibblelist.

"About who?"

"The kibblelist. Rabbi Whatsis, that holy man of yours who wears a fez. The one without teeth who's always laughing. Here in the vil-lage, we like to laugh with him."

One of the young men had a pistol strapped to his waist. A bit worriedly, the Orientalist asked the two if they were Christians or Muslims.

"That depends what holiday it is."

"How about Ramadan?"

"Then we're Muslims. But only at night when we can eat...."

They both laughed.

"Where do you know Hebrew from?"

"Nablus prison."

Yet they seemed to have taken a fancy to him, for they now insisted that he come see the skit with them. "It will be cool, man. And you don't have to worry about us. Don't worry about your driver, either.

Your Arabs in Israel won't ever leave you." They chuckled slyly. "Come on, it's not far, man. Nothing will happen to you. After that little tearjerker from Lebanon, don't we deserve a few laughs? The Arabs get theirs, too. Those two Christians, Socrates and Plato, don't give a shit for anyone. They do all the big shots in the PA, even Arafat with his shaking hands and his lips that go *gul-gul-gul-gul-gul-gul*. Just like the comics on your TV. You don't happen to have a hundred shekels on you, do you?"

"For what?"

"Expenses. Costumes and all that jazz. It's a contribution for the actors. No shit."

And so, parting with a hundred shekels for "expenses," he let himself be taken captive by two Palestinian hipsters. They walked down the hill from the church, turned into some narrow, deserted streets, and came to a structure that had served, so he was nostalgically informed, as a hideout during the Intifada. Now, it was a warehouse for plastic utensils. A small audience sat squeezed amid various sizes and colors of plastic plates, bowls, and basins, filling the dim room with purplish smoke. Rivlin recognized some of the faces from the church. Most belonged to unemployed youngsters, out of work and out of luck—who, having slept away their despair by day, had turned out for a night's entertainment in front of a small stage concealed by a red curtain.

The Arabs quickly made room for the Jew in the front row. They were so pleased to see him, though they would gladly have cut his throat in this same place several years ago, that they even turned down the Egyptian pop music blasting from an old transistor in order to enjoy his university Arabic. Waving to him from a dark corner in which, no longer droning, they sat smoking and drinking, were Suheir's four accompanists. Perhaps the Abuna was hiding somewhere, too. Yet before Rivlin could look for him, the lights went out, and the curtain was pulled to one side. Holding a candle on a small improvised stage was the kabbalist, Rabbi Kaddouri, the venerable icon of the Sephardic Shas Party. Gigantic in a loud robe and a red Turkish fez, he greeted the audience with a toothless and shyly endearing giggle.

It was Plato on Socrates' shoulders. Together the two pranksters formed a single nonagenarian dotard, who began to harangue, in the down-to-earth dialect of his native Iraq, imaginary Middle Eastern Jews on either side of him. Reproaching those on the left for forgetting they were Sephardim, he attacked those on the right for not remembering they were human, while simultaneously blessing members of the audience who jumped onstage to kiss his hand. But while the old kabbalist's head was Plato's, his arms and legs belonged to Socrates, and an amusing conflict ensued between the mouth that showered his petitioners with good wishes and the limbs that drove them off with kicks and blows.

The Iraqi dialect grew increasingly Palestinian, peppered with private jokes and innuendos served up with Hebrew gibberish and absurd Israeli military commands. Just as the huge but sprightly kabbalist was blessing an aspiring prime minister while handing him a nasty pinch, his robe opened, and out popped two more hands. Breaking into a dance to a raucous Egyptian pop tune, he whirled before the astonished audience with four-handed tai chi exercises. The cheering spectators rose to their feet, copying the Chinese movements.

Nor was this the end. As a stack of plastic basins collapsed in a corner of the stage, an actor jumped out of the disorder in an embroidered robe, a fake beard plastered to his face. Whipping out a pair of dark sunglasses from his pocket, he put them on, intoned the priestly benediction from the Torah, struck the giant kabbalist contemptuously, and cried in Hebrew: "He's innocent! He's innocent!" This was Shas leader Rabbi Ovadia Yosef, whose favorite disciple, the politician Aryeh Deri, had been convicted on corruption charges. Losing his temper, the ancient fez wearer grabbed the rabbi, stripped off his sunglasses, and swallowed him in his robe with one gulp. But this did not go down well with the kabbalist's digestion, for he immediately split into two halves—Plato, the lower half, in the form of a wheelchair, and Socrates as its occupant. He, too, now had a beard, long and unruly behind a colorful silk veil. The kabbalist and rabbi had vanished, their place taken by the crippled Hamas leader Sheikh Yassin of Gaza, who rolled his eyes heavenward and sang a dirty ditty in a squeaky voice.

And so it went. Talented mimics, the two seminarians used a small but well-chosen assortment of props to skip merrily from target to target, now a Palestinian one and now an Israeli one, each turning into and emerging from the others until all finally joined in one monstrous, pitiably conflicted figure—which, mumbling and grumbling in Hebrew and Arabic, sobbed and simpered as it struck and stroked itself and the audience called for more.

## 29.

IN THE DARK, hilarious room, in which plastic plates flew in all directions, Rivlin made out the gleam of his driver's smile. "You're back, Rashid? But where on earth did you disappear to? Come on, let's go home!" "Home? Now?" "When, then? How long do you intend to stay here?" "But it's too early, Professor." "What do you mean, too early?" "Too early, sir. The workers aren't up yet." "What workers? What are you talking about?" "Did you forget, Professor, that I have to pick up workers and bring them to Israel?" "Oh, no, Rashid, my friend! I'm not waiting for any workers. You promised to take me home when I wanted. Well, this is it. I want to go home. You can pick up anyone you want to later." "But it's too late, Professor." "What do you mean, too late? You just said it was too early." "It's too late to bring you back to Haifa and return to Jenin in time for the workers. I promised them." "But why did you disappear?" "*I* disappeared, Professor? Excuse me, but it was you who disappeared. It took a long while to find you here." "Rashid, I'm disappointed in you. You've been bugging me all day." "But how have I bugged you, Professor?" "Don't ask me how. You just did. You and Samaher and her mother, all of you." "But what did we do to you, Professor?" "I don't know what. I only know I'm no longer in my right mind." "Your mind is fine, Professor. Didn't you enjoy the Lebanese?" "Yes, and now I want to go home." "Wouldn't you like to see those two clowns do Aryeh Deri?" "For God's sake, Rashid, don't give me Aryeh Deri. Don't give me anyone. I'm tired. I'm old. Do you think we Jews are made of steel?" "Of course not, Professor. But you're not old at all. And you're a good man even if you're not made of steel. Everyone is happy to see you here. What can I do? That's the way it turned out. The night had a will of its own. Why fight it? You need a little patience, not even very much. Soon the sun will be up, and the partying will stop. If you feel you're wasting your time, I can show you some old Jewish graves that were discovered near here. They're from the time of your Temple, and now there's a little settlement watching over them. It's a good, clear night for seeing them.... No? Well, then, it's best to go back to the Abuna. He'll find a place for you to sleep. We'll start out at sunrise."

Having left the minibus at the church, they had to walk back up the hill. The Abuna, too worried about his Jewish visitor to go to bed, was wide awake. In brightly striped pajamas and a funny green turban-like nightcap, he looked as if he were dressed for a children's play. "Sweet Jesus!" he exclaimed in English. He was sweating, and his eyes would not stay still in their sockets. "What happened to you? I went to show Sister Suheir to her room, and you were gone when I came back. We were beginning to think the Islamic Jihad had taken you hostage. You need to be careful, Professor. Peace hasn't broken out here yet."

He led the Orientalist through the dark teachers' room, placing a finger on his mouth to warn him that the nun, a light sleeper, was lying behind a partition, and brought him to a little alcove that was the headmaster's room. There he swept some papers off a desktop and deftly converted a director's chair into a cot.

"Are you planning to fast tomorrow, too?" he asked gently.

The Abuna seemed relieved to hear that there would be no more Jewish concessions to Islam. His night-turban nodding vigorously, he hurried to take out a thick, hairy blanket and a small pillow in a green pillowcase.

You haven't been away from home for twenty-four hours, Rivlin mused, and once again your Israeli fatigue has met with the offer of an Arab bed. By day with Muslims in the Galilee, by night with Christians in Samaria. Off with thy shoes and onto thy cot, O weary Orientalist!

O distant woman, visibly invisible: are not the strange adventures of this day sufficient proof for you? Do you understand now, my sweet judge, that it is not disdain or condescension that you hear in my voice when I speak of Arabs, but freedom—a freedom burdened neither by feelings of superiority nor by those of hypocritical guilt? Call it a scholar's simple, bluff intimacy with his subject, for the sake of which he is willing to lie down even on a narrow cot beneath a hairy and none-too-clean blanket.

And yet how will you fall asleep when your mind is full of songs and stories—French babies afloat on poisoned horses, Arab moons plunging into seas, enormous dancing tai chi kabbalists with the squeaky voices of fanatical sheikhs? There's nothing for it but to re-convert the cot to a chair, move it to the headmaster's desk, switch on the lamp, take some paper from a drawer, and doodle a big spark of inspiration with an original idea at the center of it and a few supporting facts in its cusp.

It was the naive yet genuine and blameless belief of Algerian soldiers that shedding their blood for France in two world wars would make them French, which belief, ultimately frustrated, gave birth, fifty years later, to an orgy of violence against their descendants.

The veteran scholar quickly jotted down a few chapter headings, added references to historical events, documents, and specific Algerian officers and battalions in the French army, and followed this with a short bibliography. It would all have to be documented later.

His reinvigorated mind at rest, he folded the paper, deposited it in his pocket, switched off the lamp, and turned the chair back into a cot in the moonlight. His only regret was not having thanked the Lebanese nun for her wonderful performance. His infatuation with a woman he would never meet again kept him from falling into a deep sleep despite his tiredness. He drowsed fitfully, the vast night around him penetrating his slumber with the noise of an automobile, the sounds of shots, laughter, someone cursing. And then quiet, and the distant whinny of a horse . . .

The dawn was debating whether to awake the Holy Land when he was roused by a low murmur from the teachers' room. It was a woman's voice, telling a story that would never end. Time to get up, fold the hairy blanket, primp the pillow, smooth and button his clothes, and—still shivering from the morning cold—knock softly on the door to bid the nun an appreciative farewell.

But lying in wait for him in the teachers' room was Ra'uda, who had eluded her brother. To his relief, she did not throw herself at his feet or bang her head on the floor. She simply went on setting the table for his breakfast—which would, she hoped, fortify his resolve to bring her back, with or without her children, to her village in the Galilee. Listening to her troubles was the nun, woken by her in her anguish. The wondrous Lebanese, putting religious duty before an artist's right to a morning's sleep, had hurried from behind the partition wrapped in a blanket and now sat at the table, a small, solitary figure with big, bright eyes, listening to the homesick Muslim—who, removing a towel from a saucepan it had been keeping warm, ladled out a dish of piglet-scented rice and beans. Wordlessly, without resorting to the Hebrew of Bialik, her soft eyes coaxed him to taste her food. Rivlin thanked her and sat down, spoon in hand, across from the nun. In a French perfected from Algerian colonial documents, he carefully said:

"Mademoiselle, I hereby confirm the opportunity to express my gratitude for your marvelous voice. Never before have I looked forward to Paradise, having always feared that, without my body, my soul would be thoroughly bored. Yet if there is singing like yours there, I am willing to reconsider. I only hope it is not too late."

Her smile slight but sincere, she said in her strong, sure voice:

"*Cher monsieur, il n'est jamais trop tard pour embrasser la vrai religion.*"*

He laughed awkwardly and asked where her next concert would be held. Nowhere, she said. She was leaving for Jordan that evening and would return to her convent the following day. Yet next autumn, *inshallah*, she hoped to be in Ramallah for a Palestinian music-and-poetry festival. And she turned to say good morning to the Israeli Arab driver, who had come to announce the start of a new day.

## 30.

THE GUESTS PARTED with the Abuna, who, still in his colorful night-clothes, was jollier than ever after a few hours of sleep. Ra'uda, still

---

* My dear sir, it is never too late to embrace the true faith.

brooding over the ignominy of her fate, seized Rivlin's hand and made him swear in the name of Allah to do all he could to regain her ID. IDs, her brother assured her, pressing her warmly to his heart, would not be needed when peace came at last. "Let's go, Professor Rivlin," he said. "We have to get a move on."

They boarded the minibus, in the back of which, beside the blanket and the pillow, now clucked three hens; strapped on their safety belts; and carefully placed the photocopied material from Jerusalem, which had spent the night in the vehicle, on the seat between them.

A morning mist was lifting over the Vale of Issachar. The road grew more distinct, twisting between olive groves and fragrant fields. Rashid, taking advantage of his Israeli license plate, skirted Kabatiyeh on Jewish bypass roads, along which the checkpoints were few. A few kilometers before Jenin they were surrounded by Palestinian policemen, who prodded seven workers, hiding from the morning chill in a ditch by the road, to climb aboard.

"*Weyn Issam?*"* Rashid asked, demanding to know why one seat was empty.

Worker number eight, it appeared, having been up all night partying, had failed to wake in time.

Loath to lose the income from the empty place, Rashid offered it to the commander of the police force, a middle-aged sergeant. The sergeant accepted with alacrity. He slipped the magazine from his Kalachnikov, took off his belt with its military pouches, and handed them to his second-in-command. Then he removed his army shirt, put it on again inside out, stuck his green policeman's beret in his back pocket, wrapped his head in a kaffiyeh someone handed him, and thus completed his transformation into a Palestinian laborer looking for a day's work in Israel.

They continued northward on a new, wide, empty road toward a group of Israeli settlements. Their handsome villas, topped by cockscombs of red tiles, had names the Haifaite had never heard of. All around them the world was sweetly quiet, as if no one had ever fought a war in it. The reservists from Jerusalem manning the checkpoint on

---

* Where's Issam?

the Green Line were too busy having breakfast to bother stopping an Israeli car heading home, even if it was full of Arabs.

It was six o'clock. Good old Mount Gilboa was in its usual place, and the faithful sprinklers of the Valley of Jezreel hummed in their yellow fields, filling Rivlin's heart with an old love for his native land. All the tension seeped out of him. At Megido Junction his head fell back, and he did not jerk it back up until the French Carmel. As no driver could leave a dazed passenger standing in front of his house, Rashid came with him in the slow-moving elevator, carrying the photocopied texts.

The little space capsule carried them upward. In its mirror Rivlin noted a growth of beard that had not been there the day before. He felt compelled to return to an old question. Was Samaher really pregnant?

Unexpectedly, her cousin did not reply with his usual shrug. "Maybe not," he whispered, looking down at the floor of the elevator.

"But why does her mother keep her in bed?"

"Because she sometimes imagines or does foolish things."

"Like what?"

"Like . . . like thinking she's a horse."

He flushed hotly, the coal black eyes sad with regret. The elevator door opened. Rivlin's key was in the lock when Rashid said:

"Really, Professor Rivlin, you mustn't be angry. She really does love you. From her first class with you. Only you."

He handed the binders to Rivlin and turned despairingly to go.

This time the Orientalist did not scold him or make light of his ailing student's love. Rather, he asked Rashid to come to the bedroom and handed him two bags of his wife's old clothes for the Abuna. Hagit's red shoes he stuck into a drawer. Who in Zababdeh would wear them?

Rashid did not look surprised. There seemed to be no way of surprising him. Perhaps, Rivlin thought, he could read minds. In any case, they would see each other again soon, because there were more poems and stories to be brought from Samaher.

Picking up the phone to check the voice mail, Rivlin noticed through the open door of the kitchen that the bored housekeeper, defying his instructions not to cook, had left several containers covered with cellophane on the marble counter.

There were no messages. In the wondrous day that had passed, he had been needed by no one.

## 31.

*Dear Galya,*

*I'd like an answer to a simple question. Has your father's death, in your opinion, freed me from my vow (or promise) to tell no one what I saw (or, if you insist, fantasized)?*

*Even though I don't depend on your answer, the decision being entirely my own, I'm curious to know why you think I shouldn't be released from the silence I agreed to in the mad, vain hope that I've walked around with for the last five years—that this alone, if anything, could make you come back to me.*

*That's all. A simple question calling for a simple answer—yes or no.*

*I don't suppose my reply to your last letter made you happy. You should realize, however, that it's you who first played with fire by asking my father, quite astonishingly and unnecessarily, whether I knew that your father had died and how I had reacted.*

*What exactly were you hoping to find out? What difference did it make to you what I thought about your father's death?*

*Which is why you owe me a straight answer to a straight question. Am I or am I not absolved of my silence? Because my anger and my longing for you, which have awakened all over again, make me a dangerous man. So much so that, for my own good, I have had to put my pistol in a drawer and make sure the drawer is locked. . . .*

*Ofer*

PART IV

# A Fantasy?

*14.6.98*

*Ofer,*

*You asked for a short answer to a short question. Well, here it is. No.*

*My father's death cannot absolve you of a promise made not only to me, but to yourself. A dead man's honor is no less precious than a living one's, and there is no reason to trash him now, when he can no longer defend himself against your fantasies, old or new.*

*That's my answer to your question. It's also, if I may say so, my request (if my requests still matter to you).*

*But if you nevertheless believe that you're free to break your promise and make your fantasies known, at least do me the favor of sparing me your decision, as well as your oppressive and above all pointless letters.*

*Galya*

*20.6.98*

*Dear Galya,*

*1. Your answer was appreciated.*

*2. Your reply and its reasoning (and most of all, its request) are clear.*

*3. Even though your father's death absolves me of my commitments (which were, by the way, only to you. How could they have been to myself?), I will continue to keep silent for the time being (the last words need to be stressed) even with my parents, and especially with my father—who, I hope, will get over the frenzy that his meeting with you put him into.*

*4. I think that's all.*

5. *And again, I appreciate the fact that you overcame your negative (and to an extent, justifiable) reaction to my letter enough to answer it. Perhaps you recognized some of the old pain in my anger. I won't bother you anymore.*

*Ofer*

*P.S. For the past five years I've fought (with a resolve I didn't always understand myself) to keep my promise to you. I've told no one what went wrong with our marriage, not even those women who have mattered to me (and these were not as rare as you may—or may not—think), even though I know this may have harmed my chances for a new and honest relationship. Because while it may seem (but only seem) that a marriage lasting no more than a year can be explained by a simple sentence like "It didn't take us long to realize we weren't meant for each other," or "I thought I loved her but I didn't," or, on the contrary, "It turned out that she didn't love me back and so we decided to split before we ruined the life of some unnecessary child," this doesn't work with a woman interested in a relationship with a divorced no-account like myself. On the contrary, any serious, deeply feeling person has to be more worried by someone who divorces quickly than by someone whose marriage falls apart bit by bit, because being mistaken in the first place is more damning than experiencing the gradual attrition of love. Whoever dramatically misjudges his first partner may do so again. That's why I think highly of any woman who wants to know why my marriage didn't work.*

*The fact is that I've encouraged them to ask. Those who didn't, even if we got along well, didn't last long. (Most of them, by the way, were young, a new generation—yes, there already is one—that's quick to start up and quick to break off and doesn't care who's married and who's divorced. It surprised them, even upset them, when I insisted on telling them about my divorce on our first or second date, because they couldn't understand why this mattered.)*

*So I'm sorry—no, glad—to inform you that I've had not a few women in my life, especially in the first years after our breakup. It was as if, in leaving me, you also left me with a master key like the one I give every evening to the African woman who cleans the offices, or the one Fu'ad opens every door in the hotel with. My wanting revenge on you only increased my* masculine charms, which were assumed to come with a high degree of technical proficiency because I had been married for a year. Which is how I, who, before you and I met, would get involved in torturous love affairs with the most impossible types, now became a butterfly flitting from flower to flower for the nectar.

But I soon tired of all this, Galya. I wanted a real connection in place of the one we had had, and I believed it would come because I had proved that I was capable of it and that what went wrong was not my fault. I started looking for a lifetime relationship (with a lot of short-lived women), and the first test I gave everyone was to see who wanted to know about my marriage. After all, unless you know something about the past (ask my father: he makes his living from it), it's hardly possible, and certainly not easy, to make any headway in the present. That's what I told every woman whom I wanted and tried to fall in love with.

And so over and over I found myself harping on our divorce without being able to touch on its real cause—that is, what I saw that day with my own eyes. And although there was perhaps something noble in the discretion of a divorced man who refused to say a bad word about his ex, there was also something strange and suspicious about it, and, in the end, aggravating. After all, you can't come asking for comfort, and keep saying that you need to understand what happened before you can start a new life, while deliberately avoiding the heart of the matter. All you're doing is putting obstacles in your own way and letting the other person know that you still have hopes for the woman who said to you when you parted—

word for word—

"Perhaps in the end I'll miss you so much that I'll beg you to take me back. But if I ever find out that you told anyone, one single person, about your insane fantasy, there's no chance of that ever happening."

Word for word, right?

Not that it's so difficult to figure out what I've been hiding. Women smart enough to realize that I need to be released from some horrible scandal should be able to use their imaginations. And in fact, among the many possibilities that have occurred to them (it's amazing how fertile the imagination is when it comes to the sordid things people do), one or two of them, like little birds pecking at garbage, have come close to the truth. But even then I didn't let on that they did. "The details don't matter," I told them. "I made a promise I'm not ready to break. Just convince me that I couldn't have prevented my divorce and I can start thinking about marriage again."

Not many women are prepared to deal with such a devious neurotic.

But there was one who rose to the challenge. Not as a prospective wife, but as a friend. She was a true Parisian, a class behind me in school, who tried to free me by means of that logical French mind that hones itself on the subtleties of sex. Without knowing the details of our case, which I never revealed to her, she constructed a psychological model proving almost mathematically that despite our great love (and that, at least, you never denied), our separation was inevitable. Her analysis concluded that whether I had actually seen something or just fantasized it, our marriage never stood a chance. Even had I not (she argued), by sheer coincidence, on a Tuesday morning at eleven o'clock, left my office to look for some old building plans in the basement of your father's hotel, I was by then so involved in his project to expand the kitchen and dining room that sooner or later I would have gone down there anyway—if not to look for the plans, then, say, to check the foundations—and seen or fantasized the same thing.

That was just her initial premise. For even (her theorem continued) had I never descended to the basement, eventually I would have guessed what was going on, since anyone joining a new family, no matter how blindly enthusiastic he may be about it (as I was about yours, if only because of my love for you), develops a sixth sense that in time becomes as sharp as a laser beam. Even without my unexpected discovery, I would have begun to wonder.

In fact (continued my shrewd Parisian), who could say that the building plans were my real objective on that awful Tuesday when I left the office and went to the hotel without you? (Wasn't the whole point to be there without you?) Perhaps the real reason was a vague suspicion in my subconscious or unconscious mind. (Here in Paris, those old ghosts are still believed in. . . .)

And suppose (my Parisian friend went on) I had said nothing to you and kept what I saw and understood to myself. The whole incredible story would have come out in the end anyway, because how long could I have held it in? I was raised and educated by my parents to believe in open dialogue and in the need—no, the duty—to discuss even the most difficult subjects honestly. And although, superficially, my mother may seem the stronger of the two, my father, too, is no innocent and has his own shrewd sophistication. They were equal partners in a total intimacy—and since such intimacy, which we both believed in and wanted, was my model for our relationship, one that would only have grown stronger with the years, what chance would I have had of hiding something that was consuming me? Even in an ordinary quarrel, the most happily married couple can work itself up to a point, absurd but unavoidable, at which whole families—fathers, mothers, brothers, sisters, even aunts and uncles—are invoked in support of one person's virtues or the other person's vices. Could I have listened and said nothing, for example, if you had argued—as you sometimes did—that you were naturally generous like your father and easygoing like your mother, as opposed to my father's gloom-and-doom and my mother's prudery? Could I have resisted the temptation to shake you up with the hidden truth, which would have jumped out of me like an angry grasshopper? And then—yes, then—you would have been fully justified in regarding such a revelation, coming totally out of the blue, as not even a "pathetic fantasy" but quite simply a revolting lie invented in the heat of the argument. . . .

And let's suppose (let's!) that in spite of all this I not only tried but succeeded in keeping the truth to myself, in bad times as well as in good, without a word about what I saw that day. I still couldn't have forgotten it, especially not when it involved people I saw every day who were continuing their sordid behavior. And since I couldn't have relieved the burden by telling anyone, not even my own parents, since this would have totally estranged them from your parents, the truth would have gone on seething in me and so poisoned my love for you that in the end I would have suspected you too (why not?)—yes, you too—of knowing and hiding it from me, or even (for now that everything is possible, who knows?) of being involved in it yourself and—if only in your thoughts—even enjoying it.

I had to speak out. And immediately. The twenty-four hours that passed from the time I saw what I did until the time I told you about it seem unbearably lonely even now. And above all, you wouldn't have wanted me to keep quiet. Never, in all the harsh, bitter quarrels we had afterward—and I say this to your everlasting credit, Galya—never once did you say, "Why

did you go and tell me all this? What possessed you to do it?" You understood the obligations (yes, obligations!) of intimacy. And from your shock
when I told you, and the scene you made (you may remember how my father was attending some conference in Jerusalem that day and turned up at
our apartment and you refused to come out of the bedroom even to say
hello), I knew that you, at least, were innocent. . . .

Which was a relief. . . .

And so (argued my Parisian), concluding this part of her theorem
(there's another part still to come), the moment I realized what I had seen
was the moment our marriage was over. After that, it was only a question
of time.

### Part Two

And now let's look at it from your point of view. My Parisian is a serious
woman. Even without knowing what it was that I saw (as I say, I never told
her), she managed to prove that our marriage was doomed from the opposite end, too—that is, starting from the assumption that it was all a "revolting fantasy," as you claimed from the first. In the forty-two days that
followed, in which you systematically demolished your love for me, you
never budged from that position.

Five years have passed since then, and ultimately all will be forgotten
and perhaps even forgiven except for one thing—the insult and even the
contempt of your self-righteousness. I'll never forget you sitting tense and
pale, although perfectly patient, your feet beneath you on the couch, listening stonily, without interrupting, without asking questions, without even
turning off the radio. (Yes, I remember how grotesque it was to be telling
you such a thing to soft background music.) When I finished, there was a
moment (but too short, too short!) of silence before you reacted. I would
have thought that something so incredible needed more than that. The fact
was that, in my naïveté, I had expected only one of two possible reactions.

Either—

"I'm stunned. Give me a minute to catch my breath."

Or at the very worst—

"It's none of your business, Ofer. I'm warning you. Stop opening doors
in this hotel without knocking or asking permission. You don't own it or
my family just because you're married to me."

*But you took another line. Without hesitating, you chose to defend your family to the hilt, even if it meant destroying our relationship. You said— word for word—*

*"You have no idea, Ofer, of what you're getting us into. I'm asking you to drop this whole revolting fantasy of yours, to say you're sorry, and never to mention it again."*

*Word for word, right?*

*(Relax. This letter will never reach you.)*

*And now listen to the theorem of my Parisian (an ugly little bird, pecking away):*

*"Let's assume that your ex-wife was right and that you concocted a fantasy for reasons of your own. Let's also assume that in the end you would have been forced to admit it. Then, too, your marriage was doomed. Because to judge by your anger and obsessive behavior, your case involved two different conceptions of love. There's first love and there's second love. The experts can distinguish between them, even if sometimes they're hard to tell apart, because each has a logic of its own. They can exist side by side, not without conflict, until something comes along to turn them against each other. And then it's good-bye.*

*First love (my Parisian explained) preserves throughout a marriage the bright, living kernel of the falling-in-love that engendered it, that outgoing of the heart by which the lover recognizes, sometimes instantly and sometimes by progressive stages, the human being who can soothe or satisfy his deepest desires—the one person with whom he can redemptively re-create the primeval love for a father, mother, sister, brother, or other family member that could never be fulfilled. And though, when he falls in love, the lover may know little about the beloved, whose soul may be a mystery and whose body may hide beneath its clothes an ugly defect or scar yet to be uncovered by his desire, still he is bonded to his beloved blindly and trustingly and is ready to die for her even before he has seen her nakedness. This is the meaning of the expression "falling in love," found in so many languages, for the lover has as it were fallen into a deep pit (at the bottom of which may lurk a snake or scorpion), and there must build his love for himself.*

*And even after (my Parisian continued) the outward signs have yielded their inner promise in all its glory or poverty, its undreamed-of heights or insufferable depths, the glow of the first falling-in-love continues everywhere and all the time. Yes, even when the beloved is in a wheelchair in an old-age home, diapered and connected to tubes, even then the flash of a smile in moldering eyes, the ancient movement of a veiny hand, the heard-again lilt of a dear voice, even a single sentence containing the right words, can resurrect the first falling-in-love in a twinkling—that love that unconditionally and in advance forgives every weakness and failing, if only for the reason that in advance it knew nothing about them.*

*Indeed (in my Parisian's opinion), nothing is more democratic than this total embrace of the beloved; for just as the state, or the republic, can never revoke the citizenship of a citizen, be he a spy, traitor, rapist, or murderer, so first love forbears in all things because the first, unconditional falling-in-love persists.*

*Such (thinks my wise Parisian) was my love for you. This is why I am still stranded in it, waiting for another falling-in-love to set me free. . . .*

*(And it will—)*

*And yet, says my Parisian, who is four years older than I am even though she's a class lower—because she has a rich father who periodically treats her to a new career—"your story makes clear that your ex-wife's conception of love is of the other variety." And this is why, she explains, what happened to us was inevitable.*

*And that's precisely what I need: to understand calmly the necessity of our separation, so that I can say good-bye for good, graciously and with a light heart.*

*It seems, Galya, that your kind of love has to do with choice. That's the great difference. Perhaps yours is the more developed variety, skipping love's primitive and dangerous "fall" for what is deliberately and courageously chosen—not because it is the best choice, since there is always a better one, but because it has potential. (I once watched a nature program on television about a certain species of duck or swan that takes four years of painstaking investigation to choose a mate—the longest aptitude test on record.) Rather than marriage as a first flowering of feeling that lasts only until the next falling-in-love, the love of choice offers something less passionate but more stable: responsibility. In a moment of crisis the first kind of lover declares emotionally, "What's done is done—I fell in love with you, and so I forgive you," but whereas the second kind says coolly, "Yes, what's done is done—I chose you, and I am responsible for my choice." But—and here's the rub—*

*while love of the first kind can by its nature overlook what it doesn't
of the second kind is incapable of such evasions. And so when some
shakes the foundations, "responsible love" is too weak to support i* ....
*that point the whole structure collapses, and all that's left to say is, "You'd
better pack your things, Ofer, and go to your grandmother's."*

Once, some two years ago, a month or two after I arrived in France, in
a moment of deep sadness but also of intermittent hope (I didn't know you
were about to remarry), I decided to write an itemized account of the
horribly quick parting that you subjected me to after forty-two days of
struggle. I bought a big yellow notebook, which went well with the yellow
light of gray Paris in August '93, where I found myself after my expulsion
from the Paradise in which you lived with your father, mother, and sister
(who to this day can inspire in me, along with horror and revulsion, a
good, stiff erection).

Anyway, you and your family, even your hotel, were cloaked by my
imagination in the late-summer light that I remembered from the brambly
little hill near the gazebo under which we were married. That's how I had
imagined Paradise back in Bible class in grade school, perhaps so as to give
it a Middle Eastern touch: a lush green oasis fed by springs and surrounded
by soft, friendly desert.

And so I began to write the story of our separation, from the first moment: thoughts, conversations, facts, things we did, the weather, the political situation, even a dream or two that I remembered, such as one in which
I forced your father to let me shave him with an old electric shaver found in
a room of the hotel.

I wrote from the heart. The result was an indictment, a defense plea, perhaps even a proposal for an out-of-court settlement—but only on the left-
hand page, because the right-hand page was for your use, so you could add
your story to mine. I still hoped against hope that setting down our two versions in the same notebook might help us reach a new understanding.

I filled page after page, quickly, in less than a week. I wanted so badly to
prove that you had acted rashly that I remembered all kinds of things I had
forgotten. And I had insights I had never had before into the predicament
of your making (for example, your insomnia, which started at that time
and kept you up all night in my parents' home in Haifa). It was exciting to
put everything down clearly on paper and give my suffering a form. I was

so involved in it that I went on writing during my French lessons at the Alliance Française, to the delight of the students from Japan, China, and Indonesia, who were happy to see that the brown and yellow races were not the only ones with languages that looked nothing like French.

*I still didn't know you were about to get married—*

And then my father told me over the telephone that my grandmother had died, and I could hear the relief in his voice. She had already lost the last of her independence after falling and breaking her pelvis and being brought from Jerusalem to a nursing home in Haifa—and, as impossible as she had been when she still could stand on her own two feet, she then became such a horror that she kept having to be moved from one institution to another.

But it wasn't just my father who was relieved. So was I. Not because I ever suffered from her. On the contrary. She always showered my brother and me with love and presents, not only because she really loved us, but also because she hated to waste on us a drop of the special venom that she kept for the issue of her own womb. The relief came from my fear that in the heat of one of her daily spats with my father, she might, in order to show that I trusted her more than him, blurt out the secret I had made her promise to tell no one.

You see, Galya, the time has come for a confession. There was one person in the world (though she is in it no longer) from whom I was unable to conceal the truth. Because back when we agreed to "mutually disengage" in order to gain some perspective, I on my "fantasy" and you on your "fantasy of my fantasy," and decided to separate and move out of our apartment—you into the hotel and I to my grandmother's—my parents, although upset by our unexpected breakup, maintained (mostly at my mother's insistence) a gallant distance while hoping that the crisis (about whose cause they knew nothing) would blow over by itself. On the other hand, my grandmother had no faith in spontaneous reconciliations. Her gloomy, suspicious nature, which always made her expect (sometimes rather eagerly) the worst, led her to demand that I do something practical to restore us to Paradise Lost.

Yes, us. For as upset as she was by our separation, she was also upset by the loss of the hotel, which she had hoped, rather bizarrely, to use as a halfway house in departing this life. Did your parents ever tell you that *after our wedding she took to dropping by the hotel in the morning for coffee and cake and, sometimes, for a chat with a lounging customer, knowing that Fu'ad would not take money from a "member of the family"?*

*My three weeks with her were both sad and strange. In her old apartment in the dowdy old downtown of Jerusalem, nothing had changed: I stayed in my father and aunt's childhood room, stared at from the shelves by their old dolls and toy animals, painted weird colors by Tsakhi, and regressed, at the hands of this shrewd, bossy woman (I think my father is afraid of her to this day) to the little boy my parents used to leave with her when they came to Jerusalem on their own affairs.*

*There I was, sitting naked again in the old bathtub I once showed you, the one with those monster legs cast in lead that my father called "Mephistopheles' feet," once more throwing my dirty laundry into the big old straw basket, with its cracked, white enamel top that in our boyhoods, both my father and I had made believe was the steering wheel of a bus. Returning to her place late at night—because after work I always went first to our empty apartment on the pretext of having to get something from it—I would find her, in her nightgown, waiting tensely in the kitchen. She would serve me my supper while grilling me like a patient police detective, trying to worm out of me what had really happened between you and me—not for curiosity's sake, but in order to know how to get the two of us together again so that she could have one more dance, like the dance she danced at our wedding, with "that perfect gentleman, Mr. Hendel."*

*One autumn evening, after I had given up all hope of running into you in the apartment or of ambushing you near the hotel, and had begun to accept that we were permanently separated and that I would have to settle for my share of the apartment and find a place of my own, I was overcome by the urge to shock the old woman with the truth and make her realize once and for all what kind of "Paradise" she had lost. First, though, I made her swear on a Bible that if she broke her vow and told anyone what I was going to reveal to her, she would be personally responsible if God punished us by making something bad happen to Tsakhi in the army. (He was a junior in high school and worrying us all with his talk of volunteering for a commando unit. Who could have imagined that he'd end up in the safest place in the country?) And then, right there in her kitchen, late at night, as downtown Jerusalem was emptying out, I told her the whole story. It was* the second time (it won't be the last) that I had told it to someone else, rather than just to myself in my thoughts.

I didn't spare her any of the details. I knew she would argue with me, as she did with everyone, and I wanted to expose her to the whole tawdry reality. With a twisted pleasure, I shone a light for her on the sick roots of Paradise—roots I was willing to live with, but only on the condition that you acknowledged them.

Well, she listened to my story, right there in her kitchen, with the bored look of a mother blessed with an overimaginative child, sighed when I reached the end of it, like an old woman who has seen everything, and stunned me with her response. You would have loved it. (If, that is, you had known about it, which you never will, because this letter will never reach you.)

It went like this:

"Don't be ridiculous, Ofer. How can you dare accuse a decent man like Mr. Hendel of such a thing? Galya is right. It's all in your imagination. Whenever your parents brought you here as a boy, your grandfather would complain that you drove him crazy with your fibs. You would stand outside on the terrace and pretend that scenes from some movie you had seen were taking place in the offices of the National Trade Union Headquarters across the street, all kinds of horrible things that people were doing. It's your imagination, sweetheart. Ask your wife to forgive you and tell her that even as a child . . ."

You get the idea.

So you see, Galya, I found for you an unexpected ally. If only she hadn't been buried next to my grandfather for the past two years. . . .

"Say you're sorry, boy!"

And then I remembered, with a slight feeling of panic, how as a boy, especially on my visits to Jerusalem, I really did make up strange stories to entertain my grandfather, who lived in dread of his horrible wife. At which point I surprised her by revealing that I had already asked you to forgive me and had been, quite rightly, turned down.

I repeat: quite rightly.

(I hope you've noticed, Galya, how objective I'm trying to be.)

It wasn't so easy to explain that to her after our last meeting in that little café—when, in a desperate attempt to save our marriage, I took back everything I had said and apologized in the most groveling manner. You had four perfectly logical rebuttals, all mutually reinforcing, like four cog-wheels in a machine to crush all hope. And if your answer, which deserves to appear as a special section in The Guide to Marital Warfare, was not entirely clear to my grandmother, this was only because it was raining out and she had stuffed her infection-prone ears with absorbent cotton upon hearing the first spatter of drops on the window.

Rebuttal 1: "If you were telling an out-and-out lie, Ofer, you don't deserve to be forgiven, ever. In that case, what you did was such a low blow that I can never trust you anymore. Even if I forgave you, it wouldn't last."

Rebuttal 2: "On the other hand, if you were the victim of a fantasy, then the mind that fantasized is still there. How can you ask to be forgiven for something that's still in you and that you're still trying to prove?"

Rebuttal 3 (bravely honest to a fault): "And suppose it turns out that you've told the truth? Then it's not you who have to ask for forgiveness, but I, for involving you with such a pathological family. And why, really, should I be forgiven for that?"

I shuddered. You must remember how I answered, in a choked voice, "That's true. But I do forgive you, because I want to. And from now I'll love not only you, but whatever is yours, even your father and sister, more than ever...."

Coldly and calculatedly (after a year of marriage you knew me well enough to be prepared for such a lunatic promise), you delivered the coup de grâce,

Rebuttal 4: "I know you mean every word of it, Ofer. And believe me, it's the most disgusting thing I've heard from you yet."

I didn't go to my grandmother's funeral. My mother left the decision up to me, and my father advised against it—and not just because of the plane fare. To tell you the truth, apart from my mild and rather foolish relief that our story belonged just to the two of us again, which left me a ghost of a chance of getting you back, I felt real sorrow for the death of a woman I had spent so much time with as a child and had returned to after my separation from you for a sad yet warm and intense reunion. And because I could think of no other way to mourn in Paris, I bought a black ribbon and tied *it to my arm in the Catholic fashion that you see in old French movies. I even went around with it longer than I had planned to, in part because I noticed that it made people more patient with my bad French.*

*About half a year later, over the phone, my mother told me in passing that she had heard you were getting married and thought I should know about it, even if it was painful, since it might make it easier for me to free myself from you. I was too stunned to say anything, and so she said, "Don't take it so hard. You deserve a better and more dependable wife than Galya, and you'll find her." That helped me to get a grip on myself. "Thank you, Ima," I said. "I'm glad you told me. Even if it's only a rumor, I've been waiting for the chance to finally mourn for Galya." And I put the black ribbon back on and started wearing it again. After a week, though, when I realized I still wasn't over you, I took it off.*

*Stuck, stuck, stuck, stuck, stuck! That's frightening, because five years have gone by with nothing to celebrate. Good and stuck.*

*So you see, it's not my fault if I can't stop the words that are flowing so easily from me now, so pleasurably and without anger, onto the screen of a computer that someone forgot to turn off in the Youth Department of the Jewish Agency. I didn't even have to open a new file, but just squeezed myself in between two memos on Hebrew-speaking summer camps. There's still time to decide whether to print this "pointless and oppressive" letter or to hit Delete, just as, after my mother informed me that you really were remarried, I threw "our" yellow notebook into the oven of the Cooking Academy, which cheerfully roasted it to a crisp.*

*(I like my work as a night guard at the Jewish Agency, which occupies— a bequest from a French-Jewish Holocaust survivor—an apartment building in a fashionable bourgeois district that has a large park nearby. It's a comfortably posh, three-story nineteenth-century building with attractively oak-paneled lobbies and stairways, and old chairs and tables that were divided up among the different offices on a political basis. You have to spend time in a place like this, Galya, and use your master key to visit all its rooms, in order to appreciate that despite its bureaucratic morass there's something soothing, even comforting, about its old Jewish National Fund maps of Palestine hanging on the walls. There is a Zionism, old, innocent, and heartwarming, that will last not only another century, but another millennium, even if the State of Israel goes under in the meantime.)*

When my grandmother heard (we're back to that autumn night in her kitchen) that I had gone and asked for forgiveness without waiting for her advice and had been turned down, she was flustered. But since the logic of your four rebuttals failed to move her and she wasn't a quitter, she simply ignored them and instructed me quite shamelessly to ask forgiveness from Mr. Hendel himself. She was sure, she said, that he could talk you into clasping me to the family bosom again....

She certainly did want to dance in your hotel again!

I didn't answer her. I went to my bedroom and shut the door. I don't know whether she changed her mind, but I did manage to scare her, because her demeaning proposal was not repeated the next morning. I was running a fever that day and thought I had the flu, and I stayed in bed until noon. Then I went to the office, phoned your father, and made an appointment with him that same night.

A week later (with his encouragement, if not necessarily on his initiative) you filed for a divorce. Yet I remain confident (for some reason) that he never told you about our meeting until the day he died, which means that you'll never know about it now, either.

(Because this letter, as I've said, will not be sent.)

And yet nevertheless—

### My Impossible Meeting with Your Father

Actually, only the dreariness of those days in dowdy downtown Jerusalem could have brainwashed me into putting my grandmother's grotesque idea into practice. (In one of her nursing homes, an old staff member said to my father: "I've never in my life seen anyone like your mother. Tell me, Professor, how did you manage to come out normal?" To which, without cracking a smile, he replied: "I didn't.") I can still see her sitting in her kitchen on that revolving high chair of hers, like a pilot or an aeronautical engineer, surrounded by walls and shelves lined with knives, cleavers, ladles, spatulas, graters, mixing bowls, and appliances, all covered with the colorful little jackets she sewed for them. It was only in Paris that I realized that the idea of studying restaurant architecture first came to me, not from your hotel, whose old building plans I went looking for on that infamous morning, but from her cluttered kitchen.

Your father hesitated for a moment and agreed. Our tragic encounter had prepared him for the possibility of a private meeting, even though he had done his best to avoid it. And when it dawned on him, though he still knew nothing specific, that you were about to eliminate the threat to him by ditching me for good, he didn't have the heart to refuse me.

The truth is that although your father was not the type to cut and run, he had panicked so badly after that fateful Tuesday that he moved up a planned trip to America in the hope that it would give him, and perhaps me too, a breather in which to review the options more calmly (a sensible strategy for the stock market, but not for a Greek tragedy) before formulating his response to this stranger in his family who had never imagined that Paradise had its basements.

In the five years since our separation, Galya, I've sometimes thought about the man as much as I've thought about you. In the comprehensive dissertation on our divorce that I've composed in my head, there's a chapter devoted to the subtleties of Mr. Hendel, who ran away (yes, ran away!) to America and returned from a successful two-week business trip there with the novel notion of handling me not by pleas, flattery, threats, or sulks, but by good humor. "Why in the world did you run away that day when you saw me?" was his line. "Don't tell me you thought you had discovered some deep, dark secret! It's time that you realized a family's emotional life can be more complicated than you think."

I wonder if you remember the family dinner to which we all were invited on the Saturday after your father's return from America. It was at that nice restaurant belonging to Fu'ad's uncle in Abu-Ghosh, on a terrace shaded by a grapevine as big as a tree. Surrounded and protected by his loving family, your father thought it was the perfect place to confront the son-in-law who had caught him with his pants down.

Perhaps you even remember how he seated us around the table. He put me as far from himself as possible, but also facing him, so that he could keep me under observation while warning me with a glance not to ruin a happy family. He strained to hear every word that I said, whether it was addressed to him or not. It was at that meal that he began dropping hints that he would make me his head architect in expanding the hotel for a new clientele discovered in America: wealthy fundamentalist Christians looking not just for a place to stay in Jerusalem but also for a home away from home that would offer them, on a clear day, views of the Messiah's birthplace in Bethlehem, of his baptismal site near the Dead Sea, and of Golgotha, where he was crucified. It was at this meal—remember?—that he announced the coming revolution: no more "parasitical rabbis" checking his kitchen, no more separation of meat and dairy, no more porkless, seafoodless kosher meals. Come hell or high water, or just an ordinary Middle Eastern war, Christian pilgrims were more dependable than Jewish tourists.

And yet, little by little, as that meal went on, without anything careless being said or even hinted at, but simply by watching you and me squirm, he realized, with the intuition of a clever and intelligent father, that the thing he feared most had come to pass. The intimacy between us, so foreign to a secretive man like him, had become a wounded animal threatening to devour him.

I want you to know that to this day, at this precise moment, facing a computer in the dark office building of the Jewish Agency, I can re-create the exact shades of light, tones of voice, and smells of food on that grapevine-shaded terrace, on that day late in the summer of our separation and divorce, with its sweet light falling on the vineyards and orchards, on the restaurants, shops, mosques, and churches—that serene Jewish vision of a bucolic and uncomplaining Arab life, as sweet as baklava.

And then—do you remember?—your father grew suddenly alarmed at the prospect of my "betrayal." He looked so bewildered and hostile, and his gloom was so great, that your mother asked if he was feeling all right and Tehila, who (unbelievable!) knew nothing (and may know nothing to this day) about the drama that had taken place behind her back, said crossly, "What's the matter, Abba? Cheer up!" Even the old restaurant owner, Fu'ad's uncle, who knew your father well, sensed the shift in mood and sent us a copper beaker of Turkish coffee and a plate of yellow semolina cakes on the house. I noticed that your father, whose relationship with you had always been warm and full of love, was afraid even to look at you.

Then and there, the masks were stripped from us all. Had you wanted it (but you didn't, you didn't!), you had all the proof you needed that my version of events was as real as the Arab village we were looking at. But you, although you felt your father's distress and could easily have grasped its significance, decided to overlook it in his favor, his and not mine, because you had only one father, whereas a husband could always be housebroken or exchanged. And you knew that only by turning truth into fantasy could *you defend the honor of your family and the sweet memories of your child-hood. Right in front of me, demonstratively, you went over to your father and gave him a hug to bolster him and—isolate me.*

### My Meeting with Your Father in the King David Cafeteria

*He chose the place. You know how he liked to drop in on hotels and check their service and prices so as to know what to charge for his own rooms.*

*It was seven in the evening. The cafeteria was half-deserted. Twilight was falling on a hot, dry autumn day. He was studying the menu while waiting for me in a corner.*

*He wasn't unfriendly, although neither did he display the ingratiating anxiety he had shown me in Abu-Ghosh. He was serious and reserved throughout our meeting. It couldn't have been easy for him. He was wear-ing his safari jacket despite the heat (the beige one, not the white), and as always I had the sense (for the first time, accompanied by a twinge of envy) of a strong, impressively virile man.*

*He ordered an herbal tea for himself—did his stroke really come from his notorious high blood pressure?—and I, in a moment of weakness, asked the waitress to bring me, along with my coffee, a piece of cream cake; its tastelessness only weakened me more in what was the shortest, but most dramatic, confrontation of my life.*

*It started off in a low key. We talked about his plans for expanding the restaurant, which required a building permit. I suggested, based on my ex-perience working for Harari, that he refrain from making public his idea of bringing Christian pilgrims from the United States, and especially—at least until the plans were approved—from telling anyone that he intended to make the place nonkosher. Every official in the Jerusalem municipality, I told him, no matter how nonobservant, lived in fear of the religious parties, and there was no point in taking chances. Your father listened carefully, gripping his tea with both hands as though to warm them. He glanced at the walls of the Old City, as if checking whether the floodlights had been turned on, and then casually uttered five words that spelled an end to all my hopes:*

*"I'll really miss you, Ofer."*

*(Which is more than I ever heard from you, Galya.)*

*Just then the lights came on in the Tower of David. I went white, or perhaps red, and instead of doing the honorable thing, getting up and walking out on that pointless meeting, I bowed my head as though failing to grasp his meaning and asked ironically if he understood whose fault it was that he would have to miss me. And without waiting for answer, I said: "Yours, Yehuda, yours and only yours!"*

*He was momentarily taken aback. The surprise that made him flush seemed genuine. But after a minute, he asked in that unflappable, gentlemanly way of his:*

*"My fault in what way?"*

*And that was when I forgot all my grandmother's instructions. I only knew that this man, sitting across from me wearing a silk foulard, had already turned me out of his family. The injustice of it infuriated me. I told him he had to defend me against you.*

*In those very words. "You have to defend me against Galya."*

*This time he was ready.*

*"What are you talking about, Ofer?" he asked innocently. "We've been terribly upset by what's happened between you, but we're helpless. Galya is treating it like a top secret. She told Tehila to mind her own business and not ask any questions. It's a fact that we're fond of you. And we're sorry, too, about your parents, with whom we were proud to be connected. But how can we talk her out of it after such a betrayal?"*

*The malicious glint in his eyes said everything. The man was demonic and in full control, and although I didn't think you had dared tell him about my "fantasy," he knew that you wouldn't hesitate to break up our marriage, not only to save his honor, but also (from now on I'm going to be pitiless, Galya) because you were already thinking ahead.*

*My despair and bitterness turned to anger and hatred. In the middle of that quiet cafeteria I said furiously:*

*"What betrayal are you talking about? Yours?"*

*"Mine?" He smiled calmly. "Whom have I betrayed?"*

*I stared down at the table. I still couldn't bring myself to speak the truth. I toyed with my fork at the soft, wounded corpse of the insipid cheesecake, and I said, "All of us, the whole family. Down there in your hideaway..."*

*He was ready for that, too. Yes, your father had prepared himself well.*

"Hideaway?" The word amused him. "You call that a hideaway? It's an old office in which a cousin of ours used to work, an accountant who's been dead for years. He came from Tel Aviv to do our income taxes. I didn't understand what you were looking for down there. All you had to do was ask and I would have told you that the old plans were in the closet by the front entrance. But you disappeared without a word. What made you run away? There was no one there but me...."

At that moment I realized that before I had even thought of a showdown with him, he had figured out how to win one. If I were going to save our marriage at the last minute, it wouldn't be by cross-examining him. My only hope was a desperation measure: to offer not an apology, but my collaboration, and that would have horrified even my grandmother. "Stop right there, Ofer," she would have said. "Tell him to go to hell with his Paradise and find yourself another wife."

Find myself another wife....

But I didn't want another wife. It was you I fell in love with and you I wanted from the day I was born. And so before my final banishment, I tried one last move that only a sick spirit could have thought of:

"I'm not your judge, Mr. Hendel," I said. (Yes, "Mr. Hendel," not "Yehuda." Maybe I felt that my madness called for some formality.) "That's something I don't want to be and can't be. It's a big, strange world, full of things that seem terrible now but may be taken for granted someday. Perhaps I shouldn't have panicked. I should have assumed you knew what you were doing. I'm almost thirty years old, and I had to come a long, hard way before I learned to love as I do now. My marriage to Galya is the high point of my life, and its only hope. To lose her is to risk losing everything. That's why, although I can't pretend that I was fantasizing, I'll cooperate with you in any way I can. My love for Galya is so great that I'd look the other way even if she wanted to behave like her sister."

All at once, as if the chair beneath him were on fire, he jumped to his feet and asked the waitress for the check. He had to get away as quickly as possible, not from my being more explicit, which he was prepared for, but from the new temptation I had dangled in front of him. He would have liked to vanish on the spot, even though he was too well mannered to run out on me or the waitress. And so he stood waiting for the check with his back to me, because he couldn't bring himself to look at me. "I'll pay the *goddamned bill," I felt like saying. "Just don't leave me all alone with all the terrible things that have been said here." But I knew that one more word would drive him away and that there was still something, a last sentence, that he wanted to say. And in fact, when the waitress came back and he handed her a bill, he didn't tell her to keep the change. He waited for that too, with that virile stance of his that made two young women at the next table turn to look at him. The waitress brought some change in a dish. We were about to part forever. He turned to me and said (I would still like to believe, Galya, that these last words were uttered not just in anger, but also with concern and even compassion):*

*"Be careful, Ofer. Such boundless love will destroy you...."*

*And now he's dead. And though he wrecked my marriage, I feel (you'll be surprised to hear) that I owe him a small debt of gratitude for that warning.*

*The divorce papers arrived a few days later. Although I was expecting them, I was so sad and depressed that for weeks I couldn't even sit down to a proper meal. I simply grabbed a bite now and then on the fly, especially at night, like a Muslim on Ramadan.*

*What have I left out? Nothing. And soon there'll be nothing. I'll shade the text, hit Delete, and poof.*

*Thank you. Thank you for forbidding me to send you "pointless and oppressive" letters. The thought of printing all these pages, putting them in an envelope, and mailing them to you just to torment myself by waiting for an answer that will never come.... Thank you for wanting nothing more from me. For walking off without leaving a trail. I should have realized it was merely my father's projection to think innocently you wanted a condolence letter from me. All he managed to do was entangle me with you again. But don't worry. It won't be for long.*

*Maybe it's because he never had a daughter that he always took such a paternal interest in you. But if he thinks your father's death is an opportunity to get at the truth I've been hiding, I'll repeat my first promise:*

*The truth will not out. Mum's the word.*

*"If my requests still matter to you," you write. Well, my misfortune is that everything about you still matters. That's why I'll keep silent.*

*And even though over the past five years I've once or twice allowed myself to wonder, "Maybe, Ofer, it was just a fantasy after all," I've repressed that doubt each time, always returning to the belief that the rift between us was tragic rather than dramatic—an inevitable fate. That's why, over the years, I've rephrased the confused emotion of it into precisely stated testimony like that I saw given in court, when as a child, I would visit my mother at work.*

*Your Honor*

*Dear Ima,*
*The day was Tuesday, 15 July, 1993. It was 10 A.M. I was at work in the office of Harari, Architects & Urban Planners, 26 Hillel Street, Jerusalem (hereafter "the office"). Quite casually, I happened to mention a plan proposed by Yehuda Hendel (hereafter "my father-in-law"), the owner of a hotel at 34 Hagiv'ah Street, Talpiyot (hereafter "the hotel"), to expand its kitchen and dining room and—this was the exciting part—to have me, a beginning architect, draw up the plans. A colleague in the office advised me not to start working on the project before looking at the old building plans, which needed to be taken into account. At once, Your Honor, I telephoned my father-in-law to ask for them. But he was not (at 10:15) in the hotel, and my sister-in-law (hereafter "Tehila"), his right-hand woman, had gone somewhere, too, without saying when she would be back. I could, of course, have waited for one of them to return, there being nothing urgent about it. But in my childish enthusiasm, and my fear that my father-in-law might withdraw his generous proposal and—quite sensibly—turn to someone more experienced, I hurried to phone the Arab maître d' (hereafter "Fu'ad"), to ask him for the key to the basement so that I might look for the plans. However, Your Honor (and this is my first circumstantial evidence), Fu'ad tried to put me off, even though our relationship—in part because Professor Rivlin (hereafter "my father") liked to chat with him in Arabic—was a good one. He said he didn't have the key and didn't know where it was. Since by now my desire to surprise my father-in-law with a plan—and my fear of being preempted—had made me impatient to proceed, I phoned my mother-in-law (hereafter "Naomi") and asked for her assistance. I knew, of course, Your Honor, that this woman (a good-natured but passive and somewhat empty-headed type) was far removed from the practical affairs of the hotel, even though she had lived in it for twenty years. Still, the affection she had shown me as a member of her fam-*

*ily encouraged me to think she would talk to Fu'ad. And in fact, she turned out to be familiar with the basement—in which, before air conditioners were installed in all the rooms, the hotel's central heating system had been located. Although she hadn't been down there for years, she knew there was a storage room and an "archive" that Tehila sometimes used. And so, Your Honor, childishly eager and well intentioned, I left the office and hurried to see Naomi.*

*Does the Court wish to know what the weather was like on that fateful day? What can that have to do with my testimony? And yet, since I wish to establish my credibility with the Court, I will withhold no information. In short, it was an extremely hot, dry day, thirty-eight degrees Celsius in the shade. In the neighborhood of Talpiyot, which borders on the desert, the glare of the Jerusalem sun was blinding. Even on my motor scooter, speeding to the hotel, I felt not a breath of fresh air. Fu'ad, who must have seen me coming, slipped away before I arrived. At first I thought of going straight to the archives (the existence of which, incidentally, I had never heard of until that day). But even though, Your Honor, a year of marriage to my wife had made me one of the family, I didn't wish to step out-of-bounds. And so I hurried to the third floor, where I found Naomi, lounging in a light bathrobe over her second or third breakfast delivered from the hotel kitchen.*

*Is it possible—the Court may wish to leave the question open—that this passive, dreamy woman had a vague suspicion that the archives in the basement involved more than just the past? Was this why she encouraged her curious son-in-law to investigate them?*

*Needless to say, none of this, O wisest mother, has any relevance to the accuracy of my testimony, which is obliged to stick to the facts. Still, I wonder to this day whether the pain and disappointment that my divorce caused this amiable woman led her to guess that she, too, had played a role in it.*

*She gave me a glass of fresh orange juice and hurriedly dressed before going downstairs to ask Fu'ad for the key—which, Your Honor, I might have eventually managed to find on my own, though not without difficulty.*

*We found Fu'ad outside in the hot sun, decorating the gazebo with flowers from his village. He was so annoyed that I had enlisted the owner's wife on my behalf that he barely looked at me. "I swear, Mrs. Hendel," he* said (I'm quoting from memory), "what's the rush? Mr. Hendel and Tehila will be back soon and will show Ofer everything."

Naomi, an easygoing woman, was upset by the refusal of an old employee to obey her. She felt she was not being taken seriously. "All I'm asking of you, Fu'ad," she told him in an injured tone, "is a key." But the well-bred and soft-spoken maître d' answered her brusquely. "I'm telling you, Mrs. Hendel," he said, "there is no key." But she wouldn't yield. It flattered her that I had come to ask for her help, and she wanted to prove herself worthy of it. "Fu'ad," she said, "what are you talking about? You always have the keys with you. Come on, take them out."

Looking back on it now, Ima, I can see that this tactful, middle-aged man, who never lost his composure, was on the verge of a breakdown. He fumbled in his pocket as though looking for something that wasn't there, then changed his mind and took out a large ring of keys. Before he could claim that the basement key wasn't on it, my mother-in-law reached for it in an unusually aggressive manner. Red as a beet, he let her have it, flinging it into her hand. "You Jews," he blurted (once again, I'm quoting from memory), "want to swallow everything in one gulp, and then you wonder why it sticks in your crow." (Yes, that I remember: he said "crow," not "craw.")

The large, heavy key ring, Your Honor, was then handed to me. I had no idea which key was the right one. Mrs. Hendel, exhausted from the heat, smiled triumphantly and retired to her room. I went to the basement. The door, it turned out, was unlocked.

I descended some stairs and came to a long corridor in which an old bicycle was leaning against a wall. Next to it were a bucket of dry whitewash and a torn tire. Farther on was a closet, padlocked with an old yellow lock inscribed with the number 999. I found a small key on the ring with the same number and opened the lock at once. The closet was full of files, arranged by subject. There were thank-you letters from guests, correspondences with the municipality, and the old building plans of the hotel, which was originally (did you know this, Galya?) designed to be a school building.

And that, Your Honor, would have been the end of it, with nothing gone amiss, had I not said to myself, "As long as I'm here, I may as well have a look at the actual foundations before studying the plans for them." And so I followed the corridor as far as a metal door. Although I assumed it was *locked, I tried the handle. It yielded slightly, as if bolted from within. From the ceiling came the gurgle of running water and a clatter of pots and pans, which told me I was where I wanted to be, right beneath the dining room and kitchen. I found a light switch and continued down the corridor until I came to a dark, cold space on my left, in which stood an old boiler that looked like a predatory fossil. The bones of its victims were scattered around it: an old baby carriage, a green tricycle, and a crib with some dusty toys lying on an oilcloth-covered mattress.*

*Well, my dear Your Honor, I stood there and thought that I should go get a stronger lightbulb and come back to take measurements. But as I was about to go upstairs, I said to myself: Just a minute. If everything is open apart from that metal door, what was the Arab making such a fuss about? And I took the key ring and went to the door, which was old except for the lock. It was a standard lock, like the ones I had seen in the hotel's rooms back in the days when I was courting my wife in them. Even though I now had the building plans, I was still annoyed at Fu'ad, who had always been so friendly and courteous. That's why I took the yellow master key and turned it in the lock. The door opened. I didn't enter the room, which was lit by a hidden lamp. I stood there flabbergasted for all of five seconds, whispered "Excuse me" to my father-in-law, and left.*

*The Court may ask how much anyone can see and understand in five seconds. My answer is, worlds, especially if you're familiar with the cast— the other member of which was a woman unaware of my presence. She lay sleeping, or daydreaming, in a fetal position, her face to the wall and her long, naked buttocks, which I never would have imagined could be so pure and virginal, exposed.*

*That was all. On the face of it, it wasn't much. I couldn't tell from the surprised look of my father-in-law, who was reading a newspaper with a cozy intimacy I didn't associate with him, whether I had intruded before or after. And perhaps it was neither. I didn't stick around long enough to find out. All I wanted to do, Ima, was to tell my wife, my life's companion, the soul of my soul, how shocked I was.*

### PART V

# The Judgment Seat

THE EVENINGS SPENT on either side of the border must have left you hungry if, after a sleepless night full of surprises, you head not for bed but for the kitchen, where you remove the cellophane from the containers that have been impatiently waiting for you on the marble counter and permanently renounce, in the crystalline light of a brightening morning, a Ramadan fast half-jestingly and half-wishfully partaken of. Your resentment of the housekeeper, who so flagrantly ignored your instructions just to clean and not to cook, has dissipated your resistance even to the leftovers cramming the refrigerator, though in truth you prefer the fresh dishes that have spent the night anticipating the return of the mysteriously vanished master of the house.

And yet, what effect can the master's orders have if the mistress of the house is so intimidated by her own housekeeper that she turns to jelly in her presence? And since you forgot to tell her that the judge would be gone for several days, the housekeeper quite naturally decided to spend her leisure time preparing the judge's favorite dishes. Still, you can't be averse to them yourself, if you now sit eating them while perusing her note, which says:

Aluminum foil
Oil
Bread crumbs
Detergent
Flour
Garlic.

Beside it lies another note from her, informing you that the new owners of your old apartment have a package for you that was mistakenly delivered to your old address.

As if to spare you the pain of it, an invitation to her son's wedding has been left in a less conspicuous, though still respectable, place behind the glass door of a bookcase. You slip the gilt-edged card back into its envelope as quickly as you can and let it fall on the shelf beneath the books in the hope that it will be forgotten there, for your envy does not skip even the marriage of the thin, dark boy who, when brought to your house by his mother, sat bashfully in a corner of the living room playing with Ofer's old toys or appeared timidly at the door of your study to ask for a pencil and paper.

To sleep or not to sleep . . .

At two o'clock there's a meeting of the appointments committee, at three you have office hours, and at four you give your introductory survey course, for which you still haven't prepared. Yet having turned day into night in an Arab village, why not do the same in a Jewish duplex, even if later that will mean turning another night into day, without a wife in your bed to solace your sleeplessness?

Turn out the bedroom light, then, brush your teeth, and disconnect the phone. Under a light blanket, to the sounds of the awakening street, you think with bemused longing of a brown-robed, plain-sandaled nun in a village church, unflinching before the stare of a solitary Jew thrust at midnight into the crowd of her admirers. As soft slumber weaves its threads around you, you join a chorus of four droning, white-haired men behind an ornamented altar.

Awakening before noon, you listen to the messages left while you slept and hear the voice of an attaché in a distant Asiatic embassy struggling to inform you that the judge's return has been delayed by a day. This time, too, the new possibilities waiting to take advantage of your solitude send a shiver of excitement down your spine.

## 2.

EVEN THOUGH THE professor was not sufficiently prepared, the class he taught was absorbing. Perhaps his hyper-wakefulness had made his

usually tightly structured lecture, held in a large hall, more spontaneous. More tolerant than usual of the many questions and criticisms
of his students, Jews and Arabs alike, he responded with an equanim-
ity that led to a lively discussion. Despite its subject, the treatment of
minorities in Egypt during the Second World War, he was forced,
contrary to his habit, to run five minutes past the bell.

Outside the large windows of the lecture hall, the light was gray. An
overcast sky held the promise of a rare summer rain. His class over,
Rivlin felt his high spirits flag before the tedious prospect of a loveless,
unsmiling apartment. So when he was approached by two female Arab
students, he did not immediately refer them to his office hours, but instead steered them gently back into the empty lecture room and asked
solicitously what they wanted. They were both, it turned out, from
Mansura and had attended the "seminar" in Samaher's bedroom, with
its story of the Algerians who beat the French at their own game of absurdity. Having concluded that an acquaintance with a senior, if
slightly eccentric, professor met on a pleasure jaunt to an Arab village
deserved to be cultivated, they took the liberty of informing him that
his "research assistant," far from resting on her laurels after his departure, had translated yet another story that same night.

The Orientalist was greatly amused by these two Near Eastern
Studies majors, who were happy to reveal their names and minor
fields while coyly inquiring about his final exam. Reassuring them
that it would not be difficult, he turned the conversation back to
Mansura and its inhabitants. They giggled as they plied him, each interrupting the other, with copious details about Samaher's and her
husband's families. Samaher's cousin Rashid, they confessed with a
blush, was a fine, devoted young man. But he was wrong about his
cousin's pregnancy, for if it wasn't real, why was she in bed? "She'll be
giving birth soon, Professor. That's why you need to give her the final
grade she deserves."

His M.A. student's devious, hoarsely excited voice buzzed in his
brain. Rather than return to an apartment in which only silence
awaited him, he headed for the library, free and well rested, to look for
Ahmed ed-Danaf, whose errant name had migrated from a medieval
story to the modern Algerian tale "The Poisoned Horse." Easily found

in an index to *One Thousand and One Nights*, ed-Danaf turned out to have been a far more engaging rogue than the morbidly confused horse poisoner of the amateur author Yassin bin Abbas. Although bin Abbas may have borrowed his hero's name with the intention of giving his readers a lively and picaresque narrative worthy of the great Hārūn ar-Rashīd, the dreary reality of the Sahara had dulled the gay rascality of old Baghdad and muted its human color. The unresolved inner conflict that weighed heavily on the author had burdened his story and his hero as well.

Now, in the university library, the glowworm of his night journey to the Palestinian Authority flickered again. While a gray sky subtly shaded the silhouettes of Haifa Bay, tracing a column of flame that rose from its refinery, the Orientalist whispered to himself:

"No."

Absolutely not.

Not even the pangs of love could make a man poison a horse, just as no woman would gaily toss a French baby out the window of a speeding train because she believed in miracles, and no judge, not even an Arab one, would trample justice by freeing the moonlight murderer of a French couple. Something else was at work here, deforming and barbarizing the imagination. Could it be, he wondered, a cautious hypothesis forming in his mind, that these folktales, written in the 1930s and 1940s, long before the Algerian War of Independence, were the first foreshadowings of an ongoing dialogue between Algeria and a French conqueror-seducer that was both the country's oppressor and its object of desire? It was now 170 years old, this jumble of temptation, promise, injustice, and affront that had wreaked havoc on the soul of the country and turned its inhabitants into local strangers.

Was this the spark of inspiration that might cast light on the senseless nighttime raids that ravaged remote villages? Could it be that, forty years after the last French colons had departed and left scorched earth behind them, they still existed as a phantasm in the Algerian brain? Did the Muslim fundamentalists and army death squads imagine as they brutally slaughtered women, children, and old people that these were not their kin or countrymen, flesh of their flesh, but

Frenchmen in shadowy disguise, their ancient, intimate enemy the *pieds noirs*, the black-footed colons of North Africa—who, though long returned to their home across the Mediterranean, their great farms abandoned, still haunted a native self that no longer knew what it was?

The unexpected rain trickling down the windows of the library reminded the worried Orientalist that the window of his study, next to which was his computer, had been left open. Hastily scribbling his reflections on a notepad and sticking it in his pocket before some recalcitrant fact or sober second thought could quench the spark, he left *One Thousand and One Nights* with its red leather binding and hurried off to his old apartment.

The rain had stopped, refreshing the wadi, which clung at its lower end to a fiery sunset burning out at the point where the horizon met the sea. Rivlin knew every mark and crack on the stairs to his old home, which descended between flowering hedges. Yet not even the memory of his children running happily up and down these stairs could arouse in him the slightest regret at having moved. It was one thing to be a guest, waxing ecstatic in the living room about the sea and the wadi in bloom, and quite another to have to live in the tiny bedrooms whose walls were moldy from the salt air.

The iron gate at the top of the stairs, a gate that had served as a largely symbolic defense of a house that could easily be broken into, was wide open. The couple that had bought the place did not seem concerned that a voyeur, detouring past the front door, might cross the little lawn and peer into the bedrooms or take someone on the terrace by surprise. The doorbell, which still had "Rivlin" written by it, no longer rang. In its place, he had to use the big brass clapper that he and Hagit had bought years ago in a Cairo bazaar and proudly hung by the entrance. Its luster, like hopes for peace with the Arab world, had faded with the years and been covered by the violent vines that scaled the house. Now, however, it was back, salvaged by the new tenants. Its chime, which Ofer had loved listening to, was still delicate despite its coat of verdigris.

The wife of the couple, whom he had met only once, at the closing of the sale at the lawyer's, recognized him at once. "It's about time,"

she scolded. "We were going to return the package to the post office."
She went to get it without inviting him inside, leaving him standing,
surprised and affronted, outside his old home. Cautiously he peered
inside, searching for some memory that could be retrieved together
with the package. Just then the woman's husband hurried out of a
room, not only more friendly than his good-looking wife, but eager to
show the old tenant the changes made in the course of tearing down
and rebuilding. Though not in the least interested, Rivlin mumbled a
perfunctory expression of interest and let himself be led through the
apartment, tagged after by two small children, in order to see how the
rooms had been redivided and a little den carved out for a huge television set. The man seemed anxious to convince him that he and his
wife had made wise and even witty decisions, as evidenced by a window installed for air in the bedroom closet that offered a surprise
view of the terrace—where his wife, having bequeathed the visitor to
her husband, had resumed her conversation with a younger and even
prettier woman than herself.

Rivlin felt a sudden pang of longing for the deep wadi. Before the
new owners could renovate that too, he exercised his right as a former tenant to stride to the terrace, step into the garden, and repossess,
standing silently with his back to the women, the view of the ravine
and the smooth, pink sea beyond, on which an illuminated ship
glided regally.

"At least here it's still beautiful . . . ," he murmured.

The wife took offense. "Here? As opposed to where?"

He ignored her and addressed the beautiful woman beside her.
"Whenever my mother used to come from Jerusalem," he reminisced,
"she would sit where you are now and say: 'Well, children, you've
made yourselves a little Paradise, but what will you do when some
wild beast comes charging out of it?'"

"You had a morbid mother," the wife snickered. She seemed to
have taken an inexplicable dislike to him, as if he had left something
incriminating behind in her house.

"What's morbid about it?" Undaunted, he spoke up for his
mother. "If only you knew how many scorpions I killed here and how

many snakes I chased behind that fence! And when all the dogs in the neighborhood begin to bark hysterically at ten at night in the middle of a heat wave, you can bet that your friendly neighbor, the wild boar at the bottom of the wadi, is out for a stroll...."

The unknown beauty, who had said nothing until now, brushed back a tousle of auburn hair from a swanlike neck and asked, with teasing curiosity,

"Snakes and scorpions aside, doesn't looking at this panorama make you regret that you sold the place?"

"Regret what?" An intimate question from a gorgeous woman never failed to excite him. "At my age, you want to be closer to heaven than to earth. All the natural beauty in the world, even this wadi's, can't make up for lack of comfort. We've moved to a new fifth-floor duplex with an elevator and even a bit of a view. My only regret is not having sold this place for more money...."

"I should think that, at your age, your future lies more in the earth," the wife said, pointing to a plot of ground behind the kitchen. Her hostility was so blatant that her embarrassed husband had to excuse it with some remark about gardening being good for the elderly.

"You call that a garden?" the former owner asked, gesturing indignantly at a lemon tree and two bushes he had planted beyond a small fence. "No, thank you. Just thinking of how I had to run around shutting five doors and ten windows each time we left the house for a few hours is enough to get over the garden, the sea, and all the rest of it."

"What were you so afraid of?" the wife asked sarcastically. "Your mother's imagination?"

He turned to look at her for the first time. "Imagination? After thirty years of living here, I can tell you how easy it is to break in at any hour of the day or night. Some burglar could be entering right now, even as we stand here peacefully talking...."

He irritably snatched the little package, whose return address told him it was destined for the garbage pail, and turned to go without another word. This made the husband feel so bad that he dragged the Orientalist to the bathroom and showed him that here, at least, everything had been left lovingly untouched. The floor, the sink, the faucets, the toilet seat, the biliously green-spotted tiles—nothing had changed.

## 3.

THE NEW DUPLEX, whose distance from the ground had not brought it appreciably closer to the sky, was burning every possible light. The young intelligence officer, who had arrived from deep in the mountains on a short leave, took after his mother: lights, in his opinion, were meant to be turned on and left on. Already in civilian clothes, he was showered, shaved, and combed, and off to a horror movie in Carmel Center. Distracted by something he knew he had forgotten, however, he went from room to room, trying to remember what it was, while politely asking his father to check whether he had run the washing machine correctly. Only after he was already out the door did it come to him. Someone had called from some embassy to say that the judge was returning from Vienna tomorrow night after all. She wanted to be picked up at the airport.

"Ima is coming tomorrow? Are you sure? Think!"

Tsakhi lapsed into meditative thought. "Yes," he said after a while. "Tomorrow. I'm sure of it, Abba."

And he was off.

Though glad to be getting back his warm-bodied and gentle-souled wife, Rivlin felt a twinge of disappointment at having his solitude cut short. As of tomorrow evening, he would again be living with his other half, who would hold him responsible for every word uttered, every sentence left unfinished, and not only every passing or hidden emotion not shared, but also every one not stated with precision. Sooner or later he would be obliged to confess his night out in the Palestinian Authority and to explain why an experienced, sober scholar like himself had to consign himself to the hands of his subject matter. And yet, if the returning traveler were not too weary, he might also test out his new theories on her nonacademic but perspicacious mind.

First, though, he would have to let Hagit tell him all she could about her trip. Besides listening to her complaints about the trying and tiresome time she had had, he would solicit from her the enjoyable moments, the little pleasures and unanticipated freedoms, experienced in the line of duty.

He was already counting the hours. The kiss that her smiling eyes would throw him as she came through Customs would more than compensate for the advantages of being alone. Tidying up the house for her, he picked up the young officer's underpants from the bathroom floor, piled the dirty dishes, and systematically turned out lights, prodigally switched on even in his study. From the study window he was astonished to see leaning on the railing of the terrace across the street, not the ghost of his mother, but a heavyset man dressed in black, who watched with a satisfied look as a noisy garbage truck came up the street.

Was he a relation? A visitor? Rivlin had never seen another person on the terrace. Could the old woman have died during his day off among the Arabs, or moved to an old-age home, making the man the new owner or tenant? Since this man's gaze, unlike her downward-directed one, also wandered up, Rivlin turned off the remaining lights and stood regarding him from the darkness. Yet now, slow and bulky, the ghost herself emerged from the apartment. She had put on makeup for the visitor and was now anxiously trying to catch the eye of a thin garbage collector running before his truck. He knew perfectly well, the garbage man did, that a gleefully tossed bag of refuse would sail down at him as soon as he raised his irritable eyes to the nagging old woman on the third floor.

The man by her side, though amused by her antics, rebuked her for them. But the ghost, loyal to the memory of Rivlin's mother, whose earthly plenipotentiary she was, did not care what anyone thought of her. Switching on a fluorescent light on the terrace, she spread the little table there with a cloth, a malevolent smile on her apparitional face.

Rivlin wondered who her visitor could be. A son? A nephew? Or just some passerby? At this time of the evening her shutters were usually closed, with not a ray of light shining through them. Now, on the brightly lit terrace, the two of them sat down to play a game of cards. The Orientalist, who had never in his life played anything with his mother, watched with an astonished envy.

After the death of his father, Rivlin had tried to get his mother to move to Haifa. He did not want to travel back and forth to Jerusalem anymore, as he had done during his father's long illness. But his mother refused to budge. She would not leave her apartment in the once fashionable triangle between King George, Ben-Yehuda, and Hillel Streets in order to move from the busy capital to the distant provinces in which her son and his family lived—not when she had seen from her kitchen window, scant days before the establishment of the State of Israel, two British soldiers killed and left to wallow in their blood. And after the UN Partition Resolution, three bombs had gone off on her street, damaging the walls of her apartment—to say nothing of what had happened during Israel's War of Independence, when an artillery shell had landed on the stairs while the besieged tenants huddled in the shelter. How could she be asked to forsake so strategically located a place, especially when it also looked out on the offices of the Histadrut, the national trade union, in which—or so she imagined—momentous decisions were made on a daily basis? Nothing could make her give up such an observation post for the dubious satisfaction of staring at a mountain or the sea.

After falling and breaking her pelvis and being confined to a wheelchair, however, his mother had no longer had any choice. Rivlin remembered how stirred he had felt when her ambulance from Jerusalem arrived at the nursing home and he helped an orderly wheel her on a gurney to her new room and put her in her bed. At last I have her where I want her, he had thought, opening her suitcase and hanging up her clothes. No more running to Jerusalem. Now I can take proper care of her.

Yet even from her wheelchair his mother had fought to maintain her autonomy. "You can take care of me all you want," she adjured him. "Just don't boss me around. I'll make my own decisions." Half-paralyzed, she had launched, as his sister had predicted she would, a desperate and calculated campaign of terror that twice forced him to move her to another home. At first, certain he was squandering her money, she had demanded a receipt for every expenditure. Then she had insisted that he schedule his visits in advance, as she did not want him coming when she was busy. "Busy with what?" Rivlin had asked with an incredulous smirk that she wiped from his face at once. "You know nothing about such things," she had retorted. "You never have known anything about them. And you don't have to know anything about them. Just tell me in advance when you're coming."

All through her years in Jerusalem, she had complained about how seldom he visited her. Now his visits annoyed her, as if she feared he would take advantage of her condition to gain control of her affairs. Sometimes, on his way home from the university after teaching a last class, he would drive to the nursing home and find her drowsing in her wheelchair under a leafy carob tree in the garden, aloof from the other residents, for whom she had little patience. Treading warily on the rotting carob pods, he approached her slumped form with its thin, reddish braid of hair, while thinking of the Russian student in Dostoyevsky's *Crime and Punishment* shivering with terror and excitement as he stared at the neck of the old moneylender who was fumbling in the Saint Petersburg twilight with his pretended surety, intricately wrapped by him to engage her as he fell on her with an ax. With a shudder, he'd reach out a gentle hand to touch his mother. Never surprised by him, she would turn around and complain, "How many times have I told you to let me know before you come?"

"Believe me, Professor Rivlin," a veteran social worker had said to him after his mother's fights with the staff had forced them to ask for her transfer, "she's an incredible woman. I've never seen anyone like her. How did you manage to come out normal?" "Can't you see that I didn't?" he answered, staring at the ground.

She didn't last long in her new place, either. The loss of her Jerusalem observation post gave her no peace, and she gave none to anyone around her, so that, although her condition remained stable during the last months of her life, she had to be shifted from place to place. Finding her bed empty, he would be told by a nurse, in response to his distraught query, that the cleverly programmed computer, having revealed that morning that she had overstayed her quota of days, had spotted an available bed elsewhere and even ordered an ambulance to take her there. It was this computer, which knew more than he did about his mother's illnesses, rights, and obligations, that whisked her from hospital to hospital with the greatest of ease during the last weeks of her life. Rivlin, who remembered the endless forms he had been made to fill out for each little medical test given his father, now found the health services of the Jewish state remarkably user-friendly.

And yet not even the steady diminution of his mother's faculties, which grew fewer with each new bed, nor the competent assistance, like an energetic younger brother's, of the ambulance-chasing, bill-paying computer, could make her company more bearable. Feeling as poorly compensated for her lost observation post by the large windows of the hospitals as by the small ones of the nursing homes, she groused about everything—most of all about her son. Three hours before breathing her last, she was still threatening to dispossess him if he did not take her back to Jerusalem.

He took her back—in a hearse. Hagit wanted to ask Ofer to come from Paris for the funeral: he had often inquired about his grandmother, with whom he seemed to have formed a secret bond in his weeks of living with her after leaving Galya. But Raya, Rivlin's sister, perhaps fearing that a postponement might give the deceased a chance to come back to life, didn't want to wait. Rivlin agreed with her. "Why make Ofer do all that traveling in midsemester?" he said. "Now that my mother is gone, we can go abroad with a clear conscience—and for more than a few days at a time. Let's go to Europe after the unveiling. We'll visit Ofer in Paris and tell him about everything."

Indeed, from the minute they landed in Paris, their son wanted to know all about his grandmother. Nervously, he probed them to find out what she had told them about his separation. Rivlin was dumbfounded. "You mean she knew more than we do?" he asked. "You told her things you kept from us?" His dead mother, now entombed with his son's secret, rose in his estimation.

"You still haven't told me," Ofer persisted. "It can't be that she said nothing."

"She told us we had to be more patient with you," Hagit replied. She herself had long ago given up hope of finding out any more from him.

"Patient?" The Parisian, though surprised, seemed satisfied. Gradually, his nervousness wore off. Whereas he had cloaked himself in a heavy mantle of secrecy after his divorce, he was now eager to show his private Paris to his parents during the three days of their visit. He brought them to his cooking academy in Montparnasse, took them for a tour of its classrooms and big kitchens, and introduced them to the Jewish architects for whom he worked as an unpaid apprentice. Rivlin wasn't sure he wanted to visit his son's attic room. Who knew what state it might be in? But Ofer insisted, and the room, they were happy to see, was pleasant and not at all untidy.

One evening they went to a concert in a church. Before it, Ofer took them to the Jewish Agency building, where he was being spelled that night by an alternate—a middle-aged former Israeli sculptor who made his wooden statues on the job. While Ofer escorted his mother upstairs to show her the grand old building, Rivlin turned to the burly wood-carver, who was burnishing the large, dark breasts of a female creation. What, he asked, would he do in case, God forbid, of a terrorist attack? The sculptor left the woman's breasts, leaned down to open a drawer, and pointed at a heavy old revolver. Far from inspiring confidence, this only worried Rivlin more.

## 4.

ON HIS WAY to the airport the next day, Rivlin thought of Fu'ad's remark, "You Jews are always coming and going. It will make you sick in the end." Not that he himself was going anywhere. He was merely dispatching others and picking them up. Although he had wanted to make sure he arrived before Hagit cleared customs and looked for a taxi, he had been detained by a long phone call from Ephraim Akri, who wanted to discuss his plans for the department. At first Rivlin thought his junior colleague was genuinely interested in his advice. However, it didn't take him long to realize that the shrewd Akri was merely asking him to approve decisions already made. It was his mode of operating. No wonder that, compared to the marathon sessions of the Rivlin era, the departmental meetings had grown short.

"No question about it, Ephraim," Rivlin declared, needling his junior colleague, "you're a true political animal. It's a pity your talent is wasted on a small department like ours."

"It's the only one I belong to," Akri replied, in what was either an apology or a complaint, and promised to send Rivlin a summary of their talk. Exasperated by the pedantic nature of the man he had appointed to succeed him, Rivlin decided to goad him with the story of his visit to Mansura. The Near Eastern department head was not only goaded, he was perturbed. "You let them leave you alone in a bedroom with a sick Arab woman, just like that?" he scolded his colleague, warning him to be more careful in the future. Although it was important, even imperative, to be forthcoming with Arabs, intimacy was to be avoided. It could only lead to misunderstanding.

Rivlin was in a hurry to get to the airport and in no mood to argue. Yet no sooner had he changed to a fresh shirt than the phone rang again. This time it was an insistent saleswoman who had to talk "to your wife and only your wife." When the Orientalist asked what about, he was told that it concerned a new vacuum cleaner of such remarkable capabilities that it was being marketed only to a select clientele. Though he had no time, he felt obliged to chastise the caller for her lack of feminist consciousness, there being many men in today's world—himself, for example—who used vacuum cleaners more often than their wives. The saleswoman was delighted to hear this. In that case, she said, she would gladly discuss the new appliance with him. It was a Kirby and could vacuum anything imaginable. Rivlin thanked her for the information, adding that he was in a hurry and that the vacuum cleaner they had worked perfectly well. "One more minute," the voice at the other end of the phone pleaded, hanging on to him for dear life. "I'm only asking you to listen. There's no obligation. This is a new concept in housecleaning, a revolution your wife will want to hear about. It's called a vacuum cleaner only because our language lacks a better word." "But my wife isn't here!" Rivlin exclaimed triumphantly. "I've been trying to tell you that I'm on my way to the airport to pick her up." "Wish her a happy homecoming for me," the dogged saleswoman congratulated him. "I hope she lands safely and gets some rest. We'll be at your house for a free demonstration the day after tomorrow. How about 8 P.M.?"

"Just make sure you phone first," Rivlin warned her. And before hanging up, he repeated: "Make sure you phone."

In the new airport terminal, amid the chirping of cell phones that welcomed the arriving passengers before they had time to arrive, the pervasive smell of burned coffee, and the plashing of fountains that serenaded the crowd waiting for the returnees (who, in the seconds between clearing customs and coming into sight, had their happy-to-be-home-again faces televised on a closed-circuit screen for the benefit of their welcomers)—here, and here alone, the professor from Haifa reflected, was the erotic epicenter of the Jewish state. The Jewish heart might throb in Jerusalem, and the Jewish brain might grow sharp or soft in Tel Aviv, but the passionate focus of Israeli life was here, in the going and the coming. It took an Arab of the old school, like Fu'ad, to realize that what might seem to be Jewish solidarity, as displayed by the tall man coming over to tell him that his wife was on her way, was only Jewish hyperactivity.

Rivlin wasn't sure whether this person, who had gently put down his suitcase, was the prosecutor or the defense counsel in the mysterious trial. He himself was already looking at his wife on the closed-circuit screen. Her few seconds there were enough to tell him that something was on her mind. He hurried to take her suitcase, hoping to learn, before they joined the patiently waiting man, what it was. "Not now," she whispered, giving him a grateful hug for his powers of observation. "There's a split decision to convict, and I'm the dissenting opinion. We'll talk about it later. Did you miss me? I missed you terribly. That man is the assistant district attorney of the Northern Circuit. We're giving him a ride to Haifa. I couldn't refuse. Don't ask him too many questions. Just be nice."

Her two colleagues on the bench had stayed an extra night in Vienna to take in an opera, while the chagrined defense counsel was on business in Germany. That left the prosecutor, now ensconced in the backseat of their car. Satisfied with the results of their journey, which had tipped the case against the defendant, an accused spy he had long been trying to nail, but aware that Judge Rivlin had doubts about the testimony given in the Asiatic republic, he chatted about other things. One of these, which he mentioned in a rather snide tone, was the opening of an exhibition of oils and watercolors by former Supreme Court Justice Granot, a stroke victim who had taken up painting.

"Granot has another show?" Hagit turned, upset, to her husband. "How come I didn't know? Why didn't you show me the invitation? You know I wouldn't want him to think I'd forgotten him."

"But what makes you think I saw an invitation?" Rivlin answered. "It must have been sent to your office and got lost."

He refrained from commenting in the presence of a stranger on the chronic disorder of his wife's desk, a consequence of her inability to throw anything away.

"If the exhibition is still on, we'll go to it tomorrow," Hagit comforted herself before lapsing into a drowsy silence. She looked gray and tired in the yellow light of the road. Rivlin fell silent, too. He felt the eyes of the prosecutor, who was sitting alertly behind him, drilling into his back, as if contemplating indicting him as well.

Back in their duplex, Hagit kicked off her shoes and stretched out on their bed as if to stamp it with the impressions of her trip while he emptied her suitcase out beside her, shut it again, and slipped it beneath the bed. Before hanging up her clothes, he examined them to see which items had paid their way and which had traveled as hitchhikers. He dumped a bag of his wife's underwear into the laundry basket and carried her toilet kit to the bathroom.

"You can arrange your bathroom things by yourself," he said.

"Of course."

"So who goes first, you or me?"

"I don't have much to tell. We went to a primitive place at the end of the world to listen to the fantasies of either a psychopath or a highly sophisticated liar. I honestly don't know whether someone in the district attorney's office or the Mossad thought they could put one over on us or they're so naive that they think the man is telling the truth."

"What did the other judges think?"

"They didn't see it that way. They've been sold an opera like the one they're going to in Vienna. Not that the defendant isn't a can of worms. But you don't put someone away for fifteen years without better proof."

"Fifteen years?" His curiosity was piqued.

"It could be. There are charges of treason."

"What kind of treason?"

"Never mind. There's not much I can tell you. I'd rather not talk about it. I'm fed up with the whole trial. And I feel bad for Granot. He must think I've abandoned him."

"You exaggerate. In his condition, he has other things to think about."

"Precisely in his condition! When you can't talk and can only think, every little thing becomes crucial. I know how much I mean to him. We have no choice. Tomorrow or the day after, we'll go to his exhibition and buy a painting."

"A painting of Granot's? What for?"

"He needs the money. Why do you think he's exhibiting? His wife never worked, he has no savings, and it's hard to cover an invalid's expenses on a pension, even a Supreme Court justice's."

"I'll think about it."

"There's nothing to think about. We'll go to the exhibition and buy a painting. Now tell me about yourself. Did the peace and quiet I gave you help you to make progress?"

"Conceptually, not on paper. Are you awake enough to listen to a strange story?"

"Of course."

He paced up and down by the bed, his excitement mounting as he described his night journey among the Arabs. Hagit, eyes half-shut, lay listening to every word. She did not appear to be overly perturbed by his story.

"So! I leave you alone for a couple of days and you run wild."

He smiled, relieved by her making a joke of it. "I suppose I did..."

"Did you at least enjoy it?"

"Enjoy it? Not exactly. But it may have sparked some new thoughts."

## 5.

REMOVING HIS GLASSES, he lay down beside her in the faint hope of making love. Not that he really wanted to, but they hadn't done it for a while, and he didn't want their bodies to grow rusty. Hagit, however, smiled wearily without responding. Although he did not feel greatly deprived, he made a point of wringing from her an acknowledgment of remissness.

They switched on the TV. Rivlin fell asleep watching a program. Awakening after midnight, he found Hagit's side of the bed empty and went to look for her. She was sitting in his study, composing the outline of her dissent.

"You don't think you can change one of their minds?"

She shook her head, sadly, not only because she took it hard when her opinion was not accepted, but because her dissent would not even be made public. He stroked her hair while glancing at the little card table on the terrace across the street. Some empty bottles of beer were still on it.

"She's started to live it up, my mother's ghost," he said, telling Hagit about the man who had come to play cards.

"Are you jealous?"

"Jealous?" It never ceased to amaze him how quickly she saw through him. "What an idea! But it does make me realize how hard the last year with her was. There wasn't a moment of good feeling or enjoyment."

She sighed. "And you tried so hard to be a loving son. It's sad when an old person feels wronged. That's why I don't want Granot to think I've abandoned him."

"But he never would."

"You're wrong. I know him. He's a noble man. That makes him highly sensitive. How could I not have seen the invitation?"

"You didn't see it because your desk is such a mess. You should let your typist arrange it for you."

"That's not her job."

"But she loves you. She'll do anything for you."

"Maybe. It's still not her job. Why don't we go together one Saturday and you help me?"


## 6.

THEY WERE THE only ones at the exhibition, which was being held in the gym of a community center. The direct light only emphasized how sadly out of place the little watercolors and oils were among the parallel bars and horses. Granot's first, surprise exhibition had been held two years previously, four years after his stroke. Long the chief justice of the Haifa District Court, he had suffered a stroke a few months after his appointment to the high court in Jerusalem and had had to return to his native city. For two years he was incommunicado, then he began to speak in striking colors and compositions; this led to an exhibition for which his many friends, as well as the entire legal community of Haifa, had turned out. The present show, his second, was more modest. The mute painter seemed to be in decline. His paintings were smaller, the colors more somber, the shapes more abstract. The distorted figures looked as if they were covered by a green mold.

Hagit strode silently around the room, stopping by each painting as though it had a deep significance. Her husband, having passed through the room quickly, stood asking the guard at the door how many visitors had seen the show. The answer was, Not many. The guard handed Rivlin a sheet of paper with the titles and prices of the works.

He scanned it quickly. The prices seemed high for an amateur painter, even an ex–Supreme Court justice. He wondered how they had been determined. Yet knowing that his wife had her heart set on buying something—either to make up for the missed opening or to help her first patron and guide—he looked for a reasonably priced item that he could live with and even pretend to like.

He stood in front of a small watercolor while his wife circulated reverently among the paintings as though renewing an old dialogue with the man who had been her mentor even after her appointment to the district court. The watercolor was fairly cheap and not too gloomy, with some vague figures, little dogs or jackals, surrounding the thin, black silhouette of a woman. It could be hung one day in the room of an imaginative grandchild, and meanwhile he did not think it would bother him. Calling Hagit over, he informed her that, if they had to buy something, this was what he liked best. Everything else was too ugly and depressing.

"This?" she marveled. "These poor little children being dragged down to Hell by a black devil?"

"Children? What children?" He was mystified. "Those are puppies or jackals. And where do you see a devil? Why would Granot paint devils? It's a woman walking her dogs."

The judge took off her glasses and stepped closer to the painting. Her eyes were soft and sorrowful.

"Well, if that's what you think and you like it, let's buy it. I suppose you've checked the price."

"Six hundred shekels."

"Not too bad. Maybe we should buy two."

"Are you out of your mind? Please, even one is too much. What are we, a social-work agency?"

"All right. Don't be angry. Write down the number and we'll pick it up when we visit him. Does it have a name?"

Rivlin consulted the sheet of paper.

"Yes. *The Return of the Little Ones.*"

In their building, by the door to the elevator, stood a tall man with a black ponytail. For a moment, his heart pounding, Rivlin thought it was Galya's new husband, come to ask them about her first marriage. But it was not the bird-faced man who had told him confidently in the garden of the hotel that he knew "everything." It was a salesman, sent to demonstrate, "with no obligation," the remarkable vacuum cleaner, which stood by his side like a faithful dog.

"But I specifically said you were to call first," Rivlin protested. "You promised."

The man with the ponytail looked crestfallen. He had been misled. He had come all the way from Tel Aviv on the understanding that he would be welcome. He spread imploring arms. He was asking for only half an hour of their time, with "no obligation at all." They shouldn't put it off another day, because the price of the vacuum cleaner kept rising.

"Yes, and I suppose you're almost out of stock," Rivlin taunted him. But it was already too late, because his wife had taken pity on the man and invited him up to their apartment.

Though polite, the salesman projected a quiet authority. Informing them that, despite his hippie-style ponytail, he was a reliable type, an ex–Border Guard officer, he proceeded to tell them about the appliance's incredible success, not just in Israel, but throughout the Middle East. He had even sold a Kirby to a princess of the Hashemite royal house in Jordan. If they would kindly allow him to rearrange their living-room chairs, they could sit back and watch him demonstrate. The appliance, American-made, was called a vacuum cleaner only for lack of a better word. Its metallic gray showed that it was made from the same materials used in intercontinental missiles. Although this might sound like a stretch, it was true. He had documents to prove it. Take this hose, for example, which emptied the dirt into that container. You could crinkle it—crush it—crunch it with all your might, as he was doing now. Just look how it sprang back to its original shape, as only a noble metal could!

Rivlin, growing impatient, cast a reproachful look at his wife, who looked utterly tranquil.

"Just give me half an hour of your time," the salesman said. "There's no obligation. Say 'stop' and I'll stop. You see, you have a nice, neat house. As far as you and maybe even your guests are concerned, it's as clean as it needs to be. But our Kirby here isn't satisfied with outward appearances. It wants the full, unadulterated truth, as befits folks like you. Excuse me, but may I ask what your work is?"

"I teach at the university," Rivlin murmured rancorously. "And my wife is a district judge."

The salesman, accustomed to Hashemite princesses, inclined his head respectfully and whipped out of his valise an array of odd attachments that hooked up to one another in complicated but easy-to-grasp ways. These were designed, he said, to penetrate the most inaccessible places, from which they extracted hidden dirt that lesser machines never reached: crumbs of food in the pockets of armchairs and under sofas, dried leaves and dead insects rotting in the grooves of sliding doors and stuck to ceilings and curtain rods, dust between the lines of books or congealed under mattresses in revolting lint balls.

The judge glanced at her husband.

The salesman now swung into action. Inserting a thin, round pad into the vacuum cleaner, he ran the machine over the spotless crannies of their living room. He kept this up at length, changing the pads frequently before arranging them in a gray alluvial fan at the hastily withdrawn feet of the duplex's tenants. Just look at the filth masquerading as cleanliness that the Kirby had unmasked! "You can imagine," he said, "what your grandchildren must leave behind after they've been here for the weekend!"

Rivlin inched closer to his wife, feeling her warmth. He could feel old age creeping up on them both.

The ponytailed salesman mixed water and a fragrance in a small container and sprayed the couches with an aerosol attachment. Next he vacuumed the curtains and polished the parquet floor and asked to go upstairs to the bedroom. There, running the talented appliance over the bedspread and skimming the noduled mattress with its gleaming hulk, he removed from it yet another pad caked with a strange, white powder—the remains, he explained, of invidiously invisible mattress worms.

Rivlin glared at his wife, who seemed overcome by an inexplicable sorrow. Invited by the salesman to try out the machine and to take apart and put together its easy-as-pie components, she smiled demurely and volunteered her husband—who was soon vying to prove that he was as capable as the Hashemite royal house.

The salesman lauded the Orientalist's quick grasp.

"Maybe you should hire him as your assistant," Hagit suggested.

An hour later, as the ex–Border Patrol officer was repacking his equipment prior to departing, Rivlin told him morosely:

"All right. We understand the principle. We'll think about it. But I want you to know that I'm devastated, because you've shown me that my home, which I always took to be clean, is a repository of filth. In the end we'll have no choice but to spend a fortune on a machine that we'll never use."

"If you buy it," the salesman reasoned, "why shouldn't you use it?" Yet judging by his sly smile, such things had been known to happen.


7.

ON A QUIET Saturday morning, in a modest apartment, shaded by pine trees, whose living room was lined with books that no one read anymore, a paralyzed man sat silently in a wheelchair. Slender and erect, he wore an old blue suit with a red bow tie that was awry on his neck. Although the whites of his eyes had yellowed and faded, their blue pupils still shone with the bright chivalry of a judge who, years ago, had been compelled by moral scruples to take a purely fatherly and jurisprudential interest in a young intern with whom he had fallen in love. Even after her appointment to district judge, he had played the role of a stern teacher entrusted with her professional supervision. Now, in the methodical spirit of the German Jewry he sprang from, several low coffee tables, placed between a couch and some chairs, were set with refreshments. There were little dishes with squares of chocolate; silver bowls full of peanuts, pretzels, and petit fours; and, on an antique plate in the center of the table, a raisin cake sliced into quarters with a dollop of whipped cream by each piece. What you saw was what you got. Freedom of choice was coffee or tea.

Hagit, her cheeks hot, felt her heart go out to the old judge. While giving his veiny arm a squeeze, she seemed, in her distress at being a judicial minority of one, more in need of encouragement than he was. The former Supreme Court justice, however, though raising a yearning head toward her, could only move his lips sorrowfully, as if to say, Now, my dear friend, you're on your own. All you can do is remember all that I've told you, because I will never say anything more.

This left the conversation to Granot's wife, a slender, aristocratic woman of Yemenite extraction who had spent the last fifty years so immersed in Germanic kultur that—true freedom lying in obedience to the *kategorischer Imperativ*—she had practically become a dark-skinned German Jewess herself, though one tinkling with the antique silver Yemenite jewelry adorning her meticulous clothes. Refusing to be disheartened by her husband's stroke, she had taken it upon herself to represent him and his opinions to the world and had even begun to talk with his old voice, including a trace of a German accent. Now, she was telling her visitors about the painting they had acquired at its full, undiscounted price.

"You, Professor, see puppies or jackals, and your wife sees little children. You think you are looking at a sad woman in black, and your wife thinks it's a grotesque devil.... You never said it was grotesque? Pardon me.... Well, dear friends, the truth lies halfway between you.

Granot intended to paint children, not puppies. But what makes you think, Mrs. Rivlin, that they're being led by a devil? Really, I'm surprised at you. What would a devil be doing here? It's their natural mother, a quietly tragic woman who has gathered her children from all over the world in order to bring them home. That's why the painting is called *The Return of the Little Ones.*"

The paralyzed judge hung on the words of the woman speaking in his voice.

"Granot painted this wonderful work a year ago. Do you remember? You got out of bed that morning with the whole thing in your head. By noon the painting was finished. And it came out just as you wanted it to, didn't it? That's why it's so moving and well done. Our friends have fallen in love with it and wish to buy it. Well, what do you say? Shall we let them have it?"

The Supreme Court justice tried spreading his hands in a vague gesture.

"You see?" the Yemenite told him. "What a pity you've stopped painting this past year."

"He's stopped painting?" Hagit exclaimed sadly. Her gaze clung steadfastly to the old judge's wide-open blue eyes, which seemed unable to fathom why his old intern looked so troubled.

"Yes, yes," the woman chided, her German accent growing stronger. "Granot has stopped painting. He just sits all day and does nothing. He makes no use of his time. Isn't that so, Granot? You've become a frightful idler. That's very bad. All day he sits looking at me instead of at his easel."

A heartbreakingly guilty smile creased the silent judge's face. Honest to a fault, he nodded to confirm his wife's verdict while his eyes filled with large tears.

But the woman just went on chastising him. "Paint, don't cry! Don't you see how everyone loves your paintings?"

Back in their car, Hagit laid the unframed painting in the back. "This a good time to put me to work," Rivlin told her. "I'm in the mood to go to the courthouse and clean out your drawers. We can't afford any more missed invitations."

Yet no prospect seemed more dreadful to Hagit than having to go through her drawers, and her husband's eagerness only heightened her reluctance.

"Next weekend," she said, with a smile, as if she were doing him a favor. "Won't you be in the mood next weekend?"

## 8.

THAT TUESDAY, midway through his introductory survey course in the large hall whose very air seemed jaundiced by long hours of lectures, the classroom front door opened slowly, and in came Samaher, wearing a black dress embroidered with little flowers and a white scarf wrapped around her head and shoulders.

Well, well, Rivlin thought with a streak of meanness: the pregnancy that never was is over. He watched his "research assistant" take a seat, her sudden appearance causing a stir among the Arab students, not a few of whom were her friends or relations. Had she recovered from her illness or simply run away from her mother?

She waited patiently, after the lecture, for him to finish talking to the last student, then stepped up to inform him, rather ceremoniously, that she had more material for him. Even though the room was empty, she spoke in secretive tones, as if the subject were not amateur North African writing but a dangerous narcotic.

Rivlin regarded the slender figure. Gently but unsparingly, he asked:

"Well, Samaher. Is this the end of your pregnancy?"

She shrugged. "So it seems...." She declined to be more explicit, though her hand trembled as it gripped the edge of the lecture podium.

He felt a wave of pity for this Arab girl who was struggling to get her degree. "The main thing," he said, patting her shoulder, "is that you're back on your feet."

He pictured them, delicate, wriggling beneath her blanket as excitedly as a floating French baby.

"For the time being, Professor." She sighed glumly, unwilling to rule out future indispositions.

"Why just for the time being?" he asked sharply, reaching to take what she had brought him. "You've been sick long enough."

This time too, however, there was nothing very material about his Arab student's material. The new story, it turned out, existed only as a fever in her brain. She had read it with such excitement that she hadn't bothered to summarize it in her notebook, because she had said to herself, Hey, Samaher, this is an important story, really special, just the thing for your professor's research. Even Dr. Suissa had underlined it heavily, though his pencil marks had grown blurry from so much photocopying.

Of the stalwart bride who wrestled horses only the burning eyes, their sadness deepened by her mysterious illness, now remained.

"Then you understand what I'm looking for?"

"I think so."

"Tell me."

She gave a start, as if he were going to examine and grade her right now in the empty lecture hall:

"Maybe...I thought you wanted to find out, Professor...I mean...how it happened that the Algerian people, who suffered so much from the French, began to torture themselves...that is, to kill each other...just like that, for no reason..."

Although he had already realized it back when she was a first-year student, Rivlin had forgotten that she was really quite bright. The lecture hall was empty. It was 6:40 P.M. Soon it would be dark, and the campus would be swallowed by the shadows creeping out of the forests of the Carmel.

"But what's so special about this particular story?" he demanded, debating whether to listen to it now.

"What's special is that it's disguised. I mean, it's a story written by a woman, maybe even a young one, but signed by a man, the author. You can tell it by the style, the imagination, the feeling. That poor lecturer from Jerusalem knew it, too."

"Dr. Suissa."

"Yes, Suissa. I'm telling you, Professor Rivlin, it's a shame about him, because he was a special person, maybe really a genius—a Jew who grasped us Arabs from the inside, the way we are, without fancy

explanations. That's rare. At first I didn't understand why he wrote in
the margin that the author was a woman in disguise. But when I finished reading the story, I said, Of course! Only a woman could write
and feel such things. I can't stand thinking of the way he died, that
Suissa. Believe me, if he were alive I'd go to Jerusalem just to thank
him. I'd say, 'Thank you, Doctor, for understanding the Arab soul so
well.'"

The Orientalist felt a twinge of envy. "Well, Samaher," he snapped,
"now you know whom your Palestinians killed."

She winced at his unexpected outburst. "But what can I do about
it, Professor?" she answered stubbornly. "Every man has his fate...."

## 9.

SAMAHER WANTED TO tell him the story right away, while it was still
fresh in her mind. Although he was impatient to get home to Hagit,
who was waiting to eat supper with him, Rivlin, standing in the large
lecture hall, agreed to listen to a digest of it. Just then, however, two
Druze cleaning women entered the room with mops and sloshing
buckets of water. He had no choice but to take his excited student and
her story to his office.

They were the only ones in the elevator. Early shadows flitted along
the corridor that connected the locked offices. Without bothering to
ask about her family or the village, or even about Rashid, Rivlin led
Samaher silently down the hallway, politely holding doors for her and
ushering her into his little room on the twenty-third floor. Seating
her across from him, by the window looking out on the Galilee, he
thought of her perfume on the night of her wedding and of Ephraim
Akri's warning. At least, he thought, smiling to himself, we're not in
her bedroom this time. As he debated switching on the ceiling light or
making do with the last sweet glow of the day that still clung to the
sky, his student pulled off her white scarf and with quick, pale fingers
gathered the hair that spilled out of it into a long ponytail.

"Are you all right?" he asked with a start.

She nodded. "Then wait for me here," he said, stepping out into the
dark corridor. Leaving the lights off, he used an old key to enter his

former room, now the new department head's. With a glance at Akri's grandsons, he dialed Hagit.

"Listen," he said. "I'll be a bit late. That Samaher has just turned up with something new. She wants to tell me about it now, orally, the way she did in the village. I've become like Harun ar-Rashid in *One Thousand and One Nights*: all I do is listen to stories. Do you think I should tell her to come another time? Why don't you begin eating and I'll be there in half an hour, three-quarters at the most. She's come all the way from her village, and she's not in such good shape.... What do you think?"

"I hate to eat without you."

"You could have your hair done while you're waiting."

"My hair? What does my hair have to do with it?"

"Don't you have an appointment at the hairdresser's tomorrow morning? I thought you might be less pressured if you went now. Weren't you thinking of trimming it in the back?"

"What on earth for?"

"Then you could work on your dissent."

This was already too much for her.

"Listen, Yochi. Stop finding things for me to do. Just tell me how much time you intend to spend with her."

"None at all. Half an hour. Three-quarters at most. She's slightly mad, just as I thought. That whole pregnancy was her mother's fantasy or manipulation. Honestly, I feel sorry for her."

"If you're feeling sorry for anyone besides yourself," his wife said, "it's not an experience to miss. But keep it short. I'm hungry and I'm tired and I'm feeling low. Get it over with and come cheer me up. And don't forget to give her my regards."

"Your regards?"

"Why not? I was at her wedding."

"If I start giving her your regards, we'll never be rid of her. But fine. On the contrary. She'll be happy. Don't worry, it won't take long."

From the corridor came a muffled but familiar-sounding whisper. Could it be the department head, coming to commune with his grandchildren? Rivlin hurried out, switching on the light in time to catch a glimpse of a small silhouette, child or puppy, that passed by in the darkness. But it was already gone.

Samaher had opened the window and was standing beside it. She was staring, not at the landscape of the Galilee, in which the lights of her village glittered too, but at the paved plaza at the tower's base. Her ponytail, dark and quiet, fell down her back.

"My wife sends you her regards. Do you remember her?"

His student's suffering face lit up with gratitude.

"Who could forget your wife, Professor? Whoever likes you has to like her twice as much."

He turned red and waved a hand. "All right, let's begin. And next time, please make an appointment. You may not realize it, but I'm a busy man. What's the new story called?"

"*Er-rakid u'immo et-tarsha.*"

"The Dancer and His Deaf Mother?"

"That's correct."

The shadows were thickening in the room. The idea, given him by Tedeschi and the translatoress, of seeking inspiration in the posthumous papers of the Jerusalem genius now seemed preposterous. But I'll see it through to the end, he thought resolutely. He flicked on the ceiling light, although the last beams of the sunset were still honey clear. It would be inadvisable for a Druze cleaning woman to enter the room and imagine things.

### The Dancer and His Deaf Mother

"I already told you, Professor, that this is a story written by a woman pretending to be a man. It's about this Frenchwoman named Colette. I think the author had to hide who she was because the story appeared in a semireligious magazine called *Al-Masjid al-Zhagir,*\* which also published, if you can believe it, sermons from mosques. So how does a story like this get into such a magazine? That beats me. Even the date of publication is given according to the Muslim religious calendar. But there's a teacher in our village who can turn Muslim

---

\* The Little Mosque.

dates into Christian ones, and he told me it's May 1948. Isn't that the period in which you're looking for—how did you put it?—the black hole of identity that spawned the Terror of the nineties? If I follow you, you want to prove that it didn't come from the Algerians them- selves, but from the French...."

"From the relationship between them."

"Right. From the relationship. It's as if, if I follow you, the French left this poison behind when they pulled out."

"Something like that." Recalling that Hagit was in a bad mood, which rarely happened with her, he wished his student would hurry up. "Get to the point, Samaher."

"I thought this story could help you with your research because it's more realistic than the others. There are no miracles or poisoned horses in it. It's understated. I had tears in my eyes when I read it. And my mother and grandmother cried, too, when I read it aloud to them."

"Come on, Samaher, give us the gist of it. We don't have all night."

"All right. The woman telling the story is French. She's fifty-five years old, born in Algeria at the end of the last century on a big colo- nial farm. She writes about this Muslim woman, a Berber, who was born deaf and dumb in a nearby village. The deaf and dumb girl's parents are poor, simple shepherds and don't know what to do with their daughter. And the farmer, Colette's father, is a really good- looking man who was an officer in the French army. One day he sees this deaf and dumb shepherdess with her goats and sheep and feels sorry for her, because she's beautiful and has a good heart, even though she keeps losing her flock. That's because she can't hear its bells or make anything but funny gurgling sounds. And so he goes to her parents and says, 'Let me have your deaf and dumb girl. She'll help my wife around the farm, and we'll teach her sign language.' You see, Professor, they'd just invented sign language in Europe.

"The parents, who have nine other children, like the idea. They say, 'Why not? Take her and do what you want with her. When it's time for her to marry, we'll lend a hand.'"

"Lend a hand?"

"That's what they say. Don't look at me, Professor, it's in the story. So the Frenchman takes her to his farm to help his wife. You see, she's a weak, tired woman, all worn out by the desert and the heat, and she's always thinking of her parents in France and going to visit them. Well, you can see what's coming, Professor, can't you? It's obvious. The deaf and dumb Berber girl learns sign language, and the French-man falls for her quiet beauty. But even though he's very smart and educated, he's not careful, and he gets her pregnant. And she—not only is she unable to tell her parents, she doesn't want to, because she's happy with the Frenchman.

"Colette describes how she has grown up with this Berber woman on the farm. The woman is half a sister and half a mother, and Co-lette has become attached to her. But in the meantime, there's this matter of the pregnancy. The Frenchman goes to the Berber parents and tells them that it's time to keep their promise and help their daughter get married. It can be with anyone, he says. She'll give birth in her husband's Berber village and then come back with her child to the farm. And that's what she does. They marry her off to this deaf and dumb shepherd from a far-off village, a good, simple man who doesn't know sign language and can't talk to a wife with a French ed-ucation, and she goes back to the farm when her baby is born."

"Is there much more to this?"

"It doesn't look so long in writing," Samaher apologized. "But it's very condensed. It gets longer when I tell it. Maybe that's because I add explanations. What should I do, Professor? Should I go on?"

"As long as we're here, you might as well. You say the story was published in a religious magazine in the 1940s?"

"Semireligious." His "research assistant" wanted to be precise. "But it's always like that. If a story has the right ending, it can be about anything."

Rivlin smiled with pleasure at her insight. Samaher, encouraged, whisked her ponytail around from her neck to her throat.

"So now she's his mistress." She took out an index card and glanced at it. "It's called a *maîtresse*. That's the French word. It's the one used in the story, maybe to avoid offending readers. Colette doesn't like the idea that her father has two wives, a French one who talks normally and a Muslim one who talks sign language. But at least she has the Berber woman's child, who's like a little brother to her. She takes him with her everywhere, even to visit friends on the nearby French farms. And it's the beginning of the century, and the latest dance craze is the cancan, and they bring this teacher from Paris to give them lessons."

## 10.

THERE WAS A scratch on the door. Timidly, it was opened. A dark-skinned boy of about ten with large, horn-rimmed glasses entered, head down, and threw himself into the M.A. student's lap.

"Who is this?" the astonished Orientalist asked.

"Don't you remember him?"

It was Rasheed, Ra'uda's son from Zababdeh, whose West Bank father had deprived him of an Israeli identity. Now, while the authorities considered his mother's request for repatriation, his uncle Rashid was accustoming him to Israel by taking him around in his minibus.

"Rashid is here too?"

"Of course. How else would I get back to the village?"

"Then why doesn't he say hello?" Rivlin, livening up, ran into the corridor to look for his driver-guide and found him in the gloom at the end of the corridor.

"Is that you, Rashid?"

"How are you, sir?" came the quiet answer.

"But who are you hiding from?"

"I'm not hiding, Professor. I just didn't want to get in the way."

"Let's have a look at you."

Rashid took a few slow steps. He was wearing horn-rims like his nephew's.

Rivlin had to laugh. "What are you doing with those glasses?"

Rashid laughed, too. "It's for the checkpoints. It makes them think we're father and son."

He stopped his clowning and put the glasses in his pocket. "How are you, Professor? I owe you an apology for that night in the Palestinian Authority."

"What for?"

"For the hundred shekels those punks took from you. They had no business doing it. Here, let me return it. . . ."

"*Bikafi, ya Rashid, shu is-siri? 'lrsh birja. Es-safar wara 'l-hudud kan fazi', ma bintasa. Lissa bitghani fii ir-rahbi.*\* By the way, how is she?"

"In the end she performed in Nablus and fainted."

"She did?" Rivlin felt cheated.

"I told you she was embarrassed in front of you. But she'll be back in the autumn. There's going to be a music and poetry festival in Ramallah. Nothing political or patriotic, just love songs. There'll be Jewish poets, too. Maybe she'll agree to faint for them. . . ."

"Wonderful. Now come and join us. Samaher hasn't finished her story, and I'm in a hurry."

*The End of the Story of the Dancer and His Deaf Mother*

"The French dance teacher," Samaher continued, picking up where she had left off while her cousin's nephew snuggled in her lap and Rashid stood behind her, lapping up every word, although he had already heard it, "realizes right away that the little boy, who looks Berber but acts French, has a great talent for dancing. As small as he is, he dances with the French girls and is the star. And then World War I breaks out. Even in Algeria, across the sea, everyone is worried because the French are getting killed like flies. The dance teacher, an 'easy come, easy go' type who only likes men, is so upset that he decides to return to Paris. First, though, he asks the French farmer and the deaf and dumb mother's permission to take the little Berber boy with him. It seems he's in love with him and wants to make him famous. And so the two of them go to France, and it's wartime and hard to stay in touch. Colette describes how sad the Berber woman is, even though her little boy is now a dancer in a Paris night club called *Er-Ra'iya il-Majnuna.*[†] She's not even comforted when they send her a photograph

---

\* Cut it out, Rashid! What are you doing? I'm not taking a penny back. That trip across the border was wonderful, unforgettable. That nun is still singing inside me.

[†] The Crazy Shepherd.

of him. His real father, the French farmer, keeps promising to bring
him home as soon as the war is over. But after the war there's a
drought, and he can't leave his farm with all its problems. And so the
years go by, and one year the farmer dies, and his wife sells the farm
and returns to France with Colette, and the poor deaf and dumb
Berber woman has to go back to her deaf and dumb husband."

Rivlin tried catching Rashid's eye. But Rashid, like an attentive
bodyguard, kept his eyes on Samaher. A worried expression Rivlin
had never seen before crossed his dark, friendly face.

"Meanwhile," Samaher continued, "Colette lives in France but keeps
thinking of her Berber half brother. She even starts going to dance clubs
to look for him. She wants so badly to find him that she doesn't have
time for a boyfriend. But as the years pass she begins to realize that they
may not recognize each other even if they meet. And so—we're almost
up to World War II—she goes back to Algeria to look for the deaf and
dumb mother, because she's sure she'll recognize her son. It's not easy to
find her village, and Colette discovers when she gets there that the
woman died from heartbreak a few years before. That leaves the old
deaf and dumb husband, a simple, good-natured man who's forgotten
whatever sign language his wife managed to teach him. But he's better
than nothing, and Colette takes him to France. Maybe, she thinks, he'll
recognize his son, the lost dancer.

"And so Colette returns to France with this gray, gloomy old Algerian in a big burnoose who can't talk. She doesn't even know
whether he knows what she wants from him. But he does his best, and
Colette puts him up in her house and makes the rounds with him of
the dance clubs and fancy cabarets. Everyone stares at this elegant
woman, who's no longer young, dragging along an old, deaf and
dumb Muslim in a white robe who can't hear the music and just looks
at the dancers. And now it's wartime again, and soon the Germans are
in Paris, and no one goes to nightclubs any more. Colette is about to
give up. But one day they're in this café and a dark, fat, unshaven
Frenchman of about forty sits down next to them and keeps looking
at them. The deaf and dumb villager, who has never spoken a word,
begins shaking all over. He puts out his hand and touches the Frenchman and says the first word of his life:

"*Ibni.*"

"*Ibni?*"

"Yes. 'My son.' And that's the end of the story."

"That's the end?" the Orientalist asked, disappointed.

"Yes. There isn't any more," Samaher said firmly. "The moral is obvious. You can dance all you want—you'll still never lose your true identity."

The worried Rashid smiled with relief. Once again, as in Samaher's bedroom, their forbidden love sent a chill down Rivlin's spine. He thought of Paris, and of the loneliness of his son, who would soon be starting his night shift.

"So if you think about it, Professor," his "research assistant" said, "you'll see why I was in a hurry to tell you about it. It's an important story about identity."

Rivlin had run out of patience. He glanced at his watch, rose, patted the boy on the head, and declared:

"Ladies and gentlemen, it's time to go home."

Rashid took charge of the timid boy, while whispering something to Samaher. Reminded, she took a paper from her purse and laid it on Rivlin's desk.

"This is for you, too, Professor. It's a poem, translated."

"Another one?"

She nodded almost dreamily.

He folded the page in four and stuck it in his shirt pocket as if it were a note from someone. Then, before Rashid could say anything more, he proceeded to the door to let the two young Arabs know the meeting was over.

At a traffic light on his way home (feeling guilty and concerned for his wife), he took out the poem and looked at it. It was in Rashid's clear, curly hand. Once more it gave proof that the poetry of the Arabs was much more sophisticated than their prose.


*I Am a Prize Given in Your Name*

I will never call you by a musical name.
I will volunteer no surprises.

Your nakedness is my desire,
Because in it my reveries attain their glory.
I am a prize given in your name.
Your navel makes the world vanish
Like a whirlpool on water.
Your face is armed indolence,
And I am a one-celled animal amid your breasts.
I will call you by a name I will never forget.
There are books that smell like rooms,
And I say to them: "Books,
You smell like rooms!"
There are poems like broken glass,
And I say: "Broken glass,
I have not found you a listener."
My dream flees to your bedroom,
But your room is nothing but a trick.
Listen, I may have to call you by a different name.
Damn it! What name can I call you by?
I'll make you a new prison,
But who will help me to escape?

## 11.

### A Draft for an Introduction

It was in the early 1990s that I began work on this study of tendencies and conflicts in the national identity of Algeria between 1930 and 1960. It forms a natural sequel to my previous book, *The Reconstruction of the New Algerian Identity through Municipalism*, which dealt with the early formation of an Algerian sense of self via the institutions of local government. After I had begun the present study, a bloody civil war broke out in Algeria in the wake of the cancellation of the 1991 election results; it is still going on as I write these lines.

A historian of the recent past must choose between two approaches. The first is to write as if the present did not exist—or, rather, under the assumption that any serious and responsible examination of the present will have to wait for historians of the future, who will analyze it with the help of reliable documents and appropriate scholarly tools. In other words, any attempt to explain the flux of a hotly contested present with a methodologically responsible study of the past is doomed to hasty conclusions that will distort our understanding not only of the present but of the past as well.

Hence the warning of Professor Uriel Hed, a great Orientalist of the last generation:

"Especially in our field, in which we deal largely with recent events, we must resist all temptation to blur the boundary between scholarship and political journalism. The historian must do everything to resist the siren song of 'contemporary relevance.'"

And yet there is also, it must be said, a second approach, one that the intellectually honest and morally sensitive historian cannot simply overlook. How, after all, can the serious student of the past, taken by surprise by extreme and unexpected developments (and the writer of these lines must admit that although he has been studying the history of North Africa for nearly three decades)—how can he simply shut his eyes and engage in his research as though nothing had happened? Inasmuch as all who believe in the continuity of historic process know that every turning point has had turning points before it, does he not have a scholarly obligation to search for the connection between the examined past and the experienced present?

But perhaps there is yet a third approach (a modest footpath, it may be, yet a real one) that can be taken by the scholar wishing to trace an arc from past to present—one that will, rainbowlike, connect these two poles of his interest.

I choose the image of the rainbow advisedly, for, as both a promise and a stimulus, evanescent yet spanning our field of vision, it represents the joining of the past to the dramatic events of the present.

What has happened to the identity of the Arabs, in which the Algerians share? This question, repeated interminably in cultural and political forums, has recently become a concern of academic research as well. What has kept the Arabs from a new ascendancy in which they might reclaim their proud place in history, a place held by them for hundreds of years? Why have they responded in such self-crippling ways to the challenges of technology and liberal democracy?

What is it that brought the well-known Syrian poet Nizar Kabani to publish his notorious 1995 poem, "When Will the Death of the Arabs Be Announced?" Despite the literary and political scandal caused by this work, and the subsequent attempts to ban the Syrian poet from Egypt, there were courageous Egyptian intellectuals who rallied to Kabani's defense.

These fundamental questions, which the body of my book refrains from discussing, stand to be illuminated in this introduction by the many-hued and perhaps chimerical rainbow that I propose to sketch from the past, the proper subject of my research, to the contemporary events that hover on its horizon.

Is the covert source of Arab society's inability to internalize the concept of personal freedom to be found in its attitude toward women? Does the early childhood identification of the Arab son with his docile, marginalized, and sometimes humiliated mother seriously damage his capacity to develop a sense of inner freedom as he matures? I believe that the identification with the passive female lies in the hidden depths of his construction of his masculinity, thus producing a binary passive-aggressive loop.

And why does the memory of colonialism continue to sear the Arab mind more than that of other Asian and African peoples with similar experiences? Is it the Arab world's relative proximity to the West, or the memory of its former dominance in part of Europe, i.e., in the "lost Paradise" of Andalusia, that makes the pain and frustration of a remembered colonialism so great?

An ethereal, chromodynamic, vanishing and reappearing rainbow may suggest a number of hypotheses....

## 12.

ON SATURDAY MORNING, the Russian immigrant guard was waiting as agreed for Judge Rivlin and her husband to appear by the iron gate of a small wing of the District Court. Instead of giving them the key, he told them that he intended to keep it and lock the gate behind them until summoned to let them out. Rivlin did not like this arrangement at all. "Suppose you fall asleep?" he asked. "What if one of our telephones isn't working or you have to go somewhere? Do you want us to spend the day locked up in the courthouse?" In the end, in violation of standard procedure, the guard reluctantly left the key with them, on the condition that they return it to him personally.

And even then, as they were climbing the worn white steps of the old building, once the headquarters of the Central Intelligence Division of the British Mandate in Palestine, the judge, perturbed by her husband's eagerness to reorganize her drawers, had second thoughts. Perhaps, she suggested, they should put it off for another week.

Rivlin did not even break stride. "Are you crazy?" he said. "*Now* you think of that?"

He hadn't been in the courthouse in two years. Not much had changed in the halls of justice. Yet he was curious to have a look at the new electronic system, with its security buzzers and hidden alarm buttons, which had recently been installed outside the judges' offices and beneath their desks. He took pleasure in using the code his wife had given him to unlock the door to her office. In fact, he announced with a flourish, the protection offered by such a system, if installed in his study, might give his hobbling book a push.

"I wouldn't bet on it," Hagit said.

Her dark, cold chambers had a new feature: the desk and chair, formerly on floor level, were now set up on a low podium. Despite her husband's populist protest, the judge seemed pleased by her new elevation. Raising the heavy blinds to let in some light, she pointed to some paintings on the walls, salvaged from their old apartment, whose absence Rivlin had not even noticed. At once he proposed hanging Granot's watercolor alongside them. It might encourage her colleagues on the bench to invest in the paralyzed ex–Supreme Court justice's work. But Hagit, her loyalty to her old patron notwithstanding, thought that neither the colors nor the subject of *The Return of the Little Ones* was appropriate for her office. Since it was her husband who liked it so much, she observed, he should hang it in his study, instead of letting it gather dust in their apartment.

She went to water the little flowerpots on the windowsill. Rivlin, eager to form a first impression of the chaos of paper awaiting his sound judgment and firm hand, mounted the podium and sat at her desk. As he had surmised, its drawers were bursting with documents and notices that should never have survived the day of their arrival.

"It simply can't be that you're unable to throw out a single piece of paper," he grumbled.

"But it can be," Hagit said, with a doleful smile. "And don't forget. You're here to make order, not to destroy."

"True order demands the courage to destroy," he replied, as though it were his credo. If she was going to haggle with him over every absurd item, they might as well forget about it now.

"But you have to promise to show me what you're throwing out . . ."

Having no intention of complying with her request, which would take more time than he had the patience to spend, he murmured a vague answer. He was, after all, not only a historian who understood something about documents, but also a loving and sympathetic husband who trusted himself to decide what his wife had accumulated unnecessarily.

He began by carefully collecting all her trial files and arranging them on a separate shelf. Then he pulled out the top drawer, dumped its contents on the cleared desk, gave its empty bottom a hearty thump to rid it of cobwebs and dust, slipped it noisily back into place, pushed the chair back, and invited his wife to have a seat, while planting an encouraging kiss on her neck. Positioning himself between her and the mountain of papers, he seized on an old protocol of an inconsequential meeting and handed it to her for consideration. No sooner had she taken off her distance glasses to read it than he quickly gathered an armful of commercial brochures, invitations to already-held conferences, professional newsletters from the Judges Guild, old updates of income-tax regulations, weekly court bulletins, and pointless communiqués from the police—all of which, crumpled and compacted, were made to vanish into a wastepaper basket hidden beneath the desk.

"What did you just throw out? Show me!"

"Nothing of value. Perfectly useless drivel that you've never read and never will."

"I want to see it."

He sighed and pulled a brochure from the basket. "You tell me," he said scornfully. "Do you need this? Are you in the market for a printer?"

She took the brightly colored advertisement, turned it wonderingly around, and let it drop into his clutches without a word.

It did not take long to eliminate, to his considerable joy and satisfaction, most of the papers on her desk. Only a few were returned to the drawer. Hagit, whose helpless aversion to systematic housecleaning forced her to cooperate, found herself the object of a tender love that gradually changed to an ancient desire. Her naked eyes, staring bewilderedly at the documents that he handed her to distract her from the demolition taking place beneath her nose, reminded him of the distant days when he had fallen in love with a young soldier and future law student and introduced her to his mentor in Jerusalem as a useful appendix to his doctorate. And so, before proceeding to the next drawer, he dropped uncontrollably to his knees, showered her with kisses and caresses, and whispered soft endearments while carefully licking her little earlobe. The thought of seducing his wife here in this room, in which so many anxious litigants had awaited her pronouncements, appealed to him greatly.

His kisses grew more expert and precise. Hagit's eyes shut. She gave her impassioned husband a limp but warm embrace, which encouraged him to press his campaign by opening several buttons on her blouse. All at once, however, he was pushed sharply away with his own words:

"Are you crazy? *Now?*"

"Why not?" The idea excited him. "The building is locked, and I have the key. Just think of the good time you'll have tomorrow, surrounded by all those lawyers, thinking of the good time you had today...."

## 13.

BUT GOOD TIMES that came from crossing boundaries and mixing worlds were not his wife's cup of tea, quite apart from the fact that ever since she'd returned from her judicial junket a minority of one, her self-confidence and good nature were gone. He was thus compelled to pull out the next drawer and dump its contents too on the desk, where they were revealed to consist largely of legal circulars and official announcements. It was hopeless to conduct a separate argument about each. The trick was to convince her, in a gentle appeal to reason, that each document had its neatly catalogued double in the court library across the street. And since there was no need of it there either, why not donate the entire collection to the law library of the university for the greater enlightenment of its students?

Hagit thought it over and agreed. She even found a large plastic bag into which to put everything.

They were down to the third drawer. Out of its dense maelstrom innocently fell the invitation to Granot's exhibition.

"Tell me," Rivlin sighed, shredding the invitation into little pieces, "what will you do when I die?"

"What?"

"Who will subdue the chaos for you then?"

To his surprise, his death announcements no longer alarmed her. "Don't worry. We'll find ourselves another husband."

"But suppose he's not as talented and efficient as this one."

"We'll train him. Never fear."

He smiled, taken aback by her fighting mood yet determined to maintain his posthumous reputation.

"And if your new husband protests, quite rightly, that it isn't his job, what will you do then? Ask your typist?"

"I told you. It's not her job either."

"Then what? You'll be lost."

"Why?" She refused to accept the bitter fate foreseen for her. "I can change. What makes you think I can't arrange my own desk? I only let you do it because I know how much you enjoy ordering me around."

"*I* enjoy ordering you around?" He laughed at the affront. "Really? What, exactly, do you think I get out of it? And who could order you around, even if he wanted to?"

His enthusiasm for the task waning, he hurried to the adjacent courtroom to look for another basket before their half-joking, half–deadly serious exchange could make him despair of the remaining papers on her desk.

He had always liked passing through the narrow archway that led from a corner of her office into the dark, windowless interior of the courtroom—which, though not large, had a solemn and dignified air. Going straight to the bench, which rose massively above the rest of the cool, dimly lit room, he surveyed from the heights of justice the dock, the witness stand, and the counsels' table while deliberating in the Sabbath silence what verdict to hand down. He groped for the newly installed alarm button at his feet. It was there, shiny and ready for use. He fingered it before picking up the old wastepaper basket that stood beside it.

"How do you like it up there?"

She was standing by the witness stand, her hair mussed, a bit childish-looking from his vantage point on high.

"There's definitely something appealing about being able to look down on everyone."

"But only if you're prepared to give them your undivided attention. That's something you're incapable of."

"It depends on who it is."

"Anyone. Everyone."

"I'd give my attention to any person who was getting at the real truth, not just at some dry legal definition of it. I have endless patience for the truth. That's why I can't stand being stranded halfway toward it, either in my research or in my life."

"Stranded how?"

"I'm thinking of Ofer."

"Why on earth Ofer?"

"I just am. He's only an example. We're stuck with no understanding of what happened..."

"It doesn't matter whether or not we understand. As long as he does."

"But he doesn't. That's what you can't accept. You'd rather delude yourself. If Ofer understood why his marriage fell apart, he'd be free. It's that which gives him no peace. I'm worried about him, not myself. But who knows? Maybe now something will change..."

He caught himself, conscious of having said too much.

"Why now?" The alerted judge regarded her husband from the witness stand.

"It was just a thought."

"No one 'just' thinks anything. What made you say 'now'?"

"I just did. It doesn't matter."

"Everything matters. What were you thinking of? Her father's death?"

"I suppose. That too."

"But how is Ofer supposed to know about it?"

"How? That's obvious. Everything gets known in the end."

"Tell the truth. Did you tell him?"

"I don't think so...I mean, I may have mentioned something without meaning to."

"No one mentions anything without meaning to. Stop being afraid and tell me honestly. It's not so terrible. Did you tell Ofer that Galya's father died? Yes or no?"

"I suppose I did."

"Even though we decided you wouldn't."

"You decided. I never agreed with you. Ask my sister. I have a right to my own opinion."

"Of course you have a right. But you also have an obligation to tell me what you do. I'm your partner. We have to trust each other."

"So I happened to forget."

"You didn't forget. And it didn't just happen. You hid it from me. Maybe you asked Ofer to hide it, too."

"I would never do that."

"Why not? If you were afraid I might know, you could have done anything. Watch it, Yochi. Tell the truth. I can easily call Ofer and ask him. Don't stoop to making me do that."

"Who's stooping?"

"Then tell me what you told him."

"I suppose I was afraid. I didn't want to upset you. Maybe it's time, once and for all, to understand why I have to fear you."

"You have to fear me? Who needs your fear? You should love me, not fear me. What good is being afraid? If you are, it's because you're a coward. And a liar to boot."

"Don't talk to me that way. I'm warning you. Watch what you say."

"But I can't help it. I'm so mad at you."

His eyes now accustomed to the dim light, he stared at the wife who was upping the stakes.

"You've lost all sense of proportion. What are you making such a big deal of this for?"

"I'll tell you for what. For the truth. And I want to know it. Stop trying to wriggle out of it and tell me exactly what you meant when you said just now that, after Hendel's death, something might change with Ofer. What does Ofer have to do with Hendel?"

"Nothing. I just thought that, since he sent her a condolence note, they might be in touch again."

"Who told you he sent her a condolence note?"

"Nobody told me. Stop cross-examining me. I assume that he sent her a note. It would have been appropriate."

"You told him to do it!"

"I didn't tell him anything. And suppose I did? He'd have done what he wanted to, anyway. If he sent her a note, that's what he felt like doing. It's his right. He's not heartless like you."

"Don't call me that."

"I'll call you what I want. You started this. What have I done to you?"

"Tell the truth. That's all I'm asking. The whole truth. It's not as hard as all that."

"I'm not a defendant in your court."

"It has nothing to do with my court. I'm your wife. I'm open with you about everything. And you keep things from me like a coward."

"I don't understand you. What right do you have to be angry with Ofer for sending Galya a condolence note when you know he's still neurotically attached to her?"

"Don't change the subject. It's not Ofer, it's you. I'm asking you plainly. What did you say to him, and what do you know, and what are you up to?"

"Who says I have to be up to anything to encourage him to send his ex-wife a condolence note? But I suppose that's the kind of reasoning I should expect from someone who can't even fry an egg without burning it."

"Stick to the point. You went to the hotel, against my advice, to pry, under the pretext of a condolence call."

"No, I didn't. I went there with no such thing in mind. If I mentioned the divorce to Galya, that's only natural. You, if anyone, should
know how torn up I was by it. So I happened to mention it, so what?
It's my right."

"Everything just happens with you. You happened to do this, you
happened to do that. But you didn't happen to do anything. You're a
lot more calculating than you let on. You're not really naive at all."

"Why should I be naive?"

"You shouldn't be. You should be honest. Above all with me. Now
tell me what you know. He sent her a letter. Did she answer it?"

"I don't know. Ask Ofer."

"I will. But now I'm asking you. Did Galya answer his condolence
letter? What do you know?"

"She probably did."

"What is 'probably'? What kind of answer is that? Speak the truth,
man! Let's have it. I'm your wife. What are you afraid of? Even if you
were foolish enough to try putting them in touch again, which could
only cause more pain, that's not a crime. The crime is not sharing it
with the one person who shares everything with you. Please, don't
force me to squeeze the truth out of you bit by bit. You know I can do
it. Be honest and open. Tell me what happened. What have you done?
What have you said?"

"All right. All right. Just stop threatening me as though I were a
traitor or a murderer."

"You are. You've betrayed me. You've murdered the trust between
us."

"Don't exaggerate. The truth is more mundane than you imagine."

"Then come down from there and talk to me. What are you doing
up there anyway? Since when does the defendant sit on the bench?"

## 14.

HE CAME DOWN from the bench, hurt and sulking. But he was not
going back to her office. He refused to have this out on her turf. They
would talk right here, in the courtroom. He stopped by the counsels'
table, keeping his distance from her, looking away. Although the dim

light seemed well suited to a confession, he wasn't sure how to work his way into it. Somehow, though, he did, tersely and concisely, even telling her about his second visit to the hotel, although carefully skipping over his imaginary illness.

She listened sternly, pale with anger.

"So you lied to me when you said you went to see the Agnon House."

"I didn't lie. I had always wanted to visit it with you. You refused because you were boycotting the neighborhood. So what are you saying—that I have to live with your sick, childish pride forever? And the Agnon House really is closed on Saturdays, which is why I decided to go to the hotel."

"Don't which-is-why me. Stop playing games. Nothing which-is-whyed you to go to the hotel. You did it on purpose, behind my back—and, worst of all, behind Ofer's. I would have thought you had enough self-respect not to beg that girl to tell you what nobody wants you to know, what you have no right to know. It's unbelievable what a pathetically stubborn man you are."

"Fine, so I'm stubborn about getting at the truth. I'm willing to make a fool of myself to do it, personally and intellectually. So what? What have I done wrong? Maybe that's the reason I've got as far as I have in life."

"But we're not putty in your hands to be twisted and molded for your pathetic investigations. We're talking about Ofer. He's your son. You owe him some respect. The minute you want something, you lose all inhibition."

"Listen. If this is the style you're going to continue in, we can stop now and go home."

"First you'll hear me out."

"You can talk to the wall, not to me. Leave me out of this. You've gone totally berserk. They should never have raised your desk and chair and given you all those buzzers. You're getting awfully high-and-mighty. Well, not with me! You can be like that with your murderers and rapists. I've had it. Just shut up! This is the last time I help you to do anything. I have to be crazy to be wasting my time on you. I want silence from now on! Do you hear me? Silence! Not one word."

She stepped up to him and grabbed his hand, her eyes boring into him, and slapped him hard in an outburst of fury.

Dumbfounded, he seized the hand that hit him and twisted it without letting go.

"Now calm down. What are you..."

"Let go of me! Do you hear me?"

"I'm not letting go until you calm down and say you're sorry."

"Never!"

She tried to straighten up. His iron grip kept her doubled over.

"Watch out, Yochi. You don't know what you're getting yourself into by assaulting a judge in a courtroom. I can press an alarm and have the police here in no time. You'll be locked up in solitary before you know it. It will be a week before you can open your lying mouth to anyone...."

"You'll have me locked up?" He laughed wildly. "It's you they'll lock up. Who hit who?"

"It doesn't matter. No one will believe a word you say."

"Then I might as well give them a reason to lock me up. Here's for the slap you gave me."

He yanked her up to give her a symbolic slap of his own. But he was too careful not to hurt her. It gave her a chance, with a savage litheness he had never seen in her, to snatch his bifocals and make off with them.

"Be careful!" he cried. "You know they're my only pair."

"Then stand still and don't move until the police come."

"You bully! Who do you think you are? This is your last warning before I ruin you. Give me back my glasses. They're my only pair."

"I'll give them back if you promise to stand still."

"What for? You swung at me."

"You deserved it. You're a liar and a coward. There's nothing I hate more."

"Be careful with my glasses. You're bending them. I don't have another pair. If anything happens to them, you're ruined for good. I'll smash your computer, and you'll be fired from your job."

"You can smash what you like. You're going to jail anyway."

"Hagit, I want my glasses!"

"Stand still and calm down."

"Bully! Give me my glasses!"

He lunged at her. She backed away, light on her feet and wild, gripping the bifocals with both hands.

Once (he had been told by her sister), after a fight with the father she loved, she had broken all his work tools.

"If you don't give me back my glasses this minute, I'm going to go to your office and destroy your files."

"You can destroy all you want. There are copies of everything."

"Aren't you ashamed to be dragging us down to this level?"

"I'm so mad at your lies that I don't care if I never see you again."

He lunged again, his vision blurred, and grabbed her hair. She screamed, struggling to free herself, bent his glasses into a shapeless mass, and smashed them against the witness stand. He bent to retrieve them while she fled to her chambers through the little door and locked it.

## 15.

WITH THE REMAINS of his bifocals jammed hopelessly into his pocket, he hurried out of the courthouse and locked the gate behind him. Although he was angry enough to keep her locked up for a while, he was afraid she might hit the alarm button and make a scene. And so, returning the key to the guard, he asked him to open the gate for the judge, who still had work to do, in half an hour. The Russian took the key with a sigh of relief. He would be sure, he said, to get to the gate on time. "But you've got blood on your face, Mister," he said. He brought Rivlin a small mirror in which the Orientalist saw a long, thin scratch on his forehead. As in his childhood fights with his sister, his first instinct was to run back and retaliate. Yet he no longer had the key, and the Russian was too curious about his cut. Forswearing immediate revenge, he walked to his car and drove carefully, through the quiet and blurry Sabbath streets, to his office at the university, the best place he could think of to abscond to. Barred even from reading his mail without his glasses, he took his old key, opened the new department head's office, and sank irately into the large, comfortable armchair purchased during his tenure.

Yet after a while, his worry for the trapped judge got the better of him. Phoning her chambers and getting no answer, he tried her at home. Her "hello," quiet and friendly as if nothing had happened, told him that—as usual—she had recovered surprisingly quickly. He hung up at once, knowing that a prolonged silence was his best weapon against someone for whom conversation was life itself.

She knew it was him, of course. Soon the stubborn ring of the telephone inside his closed office reached him from the other end of the corridor. Confident, however, that it would never occur to her that he had taken refuge in his old room, he relaxed and settled back in the armchair. The photographs of Akri's adorable grandchildren bothered him less without his glasses.

He sat silently for a few minutes. His naked eyes felt huge. It was the first time he could remember being unable to read or write. The freedom this gave him was both liberating and humiliating. Going over to the large window, he studied the reflection of his cut. Although superficial, it was a good one that would take time to heal. A powerful sense of lust, aroused by the unexpected wildness of the woman who had attacked him, vied with his ignominy and thirst for revenge. Oh yes, he thought. The punishment of silence will work best if I abscond for a while.

Before deciding which of his friends was most suitable for a Saturday morning visit, he phoned his old mentor to get some feedback on his latest scholarly thoughts. The sound of his voice was a cause for joy in Jerusalem. "Where have you been?" Hannah complained. "You only come to see us when Carlo is sick. As soon as he's well, we don't exist for you."

"Carlo is well?" Rivlin teased. "I don't believe it. There must be some mistake."

"Shhh!" Tedeschi chortled, joining in. "I'm not exactly well, but who has time to be sick when the Orientalists have latched onto my old Turks again? Ever since Stephen Jones and his gang at Oxford started spreading their new theory that all the faults of the Arabs can be blamed on Ottoman rule, the whole world has been beating a path to my door. I'm the latest academic sensation. My old book, the one you were examined on, has been rediscovered, and since nobody has the patience to read it, everybody wants me to tell them what's in it. Believe me, Yochi, it's your luck up there in Haifa that you haven't been taken over yet by the new historians who are out to prove that every venal idiot and corrupt ruler in the Arab world was a victim of imperialism. I swear, they should be called the ancient historians, not the new ones. Why stop with the Ottomans? Why not blame it on the Byzantines or the Romans? Listening to them makes me sorrier than ever that you've let the Terror in Algeria hold up that book of yours. Stop being so obsessed by it. If you could come to Jerusalem tomorrow, I'd take you—for your sake, not mine—to hear a paper I'm giving at a political-science conference. You'd see I've become a new historian myself. In fact, you'd understand that your Algerians aren't killing each other off, God forbid, because they're nasty-tempered, but because the Turks oppressed them three hundred years ago. So why get worked up over it, my friend?...Ha! They're good for a laugh, these brand-new Orientalists. How I adore Stephen Jones, that imbecile of an Englishman at St. Antony's with his high table. High twaddle! O men of lovely Oxford! Stick your pipes up your arses and tell us more...."

Rivlin burst into merry laughter. The old man hadn't sounded so youthfully wicked in ages.

"What time are you giving your paper?"

"At eight in the evening. Why? Is there any chance of your coming?"

"I would come just to hear you. I really do miss the two of you. But eight o'clock is too late for me. I've broken my glasses and can't drive at night."

"But why go back to Haifa at night?" Hannah Tedeschi asked, thrilled by his unexpected declaration of longing. "You can sleep at our place. It will give us a chance to chat. If you'd like, I'll even let you look at a few new translations. And don't worry, Carlo's nightly coughing fits have stopped...."

## 16.

HE ABSCONDED UNTIL three o'clock. Then, returning in a sullen mood to the duplex, he found the kitchen clean, the dishes washed, and the pots of food cold on the stove. He couldn't tell if Hagit had eaten lunch or was waiting for him. Making it clear that he wasn't ready to end the hostilities, he stepped briskly into the bedroom, grabbed a blanket and a pillow without stopping to see whether she was sleeping or merely resting in their bed, and went to lock himself up in his study. Placing the remains of his broken glasses by the computer, where they resembled a surrealistic totem meant to ward off a premature reconciliation, he pulled out the convertible couch, took off his pants and shoes, and glanced instinctively across the street looking for the old woman, who had recently lost weight.

The expected knock was not long in coming. It was followed by an invitation, in a clear but severe voice, to come out and "talk it all over." He didn't answer. Hands behind his head, he lay staring at the ceiling.

"Please. Don't sulk like a child." The door handle rattled. "Open the door and let's talk like two grown-ups. Believe me, I'm just as mad as you are. But I promise to control myself and explain calmly why you deserved what happened this morning. Come on out and listen. Don't be such a coward..."

He turned to the wall and pulled the pillow over his ears, feeling how, despite his determination to keep silent, one more well-aimed sentence might draw his answering fire. Yet her voice reached him anyway.

"I'm sorry about the glasses, but not about hitting you. Not at all. Come on out and I'll explain."

He shut his eyes tight.

"Don't play the martyr just because your glasses are bent a little. You'll have them straightened tomorrow. Meanwhile, you can find an old pair. Open the door and I'll help you to look for them...."

He grinned, carefully gauging the scratch on his forehead. For sure! She, who always had to ask him where everything was, was going to find his old glasses. He burrowed deeper into his silence, surprised to feel it growing stronger.

"I really am sorry about the glasses, even though it's no tragedy, neither for you nor for the Middle East, if you don't write anything for a day. But believe me, you had that slap coming. It was a moral act. And if you open the door now, you'll get another one..."

As though bitten by a snake, he leaped to his feet with fists clenched, only to restrain himself at the last moment. He was pleased to note how, in spite of everything, his love and desire for this woman were unabated.

Still, if he was to avoid the new quarrel that a response would provoke, which could only lead to their making up before he wanted to, he had to fortify his defenses. And so, switching on his computer, he made it play music so loud that it not only drowned out the woman behind the door but brought the ghost across the street scurrying to her terrace, from which, gray and unkempt, she turned uncertain eyes for the first time in his direction.

He drew the white lace curtain to shut her out. It was the same curtain that, laundered for his sister-in-law's visit, had made him think of a bridal gown. He turned down the music and stretched out on the bed again, shutting the eyes that were excused from intellectual effort. A thought was running through his head.

It's true, went the thought, that my love for this woman has only grown greater with the years. Each day it's more unconditional than the day before. But if I don't sometimes put my foot down, how is our melancholy son, our flesh-and-blood image who has followed in our footsteps and learned from our love and gone beyond it, ever going to hate the woman who wrecked his marriage, or at least get over her instead of just missing her more and more?...

He switched off the music, covered himself with the blanket, and made himself rest for a while before emerging, careful to avoid any trap. None had been set. Hagit had stepped out, leaving him a note that she had gone to the hairdresser's and that he absolutely must wait for her to return, since there was an important new development they had to talk about.

Her lacerated husband, however, who was finding the world not only blurry but increasingly remote, did not want to listen to one more reprimand or scolding, no matter how subtle or sweetened by a request for forgiveness. Putting on his sneakers, he scrawled in large, baleful letters:

"I've gone out for a couple of hours. Our plans for the movies tonight are off. I don't want to talk to you when I come back. Saying you're sorry won't help. I've just begun to fight."

He was soon strolling along the beach in a southerly direction. A golden halo enveloped the ancient crusaders' castle at Atlit on its spit of land sticking into the sea. Peace talks were out of the question after a single skirmish. A resolute campaign of silence was called for. Having been punished for his lies and concealments with a slap and the breaking of his glasses, he was now entitled—no, obliged—to stalk the truth that haunted him and stood in the way of his son. Just let anyone try to stop him. They might as well try to stop a ghost. This much freedom his fight with his wife had gained for him.

He came to a halt, his helpless eyes scanning the fuzzy sea. It was not only a father's right to investigate his offspring's suffering, it was his duty, he thought, turning back northward toward the lights on the Carmel. Youngsters, wet from the sea, walked on the sand. You'll see, Rivlin whispered to his beloved. I have the strength and the patience to search on in the dark. There will be no surrender.

He came home in high spirits to find her barefoot on the couch, conversing with her sister beyond the sea. Smiling at him brightly, she signaled him to wait so that they might discuss the new development. But however clear it was that in the long run his love for her would compel him to submit to her judicial logic, this was all the more reason to abscond a while longer while their war of silence went on.

He went to his study and locked the door. From behind it came first anger, then supplication. He knew he was scandalously jeopardizing something old and precious—and since his heart would never stop loving or desiring her, he chose to imagine that the revolving chair by his desk was a wheelchair and that, right arm rigid, leg limp, paralyzed torso twisted to one side, he was, like the former Supreme Court justice who loved her, too, the victim of a stroke.

Yet at midnight, on his way to the bathroom, discovering her wide-awake in her alcove by the library, in which she was working on her dissent without looking up at him, he realized that she, too, was now at war. He shivered. Yet it was too late to retreat. Without a word he returned to his study and crawled into bed, this time without locking the door.

## 17.

IN THE MORNING, he carefully laid the broken pieces of his bifocals on the optician's counter while inventing a story about their flying off his face and being run over by a car as he sprinted to cross a street against the light.

"By a minimum of two cars, I would say," the old optician remarked skeptically. Without asking permission, he swept the remnants of the tall tale into the trash. Testing Rivlin's eyes before ordering new lenses, he discovered that the Orientalist's vision, both near and far, had deteriorated.

Although the new bifocals would not be ready for several days, Rivlin turned down, in the spirit of the warpath, the offer of a temporary pair. This did not prevent him, however, from going to his office at the university to hunt for an old pair there. Yet the drawers of his desk were bare, and in his old office he was told by Ephraim Akri that there were no extra glasses there either. The new department head did, however, have a reserve pair of his own, which he offered to lend Rivlin in the event that the two Orientalists were similarly myopic. But the assistant professor's steel-rimmed spectacles only made the world even fuzzier. Content to renew his exemption from reading and writing, which left him only the option of conversation, he thanked his junior colleague, sank into his old armchair, and related the latest exploits of the Jerusalem polymath. If Tedeschi was joining the Turkish wing of the new historians, who blamed the present on the heroes of the past, he must indeed be physically and intellectually resurrected. Actually, Rivlin said, he was giving a paper tonight in Jerusalem. Should the assistant professor wish to drive this evening to the capital, he would find in the full professor, who was setting out by bus that afternoon, a willing passenger and debating partner for the trip home.

Although Akri was not inclined to absolve anyone in the Middle East of blame for anything, the temptation of having Rivlin to argue with all the way from Jerusalem to Haifa, perhaps even to win over to his side, was great. He therefore promised to do his best to attend the lecture, even though he rejected its conclusions a priori.

A lecture by Tedeschi was hardly a reason to travel to Jerusalem, let alone to sleep away from home. But before his inevitable reconciliation with his wife, Rivlin wished to intensify his silence and abscond more seriously—something best done in a far but familiar place where he could let others do the talking. What did he have to lose? He returned home, emptied his briefcase of its books and notes, replaced them with his toilet articles, some underwear, and a pair of pajamas, and left a new, dryly factual note on the table.

He had not taken a long bus ride in ages. Unable to read or even sleep, he let old and new thoughts run through his mind and arrived worn-out and glum, early that afternoon, at the political-science conference on Mount Scopus. He was greeted with warmth and raised eyebrows. Tedeschi, he was told, had been taken that morning to the emergency room. It was not at all clear whether he would be reading his paper.

"Back to the emergency room?" Rivlin exclaimed, with genuine sorrow. "And I came to Jerusalem especially to hear him! What's got into him? I can't believe the old fox is scared of political scientists."

The political scientists smiled at the barb. "You see," one of them said, "as bland and superficial as we're thought to be, we, too, can be scary. But I know we don't frighten you, Professor Rivlin. And if the old man isn't released in time, you surely won't let his audience down—not when you, his heir apparent, are with us and can take his place..."

Surprised and even stirred to be so matter-of-factly referred to in such terms, Rivlin nevertheless turned down the offer.

"Take his place? How? With what? Besides, my glasses are broken."

"Who needs glasses to speak? Do your usual thing. Tell us what you know and what you feel."

Now he was offended. "What do my feelings have to do with it? Is that what you take me for—an understudy with a gift of the gab?"

"Perish the thought! But anyone familiar with your publications knows that you keep busy in the kitchen even when you're not serving a meal. The smells of cooking tantalize us all. . . ."

"Tantalizing smells aren't scholarship. Precision and documentation are."

"But who cares about documents any more?" the political scientists protested. "Don't be an old fogy. People want provocative challenges, paradoxes. We've made a special effort to include your Middle East in the program tonight so as not to be accused of dealing in magnificent theories while leaving the mess on the ground to you. Honestly, Rivlin, if Tedeschi stays in the hospital, we'll be left with a bad hole in our after-dinner program."

"I'll think about it," he murmured. "But that's not a promise, so don't count on me."

He entered the auditorium, in which a rising young star from the University of the Negev was juggling some highly abstract and cerebral notions in order to arrive at some quite simple and self-evident conclusions. In the row ahead of him he noticed a small, middle-aged man in an old gray fedora busily taking notes. Stepping up to him after the lecture, Rivlin tapped him cautiously on the shoulder.

"Mr. Suissa?"

"Oh, Professor Rivlin. You're here too."

"But what are you doing here?"

"What am I doing? As always, listening and learning. What did you think of the lecture? Pretty deep, eh?"

"I hope you received the material I returned to you."

"Everything arrived in good shape. It's back on my son's desk."

"But why keep it on his desk? Give it to the National Library. There are things there that are too valuable to be lost."

"Why should anything be lost?" Suissa said. "Every word collected by my son of blessed memory is sacred to me. I'm taking good care of it. God willing, I hope to carry on with his work."

"How do you mean?"

"I've been studying the material he left behind, trying to understand what such a brilliant man—may God avenge his blood—was looking for. Have you noticed, Professor, that, besides all the journalism, those old Arabic newspapers of his have stories and poems, too?"

Rivlin smiled. "I didn't know you knew Arabic."

"I don't know it well, but I get the gist of it. I can make myself understood, too. I go slowly when I read and use good dictionaries. Just sitting at his desk makes me feel his inspiration and guidance. I use his computer too. Sometimes I even write on it. . . ."

"What sort of things?" Rivlin asked, with an anxious smile, as if the man in the gray fedora were about to steal his thunder.

"I type his old notes and manuscripts. I try to imagine where his thoughts were taking him."

"Interesting. Very interesting. Could you send some of it to me?"

"Right now it's all in the computer, Professor."

"Don't you have a printer?"

"It's old and doesn't work very well. Eventually, God willing. . ."

"Listen. Why don't I come to your place and read it on-screen?"

"It would be an honor and a pleasure, Professor. Anytime."

"How about now?" The idea of plugging into another ghost took the Orientalist's fancy. "Your place isn't far from here."

"But what about the next lecture? Don't you want to hear it?"

"Your interpretation of your son's ideas, Mr. Suissa, means more to me than any lecture."

Startled by the compliment, the man took off his hat, wiped his bald head, and declared:

"All right, Professor. Let's go. I'm with you."

The little apartment on the edge of the desert had been further colonized by the dead scholar's parents. The behavior of the widow and her two orphans, worrisomely anarchistic on his previous visit, now seemed deadly serious. The same little boy who had run affectionately to greet him stood somberly to the side, a dark skullcap on his head. Seeing Rivlin bend down to his baby brother crawling on the floor, he leaped to the infant's defense and sank his teeth into the visitor.

"It's nothing," Rivlin laughed, rubbing the bite. "Please, Mr. Suissa. Let the boy be."

But it was too late. The little grandfather was already chasing his grandson furiously around the room. Catching up with him by the bathroom door, he hit him hard. The boy threw down his skullcap and spit on it before vanishing into the bathroom without a word.

They went to the bedroom. With an almost religious reverence, the bereaved father conjured up the dead scholar's thoughts on the green screen of the old computer. Unfortunately, Rivlin apologized, he did not have his glasses. But if Mr. Suissa would remove his hat, which was hiding the screen, the Orientalist would try to follow while listening to a summary such as he was used to hearing from Samaher.

There was a touching innocence in the attempt of the North African–born Suissa senior, an uneducated and academically inexperienced official in the municipal waterworks department, to read the forever silenced mind of his dead son, which he believed he could fathom by virtue of his own paternity. He had ignored, Rivlin gathered, everything in the dead scholar's texts having to do with tribal and class conflict, French colonialism, and debates about Algerian identity, in order to concentrate—culling his evidence from the stories and poems alone—on popular attitudes toward Allah, the God of the desert who had come to curb the savagery and ignorance of its inhabitants.

The Orientalist, his senses piqued by the widow's clothes, which were scattered on the double bed beside the computer, was amazed to see how intense were the religious preoccupations of the stories that Samaher had read for their social content alone. He felt a sudden affection for this man, a religious Jew himself, who, no doubt unconsciously, was seeking to overcome his craving for vengeance by exploring the divinity in the Arab soul.

"Actually, Mr. Suissa," the Orientalist said, "I think you may be onto something. The strong religious underpinnings everywhere, even at the time of the secular Algerian revolution . . . it fits in well with my own line of thought."

He felt a touch as light as a caress.

The young widow, wearing a flowery dress, had come home. Overjoyed to find the professor there, she invited him to dine with them. Rivlin, however, begged off. He had come to Jerusalem not to work on her husband's material but to hear a lecture by an old and beloved mentor who had paid a visit to the emergency room that morning with no knowledge of when he would leave. As fascinating as he found her father-in-law's research, he had to be off. But he would surely come again soon.

Mr. Suissa, greatly cheered by Rivlin's interest, switched off the computer, put on his fedora, and offered to drive Rivlin to the hospital. Yet the young widow, chagrined by her visitor's hasty departure, insisted on driving him herself. Rudely pushing away the son who clung to her, pleading to come with them, she escorted Rivlin out of the apartment in the manner of someone who had long wanted to be alone with him.

## 18.

AND IN FACT Mrs. Suissa stopped the car after a few blocks, switched off the motor, and began lamenting, as though to an old friend, about how hard and complicated her life was. Ever since her husband's tragic death, his parents had refused to leave her alone. Not that he had been an easy man himself. Yet his great love for her had atoned for his stubborn principles. He adored her so much that he had been almost afraid to touch her.

Rivlin stared down. The young woman, a bleached blond with deeply tanned legs whose polished toenails fidgeted on the stilled pedals of the car, had a sharp, strange fragrance. The street, seen through the windshield, was dusty and gray. Had he absconded or merely been newly impounded? Was this trip to Jerusalem a liberation or just an aggravation? On that wonderful night with the Arab messenger, he had been made to vanish as though by a magic trick. But here, in Jerusalem, without his glasses or his car, who would be his magician?

Perhaps, the young Mrs. Suissa was saying unhappily, the professor knew of some job for her. It could even be in Haifa. Anything to get her away from the siege she was under. Could he, as a gesture to her husband, find her part-time work as a typist or a secretary in his department, something temporary? She wasn't asking for much. As a terror victim, she received a stipend from the Ministry of Defense. She could come to Haifa without the children and rent a room there. Once she was settled, she would bring them. But first she had to have a foothold, a position at the university. She wanted Professor Rivlin, as an admirer or at least an appreciator of her husband, to take her under his wing.

The tears welled in her eyes at the thought of the man who had adored her to the point of trepidation. Carried away by her emotion, she laid a soft hand on the aging Orientalist's knee, asking not only for advice and direction, but also for comfort and warmth. She was certain that here in Jerusalem, fenced in by her husband's parents, she would never find another man.

Rivlin glanced at his watch, unable to make out the time. He nodded and asked the young widow about her own parents.

Her father had died long ago. She and her mother did not get along. Her husband's parents, on the other hand, had been nice, considerate people until his terrible death had turned them into evil little hedgehogs.

"Hedgehogs?"

Yes. Little, black, prickly things who had moved in with her to keep her children from being exposed to bad influences. Especially hers. They were worried she might give up religion. That was why they sniffed after her everywhere, the two hedgehogs. She flashed Rivlin a charmingly mischievous smile at the image that had occurred to her before her eyes filled with little tears again.

He didn't need his glasses to see what an ingenue she was. Laying his hand lightly on hers as it rested on the steering wheel, he wondered what kind of wing she was looking for. Was it for a medium through which to contact the ghost of her husband—the young prodigy who, according to the Tedeschis, had sought in an original way to revive the old Orientalism that studied not documents, speeches, protocols, and pronouncements but the literature whose intricate language revealed the secretive Arab soul?

And yet if, by her own admission, this same prodigy had been reduced to adoring her from a safe distance, what, besides frustration, confusion, and neglect, could be expected from her? The tremor of desire he had felt was already gone. He would, he promised, see what he could do to help her, not just for her husband's sake, but for her own. But on one condition. He looked her in the eye. She must take the children with her. Children must never be abandoned.

Calmed by this, she gave him a long look and started the car. But to his annoyance, instead of dropping him off by the entrance to

Hadassah Hospital on Mount Scopus, she parked and got out with him, determined to join him on his visit to the emergency room. She wanted, she said, to say hello to Hannah Tedeschi and see how her husband was.

It took Rivlin a while, without his glasses in the bustle of the emergency room, to spot the illustrious polymath sitting on a little terrace in a thin smock, quietly staring at the Judean desert while awaiting the results of his tests.

"I come to Jerusalem especially to hear you lecture, Carlo, and look what you do to me!"

"But there's nothing wrong with me," Tedeschi said. "This morning, on our way to the conference, Hannah decided that as long as we were on Mount Scopus, she might as well bring me in for a checkup. Since then we've been stuck here. But never mind, I'll soon be released. You haven't missed a thing. Your bed is already made. You'll sleep over, and tomorrow I'll give the lecture they canceled tonight. You should have brought Hagit."

"Would you believe that I was asked to fill in for you tonight?"

Tedeschi was alarmed. "To talk about what?"

"About anything. I refused. You know me. I don't open my mouth without documentation."

"And quite rightly." Tedeschi regarded his old student fondly. "Never let these giddy conference organizers talk you into anything. So what if they have a hole in their program? It's not the end of the world. They can add another course to their dinner. But where are your glasses? Don't tell me you're wearing contacts."

"That will be the day!"

"And who is the young lady you've brought with you? Do I know her?"

"You should." Rivlin introduced Mrs. Suissa, who had been standing quietly by.

The old scholar jumped to his bare feet and embraced the young widow warmly, his white chest showing through the hospital smock. "So it's you!" he said delightedly. "Just yesterday I read another article of your husband's. For the first time I fully appreciated the depths he was exploring. I stand behind every word my wife has said about him.

His loss was not just yours, but Orientalism's. Wait and see. The Arabs will yet mourn for him, too."

## 19.

THE YOUNG WOMAN perked up. She looked radiantly at Rivlin, as though asking him whether she should add the Jerusalem polymath's wing to his own.

Just then the white curtain on the window was moved cautiously aside. It was swarthy-headed Ephraim Akri, peering in to ascertain whether he had found the right patient. "What an idiot I am!" Rivlin apologized. "I talked you into coming to Jerusalem and forgot to tell you that Carlo has canceled his appearance in favor of a one-night stand in the emergency room."

"I haven't canceled a thing," the old scholar protested, thrilled to have yet another Orientalist come from afar to pay his respects. "Don't be nasty, Yochanan. You have no right to judge me until you know what it's like to be throttled to death at night by your own breathing."

"Enough of that! Leave the man alone." The rebuke was Hannah Tedeschi's. She had just arrived, waving the results of her husband's tests and his release form.

Although many years had passed since Ephraim Akri's days as a teaching assistant in Jerusalem, he remained nervous and obsequious in the presence of his old teacher—who, for his part, had nothing but admiration for the religious department head's elegantly polished Arabic. Now, sure that the keys to his promotion lay more in Jerusalem than in Haifa, Akri asked to see the test results. Using the doctor's royal "we," he pronounced with relief:

"Thank God! We're on the borderline of danger, but not over it."

An ironic smile crossed the round, childlike face of the released patient as he rose to dress. When he spoke to Akri, who was now searching for his old teacher's pants and shoes, it was tenderly. "It would be a pity, Ephraim, seeing you've come all the way from Haifa, if you missed the lecture tomorrow. Even if you don't agree with my conclusions, you'll enjoy hearing how I reach them. And don't worry about a place to sleep, because we'll put you next to Rivlin. You can hold a midnight departmental meeting."

Rivlin took Hannah aside.

"That's fine with me. By all means take Akri home with you. He'll drive you in his car. I'm going into town to do some walking and thinking. You needn't worry about me. If I'm not back by ten, lock the door and go to sleep. I'll either have thrown in the towel and gone back to my courthouse in Haifa or found somewhere else to sleep in Jerusalem. If I stay and Carlo doesn't do an encore in the emergency room tomorrow, I'll be at the lecture, listening to every word."

And before she could argue or protest, he took his stiff old classmate, the translatoress of the Age of Ignorance, in his arms, gave her a hug and a kiss on each cheek, and bade her a conspiratorial adieu.

He made his way quickly past nurses and medical instruments, certain he could tell the healthy from the sick and locate the exit even without his bifocals. In his haste, he failed to notice the young widow, loath to be abandoned by her protector, running after him.

"Let me drive you," she implored.

"I'll take the bus. Your children are waiting for you." It came out sounding like a reprimand. "Just tell me what bus to take."

"Screw the goddamn bus!" she swore. "Who needs it?"

He felt her anger melting his resistance. "But I'm going to the other end of town," he said.

"Fine. I'll drive you."

Strapped into his seatbelt beside her, he let her talk while they crossed the city from north to south. Anxious to leave her before reaching the hotel, he pointed to the corner of a small street halfway up the rise to Talpiyot and said, "This is where I get off. Thanks a million."

Yet she wouldn't part with him. "Why on the corner? Tell me the house number. I'll bring you to the door."

"It's a short street," he demurred. "The number doesn't matter. I'm going to the old Agnon house. They've made it into a museum."

"A museum?" She grabbed at the opportunity. "Why don't I have a look at it?"

Without waiting for an answer, she turned into the street, parked by the gray old building with its small, barred windows, and got out to investigate. The museum, it appeared, was closed for the day. "Where to now?" she asked, as if she had become, like Rashid, his personal chauffeur. He gave her a hard look.

"Nowhere. I have a meeting right here. Now go home and stop worrying about me."

Overcoming her curiosity to know whom he was meeting in such an unlikely place, she nevertheless insisted on a peek at the Nobel Prize winner's backyard. The gate was open. Quickly she disappeared down a narrow path that led past garbage cans and tanks of cooking gas to a hedge of dusty bushes. A restless woman, Rivlin thought. How had her husband ever managed to concentrate? After a few minutes passed and she did not return, he went worriedly to look for her.

The small yard was empty. A large, rough concrete wall, covered with water pipes, blocked one end of it. Apart from a few patches of old, melancholy grass, the ground was paved with plain, cracked floor tiles. Suissa's widow was seated on a low fence, smoking a cigarette that wreathed her in sad blue smoke. He gave her a friendly nod but kept his distance. Without his glasses, she looked none too distinct. He inquired if she knew who Agnon was.

"Of course. Who doesn't?"

Cautiously he asked, "Have you ever read anything of his?"

She exhaled a large, perfect smoke ring that floated slowly in his direction. Yes. She had read something or other. Everyone had to in school.

"What story?" he persisted, as though quizzing a student. "What was it called?"

"You're asking me to remember now?" she replied, bemused. Since her husband's death, she had forgotten more important things than Agnon's stories. Her husband had liked Agnon. He had read him a lot. He had once even told her he saw a connection between some of his stories and Arab folklore.

"Agnon and the Arabs?" Rivlin chuckled, struck by the dead scholar's boldness. "But how can that be?"

She was sure her husband had talked about it. Agnon and the Arabs. The Arabs were always on his mind.

A mixed-up woman, too, Rivlin thought, still careful not to come too close to her. Her husband must also have been a little around the bend. But now, as if his homeless status were written all over him, she turned the tables and questioned him. Suppose the person he was supposed to meet didn't show up? Where would he go? Where would he eat and sleep? Dr. Hannah Tedeschi had enough on her hands without him.

Rivlin sought to reassure her. "Don't worry. No man is ever at his wit's end in the city he grew up in."

She took a last, deep drag of smoke and ground out her cigarette with the heel of a flimsy shoe. Her earrings tinkled as she stepped toward him, her glance challenging.

"Just tell me one more thing before I go, Professor. But honestly. Do you agree with Professor Tedeschi and his wife that my husband was a genius? Was his death really anyone's loss but mine?"

The shadow of a distant cloud, floating eastward toward the desert, darkened the Orientalist's face as he explained that although his own field was Near Eastern history rather than literature or philology, he thought Suissa had been a serious and original scholar.

"Maybe too original for his own good," she remarked bitterly, surprising Rivlin with the insight.

He put a hand on her shoulder. "But why ask me? Trust Hannah Tedeschi. She's a very well-read and critical person. It's hard to get her to say a good word about anyone. If she calls your husband a genius, believe her."

Despairingly, without removing his hand from her shoulder, she opened the top button of her dress. Above the ivory crevice of her breasts was the tattoo of a face, no larger than a large coin.

She followed his glance, her mouth childishly open in a half-contrite, half-provocative smile.

"I'm confused by everything I hear about him. I'm so upset that I wasn't nicer to him that I took a picture of him and had it tattooed over my heart. You'd think his parents would have been happy that I wanted to remember him on my own body. But no, they hit the ceiling. And my little boy is mad at me, too."

The Orientalist bent to examine the tattoo, which touched the swelling outline of a hidden breast. It was strange and frightening.

When he was done, Mrs. Suissa calmly rebuttoned her dress and re-stated her original appeal:

"That's why I'm asking you and others to think of me. Use your in-fluence. Because even if you didn't know him, you're benefiting from his material. Please, get me out of this goddamned city. If you're afraid that I'll be a nuisance in Haifa, find work for me at some col-lege up north. I don't care if it's in the boondocks. First I'll go by my-self. Then I'll bring the kids. Don't worry about it. I'll never find a man with those hedgehogs hanging around."

Was this, Rivlin wondered, the place he had wanted to abscond to? The ugly backyard of an author for whom the world's beauty existed only in language and human relationships? Confident that he was old and reputable enough to behave like his old mentor, who had em-braced with the naturalness of a father this confused woman blown out of orbit by the bomb that killed her husband, he felt her slender body relax as he promised to do his best. Even had she meant to in-vite him to a different adventure, she kept within bounds and did nothing more to tempt him.

## 20.

ALTHOUGH YOU WILL never surrender your love, this is not the time to surrender to it. You know how hurtful your absconding is and how much resentment is building up against you. But if that's what is needed to free the stubborn heart that is chained to the place you are in now, you're prepared to add still more to the injury.

The daylight slowly abandons the desert, casting copper sparkles on its way to the Dead Sea. You stroll through the hilly neighborhood, in no particular hurry, even though the hotel summons you with its unanswered questions. You bide your time and wait for the twilight to turn to darkness. Only then will you make your third visit, which must remain forever sealed in your heart.

Is there any reason to hope that the truth that has eluded you in daylight will reveal itself by night? Is the old promise of a room still good even though the promiser is gone?

You approach in a roundabout way from the rear and enter the big

338 ·

garden, in which, you are surprised to see, there's no one. You pass by the tables scattered around the gazebo in the yellow light of the glittering pool, your heart twinging with the memory of a wedding held in vain. It's not just the garden that is empty. The hotel, too, is dark and deserted.

But at least, you think, grandly handing the clerk at the reception desk your ID, there will be a room. At first you don't understand why he smiles without looking at it. Then he explains that, even if no guests are in evidence at this early hour of the evening, the entire staff—clerks, waiters, cooks, and chambermaids—is on standby for a full house. The name of each guest is on a place card on a table in the dining room, next to the key to his room.

## 21.

"AH, PROFESSOR!" The maître d' hurried over. "This time you're out of luck. The heart that brought you back to see Galya did not know that she and her mother have gone abroad on vacation."

Rivlin shook the sturdy Arab's hand. Although he had been looking forward to another tête-à-tête with his ex-daughter-in-law, he was nevertheless not put out by the news. "*Ma'alesh*,"* he said. "This time I didn't come just for her. I'm stuck tonight in Jerusalem. *Fi odeh r'hiseh minshani?*"†

"*Odeh? Il-leileh? Hon?*‡ Oh, my!" exclaimed the gray-haired Fu'ad, who was resplendent in a black suit and bow tie. "You've forgotten it's high season. As honored as we would be to have you, you'd have to be a Christian, an American, and a member of an organized group to stand a chance of finding a room here in midsummer."

"*Odeh janbi, zghiri, behimmish.*"§

"There's nothing, Professor. I swear to God. Everything is filled up. You could be the size of a mouse and I still couldn't find a spare hole

---

* Never mind.
† Is there an inexpensive room for me?
‡ A room? Tonight? Here?
§ A small side room, anything.

for you. Imagine, *bas ma tihkish la'hadda*,* we're even putting up guests in Mrs. Hendel's apartment. And Tehila, though she isn't feeling well, will have to give up a room, too. You'll see the stampede begin in a few minutes. Ten busloads are on their way from the airport."

"I can't believe it."

"It's called success. There's nothing I can do about it. We're very successful, Professor. Success will kill us all in the end. As good at the pilgrim trade as the late Mr. Hendel was, Tehila has doubled our occupancy in a few months. And she hasn't even made any big changes. It's all in the details. For example, there's now free seafood at the buffet, and we pick up the tab for the cable car at Masada. We have two new Christian channels on cable TV, too. The Christians are crazy about this place. And we've done it without increasing the staff. Tehila gave everyone a raise, and *u'sirna abidha*.† What more can I tell you? She has her father's talent and brains without his heart."

"Where's her brother?"

"Tehila has—what's the expression?—kicked him upstairs. She sent him and his family to America to be agents for the hotel. It isn't nice to say, but it was her way of getting rid of him. That's life. She and her father, may he rest in peace, were thick as thieves. She never left his side. *Irfet kul ishi*,‡ she stuck her nose everywhere. That's why, when he died, she grabbed the reins right away, *u'udrub, hiyeh sarat al fars*.§ Who can stand up to her? Her poor mother, you may remember, was always a weak, spoiled woman who kept to herself and was treated like a princess by her husband. Now that he's gone, she only wants to collapse, even though I do my best to keep her going. And Galya—I don't have to tell you about Galya. Who doesn't love Galya? *Mara n'zifeh u'mumtazeh*.‖ God be praised, she's pregnant now."

"She is?" He gave a start. "In what month?"

"What month?" The maître d' smiled and spread his arms. "You'll

---

* But don't tell anyone.
† We've become her slaves.
‡ She knew everything.
§ And giddy-up, she was already on the horse!
‖ A pure, fine soul.

have to ask her on your next condolence call. Or else figure it out yourself, because she's due in the middle of January, if I'm not mistaken. She must have got pregnant in the spring, right after her father died. It's eerie. If I believed in reincarnation, I'd say it was Mr. Hendel's spirit coming back. But you, Professor—you'll say that's all a lot of nonsense."

Rivlin glanced at the big garden and at the gazebo surrounded by lanterns, nostalgic for his first condolence call, which seemed to have taken place years ago.

"Why nonsense, Fu'ad? Today everything goes. Reincarnation is big with the young folks. As long as no one gets hurt by it."

"You're so right, Professor. *Inteh bit'ul hada kul hal'ad hilu.*\* What I was thinking was, it's only natural for a father's death to—what's the word?—*b'ghazel.* . . . Right. To stimulate the daughter to be a mother. And you know, Galya isn't that young. She never gave your poor Ofer a chance. Believe me, my friend, I may be a stranger to you, and an Arab in addition, but it grieves me that you and I won't have a grandson together. I always said to myself, The Professor, he's a good man, he's never jealous. Galya is a sensitive girl. She deserves to be happy. She's the opposite of her sister, who doesn't give a damn about anyone."

A bow-tied young waitress whispered something in Fu'ad's ear.

"That's it. The buses are here. Now the fun starts. I'm sorry to have to go without helping. Listen, Professor. The next time you want to sleep here, give us a call first. I wouldn't want to disappoint you again."

But Rivlin was not going to let the night's visit end like this. Gripping the shoulder of the Arab, who appeared to know more than he let on, he said:

"*Al hal, ya Fu'ad, a'tini ishi aakul. . . .*"†

The maître d' squirmed and swore that there wasn't room for another pin in the dining room. Every table and chair was taken. The guests would proceed straight to their meal from the buses. "But I'll tell you what, Professor. I can put you in the smoking lounge next to

---

\* You put it so well.
† At least give me something to eat, Fu'ad.

the bar, where you sat with Galya. Mr. Hendel sometimes used to order a snack there with his cigar. Have a seat and we'll bring you something. The soup is on its way."

The large windows of the lobby shook as the buses flooded the parking lot with their headlights, setting the bushes of the garden aflame before lining up in a long, silent row. The elderly Christians poured into the lobby in a swift but orderly wave. Pennants were raised and hymns struck up as they marched into the dining room as smartly as conscripts in boot camp.

The Jew nearly followed them in. At the last minute, he turned and headed for the lounge, sniffing its air as though to scent the deceased's last springtime cigar. He passed through the dark, windowless bar, its counter glowing with bottles that seemed to have their own source of light, and sat in the easy chair from which his ex-daughter-in-law had dueled with him. Could he manage, without risking too much on the home front, to abscond to the very place his son had been banished from?

A heavily made-up waitress in a pantsuit brought him a large cup of hot soup and some crackers. Would he, she asked, prefer crab or a vegetarian platter for his main course?

"Crab?" He had never eaten crab in his life. "Why not?"

"Do you have enough light, sir?"

For the moment, he had all the light he wanted.

From the dining room came the voice of a woman welcoming the guests in the name of the hotel and the nearby holy sites. It took him a while to realize it was Tehila. Though down with a cold, she had made sure to be present. He wondered if Fu'ad had told her he was there.

He shut his solitary eyes and strove to return to that summer night like this one—that night that was still, despite all that had happened since then, the happiest of his life. Although he could deal with the anger of his wife, who knew he loved her come what may, he was worried that she might try phoning the home of his old mentor—where, having finished their supper, the Tedeschis were now seated with Akri in the large library, showing him Hannah's latest translations of pre-Islamic war and love poetry.

A brief, matter-of-fact grace was said in the dining room, followed by the soft chime of plates and glasses as the waiters hurried to feed the hungry pilgrims. Meanwhile, Rivlin waited for his food. But even if that Arab has forgotten me completely, he thought, I'm not going anywhere.

## 22.

FU'AD, HOWEVER, had forgotten neither him nor his solitude, which was now broken by the waitress, who returned to expertly spread a white cloth on the table and set it with silverware and wineglasses for two. Soon the curtain of the lounge parted, and in came his dinner partner, the new proprietress of the hotel. Tall and slightly stooped in her light housedress, her hair cropped short above her sallow, bony face, she planted, despite her cold, a warm but casual kiss on his cheek, as if he were still a member of the family. She wanted to thank him, she said, for taking seriously her admonition not to wait for another death before coming again. True, he had dropped in without warning on the craziest day of the year, but what of it? What mattered was that he hadn't forgotten them. She knew, of course, that it wasn't her or her mother he had come to see, but his lost daughter-in-law. Still, he was a dear and honored guest. Nor should he feel insulted at being made to dine in the lounge. Even she, the proprietress, hadn't found a seat in the dining room. She hoped he didn't object, then, to her joining him as his fellow pariah in the lounge.

The sly gleam in her little whiskey-colored eyes matched the reddish glow of the bottles on the counter.

Object? How could he, he replied, when she was the owner and he was her guest?

She sighed. She felt more like a slave than like an owner. Far from losing business after her father's death, the hotel was doing better and better, and she was coming down with more and more colds. But why complain about success when so many people could only complain about failure? How was his wife? And what had made him come again without her—and at night, of all times? She hoped the judge wasn't angry at them.

Rivlin felt a shiver. His wife, angry? Why should she be angry? She had taken Ofer's divorce more easily than he had. It was only lack of time that kept her from joining him on his visits, which had all been last-minute decisions. Take tonight, for example. He was stuck in Jerusalem without a place to sleep. Perhaps only a naive historian could have hoped that her father's promise of a room, although made long ago, still held.

The tall, pale woman, who seemed to have taken a liking to him, laid a hand on her heart and swore solemnly in the name of the new management to honor the commitments of the old one.

"Then how about a room?" His heart pounded strongly.

But there was none available. Nor, Tehila added with a naughty laugh, was there likely to be one, since she had taken to overbooking—an offense she was paying for tonight by having to forfeit a room of her little wing to an extra pilgrim, even though she was running a fever.

The waitress gracefully put on the table a gleaming brass implement that resembled a dentist's tooth extractor. From a large serving dish she transferred to their plates a boiled king crab that had been divided, eyes, whiskers, and all, into two symmetrical halves. Only the claws, reaching out toward each other over plates they were too long for, seemed unreconciled to their separation.

"Would you like more light, Miss Hendel?" the waitress asked.

"No," Rivlin answered for the second time, though the question had not been put to him. "It's frightening enough to eat this thing in the dark." Laughing gaily but apprehensively, he lifted his wineglass to toast the bony woman. She had already seized the brass implement and was cracking the legs of his crab for him, extracting white fibers of meat—"The best part, make sure you eat it!"—with long fingers.

"I'll catch your cold," he joked, taking his time about putting the crabmeat in his mouth. He could only marvel at how fast and how far his absconding was going.

"I already gave it to you," she said, her naughty eyes the same color as her deceased father's, "when I kissed you. Assuming, that is, that I ever give anything to anyone. But don't be a scaredy-cat. Eat! The marvelous meat in the legs of this crab comes courtesy of an airplane from Crete. Our hotel owes no small share of its astonishing success in recent years to the reputation of its cuisine. Our meals are as much part of the pilgrim experience as a visit to the Holy Sepulchre or a baptism in the Jordan. It all started with my father's revolution five years ago, when he threw out those parasitical inspectors from the Rabbinate and did away with the kosher kitchen. He knew he was risking his Jewish clientele, but he didn't think he could count on it anyway. He preferred to gamble on quiet, conservative Baptists from Georgia and Mormons from Utah who would visit the Holy Land come hell or high water. Ofer was still married to Galya then. It's a pity he didn't stay with us. He could have been a partner in all this...."

Rivlin flared. "What do you mean, it's a pity? It was you who drove him out."

"We?" The whiskey smiled in her eyes. "What are you talking about? Who knew anything about it?"

"You didn't know?"

"Nothing."

"A tight, loving family like yours?"

"We were. But not here. Believe me, to this day I don't know what made Galya break up her marriage. She may have been in the eye of the storm, but to us she was a closed book. Whenever my mother or I tried talking about it or suggested a reconciliation, she just grew hostile. She acted like a stranger. And when, as her big sister, I made a last attempt to ask her to reconsider leaving a man she had loved so much, she lost her temper and said she wasn't made for love that wanted to creep under your skin. That's all I know. There was no stopping her. Maybe she thought finding a better man than Ofer would be no problem with her good looks."

"Did she?"

"Find a better man? I don't know. It's hard to compare two such different types. Bo'az is Ofer's opposite. It's as though Galya wanted, not only a new husband, but one who would cancel out the old one."

"Cancel Ofer out? How?" His voice trembled with his eagerness to know. "I only met him for a few minutes."

"Bo'az is a closed, almost secretive person. He's nice, and he's thoughtful, but he's not made for intimate relationships. It isn't easy to get close to him. I'm not the right person to ask about him, because I preferred Ofer's openness and emotion. You remind me of Ofer. I liked being with him, even if he sometimes ran off at the mouth about whatever happened to be on his mind. I don't know what he's doing today. I do know, looking back, that his idea of expanding by building up rather than out into the garden was a good one. After he left, there was no one to fight for it."

"But why do you keep saying he left?" Rivlin protested. "You know he didn't. He was made to leave."

"Fine. After he was made to leave. Look, I don't really know what happened."

"Did your father?"

"No. I'm sure of that. At the bereavement, during one of those long, sleepless nights when we sat talking about him, Galya cried and said he had been very noble. My mother, you know, was against the divorce. She thought it was wrong to hurry. She wanted them to separate and give it time. But my father backed Galya all the way. He trusted her, as he always did. And he respected her too much to ask questions. He gave her complete freedom and was as generous as possible about paying the costs of the divorce."

"Generous?"

"You know perfectly well—our accountant was upset about it—that Ofer received much more from my father than he, or you and your wife, put into their apartment. Don't get me wrong. I'm not complaining. It was my father's right to do what he wanted with his money. You must have noticed that he loved and always listened to Galya more than he did to me or my brother. That's the truth. Believe me, though, I never resented it. It was enough for me to be by my father's side. No one knew better than I did every mood of his, every weakness and depression and foolish anxiety. When you work that closely with someone, it's only natural to fight at times. I wasn't like Galya, who worshiped him from a distance. So don't lump us all together. We weren't partners in the divorce. Far from it. Perhaps if you or your wife had shared what you knew with us, my mother and I—or at least I—might have encouraged Ofer to handle Galya differently. . . ."

Rivlin emptied his wineglass with a gulp and pushed the crab revoltedly away.

"But what could we have shared? We were as much in the dark as you were. We still are."

"You, too?"

"Absolutely. And if Ofer won't talk about it to this day and neither will Galya, it must have been something bad. I can't stop thinking about it. What terrible thing could he have done? If he's punishing himself by keeping silent, that only prevents him from getting over it. Or was he himself the victim of an injustice he still hasn't recovered from?"

"But what is it you want now?"

"Only to know. I have to know. That's how I am. I need to know the truth even if it's useless. It's my nature. It's what motivates any historian—otherwise he's in the wrong profession. This has been haunting me for the past five years. And the strange thing is that your father's death, rather than putting an end to it, has made it worse than ever. Just look at how I keep coming back."

"In that case," she laughed, "I feel better. At least you weren't looking for a room."

"That was only a pretext. I could have found a room somewhere else."

"And yet it was all so long ago. You're a stubborn man."

"Your sister has remarried. She's going to have a baby. But Ofer is still stuck. Even then, five years ago, something told me the separation would go badly for him. She meant too much to him. I knew he wouldn't give her up so easily. I just never imagined it would take so long. That's why I . . ."

"You what?"

"I tried talking it over with your father on the phone, without telling even my wife. I hoped that the two of us could have a restraining influence. And although you say—and I'd like to believe you—that he knew nothing, which is what he told me too, I must say I was offended by his tone. There was something cold about it. All his friendliness and good nature were gone. He sounded hard, as if he wanted to get rid of me. That's why I never came to see you afterward."

"But what did you want him to do?"

"At least to feel sorry. To be as anguished as I was that a marriage that seemed so happy was over in a year. That's all I asked of him: not to accept it so easily."

"He accepted it because he trusted Galya. That's why he was generous with Ofer."

"Yes, he was. But to tell you the truth, I didn't like his generosity either. What made him so ready to give Ofer more than he deserved? Could it have been that Ofer knew something and was being paid off?"

"What a strange thought! My father wasn't generous because he was afraid of Ofer. He wanted Galya to be able do what she thought best for herself. He didn't want to give Ofer any excuse to withhold his consent. Trust me. I knew my father well. Better even than my mother did. I knew how his mind worked. We were together on a daily basis. It was an intensive relationship. Had he known anything, sooner or later he would have dropped some hint. Listen. Look at me. I'm a confirmed single woman. I have no family apart from the one I was born in. I don't even have many friends. I was with my father all the time. I swear to you, whenever Ofer's name came up, he had only good things to say about him. 'Ofer was a nice, talented boy,' he'd say. 'The only problem with him was those strange fantasies....'"

"Strange fantasies?" Rivlin felt a chill. "What were they?"

"How would I know? Maybe my father was thinking of the plans for expansion that Ofer submitted. Or of his political opinions. He had these ideas that you couldn't get him to stop talking about. He was very attached to my father from the start. He wanted to make an impression on him. And he was very involved in the hotel. Everything about it interested him. He had his ideas about the management, about the menu in the kitchen, about the arrangement of the rooms. Maybe that's why my father thought he fantasized—was maybe even out of touch with reality. So when Galya said that she wanted to break up with him, my father's reaction was, in that case, better sooner than later...."

"Out of touch with reality?" Rivlin teetered between shock and pain. "How?"

"Never mind. Those are just words. Why get upset?"

"There's no such thing as 'just.' I want to know what your father meant. If you knew how his mind worked, then now is the time to tell me. It frightens me to hear Ofer accused of such a thing."

"No one is accusing anyone. Why do you pick on every word as though you were in court? The Mr. Hendel you knew was a polite, good-natured, smiling hotel owner, a very proper man. But the father I knew was someone who took off his jacket and yanked down his tie and could be depressed or nervous or overbearing toward those who were close to him. Even I, who was his right hand, was often hurt.... So what does it matter what he did or didn't say about Ofer?"

Rivlin was not reassured. Anxiously he studied the bony face—which, in the dim lounge, was increasingly coming to resemble the dead man's. For some reason he thought of the old revolver in its drawer in the Jewish Agency building in Paris. And even if Ofer had "fantasized" something "out of touch with reality," couldn't this have been stopped in time? Mustn't there have been some clue or lead in the young couple's silence he could have used to persuade Hendel to join him in trying to delay the divorce?

Now it was too late. Hendel was gone, and Ofer and Galya had gone their separate ways without breaking their silence. Hagit was right. He was and continued to be a coward. Yet it wasn't people or ideas he was afraid of. It was the woman who kept warning him to stay within bounds. For bounds could be crossed and new territories entered without forsaking one's love: he had learned this from a tactful but resolute Arab driver with coal black eyes. You could even abscond to a strange bed and rise in the morning wiser and richer.

He glanced at his watch. Either the dim light or the lack of his glasses kept him from making out the hands.

"What time do you have?"

"Eight-thirty."

"My wife broke my glasses yesterday. I haven't been able to read or write for a whole day. Just talk."

"Isn't that enjoyable?"

"It depends whom I'm talking with."

"Even with me."

"With you it's painful."

"You brought the pain with you. Don't blame me for it."

"Perhaps," he admitted softly. "But you've made it worse."

She regarded him sympathetically, then asked, with a flush:

"But how did she break them? She doesn't strike me as the type who goes around breaking things."

"Not unless she wants to."

Now it was his turn to blush. He snorted to play down the remark. But the proprietress nodded, grateful for the shared intimacy. Her long, shapely fingers searched for bits of uneaten crab. She did not use the brass implement, but cracked them with her teeth, sucking the hidden meat. Her whiskey-colored eyes clouded.

"You'll still need a place to sleep tonight. Don't think that will be easy at this time of year."

"I have a place. My old professor at the university has a room for me. It's just that I have to share it with a colleague who came from Haifa for a lecture. I'm not dying to lie next to him and wake up in his dreams."

From the dining room came the strains of a pilgrim hymn, blessing the Lord for the meal. Rivlin tried making out the words.

"I can save you the trouble." Tehila smiled. "I know all their hymns by heart. It's the twenty-third Psalm, 'The Lord Is My Shepherd, I Shall Not Want.' Very appropriate for wealthy American Christians."

Fu'ad entered the lounge cautiously. He emptied the last of the wine bottle into the two glasses and cleared the table with a suppressed grin, adding the decimated crab shell from Tehila's plate to the nearly intact half on Rivlin's.

"*Haruf, ya Brofesor, kan ahsan lak....*"*

"*F'il mara 'l-jay. Lazim adir bali aktar....*"†

"What did you two say?"

"It's time, Tehila, that you learned some Arabic," the maître d' said.

---

* You would have liked lamb better, Professor.
† Next time I'll have to be more careful.

She waved a dismissive hand, took out a cigarette, and waited for him to light it.

"What for? Russian is more practical."

"Russian?"

"In a few years, when Russia is back on its feet, we'll get pilgrims from there too. Why not? I once read that in the days of the czar, Russian pilgrims were so devoted that they crawled all the way to Jerusalem."

Fu'ad laughed. "They could never have afforded your prices."

Her eyes glittered.

"You know very well, Fu'ad, that I could make even a crawling pilgrim pay up."

Fu'ad nodded and reported a problem with some rooms on the second floor. Should he tell the front desk that the proprietress was in the lounge?

"No," Tehila said. "I'm sick tonight. I only got out of bed so as not to hurt the professor's feelings."

"But they're hurt anyway. We haven't found him a place to sleep."

"He knows there's nothing we can do about it."

With a snakelike movement, almost losing the dishes on his arm, the maître d' bent to whisper to the proprietress.

"Down there?" She grinned at the thought. "You can't be serious."

"About what?" Rivlin asked.

"Never mind. It was just a thought."

"I've already told you there are no 'justs.' That's what my wife says. Every 'just' has something behind it."

"Fu'ad suggested putting you up in an impossible place."

"What's impossible about it?"

"It's not a real room, just an office. There's a bed there, which our accountant used to sleep on, but I wouldn't feel right about putting you in it."

"Why not?"

"Because it's down in the basement. It's clean and well aired, but it's still a basement."

"So it's a basement." Rivlin jumped at the idea. "That's fine. I prefer it to taking a taxi to my old professor's and sitting up half the night listening to him run down other scholars. What's wrong with a basement?"

"Nothing... it's just that..."

The visitor burst into laughter.

"You know, my mother used to call your hotel 'The Little Paradise.' If your basement gets its air from Paradise, that's good enough for me."

## 23.

TEHILA, DESPITE HER real or imaginary illness, took him down to the basement herself. A small door at the rear of the kitchen, which was now hectically filling up with cleared dishes, led to a concrete staircase that descended to a narrow corridor. A bucket of congealed plaster, a dusty girl's bicycle, and an ancient tire leaned against the wall. Tehila, who clearly knew her way, found the light switch in the dark at once. A yellowish glare fell on a row of padlocked closets. He was looking, she told him, at the hotel's archives. The "accountant's room," in which he would sleep if he had not changed his mind, was farther down the corridor.

But why change his mind about a brief absconding that was less in retaliation for injury than in opposition to love's tyranny—his love for his wife and the love to which his son was chained? Here, at least, he thought, following Tehila's swift, sure steps, is a woman who needs no protector.

She passed a large iron door, checked that its handle was locked, and continued down the corridor until they came to a space in which pipes running down from the kitchen gurgled with water. An old black boiler in the middle of it brought to mind a petrified primeval beast. Strewn around it, like the bones of its prey, were a twisted baby carriage, a green tricycle, and a crib with some little toy animals on its dusty, oilcloth-covered mattress.

Overcome with sudden grief for the grandchild that had never been born, Rivlin felt as though he were mourning his own death.

"When is your sister giving birth?"

The question took Tehila by surprise.

"In early winter, I think."

"Do they know the sex of the child?

She wrinkled her brow, her little eyes naughty.

"That's a good question. I think it's either a boy or a girl. The truth is that I don't remember what Galya told me. But why should you care?"

The old despair clutched at his heart again. His vision blurred without his glasses, he watched the bony woman, whose sallow skin looked almost sickly, choose the right key for a windowless room jammed between the foundations of the building. In it was a large desk, two metal bookcases filled with file holders, and a narrow, unmade bed. Tehila halted in the doorway. She wasn't sure, she said, that the room, in which she hadn't set foot since her father's death, was suitable even for a night. It hadn't been used since their accountant, a cousin from Tel Aviv who had come every month to do their books, died seven years ago.

"Where does this place get its air from?"

She pointed to the ceiling. His naked eye made out two small, dark vents covered with rusty netting.

"You're sure it's real air?"

She laughed.

"Do you think we would have asphyxiated a wonderful accountant who saved us so much money? Relax. It is a bit strange down here, but it's clean and it's safe and I always liked it, even as a child. In summertime I came down here to get away from the heat and the sun; it was always cool at night here. And in winter it was so warm that I could take off my clothes and be totally cut off from the world, with no one to bother me or even to think of me. I tell you, if it weren't for all the germs in my bed, I'd send you upstairs to sleep in that and happily spend the night here myself."

She bent down and pulled a wooden linen chest from under the bed. Carefully choosing some white sheets, she sniffed their scent of laundry soap; then, whipping them in the dark air like the wings of two snow-white swans, she let them fall on the bed with a sharp crack, one after another, and made the bed as deftly as an experienced chambermaid. No, Rivlin thought again. This is not a woman who needs protection. This is a woman who gives it.

"Look here," she said. "This place may not be up to your usual standards, and my father would be upset to know I'd put you here, but you'll enjoy the bed. You're getting two honest-to-God starched and ironed cotton sheets such as we don't use anymore, because it costs too much money. Nothing feels better than a smooth, cool cotton sheet. Come and see for yourself."

Rivlin could not move. His absconding was getting out of hand. Despite her illness, he feared, the Circe of this cave was up to no good.

"It's strange how two sisters can be so different," he said in a subdued voice. "My wife and her sister are like that, too."

She threw him a suspicious look.

"I remember your wife very well. She has a style of her own. Your sister-in-law I saw only once, at the wedding. But you're right. Galya and I are complete opposites. My father quite thoughtlessly gave me not only his height, which is more than any woman needs, but his eyes and a metabolism that doesn't leave an ounce of fat on me. Galya's eyes are my mother's, and so is her tendency to put on weight. Do you want the blue blanket or the green one?"

"It makes no difference."

"Come over here and make up your mind."

His face felt on fire. He didn't move.

There was a knock so soft that the door opened before anyone could hear it or say "Come in." The maître d', minus his bow tie, stood in the doorway holding a big pillow in a flowery pillowcase. He did not look at the proprietress, who seem displeased by his sudden appearance.

"*T'zakart, ya Brofesor, inno el-m'hadeh hon sarlha yabseh,** so I brought another."

Rivlin let out a relieved laugh and laid a hand on the Arab's shoulder.

"Thanks. It was kind of you to think of me."

---

* I just remembered, Professor, that the pillow here isn't fresh.

*"Leysh la, iza ana kunt ili akna'tak t'nam hon e-leileh? Min hazna likbir inno hawajja Hendel ma irfish inno na'umnak hon, li'inno kan y'kul daiman inno mamnu' nist'hir hatta iza fi deif binam bi'balash."**

Tehila burst into their exchange. "What's that about Mr. Hendel? What did you say, Fu'ad? Why are you sticking Arabic into every sentence tonight?"

The Arab took the rebuke in stride.

"Why shouldn't I? When you were little I taught you many Arabic words, and you were very sweet when you used them. Why not learn them again and be sweet once more?"

"Give me a break, Fu'ad," Tehila said impatiently. "Just tell me what you were saying about my father."

"I said it's a lucky thing that the late departed doesn't know where we're putting our honored guest."

"But whose idea was it?"

"And who agreed to it?"

"Just give me a break. What's with all this Arabic? You forget I'm walking around with a fever."

"How can I have forgotten your fever when I've come to escort you to bed because of it? Just do me a favor and stop off at the reception desk on your way. There's a problem with some rooms on the second floor. Your evangelicals have run out of religion and sung their last hymn, and now they're quarreling over the rooms like little children. It takes your brains to solve this one. And you needn't worry about our extra pilgrim, because we've already put him in your wing and locked him up so that he won't bother you. He's a very old man, but a lively one and a great believer in the Resurrection."

Rivlin could feel the tall woman's agitation. Angrily she yanked the pillow from Fu'ad and stood hugging it instead of placing it on the bed. Her yellow, predatory bird's eyes strayed back and forth between the two gray-haired men, as if trying to decide whose good graces she sought. Equally aroused and alarmed by her unwillingness to leave

---

* How could I not have, since it was me who talked you into sleeping here? It's a lucky thing that Mr. Hendel will never know we stuck you down here, because he always warned us not to short-change a guest, even a nonpaying one.

him, Rivlin turned for help to the maître d', who stood there, resplendent, in his black suit. A thin smile tickled his silver mustache. With the fatherly air of a family servant taking his old master's orphaned daughter in hand, he gripped her arm, put his hand on her waist, and said, "I think, Tehila, that if you're running a fever, you should let our guest go to sleep. There's no need to leave him the key, because the door has a bolt."

He slipped the key ring from the door, opened the side pocket of his employer's dress, and slipped the keys into it as if he were in charge of a little girl. Appeased, she brushed Rivlin's cheek with her warm lips, the naughty gleam back in her little amber eyes.

"If you haven't caught anything from me yet, you won't now, and if you have, it doesn't matter," she said. "You can pass it on to your clever wife. What should I tell Galya? That you were here looking for her again? Or nothing at all?"

"Nothing at all," was his unhesitating answer.


## 24.

ABSCONDING TO THE hotel's basement was his deepest and most dangerous absence yet. Though committed in his native city and among Jews, it was entirely self-willed, an absence within an absence, for he had already absconded to Jerusalem itself, to ease the fear of his love.

He slid the bolt into place. Leaving on the light, he took off his shirt and shoes and lay down on the cool cotton sheets spread in his honor. Unable to read the yellowed newspaper that lay on the table, he stared patiently at the overhead vents as if hoping to ascertain whether the air he was breathing was real or imaginary. The deep silence around him was broken only by the gurgle of the hotel's water system.

Despite his concern that his abandoned and anxious wife might swallow her pride and find a pretext to phone his old mentor, with whom he was supposed to be staying, he had refused to send her a reassuring signal. And in any case, an expert on the criminal mind like her could easily have guessed that his erratic behavior since Hendel's death was likely to lead him for a third obsessive time to where stubborn love had chained their son.

He pulled off his pants and slipped on the pajamas he had brought, leaving them unbuttoned. All I need is a few hours of sleep to get my strength back, he thought, and I'll be off. Convinced he could fall asleep with the light on, he lay with his back to the door and his face to the wall, on which hung two old still lifes of sunflowers and a faded photograph of a young man—no, a woman—standing in shorts by the gazebo. Even his unaided eyes could see that the pointy features, cropped head, long, bony legs, and slight stoop belonged to a much younger Tehila. Beside her stood an elderly man in a dark suit and tie. The avuncular arm he had put around her conveyed that he was a friend or relation—perhaps even the accountant, who had hung the photo to look at himself while he tinkered with the books.

After a while, unable to fall asleep with the lamp on, Rivlin switched it off. He was now, together with the desk and the files on the walls, in near total darkness. Only a vague radiance shone through the vents, from which came a light, monotonous buzz. Though at first he found this bothersome, it soon made him shut his eyes and ground down his wakefulness.

His sleep was a private affair. And yet a foreign presence weighed on it. Whirled in its depths, he fought to separate the distress of the young widow appealing for protection from the fevered appeal of the bold Circe, who could not have been easily categorized even by his wife, the judge.

The first prime minister's famous four hours of sleep were granted him, too. At three in the morning he awoke. Opening his eyes, he struggled to reconstruct the spatial dimensions of the room, which had vanished somewhere inside him. A tremor, like that of a slight earthquake, appeared to bend the walls toward him, making it hard to breathe. But it wasn't lack of air he suffered from. It was surplus of desire. Being slapped by a wife who broke his glasses had made him, so it seemed, fair game for every young woman.

Rolling out of bed, he turned on the light and groped his blurry way to the photograph of the tall young lady—who, after her father's death, had built up his thriving business still more by means of small but well-calculated come-ons. Indeed, she might very well have come on to him too, had not Fu'ad appeared in the nick of time with the pillow. Yet what, apart from a low-grade fever, could he have got from it? If she, too, was unable to help him discover the secret by which he was driven, he could only be bound by her even more to this place, which was rapidly becoming dangerous.

Yes, he had gone too far this time. If Hagit were to need him, his absence-within-an-absence would badly rupture the trust he had always put before everything. And so although it was still long before dawn, he put on his pants, unbolted the door, retraced his way along the corridor past the primeval silhouette of the discarded boiler, and hurried up the concrete stairs, hoping find the door to the kitchen unlocked.

It was. He strode past rows of pots, griddles, ladles, and frying pans and emerged in the lobby, where he looked for a place to check out, even though he had never checked in.

At the reception desk was a night clerk reading an Arabic thriller. This being a land in which Arabs were accustomed to confessing to Jews all they knew, he had no difficulty in extracting Fu'ad's whereabouts. The maître d' was lying in his underwear on a cot in a small bedroom, half asleep and half awake, his black suit and white shirt on a hanger. Rivlin's noiseless appearance brought him to his feet at once.

"Well, Professor," he said, surveying his visitor blearily, "I see that all of us were wrong—I for suggesting it, Tehila for agreeing, and you for accepting. It's not so simple to fall asleep surrounded by income-tax files. Once I slept down there myself and dreamed, don't ask me why, of an earthquake. I just hope you didn't run away because you thought there was no air. There's enough air down there for an entire family. The bad smell doesn't come from the plumbing or the old boiler, but from all those files. First it was Mr. Hendel who wouldn't throw them out, now it's Tehila. They want to keep the proof that they never cheated on their country...."

"Never mind, Fu'ad, I've slept enough," Rivlin said to the maître d', who had meanwhile risen and donned a pair of gym shorts.

"If you say so." Fu'ad sighed. "An hour slept is an hour gained. Now tell me how you want your coffee—*arabi willa franji?*"*

"*Leysh ma n'ruhesh ma'a 'l-arabi?*"†

"*Heyk lazim y'kun.*"‡

He bent over a little cabinet and took out an electric hot plate, a sooty beaker, and a long spoon. Filling the beaker with water and coffee, he sat waiting patiently for it to boil.

The profound sadness of a last good-bye had the Orientalist in its grip. He sat on the edge of Fu'ad's cot, rubbing his eyes hard in the hope of restoring clarity to a world gone hazy. Uncertainly he asked:

"*Shu lakan? Bitfakirni majnun?*"§

Fu'ad was startled. "*Kif majnun, ya Brofesor?*"‖

"Because of the way I keep coming back in order to understand what happened to my son's marriage..."

The old maître d', his sturdy body looking young in its undershirt and gym shorts, did not answer. He fingered his silver mustache, broodingly watching the coffee slowly boil. As if remembering something, he asked:

"*Inteh b'tush'ur halak ahsan, ya Brofesor?*"#

"*Aa. Ahsan....*"**

"God be praised. You Jews worry too much about your health. A person can get sick just from that."

Rivlin did not even smile. He watched the Arab search for cups at the bottom of the cabinet.

"How is it possible that even you don't know what happened?" he protested.

"How? That's simple."

"But you can find out whatever you want to about this hotel, Fu'ad."

---

* Arab-style or European?
† Why not go with the Arabs?
‡ That's as should be.
§ So? Do you think I'm crazy?
‖ Why crazy, Professor?
# Are you feeling better these days, Professor?
** Yes, better.

"Perhaps I can, Professor." The Arab spoke hotly. "But I don't want to. Someone like myself, who isn't Jewish and has a master key to every room, has to be careful—very careful—not to step out of bounds. He has to make sure—really sure—that he doesn't see or hear what he shouldn't. Why do you think, Professor, that I'm still here, after starting out as a simple worker twenty years ago, when Galya was still a baby? How would I have worked my way to the top—because today I'm part of the management—if I hadn't stayed out of the family's problems? I even said as much to the late departed. And that's why I didn't argue with Tehila tonight. They respect me for that. 'Please,' I've said to them, 'don't say anything bad about one another in front of me. I don't want to know about your quarrels. I have to take orders from all of you, and I can't afford to lose my honor with any of you. *U'heyk, ya Brofesor, kult kaman li'ibnak laman balash yibki kuddami....*"*

"When did Ofer come crying to you?"

"When he split with Galya. That last autumn."

"Last autumn?"

"Yes. After they separated. He used to come here at night and lurk in the street or in the garden. He was hoping for even just a glimpse of her. I swear to God, it was hard for me too. It was hard for us all. But I didn't want him hanging around. I didn't want to have to listen to all his stories and accusations that I had no business knowing about. And that night he stepped out of line with me. I was standing at the bus stop, waiting to go back to my village. All of a sudden he drives up on his motorcycle and shines the light on me and shouts without taking off his helmet, 'Get on, Fu'ad, I'm taking you to Abu-Ghosh. Don't tell me you're afraid to ride.' You can be sure I wasn't. I have a brother with a bike twice as big. But I didn't want to talk to him, and so I said, 'Yes, I am, Ofer. I'll take the bus. I'm too old for your motorcycle.' He took off his helmet, and I could see that his eyes were on fire. And then, Professor, I swear, listen to this and tell me if I wasn't right, I said to him—I remember every word because I was

---

* And that's what I told your son, Professor, when he came crying to me.

upset—'You, Ofer,' I said, 'as much as I respect you and your parents, please don't ask me anything. If you're a man, then be a man with me too, and not just on your motorcycle. You're not getting anything out of me. Nothing. Because you'll leave this hotel, and you won't come back, and God will help you, *inshallah*, to forget your troubles. But I'm staying right here. And that's why I don't want to hear a single bad word about the family. Not about Mr. Hendel, and not about the missus, and not about their children, and not about anyone. Because I want to be honored and treated well, no matter who tells me to do what. That's why, my friend, I'm asking you to keep your problems to yourself, just as I do mine.' *Il-mazbut,** he was very hurt, and embarrassed to be crying in front of an Arab, and he put his helmet back on and drove off without a word. My heart was aching for him, but what could I do? You tell me, Professor. Nothing. That was the last time I saw him. I felt so bad I even wrote a poem when I got home."

"A poem?"

"*Ya'ani, ishi makameh z'ghireh.*"[†]

"What kind of rhymes?"

"*Makameh, b'ti'raf shu ya'ani makameh.* . . .[‡] I was always good at rhymes, even as a boy in school. Even now whole lines of them sometimes come to me, one after another. Little poems, when the heart has too much sorrow or happiness. And that night, I thought—I swear—about you, Professor . . . so I sat down and wrote an energy. Is that the right word? *Marthiyya.*"

"Elegy."

"Elegy? Isn't that what you say at a funeral?"

"That's a eulogy."

"I didn't know there were so many words. Well, I wrote an elegy for your Ofer."

"What happened to it?"

"Search me."

---

* The truth is.
† Well, it was a little bit of rhymed prose.
‡ Rhymed Arabic prose, you know what that is.

# 25.

THREE LITTLE CUPS of Turkish coffee later, Rivlin felt he had enough adrenaline to walk, not only across the city to the Tedeschis', but all the way home to his wife in Haifa. Turning down Fu'ad's offer to order a taxi, he made him promise to look for his five-year-old "Elegy for a Young Man Whose Marriage Fell Apart."

"Even if I can't find it," the Arab assured him, "I can always write another."

The Orientalist's second, underground absconding having reminded him of the first, he thought, as he stepped out into the streets of Jerusalem in the wee hours of his autonomous night out in the Palestinian Authority. Now, though, he was his own master and had no need of an Arab chauffeur. In the languorous light of the hazed orb of the moon, he strode down Korei ha-Dorot Street and headed for Hebron Road, glancing at the pine trees surrounding the sad, silent house of Agnon. Although, without his glasses, the stars did not seem as bright, making the street signs difficult to read, he navigated adeptly in his native town. His adrenaline, pumped even higher by Fu'ad's story about Ofer, kept him moving at a rapid clip, as if the faster he put the hotel behind him, the less piercing the thought of his son's despair would be. What else was there left to ask about? And whom? A stubborn scholar on a solo reconnaissance mission, he would find no one who, even if prepared to humor him, knew more now.

He was almost running as he swung into the broad, flat avenue of Hebron Road, the silhouette of downtown Jerusalem far ahead of him. Had he bitten off more distance than he could chew? But he had all night to keep on walking before the city awoke to a morning shift of Palestinian workers who, slipping past the checkpoints around Bethlehem, might abscond with him again.

He crossed from Hebron Road to Bethlehem Road, passed the railroad tracks, entered the dark side streets of the German colony until, unerringly, he came to the one that led to the Rose Garden in posh Talbiya, cut across a flowering traffic circle, made a left on Jabotinsky Street, and then, before coming to the President's house, turned and went right into Molcho, straight to the darkened building of his hyper-hypochondriac mentor. Despite the many years that had passed since he was a doctoral student awaiting the return of his seminar papers, he still felt nervous each time he climbed the steps of the old staircase.

It was a quarter to four. He let the automatic staircase light go out and peered at the crack beneath the Tedeschis' front door. Although not a sign of wakefulness shone through it, he did find there a note explaining where the key was hidden.

It was only natural, he supposed, that a woman who had spent all day in the headily anxious atmosphere of an emergency room should have forgotten that he had broken his glasses and could not read small print. Moreover, afraid that her note might fall into the hands of a passing burglar, she had composed it in Arabic, no doubt of a highly ornate nature. He had no choice, therefore, but to stick it in his shirt pocket and go back down the stairs. Perhaps a Palestinian worker hoping to get a jump on the new day might be found to read, if not the words of Hannah's note, at least the letters.

But Gaza Road was deserted. Nor was there anyone on the street named for the poet Solomon Ibn-Gabirol, at the top of which stood the modest stone house in which the first prime minister had had his office.

Rivlin soon came to the old school in which he had attended the first twelve grades. He peered through its high fence at its large, dark garden. A little footbridge, remembered from childhood, crossed a channel of water so narrow that it seemed more symbolic than real. What were the chances of finding, in the middle of the night, in this peaceful, middle-class neighborhood, someone to read an Arabic note written by a woman who, like himself, was quite possibly on the verge of going mad? Nevertheless, taking a route he had followed many times in those years, he headed up Keren Kayemet Street and along King George Street, hoping quite absurdly to come across the help he was looking for in the dowdy old downtown of the city, near the gray house he was raised in.

And find him Rivlin did, sitting on the curb by the Histadrut building, a young, sad, early rising Palestinian worker patiently waiting for a day's work. A permanent vagabond among Jews, he was no longer surprised by anything about them, not even by an elderly Orientalist now handing him, before the break of dawn, four lines by the renowned translatoress of Ignorance—the first Arabic poem of her life.

*Al-musanan al-manshud mowjud fi juz' al-nahla,*

*Muthahab wa-latif ca'amal al-nowm fi 'l kalbaka.*

*Wa-nashadak lahfuka laysa b'al-ruh ash-shaytaniya wa-laysa b'al-hawa al-ilahi,*

*Li'annahu fakat bi'hukmi 'l-Carmel tajiddu rahataka.\**

A short while later, as his fingers were still burrowing in the dry earth of a long-since-wilted dwarf potted palm, the front door opened silently, and Tedeschi, in his eternal corduroys and a blue hospital shirt taken from the emergency room, stood beaming at the old student who had not forgotten to turn up in the end. With a grand gesture he beckoned him into the large library, in which, between two windows opened to the darkness of the night, glowed a cloyingly colored computer.

"Listen!" The Jerusalem polymath leaned with confidential excitement toward Rivlin, who, drained of the last of his vitality, sank exhaustedly into an armchair. "Don't think that visit to the emergency room was wasted. I've decided to change the subject of tomorrow's lecture."

"Just a minute, Carlo. Let me catch my breath. Did Hagit try getting me on the phone?"

"No one tried getting you."

"You're sure?"

"What's wrong? Have the two of you quarreled?"

"A bit."

"Never mind. You worship her too much. The first time you brought her here, I could see you were under her thumb. You were so swept off your feet that you had to get married at once and postpone

---

\* The toothed one you long for is at the root of the palm,

As fetchingly golden as the sleep that you crave.

Your desire is not in the wind or the grave.

In the Carmel's halls of justice, there it shall find calm.

finishing your doctorate by a year, which cost you a position in Jerusalem.... But what happened?"

Rivlin smiled. The wave of warmth he felt for the old man, who read him so well, was also a warning to watch what he said.

"It's nothing. We'll get over it. So you've decided, just like that, in the middle of the night, to change your subject?"

"More the approach to it. Instead of talking about Turkish-Arab relations in a lifeless, abstract way, I'm going to do it so vividly that it may inspire even you. I want to show how the Turks saw the Arabs concretely, in terms of their literature—and especially, in terms of Ottoman popular drama from the mid-nineteenth century to the debacle of the First World War."

"There was popular theater way back then?"

"Where have you been? Have you forgotten that seminar you took with me back in the sixties? Of course there was theater. Everywhere. In Istanbul, in Ankara, in Izmir, even in the south. Little folk theaters that put on original plays, as well as European dramas and drawing-room comedies. They changed the names of the characters and places, replaced Christian allusions with Muslim ones, reworked some themes, and fed the audience a Turkish delight. Sometimes they even adapted the classics, Shakespeare or Molière. *As You Like It* and *Le Malade Imaginaire* were performed in Turkish villages. The audiences loved them..."

"*Le Malade Imaginaire?*" Rivlin grinned, giving Tedeschi a weary but loving glance. His mentor's face reddened.

"Why not? It's not a wonderful play?"

## 26.

THOUGH THEY WERE talking in whispers, the conversation of the two professors woke Hannah Tedeschi. Barefoot and unkempt, in a wrinkled nightgown, she scolded their cavalier attitude toward the remaining hours of sleep and—it being beyond her powers to drag her husband away from his computer—led Rivlin firmly away to his room. As they stood in its dark doorway, quietly listening to Ephraim Akri's light, regular breathing, Rivlin felt an old, puzzled sorrow for this once lively and talented student, the faculty's favorite, who had chosen to devote her life—first as his secretary, then as his teaching assistant, and finally as his living companion—to a professor with a mentally ill and institutionalized wife. Perhaps it was his fear of this ancient dementia still haunting the apartment that had deterred Akri, who had forgotten to bring his own pajamas, from wearing the pair offered him by the doyen of Orientalists, on whose good offices he counted in the future. He had placed it, still folded and ironed, by his black skullcap and steel-rimmed glasses and was lying starkly and swarthily naked beneath a thin blanket. His large, woozy eyes, so different without their glasses, flickered open for a moment to watch his senior colleague, a not unimportant member of the appointments committee of the university senate, open the window and lie down by his side.

Although it was a big double bed, the thought of contact with the new department head's naked body gave Rivlin gooseflesh. He put on his pajamas, wrapped himself in his blanket, and embarked on the second, academic half of the convoluted night. The familiar aroma of old journals tickled his nose. A feeling of calm possessed him, as if he were back under the aegis of his strict old doctoral adviser—who, by virtue of this position, shared the blame for his students' errors and the responsibility of defending them from their critics. A spark of inspiration flashed momentarily in the spacious room, meant for the children Tedeschi never had, neither from the wife who lost her mind nor from the lively student who took her place. I've been to this house so many times, Rivlin thought. I've learned much here, and argued much, and once even taken an exam. And yet never did I think to see the day when I would sleep here.

Ephraim Akri groaned in his sleep. To Rivlin it sounded like a general protest at the sorry state of the Middle East. Taking advantage of the break in Akri's slumber, he asked the new department head if anyone had tried getting in touch with him.

"No one," Akri avowed, his eyes shut. Discreetly turning his naked back, which was as smooth as a bar of chocolate, he added hoarsely: "But don't worry..."

In that case, Rivlin thought with fresh anxiety, she's picked up the gauntlet I threw down. She, too, wants to loosen the reins of our love.

Not, as I do, for Ofer's sake, but for her own, to keep aloof from the mistakes that I've made and will make. And if that's what she's up to, why did I bother making two nights out of one by hurrying here to see if she had called? I could have stayed in the basement. The last thing he saw, as his mind went blank and he fell into a short but powerful and delicious sleep, was the angular face of the tall proprietress.

## 27.

IT WAS APPARENT as soon as Rivlin entered the lecture hall that the postponement had been for the worse. The political-science faculty that had come to hear Tedeschi the night before, only to be told he was in the hospital, had no way of knowing, as did his colleagues in Near Eastern studies, of his propensity for miraculous recoveries. When he mounted the dais, therefore, spreading out his notes with their new approach, barely a dozen people were in the audience, and these included his wife, the two colleagues who had slept in his home, and three young political scientists, the organizers of the event, who had hurriedly mustered several secretaries and typists so that the renowned polymath wouldn't be demoralized. Tedeschi, however, was unflustered. Seeing Suissa senior enter the lecture hall in his gray fedora, along with Suissa junior's widow, he gave them a friendly wave and invited them to sit in the front row. Then he glanced at the sunlight pouring through the window, stripped off his jacket like a prizefighter—unselfconsciously baring two puny white arms riddled with yellow intravenous marks—and began in a stentorian voice to relate the story of a play produced in 1867 in a little theater in the town of Antakiyya, not far from the Syrian border.

Though punch-drunk from a night divided between two such different and distant beds, Rivlin was all concentration, as if he had instantly reverted to the loyal and eager student of thirty years ago. And indeed Tedeschi started off in fine form, using his narrative skills to introduce his subject with a concise but vivid survey of the Turkish hill town's geography, history, archaeology, and sociology, which broke down into Turks, Syrians, Greeks, Jews, and Armenians, each group with its distinctive occupations and religious and cultural institutions.

His tone growing dramatic, the Jerusalem professor invited his little audience to join him in entering a small structure that housed the town theater. The details grew thicker, as if he were now sketching not a distant century but a recent experience. Before raising the curtain on the stage, he described the layout of the little auditorium, the seats, the audience, and even the smell of grilled meats and the steam rising from the glasses of tea.

Rivlin, feeling a keen intellectual delight such as he had not experienced in ages, sensed in his old mentor's glance, which came to rest on him increasingly, that the sleepless night's revisions had been for his sake. Tedeschi had wanted to show him, the heir apparent, how a research project bogged down in dry, recalcitrant facts could be revived by a single, bold artistic stroke—at least enough to yield an article for a jubilee volume.

The curtain went up. He had never realized what a born actor his old teacher was. After reading the list of the cast, a medley of comically mangled Turkish, Arabic, and Greek names, the Jerusalem professor declaimed the opening lines with a comic leer, reciting them first in Turkish and then in a free Hebrew translation:

O despicable thief!
Where hast thou hidden my daughter?
Thou hast enchanted her, damn thy soul!
What sane man would not understand, as I do,
That, if not for thy enchantments,
No lovely maiden would have spurned such fine suitors
And fled her father for a black body,
Terrifying, not pleasuresome, like thine?

"*Othello!*" Hannah Tedeschi—who had not known of her husband's change of plans—cried with childish glee.

"Right you are, madam, as always," the lecturer confirmed, with a bow to his wife's sagacity. "Perhaps our adaptation of this famous play can help us to understand, better than historical abstractions, the shift that occurred in the Turks' perceptions of the Arabs as early as the mid-nineteenth century—a shift from an attitude of contempt, disdain, and disregard to one of suspicion, hostility, and even fear, especially among the upper classes. This is why, in the popular theater of Antakiyya, a town close to Syria, the Turkish translator and adapter of *Othello* chose to make of Shakespeare's tragically powerful black man, a figure who appears like a hurricane from beyond the bounds of civilization with no tangible national or religious identity—yes, to make of this wonderful and terrible man, whose danger-fraught life has caused a nobleman's daughter to fall in love with him—an addled, pompous, absurd general from the desert, a black Arab of unbounded ambition who joins the Venetians as a mercenary against the Turks and barbarously thinks that an accidental victory in a trivial battle entitles him to possess a paragon of Christian womanhood, even though she is culturally and psychologically worlds above him."

The doyen of Orientalists paused, his heart going out to his old student, who, though now a full professor himself, albeit at a somewhat provincial university, was sitting open-mouthed in the middle of the morning, gaping like a freshman. To help him relax after a hard night of bed-hopping, he now faced him and explained, in precise, analytic language, how the Turkish adapter had killed two Arab birds with one stone—for not only had he made an Arab of Othello, he had done the same with his treacherous adjutant Iago, now known as Yassin. The latter, however, was an Arab of a different stripe: not a black savage from the desert, but a shrewd, educated, cunning Lebanese urbanite who knew the hidden codes of his Bedouin compatriot and used them to plant in him the maddening fantasy of being cuckolded by the unworldly Christian with whom he was mismatched.

And thus, moving from play to play and theater to theater, the Jerusalem professor demonstrated how already in the middle of the nineteenth century, even though nothing had changed in official Turkish policy, the sinking empire was permeated by feelings of enmity toward and estrangement from its Arab subjects, now seen as potential traitors. Little wonder, then, that these fears turned into a self-fulfilling prophecy at the end of World War I in the form of the Great Arab Revolt—which, aided by the British, brought four hundred years of Ottoman rule crashing down. Indeed, Tedeschi concluded, with a roguish wink, the bad feeling between the two peoples has persisted to this day, giving the Jews some hope that they, too, might find a corner of their own in the Levant.

## 28.

RIVLIN CAME FORWARD at the lecture's end to congratulate Tedeschi for his original methodology and to say good-bye, nodding wordlessly to Suissa senior and his anxious daughter-in-law, who stood retiringly by her father-in-law's side.

As he was in no mood to argue with Ephraim Akri about the latter's harangue at Samaher's wedding, or even about Tedeschi's lecture, Rivlin let the department head do the talking while piloting them expertly northward. Loosely strapped into his seat, he listened with patient passivity to Akri's opinionated views, which grew most vocal at stoplights. The deeper his silence grew, the more cheerfully pessimistic about the Arabs his junior colleague became. Had the hard night rendered Rivlin apathetic toward opinions that usually exasperated him? Perhaps his strength had been sapped by Fu'ad's tale of Ofer's nocturnal prowling.

Although Akri was hurrying to a meeting at the university, he detoured to drop Rivlin off at his home to reward him for being so agreeable. He hoped, he said in parting, that his senior colleague's docility was not a sign that he was coming down with something. "I just may be," Rivlin replied with a smile. "What else could make me put up with your racism?" Yet he immediately clapped his driver warmly on the shoulder to mitigate the remark, while affirming that he had not yet said his final word.

The thought that he might actually have caught something from the proprietress was not totally unpleasant. Nevertheless, as he emptied the mailbox of mail that he couldn't read, his mood changed, and his lapsed anger at the woman who had recklessly broken his glasses flared up again.

The afternoon light was honey clear, the living room clean and tidy, and the food left in its pots on the counter by the housekeeper still warm. Although he had absconded for barely a day, his isolation from his wife, with whom he had not spoken since their quarrel, made the time seem much longer. Still unwilling to make up, however, he decided, even though he wasn't hungry, to eat lunch without waiting for her, which was something she hated. After eating, he went to his study. Unable to make out the letters on his keyboard, he took some paper and scrawled a few thoughts about the four languages that contributed to the conflict of national identity in Algeria. Now and then he paused to glance at the ghost of his mother sitting unconcernedly on her terrace in a summery green dress, her heavy arms bare and her stout, pale legs propped on a chair.

Yet reading and writing were impractical. Better, he thought, to lie down and ascertain whether he had really brought back a fever from Jerusalem. To his surprise, he found the bedroom neatly arranged, as if his wife had wished to prove she could make order without him. He pulled off his shoes and stretched out with a bittersweet feeling, then rose to lower the blinds and draw the curtain to make the room dark. He took off his trousers, unbuttoned his shirt, and tried to picture— a difficult task in such bourgeois surroundings—the dark depths of the hotel's basement.

It was not the basement, however, that he saw in the half-light. It was the tall, bony woman who had talked without inhibition while making the swan-sheeted bed with quick, snapping movements. She must have a crush on me, Rivlin thought with a start. Perhaps, despite her resentment of her dead father, she misses having an older man in her life.

Though his wife would soon be home from court, it seemed absurd to return to his study and to the old ghost on the terrace. And so, hearing the front door open, he pulled the blanket over him and turned to the wall. Hagit entered the bedroom without switching on the light. She lowered herself comfortably onto the bed and softly laid her hand on him as if nothing had happened and there were no need to ask.

"You're not going to fall asleep now anyway," she said. "Come, let's go to the kitchen. I shouldn't have to eat alone after a hard day's work."

The scent of her soft, full body bending toward him triggered his old love for her. He fought against it while trying to think of something sarcastic to say about lunatics who went around breaking glasses. Yet knowing well that any reply would lead to a conversation that—as sooner or later happens between rational people—would bring about the reconciliation his wife craved, he stubbornly clung to his silence.

Rebuffed anew, she gave him a hurt look and went to the kitchen to eat by herself. When she returned, she switched on the light, took off her dress, and put on a light robe. "I have news," she said directly. "Do you want to hear it? Or would you rather go on mourning your glasses?"

But his silence was out of control. It was stuck in his throat like a bone. Rising from the bed with a hangdog look, he buttoned his shirt and pulled on his pants with the intention of returning to his study. Hagit sat up and grabbed him. "I want you to listen," she said with a reassuring smile. "It's good news. Ofer is coming for six days. The Jewish Agency has given him a ticket to escort some youth group, but he only has to be with them on the flight itself."

Yet even this could not break his silence. As much as the news filled him with joy, it also made him realize that he feared his son's coming. With pretended nonchalance he bent to put on his shoes, conscious of how he was trying not only his wife's patience but his own.

"Will you stop it!" she cried with a desperation that wasn't like her, clutching at his shirt. "What is wrong with you?"

He shut his eyes and didn't move, to keep the shirt from tearing.

"Stay. Take off your clothes. Take them off! Lie down and rest. Don't start in again. Aren't you happy Ofer is coming?"

He didn't open his eyes or speak. He simply froze, feeling her fingers undoing, perhaps for the first time in her life, the buttons of his shirt. They touched his skin. They stroked it, clawed at it. Shameless and demanding, they grabbed at the zipper of his pants. It had never happened before. She wanted him, *now*, as her friend—her lover— her man. Shocked and thrilled by the frank desire of a woman who had always had to be courted patiently, with no end of cajoling words, he waived all rights to an apology or explanation and made his peace with a hasty, wordless reconciliation in which, slowly, the sweetness of absconding, now over with forever, faded and went out.

## 29.

When an entire people is linguistically confused, what hope is there for dialogue or communication?

Four languages mingle in Algerian life, leading to a chaotic identity:

First, there is Berber, the indigenous language of the Maghreb, spoken by close to a third of the population.

Second, there is North African Arabic, known to every Algerian. These two languages are oral media not used for writing, even though Berber once had a written form.

The two written languages of Algeria are French and classical literary Arabic. Neither, however, is a mother tongue. Both are in effect foreign languages. Classical Arabic comes with Islamization and French with Western colonialism. The first arrived as a sacred tongue, the second as a secular one.

It is obvious that, historically considered, reading and writing are forms of submission and penetration that create an intricate dialectic between the individual and the written language. To write in French is to betray. To write in Arabic is to profane.

Each of the four languages used in Algeria is thus subject to the dichotomies of the powerful/legitimate or sacred/secular. All four conflict at various levels of writing and speech. Each forms a discrete system having little significant contact with the others.

The complexity of this situation is problematic for every Algerian. Fully living an Algerian identity means knowing four languages, being at home in four cultures, and adapting to four different psychological standpoints.

Practically speaking, only 10 percent of the population of Algeria is proficient in all four languages. Such a small group is unable to bring about an integration of four different worlds. And even if such an integration were possible, it would be inaccessible to the majority of Algerians.

Rivlin scratched his head and paused before writing a last sentence.

This unique and problematic linguistic configuration has contributed to Algeria's rapid descent into violence.

## 30.

COULD HE REALLY still be wearing the same old army jacket? And had he put on weight, or was he just slower and more cumbersome, an old soldier fighting a rear-guard battle with himself? Rivlin, though happy to see his son, was worried by the figure that appeared on the closed-circuit screen above the exit from Customs. Yet Hagit, standing excitedly in the crowd of welcomers, their numbers undiminished despite its being the middle of the night, was unperturbed. She spread her arms wide to Ofer, overjoyed to see him.

"Where is the group you were supposed to escort?" Rivlin asked, after giving his son's forehead a kiss. "Aren't you still responsible for them?"

Ofer's responsibility, it turned out, had been virtual. The Jewish youngsters he was supposed to accompany for his free ticket had returned to France a week ago.

"Well, then," Rivlin laughed, "your only duty is to be with your parents."

But Ofer hadn't come to Israel to be dutiful to his parents. He had already, he informed them, phoned Tsakhi from Paris and suggested a diving expedition to the Sinai. The young officer, enthusiastic about the idea, was now working on getting leave.

"You see!" Rivlin exclaimed, crowing at his two sons' initiative. "In order to be with you, he'll pull a few days' leave out of a hat. But when we visited his base with your aunt and uncle, he didn't even have time say hello."

"Why must you always blame him for what isn't his fault?" Hagit protested, coming to Tsakhi's defense. "It will be wonderful," she told Ofer, "if you two can spend some quiet time together after having been apart for so long. I'd give a lot just to be able to see you."

"Why not dive with them?" Rivlin teased.

"Come to think of it, why not?" she said, reddening.

He awoke in the morning with the first light. Descending to the bottom floor of the duplex, he carefully opened the door of his younger son's room, in which Ofer was sleeping, his crew-cut head on the pillow. Brimming with compassion, Rivlin stood looking at him as though searching for some sign of his hopeless struggle with lost love.

Two years had gone by since they had last seen him, in Paris. The dear face so often pictured by them, now covered by two days' growth of beard, was broader and fleshier, perhaps a result of his classes at the Academy of Cooking in Montparnasse. For a moment, Ofer's eyes seemed to open. Then he turned his face to the wall. Had the father scrutinizing him been the subject of last night's conversation with his mother, with whom Ofer had sat up after Rivlin, unable to stay awake, had gone to bed? Or had he kept his grievances to himself?

Rivlin shut the door quietly and went to fetch the morning paper, of which he could read only the headlines. Then he went to the bedroom to see if Hagit was awake. Having been up half the night with Ofer, she would no doubt want to sleep. Yet, attuned to the wound-up man who tiptoed past her bed, she opened smiling eyes and promised to join him at the breakfast table.

By the time she did, he had eaten and was sitting by the unopened newspaper, which lay on the table as a mute testimony to his wife's crime. "I really am sorry," she said, picking up the paper and glancing at it. "If I had known how much you depended on those glasses, I would have been more careful. But you need to realize how impossible you sometimes are. It isn't what you do, it's what you hide."

"Please. Ofer is here. We agreed to a truce, so let's keep it. Don't be like the Arabs."

"The Arabs? Where do they come in?"

"They've always been here. After so many years of living with me, it's time you knew they're part of my mental world."

He went to switch on the electric kettle and take the toast from the toaster while she leafed rapidly through the paper as if looking for something. She found it, read it without comment, and put the paper aside.

"What were you looking at?"

"A notice that the verdict is today."

"The verdict? Today?"

"Yes."

"Well, I'm glad the damned thing is over."

"What's so damned about it?"

"It just is."

"But why?"

"I don't know. Maybe all those mysterious closed-door sessions got on my nerves."

"Why should they have mattered to you?"

"They just did."

"I wish you'd cut out all those 'justs.' Try to explain yourself. Why did this particular trial, which you knew nothing about, get on your nerves? Don't you have enough there already?"

"I do. But it did anyway. And I don't like your being a minority who can't convince the other judges."

"It's strange that you should need to feel I'm always in the right. Anyhow, the Supreme Court may rule that I was right on an appeal."

"You're that sure he didn't do anything?"

"I don't know what he did or didn't do. And I'm sure that he's a very shady type. But there simply isn't enough evidence to convict him."

"Forensic evidence."

"Yes, forensic. Don't make light of it."

"But when did you manage to write your dissent?"

"The night you ran away to the Tedeschis. Didn't you wonder why I never tried to get in touch with you?"

"As a matter of fact, I did."

"It was so quiet without you that I had all the time in the world to concentrate and finish it in one sitting."

"How did it come out?"

"It certainly convinced me." Hagit bobbed her head charmingly and took another sip of coffee.

"Will your opinion be in tomorrow's paper?"

"Only a few snippets. That's all the censor will allow."

"I'd like to read the full text."

"You'd be bored by it. There are parts you wouldn't follow. And I'd be in trouble if you blabbed about it afterward."

"Why should I blab?" he replied angrily. "To whom? Forget it. What I want to know is, what happened with Ofer after I went to sleep?"

"He talked about Paris. He loves it more every day."

"Did he say anything about a girlfriend?"

"No. I don't think he has one."

"So what will be?"

"There's nothing we can do about it."

"Nothing? I don't know about that. I suppose he criticized me."

"A bit. It's hard for him that you identify with him so much. He finds it a burden."

"I identify with him? He said that?" For some reason, this gladdened him. "But why should that bother him? I wish someone would identify with me...."

"Don't be so sure. It puts more spine in one to be opposed. And you think your identifying with him gives you the right to know things that he can't or doesn't want to talk about."

"Why can't he?"

"He just can't. You have to respect that. He was as upset as I was that you took advantage of your condolence call to quiz Galya. I don't want to say I told you so. But I did try to talk you out of going to that bereavement. All you did was complicate things."

"I didn't complicate anything. I wanted to understand."

"But you didn't."

"At least I tried."

"Look at the price, though."

"What price? Didn't you just say he said nice things about me?"

"Because he loves you."

"He does?" Rivlin marveled, as though at something impossible. "Did he really say that?"

"He didn't have to. I know it."

## 31.

YET NOT EVEN LOVE, real or potential, could wake the Parisian from his Israeli sleep. He's so used to sleeping by himself that he doesn't even dream anyone might be waiting for him to wake up, Rivlin thought sorrowfully, and proceeded to cancel all his morning appointments. He was hoping for a relaxed conversation with his son, not only to put the tensions between them to rest, but also, with the help of his night at the hotel, to uncover some new lead. Meanwhile, sans glasses, computer, notes, or reference books, he sat in his study ruminating in a giant scrawl about the Algerian language problem.

...And so we have a situation in which different sectors of social activity, having no common language, remain totally distinct. Classical Arabic is the language of religion. French is used for economic, administrative, and scientific purposes. North African Arabic and Berber are spoken in the street and in the family. This is the great curse of Algerian identity. It's not that such an identity does not exist, but that it is linguistically fragmented beyond any possibility of a synthesis. Thus French-speaking Algerians will say, "Ah, I completely fail to understand those Arab fundamentalists," while Arabic-speaking Algerians think the French-speakers are neocolonialists in the service of France. No Arabic-speaker believes anyone can love Algeria in French, no Berber-speaker believes anyone can love it in Arabic, and no French-speaker believes any intellectual life at all is possible in Arabic. Each side sees the others as an alien, hostile force. Such an Algeria is an Algeria at war.

The current civil war in Algeria is more a war of languages fighting for cultural space than it is a war between religious and secular society. The fundamentalist Arab must oppose the written civilization of the West with the Koran because that is the only sacred text he knows. The real choice facing Algeria, therefore, is: French or the Koran.

The writing flowed easily, carrying him along almost blindly, so that he forgot to keep his letters large and was soon unable to read what he had written. Although this had the advantage of making corrections or revisions impossible, such writing could not prevent him from thinking of his sleeping son. He rose from his desk, descended a few steps of the duplex, and stood midway between its floors, listening for a sign of life. But it was not until noon that the sound of water in the bathroom told him that the visitor from Paris was up.

They sat facing each other in the kitchen over a breakfast that turned gradually into lunch. Rivlin felt his way cautiously, seeking to cross no forbidden lines. Both he and Ofer avoided mentioning their harsh phone conversation, and Rivlin, afraid Hagit might have carelessly told Ofer about his second visit to the hotel, said nothing about the first—that springtime condolence call that now, at the end of a tedious summer, seemed so distant. And while he would have liked dearly to tell the spurned husband how much the new proprietress missed him and how she had lauded his architectural judgment, he knew very well that an allusion to his third, underground visit would never be forgiven.

And so, turning to the future, he tried finding out from his son when he planned to return to Israel. The night security guard of the Jewish Agency, however, was too much in thrall to the past to have any patience for the future. Dressed in old gym shorts and a T-shirt, his face unshaven and his eyes swimming from unsatisfying slumber, he replied that he had no plans. To listen to him, Rivlin remarked, one might think he was an adolescent still needing to experience life, rather than a grown man of over thirty. Not at all, Ofer replied. There were many new developments in the field of kitchen and restaurant design, both practical and theoretical, with which he ought to acquaint himself before leaving Paris. Meanwhile, gastronome that he now was, he criticized the housekeeper's pot roast, which he had eaten with relish in his benighted pre-Paris days.

"Why not make us a meal to demonstrate what you've learned over there?" Rivlin suggested.

Ofer was not keen on the idea. He and Tsakhi were returning from Sinai on Saturday, and on Monday he was flying back to Paris. That left barely a day.

"A day," his father said, "should be enough."

"We'll see," was the only commitment received.

Ofer went to phone his brother and came back with the news that Tsakhi's request for leave had been approved and that a soldier under his command, who lived across the bay in Acre, had enough diving equipment for the two of them. He would have to drive there now to pick it up.

Rivlin, thinking sadly that his son should be looking at baby carriages rather than at diving equipment, gave him the keys to the old jalopy. Soon Hagit came home from court. Setting the table for a second lunch, he allowed her to tell him about the two-to-one verdict, dismiss his criticisms of Ofer, and go to the bedroom to nap while he returned to his study in the hope of recapturing the morning's inspiration. But the writing that had gone so easily then had dried up and now felt pointless.

The front door opened and shut with a bang. It was Tsakhi. Rivlin went down to set the table for a third time. Although the young officer had already eaten at his base, he agreed to eat again for his father's sake. And in the end, still in his uniform with its officer's bars, he did so heartily.

"Listen, Tsakhi," Rivlin said. "You and Ofer will be spending a few days in another world. We're happy that he wants to spend most of his vacation with you. Ever since he went to France and you've been in the army, you haven't had a chance to be together. Now you'll have a few unpressured days on the beach. It will be an opportunity to find out what happened to him. What's bothering him. Why he can't find another woman."

His son's large eyes regarded him attentively.

"Are you listening?"

"Of course."

"All right. So you'll try tactfully to find out what happened. How and why his marriage fell apart. Maybe there was some mistake..."

"What kind of mistake?"

"Even a fantasy."

"A fantasy?" The young officer seemed alarmed.

"I said maybe. What do we know about it? Nothing. But in the peace and quiet of a beach in Sinai, you can find out more. Okay?"

Tsakhi gave no sign whether it was okay or not. He just went on listening with the same concentration, although by now looking distinctly uneasy.

"You'll have lots of time to find out—just do it unobtrusively—why he's so secretive. You should know that he loves you and trusts you without limit. You can let us know afterward, in a general way, what he told you, so that we can think of how to help him. You know I'm worried sick about him. Do you follow me?"

"Of course."

"And you promise to try?"

The young officer put down his knife and fork and said nothing. His fretful glance made Rivlin think of the rabbit he had seen hop out of the bushes on his walk near his son's base.

"Are you listening?"

"Of course."

"Then you'll do it for me? You promise?"

And still the young officer said nothing. Not wanting to hurt or embarrass his father, he kept his large eyes on him, their pain and anxiety growing. Only now did it dawn on Rivlin what his silence meant.

## 32.

ON HIS WAY to the university the next day, he stopped by the optician's to demand the speedy delivery of his new glasses. Five days had gone by since his old pair was broken. "You mean demolished," the optician smirked, promising that during his lunch break he would fetch them himself from the lab in Haifa Bay.

It was the summer-vacation doldrums, and the campus was quiet. Ephraim Akri was in Florida, at a conference sponsored by the University of Miami to mark the twentieth anniversary of Edward Said's *Orientalism*. One of the conference's organizers, having read some of Akri's articles in various semischolarly magazines, had been impressed by their metahistorical sweep and intellectual boldness. Hearing that the man was a Middle Easterner not only by birth but by looks and had a remarkable command of Arabic despite being Jewish, he had immediately invited him as a counterweight to the Palestinian professor's disciples, who were terrorizing the academic community.

Consequently, although the fall semester was still far away, Rivlin had been asked to be the temporary department head, if only to prevent the university's dean and rector from taking advantage of Akri's absence to pirate a disputed half-time teaching slot. Reluctant to use

Akri's room, Rivlin functioned from the main office, where he'd had to ask the two secretaries to read the mail to him. He was in the middle of tearing up and throwing out some routine circulars and giving instructions to the pair, who seemed glad to have him back, when in walked Dr. Miller and asked to have a private talk. He had just received, he told Rivlin, a tempting offer from Ben-Gurion University in Beersheba and had come to inquire about his long-deferred promotion. Did he have a future in Haifa, or should he accept the invitation from down south?

Rivlin refrained from revealing that he was chairman of the secret committee considering Miller's case. Promising rather vaguely that the promotion was on its way, he pointed to the window and said, with a smile:

"If I were you I'd be patient before moving to the desert—if not for the university's sake, then at least for this view's."

The promising young scholar, however, was not appeased by the bluish hills of the Galilee. Not even the gleaming expanse of the Mediterranean could make up for the delay in his promotion. And since his keen analytical mind told him that the guileful professor was on the secret committee, he had come to present him with an ultimatum. Rivlin nodded, remembering Miller's bleached-out wife, who had been pregnant at Samaher's wedding. When, he inquired discreetly, was she giving birth?

"Giving birth?" The young scholar glanced askance at him.

Rivlin felt his cheeks burn.

"Excuse me. It's just that... at Samaher's wedding... I thought that... or at least I guessed..."

He had guessed correctly, Miller told him. Unfortunately, the pregnancy had ended in a miscarriage.

"I'm terribly sorry," the Orientalist said, without feeling sorry in the least. He promised to speak to the dean without waiting for Akri to come back from Miami and asked in return, with a twinge of anxiety, whether his analytically minded colleague would care to look at a recently written first draft of an article on Algeria. Not that Algeria was Miller's field, but there were some theoretical points that might interest him.

His head felt heavy. Late last night he and his wife had driven their two sons to the bus for Eilat, after which he had been unable to fall asleep. Not wishing to usurp the department head's armchair, he took the cup of coffee given him by the secretaries and went to his room at the end of the corridor. There he shut the door and dialed Fu'ad.

"*Wallah*, Professor!" boomed the deep voice of the maître d' from Jerusalem. "I looked everywhere and couldn't find it. But if you'd like, I can write a new . . . what's the word?"

"Elegy."

"Elegy? Sorry. The same as at a funeral. That must be why I can't remember it."

Over the phone came the sound of a woman's laughter.

"Who was that?" Rivlin asked. "Let me talk to her."

"So," the voice chortled, "you ran away in the middle of the night! What happened to you? Don't tell me you were afraid of the tax authorities."

He joined her laughter. "For a second I thought there was an earthquake."

"You're not the only one who's imagined that. But believe me, all that ever quakes down there is one's heart."

"How is your cold?"

"Thank you for remembering it. It has no time to get better. Every little problem at this hotel ends up in my lap."

"That's your own fault."

"Naturally."

"You know," he surprised himself by saying, "Ofer is here from Paris for a week."

"Then tell him to come. Galya left two cartons of his things in the basement."

"Cartons?"

"Yes. She came back from abroad bursting with energy and started housecleaning. Either he takes them or I throw them out. I'm not turning this hotel into a warehouse."

"I'll tell him."

"Why don't you come, too? That will be twice as nice."

"I'll see," he said, his heart skipping a beat. "Let me have Fu'ad for a minute."

"*Aiwa, ya habibi.*"*

"*Ala kul hal, dawwar ala l'marthiyi l'adimi.*"†

"*Min shanak hatta taht al-ard.*"‡

He hung up and sat thinking of the unreal night in Jerusalem. His coffee had no taste, and he went to the cafeteria to look for a stronger brew. Although it was vacation time, the cafeteria was packed with older people who were taking summer extension courses.

He sat and sipped his coffee slowly, gazing idly at a dark-skinned boy of about ten who was circulating among the tables. Noticing a half-eaten pita, the boy stopped, looked around, snatched it from its plate, and swallowed it quickly before putting on a pair of horn-rimmed glasses and heading for the nearby library.

Rashid is here, Rivlin thought. He jumped up and followed the boy, who was stopped by a guard at the entrance to the library. "It's all right, he's with me," Rivlin said. He put a hand on Rasheed's neck and pushed him through the library door.

He was not mistaken. The boy recognized the Jewish professor who had eaten his mother's bean soup and like a hunting dog led him up and down the floors of the library and in and out of the narrow stacks. In the end they found Rashid, squatting on his haunches while looking on the bottom shelf for a book listed on a scrap of paper.

"*Lakeyt kaman el-yahudi hada,*"§ the boy called to his uncle, as though he had indeed been sent to fetch Rivlin.

Rashid did not seem at all surprised by Rivlin's appearance. Perhaps he had known that sooner or later the Jewish passenger would again need his Arab driver. Still squatting, he handed the Orientalist the catalog number.

"Can you find this?"

"What is it?"

---

* Yes, my friend.
† In any case, look for that old elegy.
‡ For you, I'd go to the ends of the earth.
§ I've also found that Jew.

"A play, *The Dybbuk*. Have you heard of it?"

"*The Dybbuk*?" Rivlin burst into laughter. "Samaher sent you to bring her *The Dybbuk*?"

This time, however, Rashid hadn't come to the university for his cousin, but only on her advice. He was in the library in connection with the coming song and poetry festival in Ramallah. It was going to be a happening, with no politics or debates. A big new cultural center, named for the prominent Palestinian educator Khalil es-Sakakini, had recently opened in the West Bank city north of Jerusalem. Well-known poets like Mahmoud Darwish, who came from Amman to give readings, had already appeared there. There would be singers from Gaza and Hebron, and Jewish vocalists too. Perhaps even the Lebanese nun, for the Abuna had gone to her Lebanese convent to ask her to cheer the Christians of Palestine again. She would sing, not prayers, but folk songs, and perhaps even have one of her fainting fits.

"If she promises to faint," Rivlin said enthusiastically, "I'll come."

"Of course you will. You'll bring your wife. Why shouldn't she hear all the wonderful music? You can bring your friends too, the more the merrier. Everyone is welcome. It's for all believers in coexistence. No politics. No debates. No history. No who's right and who's wrong. Just songs and poems in Arabic and Hebrew. They even asked us to put something on the program that would be traditionally Jewish. Samaher thought we should surprise everyone with *The Dybbuk*, because—so she says—it's the *Hamlet* of the Jews."

The Orientalist guffawed, making the somber Arab boy stare at him.

"And Samaher? Where has she disappeared to?"

"She hasn't disappeared anywhere. She's sad. In the village they think it's because of the grade she never got."

"She never got it because she never finished her work. She keeps dragging it out, as usual. Let her do it once and for all. It isn't that difficult. But it can't just be oral summaries, because then I have no way of knowing what's in the texts. I need to see at least one entire story, translated from beginning to end. I promise to give her a grade then."

"I'll tell her," Rashid said.

He reached out to pat the boy, who seemed to be trying to follow the Hebrew. It would be his second language—if he were ever allowed back into Israel.

## 33.

TANNED AND EXUBERANT, Tsakhi and Ofer returned from their diving adventure on Saturday. They showered, changed into fresh clothes, and hurried off to the Arab market to buy lamb, vegetables, and spices for a French gastronomic experience. Rivlin had no chance to be alone with his younger son or to ask him whether, between dives, he had managed to learn anything from his brother. Tsakhi, though friendly, did not seem interested in talking to his father even when he took time out from his job as assistant chef. And when dinnertime arrived, it turned out that there were guests. Ofer had invited four old friends. The older generation, it had been decided, would eat first and then go to the movies, leaving the younger one to dine by itself.

And so Rivlin sat facing Hagit over a handsomely set table, expertly waited on by their two sons. Ofer, wielding a long knife, carved the fragrant French roast into long, thin slices swimming in sauce.

"You remind me of that elegant Arab waiter in the hotel in Jerusalem," Rivlin said innocently. "What was his name? Fu'ad?"

The carving knife trembled momentarily in their divorced son's hand, which quickly regained its grip.

"What about him?"

"I was just reminded of him. I think of him as the perfect waiter. I was surprised to see at the bereavement how well he still bears himself."

"Where did you see him?"

"In that big room on the first floor."

"The library."

"I suppose so. He was made to stand, all in black, behind a table with a condolence book."

"A condolence book?" Ofer's voice filled with bitter mockery. "You've got to be kidding."

"I also thought it was a bit much. But I imagine they did it for all the Christians who came to pay their respects."

"I hope you weren't foolish enough to write anything."

"What's foolish? I had no choice."

"Why not?"

"I just didn't. I suppose that Arab waiter made me feel it was expected of me."

"What did you write?"

"I don't remember. I just did."

"There you go with your 'justs' again!" Hagit's eyes were not sympathetic. "You always remember every word you write."

"Every word? Really! That's a bit of an exaggeration. But what does it matter what I wrote? It was just something off the top of my head. A few words about his generosity. You can't deny him that. His light..."

Ofer bristled. "What light?"

"It was just something I wrote. For God's sake, let me be! What does it matter?"

He carefully cut a slice of the meat on his plate, dipped it in the sauce, and put it in his mouth. It had the perfumed tang of an exotic game animal.

"The roast is wonderful," Hagit said. "So delicate."

"Yes," Rivlin agreed. "It doesn't taste exactly like lamb, but it's delicious. Something special."

But Ofer wasn't looking for compliments. "How did Fu'ad recognize you?" he asked.

"Why shouldn't he? It's only been five years." Rivlin continued to chew while he talked. "You needn't be so hostile to them. They speak of you affectionately. By the way, Tehila called to say that Galya has left two cartons of your old things in the hotel basement. She's cleaning out her apartment before giving birth."

"Giving birth?" Ofer turned white. He laid a hand on his cheek, as if hiding something.

"She's going to have a baby."

No one spoke.

"Who told you?"

"It was my impression from Tehila." Rivlin spread blameless hands. "I could be wrong."

Hagit's furious expression, and his younger son's pained, sad look, told him he had made a mistake.

"What did you tell her?" Ofer asked, in a rough, interrogating voice.

"What could I tell her? I said I'd come to Jerusalem and take the cartons. That was before I knew you were coming."

"Don't take anything! Stay away from there. Do me a favor, Abba. Leave the hotel and the family alone."

"I'll be glad to. But don't you want to know what's in those cartons?"

"It can't be anything important."

"Because I thought that if your flight is Monday morning and I'm still on vacation, we could drive to Jerusalem to have a look. Maybe you'll find something . . ."

"That's silly," Hagit said. "It's a waste of time. There's nothing there."

But Ofer, staring angrily as his father carved another, thicker slice of lamb, muttered something no one could make out.

And so it was that, a few hours before his flight, under a torrid morning sky, they drove past the airport on their way to Jerusalem. Rivlin, at a fever pitch, almost regretted the whole thing. He leaned forward in his loosely fastened seatbelt, intently following the curves of the road as if he and not his son were driving. Ofer, on his way to a place in which, even if it was not Paradise, he had been happier than he was now, said nothing behind the steering wheel.

It was only in Talpiyot, in the clear desert light, silently crossing the large garden with its shrubs and flowers that were swooning in the heat, that Rivlin felt, like a lightning bolt, the full force of the spurned husband's excitement. A strange smile played over Ofer's tense, wide-eyed face. Certain he could find the cartons by himself, he had told no one he was coming, preferring to avoid an encounter with the woman whose love entrapped him. That could only send him back to Paris branded by more of the old pain.

He appeared to know what he was doing. The morning bustle at the hotel was over. The keys hanging behind the reception desk indicated that the guests had already set out on their pilgrim mission of frequenting the lanes of Jerusalem's Old City or the ruins of Masada. A single receptionist, a sleepy young Arab, made no comment as the nervous father and son walked past him. Rivlin prayed that they would not run into the proprietress. If she ever opens her mouth and tells Ofer how I played detective here, he thought, all the love in the world will never save me.

The kitchen was deserted. The guests' tours fed them lunch, and supper was still a long way off. Rivlin watched with amazement as Ofer led him unerringly past the big stoves and sleek worktables. It was as if he had been here yesterday. By the little door to the basement stairs he paused and asked doubtfully:

"Are you sure you want to come down with me? Wouldn't you rather wait in the lobby?"

"I'd better not," said Rivlin, his heart in his mouth. "If anyone sees me, it will mean a whole long conversation, and we want to be on time for your flight."

Ofer looked at his father as if seeing him for the first time and headed down the dark stairs, flicking on the lights one after another as though his fingers remembered where each switch was. They walked along the corridor, passed the closets and the bicycle, sidestepped the bucket of plaster and the old tire, and came to the space with the baby carriage, crib, and old monster of a boiler. As though he knew where to look for them, Ofer went straight to two small cartons in a corner. Disgustedly, hoping for nothing, he began going through them, pulling out a bare canteen, a crumpled army fatigue shirt with sergeant's stripes, a blackened copper bowl, and some old notebooks, and stopping only when he reached an old pajama top at the bottom.

"She's crazy," he muttered, offended. "What did she save all these rags for?"

"She didn't think she was saving them," Rivlin said. "She simply went through life like your mother, without noticing how many unnecessary things she was surrounded by."

Ofer stuffed everything irritably back into the carton, except for a single book, which he laid by the baby carriage. He was bent over the second carton, which looked no more promising than the first, when Fu'ad's bass voice boomed through the basement:

"*Heyk, ya jama'a, bidun ma t'salem? Zay el-haramiyya?*"*

"*Shu ni'mal?*"† Rivlin put his hands behind his ears in the gesture of Muslim prayer. "We have no time to be polite. Ofer's flight takes off in three hours."

"Still landing and taking off, eh?" Fu'ad laughed. "How will it all end? You Jews can't sit still. It will drive you crazy."

He gave Ofer a warm hug.

"The years have gone by, and you've grown into your own man. But it wasn't nice of you to forget all your friends here. If it weren't for your father's coming now and then to remind us of you, we would have forgotten you completely."

Before Rivlin could change the subject, Ofer turned to him with open anger, a new, menacing note in his voice:

"So you were here more than once?"

"Didn't I tell you?" He tried getting out of it with a sheepish smile.

"No. When? Why?"

"Because your father was stuck in Jerusalem with no place to sleep," the maître d' explained, telling the story. "He thought he would find a room here. How was he to know we're more full up than ever since Mr. Hendel's death? Just imagine: your own father, whom we respect and honor, had to sleep down here in the basement! Or at least he slept here half the night, because in the middle of it the poor man woke up and ran away in a fright. Isn't that so, Professor? *Kif fakart fujatan 'an haza ardiyya....*"‡

He clapped the Orientalist on the back and gave Ofer, who stared at his father incredulously, a conspiratorial laugh.

"You agreed to sleep here?"

"What could I do? I thought..."

"You thought what?" His elder son's voice was now a stifled cry. "What were you trying to do?"

Rivlin affected an astonished smile. "What do you mean, trying to do?"

---

* Is that how you come here, my friends, like thieves, without even saying hello?
† What can I do?
‡ You suddenly thought there was an earthquake.

But Ofer had already turned more gently to Fu'ad. "Is this room still in use?" he asked wonderingly.

"Why shouldn't it be?"

"And you still don't have the key?"

Hiding a smile, the Arab went to the baby carriage, moved the dusty toy animals, lifted the mattress, took a key, and opened the door to the accountant's room, whose shelves creaked beneath the weight of their old files.

Ofer froze in the doorway as though caught in a dream or a fantasy. His eyes were riveted to a new, large quilt that lay on the bed like a layer of frozen white foam.

Rivlin's heart skipped a beat at the sight of the quilt, foamy bright in the dark room. He wondered what made Fu'ad sound so exultant when he said:

"One way or another, it's still there, Ofer, eh?"

And with that he locked the door. "You mustn't miss your flight," he murmured.

Ofer took the book he had put by the baby carriage and started up the stairs. "You can throw out those two cartons," he called scornfully over his shoulder to Fu'ad. "Or give them to someone in your village. Come on," he said to his father. "We'll be late."

But in the empty parking lot, by their car baking in the sun, he halted and said to Rivlin:

"I have nothing more to say to you. Just shut up and don't answer me. Not one word. I don't want any explanations or rationalizations. I've had enough. Let's go to the goddamn airport and say good-bye."

"But what have I done to you, Ofer? What's wrong?"

"You haven't done anything. You're simply an impossible man. A sneaking, bossy traitor who wants to spy on my soul. Well, you can't. You're not spying on anything."

"But what have I done?"

"You know perfectly well what you've done and what you're doing. Ever since her fucking father's bereavement, you've kept coming back here to paw at my past. It's sickening, and it's pointless. God! Am I glad I'm leaving and won't have to see you anymore!"

"How can you say such a thing?"

"I can say what I like!" The stifled cry burst from him, echoing through the garden. "What gives you the right to trespass on anyone's life?"

Rivlin felt on fire. The sunlight wounded his eyes. His son's sudden anger frightened him.

"But I only wanted to help you to move on. To share your pain and find a way for you to . . ."

"You're not finding a way for me to do anything. You can't."

"But why can't I? Only because I know nothing. If you'd tell me why they drove you from here . . ."

"But I won't! Do you hear me?" He was shouting now. "I won't tell you anything. You'd better accept that. Either you stop your vile habit of poking around basements or you're not my father anymore. I swear to God, I'll have nothing more to do with you!"

"But why?" Rivlin implored, desperately trying to keep calm. "Who are you protecting? Yourself—or her too? Why keep secrets after so many years? There's a statute of limitations on secrets too. Ask your mother. She'll tell you."

Ofer's face was contorted. "I'm not asking anyone. I'll decide when enough time has passed. Not you! Do you hear me? Not you! I don't want to talk about it any more. Period. And you'll either accept that or lose one son."

Yet just when it seemed that his anguish would end in tears or violence, he looked away and out over the large garden with its gravel paths and gazebo, silent in the noonday heat. When he turned back and spoke to his father, who was watching him motionlessly, it was in a different, quiet tone. "Because if I tell you what happened," he said, "I'll lose my only chance of coming back here."

"Coming back here?" Rivlin clutched at the car door for support. "Are you telling me that you're still hoping . . . to get together again . . . *now*, when she's about to have a child?"

"That's none of your business."

"Ofer, my darling, I'll swear to you never to come back here. I'll swear never to say a word to anyone. I won't even think about it anymore. This is the last time. I beg you, don't leave me more tormented than I've been. Just say one sentence, because I have to be sure I understand. Do you really believe she'll take you back?"

Ofer said nothing.

"I beg you. Just say yes or no. Answer your father. Because maybe I misunderstood you."

"You understood me very well," his son murmured with a sudden tenderness, as though lapsing into an inner reverie. "Amazingly enough, I do believe it."

"If that's so," Rivlin said in horror, "it's because you've decided to chain yourself forever. You're destroying yourself and your future . . ."

"That's my right." He made a fist as though to strike his father. "It's my right just as it's anyone's right to live by real or imagined love. But listen here, I'm warning you. If there's one more word out of you— one word! about anything!—I'm not getting into this car. I'll get to the airport by myself, and that's the last you'll see of me."

PART VI

# The Dybbuk

ALTHOUGH HE KNEW there was no getting out of it, since not even a generous present, given in advance, would have soothed the sting of their absence, he went on hoping on that autumn evening, right up to the last minute, for something unexpected to save him from the wedding. Yet he kept his grumbling to himself. For all his criticism in recent years of their housekeeper's careless cleaning and dull cooking, he would always be grateful for her unstinting loyalty, for her love for his two boys, even for some of her meals. And so while Hagit debated what to wear, he sat in his black suit by the front door and studied the map on the invitation.

There was no Arab driver this time; there were no young parking attendants waving lanterns to show them the road, just the two of them, trying to find their way in the industrial zone of Haifa Bay. They passed garages, textile plants, furniture outlets, and appliance stores and finally reached a large wedding hall that glittered with neon magic. And even then they had to look for their wedding, since the disco music pounding inside came from several celebrations at once.

Was this the right one? Despondent and already exhausted, they stood on a palatial marble staircase that led to a reception room decorated with artificial flowers, wondering whether to slip the check they had brought into the gold-leafed box in front of them or to hand it directly to the housekeeper.

"Well," Rivlin said, deciding to deposit the check in the box, "we can go now." The sight of so many overweight cousins and aunts, escorted by little husbands in loud jackets, filled him with odium. However, as they knew none of these people and so would have no one to testify to their attendance, they had no choice but to take their seats at a numbered table with a basket of stale-looking rolls, a bottle of white wine, and a tray of wizened garnishes, there to wait, beneath the savage onslaught of the music, to see who would be their dinner mates.

Nothing had changed since the Arab wedding in the Galilee that spring. Surrounded by strangers, ordinary people with every right to celebrate and enjoy themselves, he felt only his own failure. The bile of envy rose in his gorge, as if all the weddings taking place in this building had conspired to reopen his old wound.

"Why don't we just get up and walk out?" he shouted to his wife over the violent music, which had driven a wedge between them. "Don't tell me you came here for the food."

This proposal was so undeserving of a response that the judge did not bother to make one. Only when Rivlin repeated it did she reply severely:

"Believe me, I'd rather be in bed now, too. But we have to wait for the ceremony so that we can congratulate her. Why can't you understand how much we, and especially I, mean to her?"

The ceremony did not appear to be imminent. Some members of the younger set were already gyrating wildly to the music, and new guests continued to arrive. No one joined them at their table. Time passed. "The families must be haggling over the wedding contract," Hagit remarked, lighting another cigarette while staring at the red velvet curtain from which the bride and groom were to emerge. Rivlin, though he had only a vague notion of the family feuds that the housekeeper kept the judge informed about, gave up all hope for a quick getaway and reached for the tray of garnishes, from which he began to collect the olives. His ennui was only heightened when a small, elderly man in an old brown three-piece suit sat down warily at their table. The man, who had a slight palsy, recognized the Rivlins, at whose company he seemed pleased. Contentedly reaching for a roll, he crumbled it between his fingers and held out his wineglass for Rivlin to fill.

"I'm glad to see you two," he said with a sagacious smile, brushing the crumbs from his suit. "I wasn't sure you were coming. The mother of the bride has been working for us even longer than for you, ever since she was a girl. She stayed on after my wife died, until I moved to a senior citizens' home seven years later. But we're still on good terms. When you think of the difficult background she comes from, she's an amazingly pleasant and well-adjusted person. Of course her cooking isn't exactly—what's the word the young folk like to use?—awesome. Let's hope tonight's meal was cooked by someone else, ha, ha, ha..."

Rivlin permitted himself a covert smile, which did not escape the old widower's sharp eye.

"Yes, I know all about you," he said, picking at the roll with palsied fingers. "She brings me up-to-date when she visits me—all about your new apartment, and your sons and what they're doing. She's very attached to you, Your Honor, and always says how patient you are with her. Which reminds me... if it isn't intruding... I mean, as long as we're at the same table... you see, I couldn't tell from yesterday's paper... what exactly were your reasons for acquitting that damned spy? Why, he's not even an Arab."

"Not an Arab?" Rivlin asked in puzzlement.

"You see, Professor," the widower said, taking him into his confidence, "we all know our judges go easy on Arabs. They do it even with ordinary murderers and rapists, not to mention terrorists. They're afraid—oh, yes, they are!—to be accused of something as unfashionable as patriotism. But in your wife's case, the defendant was Jewish and a big fish at that. That's why I wondered why she let him off the hook as if he were an Arab."

Pleased with his irony, the old widower took a sip of wine, broke into a cough, turned red, and nearly choked.

Hagit, perking up to the sound of a European wedding march played in a Middle Eastern style, did not even glance in the choking patriot's direction. Her eyes bright with emotion, she leaned forward to take her husband's hand and led him to the wedding canopy behind the procession that the large curtain had parted to admit. Ahead of them, accompanied by their families and a video crew, the bride and groom walked slowly and majestically.

Rivlin remembered the groom as a quiet, easily frightened boy. Now, dark-complexioned and thin, in a wide-lapelled suit and a black

hat, he looked like a pensive secret-service agent. He was holding the
hand of his father, a greengrocer, whose own suit was a summery
white. Its color matched the muslin veil of the bride, who was now
floating down the aisle between two women, one big and fat and one
slim and attractive. For a moment, Rivlin failed to recognize the slim
woman as their housekeeper. She bore herself gracefully in a bare-
shouldered yellow silk dress, her head topped by an auburn hairpiece
glittering with sequins, her heavily made-up eyes regarding the world
as if it were no longer quite worthy of her. Meeting the surprised
glance of her employer as she passed him twice, once in front of him
and once on a large screen above his head, she flashed, so he thought,
a triumphant smile.

## 2.

STANDING IN LINE at the pharmacy of his health clinic for his blood-
pressure medicine, Rivlin took a step back from the old woman in
front of him, whose blue-tinged hair he found distasteful. She sensed
his presence and turned to look at him. It was the ghost in person, her
baggy old jacket grazing his clothes. He smiled at her desiccated face,
which was heavier and infinitely harder than his mother's. Failing to
place the bespectacled, scholarly voyeur, the ghost stared blankly at
him and turned around again, shifting a long list of prescriptions
from hand to hand. As soon as a new window opened, she darted for
it more quickly than he would have thought possible at her age and
was the first to reach it. The Orientalist, amused, did not bother
changing lines.

When Rivlin was a small boy, his father kept a journal of his son's
exploits that he read aloud to whoever would listen. Sometimes,
wishing to relive his childhood, Rivlin browsed in it. The boy rather
sentimentally described in its pages was capable of great and even extreme obstinacy and was not always very clever. Sometimes, Rivlin
succeeded in dredging from the depths of memory the incidents his
father related—the time he pretended to conduct an orchestra of
children in nursery school; the time he chased a runaway chicken. Yet

the most famous of these stories, the one in which he proposed marriage to his mother, was one he had no recollection of. Perhaps this
was why, although its psychological significance seemed obvious, he
smiled mysteriously whenever he read it.

## The Six-Year-Old Rivlin Proposes Marriage to His Mother

When Rivlin attended first grade, his father walked him to school
on his way to work every day, crossing the streets of the old downtown with him. The little boy liked to take his time, especially when
he spied a pile of builder's sand or gravel, which he felt duty-bound
to climb. One day his father lost his temper at his dallying. When this
didn't help, he pointed to a neatly dressed and combed blond boy
walking with his schoolbag on his back, and said:

"That does it! I'm trading you in for that nice blond boy. From
now on he'll be my son."

Rivlin, who was standing on a big pile of gravel while regarding the
old Knesset building, was thunderstruck. Turning red with indigna-
tion, he began to call the little stranger names, even declaring that he
was Hitler's son, a cruel boy who had to be watched out for. Reaching
the school with his father, who now regretted the whole thing, he refused to kiss him good-bye.

The first-grade student—so his father's journal continued—sat in
the classroom in an agitated state. As soon as the recess bell rang, he
raced into the schoolyard to vent his feelings to his big sister. By the
time he found her standing with some friends, however, the bell had
rung again, and there was no time to say a word. Instead of returning
to class he burst into tears and ran home, dashing blindly across
streets whose dangers he had been warned of without stopping to
climb a single pile of sand. His mother was in the kitchen. Without
mincing words, he said:

"You should never have married that man. I'd make a better husband. Why don't you leave him and marry me?"

His mother, pleased by the unexpected proposal, did not reject it
out of hand. She made Rivlin repeat it and finally coaxed the whole

story from him, after which he calmed down and regained his old brashness—so much so that, when his exhausted father came home at the end of a day's work, he opened the door and said:

"Hurry up and go to Ima! She wants to spank you!"

His father ended this episode by remarking:

"Who would have thought, my little boy, that a passing remark of mine would stir up such a dreadfully strong spirit of jealousy and contention? From now on I shall never cease to worry, for if every little thing excites you so badly, what will happen when you grow older?"

### 3.

DEAR, SWEET AUTUMN, don't let us down, Rivlin exhorted the skies every morning, as he opened the shutter to study the color and shape of the clouds drifting over the Carmel. "Another rainless, stormless winter like the last two and I'll go out of my mind," he told his wife. Hagit lay self-indulgently beneath the big white quilt that he had made her take from the closet in the hope of coercing the cold weather to come.

The fall semester was about to begin, students were flocking to ask for advice, and the department head was still in America. His lecture at the conference on "Twenty Years of Edward Said's *Orientalism*" had gone so well that even exiles from Iraq and Sudan had asked him for a copy of the text, which he had delivered in Arabic as a symbolic provocation. If Akri was to be trusted, the New York–based Palestinian professor, or one of his disciples, would now have to rewrite the book, in order to defend it against the Haifaite's challenges, hot off the Middle Eastern griddle. Of course, some of the conference's participants had sought to dismiss the Israeli Arabist as simply another Western Orientalist like those accused by Said of marginalizing the Arab world—a pseudoscholar treating the Middle East as an absence to be filled by his presence, or as a shadow play waiting to be brought to life by its colonialist puppeteers. And yet how could the Middle East be absent, or a shadow, in a courageously original Middle Easterner like Ephraim Akri, a stalwart, God-fearing Levantine, albeit a Jewish one, whose brown skin and sad Bedouin eyes were those of a true son of the desert and whose command of the subtleties of Arabic put to shame the politically correct professors from New England and northern California who couldn't pronounce correctly a single Arabic curse? His bold new ideas had made such an impression that he had been invited to speak to numerous Jewish and Christian groups, who were eager to hear an Old Historian's reasons for believing that the situation in the Middle East was more hopeless than anyone thought.

And so, while Akri was enlightening his audiences in Florida and even inviting one of his grandsons to join him for a tour of Disneyland, his temporary replacement moved back into his old room, the spacious and well-lit office of a department head. Putting up with the gaze of both grandsons, one blond and one dark, he resumed his job of advising students—new and old, Arab and Jewish—on how best and least onerously to fulfill their obligations and keep the department from losing them.

He avoided serious phone talks with Ofer, the depth of whose hostility he did not dare to gauge for fear of a brutal rebuff. (On their trip to the airport, his son had kept his vow of silence, uttering a total of three inconsequential sentences.) Letting Hagit conduct their weekly conversation with Paris, he listened over the second receiver like a circumspect aide-de-camp, asking an occasional pointless question. Ofer's acquiescence in this arrangement, however artificial, allowed him to hope that his son, who had lost all self-control that day at the hotel, was taking himself in hand.

Even after getting his new glasses, he did not hurry to type his handwritten reflections on Algeria into his computer. Perhaps he feared that weaknesses and inconsistencies not apparent in the heat of composition might show up on the bright screen. Meanwhile, to the delight of the two secretaries, he spent much of his time in his old office, comfortably ensconced in the big armchair that had been his own acquisition. No one, he knew, could run the department as well as he could. Though he was only doing so on a stopgap basis, he did his best to solve the problems brought to him.

One morning he heard Rashid talking to the secretaries. Straining to listen, he learned that Samaher's cousin was on a secret, Rivlin-bypassing mission to obtain certification, at least of a provisional

nature, of his M.A. student's completion of all her course requirements for the previous year. The secretaries, remembering him as
their driver to the wedding in Mansura, asked about the vanished
bride.

"She hasn't been feeling well," Rashid said. "That's why she asked
me to take care of this."

"What's the matter with her?"

"She isn't well," he repeated. "She can't concentrate. It's the
situation."

"What situation?"

"Ours. The country's."

They checked Samaher's file, saw that she had an incomplete from
Professor Rivlin, and dispensing with further formalities, waved
Rashid in to the department head. Much to his surprise, the trusty
messenger, who had had no intention of doing so, found himself facing Samaher's teacher.

"Are you running the department again?" he asked.

"Just for a while," Rivlin apologized. "Shut the door. What's new?
What does Samaher want now?"

"Temporary certification that she's completed her requirements."

"Temporary certification? There's no such thing as temporarily
completing something. You shouldn't let her use you like this, Rashid."

The coal black eyes, taken aback, stared at him, then looked
thoughtfully down at the floor.

Rivlin felt a pang. "You didn't bring me anything from her? Not
even one story? Not a single poem?"

"She can't...," Rashid murmured, in genuine anguish. "She really
can't..." He regarded the Orientalist as if deciding whether to trust
him, then whispered in Arabic:

"*Al-hayal sar kabt, u'l'kabt b'dur ala 'l-jnun.*"*

"You'll drive me crazy, too," the Orientalist said absently, with a
bitter smile.

Rashid seemed to have thought of that possibility, for he did not
look surprised. He merely laid a defensive hand on his heart and asked:

---

* She's depressed from imagining and crazy from being depressed.

"Why me?"

"Listen here, Rashid. I want the truth."

The truth, it seemed, was a long story. It had to do with Samaher's father-in-law, the contractor, a difficult man who had insisted on hospitalizing his confused daughter-in-law in Safed, so that she could be cured of...

"...of...the horse."

"The horse?"

Rashid sighed. "Yes. She keeps imagining it."

"And she's still there?"

"Who?"

"Samaher. In the hospital."

"Just a little while longer. We have to be patient. Soon she'll get out. That's what the doctor says. She wants to very badly...."

The sky outside the window had clouded over. A bolt of lightning pawed at the bay. But Rashid, though he had never been in this room, had no interest in its views, neither of the bay nor of the mountains. Running his glance over the books on the shelves, he let it linger on the photographs of Akri's grandsons, as if committing them to memory. His silence filled Rivlin with a warm memory of their night journey. He would have liked, in obedience to an old longing, to take to the road once again with the messenger, who now reached into his jacket pocket and pulled out a crumpled white skullcap that he smoothed with his hand.

"Is that for *The Dybbuk*, Rashid?"

An Arab librarian, Rashid explained, had helped him find the play and had convinced the student at the checkout counter to let him borrow it under Samaher's name. They were already rehearsing it.

"Then the festival is really taking place?"

"Of course it is." Rashid was insulted. "When did I ever lie to you?"

Everyone in Ramallah, he told Rivlin, even the police, was organizing for the event. The date was set for a Saturday night in late November, which worked out well for Jews, Christians, and Muslims. In fact, it turned out to be on the anniversary of the 1947 United Nations partition resolution for Palestine. He, Rashid, would bring the professor from Jerusalem if he didn't want to drive through Palestinian territory himself. There would be plenty of room in the minibus. Professor Rivlin had seen how no checkpoint could stop him. And there would be no political skits like those in Zababdeh, just poems of love and friendship, some new and some old. The professor wouldn't be the only Jew there. There would be Israeli poets and peace activists, progressive people, all guests of the Palestinian Authority. There would even be a poetry contest, with prizes. The judge had already been chosen: a British professor who taught at Bir-Zeit University. It would all be in a spirit of fun. Everyone was tired of politics. Ramallah wasn't Gaza, where people loved to hate each other. The Ramallans knew how to live. And the professor should bring his wife this time. The judge would enjoy it. She mustn't miss the Lebanese nun, that divine little scamp who had promised to come on another tour of Palestine. She had even asked the Abuna—or so he said—whether the Jew would be there.

4.

AUTUMN ARRIVED AT full blast, bringing wind and rain and the promise of a real winter. Yet there were also days of warm sun and sweet light, with fleecy white clouds hanging quietly in the sky. Although her blinds were opened less often now, the ghost, dressed in two heavy sweaters that Rivlin recognized from the previous winter, continued to sit on her terrace. She no longer played solitaire. Seated at the little red table with a pad of stationery, she seemed to be—as far as he could make out from across the street—filling page after page with writing.

The semester began. The Oriental department head returned from the Occident, buoyed by his audiences of decent Christians and wealthy Jews politely worried about the future. He thanked Rivlin for filling in for him, and especially for preventing the rector and the dean from making off with the half-time teaching slot.

Relieved of the duty of substituting for his successor, Rivlin no longer had an excuse to put off typing his wildly scrawled and illegible notes, the product of his days without glasses, into his computer, to prepare them for submission to the critical eye of the brilliant young Dr. Miller, the keys to whose academic career he held. He knew that Miller was attuned to the latest winds blowing from German and American universities and that his approach to scholarship, and to Orientalism in particular, was revisionist. (Indeed, the young doctor had even announced at a departmental meeting that he refused to be called any longer by the intellectually pretentious and discredited title of "Orientalist"; he preferred the more modest description of "Middle Eastern social ethnographer.") For this reason, Rivlin, wishing to present his draft in a softer, more ambivalent light, took care to insert in more places than necessary a number of self-critical qualifications and to replace exclamation points with question marks. He then ran his remarks off on the printer, put them in Miller's mailbox with a jocular note, and postponed the next meeting of the secret appointments committee until the following week.

He thought sorrowfully of his eldest son and of their harsh exchange in the parking lot of the hotel. I won't defend myself against his accusations, he told himself. On the contrary, I'll admit openly that I should never have slept in the basement with all those superannuated tax files. Still, he doesn't have to be angry with me just because I did something foolish. If he'd told me the reason for his separation, I'd never have had to sink to such depths.

Self-pity vied with self-blame. He envied the old ghost on the terrace her outburst of writing.

His thoughts weren't only of Ofer, his face twisted with rage. He also thought of his Circe, deftly making a bed for him with snow white sheets. Had it been the brackish light of the basement or her low-grade fever that had made her skin look so translucent and virginal? It was curious. You could count on someone like her not to take a night's fling seriously or to expect anything from you afterward, her only loyalty being to the hotel. And yet what pleasure could there be in making love to such a bony, unattractive woman, who, for all her haughtiness, wanted protection, too? And how did you make love at all to a woman so much taller than yourself? Did you expand or did she contract?

And then there was Fu'ad. What had he been up to, turning up like that with a pillow? Had he come to warn him against an involvement that an ex-in-law should have known better than to risk, or was he protecting the proprietress? And in either case, why hadn't the discreet maître d' stuck to his philosophy of playing it safe and putting his own interests first?

And on the other hand, if this were really Fu'ad's credo, why write an elegy for Ofer? Why mention it? Simply to demonstrate his friendship for an Orientalist who had told him in polished Arabic that he was dying? Or was it a signal not to give up in his pursuit of a secret that he, Fu'ad, was unable to discuss?

On a whim, Rivlin called the hotel. Without identifying himself, he asked to speak to Fu'ad, who had to be summoned from the garden.

"*Anna ba'awek aleyk?*"*

"*La, abadan, ya ahi.*"†

"What's new? How's Galya?"

"God be praised. She's giving birth soon."

"And the elegy? *Al-marthiyya*? Did you find it?"

"I've stopped looking for it, Professor. So should you. What's gone is gone. Why lose sleep over it? If you want a new elegy, it's no problem. I can even write you a love poem. Lately, the rhymes just keep coming. I even wrote a little poem in Hebrew."

"Good for you."

"I don't know what it is, but since Mr. Hendel passed on I've been full of feeling. I can be in the middle of work, running the dining room or the cleaning staff, and suddenly I want to write. It's a pity it's all lost in the end, like that elegy. No one in our village appreciates a good poem. I wish I knew someone who could give me some constructive criticism. Back in the fifties we had a poet of our own, a fellow named Ibn Smih. Then he got into trouble with the law, and they took him away...."

## 5.

THAT WEEK, A movie called *Passage of Memory* was playing at the Japanese Museum. Two young lawyers, stopping their debate in Hagit's chambers long enough to discuss it, had recommended it. Whereas

---

* Am I disturbing you?
† You never could, my friend.

famous stars and good reviews could not persuade Rivlin to go to a European or American movie unless he first got a detailed synopsis from his wife, he was more tolerant of films from more exotic places. Lately, he had particularly enjoyed several Iranian ones made under the regime of the ayatollahs. "Even if the plot doesn't hold up," he explained to Hagit, "there are still new faces, landscapes, and foods... who knows, perhaps even new and better ways of making love."

Love was something he had slacked off at. Ten days had passed since he and Hagit had last made it, which meant it was time for action. Since in recent months the judge had been an elusive partner, prematurely tired at night and prematurely quick to rise in the morning, he had decided to consider other times of the day—such as before the Japanese movie, which was still three hours off. Hagit, however, was far from eager to undress or to miss the five o'clock news. It took many tender endearments, plus switching on the heater in the bedroom, to get her to take off her pants and blouse. Aroused by her half-naked body, Rivlin proceeded slowly, wary of making a false step or overshooting the intricate target zone of her desire.

And yet it went badly. Their kisses and caresses, even in places that had never failed them before, were stale and counterfeit. The room was too hot, and the tingle of passion soon turned to a thin, unpleasant trickle of sweat. Hagit, impatiently fretting and complaining, asked to be excused and even urged him to finish without her, which was something she generally hated. Though unhappy about it, he went ahead and made love to her motionless body for the sake of his peace of mind during the movie. Yet something about the way she shut her eyes, as though to protect herself, upset him at the wrong moment, and he came with a paltry dribble.

"It's all right," she said comfortingly, after he had rolled off her. "Don't worry about it. Next time..."

He didn't answer.

The Japanese Museum would have had a comfortable theater had the rows not lacked a middle aisle, thus forcing too many people to stand up for those taking or leaving their seats. The movie, though of recent vintage, was in black and white, presumably to convey its somber mood, while the English subtitles were difficult to read quickly—a serious problem in a film that had more talking than action. The film (so a flyer handed out to the audience explained) was about the passage from life to death and took place in a Japanese purgatory, where the newly deceased were interviewed. To gain admission to the next world, they had to forget everything about their lives except for one happy memory, which they were allowed to keep for all eternity.

It was storming outside. The drumming of rain on the roof gave Rivlin a cozy feeling as he watched the arrival of the interviewers. A likable group of young men and women who resembled social workers or vocational testers, they had their quarters in a small, drab office that reminded him of the former quarters of the income-tax bureau in an old building near Haifa port. Unlike other Japanese movies he had seen, in which the actors expressed simple, everyday emotions with a frequently jarring agitation, in this one they talked calmly and quietly. They, too, it appeared, were dead, stranded between worlds because they had been unable to choose their happiest memory. Their punishment was to have to help others choose.

After a long opening scene in which the interviewers chatted over coffee and cake, the first newly dead person arrived. Rivlin found the interview difficult to follow. His eyelids drooped, and his head fell to one side. After a while he roused himself and glanced at his wife. Hagit took her eyes off the screen, at which she had been staring with stupefaction, and smiled. "What do you think?" he whispered. "It's one of these intellectual art movies," she said reassuringly. "Let's give it a chance." He heard a thin whistling coming from his left. He turned to look at the attractive woman sitting next to him, whose large, bald husband was the source of the sound. She hurried to wake him, and he sat up, rubbed his eyes, gave Rivlin an apologetic look, and resumed staring grimly at the screen.

Outside, the rain beat down harder. Although the movie had been showing for barely ten minutes, to Rivlin it felt like a year. How much more of this could he take? The Japanese purgatory, though profoundly symbolic, did not speak to him. He scanned the audience of middle-class intellectuals and culture lovers, many of them known to him from concerts at the Philharmonic. Most seemed determined to

rise to the movie's challenge, while only a few showed signs of dropping out. He glanced back at Hagit. Although she was still managing
to sit straight, her eyes were closed. Now and then, as if fighting off
the sleep engulfing her, her head bobbed in agreement with the sound
track, in little Japanese bows. He nudged her. She didn't wake. He had
to whisper her name to make her open her eyes and flash him another warm smile.

"Already asleep?" he scolded.

"No. Just for a second. What's happening? Are you following it?"

"God knows. It's awfully complicated. But you can relax. No one is
going to get killed because they're all dead already."

She laid an affectionate hand on his knee and gave it a squeeze.
"Let's see what happens," she encouraged him. "Lean back. My
lawyers said it was a good movie."

A crew-cut, ornery-looking old man now appeared on the screen
and told an interviewer about his native village. He remembered the
wind and the grass. Rivlin felt cheered. The first happy memory was
on its way.

But it wasn't so simple. The ornery man couldn't decide which
memory was his happiest. And the next time Rivlin awoke, it was
only a quarter of an hour later. The attractive woman was asleep now,
too, leaning on him lightly. He tried moving away from her. But this
only made her lean more, and in the end he had to push her gently
back toward her husband. She awoke annoyed, and he turned back to
his own wife, who was now sleeping so soundly that her bowing had
stopped.

The rain had died down. A deadly quiet prevailed in the little theater. The camera panned on the industrial area of a large city, where a
dead Japanese woman was stonily describing the accident that had
killed her.

This continued for an hour and a half before the lights came on for
intermission. Rivlin, his head full of Japanese memories, awoke with
a start. Hagit greeted him brightly, while his attractive neighbor gave
him a dirty look, as if he had done something indecent to her during
their joint sleep. Her husband rose and stretched himself groggily.

"Let's get out of here," Rivlin said.

"Maybe the second half will be better."

"It won't be."

"I hate leaving in the middle. There's nothing terrible about falling asleep from time to time. The movie is made of separate episodes."

But he found falling asleep at movies and concerts embarrassing, and exhausting to fight against. He rose and made their whole row rise with them. People stood by the buffet, sipping coffee and cold drinks while discussing whether to remain for the film's second half. Those who had stayed awake explained what it was about to those who hadn't and coached them for the remainder. Rivlin, tired of happy Japanese memories, took Hagit by the arm and steered her toward the exit.

A storm-buffeted moon staggered through the sky between tattered clouds. He brushed wet leaves from the windshield of their car and said, pierced by sorrow,

"I would have been through with that interview in a minute. I could have said right away what my happiest memory was and gladly forgotten everything else."

She bowed her head. "Yes. I know."

"You know what?"

"The memory you would have taken with you."

"Which?"

"Ofer's wedding. The garden of the hotel."

"You're right," he said, a bit annoyed to have his thoughts read so easily. "Ofer's wedding. Despite, or maybe—who knows?—because of all that's happened since then."

He started the car as his wife climbed into it, then backed carefully out of the narrow parking space.

"And I," Hagit mused, "would have ended up stranded between worlds. I have too many happy memories to choose just one. Especially of things that happened before I met you."

## 6.

SEVERAL DAYS AFTER giving his preface to Dr. Miller, Rivlin found it returned to his mailbox, without an accompanying note. What did

Miller think he was doing? Was he being provocative or just stupid? Rivlin couldn't believe that the young lecturer was so unafraid of him.

At first he was inclined to say nothing until they saw each other at the next departmental meeting. That night, however, he slept poorly. In the morning, unable to restrain himself, he called to straighten the matter out.

"I was wondering if you'd read it..."

But reading Rivlin's introduction had been a piece of cake for the theoretical mind of the young lecturer. He just hadn't been sure whether the professor, with whom he had such ideological and methodological differences, really wanted to know his opinion.

"But that's just it," the Orientalist said, feeling better. "It's precisely those differences that make me want to know what you think."

Nevertheless, he was careful to set their meeting in Miller's room, a few floors above his own. That way he could get out of it any time he wanted.

Although Miller's standing at the university did not entitle him to his own office, the young lecturer, who was two or three years older than Ofer, had found a little cubbyhole between two rooms near the rector's office—a space originally intended for a coffee machine or a file cabinet—and talked his way into getting it. His sense of his own uniqueness, it seemed, made him prefer a cramped room of his own to a larger one shared with someone else.

It was late on a gray winter day. Miller's narrow window looked out on neither mountains nor sea, but on some houses of a Druze village that appeared engraved in the dust on its glass pane. Rivlin, a tense smile on his face, surveyed the tiny room's overloaded book-shelves with what was meant to be a benevolent glance. Most of the books were recently published American and German studies of political and sociological theory. Not a single Arabic volume was in evidence. Did this man demanding tenure in the Near Eastern Studies department know Arabic at all, or did he rely entirely on translations for his postmodernist opinions? Moving the empty chair away from Miller's desk so as not to have to face him like a student, Rivlin positioned himself diagonally and stretched his legs out in front of him. "To judge by your tone," he began magnanimously, "I take it that you have some objections. Well, I'd like to hear them. I'm open to criticism."

Miller ran a hand through his sandy hair and took off his glasses. To Rivlin's surprise, his light blue eyes were childishly innocent. Although the young lecturer could easily guess that the full professor was on the secret appointments committee, he did not beat around the bush. In no uncertain terms, he rejected the Orientalist's thesis that an academic study dealing with the origins of Algerian national identity could have any relevance to the current bloodshed in Algeria. His tone quiet and considered, he stressed the need to demolish not only the theoretical foundations of his senior colleague's introduction—which, Rivlin now saw, he had not only read but could remember every word of—but the premises of the still unwritten book to follow. Its reification of the concept of national identity, he contended, doomed it to failure on moral and intellectual grounds.

"Reification?" Rivlin forced a smile while concealing his anxiety over a word whose exact meaning he was unsure of.

Yes, Miller said. National identity was not a natural or empirical given, there being no such thing. It was a fictive construct used by the power structure to enslave the population it purportedly described. He found it deplorable that a senior faculty member, writing at the end of the twentieth century, should collaborate in such an anachronistic, long repudiated, and even dangerous point of view, much less base a book on it.

"A fictive construct in what way?" Stiffening, Rivlin did his best to overlook the connotations of the word "collaborate."

The young postmodernist was happy to explain. In articulate, if rather mechanical and (Rivlin thought) smugly jesuitical language, he demystified the devious concept of national identity, which served to ghettoize the lower classes and deprive them of their rights within the rigid framework of the national state, whether—for there was no difference—this was of an openly totalitarian or an ostensibly democratic nature.

"Come, come," Rivlin drawled, in what he intended to be a patronizing manner. "No difference between totalitarianism and democracy? Isn't that going a bit far?"

But the sandy-haired jesuit, now sitting in the shadow of a passing cloud, stuck to his guns. National identity was an illegitimate concept even in a country like Israel that still pretended, albeit with increasing difficulty, to be democratic. Rather than let people decide for themselves who they were and how they wished to be defined, it trapped them in a rigid category that had no room for change, development, personal experience, or multiple identities. With the full complicity of the academic community, the ruling classes sought to impose an inflexible model of reality, privileging some and marginalizing others, for the purpose of exerting total control.

Rivlin sighed. "I'd say you were the proof that they haven't succeeded," he said, wishing he could dampen the young postmodernist's ardor.

"They can never succeed," Miller agreed triumphantly. "In the end the whole system will implode." Ordinary thinking people would rebel against being labeled by the antiquated notions that the professor (sitting now in evening shadow, his head jerked back in dismay) wished to construct his book with. Those at the bottom of the social hierarchy would understand that national identity enslaved rather than enhanced them, by curbing their freedom and mobility and preventing a rich interchange of perspectives across permeable frontiers. And the moral absurdity of it was that the enslavers, the engineers of identity who locked the doors and sealed the borders, kept open these possibilities for themselves. They alone retained access to the rich interfaces of language and culture, traveling widely and associating with different peer groups while the masses, locked within the gates of the state, were chauvinistically regimented. And to what end? But that was obvious...

"Not to me," Rivlin said honestly.

"To make cannon fodder for the next unnecessary war."

"Whoa there!" he protested. "Begging your pardon! How can a political progressive like you call an anticolonialist struggle against a century of oppression in Algeria unnecessary?"

But the theoretical jesuit was unimpressed by anticolonialist platitudes. Colonialism, he maintained, was not so much a historical or political phenomenon as a ubiquitous condition that co-opted all elements of society. It was present even in countries that had never had colonies, such as Austria or Sweden, to say nothing of Israel, a colonialist entity from the start. You didn't even have to look at the Occupied Territories to see that. "Take, for instance," Miller said, with a thin smile, "the hierarchical organization of the university tower we're in, surrounded by a national park that has wiped out every remnant of the Arab villages that once were in it. Think of the internal division of the floors, with the administration at the top and the slowest elevators serving the lower and middle echelons, where the liberal-arts faculties are, while the high-speed elevators zoom up to the appointments committees and the personnel department and financial offices. That's where the real power of this university is. And what sits, disgracefully, on top of everything? A military installation, an army radar station! Of course, we pretend it's not there. Its operators are made to look like students. But let's not kid ourselves. It combs the area and sends its information to an intelligence base in the Galilee in which everything is secretly processed. That's where the legitimacy of the whole oppressive power structure comes from..."

The daylight was vanishing. So, Rivlin thought, that's what our blond wunderkind has to say.

The young postmodernist now came back to Rivlin's introduction, picking it apart like a stale roll. "National identity" was bad enough, a thoroughly dated notion. But worse yet was this business of a rainbow. Was national identity some kind of weather condition? What was the point of the whole, perfectly absurd theoretical exercise? It was only there to justify the professor's obsession with artificially linking the past to the present. But what entitled him to assume that the poor devils who murdered villagers at night and slit the throats of babies snatched from their mothers' wombs had any memory of wanting to be French? Had the more original thought never occurred to him that they might be pursuing their own authenticity, acted out by their darkly passionate souls? Surely Professor Rivlin was aware that beneath the tinsel of national identity, with which the military dictatorship in Algeria sought to distract the country, there was something more genuine and primitive. The Arabs were too fluid and unbounded to be subsumed under a single national grid.

"Excuse me," Rivlin said softly, "but I can hardly see you. Don't you have any light here?"

The little cubbyhole had no ceiling light. There was only the lamp on Miller's desk. But its bulb was burned out, and the administration had not yet bothered to replace it.

Although the Orientalist was free to beat a retreat, he remained sprawled limply in his chair, unable to tear himself away from the young lecturer, whose sandy hair glowed golden in the gloom. Dr. Miller, having finished taking Rivlin apart, now turned to the outdated profession of Orientalism itself, which had proved incapable of absorbing the new theories of multiple narratives. It was time the professor realized that the news coming from Algeria was simply one narrative among many, propagated by the corporate press to uphold the dictatorial regime....

It was getting dark. Perhaps, Miller suggested, they should continue the discussion in the professor's office.

"We can stay here," Rivlin said. "If you don't mind talking to someone you can't see, neither do I."

And as a wistful night descended on the world, lighting up the Druze houses on the Carmel one by one, he continued to offer his head to the guillotine, summoning the last of his patience to listen to the new theories whose very language he had despaired of understanding long ago.

## 7.

WINTER CAME EARLY, prolifically. After two years of little rain there were no complaints about the torrential storms and gale-force winds, only about the unpreparedness for them—especially in Tel Aviv, where streets were so flooded that they looked, at least on television, like the canals of Venice, without their gondolas and lovers. Meanwhile, the official opening of the Khalil es-Sakakini Cultural Center in Ramallah was postponed by a month and rescheduled for Christmas, which coincided with Hanukkah that year. The abbess of the Greek Orthodox convent in Baalbek had not considered a poetry contest, or even a fifty-year-old United Nations resolution to partition Palestine between two headstrong peoples, sufficient reason to send his singing nun to Ramallah and had preferred to wait for the holiday season to cast its religious aura over the event.

That Saturday morning it rained so hard that Rivlin, anticipating crawling back underneath the big quilt for an afternoon nap, did not bother to make the bed. Now, to the cozy patter of the rain and the shriek of the wind, he lay wondering whether the Palestinians of Ramallah deserved to be visited in such weather.

"I've seen enough real Arabs in the last few months," he grumbled to his wife. "From now on I'd rather meet them on my computer screen."

The judge, who had been looking forward to the event with keen curiosity, refused to hear of this.

"You've lost all joie de vivre," she accused the big gray head sticking out from the quilt. "Life with you is becoming unbearable. You're so busy controlling everyone that you can't enjoy yourself anymore. You can't even sit through a movie. At night you can't wait to go to bed, and in the morning you can't wait to get up and start eating your heart out again. I'm not calling off a trip we've been planning for so long. And you promised Carlo and Hannah that we'd take them with us."

"They'll just change their minds in the end anyway. They'll be afraid to go to Ramallah at night."

"But what is there to be afraid of if that Arab of yours..."

"Rashid."

"If Rashid takes us and brings us back, the way he took you to Jenin. What's the problem? Why are you backing out?"

"That festival can go on all night."

"Let it. I'm off from work tomorrow. We can return to Haifa in the morning. I need to get out into the world and see some new faces."

"In Ramallah?"

"What's wrong with that? Do you have a better suggestion? There's sure to be good food, just as there was at that village wedding that I enjoyed so much. And this isn't a wedding, so you don't have to envy anyone. Besides, I want to see that nun you were so wild about..."

"Don't exaggerate. I wasn't so wild about her."

"What does it matter? Live! Experience! Lately you've been pure gloom. Every day you're nursing some new injury."

"What are you talking about?"

"About that young lecturer who attacked your theories a bit. You were on the verge of a nervous breakdown. Every fly on the wall puts you in a panic."

"In the first place, he didn't attack them a bit. He attacked them a lot. And secondly, he's no fly on the wall..."

"So he's not a fly. He's a screwed-up young man who wants to be original at any cost. I knew what he was up to when I saw him at that wedding in the Galilee. It was enough to see how he put down his wife."

Rivlin smiled with satisfaction, rubbing his feet under the blanket. His mood brightened. In the west, a patch of blue sky was showing through the rain. His love for his wife, who now lay down beside him, welled within him. "All right," he said. "But on two conditions. You know the first. And the second is that we leave early and get to Jerusalem in daylight."

You couldn't exactly call it daylight. The wet city, when they arrived, was struggling with a premature darkness brought on by the storm, contravening the laws of nature by being darker in the west than in the east. As it was too early to rouse the Tedeschis from their Sabbath nap, Hagit suggested driving to the Agnon House to see whether it was really closed on Saturdays.

It was indeed, and looked gray and unwelcoming with its little window bars. Rivlin had no intention of following the trail of the tattooed widow into the dismal yard. The hometown of any famous French or German author, he thought, would do better by its native son.

He put his arm around Hagit and steered her down the little street for a view of the tail end of sunlight that was wriggling between the desert's pinkish curves. He didn't know whether he felt more glad or alarmed when she said unexpectedly, with one of her wise looks:

"All right. As long as we've come this far, I'm ready to take a look at the happiest memory of your life."

"Now? Are you sure?"

"We won't enter the hotel. We'll just have a look at the garden."

"Then let's walk."

"It's not too far?"

Even though the rain was more illusory than real, they shared a black umbrella. Arm in arm, they headed up the wet street toward the hotel, which had not yet switched on its lights, cut through the parking lot, and quietly entered the murky garden from the rear. Rivlin took a wary route through the bushes, apprehensive of encountering the tall proprietress. He had to hand it to Hagit: although she had not been in this place for years, she spotted the gazebo at once and went right to it. True, she did not notice that it had been moved from its old location by the swimming pool. But even if it was not her happiest memory, there was no denying that the night of her son's wedding had been a joyous one. Little wonder that she gripped her husband's arm tightly as he led her on a tour of the wet, fragrant garden.

The large glass door of the hotel swung open. Rivlin's heart beat faster as he saw a tall, thin figure appear in the rectangle of light, from which it looked out at the dark garden before vanishing. All at once, the little lanterns along the garden paths lit up. A young maintenance worker came out to remove the table umbrellas before it could storm some more. Although he did not wish to call attention to himself, Rivlin could not resist asking if Fu'ad was around. No, the maintenance worker said. He had taken a few days off for some festival.

"A festival?" Rivlin asked. "In Abu-Ghosh?"

No, not in Abu-Ghosh. If it were in Abu-Ghosh, the maintenance worker would be going to it too.

## 8.

AT THE TEDESCHIS', whose little street ran down from the president's house in a small but perfect question mark, he soon confirmed how well he knew his old mentor. The doyen of Orientalists had indeed decided to dispense with the trip to Ramallah on so stormy a winter night.

"At least you didn't run to the emergency room," Rivlin joked, slapping his old doctoral adviser warmly on the back. In response, Tedeschi demonstrated his resolve by putting on his bathrobe and exchanging his shoes for a pair of slippers. "*Eyri fik,*"* he said, laughing gaily at the juicy Arabic curse. His old red sweater, showing through his open bathrobe, gave him a puckish look. "*Eymta bakun hatyar hasab fikrak hatta t'sadkini fi amradi?*"† he complained.

Hagit, who could sometimes guess what simple Arabic sentences meant, was up in arms. "What is this? We were so looking forward to spending the evening with you. What's Ramallah after Tierra del Fuego? It's just a suburb of Jerusalem."

"And crossing the border, Your Honor, once in each direction, is nothing to you?"

"Don't worry," Rivlin said. "We have an Arab-Israeli driver who cuts through borders like a knife through butter."

"That makes it sound even more frightening."

"But why?" Hagit asked petulantly. "What kind of Orientalist are you, Carlo? Don't you ever feel a professional need to meet real, live Arabs?"

"Reality is what I write on," Tedeschi said affably, pointing to his computer, on whose screen saver little comic-book figures were cavorting. "Real-life Arabs, let alone real-life Jews, make me too dizzy to think straight."

"Leave him alone," the translatoress of Ignorance said morosely. "He's embarrassed to tell you that he's been up these past few nights with chest pains."

"That's because he gets no fresh air," Hagit said doggedly. "I'm telling you, Carlo, I won't take no for an answer. Come on! Don't be afraid. Do you remember that trip we took together to Turkey twenty years ago, and what a good time we had? Come! It's not like you to be such a party pooper. Let's have a good time with the Arabs like the one we had with the Turks. When will we get another chance? It's a poetry and music festival. No politics and no speeches. There's sure to be good food. And there'll be a Lebanese singer, some sort of nun, who got Yochi so excited last summer that he had all kinds of new ideas..."

"New ideas?" The Jerusalem polymath perked up. "What ideas?"

---

* Fuck you.
† When will I be old enough for you to believe that I'm really ill?

Hagit, however, stuck to the subject.

"Never mind, Carlo. Not now. Don't be such a professor. Come with us. We'll have a good time. I promise to look after you. I'll stay by your side, fair enough?"

Her eyes shone. Her cheeks were ruddy from the heated apartment. Rivlin, smitten anew by her, marveled at the youthfulness of this woman of over fifty, whose short sheepskin coat left her shapely legs uncovered. Tedeschi, flustered, rose and hugged her.

"But really, my dear, what do you need me for? I'll just begin to cough and spoil the evening. Where will you find me an emergency room in Ramallah?"

"Then at least let your wife go." The judge gave up on the stubborn old man. "Let her come with us."

"Hannah?" Tedeschi chuckled at the thought and winked at his wife, who was sitting quietly by the lamp. "I don't believe she's at all eager to go to Ramallah tonight. She's a bit under the weather herself..."

Once again the Haifa Orientalist felt his heart go out to the lovely student of former days, made old and worn before her time by an eccentric husband, so that she now stood in an old bathrobe, her hair that needed dyeing straggling onto her shoulders, ready for bed before the night had begun. He felt driven to join his wife's attack on his old mentor, who was already by his computer, running his fingers absentmindedly over the keyboard.

"Listen, Carlo. She's coming with us. Why shouldn't she? If you don't want to live yourself, then don't—but at least let live. Stop being such a killjoy. You can't keep her chained to your depressions."

"My depressions?" Tedeschi was startled by the unexpected salvo. "When do you remember me being depressed?"

"So it's not your depressions. It's your hypochondria. Or just your gloom." He could hear himself speaking with Hagit's voice. "Let there be some enjoyment in life. Give Hannah her freedom. Don't you think she deserves a rest from you?"

The Jerusalem polymath did not reply. Half fearfully and half ironically, he pulled out a crumpled white handkerchief from his bathrobe pocket, waved it like a flag of surrender with an absurdly dramatic gesture, and made a bow.

The translatoress struggled to make up her mind. She was still torn between wanting, even longing, to get out of the house, and worry for her husband—who, having dismissed the comic-book figures with a tap of his finger, was already seated at his computer—when there was a quiet knock on the door. It was the sable-skinned messenger of many devices, come with a stocking cap on his head to transport his Jews to the festival.

## 9.

IN THE COLD, dark minibus, Rivlin made out at once the coal black eyes of a small boy, who was sitting beside a woman in an old fur-collared winter coat. It was the same coat that had hung for years in their own closet because Hagit had not wanted to part with it. Amused and alarmed, he glanced at his wife to see if she recognized it on the shoulders of Rashid's sister. But the judge was busy talking to the translatoress—who, distraught over her sudden separation from her husband, had barely managed to clamber into the vehicle, where she now sat squeezed in the middle row, next to Rivlin.

He waited for the minibus to start moving before introducing Ra'uda to the two women. Though she was married to a West Bank Palestinian, he explained, she was still an Israeli of sorts and could even quote the poetry of Bialik. Rashid's sister responded with a despairing laugh while Rivlin turned around to pat her son's head. The boy did not flinch and even took off his cap and offered his head, like a pet dog.

Only then did Rivlin notice, huddled in the back on a jump seat that had been folded on the trip to Jenin, a pale young woman in a thick woolen shawl. Next to her, larger and darker than his brother, sat Rasheed. He was holding the horn-rimmed glasses meant to convince the Israeli border guards that he was his uncle's natural son.

"Why, it's Samaher!" Rivlin cried excitedly. "Samaher, this is my wife. You must remember her from your wedding."

His still-ungraded M.A. student gave him a frail and poignant smile. "Who could forget your wife, Professor?" she whispered hoarsely, nodding to Hagit. "Never . . ."

The minibus turned right on Gaza Road, passed Terra Sancta, and headed for East Jerusalem, skirting the walls of the Old City—which on this wintry Saturday night were illuminated only symbolically, as if in discharge of a formal obligation. The rain came down harder as Rashid drove through the Arab half of town. "Don't forget to stop in Pisgat Ze'ev," Rivlin reminded him. "I'll direct you." But Rashid, having rehearsed the route earlier that day, needed no directions, leaving Rivlin free to turn around and chat with his "research assistant." Her answers to his questions, though laconic, were to the point.

They reached Pisgat Ze'ev in northern Jerusalem. There, in the yellowish glare of the headlights, flagging them down at the bus stop where they had agreed to meet him—the same stop from which the murdered scholar had gone to his death—was Mr. Suissa in his gray fedora. With him was the murdered scholar's wife.

"I hope it's all right," Suissa said to Rivlin, who reddened at the sight of the young widow. "She didn't want me to go by myself. Do you have room for her?"

"Of course we do," Rashid said, jumping happily out of the car. No one even had to move. He went to the back, opened the rear door, and squeezed the widow in beside Samaher.

They drove on to the Palestinian Authority. Although a black, overcast sky hid the first three stars that ended the Sabbath, these were surely glittering somewhere above the clouds—in token of which, despite the heavy rain, the streets filled with cars as the Jews of Jerusalem, exhausted by their day of rest, emerged to see what had changed in the world while they slept. At Atarot Junction the traffic lights were rattling in the wind, which soon turned to a howling gale. In the foggy darkness, with nothing around them but dim buildings and empty lots, it wasn't clear whether they were heading in the right direction. But gradually the billboards changed from Hebrew to Arabic, and they saw that the border was close. In the end, they flew across it. The soldiers on the Israeli side, warming themselves around a campfire, showed no interest in the passengers bound for food and entertainment, while two gun-toting policemen on the Palestinian side were so eager to help that, although unaware of any festival, they piled with their weapons into the minibus, now equally full of Arabs and Jews, and guided it to the Ramallah police station.

In the stone building of the police station, the festival was better known. There were even name tags for the guests from Israel. Rivlin was told to climb some stairs to the second floor. There, in a large room whose long, curtained windows made it look like a cross between an office and a salon, sat a corpulent police officer decorated like a Russian general and surrounded by men, civilians or plainclothesmen, who made the Orientalist feel rather nervous. Taking some plastic tags from a drawer, the officer inscribed them with the names of the Israeli entourage and stamped each with a bloodred stamp.

There was a timid knock on the door. In walked a bewildered-looking Hannah Tedeschi, her thick glasses halfway down her nose. Drawn magnetically by her anxiety to the telephone on the officer's desk, she inquired in quaint seventh-century Arabic whether she could call her husband in Jerusalem. Rivlin, putting a hand on her shoulder to calm her, hurried to translate her speech into something more modern, while introducing her, complete with all her academic titles, to the astonished gathering.

"Be my guest, Madame Doctor. It's an honor." The fat officer sat up, reached for the phone, and poised a long-nailed finger on the dial.

It took many rings to get the doyen of Orientalists to answer his wife's call. While the officer and the plainclothesmen listened at one end to the shaky voice of the translatoress, the old professor at the other end was deliberately cool. He answered Hannah's questions brusquely, was vague and uninformative, and soon hung up. As though reluctant to part with it, she slowly handed the receiver back to the fat officer and took out her purse to pay for the call.

"*La, walla la, ya madam, la!*"* the Palestinians cried at once, commiserating with the strange Jewess. "Don't insult us. What's a telephone call to Jerusalem? Nothing. You can call all you like . . . even to America . . . to Japan . . . *a kul hal, b'nidfa'sh el-hasab l'isra'il.*"†

---

* Absolutely not, Madam!
† In any case, we never pay the bill to the Israelis.

There was a sense of merriment in the room. When they left it, properly name-tagged (Rashid must have told someone he had important passengers), a jeep with a machine gunner was waiting to escort them. The rain had tapered off to a thin drizzle. They traveled in a little convoy through the streets of the brightly lit Palestinian city. At the new Khalil el-Sakakini Cultural Center, teenagers holding torches directed them to a nearly full parking lot. If last summer he had crossed the border as a one-man show, Rivlin thought, he was now heading a multinational, multisexual, and multigenerational delegation. He took care to keep his five women together as they climbed out of the minibus, while saying some encouraging words to Mr. Suissa, who had sat in the car looking tense. Meanwhile, Rashid handed each of his nephews a small carton and disappeared with them around the back of the building.

They climbed some stairs to the aristocratically arched stone entrance of the Cultural Center, which looked like a wealthy private mansion. There to greet them was the festival's director, Nazim Ibn-Zaidoun, an energetic, gap-toothed, baby-faced man who in his old leather coat, Rivlin thought, resembled a trade union official. Ibn-Zaidoun shook hands briskly with the Israelis, introduced them to the British judge of the poetry contest, who towered over him like a thoroughbred horse, and urged them to help themselves to refreshments on the second floor. Tonight's festival, he assured them, was meant for body and mind alike.

## 10.

A LOCAL BEAUTY welcomed them to the high-ceilinged second floor and politely but firmly made them take off their coats, for which there would be no room in the auditorium, and hang them in the checkroom. With the thrill of old intimacy Rivlin spied, beneath Hagit's fur-collared coat, her beloved blouse and velvet pants on Ra'uda's tall, dark figure. He tried to catch her eye, wishing to share his amusement at her simulacrum from the other side of the border. But Hagit, still involved with the translatoress, who was greatly distressed by her husband's coolness, had no time for her old clothes, which now vanished with their wearer in the wake of Samaher.

Rivlin let himself be carried along by the festive hubbub of the guests, most of them young people of unclear identity. It was hard to tell the Arabs from the Jews, or either of the two from anyone else. Taking Ibn-Zaidoun's advice, he headed for the buffet, followed by Suissa's widow with Suissa senior on her heels. The murdered scholar's father, awed by the occasion despite his vengeful feelings toward its Palestinian organizers, had taken off his fedora and put on a big, colorful skullcap that might have been knit back in his North African childhood. At the buffet, by plates of stuffed grape leaves and cigar-shaped meat pastries, the conversation flowed in Arabic, Hebrew, and English, with an occasional German exclamation mark. Holding a glass and surrounded by Israeli peace activists, the most famous of Palestinian poets stood by the auditorium door. An aging, though still boyish, bachelor and full-time exile who circulated among the world's capitals reading his poetry, he was trying to follow, a bored glitter in his eyes, the singsong English of an Israeli poet of his own generation, a tall, balding, protuberant man with thick glasses, who was known for his marvelously erotic sonnets—which, though politically naive, were said to embody his lust for peace. At his side, seeking to elbow his way into the conversation, was another poet from Tel Aviv—a literary critic as well, whose brilliant but nasty essays took advantage of the Middle East conflict to settle scores with his numerous rivals.

There was a tap on Rivlin's shoulder. It was Rashid, visibly excited. "Is everything all right, Professor?" he asked softly and disappeared before the Orientalist could answer, leaving Rivlin to smile sympathetically at the sad widow—who, a glass of water in her hand, regarded him with silent resentment, as if still waiting, even though he now was entrusted with five women, for the protection she demanded.

"It seems," he said in a friendly whisper, trying to keep from being overheard by Suissa senior, who was cruising the counter in search of a kosher Middle Eastern hors d'oeuvre, "that you're getting used to your hedgehog."

The young widow, giving him the cold shoulder, merely shook her head and set her glass down on the counter.

Hagit and Hannah stepped out of the ladies' room, smiling and relaxed. Still more people were filing into the lobby, among them some country musicians in traditional costume who hurried to the auditorium with their instruments. Rivlin, his inhibitions dispelled by the noisy crowd, put two fingers to his mouth and startled those around him by shrilling his and Hagit's old whistle of recognition. At once came the judge's soft answering call. Spotting him, she linked arms with Hannah and headed in his direction. It pleased yet saddened him to see that although the two were the same age his wife looked much younger than her companion, who had been kept childless by a husband fearing rivals for her love.

"What happened to your driver?" Hannah chided him. "Don't forget that you've left your old teacher all alone. I only came because you promised I could be brought back any time I wanted."

"Any time after Rashid's performance."

"What performance is that?"

Rivlin smiled mysteriously. "You'll see. He's a demon in disguise, not just a driver."

Ibn-Zaidoun, accompanied by two policemen serving as ushers, now opened the doors of the auditorium and began shooing the audience inside. From within came the sounds of a shepherd's pipe and a three-stringed rebab. At the doorway they were blocked by a conversation, started by the remark of an Israeli that according to the latest studies Jews and Palestinians had the same DNA. Although this had occasioned much laughter, it was hard to tell whether the laughter was approving or embarrassed.

"We all come from the same monkey's ass," the erotic poet guffawed. "And should go back there."

The Palestinian poet grinned provocatively. "I trust that's one place where the Law of Return applies equally."

"Please, no politics tonight! Just love," Ibn-Zaidoun warned through the gap between his front teeth. Rivlin was startled to see a shiny pistol protruding from his old leather coat.

"*They say there is love in this world,*" quoted the Palestinian poet— who, like Ra'uda, knew his Bialik. "*But I ask: What is love?*"

He entered the auditorium.

On the spur of the moment, Rivlin decided to introduce himself and his companions to the poet, which he did while praising his verse, read by him in the original. The world-famous exile, his slim figure neat in a custom-made suit and a last cigarette butt between his yellowed fingers, listened to the Jewish Orientalist politely. He beamed when told of the accomplishments of the translatoress of Ignorance. *"Na'am, ya sitti,"* he said with an intense handshake, *"el-jahaliya mish bas asas esh-shi'ir el-arabi, hiyya kaman asas el-kiyan."** 

## 11.

THE AUDITORIUM OF THE Khalil el-Sakakini Cultural Center was designed in the best modern taste, with unadorned white walls and columns bearing a vaulted ceiling of white arches graceful as the wings of a dove. Although it was so crowded that the Haifa professor and his entourage at first had nowhere to sit, Ibn-Zaidoun soon appeared, made some young Palestinians move to the floor, and gave the Jewish VIPs their seats. These looked down on a stage covered with a checked carpet, on which stood a long wooden table and three chairs. The musicians, seated in the back, were tuning their instruments while sipping little cups of coffee.

More and more young people kept pushing into the auditorium and finding places on the floor. The warmth of so many bodies made the heated hall stuffy, and a gray-haired Arab in jeans went to a window, drew its white lace curtain, and let in some cool night air. It took Rivlin a startled moment to realize it was Fu'ad. The maître d' had taken off his black uniform and come to search for poetic inspiration among his compatriots across the border.

The first strains of hesitant melody, still lacking the firm beat of a drum, were forming from the random notes of zither, shepherd's pipe, lute, and rebab. Ibn-Zaidoun, standing by the table, signaled the ushers to dim the lights. The melody stopped, and the audience was asked to rise for a moment of silence in memory of the great Palestinian educator after whom the new Cultural Center had been named. Then all sat down again, and Ibn-Zaidoun pulled from a pocket of his

---

* Yes, madam, ignorance is not only the basis of Arabic poetry, it is the basis of all existence.

428 ·

leather coat a Hebrew translation of a passage from es-Sakakini's journals, published under the title *This Is Me, Gentlemen*. The educator's first love letter to his future wife was read aloud:

*My Sultana,*

*And so, like clouds scattered before the wind, my days in Jerusalem are over. Allow me to write you a last letter and to bid you farewell from a heart that has almost ceased to beat from so much love and that has melted away from so much suffering. I utter these words as though from the grave. Soon I will leave this city, with its people, houses, streets, and soil that I belong to, and in which I breathed love for the first time, for a place that will never be mine. How could it be when my heart is staying behind?*

*Yesterday I spent the day parting with people whose goodness and sterling qualities I will never forget for as long as I live. I thought this would be easy for me, because I had prepared myself for it ever since conceiving of my journey. But when the time came, I felt how bitter it was. All day my heart was in a turmoil. And even if I can part with friends and family, how can I part with you, Sultana? Every other parting is easy in comparison.*

*I will think of you, Sultana, each time the sun rises or sets; I will think of you when I come and go, rise and lie down, arrive and depart; I will think of you when I go to work; I will think of you when I am calm and free of worry, and when I am weary and exhausted.*

*To part with you is to part with comradeship, purity, light, and joy; it is to encounter loneliness and sorrow. The first man leaving Paradise was not more anguished than I am. You are my Paradise. You are my happiness. You are my pleasure in life, my soul's joy, my life itself. What must a man feel when he leaves his own life?*

*Think of me, Sultana, each time you enter the church to pray, or open your Bible; think of me when you are teaching your students, or taking them for a nature walk to our beloved rock; think of me when you are at home. Stand at your window, which faces mine, and say: "Fare thee well, Khalil." Ah, I would fain look at that window, for perhaps I would see you there!*

*And when springtime comes with its fair flowers and you feel a breeze, that is my greeting to you—or glimpse a flower, that is my smile—or hear the song of birds, that is my voice speaking. Should you glance up at the sky and see the sparkling stars, you have seen my eyes looking at you. If the moon peeps over the mountains and sends its silvery beams through the clouds—regard them, for perhaps I am seeing them too and our two gazes will meet.*

*Today I sat with my cousin Ya'akub, to whom I confessed: "I love Sultana, I adore her." I did not tell him that I have revealed to you the secret of my love. He thinks I should do so before I depart. When will I receive a clear answer from you? Ah, Sultana, have pity and do not let me go with an anxious heart and a worried mind. The anguish of parting is enough.*

Nazim Ibn-Zaidoun was now joined by the Palestinian beauty from the checkroom. Playing the role of Khalil es-Sakakini's beloved, she stood with a white rose in her long hair and declaimed the letter written by the thirty-year-old Palestinian in its original Arabic.

Rivlin cast a warm glance at his wife, who was listening with empathy to the words even though they were only sounds for her. The eyes of the translatoress were damp with tears behind their glasses.

"What did you think of the translation?" he whispered.

She shrugged disdainfully. "Who can't translate such simple Arabic?"

"Simple but beautiful," he said

She looked at him suspiciously, then nodded slowly and, annoyed, took off her glasses and wiped her eyes.

She was not the only one moved. Opening the festival, the simple but genuine love letter of the Palestinian educator—a revolutionary in his thoughts and a romantic in his feelings—sent a shiver through the audience and made it want more. As Es-Sakakini's last words faded and Ibn-Zaidoun signaled the musicians to strike up a sweetly plaintive tune, the first poets edged toward the stage for the contest.

The cleverly creative festival director, however, was not in any hurry. First he wished to build up the suspense, setting the bar for the young poets with classical, but still bold and lively, verse. He would begin with some eighth-century poems by "the curly-headed one," as he was known, the great Abu-Nawwas, followed by excerpts from the ninth-century poet Al-Hallaj. Both men were rebels and possibly not even true Arabs, for they were born in Persia and lived and wrote in Baghdad, where Abu-Nawwas ended his life in a dungeon and

Al-Hallaj by losing his head. Their poems, Ibn-Zaidoun announced, ratcheting up the audience's expectations, would be read by the great Palestinian poet, who need not fear their competition in tonight's contest.

The poet recited the classic verse in a voice rusty from tobacco smoke. Hebrew translations, prepared in advance, were then read aloud by Ibn-Zaidoun, who appeared to consider himself knowledgeable on the sacred language of the Jews.

*Uktubi In Katabti, Ya Maniyya*

When you write, my precious one, I pray you,
Do so with an open heart and a frank spirit and your spit.
Make many mistakes and erase them all
With it. No fingers, please.
Wet the page with the sweetness
Of your lovely teeth.
Each time I read a line you have corrected,
I'll lick it with my tongue,
A kiss from afar,
Leaving me giddy and dazed!

*Ya Sakiyyati*

O you who made me drink the bitter cup
That made a pleasant life unbearable!
Before I bore love's yoke I was well thought of,
And she, the one I love, dwelt in king's chambers.
Then some evil-wisher waylaid me with love,
And heaped upon me shame and degradation.
Her scent is of the musk of sea-dwellers.
Her smile outshines the buds of chamomile.
She laughs when friends bring gifts of fragrances.
"Does perfume need perfume?" she asks.
They say, "Why do you not adorn yourself?"
She answers, "Any jewelry

Would dull my luster.
Did I not throw away my silver bangles
To keep myself from blinding them?"

Next, to assure the Israelis—who by now had blended invisibly into the packed audience—that they, too, had a role in the golden age of the Arabs, two poems were read about Jews, who in days of old had pandered to Muslims with forbidden pleasures.

*Ind al-Yahudiyya*

I went to Kutkebul laden with gold crowns,
Eighty dinars saved by my hard work.
In no time I had blown them like flies,
And pledged a good silk shirt,
A fancy robe, and my best suit
To the Jewess who runs the tavern.
No woman more modest, more gracious, more lovely!
"My beauty," I said to her, "come, be a sport,
Give us a kiss and be done with it!"
"But why," she replied, "do you want a woman's love
When a boy,
All dreamy-eyed and smooth as a gold coin,
Is so much better?"
She went and fetched a lissome lad,
Bright as the moon, fresh-bottomed—
But I, I left that place dead broke
And down on my luck.
And though, my shirt lost to her wine,
She said in parting,
"Now be well,"
I tell you that I felt like hell.

The Palestinians roared good-humoredly. The Israelis, prepared in the cause of peace to share the blame for a cunning Jewess who had lived twelve hundred years ago, tittered politely.

Ibn-Zaidoun now put on a pair of gold-rimmed glasses and read, to the delight of the audience, another poem about a Jew.

*Jitu Ma'a As'habi*

I came with my friends, both fine young men,
To the tavern keeper at the hour of ten.
You could tell by his dress he was no Muslim.
Our intentions were good—I can't say that of him.
"Your religion," we asked, "it's Christianity?"
He let loose a flood of profanity.
Well, that's a Jew: It's love to your face
And a knife in the back, anytime, anyplace.
"And what," we asked, "shall we call you, sir?"
"Samuel," he said. "Or else Abu-Amar.
Not that I like having an Arab name.
It certainly isn't a claim to fame.
Yet I prefer it all the same
To longer ones that aren't as plain."
"Well said, Abu Amar!" we chimed.
"And now be a friend and break out the wine."
He looked us up and he looked us down,
And he said, "I swear, if word gets out in this town,
Because of you, that I sell booze,
I wouldn't want to be in your shoes."
And with that he brought us a golden mead
That knocked the three of us off our feet,
So that what was meant to be a weekender
Has lasted a month and we're still on a bender!

## 12.

THE MOOD WAS growing mellow. Who could fail to be charmed by such comic proof of the pragmatic, hard-nosed collaboration of Jewish avarice and Muslim vice in the greatest Arab metropolis of the first millennium? And now, striding gracefully to the center of the stage, the Palestinian poet invited with a flourish the illustrious translatoress of Jahaliya poetry, Hannah Tedeschi, to demonstrate her talents in the name of the everlasting fraternity of two ancient languages. His request was simple. Dr. Tedeschi, he proposed, would stand by his side and render into simultaneous Hebrew some excerpts from the mystical tenth-century verse of Al-Hallaj, "the carder"—whose thirst for Allah was so great that it drove him out of his mind and made him decide that he himself was God, leaving the authorities no choice but to behead him publicly, burn his body, and scatter the ashes to dispel his delusion.

The translatoress was caught off guard. She crimsoned, simpered with fright, and tried making herself small, while glaring at the Orientalist who had got her into this. But before Rivlin could come to the defense of his ex–fellow student, presented with an impossible task by the Palestinian poet, his wife surprised him by taking the opposite tack and urging the translatoress to agree.

"But how," Hannah protested, "can I just stand up and translate the fabulously subtle poetry of Hussein Ibn Mansur al-Hallaj? Any version I came up with could only be pitifully superficial."

Yet her even knowing the middle name of so ancient a Sufi poet only strengthened the judge's opinion. "Give it a try," she said. "What do you have to lose? No one will dare criticize you. Those in the audience who, like me, don't know Arabic deserve to know what a poet lost his head for."

The flustered translatoress threw a desperate look at the sad-eyed Mr. Suissa, as if pleading with him to enlist the ghostly authority of his son on her behalf. But Rivlin, always swayed by any show of firmness on his wife's part, now switched sides and took Hannah's hand. "What do you care?" he said. "Don't worry about subtlety. It might even end up in the jubilee volume."

It was a well-aimed shot. To a murmur of approval from the audience, which had been watching her trying to make up her mind, Hannah rose, wound her old woolen scarf around her neck, and gave her hand to the renowned exile, who gallantly led her to the center of the stage.

The lights were dimmed still more, in honor of the martyred mystic. As the Palestinian poet read the first lines, the Jewish translatoress of Ignorance, her hair in need of dyeing and her shoes of new heels, shut her eyes and let Al-Hallaj's cryptic but refined verse percolate through her.

Sukutun thumma samtun thumma harsu
Wa'ilmun thumma thumma wajdun thumma ramsu
Wa'tinnun thumma narun thumma nurun
Wa'bardum thumma zillun thumma shamsu
Wa'haznun thumma shalun thumma fakrun
Wa'nahrun thumma bahrun thumma yabsu
Wa'sukrun thumma sahwun thumma shawkun
Wa'kurbun thumma waslun thumma unsu
Wa' kabdun thumma bastun thumma mahwun
Wa'frakun thumma jam'un thumma tamsu.

Hannah Tedeschi opened her eyes and loosened her scarf. Taking the book of poetry from the Palestinian, who stood, smiling, with a fresh cigarette in his hand, she rested it on her open palms, looked up at him and back at it, and softly but surely improvised a Hebrew translation of the beheaded poet's ode.

Quiet and then silence and then stillness,
And knowledge and then ecstasy and then the grave.
And clay and then fire and then light,
And cold and then shade and then the sun.
And rocks and then plains and then wilderness,
And a river and then a sea and then the land.
And drunkenness and then sobriety and then desire,
And closeness and then touching and then rejoicing.
And contraction and then expansion and then erasure,
And parting and then union and then life.

The translatoress glowed with a new radiance. To the applause of the audience, which did not need to understand the Hebrew to appreciate its music, she returned the book to the poet. He bowed ironically, exhaled a last puff of smoke, and chose another, shorter lyric:

Wa'inna lissan al-ghaybi jalla an al-nutki
Zahrta li'halki w'altabasta la'fityatin
Patahu wa'dalu w'ahtajabat an el-halki
Fa'tazaharu l'il-albab fi 'l-ghaybi taratan
Wa'tawrann an al-absar taghurbi fi 'l-sharki.

And again the book was handed with a smile to the translatoress, who threw back her head with such concentration that it almost flew off her shoulders like Al-Hallaj's. She tossed off the five lines without batting an eyelash:

The language of mystery far exceeds speech,
Revealed to some, from others concealed.
They wonder and wander and meanwhile you are gone,
Sometimes sighted by hearts in the west,
While lost to the sight of eyes in the east.

Rivlin could not contain his admiration. Turning to his wife with a triumphant grin, he congratulated her for making Hannah accept the challenge.

The Palestinian poet bowed a second time, took the book gently, leafed rapidly through it, and found another short and enigmatic poem:

Fa'izza absartani absartahu
Fa'izza absartahu absartana
Ayaha al-sa'ilu an kissitna
Law tarana lam tufarik baynena
Ruhuhu ruhi wa'ruhi ruhuhu
Min ra'a ruheyn halat badana?

This time the translatoress was so sure of herself that she didn't even look at the text. Leaving it with the poet, she answered him:

When you see me, you see him,
When you see him, you see us.
You who would know of our love
Could not tell us apart.

My soul is his, his is mine.
Who has heard of the body
In which two souls combine?

The poet's esteem for the woman mounted. With an approving
glance at her, he recited from memory:

Muzijat ruhuka fi ruhi kama,
   Tumzaju al-hamratu b'al-ma' al-zulal.
Fa'izza masaka shai'un masani,
   Fa'izza anta ana fi kuk hal.

Back with a smile came the Hebrew:

Your soul stirred into mine:
   Into clear water—wine.
Who touches you, touches me.
   I am you in one we.

The poet bowed his head. The Hebrew he had learned in Israel as a
boy, before he chose exile, was enough to tell him how perfect the
translation was. Yet unable to resist putting the now eager translatoress to one last test, he declaimed:

Jubilat ruhaka fi ruhi kama
   Yujbalu al-inbaru b'il-miski 'l-fatik.
Fa'izza masaka shai'un masani
   Fa'izza anta anna la naftarik.

Hannah Tedeschi replied at once:

Thy soul merges with mine
   As with fragrant musk, amber.
Touch mine and it's thine.
   Thou art me forever.

Rivlin, one of the few in the auditorium to appreciate what the
translatoress had accomplished, lifted his curly head to regard with
satisfaction the Arabs around him—among whom he was astonished
to see, in the dark corner occupied by the musicians, a pale-faced,

black-hatted yeshiva student, with earlocks and a beard, whose burning eyes were none other than Samaher's.

## 13.

ONLY NOW WAS it apparent what an effort had been made by the festival's organizers to reach out to their Jewish guests. They wanted the Israelis, whether peaceniks or poetry lovers, to feel at home in their hilly city—which, freed of the cruel yoke of occupation, extended to them a strictly cultural welcome on this chilly but brightly lit winter night.

And so when Samaher had suggested producing for the half-liberated Palestinians a scene from *The Dybbuk*, "the Jewish *Hamlet*," as she called it (although she might just as well have said "the Jewish *Faust*" or "the Jewish *Tartuffe*"), the idea met with the approval of Nazim Ibn-Zaidoun, the baby-faced director with eyes of steel. These now glittered as he directed the ushers to remove the table from the stage, hang a white lace curtain in its place, and dim the lights completely.

First upon the dark stage, lit only by a few beams of wet moonlight shining through the window opened by Fu'ad, were two timid, dark-haired boys carrying candles that made their shadows flicker on the curtain. Rivlin could have sworn they were Ra'uda's sons. Soon they were joined by a serious-looking young man. This was the brilliant Rabbi Azriel, who stood between the candles staring silently at the audience with Samaher's bright eyes. Rivlin held his breath as the rabbi summoned the possessed bride:

"Leah, the daughter of Sender, you may enter the room."

But the bride refused to enter. The voice of the dybbuk possessing her, Rashid's, called from the wings:

"I won't! I don't want to!"

And a woman echoed the words in Arabic:

"*La urid ad'hul, la urid!*"

Rabbi Azriel, played by Rivlin's M.A. student with surprising aplomb, was unfazed. Turning to the wings, he said with quiet firmness:

"Maiden! I command you to enter this room!"

The figure of the bride grew slowly visible in the darkness. It was Ra'uda, still wearing the judge's old clothes, over which a long bridal veil hung past her shoulders. She stood behind the white curtain, waiting for the haunt to speak from her throat. Rashid appeared, white-bearded and wrapped in shrouds, for he was a ghost. He walked with a cane, its handle the doll-like head of a woman, illustrating his obsession for the Palestinian audience. Rivlin was startled to see that this doll had the features of his cousin Samaher.

"Sit, maiden!" Samaher commanded sternly.

The doll did not want to. The dybbuk said:

"Leave me alone. I won't."

And Ra'uda, behind the white curtain, echoed in Arabic:

"*Utrekuni. La urid.*"

Samaher: Dybbuk! I command you to tell me who you are.

Rashid: Rabbi of Miropol, you know who I am. But no one else may know my name.

(Repeated by Ra'uda in Arabic.)

Samaher: I command you again. Tell me who you are.

The little doll squirmed in Rashid's hand.

Rashid: I am a seeker of new paths.

"*Alathina yufatshuna an subul jedida,*" said the echo.

Samaher was displeased by this answer. She stroked her little beard and rebuked the dybbuk severely:

"Only those who stray seek new paths. The just walk the path of righteousness."

Rashid: It is too narrow.

Samaher: Why have you possessed the body of this maiden?

Rashid: I am her mate.

Ra'uda: *Ana zowjuha.*

Samaher: Our Torah forbids the dead to haunt the living.

Rashid: I am not dead.

Ra'uda: *Ana lastu maitan.*

Samaher would have none of it. "You have departed to another world—and there you must remain till the great ram's horn is sounded. I command you to leave the body of this maiden and return to your resting place!"

Rashid: [*Softly*] O Tzaddik of Miropol! I know how great you and your power are. I know that angels and seraphs do your bidding. But I will not. [*Bitterly*] I have nowhere to go, nowhere to rest in this world, apart from where I am now. Everywhere the jaws of Hell await me, and legions of devils and demons would devour me. I will not leave this woman! I cannot!

And Ra'uda repeated, trembling bitterly in her bridal veil:

"*La astati'u 'l-huruj.*"

Samaher turned to face the audience, sprightly in her black jacket and pants with her glued-on beard and earlocks. "O holy congregation!" she addressed it. "Do you grant me the authority to drive out the dybbuk in your name?"

"Drive out the dybbuk in our name!" the two candle-holding brothers cried, the bigger one in Hebrew and the little one in Arabic:

"*Utrud al-jinni!*"

Solemnly, Samaher stepped up to the doll held by Rashid and admonished it:

"In the name of this congregation and all the saints, I, Azriel the son of Hadassah, command you, O dybbuk, to leave at once the body of the maiden Leah, the daughter of Hannah, and to injure neither her nor anyone in departing. If you do not obey me, I will war against you with bans and excommunications. But if you do, I will find you a penance and drive away the devils surrounding you."

Rashid: I do not fear your curses, nor do I believe your promises. No power on earth can give me peace. I have no place in this world. The paths are all blocked, the gates are all locked. There is heaven and there is earth and there are worlds upon worlds, but nowhere have I found as pure and holy a refuge as I have found in the body of this maiden. Here I am at peace like an infant in its mother's lap and fear nothing. No! Do not make me leave! No oath will compel me!

Ra'uda's echo: *La, la tutruduni! La tahlefuni*!

Samaher: Leave the body of the maiden Leah the daughter of Hannah at once!

Rashid: [*Defiantly*] I will not!

Ra'uda: *La atruk!*

Samaher: [*Taking a small whip from her belt and lashing the doll while the audience gasps*] In the name of the Lord of the universe, I adjure you for the last time. Depart from the maiden Leah, the daughter of Hannah! If you do not listen to me now, I will excommunicate you and deliver you to the angels of destruction.

(A terrifying pause)

Rashid: In the name of the Lord of the universe, I am joined and conjoined with my mate and will not leave her.

Ra'uda: *Malsuk wa'mulassak ana bi'zowjati wala atrukha ila 'l-abd.*

Despairing of getting the stubborn dybbuk to depart peacefully, the Arab rabbi strode with small steps to the leather-coated Nazim Ibn-Zaidoun—who, enchanted by the performance, was standing off to one side excitedly fingering his little pistol.

"O Archangel Michael!" the rabbi commanded him. "Have seven Torah scrolls taken out and prepare seven ram's horns and seven black candles."

But either this was as far as the rehearsals had gone or Ibn-Zaidoun had forgotten his lines, because, shaking with laughter, he saluted, bowed, and went to turn on the lights. Then, to the beating of the drum, which spurred the lute, the rebab, and the shepherd's pipe to make music, he broke into loud applause. The audience followed suit. The lace curtain fell, and the older of the two boys snuffed out the candles. Samaher had tears in her eyes. Visibly moved, she pulled off her beard and earlocks and turned shyly to Rashid, who gallantly dipped the head of his doll to her. Yet when he gestured to his sister to join him for a curtain call, she fled the auditorium with her two sons, overcome by stage fright. The two cousins dropped everything and ran after her.

Rivlin, touched to the quick, turned to his wife.

"Unbelievable!" he exclaimed. "Simply unbelievable...."

## 14.

THE TABLE, RETURNED to its place, was now a judgment seat. The judge was an elderly Scotsman. As a young man he had served with British intelligence in the Holy Land, where he had learned Hebrew and Arabic in order to investigate the "terrorists" of those days. Now a pensioner, he sometimes came to the Middle East to lecture at Bir Zeit University on "The Bounds of British Democracy." It was this that qualified him to be the arbiter of the poetry contest.

He sat behind the table, a lanky thoroughbred whose eyes, too, were blue from sheer blue-bloodedness. Two panelists joined him, for balance: a pudgy Egyptian diplomat, in the area on state business, and the Tel Aviv critic-poet—who, however, could hardly be accused of bias in favor of his own people. At the last moment, the learned translatoress, having impressed one and all with her renditions of the mystical verse of Al-Hallaj, was added too. Her confidence had grown by such leaps and bounds that Rivlin easily persuaded her to accept the nomination "for the honor of Israeli Orientalism," as he put it. Hannah nodded and ran a small comb through her stringy hair before letting herself be led to the table.

One by one, the contestants were called upon to read their verse. First, however, the rule was restated that the contest was for love poems only. No entries on political themes would be accepted, even if cast in such lyric form as a Palestinian lament for a field expropriated by Jews, a Palestinian dirge for an olive tree uprooted by Jews, a Palestinian elegy for the childhood memory of a fragrant orange grove built on by Jews, or a Palestinian threnody for the tears of an abandoned horse in a village destroyed by Jews. Likewise, there were to be no refugees, no occupations, no anti-Semitism, no Holocaust, no death, and no bereavement. Only love.

The contest had attracted a large number of competitors, old poetic hands and newcomers alike. Most were residents of Ramallah or nearby villages, though some came from as far afield as Jordan, and others were Arabs from Israel, several of them equipped with Hebrew translations of their verse. The Israeli contingent was small, even after being reinforced by an overweight and bashful German woman and a slightly tipsy American, both reading their verse in their own languages.

And yet, starting with the very first poem, it was evident that the elegy and the threnody, the uprooted olive tree and the tearful horse, were not so easily forgotten in love's name. Not a few contestants sought to outwit the organizers by disguising their national grief as erotic outpourings for a stolen beloved, her splendid belly compared to a lost wheat field, the chime of her bracelets to the enemy's machine guns. One old villager wrote a poem to his wife in which a younger rival for her affections was likened to a Jewish settler.

In his seat in the murmuring, smoke-filled auditorium, the Orientalist was growing weary of the same repetitive images in the same unchanging rhymes and meters, the gist of which had to be translated for his wife. The one poem he was looking forward to was Fu'ad's— but the maître d', intimidated by so many Palestinians from across the border, passed up his turn with a wave of his hand.

Intermission came at last. The audience flowed back to the buffet, leaving the Scottish judge and his panelists to tally their scores. Arabs and Jews stepped up to congratulate Hannah Tedeschi on her translations. Flustered by so much praise, she shrugged it off by explaining in tedious detail each mistake she had made while promising to correct them all in good time. "It was a brilliant idea of yours to get her away from that tyrannical hypochondriac," Rivlin said to Hagit as he fondly watched his old classmate struggling to keep the attention from going to her head. The judge, well aware of her judiciousness, merely smiled at her husband—who, thinking he had caught a glimpse of the fluttering robe of the Lebanese nun, decided to go to the men's room before the intermission ended.

The nun, however, failed to materialize, Rashid and his possessed women had disappeared, and even the men's room proved elusive and was to be found only with the help of the poetry-reading coat-check attendant, who had resumed her position by the checkroom. Following her directions, the Orientalist climbed a staircase to the third floor. This was a loft whose wide-open windows failed to dispel the heated atmosphere of the loud young men and women gathered there, evidently more in search of love than of poetry. Several of the women had chosen to cool off by removing their shawls and letting down their hair.

There was a long line for the men's room. In it was Fu'ad, looking as athletic in his tightly cut jeans as the young men around him. Noticing the Jewish Orientalist, he turned around and said loudly in Arabic for all to hear, "Please move up, Professor. I've saved a place for you." When Rivlin, embarrassed, shook his head, Fu'ad moved back to join him.

"You look so youthful that I didn't recognize you," Rivlin said, almost grudgingly.

"Youthful?" The maître d' laughed. "How can I be youthful, Professor? Look around you and you'll see youth. I'm just without my dark suit and Miss Hendel bossing me. Come back to the hotel and you'll see the tired old Fu'ad you know."

The Jew looked at the Arab reproachfully. "How come you got cold feet?"

"How do you mean?"

"You didn't read your poem."

"You call that flimflam a poem, Professor? The poems tonight made me realize that all the juice has gone out of my Arabic. With the pepper and the hot sauce. I've hung around you Jews for so long that my Arabic is like a rusty faucet. Do you want them to think in Ramallah that that's the best Abu-Ghosh can do? Better to listen and to learn..."

The line advanced slowly. From somewhere Rivlin made out the rich voice of the Lebanese nun. His heart beating faster, he turned and spotted her on a balcony at the far end of the loft. Petite and smiling, she stood in the cigarette smoke of her choir of drones, looking bridal herself with a nun's dickey over her white robe. With her was Ibn-Zaidoun, who appeared to be telling her a funny story, at which she burst out laughing in the same throaty tones in which Rivlin had heard her lament the death of God.

"*Hadi hiyya 'l-mutribba 'l-lubnaniyya*,"* he said excitedly to Fu'ad, who made sure to remain a half-step behind him as they neared the bathroom. "You'll love her singing."

The bathroom had two urinals and a stall. Although the Orientalist would have preferred the stall for privacy's sake, a red arc above its door handle showed it was occupied. He took his place at the urinal, fumbling with his zipper. As he carefully pulled out his penis, the man next to him zipped his pants and walked away and Fu'ad slipped into

---

* There's the Lebanese nun.

his place. The Jew could not help stealing a glance at the Arab's member. It was passing water with surprising speed.

Rivlin felt anger. He couldn't relax enough to pee.

"It's not the Jews who have ruined your Arabic, Fu'ad," he said despairingly to the flower-patterned tiles in front of him. "It's surrendering your freedom to the hotel."

The plash of water stopped beside him. He continued, still looking straight ahead:

"When I beg you to tell me what happened with Ofer and Galya, and who was to blame, you just clam up. But I know you know, *l'inno inta, ya Fu'ad, mowjud fi kul mahal.*\* You don't give a damn how I'm suffering because you only think of yourself and of getting ahead. But where to? If you're not free inside you'll never get anywhere. You'll end up writing elegies for yourself."

The water flushed in the stall. Yet the door remained closed, and the next man in line lost patience and moved up behind them, waiting for someone to finish. Fu'ad, pale, looked stunned by the Orientalist's words. He went to the sink, washed his hands quickly, and left.

Rivlin shut his eyes fervently and waited for the painfully slow trickle of his urine to increase. He had finished and was washing his hands, slowly squeezing detergent from a plastic bottle, when the door of the stall opened and out stepped Mr. Suissa. Had he overheard the conversation with Fu'ad? But what if he had?

"Well, what do you think of the festivities?" Rivlin asked. "Wasn't I right, Mr. Suissa, that it was worth coming tonight?"

"Yes," Suissa replied, "there's always something to be learned. Those Sufi lyrics were golden."

"And Hannah Tedeschi's Hebrew translations? Marvelous."

"They were. My son always said to me: 'Doctor Tedeschi outranks her husband.'"

"And this Center—would you have believed it of the Palestinian Authority? Such a pleasant, elegant place!"

"I suppose so—if visiting a vipers' nest can be pleasant."

"A vipers' nest?"

---

\* Because you, Fu'ad, are everywhere.

"Make no mistake about it, Professor Rivlin. They can stand and recite love poems all night, but they're still vipers. Even that Arab you were just talking to."

Rivlin, nettled, came to the maître d's defense. "What do you know about him, Mr. Suissa?"

"Nothing, Professor," Suissa replied, his face betraying no emotion. "Since my son was killed, I don't know a thing. I'm listening and learning, just like your friend."

Yet encountering Fu'ad waiting for them outside, Suissa dropped his eyes deferentially and headed for the stairs leading back to the second floor.

The top floor was emptying out. Even the young people who had ignored the poetry contest wanted to hear the Lebanese singer, whose white robe was still visible on the balcony. Her male chorus was gone, and she was alone with the festival's director, who regarded her admiringly while smoking a little pipe.

Rivlin, convinced that the nun not only would but should remember him, set out in her direction. He was intercepted by Fu'ad, anxious to smooth things over.

"Don't be angry, Professor. It's been so many years.... Why should I be a tattletale? I wouldn't even know what tale to tell."

Rivlin just kept walking. "The truth is," he said venomously, "*bas al-mazbut—inta hiwif.*"*

And he hurried to the nun without paying attention to the gray-haired Arab's distress.

She remembered him. Who could forget a lone Jew in a village church in the middle of the night?

"*Inti shaifi, ya Madame, ana anid k'tir,*" he said to her with emotion. "*Jit kaman marra ta'asma' eish bighanu fi 'l-janneh. Bas hal marra jibt el-mara kaman....*"†

She smiled gently. "*Ahlan u-sahlan.*"‡

---

* But the real truth—you're a coward.
† You see, Madam, I'm very persistent. I've come to hear once again what they sing in Paradise. But this time I've brought my wife too.
‡ You're welcome.

He glanced at her bare feet in the plain sandals worn by her even on this cold, rainy night. Speaking in French to avoid embarrassing her in front of Ibn-Zaidoun, he said:

"I told my wife how you wouldn't faint for me last summer. She joins me in hoping that this winter you'll be more forthcoming...."

If shocked by the Israeli's forwardness, the nun was too well bred to show it. She merely gave him a lucid Christian look and said, with a hint of irony:

"*Inshallah.*"*

## 15.

THE AUDITORIUM WAS twice as full as before. It took considerable effort for Rivlin, one of the last to reenter it, to make his way to his wife over the Palestinians on the floor.

"I thought you'd been kidnapped," Hagit said, more curious than concerned by his absence.

"Where to?" Rivlin said, stroking her hair. "Anyway, we're kidnapped already." In a whisper he told her of his encounter with the nun, who now entered to stormy applause. On the floor at his feet, he noticed Ra'uda in his wife's old clothes with her two boys.

"*Feyn Rashid?*" he asked. "*Feyn Samaher?*"†

"'Round," she said, using what Hebrew she remembered. She seemed worried by their disappearance.

The second half of the program was entitled "Christian Arab Song." More folkloristic than the performance in Zababdeh, it was all in Arabic, with no Greek Passions or Resurrections. He glanced at the words of the lyrics, obtained by the translatoress. Although they abounded in religious references—how else would the convent in Baalbek have agreed to send the nun to the Holy Land?—the emphasis was, in the spirit of the festival, on God's love. The musicians, too, were more richly polyphonic than the monotonous droners of Zababdeh, whose four male singers, now taking their place by the band, were

---

* Please God.
† Where's Rashid? Where's Samaher?

augmented by three more hefty, gray-haired men in dark suits indistinguishable from themselves. Rivlin hoped that this ensemble, backed by a small but vigorous drum, would force the Lebanese singer out of her angelic bubble and into a confrontation with the world.

And it did. At first every line warbled by the little nun was resoundingly seconded with all its grace notes by the lute, rebab, and drum. Then, however, these were joined by the shepherd's pipe, whose plaintive tones turned their agreement into a protest or question to which the Lebanese was forced to reply—which in turn forced the male choir to stop its droning and rebel, pained and incredulous, against the white-robed singer's unshakable harmonies. It was hard to tell what was rehearsed and what was improvised. At times, despite her great vocal resourcefulness, the nun was surprised and thrown off her stride. Yet she not only recovered quickly, she rose to the challenge and added still more quavers to her answer until these lengthened into a single long appoggiatura that brooked no response.

Was this her way, assisted by the musicians, of preparing for the swoon that Rivlin was looking forward to? Were they wearing down her resistance with their repeated phrases until its precise point of collapse was reached, not by calculation, but by a true intoxication of the spirit? Or did they, on the contrary, fearing that too quick a loss of consciousness might end the concert prematurely, engage her in this complex dialogue to keep her from passing out from sheer boredom?

The Orientalist felt a tug on his pants. It was Ra'uda, drawing his attention to the rear of the auditorium. There, in its crowded last row, was Samaher in a scarf, and behind her, her handsome cousin. His gaze zeroing in on the Orientalist, Rashid flashed him a V sign like the one Rivlin remembered from Zababdeh. Yet this time, he felt, there was something proud and debauched about it. Ra'uda, he saw by her frightened face, had the same reaction.

The nun's singing had now infected the Ramallah audience, which swayed in its seats as if straining to join in. The musicians, prepared for such an uprising, changed tempo to nip it in the bud. Rivlin turned to his wife, wishing to share the experience. Her ironic smile left him uncertain that she was enjoying it. "Well, what do you say?" he asked excitedly, as if he were the nun's impresario. "Doesn't she have a wonderful voice?" Hagit gave her husband a pitying look. "I wouldn't exactly call it wonderful," she answered judiciously, while smiling at the Arabs bouncing up and down to the insurrectionary beat of the drum. "But it is special."

Disappointed in her, Rivlin surveyed the rest of his entourage, hoping for greater enthusiasm. Hannah Tedeschi, bent over the lyrics that she was no doubt translating in her head, did not appear to be listening to the music. Mr. Suissa, on the other hand, had a look of wary satisfaction on his face, as if he had discovered here in Ramallah the Arab music he had been deprived of in his North African Jewish childhood.

> O my Lord, who spreads the heavens,
> We are purged of our carnality,
> And the earth quivers with love.
> Your long arm
> Summons us to the Redemption.

The nun now began a new exchange, with a tambourine—which, however, rather than following her, took the lead. Its percussive rattle rising above the diminuendo of the musicians, it, too, sought to throw her off balance, forcing her to cling to more and more sobbing grace notes of an increasingly Oriental character. Supposedly above it all in her Lebanese cloister, she now seemed, like the oppressed Palestinians of the Holy Land, to be fighting for an existence that vibrated with them on one wavelength.

Rivlin felt one of Ra'uda's dark-haired boys slump sleepily against his knee. Laying a hand on the warm little head, he tapped the rhythm of the drum on it. He gave his wife a loving look, glanced fondly at the translatoress immersed in her lyrics, and was surprised to see, out of the corner of his eye, Mrs. Suissa junior, who had not said a word to him all evening, crying as he had cried for Jephthah's daughter.

## 16.

BUT WHEN WOULD the promised fainting take place? Was it possible in front of such an openly non-Christian audience? And who, apart from Rivlin and Rashid, even hoped for it?

Song followed song, and the little nun showed no signs of tiring. The lute and rebab kept pace with her, their ancient erotic rhythms luring her so far from the sacred that there were times when she could have been performing in a Cairo cabaret.

A thin, reddish gas drifted upward near the musicians. Produced by a secondhand smoke machine bought by Ibn-Zaidoun from an Israeli disco club, it thickened and spread, forming a mist that enveloped the choir and curled around the plain sandals of the nun. From there, like a friendly animal, it crept toward the Palestinians sitting on the floor near the stage. At first they backed away, as if from a tear-gas bomb. Yet seeing that the odorless substance did not burn or make them cry and was no more than a symbol of the world's insubstantiality, they began to laugh and to try to get a whiff of it or even catch it in their hands.

The Lebanese nun, startled by this special effect, which seemed about to turn her performance into a rock concert, stopped singing. She shut her eyes and hugged her shoulders as if fending off the audience's clapping to the rhythm of the drum. Now is the time, Rivlin thought. He tugged at his wife and whispered: "Watch her. She's going to faint. I just hope she doesn't blow it."

The judge looked at her husband as if he were deranged. "But what good does it do if she faints?" she asked.

The Orientalist did not expect such a question. Automatically, however, as though from the depths of a trance, the answer came to him. "It's a warning," he said. "A warning of the abyss we're all about to fall into."

Yet the nun was taking her time. Indeed, if she had been supposed to faint at the point of her hushed climax it was already too late, because the music had resumed and passed the point of no return. Even Ibn-Zaidoun's smoke machine was now out of control and rapidly fouling the auditorium, in which several veterans of the Intifada had risen to their feet and were shouting the nun down with nationalist songs.

She turned pale and retreated to the rear of the stage. Something unpleasant, a serious and perhaps even violent misunderstanding, was in the air. In another minute, it seemed, she would have to hide behind her choir of hefty drones. And yet oddly, so loyal until now, they were doing nothing to protect her. Droning and clapping, they pushed her almost comically back, as if holding her to the terms of her contract. Rivlin was on his feet, trying to sight the white robe, which was surrounded by a crowd that had burst onto the stage. At its head, talking to the still-singing nun, was Rashid. He made a gesture, and suddenly, with no warning, she collapsed at his feet and disappeared from the sight of the Jew.

## 17.

IT WAS AFTER midnight when the audience dispersed, in high spirits. The Lebanese nun's fainting fit had met with sympathy, and numerous well-wishers had come up to her once she regained consciousness. Despite their repeated requests, however, she declined to go on with her performance—which was just as well, since anything more would only have been anticlimactic.

Rivlin and his entourage took their coats and umbrellas from the checkroom and said good-bye to Nazim Ibn-Zaidoun and the blue-blooded judge. The Scotsman, against the advice of his panelists, had awarded first prize in the poetry contest to an elderly village bard who had written his first verse in the days of the British Mandate. The famous Palestinian poet had already departed for Amman, where the air of exile was purer, setting out in a taxi for Jordan as soon as the nun fainted. Ibn-Zaidoun bade everyone farewell for him, especially the Jewish student of the Age of Ignorance, his mystical dialogue with whom he would long remember.

It was bitterly cold when they left the large stone building. The skies were clear, with no sign of more rain. The orange moon that had barely cleared the mountains earlier in the evening was now floating palely and effortlessly among the stars.

They all took their places in the minibus except for Ra'uda, who was given a ride back to Zababdeh by a Christian family. Her two boys remained with Rashid, the older of them sitting by the young widow, whose eyes still shone with emotion. Samaher, bundled up in her shawl, sat self-consciously in the back as if anxious to forget her role as a Jewish rabbi. But Rivlin would not let her. Stooping to enter the vehicle, he said loudly:

"Samaher, you were marvelous! It was a fabulous idea to do a scene from *The Dybbuk*. I told my wife that the way you got into your part was incredible."

"Well, Professor," Rashid said, his dark face smiling at Rivlin in the rearview mirror as he pulled out of his parking place with a honk of the horn, "maybe that's a reason to give Samaher her final grade tonight."

"Her final grade?" Rivlin chuckled. "It's a bit too early for that. But if it's a question of extra credit for her Arabic translation of *The Dybbuk*...yes, I suppose that's possible."

Deep down the Haifa professor had to admit that not giving Samaher a grade was more than just a matter of maintaining academic standards. The fact was that he did not want to part with these two young people, whose love traced an invisible arc in the bulky van.

They joined a convoy of Israeli cars, its peace and poetry lovers escorted by a Palestinian police jeep to the military campfire at the border. This time, the soldiers—unwilling to rely on their instincts to tell an Israeli physiognomy from a Palestinian one in the dead of night—asked for IDs. Through the window of the minibus Rivlin saw Fu'ad led off to the campfire, as if to be examined by its light. Feeling responsible for the maître d', he climbed out of the minibus and hurried over. The intervention of the aging Jewish professor had its effect, and Fu'ad—perhaps singled out because of his singularly crumpled ID—was allowed to proceed. Meanwhile, however, the car he'd been in had driven off without him, leaving him hurt and bewildered. Still smarting over Rivlin's remarks, he accepted his offer of a lift to Jerusalem without knowing what to make of his sudden protectiveness.

The drive back to Jerusalem was a short one. Hagit laid her head on her husband's shoulder and was out like a light, sleeping through Hannah Tedeschi's impassioned recitation of an elegy written by the

great Syrian poet Adonis for the same Al-Hallaj whose verses she had
translated. Rivlin, a captive audience, listened to her declaim it:

> Your poisoned green quill—
> The veins of its neck bottled flame
> In which a star rises over Baghdad—
> Is our bright past, our resurrection on earth,
> Our death that returns to itself.

Rivlin, exhausted by the night's impressions, nodded ironically at
this woman who gave birth to translations instead of children. "Well,
Hannah," he demanded, "aren't you going to say 'thank you'?"

"'Thank you'?" She looked askance at him. "For what?"

"For making you come tonight."

"Just wait," she grumbled, turning color. "We haven't yet seen
what it's going to cost me."

They dropped a pensive Suissa and his widowed daughter-in-law
in Pisgat Ze'ev. The translatoress, as anxious as a student before an
exam, asked Rivlin to come upstairs with her to help bear the brunt of
the abandoned Tedeschi's anger. But the Haifa Orientalist was in no
mood to climb three flights of stairs just in order to listen to the old
man's complaints. In the end, they agreed on a compromise proposal
of the judge's that she and her husband wait down below for five minutes to see whether they were needed.

Hannah Tedeschi said her good-byes. All the pent-up emotion of
the evening came out as she hugged and kissed Hagit affectionately
before turning on the entrance light and starting up the stairs. The
Rivlins said good night to Rashid, Samaher, and the two boys, and the
Orientalist unlocked their parked car, turned on the heating for Hagit,
and went to stand outside the Tedeschis' building.

The minibus drove a distance down the street and stopped in a
little square, waiting for the Jews to be safely on their way. Rashid's
silhouette, seated stiffly by the wheel, was limned by the yellowish
glare of a streetlight. Samaher, still in the backseat, looked like a sad
mummy. Something that had happened across the border, Rivlin felt,
made them afraid to sit close to each other.

The judge, full of the evening's music and ready for more sleep, leaned her head back in the car. Rivlin stood reading the names on the mailboxes, trying to remember which of them had been in this building thirty years ago. Before he could finish, the stairway light went out. A minute later he was approached by Fu'ad. The maître d' wished to know whether, on their way back to Haifa, they could drop him off in Abu-Ghosh. Rivlin look at his watch and nodded. He cast a weary glance at the Arab, who took a last, thirsty drag on his cigarette, ground the butt out with his shoe, and whispered underneath his mustache:

"*Bas kan biddi ha'ul, ya Brofesor,** that if you're wondering whether he cheated on her, you can be sure he didn't."

The Orientalist's battered heart twinged.

"That's what I thought." He made two fists. "And that's why it kills me that..."

The light came back on in the stairwell. They heard hurried steps. Hannah Tedeschi, looking pale, appeared without her coat and signaled Rivlin to follow her.

"But what's wrong?" he asked. "What does he want? Didn't fall asleep in the end?"

"In the end..." She repeated the words as though hypnotized. With an abrupt gesture, she signaled the Arab to join them too.


## 18.

"BUT WHY IS it so dark in here?" Rivlin complained, following Hannah Tedeschi down the hallway with its shelves of novels and thrillers in many languages, bought in airports by the Jerusalem polymath to pass the time on international flights. Hannah didn't answer. With a stride that seemed to have grown swifter, she led him through the dim guest room to the door of Tedeschi's study, beneath which crept a beam of light.

Even though Hannah had said nothing, he was prepared for what

---

* I just have to say, Professor.

awaited him and turned around to make sure the maître d' was behind him. A man who had spent his life going in and out of the rooms of strangers could surely cope with the warmly lit study that the translatoress now ushered them into.

Tedeschi, dressed in his pajamas, had apparently risen from bed and gone to his desk to do something at his computer. His arms embraced its lit screen, and his puckish face nuzzled its ivory keyboard, leaving the wife fifteen years his junior to guess whether he had been slipped an Ottoman sleeping potion, fainted from fright at her absence, or decided to bid a fond adieu to the world of scholarship. From the way she stood, tall and grave, without approaching for a closer look, it was evident which of these possibilities she believed in.

Rivlin felt weak-kneed. His heart went out to this grave woman, his loyal former classmate—who, surprisingly, did not seem to blame herself for her sudden liberation from the teacher who had trapped her. And since the latter was in no condition to tell anyone what to do with him, Rivlin asked the maître d' to help pry his old mentor loose from the computer, on which he had vomited in a last act of desperation.

Not that Fu'ad owed Tedeschi anything. Still, many years of experience at entering and even breaking into hotel rooms made him a competent assistant. "Let's lay him on the floor," he said softly to the Jew, stepping nimbly forward to grab one end of the dead man. It wasn't easy. The Jerusalem scholar was stronger in death than in life, and it took no little force and ingenuity to wrestle him from the computer screen, on which his favorite comic-book figures were still cavorting, and carefully straighten him out. Undeterred by the pity he felt, Rivlin seized his old doctoral adviser's skull and pulled it from the keyboard without checking whether the eyes were closed.

Only now, as the maître d' expertly eased the pudgy body, undeniably a corpse, onto the floor and rather illogically moved the heater closer to it, did it dawn on Rivlin that he would never again sit in this room discussing the Middle East or having new ideas about it run past him. He glanced at Hannah Tedeschi, who was watching sternly and aloofly from the other side of the room, as if the horror of what had happened were a moral boundary she refused to cross. It saddened him that obsessive worry about his son had kept him from promising his old mentor that, come what may, he would write something for the jubilee volume.

"Just a minute, I'll get a blanket," Hannah whispered. She actually looked younger, as if the death of her husband had taken years off her age. Since he actually had been parted from his computer and laid down in repose on the Persian rug, no cry of grief escaped her. "Better a sheet, ma'am," Fu'ad said. "That's what's usually used." The quiet confidence of his movements suggested that he had done this with more than one hotel guest. The translatoress looked searchingly at the Israeli Arab, who was not yet a Jew and no longer a true son of the desert; then she nodded and went to fetch an old, starched cotton sheet. This was taken from her by Rashid, who had turned up as if it were only natural to be offering his services at such a time. Having recently worn sheets in his role as the dybbuk, he expertly unfolded this one and handed one end of it to the maître d'. Working in comradely tandem, the two men whipped it in the air like a great white sail and let it settle over the face of the doyen of Orientalists.

Now that Tedeschi had disappeared from sight for the last time, Rivlin remembered his wife, who was probably still asleep in the running car on the deserted nighttime street. Worriedly, he headed for the front door. The trusty messenger—who, since the wedding in the Galilee, seemed able to read the mind of the teacher who still owed his cousin a grade—stopped him. "You don't have to run, Professor," he said. "I hear her coming up the stairs."

She was already in the doorway, his pleasantly plump beloved in her short sheepskin coat. Her untroubled face, the face of a lover of the Just and the Good, showed no suspicion. "Is anything wrong?" she asked softly, with a smile, and advanced innocently toward the study, where she saw the corpse beneath its white sheet. Fearlessly she knelt and pulled back the sheet for a last look at the man who had taken a fancy to her on her first visit to this apartment, thirty years ago, as a young soldier, aspiring law student, and future bride.

She began to cry, her silent tears breaking the heart of a husband who had been sure that here was a death that left him cold and unmoved. Still relentlessly aloof, the translatoress turned in alarm to the two Arabs, as if it were their duty to keep this self-assured woman from introducing grief into the deceased's study. But they, unaware that the dead man had thought he understood Arabs better than Arabs understood themselves, declined to involve themselves in a Jewish matter, thus forcing the translatoress to drop her mask. At long last she uttered a sound that was somewhere between a groan of pain and a curse of despair, went over to the computer, and tapped a key. The comic-book figures vanished. Tedeschi's last article appeared on the screen in all its rich complexity. She reached out to touch it, in a final, merciful caress.

### PART VII

# The Liberation

HAD THERE BEEN advance signs of this death?

Rivlin lay waiting for the dawn under an old woolen blanket in the unborn children's room. The Jerusalem polymath, wrapped in a sheet on the Persian rug in his study, awaited the same dawn, which would bring a doctor, a family friend, to confirm his final adieu. Meanwhile, in the living room on the other side of the door, the translatoress sat up talking emotionally to the judge, seeking guidance.

The two Arabs had left, each for his own destination. Or had they gone off together?

They had spread the sheet over the doyen of Orientalists with such perfect coordination that they might have been trained for it.

But what were the signs? For it now appeared that behind the hypochondria and the false alarms a real death had been hiding, waiting to catch the translatoress of Ignorance off guard before striking.

And yet...

Rivlin thought about the pajamas Tedeschi was wearing when he died. They indicated that he had gone to bed and tried to sleep. Had some new idea made him jump up and go to his desk? Or was it the terror of dying, against which he had sought comfort in something he had written?

Had he found it?

Or his adamant refusal to spend the evening in the Palestinian Authority, where he would have died among Arabs—was that a sign? Or his battle to keep his wife from going without him, which had ended with a white handkerchief of surrender telling death that the way was now clear?

And how about his lecture that strange morning on the Turkish *Othello*? And his new interest in imaginative literature as opposed to speeches and protocols?

Two years previously, on a trip to the Dolomites, the Rivlins had found themselves floating skyward, late one summer afternoon, in an orange funicular bound for a restaurant on the heights of Mount Cortina. Although in winter the site must have swarmed with skiers, it now had few visitors. In the restaurant, at a table next to theirs, looking down at the fertile valley below, sat a quiet, polite couple with two small children; on the Rivlins' other side, facing the bare mountain, was an elderly, stocky man in an old-fashioned summer suit that appeared to have come straight from a 1930s European movie. He was sipping champagne while talking seriously with a man of about thirty who was wearing sporty designer clothes.

The two Israelis watched the children lick their ice cream, then gradually shifted their attention to the ruddy-faced old man. He looked German or Italian and might have been a banker or an architect, or perhaps a local politician. His young companion, to judge by the deference he showed, was not a relative or friend, but, more likely, a student or assistant.

After a while the man rose with the help of a gold-handled cane, donned a Panama hat, paid the bill, and left with his companion. But instead of heading downhill for the cable car, he took the younger man by the arm and set out for the bald peak. Although the sun was already low in the sky, he strode slowly onward, leaning on his cane while continuing his conversation, as if fulfilling some obligation toward nature or the mountain, the distant summit of which gleamed with a last crown of snow.

The two Israelis regarded the elderly gentleman intently, expecting at any moment to see him tire and turn back. The path he was on zigzagged at a gentle grade up the mountain's bare, arid flank. He kept walking up it, the younger man at his side or falling slightly behind. Unhurriedly he climbed, in a purpling light that the setting sun would soon take with it.

"Doesn't he remind you of Tedeschi?" Rivlin had mused aloud.

Hagit's eyes lit up. "Yes," she said. "I was thinking the same thing."

The elderly gentleman and his young companion vanished in the late-afternoon haze. Were they still heading up the mountain? But where to? The minutes passed and they did not return. The two Israelis looked around them. It was time to take the funicular back down to the darkening valley. "Imagine," Rivlin said to his wife as they skimmed the treetops between sky and earth, "what would have happened if there had been no Fascism or Nazism and no Second World War. Carlo would have remained in a peaceful Europe and ended up looking like that man—a bit recherché but perfectly respectable, ruddy with health and well-being, strolling in the Dolomites in a summer suit, with a gold-handled cane, until he vanished in the haze. Arabs and Jews would have been the furthest things from his mind."

Was that a sign, the haze at the bend in the path two years ago?

THE FUNERAL, set for 5 P.M., was postponed until six because of a logjam at the cemetery. The Rivlins spent the day in Jerusalem. The Orientalist helped with the funeral arrangements while the judge stayed on the telephone, calling the Tedeschis' friends and acquaintances and urging them in a quiet but authoritative manner to come pay their last respects. Later in the day she went to buy flowers and food, and fresh socks and underwear for herself and her husband to wear after showering. Rivlin, however, was repelled by the old, peeling bathroom with its assorted toothbrushes and shaving implements, and untidy laundry basket and medicine chest. Picking up a broken comb to which still clung some old hairs, he dropped it in a fright, quickly changed his underwear, sprinkled himself with aftershave lotion from an old bottle, and said to his wife:

"Don't expect me to shower. It's too much for me."

Soon after arriving in Palestine at the start of World War II, Tedeschi, as a statement that he would never return to Europe, had purchased a burial plot in a small cemetery in Sanhedriya, then an ordinary Jerusalem neighborhood. Subsequently, it had turned into a crowded ultra-Orthodox ghetto, in which the cemetery, grown larger, remained the only open green space. Now, obeying judicial authority, a sizable crowd had gathered and was making its way in falling darkness along the congested aisles between the tombstones, or else cutting through or climbing over them. At its head walked the president of Hebrew University with the rector and the dean, followed by Tedeschi's fellow faculty members, some senior librarians, and Orientalists from other institutions and organizations—including the Mossad, representatives of which had sometimes consulted the Jerusalem polymath about the lessons to be learned from Arab history. Missing were only the Arabs themselves, not one of whom was in evidence, although Tedeschi had liked to boast of his Arab friends.

Rivlin, standing by the fresh grave, noted that it was the last empty one in its row. Tedeschi, in planning for his own death, had forgotten to think of his wife's. The liberated translatoress, Rivlin thought sadly, would have to fend for herself. Although she had wanted him to give the eulogy, he had begged off. "Let the president or rector do it," he told her. "In cemeteries they outrank me. There'll be other chances to eulogize Carlo. Today I'll recite the mourner's prayer. And you should think of some parting words to say yourself."

Indeed, Rivlin enjoyed the hush that descended on everyone, from the president down, as he read the kaddish in a strong, clear voice from an imitation-parchment scroll handed him by the undertaker, who shone a little flashlight on it. The translatoress, though freed at last from her marital bonds, was too flustered to speak. Taking the flashlight from the undertaker, she pulled from her pocket an ancient elegy from the Age of Ignorance, recently translated by her. "You'll forgive me," she apologized to the distinguished gathering. "This is what I know how to do."

In hard, quick tones she read some lines by the sixth-century Arabic poet Thabata Sharan, put in the mouth of his mother after the death of a son:

You traveled far to run from death, but it caught up with you.
If only I knew how you fell into its hands.
Were you ill, alone without a friend,
Or did your enemies trick you into it?

How harsh the world
In which you may not answer me.
Your silence makes me
My own comforter.
O my heart,
Stand still a while!
I grieve that my soul
Was not taken forever
In place of yours.

## 1.

EARLY THAT WINTER the Rivlins were informed by Ofra and Yo'el that the two of them were planning to be in Israel on their way to a UN conference in Singapore. It would be a brief stopover, made possible by a ticket from Europe to the Far East.

The stopover was originally planned for five days. While the judge looked for ways to lessen her caseload, Rivlin hurriedly reserved a hotel room on the Carmel and obtained a list of that week's concerts and performances from a ticket agency. Yet in the end, various constraints and obligations shortened the five days to three.

"Well," Rivlin said generously, "if it's only three nights, let's cancel the hotel reservation and give them my study. We'll want to spend as much time with them as we can."

But the three nights did not survive intact, either. The visit was cut again, this time to twenty-four hours.

"If that's the most your beloved sister can afford to give you," Rivlin told his disappointed wife, "let's take a day off from work and spend it and the night by Lake Kinneret."

Two weeks before his in-laws' arrival, however, a change in international flights scotched this plan too. The stopover was reduced to a few hours.

"This is already an insult," Rivlin proclaimed, with an odd gaiety. "Not to Israel—it will manage without them. But what about us? Is that how little we mean to them? I intend to lodge an official complaint at the airport."

"Just don't say anything to spoil their visit," warned his wife, who had no sense of humor when it came to her sister.

Once again they were in the arrivals hall of the airport with its plashing fountains. The two globe-trotters, tired but traveling light with only their hand luggage, were the first of their flight to emerge from customs. "It's marvelous, even spiritual," Yo'el said, giving his welcomers a big hug, "to enter Israel with only a light bag."

"Yes," Rivlin agreed. "Unfortunately, that's the bag we're left holding when you leave."

"Stow it," Hagit said, embracing Ofra.

Ofra, thin, pale, and guilt-ridden, threw her arms around her sister and promised that on their way back from Singapore they would come for longer. Meanwhile, they had decided to spend their few hours in Jerusalem, if only for the sake of the venerable aunt, whose survival from one stopover to the next was far from assured.

It was storming. Rivlin, wanting to make sure no one complained about the weather, praised the badly needed rain. They debated stopping for lunch in Abu-Ghosh at Fu'ad's uncle's restaurant, which was such a favorite of Yo'el's that it almost seemed that the entire stopover had been planned with it in mind. Yet since everyone had already eaten, the visitors on the plane and the Rivlins at the airport, it was decided to postpone the restaurant meal until supper and make do with coffee and cake at a roadside diner.

Although the two sisters spoke regularly over the telephone several times a week, not even the longest and most audible of long-distance calls could compete with a face-to-face talk by the roaring fireplace of a diner. The conversation touched on everything, old, new, remembered, and forgotten, and when his in-laws asked about Ofer, Rivlin replied by bewailing his eldest son's solitude in Paris. Ofer, he said, was still not over his divorce. Before he could proceed any further, however, Hagit changed the subject to the festival in Ramallah, her account of which—especially of the Lebanese nun's fainting fit and the Arabic production of *The Dybbuk*—fascinated the visitors. "From now on," Yo'el said, shaking his head with sorrow at Hagit's description of Tedeschi's death, "you'll have to live your married life without its best man." They smiled bittersweet smiles, and a tear shone in Ofra's eye.

She went on dabbing at her tears until, eternally thin and pale, she gave Hagit a last, clinging embrace by the departures gate. So guilty and upset was she over their short visit that Rivlin forbore to comment. Why rub it in?

There had been more tears at their aunt's, who was bedridden with a bad cold. The old lady, though her usual lucid, ironic self, told her beloved niece not to kiss her and concentrated on Yo'el, whom she had not seen in years, while sparing Rivlin her usual third degree. Perfunctorily expressing her sorrow at the death of his old teacher, she turned to the UN consultant and quizzed him about his conference in Singapore and the names of the participating countries.

Yo'el patiently reviewed the entire list of them. The old lady nodded her white head to confirm the existence of those countries she had heard of and inquired about those she had not. "And you, Yo'el?" she asked with a faint smile. "Will you be representing little Israel?"

"No," the Third World expert replied. "My clients are ideas. Israel will be represented by its foreign ministry."

The old lady frowned with disappointment. "What a shame!" she exclaimed. "You still look so Israeli with your khaki pants and your sandals. And that old safari jacket! I remember it from before I was taken ill...."

Yo'el beamed at her. "I'll still be Israeli even when there's no more Israel," he declared. And regretting the remark at once, he bent to kiss her, cold and all.

"All right," Rivlin said, interrupting the patriotic scene. "Let's leave the women to their own devices and come back in an hour."

## 2.

IT WAS 4 P.M. The rain was still coming down. "What would you like to do?" Rivlin asked his brother-in-law.

"It's up to you, Yochi," Yo'el said. "I haven't been in Jerusalem for so long that anywhere you take me will be new."

Rivlin thought for a moment. "In that case," he said, "let's go to a place I haven't seen either. Whenever I've been there, it's been closed. Maybe it will be open in your honor. An hour is all we need."

They drove to Talpiyot, parked near the hotel, and walked to the gray Agnon House with its barred windows. Though it again looked deserted, it was, to Rivlin's surprise, open to visitors. The person in charge, a small, vivacious woman of about forty, was standing on a stepladder in the kitchen, painting a wall.

"A living soul at last!" the Orientalist declared. "What is this? Just because the city doesn't charge admission, does this place always have to be closed?"

"For you, we'll even charge admission." The woman, who wore her hair in an Orthodox-style puff, grinned at him.

"Admission to an author's house?" Rivlin was in a fighting mood. "What for, to pay your salary?"

She laughed. "Good Lord! If my salary came from admission fees, I'd have starved to death long ago."

Rivlin paid thirty shekels for himself and his guest and declined the offer of an information sheet. The two men walked silently around a large, nondescript room, the famous author's salon that was now used for lectures about him, and climbed a steep staircase to his study. Its walls were lined with books, mostly large rabbinic volumes. Standing on a worn rug was a small, old desk with an antique typewriter, a museum piece in its own right. The room was cold, and an elevated, built-in fireplace, though its blue tiles enlivened the gloom, did not look to Rivlin as though it had been used even in the author's lifetime.

The room had a single window looking out on the yard. Beneath it, bulky and graceless, was the renowned lectern on which the Nobel Prize winner—in awe, it was said, of the Hebrew language—had written his prodigious output of novels and stories standing up. A sheet of paper covered with his tiny, nebulous script lay on its slanted top. Beside that were his eyeglasses. Rivlin, not daring to try them on, picked them up and immediately put them down again.

The rain outside beat down harder, casting a thick pall. The lamp in the room shone feebly. Yo'el took out his reading glasses and perused the titles on the shelves, now and then taking down a book to look at it. An expert on Third World agriculture and the effects on it of global warming, he had a wide range of interests and encouraged Rivlin to send him Israeli magazines and periodicals, as well as new volumes of Hebrew fiction and poetry, which he avidly read on his long flights. It was his way of keeping in touch with the country, his up-to-date knowledge of which often surprised people.

"How Spartan it is here," he remarked.

"Yes," Rivlin said. "Agnon was said to have been a great miser."

"That's not what I meant." Yo'el came passionately to the author's defense. "It's not a question of money. It's an attitude toward life. Look at these books. Some were expensive. There are even rare manuscripts. It's not miserliness that you're looking at. It's a radically modest way of life. I've seen the same thing in the houses of other real intellectuals, East and West. I have the greatest respect for it."

Rivlin took a large, heavy volume from a shelf, glanced at it, and put it back. "Just the title page puts me to sleep," he said.

"What can you expect? An eternal people like the Jews didn't go around producing best-sellers. But don't think that the sacred literature of other peoples is any more lively. And if you look at where all these books come from, you'll find an amazing variety of periods and countries. Some were printed in places that even the geographers have never heard of. They may seem tedious now, and perhaps they always were, but for better or for worse they're still the context for many things—including the great works of the man whose house we're in. That's why he preferred to spend his money on them and not on rugs or paintings."

"Far be it from me..." Rivlin left the sentence unfinished. His brother-in-law, whose nationalist ardor was satisfied with seven hours in his native land, sometimes baffled him.

"Especially when I'm in places where no Jews ever lived," Yo'el continued, "I think of the rabbis, who purged their discourse of all historical concreteness to make a distilled, abstract essence of it even when dealing with the petty details of life. It transcends time and place, which why it fits together so naturally in a library like this, assembled to meet the specifications of its owner."

"Which were?"

"I don't know. I only know that the man who worked in this room and consulted these books knew how to get the most out of them and to make the connections between them. He wasn't interested in history, but in something else . . . something more important . . ."

"More important in what way?" Rivlin picked up the gauntlet. "All these books, with their endless hairsplitting commentaries, never helped the Jews to survive, let alone to prepare for the next catastrophe."

"And those Jews better anchored in history or reality were better prepared?"

"Yes," the Orientalist said. "I think so. It's a fact."

"Would you say that about the Israelis?"

"Why not? As long as we're able to free ourselves from our own myths. . . . But we'd better get a move on, Yo'el. Hagit and Ofra's aunt is sick, and they can't spend too much time with her."

And seeing that his brother-in-law was loath to leave the great author's room, Rivlin added:

"The reason you've developed such a nostalgic, sentimental attitude toward Judaism, Yo'el, is that you spend all your time at international conferences. You inhabit a bubble of virtual reality. If you lived in this country and saw all your tax money go to support parasitical yeshiva students, most of whom don't even study, you'd talk differently."

"You're wrong." Yo'el's smile was tolerant. "I'm not nostalgic about Judaism, and I'm perfectly realistic. I have no illusions that what's written in these books has any answer for the suffering and the hardship that I see all the time. I'm talking about something different. Not the content but the template—a style of thought such as you find in a wonderful, if sometimes wearisome, book like Agnon's *The Bridal Canopy*, which I read last year in Laos and Cambodia. It gave me more insight into the Third World than no end of documents. That's what I'm looking for: a template that Israel—and you know how attached I am to it—has lost. . . ."

"But a template for what?" Rivlin asked impatiently.

Yo'el paused by the old lectern and glanced at the page of writing. His glasses, which resembled the author's, had slipped down his nose, giving his broad, strong face a spiritual mien.

"For giving Israel more of what Judaism once had."

"What are you talking about?"

"About how Israeli identity might be freed from its provincialism and given wings. How it might adopt a more spiritual attitude toward a world in need of new ideas. It should be possible to combine the Jewish genius for ahistorical abstraction with Israel's scientific accomplishments—with the curiosity, the collective solidarity, the ability to improvise, that so many Israelis have...."

"Mostly to improvise unnecessary problems," the Orientalist opined.

"Don't lose your sense of proportion," Yo'el corrected him. "Believe me, I know the problems of other peoples. Real ones of hunger and civil war and terrible natural disasters. I'm tired of spoiled Israelis whining all the time, as if the only point of comparison with their situation were the tranquillity of Europe—as if Europe itself hadn't been within living memory the site of the most horrible of atrocities, not to mention what just happened in Bosnia...."

Rivlin smiled. "Yes, I say the same things in defense of the Middle East when I hear it attacked. But it doesn't really do any good."

"What I'm saying," Yo'el continued, removing the glasses from his nose and laying them absentmindedly on the lectern, "is that it's time for Israel to look beyond its local squabbles. Globalism, with all that's frightening and fascinating about it, is our business, too. We have to think of ways to cope with it. We should learn from the way we were in the 1950s, both more modest and more driven by a sense of mission."

"What mission could we have?"

"But if we believed forty years ago that we had one—that we had something important to contribute to the world even though half of it didn't recognize us—why not now, when everything is so much more open and interconnected? Just think of what it does for our pride when an Israeli rescue team or field hospital saves lives in an earthquake or a flood somewhere. And that's just a fraction of what we could do. It would give us a better perspective on ourselves."

"A better perspective..." Rivlin sighed. He had a great liking for his barrel-chested brother-in-law, whose old safari jacket brushed against the lectern. "Yes, that's what we need. But we'd better get going. You've forgotten you have a flight tonight. Just be careful not to switch glasses with Agnon. It won't bother him to have yours, but what are you going to do with his in southeast Asia?"

They returned to the little street. Although Rivlin would have liked to take his brother-in-law to the hotel and show him how the garden had changed, he thought better of it. The garden meant nothing to Yo'el. It's my own open wound, he told himself.

It was getting dark. The rain had eased up. Above the restaurant in Abu-Ghosh the clouds had parted to reveal a dark swath of sky in which, lost and distant, errant stars glittered. Yo'el was in a buoyant mood. Hungry, he went to the kitchen to seek inspiration before ordering.

"They'll serve you dinner on the plane," Ofra reminded him.

"I'll skip it."

"You know you won't."

"So I won't. So what? Who knows when we'll be back here?"

An elderly waiter, amused by the broken Arabic of the Israeli who had stopped for dinner on his way to Singapore, soon covered the table with dozens of colorful appetizers in dishes so small that the international consultant had no qualms about finishing all of them. But the gloom of parting hung over the two sisters. Moved by his sister-in-law's strained face with no makeup, Rivlin turned to his wife and urged her to relate a strange dream she had had that week.

Hagit did not want to. "Then I'll tell it," Rivlin said, starting to describe what he remembered. "You can stop right there," Hagit said, taking him aback with her sternness. "It's of no interest. And anyway, since when do my dreams belong to you?" Hurt to the quick, he stammered something in his own defense. The judge patted his knee under the table, to let him know that she was annoyed not with him but with her here-today-gone-tomorrow brother-in-law, who was still heartily polishing off dishes that were now so small that their contents looked more like medicine than food.

RETURNING HOME AT MIDNIGHT, Rivlin had an anxious feeling about Ofer and telephoned his attic apartment. As there was no answer, he dialed the emergency number of the Jewish Agency. There he was told, in a French-accented Hebrew, that Ofer had been sick for the past few days and that the speaker was filling in for him. Rivlin dialed the apartment once more. Again no one answered. "He must have felt better and decided to go out," said the naturally optimistic judge.

But Rivlin slept poorly. When there was still no answer in the morning, he phoned Ofer's landlady. Ofer, she told him, had come down with such a bad case of the flu that, having no one to take care of him, he had gone to the hospital. Yesterday, he had called to say that his condition had improved. Asked what hospital he was in, however, the landlady said she didn't know. Perhaps it was just French discretion.

"You see?" Rivlin said to his wife. "He's been in Paris for five years, and he's still all alone. And who would want to take care of him when his heart is far away?"

"And suppose it is?" Hagit replied. "Is it up to you to decide where his heart should be?"

## 3.

WAS IT AN INDICATION of the position he would take that Rivlin convened the secret appointments committee in his own office rather than in the conference room next to the rector's office, which was on the same floor as Miller's alcove? He did not wish Miller to see them and guess what it was about.

Yet until the last minute he was undecided and open to persuasion. Despite his hostile feelings for the young lecturer, who had arrogantly torn apart not only his introduction but the entire book that was to follow, he admired Miller's courage and honesty. Whatever one thought of his beliefs—which, Rivlin hoped, did not have to be taken too seriously—he had risked his promotion by being so outspoken.

The appointments secretary, a middle-aged woman who had been in charge of such meetings for years, was unhappy with Rivlin's decision. "How am I going to bring all the refreshments down to your office?" she wanted to know.

But Rivlin was adamant. "You've dealt with bigger problems," he told the appointments secretary, who had once worked in the Near Eastern Studies department.

And indeed, coffee, tea, cakes, and sandwiches were on hand when the committee convened to review the secret file. The other two members were the head of the Political Science department, an assistant professor from America, and a fellow Orientalist from Bar-Ilan University. Rivlin felt a comradely kinship with this man, a pleasantly bashful and reliable associate professor his own age whose field, nineteenth- and twentieth-century Sudan, was every bit as thorny as Algeria. Occasionally, the two had long telephone conversations in which they compared the form fundamentalism took in each of the two countries and argued which was worse. Rivlin had persuaded the dean to put the "Sudanese" on the appointments committee, both because he enjoyed talking shop with him and because he needed an ally to implement his plan, which was to block Miller's advancement in Near Eastern Studies by shunting him off to the Political Science department, the American liberalism of which could better cope with the young lecturer's revisionist theories.

The committee had already discussed, in a previous session, Miller's curriculum vitae and publications—which, though not numerous, had appeared in a number of prestigious American journals well known to the political scientist. Now they had to review his academic references and to discuss whether the fact that some of them had not been received was due to negligence or disapproval. Rivlin chose to read the recommendations aloud and to parse them sentence by sentence, dwelling especially on any reservations expressed between the lines.

He was cut short by the head of the Political Science department, who did not think this was necessary. He, too, had heard of the tempting offer made to the young lecturer by the University of the Negev, which had a reputation for body snatching, and suspecting Rivlin of setting a trap, he warned against permitting the provincial nitpicking so prevalent on their campus to lead to the loss of a promising talent.

Just then the door opened. An unfamiliar fragrance wafted into the office. Before the door could be shut again, Rivlin spied a woman in a silk shawl.

It was Afifa. "Professor," she said. "If I could have just a minute with you, please..."

He hurried into the corridor, leaving the door open for the committee members to see him take the hand of the flustered woman and ask, with concern and in Arabic, about his M.A. student.

"She'll be fine," Samaher's mother answered in Hebrew.

But Rivlin insisted on continuing in Arabic, his voice echoing loudly down the corridor.

"*Le'inno hunak fi Ramallah kunt kalkan min shanha, ba'd-ma shuft kif kanet mujtahida kul-halkad fi 'l-masrahiyya ma'a hada 'l-jinni. Le'inno hada kan ra'i'. Samaher mitl hahim yahudi... bitjanin! If-takaret inno fakat b'ilnisbi lahada b'tistahik h'al-alameh.*"*

"That's just it," Afifa said excitedly. "I've brought another story. It's time to give Samaher her grade."

"*Shwoy-shwoy. Kul shi biji fi 'l-nahayeh. B'halmuddeh stanini hon. Ba'd shwoy bantihi 'l-jalseh u'nu'ud b'il nisbi lal-hakayeh.*"†

He returned to his office, sank pleasurably into his armchair, and declared with a deep sigh:

"I'd be the last to deny that Miller is a solid and independent-minded scholar who's up on the latest approaches, which may yet—who knows?—turn out to have value. That isn't what bothers me. The problem is something else. I must say that I don't understand what Miller is doing in our department. When I look at the bibliographies of his publications—and they're very impressive, very up-to-date—I can't help asking, where are the Arabic texts? Where are the original sources? I'm concerned about the systematic absence of such references. Does he think that nothing written by Arabs is relevant to what he writes about them? After all, one has to assume the man knows some Arabic. I don't mean that he knows it like Akri—none of us do, not having had the good fortune to be born in Iraq. But he must know how to read it, and perhaps even to write and

---

* Because I was worried about the way she threw herself into that play about a haunt in Ramallah. Not that it wasn't wonderful. Samaher as a Jewish rabbi—fantastic!... I remember thinking, She deserves a grade just for that.

† Easy does it. Everything in good time. Meanwhile, wait for me here. I'll soon be finished with the meeting, and we'll have a look at the story.

speak a bit. Why, then, doesn't he do something with this knowledge? Does he find Arabic texts so tedious and uninteresting that he prefers to rely on second- and thirdhand Western translations of them? Perhaps he thinks the Middle East is not the subject of a separate discipline but simply grist for his theoretical mill. He's even implied as much in his conversations with me. For his purposes, any other area—Southeast Asia or South America or Africa—would do just as well."

"And suppose it would," the political scientist said crossly. "What of it?"

"Nothing. It's perfectly legitimate. The only question is why he needs to be in our department. Here, take this article of his. It appeared in a journal that's apparently reputable, though it's one I've never heard of. It actually contains an Arabic quotation—full of errors. Have a look..."

He handed it to the associate professor from Bar-Ilan.

"That's not so serious in itself. But it's typical of a certain kind of scholarship. You might call it the global approach. I don't say it isn't important—but it belongs in a different department, in political science, say, or sociology or international relations. It's more interdisciplinary, and less appropriate for a historically oriented department like our own. Here in Near Eastern Studies we deal with pedestrian topics like 'The Political Strategy of the Wakf Party in Egypt Between the Two World Wars,' not with theoretical models."

"Just what are you suggesting?" the political scientist asked.

"I'm suggesting that, for Miller's own good, we return his application to the dean with a request to appoint a new committee, or at least a new chairman for this one. Let him be promoted somewhere else, perhaps in political science. After all, he speaks your language."

"I'd grab him immediately," the political scientist said eagerly. "I just don't have an available slot."

"Then why not work something out with Sociology? I've heard they have a part-time slot in their B.A. honors program. You might look into it. And there's always the possibility of a position in our foreign-students program. You could create a genuinely interdisciplinary track..."

The secretary felt the ground slipping out from under her. "But what will we do?" she asked in alarm. "Start the whole process all over?"

"Why all over? Miller's file is complete. It has all his recommendations, or at least all those that will arrive. It simply needs to be transferred to another department."

The political scientist exploded. "Hold on there! We'll just lose him that way. He'll leave us for Beersheba."

Rivlin clapped his hands in pious distress.

"How unfortunate! Still, it's not a national tragedy, seeing that Beersheba is part of the state of Israel. I understand your concern. But you have to realize that we in Near Eastern Studies don't have many positions and have to think of the future. I'm not so young anymore. My retirement is approaching, and some little heart attack or stroke— I had an in-law who recently went in a day—could keep me from reaching it.... And then what? Be left without a North African specialist? I have nothing against Miller. Not that I always know what he's talking about, but that's no doubt my own problem. But a promotion would give him tenure and leave our department full up. It's my obligation to think of a successor for myself. Take our greatest Israeli Orientalist, Professor Tedeschi, who died a week ago in Jerusalem. His mind was at rest, because he believed, rightly or wrongly, that I would carry on in his place. But Miller isn't really interested in the Arabs. He'd never waste his time like the two of us here—two Orientalists of the old school—on such drudgery as examining old religious court records from Algeria or ink-stained stencils of the harangues of Sudanese imams. That's the truth. Which isn't to say that my colleague from Bar-Ilan and myself may not be old fogies for believing that dull spadework is crucial for the advancement of science..."

## 4.

HIS COLLEAGUE FROM BAR-ILAN joined him in recommending that Miller's file be transferred from the department. The meeting was adjourned, and Rivlin hurried to invite Afifa into his office.

"Have some cookies," he said. "Perhaps there's some juice left, too."

She shook her lovely head, from which the silk shawl slowly dropped. Without warning, as on her previous visit, she let out a hot, overwrought groan.

Rivlin said nothing, curious to see how deeply her distress stirred him. Cautiously, he offered her a box of tissues. She took one, wiped her eyes with it, and left it soggy with tears on his desk.

"Did Rashid bring you?"

"Rashid!" She waved Samaher's cousin away with both hands. "He's too involved with the family. They're all like that, those Arabs who..."—she groped for the right phrase—"...who lost their villages. They don't know who they are or where they belong, and they don't let a body be. He's always fretting about Samaher, as if she didn't have a husband to do that. And about that sister in Zababdeh he wants to bring back to Israel.... Even Grandmother, though she cares about that sick Christian, too, told him, 'Enough, give us some peace! *Shu hada? Hada zalameh hatyar u'nus, musn, leysh la y'kun l'halo?*'"*

"The man's a jinni," Rivlin said, half to himself, as if remembering.

Afifa's big, bright eyes shut unhappily.

"*U'shu 'l-aaher?*"† He switched gently back to Arabic. "*Rah el-habl, ow yimkin inno ma balash b'il-marrah?*"‡

"The doctors were wrong." She resisted the intimacy of switching to her own language. "We thought having a baby would bring her some peace of mind, so we believed it..."

"Never mind. *Min nahitkun el-iman k'tir kwoyis.*§ But where is Samaher? At home?"

"Yes. She's still resting. That's why I've brought you the last story, so that you can give her—but really, Professor—her final grade. It's terribly important to her husband's father that she get her degree."

Her broad, clear face moved him to compassion. Pleased with having blocked Miller's tenure, he thought languorously of bathing in her tub in the Ramadan twilight. He glanced at his watch. "All right, let's begin," he said, trying to sound impatient despite his smile.

---

* What is this? The man has one foot in the grave already, why can't he be left alone?
† What's the story?
‡ Is the pregnancy over, or hasn't it begun yet?
§ It's good to have something to believe in.

This story, too, was a strange one. Outwardly, it was an animal fable, one of a series written during World War II by an Egyptian veterinarian named Shauki ibn Zamrak. Invited to Algiers by the Vichy government after the fall of France to serve as a consultant for a new zoo established for the amusement of French children, Ibn Zamrak, who called himself "the Arab Dr. Doolittle," also wished to educate young Arabs about the animals brought in cages from the interior of Africa. And so he began publishing stories in the local Arabic press, in which, being a broad-minded man, he did not shrink from describing even the most dislikable beasts. His fable of the snake and hyena who became friends, translated into Hebrew by Samaher and typed up, was now held by Afifa—who, putting on a pair of gold-rimmed glasses that gave her a rather intellectual look, insisted, as if the Orientalist were illiterate, on reading it to him.

### The Snake and the Hyena

Once upon a time there was an old hyena named Abu-Maher who had trouble finding carcasses to eat. In part this was because of a drought, which made the leopards and wolves less generous with the meat from their kills, and in part because younger and spryer hyenas than Abu-Maher were getting to it before him. One way or another, he grew thinner and thinner and more and more depressed. His laughter at night was bitter and strained, and life was a burden to him. All hyenas hang their heads, since they are ashamed of eating what others have killed, but Abu-Maher's head hung so low that although he was tall for a hyena, his tongue practically licked the ground.

One night, as Abu-Maher was nosing around some rocks in the desert, he encountered the wary old viper Ibn Sa'id, who was busy digesting inside his long striped stomach a young field mouse eaten two days earlier. Abu-Maher was so hungry that even though fresh meat disgusted him, he thought of eating Ibn-Sa'id. His cast-iron stomach could digest the worst offal; however, his parents of blessed memory had never taught him whether a snake's poison is found only in its fangs, or in its veins as well. And so before undertaking so risky an enterprise, as he bent over the coiled viper and opened his jaws, which glistened with good, strong teeth, he said, without beating around the bush, "Would you mind telling me where you keep your poison? And also, does it lose its power when you die, or does it remain deadly?"

Ibn-Sa'id had never been asked such a searching question about himself, let alone by an experienced and desperate pair of jaws located so near his head. Though brave and honest to a fault, he was afraid to tell the truth, which was that all his poison was concentrated in a gland behind his fangs. And so he lied and told the old hyena that the poison was everywhere in his body, even in his tail, and that it was best to leave him alone.

The old hyena Abu-Maher, not knowing any better, found the snake's answer logical, sadly snapped his jaws shut, and went off behind a large rock to lie down and pray for mercy.

The snake felt sorry for the hungry but fair-minded hyena, who could have killed him from sheer disappointment. Having digested the field mouse and passed what was left of it, he crawled quietly over to Abu-Maher, coiled himself gently around his neck, and whispered a surprising proposal:

"You know as well as I do that nobody likes snakes or hyenas. Even though we work hard for our livelihood and are no worse than other animals, we aren't well thought of. Frankly, I see no hope of changing such superstitions in the near future. Yet if the two of us get together and become friends, perhaps others will think better of us, too."

Abu-Maher listened to the snake's hisses and replied:

"But there is a great difference between us. Your bad reputation comes from God and is very ancient. Mine comes from holding up a mirror to mankind, because I eat dead meat and laugh, just as men do."

"Indeed," the snake admitted, "my reputation is worse and more frightening than yours, since I have been cursed by Allah himself. And as I need your help to improve it, I'll do more for you than you need do for me. Not only do I require less food than you, I'm a better hunter, especially in times of drought. If you let me ride on your back, we can easily approach animals that have no fear of you, since they know you won't eat them until they've been killed by another animal. I'll slip off your back, kill them by surprise, and then you can feast on them."

And so the cunning snake and the hungry old hyena became friends. Hated by everyone else, they learned to like each other and formed a single monster that the beasts of the desert were soon afraid of. This great fear of them led to their being held in awe, and awe is the mother of glory.

## 5.

RIVLIN LISTENED ATTENTIVELY, his chin in his palm. Despite his efforts to find some social or political moral in the Egyptian veterinarian's fable, all he could think of was Samaher in her beard, dressed as a young rabbi and pulling out a whip to lash the doll held by her cousin.

He took the translation from her mother and put it in her file. "Very good," he said. "There's food for thought here. These old stories collected by Dr. Suissa are treasure troves." And while Afifa, plump and bejeweled, regarded him with big eyes, waiting to see whether Samaher had completed her seminar requirements, he added, "The translation is excellent. Did you help her?"

He could not tell whether her hot flush meant "yes" or "no."

"It's a pity you never finished your studies," he rebuked her. "You should ask one of the secretaries if your university entrance-exam results are still valid."

She spread helpless hands. "Valid for what?"

"For continuing your studies."

"But why should I continue them? It's Samaher who needs her degree."

"And she'll get it. Just keep her cousin away from her. He hangs around her too much."

"It's not her fault, Professor. It's yours."

"Why mine?"

"He's always talking about you. He thinks that if he can get you to like him, you'll help his sister return to Israel."

"But that's crazy."

"He's even found some official in the General Security Service who's an old student of yours. Do you have a student in the GSS, Professor? What is he doing there?"

"What kind of question is that?" The Orientalist chuckled. "I have old students in the GSS, in the Mossad, in the foreign office. Why do you think there's a demand for Near Eastern Studies? To hear about hyenas and snakes?"

Afifa reddened again. "Well, there's a student of yours there who thinks a lot of you. Rashid says he could take care of everything if you'd talk to him. Believe me, that's the only reason he hangs around Samaher. It has nothing to do with her."

"Then why doesn't he speak to me?"

"He's afraid to."

"Afraid of what?"

"Of your having thought he was making fun of the Jews in that play in Ramallah."

"But it's his right to make fun of us. His *Dybbuk* was marvelous."

"Well, I'm telling you, Professor, you're all he thinks and talks about."

"Honestly, Afifa, would it make sense to separate Ra'uda from her husband by bringing her back to Israel?"

"But of course it would, Professor. She's Israeli. And this husband of hers, he's from the West Bank and a Christian and sick. He could die at any time. Where will that leave her?"

"I suppose so." Rivlin felt exhausted. He rose, stretched, led Afifa to the departmental office, and asked a secretary to look for her old file and tell her what credits she could get for courses taken twenty years ago.

Afifa, who had no intention of going back to school, stood embarrassed in a corner. Rivlin went to check his mailbox. As he emptied it, he smelled the scent of Miller's aftershave. The young lecturer was in the middle of sealing an envelope, doing a thorough job of it. Rivlin gave him a friendly smile and invited him to speak at a one-day Orientalists' conference soon to take place in Jerusalem, on the first month's anniversary of Tedeschi's death.

## 6.

THE WINTER, HAVING BEGUN at Hanukkah with an impressive display of wind and rain, had petered out. Days of unseasonably high temperatures arrived and parched the earth. "If the summer has no bounds," Rivlin said to Hagit, "I may as well take some vacation." He intended, he told her, to take all the shopping coupons accumulated over the past year and exchange them for gifts. "They lose their value after December 31," he explained. "Pick what you want from the catalogs, and I'll get it."

Equipped with the coupons and Hagit's instructions, he set out. His first stop was a shopping mall, where, after climbing up and down many flights of stairs, he came to a small office near the washrooms, signed a form in triplicate, and was given a large, green plastic carrying bag. Next, in a department store, he received a beach towel and an apron. From there he went to a supermarket and after patiently standing in line was rewarded with two small bottles of olive oil and—for only two extra shekels—a bottle of detergent.

A second shopping mall, at the southern edges of the city, was his next-to-last destination. Here they were out of Teflon frying pans and offered him a choice between a saucepan with a transparent cover and six flower-patterned Turkish coffee cups. Lacking clear directives, he phoned the courtroom and found Hagit between trials. A brief discussion ended in a decision to take the saucepan. "When do we ever drink Turkish coffee?" Hagit asked. Finally, he went to a store where, although his coupons for it had become invalid, he obtained a rather odd-looking desk lamp as a premium for buying a cookbook of pasta recipes. Burdened with his acquisitions, he returned home in time for lunch and wrote the following letter to the municipality:

*Traffic Department*
*Municipality of Haifa*
*Re: U-turns at the intersection of Moriah and Ha-Sport Streets.*

*To Whom It May Concern:*

*I wish to propose a way of facilitating U-turns at the intersection of Moriah and Ha-Sport Streets. Such turns, though legal and unavoidable for drivers heading from Carmel Center for the shops and cafés on the east side of the street, are impeded by the unnecessarily wide sidewalk. As a result, even cars with power steering, like my own, must make a broken U-turn, reversing in the middle of the intersection and in the face of oncoming traffic.*

*A careful examination has led me to conclude that, were the unnecessary pavement on the left-hand side of the entrance to Ha-Sport Street (which is of little use to anyone, since it slopes and is fenced off from the street) to be reduced, it would be possible to execute a U-turn in a single maneuver, making it easier and safer for drivers in both directions.*

*I would greatly appreciate your giving this matter your careful consideration. I would also be happy, should it be deemed helpful, to come to the municipality in person to explain my plan.*

*Sincerely,*

*Professor Yochanan Rivlin*
*Department of Near Eastern Studies*
*University of Haifa*

7.

HANNAH TEDESCHI TELEPHONED EVERY day to consult with Rivlin about the memorial conference in Jerusalem. If Hagit picked up the phone first, Hannah took advantage of the opportunity to ask for legal advice regarding Tedeschi's first wife, never divorced by him despite her many years in an institution.

Ever since Tedeschi's retirement from teaching eight years previously, his connection with the Near Eastern Studies department at Hebrew University had grown tenuous. Hannah was concerned, therefore, that if the conference were left to the department to plan, it would become a dumping grounds for second-rate papers unpresentable elsewhere. And so, making Rivlin her adviser, she chose the lecturers herself, leaving only the administrative details to the university. She asked Rivlin to give the main lecture, on the subject of literary sources of the Algerian Terror.

"I'm sorry, Hannah," he excused himself. "Carlo knew this was a subject in which I was still groping in the dark. I'm still not prepared to lecture on it. But I will give a eulogy. I'd like to talk about Carlo's humanity."

"What is that supposed to mean?"

"That's my secret."

"Be careful, Yochanan. There are sensitive areas..."

After much debate and changing of minds, the program was decided on. The morning would begin with two Ottomanists, one discussing the age-old relationship between Turks and Arabs, and the other, Ataturk in retrospect. They would be followed by a scholar with some new ideas about the period of the great Abbasid caliphate, on which Tedeschi had written his doctorate, after which the translatoress would present several Sufi texts by Al-Hallaj, polished versions of her improvisations in Ramallah.

The afternoon session would begin with Dr. Miller and a provocative lecture in the spirit of Said's *Orientalism* (a book Tedeschi had been surprisingly tolerant of) on the profession of Near Eastern Studies. Then would come two traditional scholars, the "Sudanese" from Bar-Ilan and an "Iraqi" from the Dayan Center, who would defend their approach against Miller's revisionism.

In the evening, as dusk appropriately fell, the Orientalists would be joined for the last, memorial session by a number of prominent Jerusalemites and members of the city's Italian-Jewish community. There would be a violin and flute duet and three eulogies. The first of these would be given by the head of the Near Eastern Studies department in Jerusalem, who would review Tedeschi's scholarly work; the second, by a speaker from the Truman Institute, who would talk about the Jerusalem polymath's public activities; and the concluding one by Rivlin, who, if not as the dead man's successor then at least as his close friend, would mourn Tedeschi's passing and reveal a secret.

"But what kind of secret?" Hannah asked again.

"Wait and see."

"Just be careful you don't say anything you'll regret, Yochanan. Don't be carried away by truths no one needs to hear. I'm still living, remember?"

"How could I forget?"

Meanwhile, the winter that had petered out returned full force. The skies clouded over, and fierce winds blew. Three days before the conference, the forecasters predicted snow in Jerusalem. Hannah Tedeschi now phoned several times a day. What should they do? Should the conference be postponed? Who of Tedeschi's elderly Jerusalem friends would brave the heights of Mount Scopus in a snowstorm?

Rivlin pooh-poohed the snow warnings. If it snowed in Jerusalem every time somebody said it would, he joked, the city would be known as the Geneva of the Middle East rather than as its disaster zone.

But the warnings came faster and more furiously. Snow had blocked roads in the Galilee and a blizzard had closed the ski slopes on Mount Hermon. Hannah's telephone calls were more and more hysterical. Perhaps, she said, the event should be moved to a hall in town. "On the contrary," Rivlin replied. "Snow on Mount Scopus will tell us who Carlo's true friends were."

Yet on the day before the conference, as he was putting the finishing touches to his eulogy, the news bulletins announced that the capital had been closed to everything but buses and vehicles with four-wheel drive. The translatoress, afraid of losing him too, phoned at once. Rivlin turned to Hagit and said, "Why spend a day on buses when I have a better idea? I'll hire Rashid. How much could he ask for?"

## 8.

HE PHONED RASHID AND got straight to the point:

"Does your van have four-wheel drive?"

"For you, Professor," Rashid said, "I'll have four-wheel drive."

"What do you mean?" Rivlin asked.

In a village near Mansura, the messenger told him, was a hunter who rented out his jeep.

"Then let's hunt for Jerusalem tomorrow in the snow," Rivlin asked. "Just tell me what the pleasure will cost me."

There was silence. Then Rashid almost whispered:

"What have I done to you, Professor, to make you insult me?"

"Either I pay you, Rashid," Rivlin said, "or we don't go."

Hotly, however, the Arab explained that he had been intending to visit Jerusalem anyway. He wanted to apply again at the Civil Administration Bureau for an Israeli identity card for his sister, and there was no better day than a snowy one, when the lines would be short. Rivlin relented. "But only on the condition that I come with you and try to use my influence," he said. "I heard from Samaher's mother that there's a GSS official in the Bureau who's a former student of mine."

"Not one student, Professor," Rashid said. "Three. A person might think no one joined the GSS without first taking a course with you . . ."

And so on a gray, cold, misty morning, a big old jeep pulled up in front of the Rivlins' building on the French Carmel. It was still full of hunting gear, including a harness seat, a large flashlight, some nets, and a partridge snare with a long, shiny knife in it. Although it had a sturdy top, Rashid covered the Orientalist with a woolen army blanket. "The canvas," he observed, "isn't windproof."

The weather forecast had been taken seriously, for the road leading up to Jerusalem was almost empty. The snowflakes drifting down on the large cemetery at the city's entrance were no sign that the storm was letting up. Unplowed snow caked the city's streets, and Rashid shifted into four-wheel drive at Rivlin's request, though even without it the jeep's big wheels crunched easily over the white powder.

They talked little on the way. The blanket made Rivlin pleasantly drowsy, and Rashid, concentrating on driving an unfamiliar car in bad weather, was uncommunicative. He inquired briefly about Hannah Tedeschi, wanted to know how important the husband had been whose face he had covered with a sheet, and then lapsed into silence. He did not even respond when, as they started the ascent to the capital, Rivlin awoke and praised his double-brided production of *The Dybbuk*. Nor did he mention Samaher. The Rabbi of Miropol's exorcism, the Orientalist thought with a grin, had worked. The jinni had been banished—and not only onstage . . .

Yet once he had killed the motor upon reaching the Civil Administration building in north Jerusalem, the Arab abandoned his reserve. Sitting with Rivlin in the jeep, in teeth-chattering cold amid European-sized snowbanks, he explained the bureaucratic obstacles that kept his sister from returning to her native village with her children. The officials, he said, acted as if they were dealing with an intercontinental border. And why? Solely to protect the rights of the sick father, who might miss his sons and complain to the Red Cross that he wasn't allowed to visit them.

"How odd," Rivlin said. "I never would have imagined they'd worry about such a thing."

"They don't. It's just an excuse to turn my sister down. You know Ra'uda's husband, Professor. He's a sick old Christian who eats from a soldier's mess kit. Does he look the type to complain?"

"But what should I say to them?"

"That you'll be responsible."

"For what?"

"For no one complaining."

"How can I be responsible for anyone's complaints?" Rivlin smiled and pulled the blanket back up over him. "I can't always keep myself from complaining."

But Rashid hadn't come this far in order to back down.

"You could at least promise—to the GSS man, say, who was your student—to handle the human-rights organizations."

"Human-rights organizations?" Astonished by the sophistry that went on inside the white building visible through the fogged windshield, he regarded the agitated messenger. "Don't tell me the GSS is afraid of the Israel Civil Liberties Union!"

"They're afraid of whoever they want to be afraid of."

Yet on this snowy morning at the Civil Administration Bureau, not only was no one waiting in line, no one was waiting to receive anyone either. Even his old student had chosen to stay in bed. Rivlin, worn-out from the drive, followed Rashid down a long corridor in which the Arab knew every door. He tried opening them one by one while asking where everyone had disappeared to—which might have gone on forever had not a woman cried out a surprised hello. "What did I tell you, Professor?" Rashid crowed. "They all know you here. I'll bet that lady was a student of yours, too."

The woman, who was roly-poly and henna-haired, came hurrying toward them up the dark corridor. Although Rivlin had forgotten her name, he was quite sure she had once taught introductory Arabic in Haifa. "What brings you here in a snowstorm?" she inquired. Pointing at Rashid by way of explanation, he was invited to warm up in her room. This did not look like a government office. With a sofa uphol-stered in flowery fabric and a large flowerpot with a dwarf tree that would, the woman said, bear fruit in the spring, it looked more like a comfortable residence.

Rivlin let his weary body drop onto the sofa with an odd relish, toasting his feet by the mock flames of an electric fireplace while signaling Rashid—who, standing in the doorway, seemed to be debating whether the woman could be of use—to join him. He now recalled, watching her put up a kettle to boil in a kitchenette, that she was an Egyptian Jew who had learned her Arabic in the streets of Cairo. He grimaced with the almost physically painful effort to remember her name, but in the end had to ask her for it apologetically. "Georgette," she replied, wagging a finger. "How could you forget such a nice name?" Rivlin clutched his head." "Of course," he said. "My mind just doesn't work well when it's snowing so early in the day."

The snow was piling up in thick, heavy flakes on the windowsill. Georgette, it turned out, had heard of Tedeschi's death and of the conference that brought Rivlin to Jerusalem. While she had never studied with the Jerusalem polymath, she had had the greatest respect for him and was thinking of attending the closing session to hear the eulogies and meet old friends, some of whom she began discussing with Rivlin.

The Orientalist, however, mindful of his mission, was more interested in what Georgette did. The answer was that, having changed not her profession but only her students, she still taught Arabic. Yet her salary was better, for she was now paid both to improve the Arabic of the young GSS investigators and to teach them her linguistic methods for detecting lies in that language. A divorcée with children living abroad, she was so devoted to her work that she sometimes slept in her office. Hence, its resemblance to a private apartment.

Rashid just stared at her.

They chatted for a while before Rivlin disclosed why he had come and asked Rashid to produce his documents so as to be advised by Georgette as to who in the GSS might be suitably softhearted. Flattered and amused to be asked, she leafed through a packet of Palestinian birth certificates and tattered old Israeli passbooks in which Rashid and Ra'uda were listed as brother and sister. When she was done she said that although she was no expert on such things, she imagined that to turn little Palestinians into Israelis more was needed than a mother's longing for her native village.

"Such as?"

An intelligent woman, she stopped to think. Did any of his sister's children, she asked Rashid, have a chronic disease or rare health problem that called for treatment in Israel? A medical reason, she explained to the Orientalist, who nodded while stretching his hands out to the electric flames, was better than an emotional one, perhaps because the Jews thought their curative powers made the Arabs more trusting and less dangerous....

An enigmatic smile played over Rashid's lips.

Rivlin turned to him. "Well?"

He shrugged. As far as he knew, both of his nephews in Zababdeh were healthy. If there were no other choice, however, he would try to find something wrong with them.

"The problems people have," Rivlin sighed as the messenger gently shut the door and headed for the ground floor to obtain application forms for medical treatment in Israel. He took another sip of his tea.

Georgette shot him a distrustful look. "What do you want us to do, open the gates to all of them? Don't we have enough of them already?"

"Excuse me," he said, turning crimson as if accused of high treason. "Those children are half-Israeli."

"So is the West Bank, which is why it should be good enough for them. I see no reason to separate them from their father. Tell me, Rivlin: how did you get involved with this Arab in the first place?"

"He's sometimes my driver. And also..."

"Also what?"

"*Jinni 'l-aziz alay....*"*

## 9.

FOR A SECOND, the falling snowflakes wavered between turning to sleet and keeping their pristine whiteness. Yet those falling quickly be-

---

* My favorite jinni.

hind them stiffened their frozen resolve, and the white carpet outside the window grew thicker. Under a large umbrella they stepped back onto it, the careful Jew and the glum Arab, whose pockets were stuffed with useless medical forms. It took a moment to spot the jeep, now a white mass like the cars around it. Perhaps, Rivlin thought amusedly as he directed his driver toward a majestically white Mount Scopus, the snow was Europe's farewell salute to the young man it had tried to murder sixty years ago. The idea so appealed to him that he decided to include it in his eulogy.

In the university parking lot, he sought to part with Rashid. "Why waste the day waiting for me?" he said. "Start back now. I'll make it to Haifa on my own. I'm sorry I couldn't do more for your sister's children. We have to sit down and work out a plan."

"No plan will work if no one has a heart," Rashid said. "But thanks for trying."

He put a gentle hand on the Arab's shoulder. "Don't give up. It's not like you."

"It may not be like me, but it's how I feel."

"It's not like you at all," the Jew repeated reprovingly.

Rashid turned a dark, stubbled face full of anguish toward the road. His profile against the snow made Rivlin think of the dybbuk's white shrouds. "If this snow keeps up, Professor," he said, "you'll need a jeep to get out of Jerusalem."

"Don't worry," Rivlin said. "I'm tenth generation in this city. I know these Jerusalem snows. By this afternoon the sun will be out and it will all melt."

But even if Samaher's teacher was holding up his cousin's grade, the messenger insisted on sticking by him. He had no other work lined up for the day, which he would spend in Jerusalem, returning for the Orientalist's eulogy at the end of it. An Israeli Arab in a jeep could go where he wanted in this two-part city. Perhaps he would visit Fu'ad at his hotel. The two of them had got along well on the night of Tedeschi's death. He had even stopped in Abu-Ghosh on his way back to Mansura because Samaher hadn't been feeling well.

Rivlin felt a sweet frisson.

"Don't worry about me, Professor," Rashid said. "The ride to Jerusalem was my treat, and the ride home will be too. Your wife will feel better if she knows you're with me."

Rivlin smiled at Rashid's intuition. "Listen," he said, reminded by the gurgle of melting snow in a nearby drainpipe of the basement of the hotel, the symbol of his lost and longed-for happiness. "Come back at lunchtime and we'll go together. Fu'ad will feed us."

He took an invitation to the conference from his pocket and handed it to Rashid, showing him the building and the number of the room in which he would be.

The auditorium was empty. Hannah Tedeschi was pacing irritably up and down, her eye on the white maelstrom outside the window. The dark, masculine suit she had on looked as though it might have been Tedeschi's. Though they had spoken often by telephone since the day of the funeral, he was surprised to see how she had changed. Thinner, and with a new, short haircut, she suggested, despite her makeup and high heels, a melancholy youth. "I warned you!" she scolded Rivlin despairingly as soon as she saw him. "We should have postponed it or moved it to town, where at least the streets are plowed. You forgot, Yochanan, that Jerusalem can cope with war, siege, and terrorism but not with snow—and especially not on Mount Scopus."

Rivlin defended himself calmly and logically. In the first place, there was no guarantee that a more suitable place in town would have been available at the last moment. Secondly, even if one had been, there hadn't been time to inform the public. And thirdly, what would Carlo have said had he known that a little snow would make them forsake a campus that meant so much to him? After all, not only had his entire career taken place on it, he was almost killed trying to break through to it in a relief convoy during the 1948 war.

"A little snow? Yochanan, don't you see what's going on out there?"

Once again Rivlin trotted out his Jerusalem pedigree to make light of the snow. By noon, he promised, the skies would clear and there would be nothing left but a white frosting. The timid souls who missed the morning session would surely have enough northern blood in them to turn out in the afternoon.

"You wait and see," she accused him. "This snow will be an excuse to trample on his memory. We're in for another disaster like the *Othello* lecture. He never said a word about it, but I know how hurt he was."

"But what made you take him to the emergency room?"

"He was afraid."

"Of those political scientists? You're kidding."

"But he was. All those theoreticians frightened him. He didn't know what they were talking about."

"Neither do I. So what?"

She looked startled. "You don't?"

"Not always. But to hell with them. You have new glasses."

"Just the frames. Was it wrong to change them?"

"Of course not." He moved closer to her, feeling pity. "On the contrary. Since his death, Hannah, you're even more lovely."

She flushed, hotly. "Don't be silly. The things you say! I feel so lost . . ."

Her eyes filled with tears.

Yet not even her tears were an incentive to come to the morning session. Although one of the two Ottomanists managed to make it through the snow, he had to speak to empty seats. If not for Suissa senior, who—his fedora covered in plastic against the rain—turned up at the last minute as a gesture to his son's admirers, there wouldn't have been a dozen people in the hall. The dean of the liberal-arts school, an art historian who couldn't have cared less about the Turks, delivered a few welcoming words, shut his eyes, and fell asleep, chin in hand, on the podium. Fortunately, the secretary of the Near Eastern Studies department, who had always been fond of Tedeschi and his witticisms, handed the dean a note summoning him to an imaginary meeting, thus sparing him further embarrassment.

Rivlin sat through the lecture with a sense of tedium. It didn't help that the lecturer let himself be sidetracked from the complex subject of Turkish-Arab relations to a discussion of Kurdish nationalism and its "historic," as opposed to merely "emotional," roots.

"Be careful, children," his mother would tell Rivlin and his sister on snowy days in Jerusalem, on which she had made them stay home.

"Snow lulls the brain to sleep." So that they might enjoy the snow anyway, she would send their father out to fetch a bowl of it, which they were allowed to play with, under her supervision, in the bathroom. Now, feeling his eyelids droop, he wondered whether she hadn't been right. Others around him were yielding to the same effect. Although the lecturer, a delicate homosexual once labeled by Tedeschi "the True Turk," was struggling valiantly, in the extra time provided by the absence of the second speaker, to return to his original theme, the Kurds, whose muddled identity was typical of the minorities of the Ottoman Empire, kept distracting him. Now and then, in a concession to the occasion, he mentioned some old idea or forgotten publication of Tedeschi's. But the audience was too sleepy and too small for it to matter.

Rivlin, despite his sympathy for the Kurds, could barely keep awake. He went on repeating his mother's words like a mantra. And indeed the snow soon stopped falling, and a first patch of blue gleamed through the windows. Slowly the sky grew calm and clear, just as he had predicted in the name of his ancestors. He nodded encouragingly at Hannah, as if to say, "See, things are looking up." By evening, he was sure, there would be a full house.

The rear door of the auditorium opened. Rivlin turned around to see who was there. It was his trusty driver, the dybbuk.

## 10.

ALTHOUGH THE CONFERENCE ORGANIZERS had given the lecturers meal tickets for the cafeteria, Rivlin excused himself.

"I've been up since early morning, and all this snow has made me sleepy," he told the disappointed translatoress. "I need some fresh air, not more academic chitchat. You'll manage without me. I'll give my ticket to Mr. Suissa."

And going over to the bereaved father, he clasped his hand with his own two and said, "It's wonderful to see you following in your son's footsteps." Suissa accepted the voucher gladly. "How is your daughter-in-law?" Rivlin asked. "She's left Jerusalem and gone to look for work in Tel Aviv," the father of the murdered scholar replied. "And the children?" "For the time being, they're with us." "I thought she and you were getting along better." "I thought so, too," Suissa said sadly. "But there's nothing to be done about it. She's a young woman in a hurry to live." "How old is she?" Rivlin asked, blushing as if he had committed an indiscretion. "Twenty-five next spring." "That's all?" He had thought she was older. "With all she's been through," he said, "you wouldn't think she would be hurrying anywhere."

In the garden of the Hendels' hotel, the snow lay fresh and virginal on the paths and formed frisky little snow cubs of the bushes. Rivlin walked ahead, with Rashid following carefully behind him. Stopping to inspect a fringe of ice gaily trimming the old gazebo, he yielded to temptation and mentioned the wedding. Only six years ago, he told his driver, they had all been standing here. And as if to make up for the disappointment of the Civil Administration Bureau, he related the story of the unexpected and difficult divorce.

"They were only married a year?" Rashid asked, a sardonic glint in his coal black eyes.

"To this day, I don't understand what happened."

"It must be painful for you to come back here."

"It is. But real knowledge, Rashid, is born of pain."

"And what do you know?"

"That's just it. I can't get an explanation from anyone. Not even from Fu'ad, who knew exactly what went on here."

"Fu'ad?" Rashid read his mind. "*Hada ma bihki k'tir. Hada arabi kadim, b'tist'hi k'tir.*"*

The Orientalist smiled. "*B'tist'hi min sham eysh?*"†

"*B'tist'hi yehin el-yahud.*"‡

"But why should anyone be offended?"

"There's no reason. *Bas ahyanan, b'kulu andna, el-yahud biz'alu min el-hakikah ili bifatshu aleiha b'nafsehum.*"§

A few minutes later, the old-fashioned maître d' was surprised to

---

* He's not one to talk. He's a bashful, old-fashioned type of Arab.
† What is he bashful about?
‡ Offending the Jews.
§ But sometimes we say that the Jews are offended by the truth that they themselves go looking for.

find the two uninvited Israelis in his dining room, standing in line among the Christian pilgrims at the buffet with large, empty plates in their hands.

"What are you doing here in all this snow?" he asked, startled to see them. "*U'sayara ma t'zahlakatesh*"?*

"*Ahadna jeeb bit'harak min el-amam*," the Arab explained to the Arab, "*u'safarna mitl ala zibdeh.*"†

But though the Jerusalem snow was child's play for the pious Christians from the American Midwest, it had blocked roads and canceled tours all over Israel, so that, as on Rivlin's previous visit, the dining room was full up. Rather than wait for Fu'ad to apologize, he filled his plate and headed for the smoking lounge favored by Mr. Hendel, whose death now seemed to belong to the distant past.

"You see," he said as Rashid sat down next him, "I'm still family despite my son's divorce."

The unexpected crush kept Fu'ad running back and forth from the kitchen to the dining room. Still, he found a few minutes to drop by the lounge and even to smoke a cigar, reminisce about the eventful trip to Ramallah, and ask about the scholar who had died.

"As a matter of fact," Rivlin said, "I'm in Jerusalem on a snowy day like this is for a memorial conference in his honor."

"Don't tell me it's already been a month!" the maître d' marveled. It seemed to him just a few days. Sometimes, falling asleep at night, he still thought of the face he had covered with a sheet. "And how is the widow?" he asked. "What a poet!"

Rivlin clucked with sympathy. "She's coming around slowly," he said.

The maître d' asked to be remembered to her. He could still hear her declaiming Al-Hallaj's lines—*My soul is his, his is mine. Who has heard of the body In which two souls combine?*—as if they had been written in Hebrew. He was so moved by the great Sufi poet that he had even tried writing a few mystical poems of his own. But who had patience for such things? "*Ya'ani, el-hawa ma bikdar yimsikha.*"‡

---

* Didn't your car skid?
† We took a jeep with four-wheel drive. It was like driving on butter.
‡ I mean, the air isn't right for it.

"*Kif el-hawa?*" Rashid asked.*

"*El-jow.*† Mysticism needs peace of mind. In this country everyone just wants to hear the next news bulletin."

He stubbed out his cigarette, cleared the dishes from the table, and suggested dessert. He would bring them ice cream and coffee.

"We'll have neither," Rivlin declared, getting to his feet. "We just came to see if you were still alive. It's time we got back to the memorial."

"But what do you mean, Professor?" Fu'ad said, taken by surprise. "Aren't you going to say hello to the management?"

Rivlin felt a ripple of unease.

"We can't today. Another time."

"But how another time? I've told Tehila you're here. And she said I should keep you here until she's free, because she's busy with all the guests whose tours were canceled. *Bihyat Allah, ya Brofesor, hatta la y'hib amalha minnak.*"‡

Something gnawed at him.

"Tell her another time. I'll be back."

Yet even as he said it, he knew he would never be back. The chapter of the hotel had ended.

"I can't do that," Fu'ad said.

"Of course you can," Rivlin told him. "We came for you this time, didn't we, Rashid? And for you only."

"I'm honored, Professor." Fu'ad put down the dirty dishes on the table and pressed his hands to a grateful heart. "I appreciate it. But that isn't something I can tell Tehila."

"And Galya?" The image of the lost bride flashed before him as though in an old dream. "Why isn't she here?"

"In a snowstorm in the ninth month of pregnancy? She's enormous. You could visit her, but I wouldn't recommend it. She rests in the afternoon. This is her first child, and she's nervous. You'll see her at the circumcision."

---

* How the air?
† The atmosphere.
‡ I swear, Professor, don't disappoint her.

"All right," Rivlin said impatiently. "Rashid and I have to go."

But Rashid didn't move. The always polite and reserved maître d' was physically blocking his path. As though pleading for dear life, Fu'ad said:

"I can't let you go, Professor, without your at least saying hello to someone in the family. Go see Mrs. Hendel. I'm sure she's up by now. You haven't spoken to her since the week of the bereavement."

"Next time," Rivlin replied, laying a friendly hand on Fu'ad's shoulder. But the maître d' stubbornly stood his ground. "I mean it," Rivlin said more softly. "How is Mrs. Hendel doing?"

"Still falling apart," was the cruelly candid answer. "There's nothing left for her here. Her son is in America with his family, and if we didn't find someone to play cards with her now and then, she'd have only her own depression to keep her company. Maybe the new grandson will cheer her up. But that will be no substitute for a man who treated her like a princess. And she's not going to find another one in this hotel, because there's no one here but Christians looking for God."

Rashid grinned.

"Come," Fu'ad said, grabbing the Orientalist by the hand. "Do me a favor and say hello to Mrs. Hendel. She'll be grateful that you haven't forgotten her like so many of her old friends. I'll send up coffee and cookies. Tehila will come if she has time."

"All right." Rivlin blinked anxiously. "But only for a minute. And leave Tehila out of this. Another time..."

And again he knew there would never be another time.

From the stuffy, overheated room on the third floor, the snowy garden looked like a fairy tale. Gently he gathered the widow, delicate from falling apart, in his arms. Her new, unresisting gauntness made her large eyes that demanded his sympathy shine more brightly than ever. Although it was afternoon, her bed was unmade. Her hardly touched breakfast was still on the table. A black silk nightgown sticking out from beneath the quilt made the Orientalist feel a slight sexual qualm. His amiable smile gone from his face, Fu'ad quickly restored order, carrying the dirty dishes to the hallway, deftly making the bed, and folding the nightgown and putting it in a drawer.

"It's the professor, Mrs. Hendel," he said as he exited. "He's come to say hello and have coffee with you."

She offered him a small chair by her side. "I suppose I should be insulted that you forgot all about me while coming to visit my daughters," she said.

"All in all," he answered, turning his chair to face the garden, "I've been here twice since the bereavement. The second time, you weren't here."

"I wasn't?" She seemed astonished to hear it.

"You were in Europe with Galya."

"Oh, yes," she remembered. "That was when you tried to sleep here."

He smiled. "You see?" he said. "You know everything."

"Everything?" She bowed her pretty head sadly. "Far from it. I only know what I'm told."

"Well," the Orientalist said, "I had no place to sleep in Jerusalem, and I remembered Yehuda telling me that I could always have an available room. It was foolish of me."

"Not at all!" Moved by his mention of her husband, she regarded him with bright, solicitous eyes. "He meant it. And while he lived, he was as good as his word. The promises he made, he kept. He didn't want this hotel turning into the railway station it's become. Of course, he wanted to succeed and make money. But he also wanted this place to be about more than just work. That's why he always left an extra room for family or friends. Now that Tili is in charge, all that has changed. You've seen how full the place is. She overbooks so much that she has to put up guests in her own wing."

"Yes." Rivlin grinned. "I got the basement."

"I heard about it. And about how you ran away in the middle of the night. It made me mad. I said to her, 'Tell me, Madame Manager, have you no sense of shame? If you can't treat an important guest well, it's better to turn him away.' But nothing fazes her. She's as tough as nails. And her father's death only made her tougher. He would never have dreamed of risking the hotel's reputation. Tehila couldn't care less. I sometimes wonder how I ever gave birth to someone so brash. She'll ride roughshod over anyone."

"Yes." Rivlin nodded. "My wife is sometimes like that, too."

"Your wife?" The revelation startled her. "Perhaps...." She thought it over. "I suppose I did feel that kind of backbone in her, even though you never gave us the chance to get to know her. But she's more gracious about it, a true lady. She's cultured and has boundaries. Tili is a wild woman. You wouldn't believe how afraid I've always been of her, even when she was a child..."

"I assure you, I would." Rivlin laughed candidly. "I'm afraid of my wife sometimes, too. Not that it stops me from loving her."

Mrs. Hendel's face darkened with sorrow. The thought of her former in-laws' love for each other, so palpable the first time she met them, made her feel the loss of her husband even more keenly. Only lovers, she told Rivlin, know love when they see it. "That was something I used to say to my husband. 'I trust Galya's choice of Ofer,' I told him, 'because his parents are like us. They're loving and close. Ofer and Galya won't have to improvise, because they have models.' Only..."

"Only what?"

"Only then..."

"Then what?"

"You know."

"No, I don't!" he said heatedly. "And none of you will tell me. And that's why I can't help Ofer to get unstuck..."

"But I don't know anything, either. I asked Galya a thousand times and never got an answer. Even on our trip to Europe, when we shared a double bed at night. I said to her, 'Gali, maybe you were embarrassed to tell your father, but now that he's gone, learn from your sister, who's embarrassed by nothing. Tell me what happened...'"

"And?"

"Nothing. She clammed up. But what does it matter? They're not the first couple to have fallen out of love. At least it happened before it was too late. She knew how much I liked Ofer. But it wasn't me who had to live with his fantasies."

"Fantasies?" There was that word again.

"That's what she called them."

"But fantasies of what?"

"She wouldn't say."

"You never asked?"

"No."

"But it isn't possible!" He flung the words at her angrily. "I don't believe you."

"You don't believe *me?*" The delicate woman was hurt.

"Don't take him seriously, Mother." Tehila had entered quietly through the door left open by Fu'ad. "He keeps thinking we're hiding something from him. But at least that gives us a chance to see him."

He sat up in his chair, the afternoon sun in his eyes. The proprietress, in whose cropped hair he noticed the first streaks of gray, was not content with a handshake. Tall and stooped, a chambermaid's apron tied by its strings around her waist, she bent to plant a ministering kiss on his forehead, as if he were a small boy with a fever.

"Your coffee, Professor," she said, with a hint of mockery, "is waiting downstairs."

"But Fu'ad said he would have it sent up," Mrs. Hendel complained.

"So he did. But I told him not to, because I didn't want you to miss your lunch. We're closing the kitchen soon."

"You can send my lunch up too."

"No, Mother. I have no one to wait on you today."

"Then I'll skip lunch."

"No, you won't. You think you will, but at three o'clock you'll decide you're hungry, and I'll have to wake up the chef and make him light the oven. You need to show some consideration, because it's been a crazy day even without the snow. And don't worry about our guest. He'll be back—won't you, Professor? Just because we tell you we know nothing is no reason to believe us, is it?"

## 11.

TEHILA DESCENDED THE BROAD, old-fashioned staircase ahead of him to the ground floor. Her long stride made her look like an ungainly bird that had forgotten how to fly. If Ofer knew to what depths I've descended to look for the fantasy he's marooned by, Rivlin thought, he'd wipe me from his mind instead of just cold-shouldering me. In the large lobby he halted, stuck out a hand, and said:

"Thank you. I'm afraid I'm running late. I'll have my coffee on Mount Scopus."

"But why?" She gave him a whiskey-colored glance. "The coffee is ready. What can you be late for? You have plenty of time until your talk."

"How do you know?"

"I saw an ad for the conference in the newspaper. The afternoon session starts at four, and your eulogy comes at the end of it. You're in no hurry. And where are you going on a day like this? Don't let the sunny skies fool you. The temperature is dropping."

"I see you've decided to manage me too."

"Let's say I'm giving you a bit of friendly advice. Not that you couldn't use some managing—especially when you're away from your wife, with no one to keep an eye on you."

He recoiled. "My wife," he said softly, "keeps an eye on me every-where—from within me..."

There was an awkward silence. Her birdlike face, sharp, hard, and offended, lost its teasing look. He felt suddenly sorry for this ugly Circe of the hotel, her bright apron perched absurdly on her hips like a chambermaid's in an Alpine inn.

"All right," he relented. "Let's have some coffee. I wouldn't want to hurt Fu'ad."

The little table in the smoking lounge was set with elegant cups and saucers and a plate of cookies. Rivlin looked for Rashid. "I gave him a bed to rest in," Fu'ad said, pouring their coffee. "He's feeling low be-cause of all those forms for his sister's children. Why does an Arab have to be sick to be allowed back into his own country?"

"What's wrong with having to live in a village near Jenin?" Tehila asked, warming her ivory hands on her coffee cup. "Isn't that Pales-tine too?"

"But Ra'uda grew up in the Galilee."

"So what? Why must every one of you live where he or she was born? What babies you are, missing Daddy and Mommy's home when you're parents and grandparents yourselves! I swear, you deserve a spanking, not a state."

Fu'ad glanced at Tehila and then down at the floor, unsure what to make of her barb. His arm in the sleeve of its black maître d's jacket trembled as it lifted the cover of the canister to see how much coffee was left. "*Afay'o, ya Brofesor?*"* he glumly asked of Rashid.

"Give him a few more minutes," Rivlin replied. "He needs to rest. *Sar majnun u'murtabir min kul el-ashyaa illi hawil yi'milha.*"†

"*Mitl el-masrahiyya,*"‡ Fu'ad said. "*Hada el-dibbuk illi mat.*"§

"A jinni," Rivlin said. He looked wearily at the proprietress, who was nursing her coffee in slow sips. Sallow and sickly-looking, she sat plotting her next move while trying to follow the Arabic conversation—until, with a gesture of impatience, she signaled the maître d' to be gone.

"As long as your driver is resting, you may as well, too," she said to Rivlin when they were alone. "Is your eulogy ready?"

"More or less."

"Will you read it?"

"I'll speak from notes."

"Good," she said approvingly. "That way you can cut it short if you're losing your audience."

He regarded her sardonically. "Don't worry. That's never happened to me."

"I should hope not. But tell me, what made this Tedeschi such a big shot that he's getting a whole day in his honor?"

"You don't have to be such a big shot to get a day for dying. But he was an important scholar. And a dedicated and much-loved teacher."

"Ah, yes," she said, with a sly gleam. "Yours is a generation that still loves its teachers. Nowadays, I'm told, university faculties are full of dumb women."

---

* Should I wake him, Professor?
† He's going crazy from all he has to do.
‡ It's like in that play.
§ He has a dybbuk in him.

"That's ridiculous." He felt a chill of fatigue. "You've never even been to a university."

"What if I haven't?" She took another calm sip of coffee. "It's not because I couldn't have, as you seem to think. It's because I went to work for my father, helping him to put the hotel on its feet. Believe me, I've learned more from life here than I could have at a university. But you're cold!"

"Something is wrong with the heating."

"Nothing is wrong with it. Fu'ad likes to save electricity, especially when he's mad at me. As soon as the dining room empties out, he turns the heat off. This part of the building cools quickly. Down in the basement, where you were the last time, you wouldn't know the difference, not even when it was freezing out. There's natural heat down there."

"Natural heat?" He scoffed at the idea. "It must come from those old tax files."

"Perhaps," she said with a hearty laugh, throwing back her head as though remembering something. "I wouldn't be surprised if it did."

"So you want to stick me in that hole again?" He met her small, eagle eyes, their gaze fearful with anticipation.

"You can rest there undisturbed, polishing your eulogy beneath a warm blanket in perfect equilibrium."

He smiled uncertainly and glanced at the thick curtain on the window. A ray of blue light slipped through the space between the hooks and the curtain rod. Why was it, he wondered, that during the year of his marriage Ofer had hardly ever mentioned Tehila? He had only enthused about Galya's father and the hotel. Had he paid no attention to his wife's shrewd sister, or was she, too, part of his "fantasy"?

"*Yallah, ila 'l-amam.*"* He rose and touched her bony shoulder. "*Ta'ali nitdafa shwoy bil-kabu.*"†

For the third time, he found himself walking through the hotel kitchen. In the between-meals silence, the carving knives and cleavers gleamed above the big, clean vats and the empty tables and cutting

---

* All right, forward march!
† Let's warm up a bit in the basement.

boards. They passed the large freezer and came to the little door whose concrete steps led to the underground corridor with its broken bicycle, torn tire, and bucket of hardened whitewash. A new broom was the one addition to this display. In the space at the corridor's end the baby crib stood beside the old boiler, whose chimney was rammed into the ceiling like the tooth of an ancient, petrified mammoth that still gave off its secret heat.

Rivlin watched the tall woman search in vain for the key to the accountant's room beneath the oilcloth mattress of the crib. The door to the dark room was open. Sound asleep on its bed was the protean driver-messenger-brother-cousin-uncle–displaced citizen–and–dybbuk for a day. Undressed, he lay dead to the world with his face to the wall, the splendid rear of his dark, smooth, naked body pointed at the door.

The proprietress was startled by the liberty taken by the maître d' Yet touched by the sight of the naked Arab, who had instinctively availed himself of the freedom offered by this subterranean grotto, she asked Rivlin for his name, knelt by his side, and gently poked him as if he were a soldier being awakened for guard duty. "All right, Rashid," she said. "You've slept enough. Give someone else a chance."

His name spoken by an unfamiliar woman, followed by her gentle touch, caused the sleeper to bolt to an upright position and wrap himself in his sheet, the hot coals of hastily extinguished sleep still glowing in his eyes. As if he were in the midst of a dream whose interpretation they were, he groped with a beseeching hand toward the two Jews. Before he could utter an apology, if not for his sleep itself, for which he had permission, then at least for his nakedness, he was fully clothed and holding a folded sheet beneath his arm, with which he departed, to return it to Fu'ad.

"Wait. Don't turn on the light," Rivlin told the proprietress, who had shown no sign of doing any such thing. In the gloom pierced by a few murky rays coming from the direction of the staircase, he moved the accountant's chair to the desk and sat down with his arms on his chest. He did not look at his Circe—who, instead of remaking the evacuated bed for him, sank onto it like a white ghost. It's hopeless, he told himself, and there's no time for it anyway, but if I don't ask her now I never will. And although she had still made no move to do so, he said again, "Don't turn on the light. Maybe it will be easier in the dark to tell me what you know about your sister. You can see how I'm suffering. Be kind just once."

She said nothing. Unable to make out her expression in the dark, he did not know what she was thinking. One after another, her shoes dropped to the floor. The bed creaked. Only then did she say:

"You're a hard man, Yochanan Rivlin. Really hard. Your Ofer was much nicer. What a pity you didn't make a career in the police or the secret service instead of wasting your time teaching. You would have felt at home there, looking for the truth in all the wrong places. It's too bad, because I thought you wanted something else from me—something I could have given you."

A shiver went through him.

"Come to think of it, why not ask my sister? You can go on giving her the third degree. If anyone knows what happened to her, she does."

"She refused twice," Rivlin said. "I couldn't get anything out of her."

"And so you've decided to pick on me?"

"You're a liberal woman. You're open for a relationship. And you've chosen, if I may say so, an uninhibited single life that lets you be frank and do what you want despite your loyalty to your family and the hotel . . . or am I wrong?"

She sat up on the bed. His eyes, now accustomed to the dim light, discerned the shadow of a smile as she pulled off her sweater, unfastened her apron, and opened the linen drawer beneath the bed. She took out a sheet, spread it on the mattress, and lay down again.

"Thank you for telling me how liberal and open I am. But it won't do you any good, because I really know and understand nothing about my sister and Ofer."

"But you must!" he burst out, placing professorial hands on his heart.

She laughed out loud. "You don't believe me, do you?" she said easily. "And maybe you're right not to. In a family, after all, everything is connected, even what no one understands. But there has to be some closeness before one can talk about such things. And if you're really such a big-time sleuth, I have a proposal, or rather a condition, to make... yes, a condition. That's the right word for it. Before I can loosen up with you, I need some love. I don't suppose you would mind a secret little bedtime adventure, would you? We might as well start now. After all, you're a busy man—and you must realize by now how uninhibited I really am...."

His arms stayed crossed. Although he wasn't sure whether he was being challenged to a test of his determination or a battle of wills, he knew deep down that he had expected this—that his unforeseen visit had been made with it in mind.

"If such is your condition," he said with mock formality, "I am prepared to surrender my precious faithfulness to my wife. But what is it you look forward to in an old man like me?"

She smiled. "Leave that to me. You already made me curious at the bereavement, when I saw how lovingly you embraced my mother. That's why I insisted you wait for Galya. And when I saw you pleading with her in the garden, I said to myself, this is a man who will come back. And you did...."

"But curious about what?"

"About what you're like when you're turned on."

"But what good to you is my pretending to be turned on?"

"As good as my pretending to know something is to you."

"Then you don't?"

"Don't know and don't care. I'm not like you. I respect other people's boundaries and wills. I've never understood how you dared snoop on your son's life, poking into his affairs while pretending to save him. If I were your daughter I'd have murdered you long ago."

"*Murdered* me?"

"With my own hands."

"Then how lucky I'm not your father." But the feeble joke fell flat. Her hard face jutting with disappointment, she turned to the wall, curled up her long body, and withdrew. At that moment he knew that, in a basement full of files, he had lost his last link to a world that would forever keep his son's secret. Reluctantly he rose, wanting to touch the long body one last time. But he lacked the courage to do so and only said a weak good-bye that was not acknowledged. He walked past the silent stove, running his fingers over the crib, then traversed the corridor and climbed the stairs to the kitchen, in which a solitary chef was concentrating on beheading a large fish.

The two Arabs were in the smoking lounge, talking quietly like old friends. Fu'ad was smoking a cigarette while Rashid twirled a cigar between his fingers as if uncertain what to do with it. They looked at him accusingly as he entered. For the first time he felt that neither of them liked him. "*Shu hada, ya Brofesor?*" Rashid asked in a cold voice. "*Kul halkad b'sur'ah hillis nomak?*"*

## 12.

IT WAS CLEAR AND getting frostier outside. The snow had been cleared from the streets. Here and there, in the afternoon sun, rosy icicles gleamed on the roofs.

Rashid was in low spirits, disappointed by his failure at the Civil Administration Bureau and embarrassed to have been found naked. He drove silently, with his eyes on the road, passing in front of the walls of the Old City and heading for the underground parking lot on Mount Scopus. Bluish clouds were stamped on the skies above Hebrew University. To the east, over the desert, hung a thick haze.

The guard at the entrance to the parking lot found an Orientalist in a hunting jeep suspicious and insisted on seeing Rivlin's invitation to the conference. This, however, was not to be found, having been lost in the hotel or the basement. Not even a faculty ID card from Haifa could persuade the guard to let the car through. Rivlin felt he had had enough of Rashid. Why not, he suggested lamely, start back for the Galilee without him? He would probably find someone to give him a ride back to Haifa.

Rashid demurred. "I'll come for you at the end of the session," he said. "Your wife won't like it, Professor, if I leave you here in Jerusalem." Despite the anger in his voice, he still held the judge in high esteem.

---

* What is this, Professor? Don't tell me you've already finished sleeping?

In the reception room of the Truman Institute, a large gathering was crowded around the refreshment-laden tables. The translatoress of Ignorance, circulating excitedly, lit up when she saw Rivlin. "Where did you disappear to?" she scolded. "Everyone has been looking for you. Hagit called, too. She said not to try calling her back— she'll try again. Look how many people came in the end! Do you think we should move to a bigger auditorium?"

"There's no need for it," he assured the happy widow, explaining that the more crowded the audience, the better the lectures, since packed rows of listeners were an erotic stimulus to an intellectual.

The rows of the little hall were indeed so full that a janitor had to bring extra chairs. Although many of those present were unfamiliar to Rivlin, he had a good idea of who they were. Apart from university officials and administrators, there were members of the small Italian-Jewish community of Jerusalem, most of them slight, elderly women in high heels and black dresses set off by colorful scarves, who took pride in their scholarly compatriot and hoped to hear stories that would remind them of their childhoods in the beautiful land of fascism they had fled. There were also Arabists from various universities and colleges, and, to his surprise, quite a few young M.A. and Ph.D. students, as well as strange hybrids spawned by pseudoacademic think tanks and research institutes. These, in the spirit of the times, were confusingly interdisciplinary, their Orientalism combined with sociology, law, literature, political science, philosophy, education, Jewish history, computer science, and other things. As he was wondering what they were doing at a memorial for Tedeschi, who had done his best scholarship before most of them were born, he noticed a group of them swarming around Dr. Miller. With a mixture of amazement and consternation, it dawned on him that this pale, quiet man whose promotion he had foiled had disciples. One day, no doubt, they would take their revenge on their guru's nemesis.

Yet his envy had no time to linger on Miller, because it had already shifted to the dead man himself and his well-attended memorial. For a moment, Rivlin even begrudged Tedeschi his own eulogy. Who, he lamented, would mourn him? Would he have a successor, in this generation that did not want to succeed anyone because everyone wanted to be his original self? Going off to a corner, he reviewed his talk in solitude, ignored by the colleagues invited according to a list drawn up by him.

The afternoon session was opened by the university rector, a vigorous, middle-aged mathematician who, too old to discover new theorems, had embarked on a second, administrative career. Since he had never known Tedeschi, the doyen of Orientalists having retired before his time, he chose to say a few words about peace with the Arab world and invited Dr. Miller to give the first lecture, the topic of which was "Colonial Desire."

The young lecturer strode unhurriedly to the podium. He wore new eyeglasses with clear, light frames so transparent that they seemed not to be there at all. In a soft voice, he read from a prepared text.

"In his book *Colonial Desire*, published in 1995, the British cultural historian Robert Young writes about the longing for the cultural Other as an escape from one's own cultural world. One subject he discusses is the active, sometimes even erotic, desire for the Other that informs all cultural crossovers.

"Such cross-cultural contacts, as has been observed, leave their perpetrators in what the University of Chicago's Homi Bhabha has termed 'an in-between space'—or as Kipling put it, they are 'East-West mongrels.'

"The existential plane of this androgynous hybridism is the European colony, whose inner cultural dissonance creates a fractured and divided self..."

Rivlin felt exhausted. In the end, he thought bitterly, his Circe had not let him rest for a moment. At least he would not have to do the driving back to Haifa.

"Young, like other students of culture, argues that following Sartre in 1960, Mannoni in 1964, Franz Fanon and Albert Memmi in 1967, and Aimé Césaire in 1972—the founding theoretical fathers, as it were, of postcolonialist theory, that theory has emphasized the dichotomy between the binary forces of the colonizer and the colonized.

"This dichotomy treats the colonized as the Other of the colonizer, knowable only by a false representation that reinstitutes the same static, essentialist categories it wished to do away with. By contrast, the multiculturalist outlook has encouraged many populations to assert their separate individualism. Thus, both Floya Anthias and Nira Yuval-Davis maintain that even extremist groups need to be encouraged in their struggle for representability.

"Historically speaking, we can, therefore, say that only recently, in the final decade of the twentieth century, have critics and scholars grasped the significance of cross-cultural contact as a mapper of the full complex of constructive and destructive social forces. And yet the available models for describing this complex are far from satisfactory."

Rivlin noticed that some members of the audience were taking notes. Pleased by this, Miller slowed his pace to enable them to keep up with him.

"We can say that the main theories of cross-culturalism have been based on the three models of diffusion, assimilation, and isolation. None of these, however, takes into account the effects of interaction, even though historical studies have shown the importance of cross-cultural stimulus and response in such areas as religion, commerce, epidemiology and health care, and so on. The most productive paradigm to date has been the linguistic one."

Someone tapped Rivlin on the shoulder. "Your wife is on the phone."

He hurried outside to the telephone at the entrance. "Where are you?" asked Hagit.

"Right here."

"Your sister called two hours ago. She's in the hospital."

"What happened?"

"Nothing serious. She'll need tests. There's a problem with her eye. I'll tell you in a minute. But first I want to know where you ran off to again."

"Where do you think? I had lunch off-campus to get away from Hannah and her hysterics. Now I'm back keeping an eye on things and waiting for the memorial session."

"Hannah complained there were very few people this morning."

"She should stop whining. What does she want? There were as many people as could be expected for a conference in honor of a dead old professor. And it was snowing. But now a whole Italian contingent has arrived, and the place is packed."

"Then you're happy?"

"Happy? What for? It's not a memorial for me."

"You're unbelievable. You even envy the dead."

"I can envy anyone. But tell me what happened to Raya."

"She has a torn retina in three places in her left eye."

"For God's sake! That's exactly what happened to my father."

"Except that the treatment nowadays is much simpler, provided the retina isn't detached. They use lasers at low temperatures. We'll know more when the head eye doctor examines her tonight. Meanwhile she has patches on both eyes and is feeling low. She keeps thinking of your father."

"Is anyone with her?"

"Noa was, but she had to leave at seven to relieve the nanny. And Ayal won't come before nine. That's why I thought that, if you weren't too tired, you might drop by the hospital on your way home. Your sister is all alone there....Do you hear me?"

"Of course."

"Is Rashid still with you?"

"Yes. I'm lucky he tags after me everywhere, even though we accomplished nothing at the Civil Administration Bureau."

"I'll take a look at what the law says. But what's up? Do you feel ready to give the eulogy?"

"Pretty much."

"Put some feeling into it. Carlo deserves it."

"I'll do my best. I'll see you tonight."

"Just a minute. Why are you so remote?"

"I'm not. I'm just tired."

"Do you still love me a little?"

His felt his heart turn over.

"What do you mean? You're my whole life..."

# 13.

THE LAST GLIMMERINGS OF daylight sifted in among the audience, which had not diminished the second session. Although neither the "Sudanese" from Bar-Ilan nor the "Iraqi" from Beersheba had directly challenged Miller's conclusion that Orientalism was a meaningless concept, each preferring to make a modest point in his own field, the two had demonstrated that Orientalist research was on solid ground. Disappointed by such evasive tactics, a number of Miller's followers left at the session's end. Yet the auditorium remained full, since the empty seats were taken by an Italian consular delegation and some Italian priests and nuns, come to pay their last respects to the fellow countryman who had often lectured to them on various subjects.

The memorial session began at five-thirty. A black lace shawl around her slender shoulders, the widow stepped forward to place two large framed photographs on the podium, one of the young Tedeschi in the Israeli desert and one of an older man getting an honorary doctorate from the University of Turin, the city he had fled on the eve of World War II. The green-ribboned mortarboard above his heavy academic robe gave his nose a pinched and ugly look.

Two young musicians played a lively Rossini serenade for flute and violin. When the applause died down, the chairman of the Hebrew University's Near Eastern Studies department delivered a brief review of Tedeschi's scholarly achievements—which, he declared, were a guiding light to an entire generation. He was followed by the director of the Truman Institute, who regaled the audience with recollections of Tedeschi the public figure. The Jerusalem polymath, he related, had never refused to put aside his scholarly pursuits for a luncheon or dinner in honor of the university's Middle Eastern guests—Turks, peace-loving Jordanians, Arabs from the Persian Gulf, brave Pakistanis—and to teach them a thing or two about their own history.

The two musicians returned to play a modern work by an Italian composer, an intricate and unmelodic dialogue that left everyone relieved that it was over. A hush descended on the hall, where the elegiac mood was heightened by the twilight that was its sole illumination. It was time for Rivlin, the deceased's protégé and real or apparent heir, to rise and go to the lectern, where he shut his eyes for a moment with such force that he seemed about to burst into an aria. Outside the large windows, at the foot of Mount Scopus, the Old City, bounded by its ancient Turkish wall, merged in the dusk with the neighborhoods around it. Patches of snow gleamed on its golden domes.

Rivlin felt a wave of despondency. The hopeless Rashid and the amorous Circe nagged at his mind. His stubborn, patient pursuit of the mystery of his son's marriage, begun last spring in the garden of the hotel, had ended in a basement on a snowy day in winter by shelves filled with income-tax files.

He took his notes from his jacket pocket, placed them on the lectern, and began to read the opening paragraphs, which he had written out in full to get himself off to a good start.

"Two years ago, my wife and I were on a summer vacation in the Dolomites of northern Italy. One afternoon we took a funicular to a well-known ski site. It let us off on the slope of Mount Cortina, where there was nothing except for a small café. Sitting there was an elderly Italian gentleman, a stocky man with a distinguished if slightly recherché appearance whose face and body language were remarkably like those of Professor Tedeschi. Yes, my friends, he was the very image of our dear Carlo. We were so struck by it that we couldn't take our eyes off of him. He drank his coffee and ate some cake while conversing thoughtfully with a young companion who—to judge by the deference he showed the older man—might have been his private secretary or student. After a while the gentleman rose, paid the bill, took his burnished, gold-handled cane, and left the café. Yet instead of heading downhill on the funicular to the little valley below, he took the young man's arm and pointed amiably but firmly with the cane at a bare path that wound toward the summit of the mountain, bald except for a crown of snow. The two of them walked slowly, halting now and then to exchange a few words or look at the scenery, until they disappeared in a sudden haze.

"The elderly gentleman's resemblance to Professor Tedeschi affected both me and my wife. We wondered where he and his young companion had been heading. And it was then that a thought occurred to me. 'Imagine,' I said to my wife, 'that there had been no Italian fascism or German Nazism and no Second World War. Carlo Tedeschi, who was born to an assimilated Jewish family and considered himself an Italian in every respect, would have finished his medical studies in Turin. A successful, amiable physician, he would have gone hiking from time to time in the mountains near his native city

and might have been the man we just saw. It never would have occurred to him to study Arabs or Turks, whom he would have known
only as an occasional item in the newspapers.'

"Yes, ladies and gentlemen, Tedeschi's Orientalism was a by-
product of the tragedy of World War II. Even after the war, he could
easily have returned to Italy and resumed his medical studies. But the
fate of Europe's Jews caused him to burn all his physical and spiritual
bridges to his native land. He sold his parents' home in Turin for less
than market value, renounced his Italian citizenship, and began a new
career on Mount Scopus as a student of Near Eastern history. His
mentors, great Orientalists from Germany and Central Europe, had
turned to the field for similar reasons. But Tedeschi was not satisfied
with their classroom learning and decided to polish his spoken Arabic
with a strict old Arab instructor known for his rigor in inculcating a
proper accent. The young Italian threw himself into his new field with
total dedication. It was more than a career for him. It was a calling, his
contribution to integrating the Jewish people into the region they had
chosen to live in—a crucial task if they were to survive there."

There was wonder on the face of the translatoress, who had never
heard Rivlin's vividly told story of her husband's doppelgänger climbing Mount Cortina in the sunset. He smiled at her tenderly. Getting
no response, he turned to the consular officials, who were listening to
his Hebrew with attentive incomprehension.

"In recent years," he continued, "the field of Orientalism has been
under unremitting attack. Edward Said's renowned book, published
twenty years ago, is but one illustration of this. Even though the radi-
cal accusations of this literary and intellectual critic living in New York
were rejected out of hand by most scholars, among them such serious Arab academicians as Jalal el-Azem, Nadim el-Bitar, and Fu'ad
Zakariyya, they have served to legitimize the ongoing criticism leveled
at their own profession by many young Orientalists. So dubious are
they of the scholarly integrity of their field that they would deny it its
very name. Suddenly, a time-honored belief in the capacity of rational
Western thinkers to understand the history and reality of the Arab
world has been called into question. At the end of the twentieth century, we have been asked to adopt a postmodernist sensibility—a

rather nebulous concept, I must say—characterized by a more flex-
ible, relativistic, multicultural approach. This alone, we are told, can
get us to the heart of an elusive essence that—so forthright Arab writers like Fu'ad Ajami lament—even the Arabs have despaired of
understanding.

"The problem is especially severe for Israeli Orientalists, who are
caught in a double bind. On the one hand, they are suspected by both
the world and themselves of being unduly pessimistic about the Arab
world because of Israel's conflict with it. And on the other hand, they
are accused of unrealistic optimism because of their deep craving for
peace. For the Israeli scholar, whether he likes or admits it or not,
Orientalism is not just a field of research. It is a vocation involving
life-and-death questions affecting our own and our children's future.
This is why we have a greater responsibility to be accurate in our
work. Just as we must refrain from all condescension toward the Arabs,
so must we avoid all romanticization of them. We are not German
philologists, retired British intelligence officers, or literary French
tourists, who can afford to be deluded about who the Arabs are or
should be. We are the Arabs' neighbors and even their hostages—
participants in their destiny who are unavoidably part of what we
study. We are the old and yet new stranger in their midst, the constant
shadow of the Other that, by their own testimony, has become their
twentieth-century obsession. The problematic indeterminacy of Jewish identity undermines the old stability of the Arab world that slum-
bered peacefully for centuries in the desert."

From the throes of Israeli Orientalism's double bind, the eulogist
gave his worried audience a sorrowful, we-must-carry-on-nonetheless
smile. Even the Italians who did not understand him nodded trustingly at his impeccable logic.

"And here," Rivlin continued, pointing to the photograph of the
Jerusalem polymath in the desert, "lies another of Tedeschi's unique
contributions. Growing aware many years ago of the dangers posed
to Israeli Orientalism by this symbiotic relationship with the Arabs,
he decided to draw a clear boundary. 'Let us,' he declared, drawing on
his fund of knowledge, 'learn from the Turks how to belong and not
belong to this region at one and the same time.' And so turning away

from Iraq, putting Sudan aside, and even abandoning great Egypt, he traveled northward to Turkey, in whose relations with the Arab world he saw a paradigm for our own."

The eulogist regarded his audience. It suddenly struck him that the elegant young woman seated several rows behind the eternal fedora of Mr. Suissa, her eyes riveted on him in the dim auditorium, was not an Italian consular worker but Mrs. Suissa junior, who had come to express her sympathy for a colleague of her murdered husband and for a newer widow than herself. The sight of this restless soul, looking calm and pretty with her hair pinned up, a new life ahead of her now that she had freed herself from the clutches of her in-laws, should have gladdened him. Instead, however, he was flooded with such sorrow for his own son that an involuntary groan escaped him. Seeking to obey his wife's bidding, he fought to concentrate on his feelings for Tedeschi. The dead man deserved no less.

"Nevertheless," he continued, "though the Turks, ancient and modern, became Professor Tedeschi's main concern, he did not neglect the Arabs completely. Indeed, having reached a stage in his career in which he could afford to take a panoramic view, he grew increasingly worried by our inability to understand the Arab mind. While he did his best to conceal it, he was fearful that we Jews, having failed catastrophically in Europe, were about to fail again in the Middle East—that the new homeland meant to be our final destination could become another bloody trap. Despite the natural optimism of a man who had taken his fate in his hands and saved his own life by coming to this country, he felt torn, as Israel's leading Orientalist, between his responsibility to warn his colleagues of the pitfalls of wishful thinking and his reluctance to sow despair by declaring—he, who had educated generations of Arabists!—'It is hopeless to try to understand the Arabs rationally. Back to their poetry, then, for that is all we have to go on!'

"Ladies and gentlemen, from this inner rupture came Tedeschi's many imaginary illnesses, whether they were an escape from the harsh truth of reality or a cry for help to his friends, asked to come still his fears."

The profound silence told him that he had said something unexpected and true. Reaching for the glass of water on the lectern, he took a slow sip while summoning his strength for the love and compassion he had promised his wife. It surprised him that no one had turned on the lights to dispel the darkness that had become almost palpable. Perhaps this was because Rashid, an anguished look on his face as he strained to hear the eulogist's painful words from the back of the hall, was standing in the way of the light switch.

## 14.

DESPITE THE PATCHES ON her eyes, she knew it was her younger brother even before he opened his mouth. The intimacy of a childhood shared in one room in their parents' small Jerusalem apartment had taught her to sense him from afar.

"You shouldn't have come," she said. "I told Hagit it was too much for you."

"It's all right. It was on my way."

"Did that Arab at least drive you?"

"Yes. I'm lucky he sticks by me."

"But why does he? I've heard you don't even pay him."

"Don't ask me. It's he who doesn't want to take anything."

She lay, small and thin, on a couch in the head eye doctor's office, a black patch on each eye, waiting for the doctor to finish an operation and determine whether the low-temperature laser suture performed that afternoon had repaired her retina and made surgery unnecessary.

"In which eye did it happen to our father?" he asked.

"The same one. The left one."

"Couldn't you think of a better way to take after him?" He couldn't resist teasing his sister, even while she lay dismally in the dark, with her good eye covered too—a precaution taken, she told him, not on orders from the doctor, but on the suggestion of a nurse. Although her son's kindhearted wife had spent the afternoon with her, she had only made Raya's fears worse by overidentifying with her condition. Now Rivlin's sister lay waiting for her son to appear with his calming presence. Her brother, glum and tired, was not having a reassuring effect. On the contrary, he soon lapsed into a listless silence, from which she tried to arouse him by changing the subject to the snow in Jerusalem.

"That old bitch!" she declared of their mother, as angry at the age of sixty as if she were still a teenager. "All the kids were outside having fun while we were protected from pneumonia by having to ski a doll in a bowl of snow in the bathtub."

"What doll are you talking about?"

"Don't tell me you don't remember!" Just because she couldn't see she was not about to give up on her never ending struggle to keep her childhood memories alive in him. "That little black doll you went with everywhere..."

His silence only deepened as he tried remembering the black doll. He had no wish to rage with his sister against their mother. He hadn't seen her ghost for ages. Would he end up having to eulogize her too?

Two hours ago he had been speaking in honor of Tedeschi. The lights in the auditorium had come on, the light switch behind Rashid having been discovered, just as he was describing in a tremulous voice how the translatoress of the Age of Ignorance, that pre-Islamic period so crucial for understanding the Arabs, had combined scholarship with her love of poetry and devotion to her husband's health. But had it been fair to say what he had about Tedeschi's illnesses, or had this been cheap psychologizing on his part? Before he could answer that, his son's dreary solitude again pierced the twilight of his mind. For the first time, he felt no sympathy for Ofer, only anger. That's it, my boy, he addressed him in his thoughts. I've failed just as you hoped I would. There's no more hotel and no more Arabs to help me.

As in a dream, this, too, quickly faded. Now he saw his pale, lanky Circe, curled on the basement bed like a long fetus, osmosing into her own freedom.

"Listen," he said to his sister. "I'm getting hungry. Shall I bring you something to eat too?"

"I'm too worried to eat. But I can feel how edgy you are. Why don't you go home? It's late."

"It's all right. Hagit made me promise to stay until Ayal comes."

His sister smiled, reaching out a blind hand toward him.

The corridor outside was empty. The visitors had gone home. The nurse on duty sat reading a book. There was no telling whether the patients, lying in their rooms with bandaged eyes, were awake or asleep. A large figure was blocking his path.

"What's up, Professor?"

To his amazement, he found himself looking at his sister's former husband, a tall, thin, balding ex-playboy. Hearing from his son that Raya was in the hospital, he had come to have a look Although he was a strange, difficult man who had given his wife a hard time, Rivlin felt a nostalgic affection for him.

"Look who's here!" he said, giving him a friendly slap on the shoulder. "I don't believe it! Come, say hello to Raya. She'll flip when she sees you."

"Shhh," his ex-brother-in-law said. "If she does see me, she's liable to detach her other retina."

"But isn't that what you're here for?" For some reason, his encounter with this man, whom he had not run into for years, had improved his mood.

"To see Raya? What a thought! The head eye doctor is my tennis partner. Ayal asked me to speak to him."

"But as long as you're here," Rivlin persisted. "why not look in on her? Don't be childish. What are you afraid of? She won't even know it's you. Her eyes are covered."

"They are?" The temptation to be invisible in his wife's presence was too great to overcome. Silently, he followed Rivlin to Raya's room.

She was still lying on the couch, small and thin. A lamp, buzzing softly on the table, lit her face. The black patches over her eyes gave her the look of an airplane passenger trying to get some sleep. For a moment, Rivlin thought she was drowsing. But sensing her ex-husband, who was standing in the doorway with a crooked smile, she raised her head and asked anxiously:

"Yochi, is that you?"

"What's up?" Rivlin asked quietly.

"Did you eat so fast?"

"It seems I did..."

"But there's someone else with you," she said worriedly. "Who is it?"

He dodged the question. "Who could it be?"

"But there is!" She sounded fearful. "Someone is with you! Is it your driver?"

"My driver?"

The unseen husband smiled ironically. His blue, froggy eyes darted with amusement, as if reconfirming the oddness of the woman he had married and suffered with. Putting a finger to his lips, he turned and left.

Ayal arrived at last, tired but in full possession of himself. When told of his father's visit, he said angrily to Rivlin, "You shouldn't have let him come near her," as if he were talking about two disturbed children.

It was ten o'clock when, back in a wet, glittering Tel Aviv street full of strollers taking the air after the storm, he climbed into the jeep and woke Rashid—who, having filled the vehicle with smoke from one of Fu'ad's cigars, now lay fast asleep beneath a blanket.

"Look here, Rashid," he said. "It's turned into such a long day that I'm not driving back with you unless you let me pay you."

"Pay me?" The messenger's coal black eyes regarded him blearily. "You couldn't afford what a day like this costs."

"I wouldn't say that," the Orientalist said, offended. "I'm not a charity case. I can afford whatever you would normally take. Just tell me honestly what that is."

"Normally?" Rashid smiled to himself, as if at a new thought. "For a long, hard day like this with a four-wheel drive vehicle, I'd take... at least... at least fifteen hundred shekels."

"Fifteen hundred?" Though unable to conceal his shock, he quickly recovered and laughed derisively. "If that's the going price, fine. Why not?" Grandly he pulled out a checkbook and wrote a check, while promising Rashid that his wife would read up on the immigration laws dealing with the reunion of families.

The Arab jammed the check in his pocket and replied in a half hopeless, half newly dismissive tone:

"You can tell the judge not to try too hard, Professor. Laws have got nothing to do with it."

15.

> I have a strange pet, half kitten, half lamb. It's a hand-me-down
> from my father, but only now has it begun to grow.
>
> —Franz Kafka

THE HEAVY RAINS, WHICH went on falling in the north for another week, turned the dirt roads of the Israeli security zone in southern Lebanon into treacherous bogs. After a Bedouin tracker was killed by a mine concealed in the mud, Central Command suspended all foot patrols and kept the roads open with armored vehicles. The Commanding Officer of the trackers' platoon, a lieutenant whose name was Netur Kontar, hurriedly applied for leave and was granted it.

The CO was a Druze of about forty, a heavy man with a big mustache. Before leaving his base, he informed his family on the Carmel that he was going first to the village of B'keya in the Galilee, where he had promised to let his Christian dentist friend Marwan pull an infected wisdom tooth. If the weather improved, he might also join him and his friends for a night of hunting.

Kontar had been an avid hunter since he was a small boy. His father, discovering early that he had a natural instinct for finding his way at night without getting lost, took him along on his hunting trips, during which young Netur sometimes spent entire nights perched silently in the treetops. It was so hard to wake him the next morning that he was almost expelled from school. If it hadn't been for his older sister, who did all his homework, he would never have graduated.

It was in the army, however, that his abilities became fully appreciated. As a recruit in boot camp, he so impressed his officers with his navigational skills that they vied to take him on their nighttime maneuvers. When his three years of conscripted service were over, the Northern Corps, loath to lose an ace tracker, made him the unusual offer of a commission, without requiring him to take an officers' training course, and immediate command of a platoon in southern Lebanon.

The young Druze accepted, not only because the conditions were good and the job was a feather in his cap, but also because the army was a first-rate base from which to pursue his life's passion. Throughout his long years of daily exposure to mines, bayonet charges, and booby traps, he took comfort in the regimental armory, out of which he enhanced his collection of weapons with an array of silencers, telescopic lenses, starlight sensors, and other devices, to say nothing of camouflage nets, which made excellent snares, and stale bread from the kitchens, which was good bait for wild boars. After losing his right thumb to a mine blast, he was afraid he had impaired his trigger finger, and for a while he suffered from depression. But the impediment was overcome, and the old army jeep that he was given in compensation, which he quickly filled with the equipment that now went with him everywhere, made him a legendary figure among the hunters of northern Israel and even of southern Lebanon.

Today, however, as he knocked on the door of the dental clinic in B'keya, Netur Kontar was in a troubled mood, both because of his painful wisdom tooth and of a strange story told him by his father. At first he didn't mention it. Leaning back in the dentist's chair, he opened an uncomplaining mouth and let his head be jerked this way and that while his friend gaily pulled his tooth and told funny stories to distract him. Yet once Netur Kontar had spat out the last of the blood, rinsed his mouth thoroughly, admired its new hole in a hand mirror, and taken off his bib, he asked the assistant to leave him alone with the dentist so that he could speak his mind.

Netur Kontar's father, the renowned hunter of his childhood, was now an octogenarian. Yet several nights ago, Netur told the Christian dentist, the old man had gone hunting in the hills near Megiddo—where, in the moonlight, he spied a creature like none he had ever seen before. It had the height and shape of a large lamb and the head and claws of a cat, and it moved by alternating wriggles and skips. Its round, green eyes, wild and roving, were catlike and lamblike at once. Instead of cat's whiskers it had heavy muttonchops that gleamed pink in the light of the moon.

Surprisingly, the old hunter told his son, this strange mongrel made no attempt to flee. Curious and frisky, it let out a sound that was neither a meow, nor a purr, nor a bleat, but rather a hoarse groan, and approached the old Druze in a friendly manner, nuzzling him and sniffing at his clothes as if they were on the best of terms. Yet as the old Druze was wondering how best to trap the animal and bring it back to his village, it seemed to guess his intentions and sprang from his arms, scratching his forehead and disappearing on the bushy hillside.

The old man was determined to pursue the matter. Although being clawed by an unidentified beast required medical treatment, he spent the next day secretly making a large rope net, with which he returned to the scene of the encounter the following night. He set out a bowl of milk and a chopped fish, sprinkled them with fresh alfalfa, and hid in the branches of a tree to see what would happen.

It was only toward dawn, as he crouched in the tree half-asleep and half-shaking from cold, that the mongrel appeared again. This time it resembled neither a cat nor a lamb, but a cross between a goat and a German shepherd. It sniffed at the food, consumed it all, and glanced fearlessly at the old hunter as he slipped slowly down from his tree. This time, too, it let itself be petted and even turned over on its back, enabling him to see that it was sexless—neither male, female, nor in between. "Well, then," Netur Kontar's father thought, his desire to show the strange animal off to his friends and family growing stronger by the minute, "this is a pure miracle, a one-time creation of God's that will never reproduce itself." Yet as soon as he spread the large net he had brought, the animal gave a great leap and—before bounding off toward the Valley of Jezreel—nearly tore out the eye of the old Druze who had planned to catch it.

Even now, however, the old hunter refused to give up. Despite his eighty years, he set out in pursuit of the fleeing beast, at first on foot, and then, seeing that it was following the road to Afula, in his old pickup truck. Near Mount Gilboa, not far from the Jordan, the mongrel vanished from sight.

"And then?" the dentist asked. He had listened with no sign of emotion while disinfecting and arranging his tools.

And then a week went by. The old hunter's wounds were treated by a doctor, who gave him anti-tetanus shots. Fearing to be made fun of by his family, he said nothing about the beast that had clawed him and waited for his son to come home from the army. He was prepared to tell his story to him alone.

The dentist felt concern for the Druze officer still sitting in the revolving chair, his eyes red from lack of sleep. Not only had he just had a tooth pulled, he had lost a tracker earlier in the week. "With all due respect to your father's wounds," said the Christian dentist, who had heard his share of Druze tall tales in his life, "don't you think he might have imagined it?"

Netur Kontar frowned. He knew his father well. He had learned to hunt from him. They had spent long nights together in the mountains. Although he questioned the mysterious lambcat's sexlessness, he didn't doubt that the beast existed. His father, though possibly confused, was not making it up. He had been hunting since the days of the British Mandate and had seen every animal there was, and if he said at his age that he had found a brand-new one, he was to be taken at his word. Indeed, it was the duty of every hunter to bring the lambcat alive to the Nature Authority, or else to the University of Haifa or even the government in Jerusalem, since it was sure to be named for its discoverer, thus bringing scientific glory to the Kontars and the entire Druze community.

"But where do you suggest looking for it?" the dentist asked gently. He was beginning to wonder whether his old friend was in his right mind.

"On Mount Gilboa. That's where it was last seen."

"But where on Gilboa? It's a big mountain."

"It's not as big as all that."

"It's also a nature reserve on which hunting is forbidden."

At this the Druze officer turned livid. Forbidden? To whom? To an officer like himself who risked his life day after day for the State of Israel? You might think he was proposing to kill the animal and eat it in revenge for its having clawed his father. All he wanted was to further scientific knowledge of the country's wildlife.

The dentist feared his friend might burst out crying. He would think about it, he said. Meanwhile, he urged Netur Kontar to wash up, change his clothes, and lie down in a little side room of the clinic.

The Druze officer took the dentist's advice and was soon fast asleep. Going to the telephone, Marwan called his fellow hunter Anton, the lawyer in Nazareth, to ask for his opinion of the story. The lawyer tended to agree that it was all the old man's fantasy, taken seriously by his son out of filial loyalty and mental exhaustion from his long service in Lebanon. Still, he, Anton, would be happy to hunt the lambcat together with them tomorrow night. "Don't worry, Marwan," he laughed loudly. "Even if we're arrested for poaching, I'll file such an appeal with the Supreme Court in Jerusalem, arguing that we can't be convicted of hunting a nonexistent animal, that the judges will pee in their pants. So why not spend a night on Gilboa protected by an army officer? While we're looking for Netur's animal, we may bag a boar or a nice juicy gazelle. In Nazareth we say, 'The Arab harvests the Druze's dreams.'"

## 16.

AND THEN YOU KNEW it. Calamity burst from you like a dream become a reality, and though you leaped barefoot in the dark to head it off, it was too late. Its swift shadow passed through the room you had prepared and merged outside the window with the certainty awaiting it, gathering speed along roads of awakening light, rolling as all calamities do to a place you had never imagined. The lamb fled to the hunter who dreamed a dream.

Now they all say, "Enough, stop blaming yourself! It was Fate. Only God knows the reason, and God will make good on it." Idiots! Go explain to them that Right is stronger than Fate and mightier than God because it alone promises sweet Justice.

It found you outside the Civil Administration building, hopelessly stuffing your jacket pocket with forms as though it were a garbage pail for hope. "Take me with you!" it cried. "Take me from this Jerusalem slush. Even the Jew, though you led him here through a blizzard, can only go *tsk* and mumble vague promises. Take me with you, Rashid! If not now, when? I'm light and I'm clear and I won't weigh you down. Enough of the hypocrisy of colored forms—forms for the government, and forms for the army, and forms for tired bureaucrats and officers with their games. 'Yes, by all means, bring your sister and her children, just make sure they're dying of some illness'—as if any illness could be fatal enough. Take me with you, O Arab of Israel, O displaced citizen who has his rightful place!"

And so you threw away the forms, and Right jumped into your arms like a lion cub, emboldening you so that you asked for your full pay, and the shocked Professor laughed but forked up. And that night, when you reached the village, even the horse sensed that Right was with you and backed away from the gate. Samaher and Afifa turned over in their sleep, hearing Right pass down the hallway, and Grandmother lay with open eyes by Grandfather and smelled it as if sniffing fresh vegetables. "Careful, Rashid, my love," she thought. "Don't do anything crazy with this Right you've brought home." Yes, Grandmother. The Law blows up in the lawmaker's brain, and Right stabs the hearts of the righteous. But what else can I do when it and I have embraced and there is no turning back?

That night you began clearing out your room for Ra'uda and her children. You felt sad giving up the place that had been yours since childhood, the solitary room of your hopes and dreams, of your books and self-abuse and love for the young cousin you protected. It was hard to empty out the drawers, collect the books, and fumigate the same mattress the Jew slept on. But when you took down the colored memos and the pictures, baring ugly patches on the faded walls, you realized that childhood had gone on long enough and love had grown too entangled. It was time, O wise one, to choose exile.

You spent the day painting and plastering. And in the evening, when all came to see, the village informer came too, for who knew what juicy bit of information the police might pay for? But Right was stronger than all payment, and even the old informer could only say "Well done" and depart. Your old enemy alone, Samaher's husband, was gloomy and nervous and refused to believe that anything had changed. "O husband of my beloved cousin," you should have said to him, "are you not glad the jinni is leaving?" But he knew that the return of Ra'uda and her children would only strengthen your foothold in this house, even though you had moved to the far end of the village.

Was it he, in desperation, who informed on you that night?

Yes, Calamity burst from you like a dream become a reality, and though you leaped barefoot in the dark to head it off, it was too late. Its swift shadow passed through the room you had prepared and merged outside the window with the certainty awaiting it. Over the hills, in the awakening light, it rolled as all calamities do to a place you had never imagined. O rash Rashid, how could you deliver the boy into the hands of poachers?"

It was afternoon when you arrived in Zababdeh. The winter sun was mild. As on the night of Paradise, you crossed the fields and—noticed only by Calamity, which followed you—kicked down a section of fence. You suspected nothing, happy to see the children in the churchyard looking so nice in their clean clothes, dream-Israelis about to become real ones. Ra'uda was wearing the Jewish judge's hand-me-downs in honor of her return. You gave her sick old Christian husband a package of your old clothes, too, and some books to pass the time with when his children were gone, and you went to say good-bye to the Abuna, who showered you with twice as many blessings as usual because he sensed that Calamity was on its way. After that you went for a last meal in the basement. The Christian sat silently at the head of the table, eating his soup from his army mess tin in a mood of great fear, as if Calamity were directly overhead. You alone were not frightened or confused. You were as pleased with yourself as if Right and you were now bedfellows.

At three that afternoon you folded the backseats of the minibus, loaded the bundles and kitchenware, and hid the children among them. Ra'uda sat up front with the baby. Ismail and Rasheed put on their big glasses, so that whoever had seen them in the Jewish state would recognize them. Their father gave them some farewell gifts, and they parted with a few words. It had clouded over and begun to drizzle, and you were in a hurry to get back to Israel before dark. The Palestinian police in Kabatiyeh and Jenin knew you were on your way. "Good luck," they said to your sister. "We too will return some day." But cutting across the field, you saw a new checkpoint that hadn't been there before and two soldiers waiting for something, perhaps for you—and you panicked. In fact, you did the worst possible thing.

You stopped the car and turned around. And Calamity thought: if one checkpoint with two soldiers can make this Israeli Arab turn and run, how much Right can he have?

The report of the vehicle that had turned back spread like an ink stain. More and more checkpoints went up. You headed east toward Mount Gilboa and reached it at twilight, hoping to find an unguarded path, only to run into a roadblock there too. And yet Calamity was still preventable. The three soldiers, all middle-aged reservists, had no idea what to look for. They checked the bundles and suitcases, searched for explosives and drugs, and lined the children up in a row and demanded to know the history of each. You kept calm. The children, you explained quietly, were all little Israelis who had been visiting their cousins in the Palestinian Authority with their mother. Now they missed their village in the Galilee, which was why it was wrong to detain them, because they were hungry and wanted their Israeli supper.

The dark Arab's light manner did not entirely assuage the Jews, who failed to grasp what so many ID-less little children were doing at the foot of Mount Gilboa at dusk on a winter day. And yet their commander, a sergeant in his forties whose hair was streaked with gray, was not looking for problems. He had a family of his own, which was sitting down to its supper now, too, and he felt sorry for the children, especially for the black baby sleeping in the arms of its curiously well-dressed mother. He was ready to turn a blind eye—but only one. He would let them all through except for the two older boys, the ones with the funny glasses, who would have to wait for their ID's.

And then, Rashid, you made your second mistake. You should have noticed the fear in little Rasheed's coal black eyes and insisted, "Hold on there, my fellow citizens. I have too much Right on my side to compromise. I'm not going anywhere without the two boys. Their grandmother is waiting for them too."

But you didn't. You were rattled and started to squirm, afraid the sergeant would open his blind eye too, and you turned tail and headed for the village of Arabuna to find a place for the two boys for the night. Bolts of lightning sliced the air, and you heard a boom of thunder and thought, "I have to hurry," and you knocked on the door of the first house. The old woman who opened it looked as ancient and used as a ghost from Turkish times. And then you made your third mistake. Instead of saying, "Sorry, I've come to the wrong house," you appointed her temporary grandmother in charge of the two returnees. You even gave her twenty shekels for milk and eggs and told the *Dybbuk*'s two candle bearers to wait for you, making the younger one promise to obey the older and the older one swear to look after the younger, so that Grandmother Ghost, who had by now awakened Grandfather Ghost to help her, would not be annoyed with them.

And now, sitting day and night by the boy's bed, you wonder how Calamity took over that night and Right stabbed you in the back. Because Rasheed freaked when you didn't come back. He didn't even take off his funny glasses, because he was sure you would return in a minute to bring him to Israel. He must have thought you loved him best of all because his name was just like yours. And you did, because he was the most darling. But when the two old folks gave him his supper, he began to cry and scream at the old lady that he didn't want to be left behind in Palestine. And even then she might have calmed him if only Ismail, a moody child in the best of times, hadn't slapped him and made him cry even harder for his mother. And at night, when they were all asleep with the windows shut and the door locked, he wriggled through a transom in the bathroom. Although at first he meant to wait for his uncle, he was lured on by the lights of Israel in the distance. He was sure that once he reached them, no one would ask him for any ID. He didn't know that Fate prowled on the mountain, disguised as the hunter whose gun would fill out the forms you had thrown away.

## 17.

'CAUSE WHY NOT TRY? The lights are bright and near and I can reach them. Why be afraid of the soldiers if my mother was born there and can speak their language? The village is called Mansura. We were there twice. Grandmother gave us candies and told us to come back. What made Mamma leave? She shouldn't have done it for Babba. He's sick. Let him die in Jenin, where he was born.

But why does this path keep going up? I thought it was just a little mountain. Now I see it's a big one. And there's nothing on it. I should have slept in that old witch's house. But I made a mistake and I can't go back.

THE DRUZE OFFICER SLEPT all day and all night in his friend's dental clinic, woozy from the painkillers he took for his pulled tooth. At dawn he arose, amazed and contentedly refreshed by his long slumber. He phoned headquarters to make sure his leave had not been canceled, went to his jeep, which was stocked with six battle rations, two canteens of fresh milk mixed with grated cheese, and a carton of stale bread, and took out a military map of Mount Gilboa. Spreading it on the floor of the clinic, he studied it carefully. Then he picked out a route and some good spots for hunters' blinds, committed them to his photographic memory, and folded and put away the map. The dentist, none of his patients protesting, called off his appointments for the next day; the lawyer postponed all his meetings, giving each client a different excuse; and the two Christian hunters sat down to clean and oil their guns in preparation for the Druze extravaganza.

A light rain was falling in the glare of their headlights as they set out. They stopped in a field, to pick some alfalfa for the lamb half of the lambcat, and arrived at evening, fully armed and bundled in their windbreakers, at Netur Kontar's father's house. There, over a cozy supper, the old hunter described what he had seen. The main thing, he warned, was to catch the animal alive. This was important not only for science, but also for tourism, especially if—though the task seemed impossible—the sexless lambcat could be made to propagate.

It was nine o'clock when the three hunters returned to their jeep and set out for Mount Gilboa. Parking by a spring chosen by the Druze officer, they spread the alfalfa on a rock, poured the milk and cheese into a bowl, and added a fish head given them by Netur's mother, who knew nothing of the strange beast that had frolicked with her husband. The Druze positioned his two friends and climbed a tree that looked down on the bait. In the next few hours the bait drew partridges, conies, and even a wary young fox, who left nothing for the lambcat. The rain beat down harder.

IT WAS RAINING SO hard that I couldn't even see the darkness and had to take off my glasses. As soon as I did, I lost them. That's too bad, I thought, 'cause now no one in Israel will know me, and I'll be like Babba, without a right to return. It's best to cross now in the dark when the soldiers are asleep, 'cause if they see that I don't know any Hebrew except for "Hello" and "Screw you" they'll bring me back to my sick father in the basement.

I was getting hungry. Between Ismail and the old woman, I didn't eat any supper, so I broke off a leaf and chewed it and thought, maybe it's poison and I'll die before Babba. I felt sorry for leaving him all sick and pale in the church. What if the Abuna forgets to take care of him? And I felt bad that I hadn't opened his present or said thank-you, so I looked in my pocket and there it was, wrapped in some newspaper, and I took it out and it was a little pen, and I wondered what would happen when Babba died, and I missed him and wanted to cry and go back.

There was a fishy smell. I went to see what it was. A flashlight shone on me. "There he is," someone whispered. That's right, I thought, here I am, but why are you talking in Arabic?

AFTER THE SMALL GAME of Gilboa had eaten all the bait and vanished without a shot being fired, Netur Kontar decided to leave the spring for a new spot on Brave Men's Hill. They drove over Buttercup Pass and down the Old Patrol Road for five hundred meters. Once again they spread the alfalfa and put out the milk and cheese, into which they now tossed the fish's tail. This time the Druze remained below and told the two Christians to climb trees.

The more the night progressed, the more temperamental Netur Kontar became. He began to order the doctor and lawyer around as if they were trackers under his command, barking at them what to do and demanding such silence that not only laughter but smiles were forbidden. "Who does he think he is?" the lawyer whispered indignantly to the dentist. "We didn't stay out of the Jews' army in order to serve in a Druze's. We haven't caught a damn thing tonight."

But as Netur was determined to trap the lambcat, and the keys to the jeep were in his pocket, there was nothing the two Christians could do but climb into their harnesses and up two wet-branched trees. They perched there in their windbreakers, the victims of Netur Kontar's father's fantasy. They would, they decided, give it until three in the morning. If the lambcat had not turned up by then, they would look for other game.

The silence was total. Although the rain picked up again, the dentist and the lawyer soon fell asleep in the branches. They were half-dreaming when the Druze shone his flashlight on the bushes and whispered, "There he is." By then it was too late to stop him.

AND I THOUGHT, if they're talking Arabic, I haven't reached the border and it must be Ismail coming to spank me. "Don't," I wanted to beg him. "Go easy. Don't spank me too hard, 'cause I'm worried about Babba, who's sick and all alone, and I'm mad at Mamma for leaving him." It was wet and cold and dark and I ran and I ran until I couldn't run any more and I heard my brother growling beneath a tree. He wasn't shouting or cursing, just making these crazy animal sounds. I was good and scared. So I ran some more and my present fell from my pocket and I bent to pick it up and something whistled and I felt an awful pain as if Babba's pen were stuck in my back.

AN EXPERIENCED HUNTER LIKE Netur Kontar knew at once that no animal moved or made sounds like that. Perhaps, he thought, the beast that had fired his father's imagination was a werelamb. Waking the two Christians in the treetops, he signaled them to slip quietly down and execute a flanking movement and—though he had been warned by his father to catch the lambcat alive—opened the safety catch on his shotgun and took off in hot pursuit.

It was too dark to see anything. Yet the Druze hunter was used to such nights and tracked the animal by ear. Now and then, glimpsing a silhouette that didn't match his father's description, he wondered if it might have changed shape again.

But it was too quick for him. And so after a while, fearing to disappoint his father, he stopped running, dropped to his knees, and began making friendly animal noises, yowling, bleating, purring, and sighing to convey his good intentions. Yet the beast that had been so playful with his father refused to approach his father's son, though it did pause for a moment in the bushes to stare curiously at him with its coal black eyes. That was when, desperate, Netur Kontar menacingly shouldered his shotgun. The doctor and lawyer, running up to him at that moment, barely had time to say "Hold it," as he pressed the trigger in spite of his father's warning...

It wasn't my brother or the pen. It was some metal in my back that knocked me down and didn't let me move. I couldn't talk. I couldn't hear. I couldn't see. All right, I thought. I'll forget about Grandmother in the village. Just let me go back to Babba, 'cause he's sick in the church and I want to be with him. But I couldn't make a sound, not even a whimper, and my head hurt real bad. Something heavy pressed on me and pinned me down. I wanted to go to sleep and die. Oh, Babba, Babba, oh, Abuna, help me, help me and save me from this earth.

## 18.

Midway through your class, the door at the top of the lecture hall opened, and a bulky woman with an overnight bag walked in and sat down in the last row.

Startled, you lost the thread of your lecture for a moment. Since it wasn't the origins of French colonialism in North Africa that had brought this very pregnant woman to the last class of the winter semester, she had to be a former student coming to display her condition before asking for an extension on a term paper. Yet a second later, your heart did a flip-flop. It was Galya, the lost bride herself. You waved to let her know she should wait for you after class, then resumed your lecture.

The lecture ended. She struggled toward you with her bag down the tiered rows, carrying her pregnancy as though it were a gift for you. While the students crowded around you to ask about their final exam, she sat again and waited for them to leave. Gone from her glance were last spring's haughty impatience and anger at her father's death, their place taken by a wistfulness that verged on defeat. She made a move to get to her feet. You told her not to and hurried to her from the lecture podium. "I almost didn't recognize you," you said, bending to embrace her before she could reply. Her body yielded willingly, soft and unresisting like her mother's. She seemed not to know what to say. It was as if, having come all this way and received a warm welcome from you, she no longer remembered the reason.

But you weren't asking for it. You treated her sudden appearance as a perfectly normal family visit, gave her big belly a fatherly appraisal, and asked when she was giving birth. The due date, she answered with some embarrassment, was this week, perhaps even today or tomorrow.

This was already too much for you. Was she planning to have her child in your lecture room? "What kind of time is this to be running around the country?" you rebuked her mildly, as if the baby in her womb were partly yours too.

Her overnight bag at her feet, she tried to defend herself. First births were usually late. She was counting on that. She had come to see your son. She needed to speak to him immediately, if possible before she gave birth. Of course, she could have got his telephone number from you. But she wanted your help in persuading him to come to Israel. After all, you were also responsible.

"I am?"

Yes, you were. She was firm about that. That's why you had to help her. She would pay for Ofer's ticket. She had already reserved a seat for him on tomorrow's flight from Paris. She had a face-to-face confession to make, and she needed to ask his forgiveness, if only for her baby's sake. She had sworn to herself that she would do it.

Her voice echoed emotionally in the empty lecture room. You were beside yourself with joy. At last, though you had no idea what it was, the truth sought by you for nearly a year was about to materialize. You asked, not recognizing your own happiness:

"Forgiveness for what?"

## 19.

SEATED IN THE EMPTY lecture room like the last student to finish an exam, Galya realized that this man who had pursued her with his frenzied questions hadn't a clue. As much as she needed his help, she wasn't about to give him one now. If Ofer wanted to tell him, that was his business. He had had the past six years to do it in, even though she had asked him not to. She respected him for that. He had acted not from weakness or guilt, but from gallantry toward a woman he loved. She would never compromise him.

As in their meetings at the hotel, Rivlin felt that his ex-daughter-in-law still harbored a resentment against him. He had to nurture the new trust between them if he didn't want to lose her again. He reached for her bag, surprised to feel how heavy it was.

"But why are we standing here?" he asked, adopting a light tone. "Giving birth in this lecture room won't get your child free tuition in the future. Let's go to our place. We'll call Ofer and tell him you're waiting for him. Believe me, he would have come running even without the ticket you bought him. It's his attachment to you that's made me so worried about him. That's why you mustn't be angry at me for saying that, quite apart from forgiveness, the truth matters, too."

She bowed her head, as if the truth he saddled her with were too heavy for her. Carefully, she eased her way out of her seat. How strange, Rivlin thought, that of all the women, Jewish and Arab, who had asked to be taken under his wing this past year, she had waited to do so until now, in the final days of her pregnancy. Yet in spite of everything, he would grant her wish and be the father she had lost.

Gripping her arm lightly but firmly, he led her through the gloomy corridors of the building, which had been designed without any provision for letting in the copious sunlight from outside. Passing the large show window of the library, in which were displayed new works by the faculty, he thought sadly of his own book, held up by this, his parallel quest for the truth. The university, he told the perfunctorily nodding Galya, had grown enormously in recent years. Her steps faltered as they entered the dark underground parking lot, along a wall of which some cartons with old files were waiting to be thrown out. But they were already at his car, stowing her bag and his briefcase in the back. He adjusted the front seat for her, as if to let the baby know that the world was making room for it.

The late winter day was bright and crisp, the rainstorms of the past months now a pleasant memory. It was Galya's first visit to Haifa since leaving Ofer. "I forgot how beautiful it is," she said, gazing at the sweeping view of the bay and sea. "Well," he answered, half in jest and half temptingly, pointing at a large hospital on a ridge of the Carmel, "if you feel like it, or don't manage to get back in time to Jerusalem, you can always give birth up there, with a nice view. Does the baby have a name?"

The question seemed to upset her. It had had one, she told him, and then fell silent, as if she had begun to say too much and had changed her mind.

Rivlin lapsed into silence, too. He did not wish to risk losing his mysterious stake in this child with a careless word. In the parking space of his building on the French Carmel, he backed into a spot and exclaimed when Galya went on sitting in her seat belt:

"But I haven't told you that we moved!"

"To here?" She looked disappointedly at the discolored brick paving and the old houses farther down the narrow street. "How could you have given up your beautiful wadi?"

"If you hadn't left Ofer," he said, with dark humor, "you might have talked us into staying. But don't make snap judgments. Our new apartment is quieter and has more light. And it has another advantage for old people like us or pregnant ones like you..."

He pointed to the elevator, which brought them slowly to the fifth floor. The sight of the spacious apartment, with its familiar couches, armchairs, rugs, and bookcases, was reassuring to her. So was Hagit's not being there.

"She's at the beauty parlor," Rivlin said familiarly. Taking advantage of this to establish facts on the ground, he took Galya to his study, placed her bag by the couch, and asked discreetly if she wished to wash up first or call Paris at once. She chose the former, and he led her to a large, colorfully tiled bathroom, asking wryly whether she remembered the WC in their old apartment, small and dark despite the glorious view outside. Her smile, which he had forgotten, made his heart twinge. He handed her a towel and a fresh bar of soap, as befitted an honored guest, and went to make her bed in his study, pulling out the convertible couch and spreading sheets and a blanket on it. Although the results were less grand than the royal bed made for Hagit's sister, he regarded them with satisfaction. Now that the truth had arrived at his doorstep of its own accord, he meant to take good care of it.

Washed and refreshed, Galya gave the bed an approving glance and sat in the chair Rivlin offered her by the telephone. He wrote Ofer's number for her on a piece of paper, then wondered out loud whether he shouldn't speak to him first. After all, he said, he didn't want his son to think he might be fantasizing again. She reddened at that, but agreed. She would get on the line if Ofer wished.

"I'll leave you alone as soon as you do," he promised her.

He dialed Paris. His son wasn't in. There was no longer a Hebrew announcement on his voice mail, just a laconic French one, as if only routine calls were expected. Rivlin, however, chose to leave a complicated message. With one eye on the terrace across the street, on which now appeared his mother's ghost with her bag of garbage, he told Ofer of Galya's arrival and imminent delivery, and of the ticket to Israel awaiting him. He was still talking when a beep informed him that he had used up his recording space. "Did I say too much?" he asked his ex-daughter-in-law, who had been listening intently.

"You were fine," she said, regarding him as if for the first time. Her old beauty, Rivlin saw, thought by him to have been lost, was still there. He glanced with amusement at the old woman across the street, her ear pressed to empty space to catch the sound of the approaching garbage truck. Did Galya remember his mother? She nodded slowly. "Would you like to see her?" he asked.

"But..." She shivered. "I thought..."

"Yes, she's dead. But I've brought her ghost from Jerusalem. She's across the street. I put her there to keep an eye on her...."

Galya did not smile. Apprehensive, she shifted her gaze from the old woman with the garbage bag to the idiotically grinning man at her side.

"But how are you, Yochanan?" she asked. "Are you better? You had us all worried at the bereavement."

"Yes," he confessed awkwardly. "It was a false alarm. But who is 'us all'? You're the only one I told."

"You also told Fu'ad."

"Did I? That seems unlikely." Although he found it hard to believe that he could have made such a fool of himself with the maître d', his memory forced to him to admit otherwise. "You're right," he said softly, chagrined. "I must have wanted him to know how desperate I felt. Well, suppose I did? Did he run to tell his boss?"

"Tehila? She's not his boss any more."

"How is that?"

"He quit his job a week ago. For good."

"Fu'ad quit? But why?" He felt there was more to it than met the eye. "He was so proud of that job. How will Tehila manage without him?"

"Why can't she? You know her by now. She's become so strong-willed since my father's death that it's not only the staff she can manage without. It's..." Galya paused, as if surprised by her own words. "It's her own family too..."

## 20.

THE FRONT DOOR OF the duplex opened. Before it could shut again, Hagit's voice traveled through the house in search of his. He quickly closed the study door and hurried downstairs to tell her about their surprise guest. Seductively painted by the beautician, her eyes regarded him with the infinite patience of someone used to assembling the facts before passing judgment. Not even the news that he had made the bed in his study could shake her repose. Not until he told her about the message he had left for Ofer did she turn on him.

"You knew I'd be home soon. Why couldn't you have waited to ask me what I thought?"

Refusing to be put on the defensive, he threw his arms around her and passionately pressed his lips to hers. "Be careful," he pleaded in a whisper. "She can hear us from upstairs. Have pity on her. And on me. What does it matter what message I left him? This isn't in our hands. And neither of us can stop it. Why shouldn't Ofer come? The truth will free him."

She slipped gently, as though not to hurt him, from his pacifying arms. "The truth doesn't always free. Sometimes it entangles. I wish you'd think more of Ofer and less of yourself."

Stung by her rebuke, he hugged her even harder. A squeeze of her hand told him that Galya was standing at the top of the stairs. There was no telling how much she had heard.

Hagit hadn't seen her since the divorce. Now, pale and big with child, she was gripping the railing as if warding off an attack of vertigo. It was no time to be critical. Hagit invited her downstairs, gave her a quick hug and kiss, and suggested she sit with her swollen feet on the low table. Galya asked for some coffee, which Rivlin went to prepare, leaving the judge to cross-examine her about the course and medical history of her pregnancy. She compared it to her own two pregnancies and asked warmly about the Hendels. How was Galya's mother holding up? She would never forget her great love for Galya's father. Although her courtroom experience had taught her never to trust appearances, this had seemed real. Of course, the most loving couples could be problems for their children . . . just look at Ofer. Or at Galya's sister. Was she still unmarried?

Rivlin, having discovered that the milk was sour, came back from the kitchen to propose tea.

"But why tea?" Hagit protested. "We need fresh milk, for tomorrow too. You should run down and get some. And while you're at it, pick up a cake, because something tells me we'll have more guests from Jerusalem. . . ."

Galya, the judge had discovered with her usual knack for ferreting out the truth, had not informed her family or even her husband of her trip. She had set out for Haifa without telling them.

For a moment, no one spoke. Hagit gave Rivlin, standing by the door with a shopping basket, a reproachful look. Uncharacteristically fumbling for words, she probed for the hidden logic of her ex-daughter-in-law's actions.

"But how could you, Galya? Not that it's any of our business . . . but still . . . and now of all times . . . are you aware of what you've done? How could you just go and disappear in your condition? Suppose you should ... of course, you're not alone ... we're here with you ... but you're not registered at any hospital ... and your husband must be frantic with worry ..."

"Don't worry about Bo'az," Galya reassured them. "He's not the frantic type. He's calm and collected and takes things as they come, sometimes a bit too much. He's not like Ofer, who'll run to the end of the world to find something to worry about. I suppose I've gone to the opposite extreme ..." She laughed strangely. "Maybe I'll need a third husband to find the golden mean."

But Hagit had no patience for jokes. "Please," she told her stunned husband, "the grocery is closing soon. And don't forget we have a concert tonight."

"Why not skip it?" Rivlin suggested.

"What for? If you don't feel like going for milk, I'll do it."

He went for milk, making an agitated reckoning of how many of the bounds breached since Hendel's death he was responsible for. Afraid Hagit might talk Galya into returning to Jerusalem, he hurried back with his purchases and was relieved to find his ex-daughter-in-law where he had left her, her feet on the coffee table.

"Ofer phoned," Hagit informed him, her annoyance replaced by a new tone of complicity. "Your message confused him, but I set him straight. He's coming tomorrow. Galya talked to him, too. He didn't stay on the phone for long, as if he were afraid to spoil things."

"What did I tell you!" Rivlin crowed to the bulky young woman, who seemed to have taken refuge behind the baby in her stomach.

"You and I will pick him up at the airport tomorrow afternoon," Hagit said. "Unless you have more important things to do."

"What could be more important?" he protested.

Yet as afternoon turned into evening, a brooding silence settled over the duplex. Only when Galya agreed to notify the hotel of her whereabouts did Hagit relax and go to dress for the concert. Rivlin, resigned to going, paced moodily while she changed before the mirror. What else, he asked, had she discovered while he was buying milk?

"Nothing. I didn't ask, and I don't want to know."

"Not even now? I still can't get you to budge, can I?"

"Why should I budge when I'm where I should be?"

## 21.

THE PHILHARMONIC CONCERT WAS an all-Haydn one. Although he didn't question the greatness of the classical composer, Rivlin feared a whole evening with him might be dull. But after leafing through the program notes, from which he learned that the four works to be performed took no more than an hour and a half, he felt reassured. Even if she went into labor, Galya could hold out until they returned. And the opening piece, the C Major Cello Concerto, gave him unexpected pleasure. Its soloist, a guest performer from abroad with an enormous mane of hair, played without glancing at his instrument, as if it were part of his body. His hands flowed in and out of the strings of their own accord, his mane tossing as he kept practiced eyes on the audience as if to forge a connection or even a friendship with it.

During the intermission, perhaps to avoid an argument, Hagit and Rivlin did not discuss their guest. Instead, they reminisced about the birth of Ofer, lovingly recalling every detail of the thirty-three-year-old memory.

The concert ended with the *Clock* Symphony. Haydn, Rivlin had to admit, had not subjected him to a dull moment. Yet finding the duplex in darkness upon their return, he felt a current of anxiety. Had someone spirited their miraculous visitor back to Jerusalem?

He opened the door to his study carefully. The orange reminder to be of good cheer twirled over the screen saver of his computer and lit the face of the sleeper on the couch with a tender light. She lay as peacefully beneath the mound of her pregnancy as if she were where she had always wanted to be.

He and Hagit exchanged smiles, like the parents of a naughty child, and shut the door softly. They undressed in silence, getting into bed and turning out the light without the TV news. Although for a moment he thought his wife wanted to make love, he didn't dare put it to the test. He gave her a last hug, stroked the face he had kissed, and turned to the wall.

In the middle of the night, the telephone rang and stopped before he could answer it. Curling up again beneath the quilt, he realized that his sleep had fled and would have to be hunted down in the apartment. He went first to the bathroom and then, cautiously, to his study. Although the lights were still off, a voice was speaking as though to itself. Going downstairs to the guest room, he gently picked up the receiver of the telephone. Now there were two voices, Galya's plaintive, her husband's quiet and restrained. He hung up and sank into a chair, his wakefulness growing. Let it. Keeping watch over his ex-daughter-in-law's last hours of pregnancy seemed the right thing to do.

After a while he went to the kitchen, poured himself some wine, and sipped it with slow ceremony. When he picked up the receiver again, the conversation was over. Content with the world, he went to the terrace for a look at it. From the bottom floor of the duplex, he had no height advantage over the ghost. Her apartment was dark. She slept better than he did.

The narrow, quiet street below was filled as usual with the cars that occupied every inch of parking space at night. Even ordinarily, this made it hard to get in and out of their building. Now, though, a large car blocked the entrance completely. If Galya went into labor, he thought worriedly, he wouldn't be able to drive her to the hospital. Yet a second look revealed someone sitting beside the empty driver's seat. They had come to get her, without even waiting for the new day.

He heard footsteps. They must be Bo'az's, he thought, coming up the street from the pay phone around the corner. In the glow of a streetlight he made out the ponytail of the man who took things as they came, perhaps because he thought he knew all about them. And yet, in the middle of the night, in the silent street of a strange city, the knowledgeable husband seemed at a loss. Bending over, he spoke to the occupant of the car. Rivlin, looking down from above, had no doubt that this was the proprietress, come to restore her sister to her senses. Soon her lanky frame appeared in the street. Heart pounding, he shrank back as her birdlike head swiveled upward to look for his floor.

What now? The taker-of-things-as-they-came and the thumber-of-noses-at-them had joined forces to rob him of the confession he had yet to hear. He had to stop them, to turn them back at the entrance to the building. Stepping into full view on the terrace, still in his pajamas, he signaled that he was coming down.

They met in the parking lot. Tehila planted a sisterly kiss on his cheek, and Bo'az gave him an affable nod. How close he had come, Rivlin mused, to disgracing himself in his passion for the truth—and now here it was, upstairs in his home, waiting to be deciphered. Shivering from the cold of the winter night, he brought the Jerusalemites up-to-date on the day's events, starting with Galya's intention to confess.

"To confess what?"

"Don't ask me. Ask her."

"She's out of her mind," Tehila snapped, narrowing her whiskey-colored eyes.

He stuck up for the shelterer in his study, who was definitely in her right mind. Although feeling sad, even miserable, she had a plan that she meant to carry out. It would be best to let her do it.

He took a long look at his watch to remind them of the hour. He was sorry, he said with a remote smile, that he had no basement to put them in. On the next ridge of the Carmel, he told them, pointing at a building rising starkly in the moonlight, was a hotel he could recommend, even though he had never stayed in it.

But the proprietress had her own hotel, where at this time of the night when the roads were empty she could be again in two hours. And so, with a friendly handshake, she promised to phone in the morning and was off with her brother-in-law while Rivlin, returning to bed, found his escaped sleep waiting for him there.

The new day dawned filled with the anticipation of discoveries. Hagit left early for the courthouse, and Rivlin stayed behind to wait for Galya to awake. She rose late and took a while to arrange her new room, in which she had made herself at home. She was already in the kitchen, glancing pregnantly at the morning paper, when the housekeeper arrived and was struck dumb. But Galya preserved a demure silence, while Rivlin, who felt so much and understood so little, made no attempt to explain what looked like the backward flow of time.

His study commandeered once again, he drove to the university and circulated aimlessly. From there, unable to contain his excitement, he continued to the courthouse. Entering his wife's courtroom, he sat in the last row, behind the defendant, several attorneys, and the usual spectators with nothing better to do. The black-robed wife-judge conducted the proceedings with dispatch. When they were over, he waited until she was alone in her chambers and embraced her with inexplicable love.

They returned to the duplex at noon. Their guest, having installed herself as thoroughly as if she had rejoined their family, had made a list of their telephone calls. She said nothing about her husband and sister. "They can wait in Jerusalem," was her sole reference to them, as if it were no longer her city. Meanwhile, she would appreciate being stayed with until Ofer arrived—preferably by Hagit, who could help interpret the stirrings she felt.

FOR THE FIFTH TIME in a year, Rivlin found himself standing by the fountains in the arrivals hall of the airport. Yet this time, he thought as he watched Ofer stride out of customs with only a small bag on his shoulder, was the most remarkable.

They stood warily in the place where they had parted so painfully last summer. Avoiding his son's eyes, Rivlin put his arm lightly around him. Ofer's suffering face, on which a narrow French beard now grew, had a new, almost exalted look.

"You're becoming like your aunt and uncle, who visit Israel for a few hours at a time," Rivlin joked when informed by his son that he was returning to Paris the next day for an exam at his cooking school. Ofer took the jibe in stride. He saw nothing wrong in using Israel as a stopover.

Rivlin told him about Galya, choosing his words carefully. She had confided very little in them, he said. The news that she did not want to see her family or husband brought a tight, malicious smile to Ofer's face. In no mood to talk on the drive back to Haifa, he let his father describe his book on Algeria and the memorial conference for Tedeschi.

"Did you really love him that much?" he asked, hearing for the first time of the Jerusalem polymath's death.

"I'm not sure what you mean by love," Rivlin answered. "But missing him so much makes me realize how attached to him I was..."

Yet when it came to attachments, this admission could not hold a candle to the deathly pallor that suffused Ofer's face as he entered the house in which his ex-wife, encountered only in his imagination for the past six years, was waiting for him. Even now that she had taken refuge with his parents, he could hardly bring himself to look at her or at her swollen stomach. With a few curt words, he invited her upstairs to his father's study.

"Are you sure you won't eat or drink something?" asked his mother, who barely had time to give him a hug. He shook his head. Like a sleepwalker, he followed the pregnant woman up the stairs.

## 22.

"I COULDN'T DECIDE WHAT to do. I didn't know if I had the right to ask you to come. If I hadn't been about to give birth, I would have gone to Paris. Because suddenly, three days ago, it struck me that before I brought a child into this world, I had to cleanse myself of what I did to you. And to myself. I wrecked a love that made me happy, forever and for no good reason."

Why forever? he wanted to ask. But the words stuck in his throat.

"And even if you came, I knew it would be wrong to meet you in Jerusalem. Certainly not in the hotel. I only now realize how the place weighs me down. And so I decided to come to your parents—that is, to your father, because he's the only one who kept fighting to know the truth. I thought you'd agree to meet me here, not just for the sake of the love we once had, but because it would be a revenge for you. But I never dreamed, Ofer, that you'd come so quickly, with no questions asked. Maybe you were waiting for this all along. Were you? Did your father tell you something? But unless I'm wrong, he doesn't know the truth to this day."

"You're not wrong. He doesn't."

"And it's up to you whether it stays that way. I mean, whether you go on keeping the promise you made me..."

"If it's up to me," he said eagerly, his answer cutting through the dense air, "the promise will be kept. I swear to you, Galya, he'll never hear from me what he wants to know. But how about you? Can I count on you to keep, if not the condition, then at least the hope behind that promise . . . I mean . . . that you'll come back to me one day?"

Her face shone. A married woman about to give birth, she made no attempt to disabuse him. It was as if every sign of living love that he gave her was part of the cleansing she had come for.

Ofer sat in his father's revolving armchair, into which he had thrown himself with stiff distraction, his back to the computer and his hungry eyes feasting on his pregnant ex-wife. Galya, for lack of a chair, sat on the convertible couch, her hands supporting the burden of her large belly.

It was nearly evening. A thin, melancholy dusk descended on the voices of the children playing in the street. No lights had been switched on in the Orientalist's study, in which a folded blanket and sheets were set by the books on the shelves. The pale twilight suited their encounter.

"I know," Galya continued, "that you're angry at your father, just as I am. He's gone beyond all bounds since my father's death. Still, now that I accept your 'fantasy' as fact, shouldn't the two of us forgive him?"

He looked with amazement at the woman he still loved like an old dog faithful to its master. Though he might try remembering her as she was now, swollen and ugly with another man's child, to tide himself over the sad, lonely days ahead, he knew she only had to touch him with a finger for all his feelings to flame up again.

"So my 'fantasy' is now a fact?" He regarded her with sarcastic wonder. "Are you sure of that, Gali?"

She quailed. Was it possible that, after what she had done, risking anger and uproar by running off to Haifa to see him, he was brutally about to turn the tables by admitting he had imagined it all? But this was the way he had always argued, deliberately playing the devil's advocate. Reassured by this knowledge, she rebuked him with a smile, kicked off her shoes, loosened her sweater, put a pillow behind her back for support, tucked her legs beneath her, wrapped her arms around herself, and sat on the couch like a great ball.

"Yes, Ofer," she said, her voice soft but firm, "I'm sure." Her belly swayed in a supplicating movement, as if comforting the infant about to emerge into a world of human sorrow. "Absolutely sure..."

She was sure enough to tell him what she knew. It went back to the beginnings of the hotel. That whole first year, in the chaos of getting started, when her parents were occupied with the staff and the guests every moment and her older sister, too, was totally involved in the work, a young Arab from Abu-Ghosh—whether to please his employers or because he felt sorry for a little girl who wandered all day around the many floors and rooms of her new home—took her quietly under his wing. In his spare time he went with her for walks in the neighborhood and bought her the falafel that she loved, and he sometimes asked permission to take her home to play with his nephews. She still remembered her games with them, though not what they themselves looked like.

As she grew older and went to school and made friends, who were thrilled to know someone with her own hotel—to which they invited themselves to play hide-and-seek in the garden and tag in the hallways or to ride up and down in the new elevator and bang on the big pots in the kitchen—she remained buoyed by the knowledge that there was someone who, in his quiet and chivalrous way, always knew where to draw the line with them. And thus the years passed, and even as she learned to accept that the hotel could never be a real home, he remained a dual figure of intimacy and strangeness, a family member whose degree of kinship no one knew. Although she was never sure what he was thinking, she felt certain that he would always be there for her, if only fleetingly and from afar.

The more the hotel grew, the higher the Arab climbed the ladder of advancement and the more indispensable he became. He was a gardener, waiter, bellboy, and custodian all in one, a maintenance man who doubled as a tourist guide. Sometimes, coming home late at night, she found him in a tuxedo and bow tie at the reception desk; other times, in the middle of the day, she spied him through her window in nothing but his gym shorts, unloading fresh produce—fruit, vegetables, eggs, and poultry—from a truck. Once he brought her a week-old lamb, which was her pet until it went to the slaughterer.

No one ever met his wife or knew her name. She was said to be childless, a sickly older woman with whom he remained because she stood to inherit a large orchard of olives and figs. His real home was the hotel. He served it loyally and in a spirit of harmony and was often consulted by Galya's father, who treated him more like a partner than an employee.

And then one day, while Galya was doing her military service, Fu'ad suddenly resigned. There had been no argument with Mr. Hendel, no demands, no reason given at all. He had simply announced one afternoon that he was leaving, and the next day he had a new job at a rival establishment nearby. Although everyone, especially Mrs. Hendel, was greatly upset by this and called for an explanation from Galya's father, he himself, though failing to provide one, did not seem overly perturbed. And yet slowly it dawned on him that the Arab who had mysteriously abandoned the kingdom he had penetrated so deeply was dangerous.

At that period of her life, Galya had been living away from the hotel and had taken little interest in the incident. Only now, after leaving again and for good, had Fu'ad revealed to her what had happened the first time. Hendel, he told her, had lured him back with an offer that hinted at taking him into the business.

Even now, knowing what she did about her father, Galya told Ofer she could not but feel deeply for him. She still loved and even identified with the tall, lanky man who arrived one winter evening in Abu-Ghosh dressed not with his usual elegance, but disguised in jeans and an old jacket and hat. There, in a little coffeehouse in the square in front of the village church of St. Joseph, he coaxed Fu'ad into coming back. Convinced that the Arab had quit after uncovering his secret, he chose to confess all to him, the intimate stranger to whom alone the truth could be told.

Hendel, according to Fu'ad, displayed no feeling of guilt about what he revealed. He seemed less contrite than annoyed at the weakness, having nothing to do with sex, that had got him into his predicament. He had simply, he said, wanted to be nice to the daughter who had helped put the hotel on its feet. Though young, she considered herself his second-in-command and refused to share her ambition with anyone else. She did not want other men or love affairs in her life, which was dedicated to her work. This was why it was his duty, she told him, to make her less lonely, with an adult form of the love he had shown her as a child.

And so, Hendel told Fu'ad, he gave in, thinking it was just for one time, and became Tehila's prisoner.

Fu'ad sat in the square of St. Joseph's, listening silently to this confused and unbelievable account by a man he had once greatly respected. At first, determined to put more distance between them, he refused to reconsider his decision. Yet his former employer now made him a proposal so bold that it took his breath away; namely, to return to work, for double his old pay, as maître d', future partner, and guardian of the secret which he was entrusted to make unknowable by both protecting and keeping in check what he alone knew.

For the first time in his life, Fu'ad could do something for a Jew other than serve him. *At last,* he thought, *I can help the Jews without having to defeat them.*

"Without having to defeat them?" Ofer asked in astonishment. "What does that mean?"

Galya spread her arms helplessly to acknowledge that she didn't know. She shut her eyes with a grimace, as if the child inside her, too, were demanding to be told. In a frail voice, she asked her ex-husband to change places with her. She had felt what might be a first labor pain and needed better support than a pillow.

"God knows," she said, easing her way into the Orientalist's revolving chair. The computer at her back, switched off by Ofer, no longer radiated good cheer. "I didn't ask him because I was afraid if I did he would never get to the point—which was, you'll be surprised to hear..."—she paused to look at Ofer, hunched on the couch like a big rabbit preparing to jump—"...you."

"Me?"